Memory

A Tale of Pride and Prejudice
Volume 2: Trials to Bear

Linda Wells

To

Catherine and Tania
Bill and Rick

And to all of the readers at the Meryton Literary Society and Austen Underground, thank you for your exceptional support.

Main Cast of Characters Volume 2

Darcy
Fitzwilliam b. 2 October 1784
Elizabeth b. 16 August 1791
Married 21 June 1809
Georgiana b. April 1796

Fitzwilliam
Lord (Henry) & Lady (Helen) of
Matlock married 1774
Stephen (Viscount Layton) b. 1776
married 1806 to Alicia
Richard b. 1783
Audrey b. 1785 m. Robert
Singleton

Bennet
Thomas and Francine
Jane b. 1789
Elizabeth b. 16 August 1791
Mary b. August 1793
Catherine b. August 1794
Lydia b. June 1796

Gardiner
Edward and Marianne
Benjamin b. 1804
Amy b. 1807
Paul b. 1808

Bingley
Louisa b. 1785 married to Gerald
Hurst 1805
Caroline b. 1787
Charles b. 1788

De Bourgh
Lady Catherine
Anne b. 1786
Captain Peter de Bourgh
Mrs. de Bourgh
Michael de Bourgh

Others
George Wickham
Dorothy Younge
Lord and Lady Creary
Victoria Gannon
William Collins

Lucas
Sir William Lucas and Lady Lucas
Charlotte b. 1785
Robert b. 1786
Maria b. 1793
Two other brothers

Friends of the families
Jeffrey Harwick (wife died mid-late
April 1807)
Evangeline Harwick Carter b. 1784
widowed 1806
Lord and Lady Moreland (Stewart)
Daniel Stewart b. 1784
Laura Stewart b. 1788
Mr. and Mrs. Robert Henley
Julia Henley

Servants
Mrs. Somers (Nanny Kate)
Mr. Foster (butler, Darcy House)
Mrs. Mercer (housekeeper, Darcy
House)
Mrs. Reynolds (Housekeeper
Pemberley)
Mr. Nichols (Steward, Pemberley)
Adams (Darcy's Valet)
Millie (Elizabeth's maid)

Chapter 1

On the fourth day of his homecoming to Pemberley, the twenty-third day of his marriage, Fitzwilliam Darcy finished the afternoon interview with his steward and closed his eyes to fight the headache that was beginning to bloom. It was not the quality of the news, simply the abundance of it that inspired the pain. He glanced at the clock when it chimed and rubbed his temples, "Three hours!" He moaned and looked at the stack of correspondence that cried for his attention, and the pages of notes he had taken as he spoke to Nichols. "This is not what I had planned for today." Frustrated, he reached for an envelope covered with splotches of ink, and tearing it open tried in vain to read the contents, then threw it down in disgust.

From the open study door he heard the sound of the pianoforte drift inside. A smile came to his lips and he sat back to listen. It was not perfect, yet it was not imperfect either. The performance held a quality entirely unique to the woman who touched the keys, but then her voice was added to the melody . . . and Darcy was lost. He did not move, only closing his eyes and drinking in the sound as she sang of love and beauty, of homecoming and longing. He relaxed and let it play over in his mind until he caught the soft scent of her perfume when she leaned down to brush her lips over his mouth. Darcy's hand came up to hold her cheek and they kissed slowly. "Will you play and sing for me every day?"

"Shall I add that to my charge to laugh as well?" Elizabeth Darcy smiled to hear his low chuckle. "What else would you like?"

"Oh, I do not know. I am regretting not taking you on a proper honeymoon, somewhere far away." His eyes opened to find her smiling. Noticing the open study door, he rose and walked past her to close and lock it, then turned to see her standing by his desk with her brows raised and fighting to contain her laughter. "Now, where were we?"

"I have a feeling that you were about to complain about all of these letters you need to read." She darted away from him and settled in a chair. "If I help it will be finished sooner, and then we can go play without guilt."

Darcy sighed. "It is not fair how well you can read me."

She picked up the discarded letter. "I have a feeling that you were having difficulty reading this."

"Bingley." He came to lean against her chair. "Go ahead; see if you can decipher it."

"It is for you, dear, what if there is news of a personal nature inside?"

"Then it will remain unknown because I refuse to strain my already weary eyes further. He deserves to have his laundry aired to any who can understand these hieroglyphics he calls letters."

"You are tired." She smiled and raised her brows. "And unkind."

"He is old enough to make his writing legible." Darcy spoke to his folded hands. Elizabeth cleared her throat and he glanced up at her pursed lips. "Forgive me. What does the great artist say?"

13 July 1809
Grosvenor Street
London

Dear Darcy,
Well Caroline has surely put her foot in it this time. Her little announcement of her availability and end to her non-existent engagement to Wickham has made her the laughing stock of our society. I can barely walk into the club without some wit approaching me and asking if she has had any takers since she put herself on offer. I am sick. They are correct you know, she may as well have gone to sit in a merchant's window with a bow around her middle and a price attached to her head! Her suitor of the past has expressed no interest, even with the additional dowry, so we are back at the beginning.

Hurst's parents got wind of the situation and they refuse to welcome her to their estate, and left it to me to do something with her when they leave London. What do you suggest? I am at a loss.

I hope that you and Mrs. Darcy are well and are enjoying Pemberley. I cannot wait to join you there.
Sincerely,
Bingley

Darcy rubbed his temples. "Cannot this man make one move without my advice?"

"Have you trained him to wait for your word before doing anything?" She tilted her head. "He is too afraid of making a mistake, especially now when he is just being accepted."

"I know." Darcy sighed. "I did not mean to make him dependent on my every thought; I just wished to guide him. He latched on to me."

"You needed him, and did not let him fly on his own." She said softly.

"I needed him, but this situation with his sister came about because I *did* leave him alone. If I had not been preoccupied with a certain bewitching woman . . ."

"So it is my fault now?" She smiled and he laughed softly. "Very well, there are many to blame here, and of course most of it should lie with Miss Bingley. Should we invite her here . . ." Darcy's horrified look made her burst into laughter. "I was not serious, dear. I do not wish for her presence any more than you do. She was looking at you with entirely too much gratitude when we last saw her."

"*Entirely* too much." He said emphatically. "No my love, I will suggest that Miss Bingley return to their relatives in the north if she is not permitted to travel with the Hursts or stay in their townhouse." He sighed. "And I will contact a few acquaintances in want of a wife."

"That seems so cold." Elizabeth said softly.

"We are the exception dear, not the rule." Darcy smiled a little and caressed her jaw. "You know that."

She smiled and leaned into his hand. "Come, sit down and let us see what else is here. Then perhaps we can take a long walk? We still have time before the sun sets. I was looking at the lake, there seems to be a very well-tended path there."

"Yes, and I know so many places where . . . Well, you will see." He fixed a fiery gaze upon her. "You will not be shy?"

"Oh."

"Elizabeth?"

"No, Fitzwilliam, I will not." Blushing, she reached for the pile of letters while he let out an unsteady breath. She giggled and seeing him grinning like a pleased cat, laughed. Between the two of them they had nearly everything opened and sorted quickly, then Darcy saw a letter from Mrs. Jenkinson. He opened it and Elizabeth noticed his brow creasing. "What does she say?"

"Anne has begun driving her phaeton again."

"Well that is good news, is it not? She must be feeling stronger. Her mother must have employed a very poor physician, and it is fortunate that your uncle found someone who was able to help her."

"Yes." He read on. "She is really leaving the driving to de Bourgh or his sisters, but at least she is enjoying the fresh air for short periods. Mrs. Jenkinson hopes that her final days will remain pleasant."

"So despite her improvement Mrs. Jenkinson holds little hope?

"So it would seem." Darcy looked up to her. "I realize that it was Anne's delusion and her mother which were more to blame for what occurred, but I still have dreams about it, and what might have happened."

"I know."

"You do?" He tilted his head. "What do I do?" She shook her head and smiled. "Is this why I wake with you holding me?" Her smile grew and Darcy kissed her hand. "Have I ever thanked you for not wishing to sleep separately?"

"I believe that you have yet to miss a morning."

His eyes twinkled, "I hope I never do."

"I suppose that it is not something that your family would approve of?" She lifted her chin and met his twinkle with a sparkle of her own.

"Hmm, that is difficult to say, but I suspect it would surely raise some eyebrows if it were known, although I can imagine Richard applauding thunderously. He is an unconventional lout." Darcy grinned.

Elizabeth laughed. "I wonder how he was with his men, all business or a great cheerleader, rousting them to fight on bravely. I can see him taking pleasure is speaking of his exploits."

"No, no, Richard never speaks of battle." Darcy said quietly and looked down at their clasped hands. "He has confessed much to me but I know that it barely scratches the surface of the hell he experienced."

"I am sorry, Fitzwilliam, I did not mean to offend."

He looked up and smiled reassuringly. "You did not, dear. He works very hard to hide his injures and pain. He certainly stared death in the eye."

"Have you heard of how he gets on with Mrs. Carter?"

Darcy smiled and picked up a letter. "Very well, actually. He was pleased that she has been more welcoming; I believe that her wariness is understandable, especially following her miserable marriage. I think that she needs to learn to trust again before giving up her independence."

"I hope that they can help each other." She held his eyes and he began stroking his thumb over her wrist. "Shall we invite Mr. Harwick and Mrs. Carter here this autumn? I remember Richard saying that he would have a great deal of leave in October and November."

"Would that be difficult with Jane here?"

"She does not regret him, and he is your friend, Fitzwilliam. I will ask her if she would object and then you can write to him." She smiled, "And perhaps we could invite Mr. Stewart and his sister as well."

"Matchmaking again, Mrs. Darcy?" He chuckled. "We were so successful the first time."

"Well I am an old married woman who has nothing better to do . . ."

"Oh, I can think of any number of things that are better to do." Darcy tugged her hand and she stood to come around the desk and settle in his lap, and he drank in the scent of her hair. "mmm, much better. I have become very fond of this."

She snuggled into his arms. "There is certainly no reason for it to end."

"At least not here."

"Where?"

"In the trees, my love, in a private glade. In the cool of the shade, upon some long soft grass . . ."

"And what will happen there?" Darcy whispered in her ear and she hid her face against his neck. He whispered again and she nodded, and he stood, lifting her with him, then set her down on the floor.

"Come." He commanded and taking her hand led the way out of the study and to the front door. A waiting footman handed him a basket and he nodded, then smiled at her.

"What is this?" She tried to peek around him and grab the folded cloth from the top, but he held it well away from her reach. "Fitzwilliam!"

"You asked for a picnic. Now there is no reason to hurry back, is there?" He laughed happily.

"How long do you plan to stay out on this adventure?"

They stepped outside and pausing for a moment on his front step, surveyed the view. "Until the stars are well in the sky."

"Are they not always there?" She asked and felt her hand squeezed tight.

"You are spoiling the mood, Mrs. Darcy."

"I sincerely doubt that anything could do that." Elizabeth met his smile as they strolled off towards the lake. "I had an interesting interview with Mrs. Reynolds. I do believe that it was she who was doing the interviewing. That woman is fiercely protective of you."

Darcy sighed. "What did she do?"

"Oh nothing, Fitzwilliam. I think that she was concerned about my youth. She wished to be assured that I knew how special you and Pemberley are."

"I will speak to her."

"Please do not; I want her to trust me." Elizabeth smiled up at him. "I can understand her hesitation, after all, she has cared for this mansion for twelve years, and here this girl appears and takes away everything in one day." Darcy frowned and she hastened to add, "No she did not say that, but I must prove myself to her. I have started with the accounts."

"You have begun already?" He looked at her in surprise.

"You were long at work, dear. I could hardly sit and sip tea when I have an education to receive." She smiled when she saw the pride shining from his eyes. "You are pleased?"

"Indescribably." He kissed her hand. "Thank you." They reached the lake and he pointed out the stream that fed it, and the ancient dam that formed it generations ago. Steadily they walked along, and entered the trees, following the path until they came to a bend, here they made their way along a trail, forged by deer rather than men, and eventually reached a clearing where the sun shone through the sparse trees and long grass grew.

Elizabeth looked around in wonder. "What is this place? Why are there no trees here?"

"I found this when I was a boy, and realized that the deer come to sleep here." He pointed at places in the grass where there were depressions. "Something must have cleared it long ago, but whatever seedlings attempted to grow were either eaten or trampled by the nightly visitors." Walking to a spot where the grass was undisturbed, he set down the basket and spread out the blanket. Elizabeth took the other end to help, then remained on her knees while he sank down beside her. "I have spent many hours here."

"Why? There is no view like there is up on the ridge."

"Mmmm, yes there is." She watched him remove his coat and waistcoat, then his neck cloth. He leaned down to kiss her. "Do you feel safe here?"

"Yes." Elizabeth opened his shirt, pulled it free from his breeches, and off. "The only prying eyes are the deer."

"Perhaps a bird or two." He kissed her and then sat up, tugged off his boots and turning to see her struggling from her gown, he grinned. "Let me help you."

"I was hoping you would offer." She held up her hair and he quickly unbuttoned the back, sliding the sleeves down while nibbling on her neck. "mmm." Elizabeth smiled back at him while his hands pushed the dress away. Rapidly he untied her stays, and finally pulling the chemise over her head, lay her back down on the blanket and stared happily at her partially clad body.

"A feast!" He declared and with one movement, took hold of the dress and pulled it off, then just as quickly stripped away his breeches. "Now, Mrs. Darcy, I have you where I want you." He growled and hovered above. His intense stare was boring into her when suddenly he jerked and his passion was replaced by surprise. He looked to see her hands had wrapped around his arousal and were stroking him lovingly. "What . . .what are you . . . Ohhhhh."

Elizabeth slipped away and easily encouraged him to lie back, then kissed his throat and slowly down his chest, following the trail of dark hair over his stomach to finally caress his arousal with her lips. Darcy groaned and she bit her lip then whispered, "Remember? I said that I wished to kiss you the way you kiss me, that I wished to taste every part of you?"

"yes." He said shakily.

"Then relax, my love, it is my turn."

Darcy closed his eyes, and gasped with the breathtaking sensation of Elizabeth's tongue and touch flowing over him. He swallowed and moaned, not knowing where to put his hands, not knowing how to relinquish control, and relishing every second of her touch. "Ohhh." He moved his hips and grabbed the blanket tightly. "Eliz . . . Liz . . . ohhh." He panted then opened his eyes to watch and groaned loudly, "Ohhhhh!"

Elizabeth felt so powerful, so gloriously happy to finally give him this feeling that he had gifted her countless times. She discovered him watching and stopped, smiled, and crawled over him, her breasts brushing over his chest, until she was crouched above, her hair a curtain that surrounded their faces. Darcy's eyes widened as he silently questioned her, and lifted his hands to caress her hovering hips. "More, my love?" She whispered invitingly, and stopped to nip and lick his mouth. "More Husband?"

"You temptress." He whispered hoarsely. "Yes, oh Lord yes, please do with me what you will." His eyes closed and his lips parted, giving himself over to the exquisite pleasuring of her tongue as she savoured all of his body. Before long, the sounds of passion overtook the sounds of nature, and that was soon replaced by laughter as they made this place their own.

"ENOUGH WICKHAM!" Dorothy Younge pushed him off of her. "Do you never get tired?"

"No, I do not." He smirked and used her discarded nightdress to wipe himself clean. She got up and glared at him as she walked across the room. "Do not go far. I will want you again before very long." He laughed and stretched out on the bed, closing his eyes and rubbing his hand over his well-dipped tool. "Ah, you have always been a good lay, Dotty."

"At least you have appreciated it." She said from the dressing room. "My husband certainly did not."

"Your husband never lived long enough to get a good taste." He rolled over and snatched a half-smoked cigar, relit it, and fell back on the pillow, puffing with one hand and fondling with the other. "What will you do now?"

"I have these rooms for a few more months." She returned and stood before him. "I told you not to smoke that in here! If you start a fire . . ."

"Then keep me occupied." He patted the bed and held up his limp member. "Give us a kiss."

"Pig."

He laughed and took another long draw. "I believe I was called a stallion last night."

"Now you are a worm."

Wickham snorted. "A one-eyed worm." He relaxed and looked at the paper he had thrown to the floor the night before. "Insufferable bitch."

"What?" Dorothy glared.

"Not you. Caroline." He spat her name. "Now what am I supposed to do? My name is known in every circle as one to be avoided thanks to her."

"Can you blame her?" She picked up the nightdress and put it on. "I am surprised she did not ask more questions and find you out sooner."

"Well that was the beauty of it, I think that she knew something was not quite right with me, but that connection to Darcy, that was what drove her." He puffed again. "Prig."

"She would marry you to get revenge on him?"

"No, no, she thought it would get her into Pemberley, the first circles, she thought we were the best of friends. What her plans were from there is anybody's guess. I do not know if she planned to just use the connection to move up in society or if she actually thought she could seduce him." Wickham snorted. "As if that would happen, that little girl he married is quite the tasty morsel. Caroline had nothing on her; of course, I never got to taste her . . ."

"Too bad, you could be a married man now." Dorothy grinned.

"I would have dropped her the second I had the dowry." He laughed. "I was hanging on for that, God I wished I could just once have told her to shut up and stop her yammering about Darcy! Damn him! That is the fourth time he has crossed me!"

"Fourth?"

"The inheritance, the extra funds, the club, and now the wedding, throw in his damned wife on top of it. The bastard gets everything he wants. It isn't fair; everything is handed to him on a salver."

She laughed. "What do you expect? He is the *HEIR*!"

"Heir my . . . I want what is mine."

"Yours?" Dorothy shook her head. "How many years did you fleece his father? Poor bereaved man; and you got that education from him! Weren't you presented at court?"

"No, he died, and I could never talk him into it before then, he didn't forget that I am no gentleman." Wickham sighed. "The best time was when Darcy was gone on his Grand Tour; I was the favoured son then. I spent hours in his study listening to him reminisce, and entertaining his daughter."

"You did not. You visited when your pocket was light. You are no man to hang about for no reason."

"I did sit with him, well for a short while until he tossed me a coin. I still say that Darcy owes me more, but fat chance of prying it from him now, not after Caroline." Wickham eyed her. "You know too much of me."

"You mean that I know enough not to be taken in by your charms." She laughed.

He shrugged and waved his growing member at her. "I have to find somewhere to hide out until I can reappear with a new persona. Care for a husband for awhile? I could be Mr. Younge."

"Tempting, but I accepted a position in a girls' school this autumn." She smirked. "No men allowed."

"Not a companion? Or was it governess?"

"Maybe I will try that next. For now I am the sewing mistress." She shrugged and he rolled his eyes. "Well it will be payback for all the lessons I had to endure. I look forward to bossing around the little heiresses."

He grabbed her and dragged her back into the bed. "Hmm, well until then, I will remain here, and you can endure me."

21 JULY 1809

Three days ago would have been our wedding day, and today we would have just arrived at Pemberley. For all of the reasons that the 18th of July is not to be our anniversary, as difficult as they were to bear at the time, I am grateful that we married sooner. How could I have missed these weeks as the husband of Mrs. Darcy? I wonder even more so how we could possibly have remained chaste, although admittedly the past five days have been a miserable reminder of the time before we were married. Elizabeth promises that it is over today. I intend to celebrate that fact enthusiastically.

Elizabeth giggled when she read his entry then walked back into the mistress' bedchamber and headed for her dressing room. "Poor dear man. First he is terrified that I am dying, then when I am not, he is so miserable to be without me."

Hearing the sound of boots striding across the chambers, she looked up to see him standing in the doorway with her journal in hand, his finger stuck in the page. Darcy held the book out to her. "It is over? You said that it is over!"

"You read my journal?" Elizabeth lifted her hand to her breast in mock horror. "My private thoughts and feelings? Why Fitzwilliam, how could you?"

"Do not toy with me Wife!" He growled and entering the room, scanned over her dressing table, scooped up a handful of ribbons, fashioned a hideously misshapen knot out of them, kissed it, and stuck it into the book. "There! Now you know I read it!" Darcy dropped the book and grabbed her and held her tight to his chest. "You are free of this . . .malady now?"

"I am."

Darcy kissed her hard; there was no hint of romance, only raw desire. "You are well? You are able to . . . we can . . ."

"Yes." Elizabeth squealed when he immediately picked her up and carried her to the bed, laying her down so that her legs dangled over the edge; and spread open her robe. "Will . . . what . . . ohhhhhhh." Her eyes closed when he leaned over and magically grew a hundred hands that seemed to touch her everywhere at once while his mouth devoured hers, then found its way to the wildly pulsing spot on her neck. Elizabeth's back arched under his relentless care and when he thrust into her, she gratefully wrapped her legs around his waist. Darcy braced himself on the bed and stared down at her, his mouth slightly open, and his heavy breath blowing wisps of hair around her face. It was not long at all before his eyes squeezed shut and they both found release. When the shudders ended, he opened his eyes to find the soft expression that always came over Elizabeth's face after they had loved. He leaned down to kiss her gently.

"Dearest."

"What came over you?" She smiled then laughed at what greeted her when she opened her eyes. "You are still clothed."

"You just noticed?" He chuckled and kissed her again before standing and looking down at his sorry appearance. "Oh Lizzy, I am hopeless, surely you know that by now? I have warned you of my feelings."

"If your feelings continue this way, we will not have episodes like this to endure for long." She smiled and stood. "Let me get a cloth."

Darcy watched her go, and feeling fingers of fear wind around his heart, followed her into the dressing room where she was wringing out a damp cloth. She began to clean him, but he stopped her movement and held her hands. "What do you know of becoming with child?"

"What . . . Well, that they come when . . . Well, what we just . . . Why do you ask? Surely I do not need to explain this to you?" She tilted her head and smiling, caressed his cheek. "We have only been married a month, please do not become discouraged already, Fitzwilliam. We will have our babies. Do not worry."

She found herself inside of his arms in a moment, and his face pressed onto her shoulder. "I love you."

"I love you." She said softly, and embraced him every bit as tightly, and quickly deduced the problem. "Are you hoping that I go on suffering my . . . malady forever?" She felt his nod and stroked over his back. "But then we would not have the joy of seeing our children grow. I want to know if our son will have your solemnity or be an unending source of worry when he wanders off to chase a whim. I want to know if our daughter will be a handful, challenging every convention or if she will be the perfect example of the proper miss. I want to see our children wrap their stern father around their fingers and make him laugh with joy. Why would you want to wish this away? As much as I have come to admire your mother for producing you and for all I now know she did for this home and wish to be like her, I am not she."

"You will not leave me?" He said into her hair. "Do you promise? I cannot bear the thought, let alone the reality if it would happen. Perhaps, perhaps we should not . . ."

"Do you truly believe that you could never love me again? I could not bear to be without you any more than you could stand to hold back from me." She hugged him. "Oh Will, what has come over you today?"

"You are so young, it only means that the chances of you becoming with child are so much greater, and it will happen so many more times. Every time will be another risk. Every time I might lose you, and it would be my fault for putting you in danger because of my desires."

"So you made a mistake, did you not? You should have married an old woman who you could not stomach touching." She listened and heard nothing but his sniff. "What are you thinking about?"

"The day we finally met, in the park?"

"Yes."

"I came back to learn your address, and you were talking with your aunt and sister. You were holding your cousin Benjamin's hand, and Amy was peeking around your skirts. Do you remember?"

"Yes, I do." Elizabeth rubbed his back. "Did that make you think that . . ."

"One day that would be our children. It struck me so forcefully then."

"Then do not be afraid."

"Are you?" He asked softly. "Honestly dearest, are you?"

"Not yet." She laughed and at last he lifted his head, and rested his forehead on hers. "I cannot fear the chance of something happening; ask me again when I am in the throes of labour and cursing you ever touching me."

Darcy smiled a little and chuckled. "Would you really do that?"

"I have heard tales of it, but of course they were from Mama so again, you must consider the source." She smiled and caressed his face. "Please do not worry until there is reason to, and please, do not hold back from me."

"I do not think that I can." He kissed her and hugged her tightly. "I am a mess." Elizabeth laughed and he drew away to smile. "What is it?"

"Well, you are a mess, as am I. Shall we continue what we started?" She held out the damp cloth that was still in her hands.

He took it from her and put it down, then untied her robe and began to caress her curves. "I do think that we need to continue what we started."

"Fitzwilliam, we are due at the Henley's home in two hours!" She protested.

"It takes an hour to travel there." He murmured and began to suckle her throat.

She squealed and batted him away, "NO! I will not meet the neighbours with . . . with love bites on my neck!"

"Just one?" He grinned and kissed her again. "A little one. Just for show?"

"Infuriating man!" She cried and wriggled out of his grasp. "I must dress, Millie must do my hair . . . you, you sir are in need of a razor, and a clean pair of breeches!" He walked determinedly forward and she dashed out of the way. "Fitzwilliam!"

"Com' on lovie." He cocked his head. "Give us a kiss."

"I do not even want to *think* of where you heard that."

He stopped and grinned. "Where do you think I heard it?"

"Some . . . Some cesspool that your roughish cousin introduced you to, I presume!"

"What do you know of cesspools of bad behaviour?" He now crossed his arms and stood straight, glowering down at her. "Have you been a frequenter of such places? Have you visited Bond Street after dark?"

Elizabeth's eyes grew wide. "ohhh, what happens after dark?"

Darcy laughed and drew her into his arms. "Nothing that either one of us needs to know." He kissed her then dipped his head down to nip her breast, and smiled at the small strawberry he left behind. "There, that is all I wanted."

"I find that hard to believe, but I will accept it." She sighed and patted his bottom. "Go on, get dressed, and let us meet your friends."

"Yes dearest." He buttoned his fall and walked rapidly from the room, calling. "Hurry now, we are going to be late!"

"WE ARE SO HAPPY FOR YOU, DARCY." Benjamin Henley nodded over to the group of ladies in his drawing room. "You have had a rough time of it these past years, and it is good to see that you found a girl to lift your spirits."

"She has indeed, sir." Darcy smiled a little and Elizabeth tilted her head and lifted her eyes to the ceiling for a moment. He hid a chuckle by taking a drink, then returned his attention to his host. "I am happy for your invitation, sir. I was surprised that you are returned home so soon."

"We had enough." He indicated some chairs and they sat down. "Julia was discouraged and there is only so much you can do to cheer a girl when she gets that way. It was best to just come home for now. Perhaps we will go back for the little Season, but I would just as soon wait for next year."

"Were there no interested suitors?" Darcy asked. "She is beautiful girl."

"She is; I had my hopes for you taking a liking to her." Henley laughed when Darcy sighed. "No, no, I am not chasing after you, not that it matters now. But it would be a bit of a farce to say it did not come up in conversation. I tried it on your father once and he said he was determined to stay out of your affairs of the heart."

"I am grateful sir, that he in fact did not." Darcy said softly, but did not elaborate.

"Hmm, is that so?" He looked at how the newlyweds gazed at each other and raised his brow. "Well then, Julia had plenty of men buzzing about, but she has very set ideas on what she wants. She is young, there is time."

"Well, my wife and I," Darcy paused to savour the novelty of that phrase for a moment, "we are planning a house party in October. There will be several eligible gentlemen invited."

"A house party!" Mrs. Henley heard and turned to her daughter. "I cannot remember the last time Pemberley held a ball, will you host one, Mrs. Darcy?"

Elizabeth's eyes grew wide and she looked to Darcy who looked equally uncomfortable. "Oh, I do not know, we had not discussed it. I was thinking perhaps we could have a dinner, and invite some of Mr. Darcy's closest neighbours, and we have the Harvest Home in September."

"You simply must have a ball." She said positively.

"Mama, do not press her, she is only just married." Julia said quietly. "You must forgive my mother, Mrs. Darcy, she is thinking of matchmaking, not dancing."

"I understand that very well, Miss Henley, I assure you." Elizabeth smiled and thought of her mother's machinations. "We will have several unattached gentlemen visiting."

"Who?" Mrs. Henley pounced.

Elizabeth saw Julia's eyes roll and remembered the feeling too well. "Mr. Bingley, Mr. Harwick, Colonel Fitzwilliam, and Mr. Stewart."

"Daniel Stewart?"

"Why yes." Elizabeth smiled at Julia who was suddenly sitting up straighter. "He is a friend of both my husband and myself. His sister Laura will come as well. Do you know her? She is a delightful woman."

"I have seen her about town." Julia glanced at her mother then to Elizabeth. "Mr. Stewart seemed distracted this Season, I even heard that he might have been interested in a woman." She stared straight into Elizabeth's eyes.

"No, he was a friend, nothing more to that woman, a very dear friend. She has a love match, why would she look for less with another man? He looks at her like a sister, and her husband as a brother."

"Who?" Mrs. Henley demanded.

Julia smiled and nodded at Elizabeth. "I had heard that Mr. Stewart was attached, but I was mistaken Mama."

"Well!" Mrs. Henley beamed. "The son of an Earl! Now that would be a very fine match, my dear! We must pursue it! You seemed to get along well when he visited last year."

Elizabeth studied Julia then turned to Mrs. Henley. "He is the second son, does that bother you? I have heard that second sons are not as desirable as first."

"Naturally, my dear, but my daughter has been left property by her grandmother, so she is not in need of a man with an estate, but to marry the son of a peer! Well! That would be something!" She patted her hand. "Leave it to Mama, dear."

Julia looked at Elizabeth with wide eyes, and she understood the embarrassing machinations of a determined mother all too well. "Do you ride, Mrs. Henley?"

"Oh no, my dear." She laughed.

"What a shame, I will be inviting many neighbours to visit when our guests come and we ladies intend to do a great deal of riding while the gentlemen enjoy their sport. Miss Henley, I do hope that you will join us frequently? I am sorry that your mother will not be able to join us, but perhaps you can help me to know our neighbours?"

Julia nodded and smiled. "I will, Mrs. Darcy, I will be delighted to be of help. Thank you."

Elizabeth looked up to Darcy who was watching her with a tiny smile that highlighted the crinkle around his eyes. Pursing her lips, she raised her chin, and he did not try to hold back his laugh.

Chapter 2

"*I* appreciate this Mr. Gardiner." Bingley said sincerely and settled into a chair opposite the man's desk. "When Darcy wrote with his advice that I seek you out, I was ashamed I had not thought of it myself."

"I imagine that you had quite enough on your mind. Darcy wrote to me as well in case you called." Mr. Gardiner sat forward and clasped his hands. "I understand that your sister has very well ruined herself in the eyes of upper society?"

"Yes and no." Bingley sighed. "Although she is currently a laughing stock, I imagine that will all be forgotten by next spring and she could start anew, but, well frankly sir, I do not know what to do with her. I have no home of my own, and my brother Hurst is anxious to close up his townhouse and return to his father's estate. Grouse season will open soon and he is quite fond of his sport. I have an invitation to Pemberley, but, well, I suppose that Darcy was not joking when he said that my sister is never to be invited."

Mr. Gardiner chuckled. "No, I have no doubt that Darcy spoke the absolute truth, he is a man not given to falsehoods." Bingley shrugged and nodded with a small smile of agreement. "My niece told me of Miss Bingley's reaction to Darcy's exposure of Mr. Wickham. She described it as worshipful. Am I incorrect?"

"No, no, that is precisely it. She had such hopes that my connection to him would win her the prize; it was a foolish scheme that I tried to discourage. I knew there was no chance of that happening. As much as he flaunted society by marrying Mrs. Darcy, she is still a gentleman's daughter, where my sister is decidedly not."

"Yes, but I have noticed that more frequently gentlemen are marrying tradesmen's daughters with substantial dowries. Just listening to my wife talk about the ladies and their latest efforts tells me that a good dowry will override bad personality quirks. Forgive me." He added apologetically.

Bingley laughed resignedly. "You are not telling me anything that I do not already know, sir."

"So what will you do with her?" Mr. Gardiner raised his brows and chuckled at Bingley's groan.

"I suppose that I have no option but to send her home to our relatives in the north. Perhaps the reminder of her roots would be good for her and perhaps let her lower her expectations." He looked up hopefully. "Do you have any other ideas? I would rather avoid this conversation with her."

"I am afraid that you will have to speak to her regardless, however, I do know of a few tradesmen who are about my age, perhaps a hair younger, who have worked hard and made substantial fortunes, and are now ready to marry. They would not look askance at your sister, especially with her dowry."

"She would not accept it. Her sights are set far above our origins." He shook his head.

"If it means the difference between marriage and not, what is her choice?" Mr. Gardiner looked him in the eye. "Are you ashamed of your roots?"

"No, not at all. I am no more ashamed of mine than . . .well Darcy could be ashamed of his." Bingley smiled.

"Excellent. Then perhaps we could arrange for your sister to meet these gentlemen and see if anything comes of it. If she makes a favourable impression she could be off of your hands fairly quickly. I remember that she is not without appeal, and frankly these men would tolerate quite a lot for a handsome wife and dowry to match." He chuckled to see Bingley's face reflect his hope. "Of course, she would have to cooperate."

Bingley grimaced. "I think that the choice of winter with our relatives or marriage to a wealthy tradesman will help her make a sound decision. I cannot help but feel guilty for my part in this. I should have been more vigilant."

"Your brother Hurst is far more experienced, he should have spoken. Surely he sensed that something was amiss?"

"He did, but . . . Well, I suppose that my sister has hardly ingratiated herself with him."

"I can well imagine his desire to rearrange his household." Mr. Gardiner's lips twitched and Bingley looked down at his hands to cover his smile. "Every family has members that you would prefer were not, Son. I have a difficult sister myself." Their eyes met and Bingley nodded.

"Thank you, sir."

"I am pleased to help. I know of several dinners scheduled for the coming week, I will speak to the hosts; or rather I will have my wife speak to the hostesses to assess which event holds the most promise. Your duty will be to speak to your sister and determine if you will be attending at all. Now, when do you plan to visit Pemberley?"

"I expect to arrive by early October, and stay as long as they will have me." They laughed. "I planned on taking my sister to our relatives' home and meeting with the board of directors for the factories, then going south to Pemberley. Perhaps with your help I will be travelling north alone."

"I understand that they will be coming to town to deliver Miss Darcy and my niece Mary to school then retrieving Jane from Longbourn for the trip back to Pemberley."

"Yes." Bingley smiled. "I look forward to meeting Miss Bennet again." His brow creased when Mr. Gardiner seemed to study him. "She is not like my sister. After her disappointment with Harwick, I hope that she finds much happiness in marriage one day."

Mr. Gardiner nodded slowly. "So do I."

JANE CLOSED HER EYES and attempted to drown out the incessant sound of her mother's voice. *What would Lizzy do?*

"That Mr. Harwick!" Mrs. Bennet exclaimed once again. "How dare he treat you so poorly! I have written to my brother and told him how angry I am that he failed you so! Giving permission for such a man to pay court! He should have known that Mr. Harwick was a good-for-nothing!"

"Mama, please, Mr. Harwick did what he felt was best for everyone concerned." Jane murmured tiredly.

"Best?" She cried. "Leading you on and then leaving you unmarried is not the best! I am so embarrassed! All of my friends are sniggering behind my back! I told them what a great match you made, but here you are at home again!"

"But Lizzy made a fine match, Mama. Your friends should be impressed with that." Mary said quietly. Jane caught her eye and smiled gratefully.

"Well, there is that." Mrs. Bennet considered. "Mrs. Darcy! How well that sounds! We must go and visit them!"

"Mama they are on their honeymoon, and Mr. Darcy told you that they would prefer to be on their own."

"Nonsense! What can they possibly want to do alone all the time?" She declared then her mouth shut. Her two daughters stared curiously at her and she blushed. "I have work to do, I cannot sit here talking to you all day!"

"I am glad to hear that Mrs. Bennet." Mr. Bennet appeared in the doorway. "I have let you vent your spleen long enough. Unfortunately I do not possess Mr. Darcy's talent for silencing you with a look, however I do have a tongue and Elizabeth has encouraged me to use it."

"What are you speaking of?"

"Your inability to curb *your* tongue is why you are hearing the sniggers of your friends. You were told that Mr. Harwick's decision was hardly set in stone; you should not have gone about the countryside crowing about it. Your behaviour drove him away. It is my fault for not correcting you; it is my fault that Jane was rejected."

The three women stared at him in stunned silence. Never had Mr. Bennet taken ownership of their behaviour. He felt their attention and cleared his throat. "Now, what are you doing to improve your situations? Go . . . Go read. Where are Kitty and Lydia? Set them to . . . to work, Mrs. Bennet." He turned and disappeared into his bookroom.

Mrs. Bennet's gaze went to her girls. "Did I really drive him away?"

"He was displeased with all of us, Mama." Jane said quietly. "He is no monster. I wish that you would stop speaking of him that way."

From another room the quarrelling voices of Kitty and Lydia could be heard. "Good heavens what are those two arguing over now! Mary! Give me your book!" She grabbed it and ran from the room, and the two girls sat and drank in the blessed silence.

"Why did you come home, Jane? You surely knew what Mama would be like after Lizzy and Mr. Stewart, although I think that Mama blamed Lizzy for everything."

"She did, but I felt that I deserved to hear whatever she says. I am partially to blame for what happened." She smiled to see Mary's confusion. "I drove him away as surely as Mama and Papa did, I was not welcoming at all. I have learned a lesson though. When I do meet a man who I like, I will let him know."

"But Doctor Fordyce . . ."

"Is incorrect. Lizzy was correct. She rarely saw Mr. Darcy, but when she did, she made such an impact with her admiration that he never forgot her, so when they met in truth, they barely hesitated." She tilted her head at Mary. "I thought that you were not allowed to read Fordyce's sermons any longer."

"I am not, but I still remember what I read!" She said obstinately. "Papa is making me read the books that Lizzy used to study, but I suppose that I do not find them as satisfying as theology."

"You should marry a reverend." Jane smiled. "There must be a good parson in want of a wife somewhere."

"I am far too young to think of such things!" Mary blushed scarlet. "I am so glad that Papa will not let Mama put me out until I am seventeen!"

"I am so happy that nobody wanted me at fifteen!"

Mary thought of her sister. "I cannot imagine being the mistress of such a home as Lizzy has at my age let alone hers. We must send her a note telling her all about Charlotte dancing with Mr. Hugus at the assembly; only her brother danced with her before. Mr. Lucas even danced with me!" She smiled shyly. "My first assembly and my first dance with a man. Well, my only dance."

Jane squeezed her hand. "Mr. Lucas is very kind, we should be so fortunate to have such a brother." She smiled with the memory of his nervous request for a dance with her.

"We do have a brother, now! Perhaps Mr. Darcy will dance with me someday, he is so handsome." She sighed at the thought and blushed. "Listen to me, I sound like Kitty!" She saw Jane shake her head and shrugged. "Well a little. Talking of Lizzy makes me livelier, I guess. I miss her so much. I wonder if Mr. Darcy will dance with Lizzy at the assemblies in Derbyshire."

Jane looked down at her hands. "I have no doubt at all that he will, although I suspect that they will attend private balls rather than public assemblies in his home county."

"Not if Lizzy has anything to say about it!"

"You have a letter, miss." Hill entered and handed it to Jane.

"It is from Lizzy!" Jane exclaimed.

"Oh look at the paper!" Mary touched it. "I have never seen such fine stationary."

"I think that the paper is only the first thing we will have to marvel over when we someday see Pemberley." Jane carefully broke the wax seal stamped with Darcy's mark, and eagerly opened the sheets.

17 July 1809
Pemberley
Derbyshire

Dear Jane,
Forgive me for being so slow to respond, I have barely time to scribble a few lines in my journal, let alone write a letter. My husband endeavours to capture my undivided attention! I had to wait for a morning when his steward stubbornly refused to leave his study and at last he gave in to duty. Now do not think him negligent, he is hardly that, but he wishes to make the most of our solitude before Georgiana returns and the harvest begins.

I am slowly becoming acquainted with my duties, or rather with all the mistress should command. I have decided to tackle them by learning a new item each week. I have a list, and I think that by the time our guests arrive in October, I will be in a fair way of knowing the greater portion of them. Fitzwilliam is nervous about having so many here; the most he has entertained were his relatives last year for a few hunts. We will begin visiting the homes of Pemberley's tenants tomorrow. Fitzwilliam assures me that I have nothing to fear; and he wants them all to know me. I can only trust him, and of course I do. I hope that they will accept and trust me to do what I can for them.

Now tell me Jane, how are you withstanding Mama? If her pronouncements are anything close to what I heard, I know that your head is spinning. I would not hesitate to board a coach to London if I was you, but of course you will not. I highly recommend walking. I know that it is not your favourite activity, perhaps take Nellie out for a ride? Escape is your only hope, that or becoming suddenly engaged! Is Papa at least trying to curb her?

How are our sisters? Have they become studious with Papa's new edicts? I only say that half in jest; I sincerely hope that he will do well by them. Fitzwilliam is hesitant to believe that anything will change. Please assure me that he is mistaken! I have no concerns for Mary; she will soon shine in her new school.

We heard from Mr. Bingley, poor man. I know that he will be so happy to be here with us and away from his sister! Note that I did not describe her as miserable! I may have thought it but I did not write it down. Well, perhaps I did. I am not you, Jane. I cannot see the good in everyone. Unless it is Mr. Bingley, he is a very good friend to us all.

Please give my love to our family, and please write to me soon!
Elizabeth Darcy

"Marriage has not changed her has it?" Mary said thoughtfully as she read. "I think she is happier, if that is possible."

"I think so as well." Jane sighed and glanced at the last lines again. "Mr. Bingley is a good friend to us all." She said softly.

"I am sorry, did you say something?"

Jane blinked and smiled. "No, nothing at all."

ELIZABETH REACHED OUT and brushed Darcy's forehead with her fingertips, moving the fringe of hair away so that his entire face was revealed. She tucked her hands back under the pillow and watched his lashes flutter, and heard a soft sigh. It had been six weeks, and the sight of her sleeping husband had lost not one bit of its fascination, and she suspected it never would. She knew by now that waking him when he was this deeply asleep was nearly impossible, although, admittedly, she had not tried very hard. Likely it was a combination of not wishing to disturb and the pleasure of simply looking upon him in such a relaxed state that held her back. She could touch him, glide her hands from his shoulders, down his back, and over his sweet round bottom and return, and he would smile in his dream, sometimes whisper *Lizzy*, sometimes hug his pillow or her tighter. It was all the same; to her he was saying he loved her.

This night, the eve of his sister's return, they had spent walking under the light of the full moon, hand in hand, until they reached the lake and sat together, their bare feet dangling in the cold water, and talked. Darcy at last spoke of his mother, and how her sudden loss had nearly paralyzed him. Then he spoke of his father, and how he now understood the depth of his despair. Elizabeth understood already his fear of losing her, but now it was spoken coherently and they discussed it openly. She had been waiting for him to say more, she knew him well now, and knew it would come when he was ready. Darcy had been dwelling on the subject when he was alone. She had reassured him the best way she could, and told him that she did understand the risks of pregnancy and childbirth. They discussed all that they understood of their religion's teachings, and how different the expectations of their society was from those below them, and ultimately they agreed that despite their worries, children were imperative to Pemberley's future. Clearly his fears would not be resolved with one hug. He would need to talk about it frequently. She learned that each of them had roles to play in this unusual marriage, and in this subject she was to be the strong and reassuring partner. It was only fair; he was the strong one for nearly everything else.

"You are a complex gentleman." She whispered to him and kissed his slightly parted lips. He smiled and his eyes opened to see her for a moment, then he fell back to his dreams. Elizabeth smiled. "aha!" She snuggled against him and thought over the end of their conversation at the lake.

"Will you be happy living here, do you think? More than in town?" He smiled and ducked when she kicked some water at him.

"What a ridiculous question! How could any woman say no to that?"

"I can imagine a few."

"I imagine you have met a few."

"So you answered your own question, will you answer mine?" He kicked a little water back at her and turned when she wetted her hand to flick droplets at him.

"Of course I am happy here. Do I not appear that way?"

"You are always happy."

"And that is so terrible because . . ."

He chuckled. *"Dearest I am still a dour fellow; your light is what draws me out. It is my desire to always see you happy."*

"So that you will keep feeling as wonderful as you do now?" She tilted her head at him and saw his nod. *"Fitzwilliam, why not simply say that you need me?"*

Darcy smiled. *"Because when I do, you become shyer than I."*

"So you force me to debate philosophy with you to make a point."

"Precisely. I knew you would understand, you do understand, do you not?"

"Yes, everything that we have spoken of tonight makes that perfectly clear."

"So my dear, are you feeling shy, out here in the dark with the crickets and the owls?"

"What do you have in mind?"

Keeping his eyes on her he pulled off his shirt, and breeches, then stood before her nude and holding out his hand. *"Come."*

"Where?" She laughed, and while running her hands over his admirable thighs, heard a groan and was pulled to her feet. He began to unbutton the simple morning dress she wore. *"Fitzwilliam!"* Elizabeth exclaimed and hid against his chest when her clothes dropped to the ground.

His arms came around her waist and held her close. *"WE are going swimming."*

"No!" She turned her head to stare at the inky black lake. *"Oh no, not in the dark!"*

"So you would prefer to swim the lake in the daytime? Very well, tomorrow morning when the boys are out exercising the horses . . ."

"You would never . . ."

"No, but I do wish to . . . Oh Lizzy, I want to feel you hold onto me while I . . . let me show you." He scooped her up and strode down into the water. When his feet slipped she squealed, when the cold water touched her she nearly swore, and Darcy, delighted with her discomfort, naturally dropped her into the water.

"Fitzwilliam Darcy!"

"Yes my love?" He lifted her back up and kissed her soundly. *"I never let go."*

"You are determined to scare me to death!"

"Why would I want to do that? I just said that I needed you."

"No you did not."

"Why are we arguing semantics when we could be enjoying passion?"

"And what sort of passion do you expect in this cold water?"

"I just wish to kiss you, love."

Elizabeth sighed and thought over the glorious demonstration of devotion her reassured Fitzwilliam had displayed in his kisses, and giggled when she remembered her disastrous swimming lessons. She caressed him again and held his waist, then fell asleep.

Darcy awoke many hours later to find Elizabeth burrowed against his chest, and rested his face on his pillow to watch her sleep. He dared not move, for as soon as he did, he would be lost in her eyes. She always woke when he caressed her. Instead he thought about the past weeks together, and wrapping a long curl around his finger, thought about how many things had changed between them.

She was becoming more confident in her duties, and, he smiled, in her expressions of love to him. It was not surprising now that he thought about it, that she was so much bolder with her teasing and kisses when they were engaged, and how she became so shy once they were married. In his eagerness to be with her, he often needed to slow down and remind himself that she was very young, and very inexperienced. He laughed softly, "But you are a willing student my love, as am I." He kissed her hair and heard her sigh. Darcy thought how his shy wife, when absolutely assured of their privacy, had become almost wanton in her behaviour, happily accepting and encouraging breathless and satisfying trysts, passionate or gentle, in so many rooms of their great house.

Darcy groaned with the memories and closed his eyes. "Lizzzzzzzzzzzzzy." He held her closer and rubbed against her. "Dearest." He whispered and began kissing her face.

"mmmmm." Elizabeth's eyes fluttered open to find Darcy's nose touching hers. She laughed, and stretched, leaving her exposed to his caressing hands and mouth. "Good morning."

"Good morning." He smiled and looked down to find her lovingly fondling him. "Care to start it off well?"

"You are not too sleepy? We were out very late."

"Never." He growled. "I mean to take advantage of my wife's scandalous presence in my bed now since I did not do so last night."

She walked her fingers up his chest and teased, "Perhaps I should stop sleeping here, with Georgiana returning . . ."

Darcy immediately rolled to hover above his laughing wife. "Bite your tongue! Or better yet, let me do it for you." Quickly they joined in an intense frenzy of movement, and gasping, fell apart not so very long afterwards, both on their backs, holding hands tightly and staring at the canopy. Eventually Darcy drew a long contented breath and turned his head to grin widely at Elizabeth. "Now *that* is the way to begin a day!"

She laughed at him. "We do certainly get the blood flowing."

"To all the proper places, my love." He kissed her hand. "You are not serious about sleeping apart, are you?"

"No of course not, but we should probably not speak of our arrangement. Should we moderate our enthusiasm?

His brow creased. "How so?"

She whispered as he caressed her cheek, "Is it wrong for us to enjoy each other so often?"

"I thought that we resolved this last night." Darcy said quietly and studied her. "We already abstain on Sundays and we certainly are not constantly lovemaking, even if it seems that way. This is our honeymoon, love. When will we ever be so free to demonstrate our feelings again? Are you trying to assuage my fears? Have you thought more on this? Do you wish for less of me? Am I too demanding? I do not wish to be a husband you come to dread."

"No, dear, no to all of those questions." Elizabeth smiled and kissed him. "You have heard the same sermons I have."

"Yes. They sound so practical and easy to adhere to until . . . Until I have you beside me." He gave her his little smile, and looked down. "What concerns you?"

She studied his expression and wholeheartedly agreed with it. They had thoroughly discussed the risks that came with their conduct, he remained immovably anxious, but they both knew that it was inevitable, so why hold back? *Very well then, in this we shall also forge our own path. If I am not with child soon, I will be amazed.* Running her hand along his temple, she confided, "We are noisy, dear." She laughed and kissed his jaw when his head came up quickly to look at her with a smile. "And we may have to stop our activities throughout the house."

"Oh no." Darcy's head shook emphatically. "No. With people here it will only become more important that we steal our moments when we can. I can be quiet if necessary." He grabbed her around the waist and drew her up to lie on his chest. "We will have to increase our creativity to combat the presence of guests."

Elizabeth kissed his nose and he grinned. "I see, so lovemaking is the solution to stressful family members."

"It is a theory worth exploring." He kissed her and ran his hands down her back to cup her bottom and knead her firm cheeks with his hands. "mmmm, riding is doing wonders for your assets, my love."

"I only wish to emulate yours." She licked his lips and was rewarded with his moan.

"I am feeling the need to be ridden now." He met her eyes. "Will you exercise your favourite mount this morning?"

"Oh yes, she is in the stables waiting for me, the new saddle is just perfect, I . . ." Elizabeth squealed when her hips were lifted and she found herself speared on Darcy's shaft. She caught her breath and holding his shoulders laughed, squeezing the arousal buried deep within her. "Oh, *you* are my favourite?"

"I am." Darcy pushed her hair over her shoulders, then lifted his hips to seat her firmly in place. "Now, work your mount hard, he needs the exercise."

ELIZABETH HUMMED as she walked through the house, pausing to look into the bedchambers and be sure that all was well before Georgiana and the Matlock party arrived. She was nervous about this first true test of her position as mistress, but the master had certainly done an effective job of thoroughly relaxing her that morning. "Of course that was what he was about." She said softly when she stopped in the gallery to smile up at his portrait. *Well, his own gratification was undoubtedly involved, but I know my Will, he was trying to assure me of his love, knowing that would give me confidence today. And as always, he was correct.* She kissed her fingers and held them up to his image, then walked on, finally descending the stairs to enter the mistress's study she used only when he was out working on the estate or busy with his steward. A knock on the door made her look up from her work and she smiled at Mrs. Reynolds.

"Mrs. Darcy, the rooms are all prepared for the guests and their servants."

"Thank you so much, Mrs. Reynolds. I was just looking over the menus. Is it typical to have such elaborate meals when the family comes? This seems to be so much more than what Mr. Darcy and I have enjoyed since our arrival."

"Mr. Darcy is not fond of elaborate displays." She said stiffly.

"Then why change his preferences when guests come?"

"Because this is Pemberley, madam, and Pemberley must be shown to its greatest advantage whenever a visitor arrives, whether it be a day tripper or the King." She looked at her hands.

"I see." Elizabeth's hand travelled upwards to hold her locket while she considered the older woman. They had been walking a tightrope for weeks. Elizabeth had been very considerate and accommodating, accepting the woman's advice and lessons, and Mrs. Reynolds had been wary, teaching the young woman the complicated requirements of the mistress. Their common goal was Darcy's happiness. Elizabeth knew full well that his newfound smile was what made Mrs. Reynolds happy, and if Elizabeth was the cause, then she would accept her. However, Elizabeth instinctively knew that the moment had arrived to assert herself as mistress or forever play second in command to this exceptionally loyal servant.

"I believe, Mrs. Reynolds, that Pemberley is capable of being shown to its best advantage in any number of ways, nevertheless, treating every evening where guests are present as a dinner party is not one of them. To do so would make an actual dinner quite ordinary, do you not think so?"

Mrs. Reynolds eyed her. "Pemberley is never ordinary."

"I appreciate that very much, I assure you." She paused and rubbed her locket. "When was the last dinner held here, not for family, or after a hunt, I mean a formal dinner with many guests, or even a ball?"

She considered the question. "No ball has been held at Pemberley for close to thirteen years. Mr. Darcy senior had no desire for one without his wife. He did occasionally host dinners for the neighbours. But the present Mr. Darcy has held nothing at all."

"So perhaps your desire to show off Pemberley to any guests is simply your wish to put some life back into the house? You create a festive atmosphere in the hope that it will continue once they depart?" Elizabeth cocked her head to see Mrs. Reynolds' forehead crease. "May I ask; have you felt a change in the atmosphere since Mr. Darcy's marriage?"

"I have madam. He is happy, and the staff is very pleased." She looked at Elizabeth's lifted brow. "What are you saying, madam?"

"I am saying that there is no need to create an event to inject life into this home, the people who live here will do that themselves." She picked up the menu and began crossing off unnecessary courses, simplifying the meals to ones that would not put out the staff on a daily basis, and handed them back to her. "Please see that Mrs. Harris receives these and revises her plans. I did leave the meal for the family's last evening as it had been intended."

"Yes madam, I will do that." She looked at the menus and back up to see Elizabeth's smile. "Would you like to inspect the rooms for the guests?"

"I already have, everything is in order. I also finished reading the monthly accounts. Now, I understand that there are some maids who are squabbling? Shall I speak to them or would you like to handle the situation?" Elizabeth looked her square in the eye. "Perhaps threatening them with the mistress should be the last resort before dismissing them?"

Mrs. Reynolds smiled and nodded. "Indeed madam. I will see if I can calm them, but I will tell them that you are not pleased."

"Thank you, Mrs. Reynolds. Do you need me for any other decisions?"

"No madam." She nodded and started to turn and stopped. "It is good to have a mistress in the house once again."

"Thank you." Elizabeth watched her go then opened her locket to touch Darcy's hair. Closing it up again she closed her eyes before letting a shaking breath go. "Well Lizzy, perhaps the tide has turned your way."

"FITZWILLIAM!" Georgiana squealed as Darcy picked her up and spun her around the courtyard. "Put me down!"

He grinned and set her down. "You are not pleased to see me?"

"I am; I just am overwhelmed at your . . . What has happened to you?" She beamed at him and held his hand tightly. "Please change nothing! This is Elizabeth's doing!" She turned to see her sister who was being hugged by Alicia. "Oh Brother, I am so happy! We must take care of her; you must tell me how to make my sister happy, too."

"I think that is very simple, dear. Just be yourself, she will appreciate that more than any show you put on for her." He kissed her cheek and extracted his hand to finish meeting the rest of the family.

Elizabeth turned to see Georgiana fairly bouncing up and down by her side and laughed. "Calm yourself!"

"I cannot! Oh Elizabeth, I have been counting the days until we returned to Pemberley! Fitzwilliam was so changed and happy when you left London, and I was sure that when we came here he would be even happier. I . . . I have wanted to see him so much! I have never in my life known him to smile so!" Georgiana grasped her hands. "Thank you for loving him!"

"Georgiana, please." Elizabeth blushed and squeezed her hands back. "Your brother is a dear man as you well know. How can we not help but love him? Now, I will need your aid, I know so little of his favourite things, he does not like to speak about himself."

"Oh I know." She nodded emphatically and whispered loudly. "But I know many of his secrets."

"Well then we shall have to conspire together." Elizabeth whispered back and catching Darcy's eye, laughed as his eyes lifted to the heavens.

Elizabeth moved on to embrace Lady Matlock and suffer a hug from her husband, and Darcy at last shook Layton's hand. "The journey was easy, I hope?"

"No trouble at all, oh and I mentioned your name at the last inn, and the owner did not flinch." Layton winked at him and Darcy blushed. Elizabeth looked at him with wide eyes and he took her arm and cleared his throat. "Come inside and refresh yourselves, I am sure that you are ready to be free of your dusty clothes."

He led the way and felt his wife's insistent gaze. Eventually he gave in to the stare. "I asked Layton to casually say where he was going to the innkeeper just to see if he . . . remembered us." Darcy glanced down to see Elizabeth was blushing madly. "I would hate to be embarrassed when we return and . . . It *is* a very good inn."

"So we left no lasting impression?" She looked at her toes.

"It seems not." He covered her hand and squeezed. "Perhaps it is not so uncommon?"

"Please do not talk about it now!" She continued her studious examination of her shoes and heard Darcy's quiet chuckle.

"You become shy so quickly, Lizzy."

"You are one to talk, Will." She finally looked up to see his twinkling eyes and relaxed. They had entered the house and reached the stairs. Elizabeth led the ladies up to their rooms and Darcy invited the men to sample some port before joining them.

Lord Matlock sipped and sighed with satisfaction before dropping into a chair. "Your Elizabeth glows." He considered the proud expression on his nephew's face. "And you Son; are ready to burst."

"I am happy, sir." Darcy smiled and thought of Elizabeth's blush. "Very happy."

Layton started laughing. "I do not know about you Father, but I have the distinct impression that our hosts are in no way ready to be entertaining us. I think that you need another month."

"I would not object at all." Darcy nodded. "But it is good to have Georgiana home again. I will be working on the estate quite a great deal for the next month and I am happy that Elizabeth will not be left alone."

"To get into trouble?" Layton smiled. "How goes the riding?"

"Very well." Darcy smiled at his boots, thinking of a recent adventure they took. "She has responded well to my lessons and has not argued too much with my methods."

Lord Matlock laughed. "I thought she would be a feisty one, just wait until she gains her confidence with age. How is she doing with the staff?"

"They like her, although she has had to assert herself to make them respect her in some cases. She has absolutely refused to let me step in. She says that they must respect her as mistress on her own, and not see her as a weaker link to me."

"She is establishing that the house is her domain." Lord Matlock nodded. "That is admirable and wise."

"Alicia is fortunate that she will not have to go through such an experience." Layton mused.

"Speaking of establishing authority, Peter has replaced nearly every servant at Rosings. His mother is running a tight ship there, as is only appropriate for a navy widow." Lord Matlock laughed. "He has no worries about servants accepting him."

"How is Anne?"

"We visited there for five days before we left for here." He stretched his arms over his head. "It was honestly the most pleasant visit I have had to Rosings since Lewis died, what is it, some twenty years ago? Well Peter and his family, for people who have absolutely no experience in the operation of an estate, have really done a remarkable job. Naturally the staff is doing the work, but this man is astonishing in how he is throwing himself into learning everything he can. He is shadowing the steward's every move. I am in no doubt as to the gratitude he has for this extraordinary opportunity." He noted Darcy's smile and nodded in agreement. "Mrs. de Bourgh has taken on Anne's care and is treating her with the utmost respect, and defers to her opinion everywhere that is reasonable, particularly in the redecoration of the home. She is waiting for you to come home, still." Darcy's eyes closed. "I am sorry, but you may as well know. She is calmer, and I think that she is happy, anticipating

. . ." He stopped and glanced at Layton who was shaking his head. "We visited with Catherine."

"And?" Darcy said softly.

"She had nothing civil to say on any subject. She finally admitted that while she cannot dispute Anne's right to remove her from the house, she refers to Peter and his family as *The Squatters*." He chuckled. "I am rather enjoying her downfall."

"Moving to the dower's house is not a disgrace, Uncle. Women do this every day."

"She has it too good, you think?" Lord Matlock asked with his head cocked.

"I will defer my opinion. It does not matter." He looked up and smiled at Layton. "Will you remove your mother when the time comes?"

Layton looked at his father who was chuckling. "Do not look at me for advice, Son. I will be safe in my grave."

"Perhaps I will leave it to Alicia to accomplish." He muttered.

"How is Audrey? Is she healthy?" Darcy asked quietly.

Lord Matlock exchanged a quizzical look with Layton. "She is very well, about five months to go. They are returned to Singleton's father's estate. They seem to be pleased with each other."

"No problems then."

"No, Son. It is going well." Lord Matlock smiled to see Darcy relax, and realized his worry. "She is a strong girl."

"Yes sir." Darcy looked back up and smiled. "And what news is there of our soldier?"

"Ah, our cow-eyed soldier." Layton laughed. "He has it bad, Darcy. He is certainly putting in the time with Mrs. Carter, but I am not sure if she will budge."

"Has he proposed?"

"No, no. He cannot even get her to admit that they are courting, although that is certainly what is happening. We have invited her to dinner at Matlock several times over the past month. She is very good for him, I think."

"Well if nothing else he has a good friend. He has moderated his habits quite significantly." Layton raised his brows to Darcy, who smiled then laughed outright.

"My, my."

"Indeed."

"Besotted."

The three raised their glasses in toast. "To my warrior son, brought down by cupid's arrow."

"To Mrs. Evangeline Carter, for resisting him!" Layton grinned.

"To the happy couple, may it be inevitable!" Darcy drank and they all laughed.

Lord Matlock accepted the refill that Darcy offered and settled back in the chair. "Richard swears that he saw that Wickham character nosing about Darcy House when he passed the other day. I am sure it was his imagination. What reason would he have to be there? He is certainly no friend of yours."

"No he certainly is not." Darcy's brow creased. "Of course, it likely was not him."

"Are there an abundance of dissolute men hanging about your neighbourhood, Darcy?" Layton asked seriously.

"Stephen."

He looked at his father. "I am just saying that Richard was shot in the leg, not the head. I trust his powers of observation."

"Most of the homes are probably emptying out now; I imagine that thieves are looking at them with anticipation." Lord Matlock mused.

"I will send a note to Mrs. Mercer to be on guard."

Layton held up his hand. "I already spoke to them Darcy, and Richard proposed staying there himself."

"Oh." A smile appeared on Darcy's face. "I understand now."

"What?"

"My cousin has created an urgent need for his presence so that he might sleep in my rooms and drink my port. And perhaps have a convenient place to entertain?" Darcy relaxed. "He should have just asked."

"He was very convincing, Darcy."

"Well I cannot imagine what Wickham would be doing there. I think that my last *no* was fairly convincing. If it was he, it is possible that he might have ingratiated himself into the bed of a new widow in the neighbourhood. Not everyone in town would know his story."

"Well that is true enough. Handsome and charming." Layton noted and smiled at Darcy's glower.

"I never saw it myself."

"You are remembering your father's favour." Lord Matlock tilted his head to read his face. "I will be honest with you; I did not like it either. Particularly when you were away."

"What do you mean?" Darcy's brow creased. "He visited my father?"

"Of course, and always with his hand out." Lord Matlock sighed. "He came by when your father was showing me the jewels he bought for Georgiana, the ones that are saved for her coming out, wedding, and first child?"

"Yes." Darcy thought of that afternoon when she had tried on the Darcy jewels and eyed the three unopened boxes so curiously.

"Wickham had the audacity to enquire after Georgiana's dowry, laughingly suggesting that he would be an ideal husband."

Darcy startled. "He what?"

"Your father was not amused, I am happy to say. Wickham charmed his way out of that uncomfortable conversation, and after a bit more time, your father handed him a note and he was gone. We spoke at length about him after that, and how careful we will have to be with unscrupulous men interested in your sister's dowry. I will certainly talk to you about this at length when she is to come out. She will be the subject of a great deal of attention one day."

"I know; it frightens me to the bone. I pray that she finds what I have, but I am not blind to the rarity of that. I do believe that I am capable of protecting her from the wiles of a man like Wickham. My sister would never sink to such charm." Darcy said positively. "She knows her heritage and what is expected of her."

"Miss Bingley fell for him." Layton reminded him.

"Miss Bingley wanted him for much different reasons." Darcy sighed.

Lord Matlock laughed. "Well hopefully Bingley has learned his lesson and will do something about that."

"Hopefully my new uncle can give him the fatherly guidance he needs." Darcy smiled at his uncle. "I certainly appreciate yours."

AFTER DINNER THE LADIES left the gentlemen and Elizabeth led the way to the music room. She felt Darcy's eyes following her; he had barely looked anywhere else during the meal. "It must be a relief to be free of Darcy's scrutiny, Elizabeth." Alicia whispered as they walked. "Does he always watch so carefully?"

"Do you think that he was looking for fault? I thought he was pleased." Elizabeth asked worriedly. "I was trying to emulate the hostesses I have observed this Season."

"Oh no, Brother would not look at you with anything but admiration!" Georgiana declared.

"I . . . I assumed he was curious, this was your first dinner." Alicia looked at her mother-in-law for help.

"My dear, Darcy was most certainly not looking for fault. He was likely unhappy having to share." Lady Matlock smiled to see Elizabeth bite her lip. "Tell me where did you sit before we arrived?"

"By his side."

"There, you see? It is the different seating arrangement that bothered him, if indeed anything did. I imagine that Elizabeth's assessment was correct, he was pleased." They entered the music room and took seats while Georgiana went to the pianoforte and began looking through the sheets. "I noticed that the dinner was not nearly as elaborate as it usually is when we visit."

"Are you disappointed?" Elizabeth asked quietly. "Mrs. Reynolds presented me with Mrs. Harris' menus and I felt that such a display was not necessary for a family meal. Ostentation is the direct opposite of everything that Fitzwilliam is. I . . . I had a disagreement with her over our views. Was I wrong?"

Lady Matlock shook her head emphatically. "No. You know your husband. I would say that you know him better than a servant who has lived in the same house with him for more years than you have been alive."

Elizabeth glanced at Georgiana who was quietly playing then looked at her hands. "I am trying so hard. I am so frightened of failing and . . . The responsibilities that I have here are nothing to what I watched my mother address at home. I . . . I know that I am young and that the staff looks at me warily. I . . . I think that Mrs. Reynolds has been won, at least as long as Fitzwilliam seems happy, but I cannot stop feeling that they regard me as a . . . little girl playing house, and they are my dolls to do as I say. Mrs. Mercer was so different with me at Darcy House."

"Mrs. Mercer had the opportunity to witness your engagement and Darcy's transformation firsthand. I wonder how much of what occurred in town was told to Mrs. Reynolds. Beyond that, I saw no evidence of the staff here regarding you with anything but respect. Every servant responded to your direction efficiently. I would say that they were eager to show you to your best advantage. The mistakes you made were covered by their service."

"I made mistakes?" She cried and closed her eyes. "I knew it! Oh I am not fit for this!"

"Nonsense!" Lady Matlock took her hand. "The dinner at Matlock House was the first that you ever prepared, and we never even ate it properly! My dear, you are doing remarkably well!"

Alicia moved to sit next to her and patted her shoulder. "I do not know that I could have done as well, and I have all of this schooling behind me. You only had your mother and what Lady Helen has taught you."

"And Aunt Gardiner." Elizabeth sniffed and dabbed at her eyes.

"Have you spoken to Darcy about your fears?"

"No. He has enough. I am increasingly cognizant of the burdens he carries, and I am trying to determine how I might ease them." She looked up to them. "He does not need to know of my worries. I do not want him to ever feel that he made a mistake."

"My dear, if my husband looked at me the way yours does, I imagine I would have been testing him to see just how many mistakes I could make before he noticed." Lady Matlock laughed quietly. "You truly have nothing to fear from Darcy."

"I just know that if I tell him my struggles that he will swoop in to make it all right, and . . . I must not let him do that!" She said fiercely. "As wonderful and easy as that would be, it would undermine my position, would it not?" Elizabeth looked quickly between the ladies, hoping that they would agree.

Lady Matlock sat back and took her hand away. "How old are you, Elizabeth?"

"I . . . I will be eighteen in two days."

"I would swear that you were eight and twenty to hear you speak. I wish that girls were taught how to think this responsibly instead of worrying over the length of sleeves. You will be just fine, my dear."

The men appeared at the door and Darcy's smile fell away when he saw Elizabeth. He ignored the ladies by her side and leaned down to take her hands. "Your eyes are red."

"Yours are blue." She smiled and his brow creased. "I am well, dear. Truly."

He studied her silently and kissed her hands. "We will discuss this later, I think. Agreed?"

"If you insist."

"I do."

"Am I in your way, Darcy?" Lady Matlock smiled. "Shall I move to another seat?"

"That is unnecessary, Aunt. I shall move my wife." He tugged and Elizabeth laughed while he pulled her up to stand. "Where shall we sit?"

"Well, Georgiana is going to perform for us, shall we take a seat near her?"

They settled on a sofa near the pianoforte. Lady Matlock whispered to her husband and he whispered back. They laughed with their shared observations. Layton and Alicia sat side-by-side and watched their cousins.

"Are you well?" Darcy said softly, sending shivers down her spine with his warm breath upon the nape of her neck.

"Stop that!"

"What did I do?" His voice smiled and he leaned closer to whisper again. "I only wished to be sure of your comfort."

Elizabeth closed her eyes against the sensation, only to feel his thumb stroking endless circles over her palm. "My discomfort is more like it."

"You are shivering, how can that be on such a warm evening?" Darcy kissed her ear.

"I . . . I am containing my ire. You are preventing my enjoyment of Georgiana's performance."

"She is playing scales, my love." He kissed her hair. "Your scent is intoxicating."

"So is yours." Elizabeth sighed and leaned against his shoulder. Their fingers entwined and Elizabeth looked up to see his smile. "You look far too pleased with yourself."

Darcy chuckled. "While I admit to enjoying seeing the fire when your hackles are raised, I am happier still to see you relax." He raised her hand to his lips to kiss her fingers, then tucking her hands within his grasp, looked to his sister. "What shall you play for us, Georgiana? We have been anticipating your performance."

"Oh!" She startled and blushed.

"Come on Cousin, stop staring at the lovebirds and entertain us." Layton called.

"I am sure that the sight of their absolute lack of appreciation for decorum will become quite familiar very quickly." Lord Matlock laughed. His wife poked him and he laughed harder. "Helen! You do not agree?"

Layton spoke up. "Oh she will give Darcy a pass on behaviour just as she would Richard, but me or Audrey . . ."

"I will not dignify that accusation with any attention." Lady Matlock huffed. "I did not play favourites! Remember that when your child is born, Stephen!"

"I will, whenever that happy event comes about." He smiled at Alicia, but she only blushed.

Darcy looked worriedly at Elizabeth then to Alicia. "Is there something that we do not know?"

"No, not yet." She said quietly and looked to Lady Matlock expressively.

"No, not yet, but of course we have great expectations."

"Oh." Said Darcy who smiled and relaxed again.

"Oh." Said Georgiana, deflating from the prospect.

"Oh." Said Elizabeth who looked to Alicia and saw a tiny nod.

"Oh ho." Said Lord Matlock who read his wife's pleased smile.

"Oh yes." Layton took Alicia's hand and kissed it. "Great expectations indeed."

15 AUGUST 1809

Tomorrow I will be eighteen. Never in my wildest imaginings could I have conjured the location where I find myself on this day. I am sitting in my husband's study, in his chair, before the desk that seems nearly as large as the bed we share. Everywhere I look there are neat piles. Letters to be opened, answered, or ignored. I am continually amazed with the sheer volume of the letters of congratulations that continue to flow in, but Fitzwilliam makes a point to tell me exactly who these people are and just what their motivation is for knowing him.

Some sit on boards for charities that want his benevolence. Some are schoolmates hoping for a loan. Some are merely hoping for a connection and his attendance at their events now that he is married. And then there are a few, a very few, who he truly considers to be friends. Add to that the letters of business, and the demands from the tenants, parson, magistrate; how my husband has time to smile at me is miraculous.

My petulant worries over inadequacy for my position seem petty in the extreme. I am grateful that I may ease this burden from him, although he constantly reminds me that he never took this particular duty on. Of course he wheedled his way into goading me to talk about it. It is infuriating the way he never forgets things! Just when I think that I have him sufficiently distracted from a subject, out of the blue he will open up the discussion. And what is even more infuriating is that there is no pattern to it! I can no more tell that a kiss on my throat will lead to an interrogation or if it will begin with him towering over me with that frustratingly endearing frown he wears! How can I combat such a stern expression? I believe that if he ever was justifiably furious with me, I would only feel his chastisement for a short while before I would wish to smile at how ridiculously attractive he is with that furrowed brow and want to kiss it away! Oh this man!

I have no idea what set me off on this subject. Now I remember. I am sitting in his study, somewhere I do not usually come when he is absent, but today he is off touring the estate with his uncle and cousin, Alicia is taking a rest for some unidentified illness, Georgiana is joyously playing the new pianoforte that Fitzwilliam purchased for her a few weeks ago, and Lady Matlock sat me down to go over in excruciating detail my duties as mistress. EVERY single one. It was exhausting, and when I was at last released the first thing I thought to do was come to sit in the embrace of my husband's chair. It is here that I feel so safe that I am free to rant on about nothing at all. How he tolerates me is a mystery, but I remain grateful for it daily!

I hear Georgiana calling so I must end this now. My new sister is so happy to be home, and I look forward to our guests departing so that we might truly form the bond that she deeply needs. I shall embrace my Fitzwilliam's chair and return to my work. Thank you dearest, even in your absence you comfort me.

Darcy set down the journal and moved his knotted ribbon to the page before sitting back and listening to the laughter drifting down the hallway from the general direction of the music room. He smiled to hear their happiness and closed his eyes to drink it in. His eyes opened when Lord Matlock knocked and took a seat across from him.

He gestured to the hallway. "The house is alive again, Darcy."

"It is." He sighed and smiled. "All due to a slip of a girl."

Chapter 3

"*Y*ou are serious? I refuse to accept this!" Caroline declared. Bingley closed his eyes, steeled himself, then faced his infuriated sister again. "That is your only choice, Caroline. It is your performance that put you into this position. If you had just kept your business out of the papers all would be well! I was having a hard enough time moving about in the first circles without Darcy's presence, but add in your behaviour and I . . . I am an amiable man Caroline, but for the first time in a very long time, I find that I must use all of my strength to conjure a smile! I feel as lost as I was when I first arrived in town with a pocketful of money and no idea how to proceed! The inroads that I have made into society are . . . Do you know how it feels to have people perpetually snigger at you behind your back?" Bingley paced. "I must repair the damage to my name, and I must do it on my own. If Darcy were here undoubtedly all would be smoothed over quickly, however, I realize that I cannot be labelled as Darcy's puppy forever." He stopped and looked her in the eye. "That is what they call me. I must be my own man."

"What does that have to do with me?" She sniffed. "You failed me!"

"I?" Bingley stared. "I admit that I was completely taken in by Wickham, and I wish that I had listened to Darcy's counsel, but it was your machinations that encouraged him in the first place. I cannot believe that you thought marrying Wickham would get you the first circles!"

"I thought that he was . . . It does not matter now. It was clear that I would not get to the top through marriage to any other gentleman who was available to me." Caroline sank down on a sofa tiredly. "I have been through two Seasons, Charles. I am not blind. I know that I am undesired by the first circles. I had such hopes when Mr. Darcy befriended you. If you had just encouraged him my way . . ."

"Darcy's heart was taken before you ever met him." Bingley pulled out a chair and sat down heavily.

"So I *did* have a chance with him!" She cried.

"No Caroline, when I was first befriended by Darcy, before I knew the man he truly is, I thought it was a possibility, however remote, simply because of your dowry and he, I expected, would be like so many other men I have met and would accept a woman for the financial gain. But he made it very clear to me that he was not interested in you from the start. I thought then that it was our origins alone, but . . .it does not matter. He was not interested at all, and I might add, the more he heard of you and saw you, the less he liked you."

Caroline bristled. "What do you mean? I am the perfect example of a proper woman."

"You learned your school lessons but nobody taught you kindness. And you aspired to be far above yourself. You could have easily won a man from Hurst's level if you had been the slightest bit accommodating. I told you to give Darcy up."

"I do not know what you mean; I am kind to all who deserve it. I realized that Mr. Darcy was taken, and when Mr. Wickham came along I believed his tales, and thought if he was such good friends with Mr. Darcy, at least I would go to Pemberley that way. Mr. Darcy has everything that I have ever wanted. And then he rescued me."

Bingley regarded her dreamy countenance with fascination. "How could you become so obsessed with a man who not once gave you the slightest hint of encouragement? What exactly did you expect to happen at Pemberley?"

Caroline startled. "I was sure that if I just had the time he would see how perfect I was for him, not that little country chit! What does she know of society?" Her eyes flashed and Bingley glared at her.

"And then what? He is *married*. That is *forever*! What did you hope for, to see him chase after you? To what end? Did you think that he would abandon his supposedly incompetent wife? Surely you did not hope to be his mistress and be kept in Town for when he visited?" He stared at her incredulously. "You did! Good Lord! You would accept selling yourself for the chance to be in his society? Have you not brought enough shame on our name?"

"I wished no such thing." She sniffed. "Mistress. I am no refugee from France."

"What did you hope for, then?"

She met his eye and said clearly, "I knew that all was lost after he married, but if he had been with me and realized his error, he could have recommended me to one of his equals." Bingley's mouth dropped open. "Of course this was before I thought I would be married to Mr. Wickham. After we met, I thought that Mr. Darcy would have seen me in Pemberley, seen how perfectly I belonged in his circle, and he would have welcomed the both of us. This is what I hope for still . . ."

"Darcy finds nothing about you appealing, Caroline! You will never be invited to Pemberley! Stop this foolishness now! And do not ever speak of Mrs. Darcy without respect again!"

"What are *your* feelings for her?" Caroline accused. "I think that you are in love with her!"

"Caroline, stop trying to change the subject. We are discussing *your* future, while you still have one." He sighed then continued. "Now, Mr. Gardiner has arranged for you to meet two gentlemen at a dinner next week. They are both very successful and wealthy tradesmen. Either of them could give you a comfortable home and life. Your other choice is to travel north to remain with our relatives until the Hursts return for the little Season, or return in the spring to try again. If you begin a courtship with one of the men, I will remain in town in this house for as long as is necessary before you wed, but I will be going to Pemberley in October. Without you. So your decision must be made before then."

Caroline eyed him in silence. "You have changed."

"How so?"

"I cannot . . ." *Manipulate you.* "You have confidence."

"I have watched my friend transform and through him I am now surrounded by people who give me direction. Now, what is it going to be? Dinner with the Gardiner's or shall I begin arranging our travel?"

She conceded unhappily. "I will meet these men, and then I will decide."

"That is fair." Bingley rose to his feet. "I will inform Mr. Gardiner."

She watched him leave the room, then opened up a locket containing a likeness of her mother. "I had such hopes and now I will be no better than you."

"I HAVE NOT BEEN HERE FOR SO LONG." Evangeline smiled and took in the sights and sounds as she and Fitzwilliam strolled the paths of Vauxhall. "When my brother was courting Ellen and after they married, we would come to enjoy the summer evenings. It was a wonderful time."

Fitzwilliam tilted his head and smiled to see her happiness in the memory. "And what did you enjoy the most?"

"Oh, so many things!" She laughed. "I am being silly, I feel like a little girl, not a grown woman."

"I like seeing you silly." He grinned. "Did you dream of being a tightrope walker? Or did you want to be one of the ladies dancing around the pavilion?"

"I certainly will not tell you." Fitzwilliam chuckled and lifted her hand from his arm for a kiss. "Colonel!"

"Oh come now, you are quite old enough to receive a kiss on your hand." He shook his head. "You are quite old enough to receive a kiss to your lips, as well." Their eyes met for a long moment, and Fitzwilliam steered them off of the crowded path to a quiet darkened one. He came to a stop, then cupping her face with his hands he leaned down to gently brush their mouths. Feeling her hands clutch his coat, his stroking lips deepened the kiss, finishing at last with the briefest touch of their tongues. Fitzwilliam swallowed and drew her into his arms. "Eva."

"What have I done?" She whispered, but did not pull away; she instead clung to his solid form and closed her eyes.

"You have assured me at last that all I have been feeling does not exist only in my head." Fitzwilliam kissed her hair and ignored the whistle of a man leading his lady down the dark path. "Please tell me at last that you care for me."

"Colonel . . ."

"Richard."

"I . . . I do care for you." Fitzwilliam began to rejoice but stopped when she put her hand to his cheek. "But please do not ask for more."

"Why not?" He stepped back and stared at her. "Surely you do not wish to live your life alone?"

"I am not alone; I have Jeffrey and the girls. I will return to Meadowbrook with him tomorrow."

"Eva, I understand your attachment to your brother and his children, but Harwick wishes to marry again; surely you do not mean to remain at his side then? His wife will not want you there."

"I know, and . . . I intend to come to London when he does remarry. I have the townhouse."

"So why not go to visit the girls and then come back here? Eva, your acceptance of my kiss tonight tells me that your feelings are just as deep as mine!"

"I am hesitant to give up my independence." She said clearly.

"*You* are afraid of being caught with another dissolute husband!" Fitzwilliam cried and let go. "How can you possibly compare me to Carter?" He paced off for several yards and turned to see her standing alone. "I am hardly perfect but I assure you, my dear, I am as much a gentleman as your brother is."

"I did not call you a cad!" She exclaimed, then glared at another couple who had passed hurriedly by. "This is not the place for this conversation."

"Where do you suggest we have it? Shall I ride alongside your carriage and shout to the windows as you escape my clutches and run away?"

"I am *not* running away! I have a duty to my family."

"And what of *your* family, Eva? Do you want one of your own? Or do you wish to spend your life forever the widow, and never enjoy your dreams? You must have been full of them the day that you wed."

"I do not wish to lose control again!" She cried. "I . . . I never wish to . . ." Her voice was silenced when Fitzwilliam strode quickly to her side and wrapped her tightly in his arms.

"You can trust me, you can." He whispered fiercely. "Think about it, please. Go to your brother's home, see his children, decide if you would like a family of your own. We will meet at Pemberley in eight weeks. I pray that you will know your mind then."

"I can make no promises, Richard."

"I have not asked you any question yet." He kissed her forehead and felt her tremble. "I understand more than I can say, truly, but you *can* trust me. I have not seen another woman since meeting you."

"Well we are not courting; you are at perfect liberty to see . . ."

He took her face in his hands and looked into her eyes. "You are not listening. I have not *seen* another woman, I have not noticed, been attracted to, desired any other woman but you."

"Oh."

"You will write to me."

"It is not proper . . ."

"Damn it, Eva! You are no maiden, and I am no . . . young dandy. We are both old enough to exchange letters. Who is to know or care? Will your brother take you to task? Of course not. And I live in a barracks with a group of boys. If you will not give me your hand, then give me your pen."

Evangeline blinked back the tears that his impassioned speech brought to her eyes. "You have not asked for my hand."

"If I thought you would give it to me I would be on my knee right now." He blinked hard and kissed her. "Please write to me."

"I will." They stood embraced in the pitch dark, listening to the crowd passing by on the brightly lit path above them. Suddenly the boom of fireworks filled the air and the night sky was ablaze with light. Fitzwilliam took her hand and placed it on his arm. She looked up to see him try to smile.

"Come let us enjoy our last evening."

"Not our last, Richard." He nodded and they moved to rejoin the crowd.

16 AUGUST 1809

Well I have learned my lesson today. When Elizabeth tells me that her birthday, or I assume any other significant date, is unimportant and that it should be acknowledged with no more than a smile, I should ignore her. Although I never had any intention of not celebrating it joyfully, I decided to take her at her word, and began the day with a kiss, a quick congratulations to her achieving the healthy age of eighteen, and a wave goodbye. The crestfallen expression on her face as I exited our chambers haunted me all morning as Uncle and Stephen joined me to inspect the new cider mill we are building on the grounds. I wanted to run back and reassure her that I had magnificent plans for her that evening, but if I had, she would not be surprised, and I so wanted to surprise her. So cruelly, I left her alone. I suffered for it, and she, I discovered, has quite a talent for spite.

We returned home to a meal with a roomful of silent, cold, women. I have never felt so intimidated in my life. Any and all attempts at conversation were met with terse replies. I tried to kiss her and I was greeted with lips that neither welcomed nor rebuffed. They were simply tightly closed pieces of flesh, and her eyes looked at me with no emotion at all. It was every nightmare come to life to be so unwanted and again, my resolve was tested. I admit to feeling angry, after all, she was the one who said not to do anything for her, she was the one who said that her birthday had traditionally been a day where Jane would give her a handkerchief, her father might give her a book, her younger sisters might give her a bouquet and her mother would forget. But that is when it struck me. Only Jane could be counted on to remember her birthday before, to remember anything about her, and now she has me, and I devastated her. When she said that she wanted no recognition, she was hoping that she would not have to ask for it, that I would act on my own. It was clear as day that this is not simply a request for her birthday, but one for every day. And I, dense fool that I am, thought I was being playful by keeping her guessing.

Apparently I am not alone in this malady of thoughtlessness, since my uncle and cousin struggled to understand the workings of our ladies' minds as well. All we knew was that we were in this boat together now, although I cannot help but suspect that my uncle was not as uninformed as I and let me founder to teach me a lesson. At last I cornered my sister and demanded an explanation. This girl has learned a thing or two since going to Matlock House. I am not sure yet which lady she is emulating, but for a while I swore I was speaking to Aunt Catherine. At last she relented and intimated that Elizabeth was hurt.

I could keep my secret no longer once having the positive assurance from my sister of my error. I immediately found my wife, who was writing rapidly in her journal, lifted her to her feet and kissed her as soundly as a man in search of forgiveness can, then taking her by the hand, led her outside, down the garden path, past the lake, and to our secret glade, and showed her what I had done. She burst into tears, and we loved. We must have sounded ridiculous to the birds and the deer, apologizing and kissing while wrestling with our clothes, and never did succeed in removing them completely before succumbing to our need to make amends. When the shadows became long I roused her from our hideaway, and we returned home. Nobody mentioned the grass clinging to our clothes, and we changed to enjoy the dinner of her favourites I had ordered. I gave her my other gifts, and Georgiana played so that we could dance. The ladies were all speaking to us gentlemen once again. And then when the sun set, I led the way outside to watch the fireworks I had purchased exploding over the lake. My dear love is still afraid of the noise, and she clung to me tightly while we watched. I confess I hoped she would. She whispered that it was a day she would never forget. Neither will I.

"Do you know how difficult it is to read when you are being nibbled?" Elizabeth closed her eyes as Darcy stood behind her and caressed her throat with his lips down to her shoulders and back up to her ear.

"As a matter of fact, I do." He whispered and kissed his way back down to her shoulder.

"Spiteful?" She said softly and moved her head away and sighed as his hair brushed her cheek. "I did not take revenge."

"Yes you did." He nipped her skin, then immediately bathed the spot with his tongue when she protested.

"How?"

"You would not kiss me; you denied me your smile and laugh. You hid yourself from me."

"That was petulance, not spite."

"Children are petulant; you my love are a woman." His hands drifted up her torso to caress and fondle her breasts through her night dress. "A very enticing woman." Darcy's hands moved down to her hips and pressing himself against her back, nipped her again. She gasped and fell back against his chest. "I have one more gift for you." Darcy nudged her cheek with his nose and she turned her head to receive his kiss and smiled to see the twinkle in his eyes. "The way I shall begin your birthday from this day on."

"WHAT HAVE YOU DONE IN HERE?" Lady Catherine's shrill voice demanded as she toured a renovated sitting room.

"We have replaced the rather hideous paper that adorned the walls with something far more palatable." Mrs. de Bourgh looked around at the softly patterned Chinese print. "The room no longer resembles the setting for a throne from some medieval castle." She glanced around. "The armour has been sold."

"*Sold!*" Lady Catherine huffed. "How dare you . . ."

"Sister, it is not I who suggested it, but your daughter. It was quite the sensible plan to finance the project. Unless you envision an army invading from the sea, I sincerely doubt the usefulness for such decoration. My son assures me that the animals and foils strewn around the master's study and library provide quite enough masculinity for Rosings." Her lips twitched and her eyes narrowed. "Surely your daughter's opinion must be correct? She is the mistress."

"Mistress." Lady Catherine sniffed. "With no husband."

"Yes, but you see, in her mind she has a husband." Mrs. de Bourgh fixed her with a cold glare. "Thanks to your games. Sister."

"I wish that you would refrain from calling me that. I am Lady Catherine de Bourgh!" They moved on to view a newly-redecorated bedchamber. Lady Catherine eyed the bright room unhappily.

"You are still my sister." Mrs. de Bourgh smirked as she watched her reaction. "And I am very fond of the connection."

"Because you are taking advantage! How you can think of taking up residence here . . . sitting and waiting for my daughter to die! She is growing healthier by the day!"

"Yes, and no thanks to your attention." Mrs. de Bourgh opened the door to a closet. "We removed the shelves in here. They made no sense whatsoever." She turned to encounter a glare. "Would you prefer to see your daughter wasting away again?"

"I would prefer to see her married and you gone!"

"She could marry my son."

"That is not what I mean!"

"Then I am afraid that I do not understand." Mrs. de Bourgh smiled. "Who would you prefer? It does not matter; you were always destined for the dower's house. You are a fortunate woman to have such a home provided for you when your husband died. Some ladies have very little and are left to scratch out a living or hope for the kindness of their kin." She fixed a fiery gaze on Lady Catherine. "I certainly appreciate the plight of a widow cast from her home. And I appreciate the benevolence of family. Perhaps it is time that you learn humility. Sister."

24 AUGUST 1809
Grosvenor Street
London

Dear Darcy,

Darcy looked up from deciphering the much-splotched letter across his desk to where Elizabeth sat, failing completely from holding back her laughter while reading hers. "What does your aunt have to say?" He smiled to see her eyes dancing and bright with tears of amusement.

"Oh Fitzwilliam! I can only imagine what Mr. Bingley had to say about this dinner he attended with his sister!"

Darcy sighed and looked at the sheets. "Me as well." Their eyes met and he smiled, placing the letter in her outstretched hand. "I made out some of it; he seems to think it was a magnificent success, and that she will be delighted to walk down the aisle with one of these fine gentlemen. I hope that it is not his eternal optimism clouding his perception. He says that she was admired by men and women alike."

"And Aunt said that the disdainful smirk on her lips gave every person in the room the impression that she felt none of them had bathed in months." She met his raised brows and handed him her letter.

"How can she possibly feel herself to be above that company?" Darcy read with interest. "She actually sought to lecture these women on their choice of clothing and deportment?"

Elizabeth looked up from Bingley's letter. "Yes, she seems to feel that women need to possess something in their air and manner of walking to show themselves to their best advantage, and clearly none of those ladies had attended the school she did."

"Extraordinary."

"Mr. Bingley spoke with the gentlemen, Mr. White, who owns a perfumery, and Mr. Brewer who is, ironically, a brewer." Elizabeth's laugh brought on Darcy's smile. "Oh dear, he said that both men found her handsome and were curious if she was always so . . ." She squinted and bit her lip. "It looks like it says superior." She looked up to Darcy. "Does Mr. Bingley know that is not a compliment?"

"Apparently not." Darcy sighed. "I was once called something similar to that."

Elizabeth put down the letter and took his hand. "I find that hard to believe."

"Thank you, dearest, but it is true, and you have witnessed it from time to time." He kissed her hand. "I am fortunate that my descent was halted before it became ingrained." They smiled at each other then he picked up Mrs. Gardiner's letter while still holding Elizabeth's hand. "Your aunt seems to have taken Miss Bingley aside and reminded her of her position."

"Yes, my aunt has a talent for that; I hope to be like her someday." She smiled as Darcy's eyes began to twinkle. "What are you thinking?"

"I believe that you are well on your way." Darcy laughed when her brows rose. "Well, in any case, the tradesman's wife seems to have informed the tradesman's daughter that she is nothing special and to get her priorities in order, which should be security."

"Which means marriage."

"Which means, Miss Bingley has reluctantly accepted the offer of courtship from Mr. White."

"Well, she will always smell nice, and she will have a home." Elizabeth offered.

"You are too good."

"As long as she is not visiting us, I give her all the goodwill I possess."

"That is a great deal." Darcy's fingers entwined with hers. "I need to have a portrait of you made. I need to see that sparkle in your eye captured on canvas."

"Would it be similar to the one of your parents'? The two of us together? I would like that very much, and maybe . . . maybe the artist could paint a miniature for me."

"Of us together?" Darcy's thumb began stroking her wrist.

"No, just of you." She smiled shyly.

"May I have one made of you? I need you to sit here on my desk to keep me company when I am working." He smiled and she looked down to nod. "Thank you, love."

"Oh!" Georgiana entered the room to see Elizabeth's head down and Darcy grasping her hand. "Is something wrong?"

"No, not at all dear, come in." Darcy smiled and Elizabeth looked back up. "What can we do for you?"

"I have a letter from Mrs. Somers." She held it up. "She asked me to thank you again for your generosity."

"It was the least I could do. How fares her father?"

"He is not well at all." She looked at the letter. "She is grateful that she will have a little time with him before the end. Fitzwilliam, if her father dies soon, could she come back to us?"

"There would really be no reason to, Georgiana. You will be leaving for school in a matter of weeks."

Elizabeth touched a letter. "I heard from Mary, she is so happy to be going to school with you. She is very nervous."

"So am I." Georgiana sank into a chair and watched her brother's thumb as it continued to move on Elizabeth's wrist. "Audrey told me what to expect, though she is a lady and I am not."

"Does that frighten you? Do you think that the peers' daughters will treat you unkindly?"

"I do not know. Audrey said that most of the girls are nice and that there is a mix of them. The snooty ones are girls we would not like anyway." She smiled and lifted her chin. "So I will ignore them."

"Good for you." Darcy cheered.

"Elizabeth taught me that." Georgiana smiled at her.

"They will probably leave you alone but I fear for Mary there." Elizabeth confessed and felt Darcy's grip tighten. "She will be so low compared to the others. They will not be kind once they know her circumstances, and they might even challenge you to explain your favour."

"There is nothing wrong with her! Besides, she is my sister now, so she is the same as me."

Darcy and Elizabeth exchanged looks. "I am pleased to hear you say that. Keep in mind that she is just like I was, even worse since she never came to stay in London with our relatives. She cares little of fashion, and is very studious."

"Oh." Georgiana looked to her brother. "What should I do?"

He smiled. "Could you do what Father asked you to do for me? Could you look after her?"

"But she is two years older than me! She should be the one caring for me."

"But she does not know how. You must educate her." Elizabeth smiled. "We shall begin with taking you both to Madame Dupree to purchase your wardrobe."

"We will have to go early then." Georgiana looked at Darcy. "In the middle of September?"

"We will leave in two weeks, dear. We will stop at Longbourn to collect Mary, and she will stay with us until school begins."

"And then after we leave, just remember that Aunt and Uncle Gardiner will come to you should you need anything at all. And we will come to London for your school holidays."

Georgiana nodded and stood. "I will write to Mary and tell her our plans and reassure her."

"She would appreciate that very much Georgiana." Elizabeth smiled.

Darcy watched her leave then squeezed Elizabeth's hand. "She is growing up. I am pleased with the changes that are coming over her. She seems to be less self-centred. This is your doing."

"Oh, I cannot claim credit for that, Fitzwilliam! She has only been home for a month. I am sure that your aunt and cousins had more influence than I."

"No, I disagree. Her time at Matlock House taught her proper behaviour and the expectations of our class. Her time with you, watching you learn your role, seeing you interact with the staff and the tenants, witnessing our love, has taught her humanity. That is a rare quality for someone of our circle to possess, and I am so happy that you have given it to her."

"Thank you, Will." Elizabeth said softly. "But you are the same; I think that she watches you as much as me." Darcy blushed and tried to cover his embarrassment.

"Are you sporting for an argument, Lizzy?"

"I would win."

"I would let you."

"You never let me win."

"When it would work to my advantage I do." His eyes twinkled at her.

Elizabeth's flashed. "Oh? And when is that? Do you consider me incapable of making my point and backing my assertions with proven fact?"

"I said nothing of the sort, I merely state that I know when to let my obstinacy go."

"Because you feel that you are always correct."

"Not always."

"Oh! But most of the time?"

Darcy pursed his lips and smiled while shaking his head. "I will not satisfy you with an answer to that."

"Why not?"

"Because you have a long memory and will undoubtedly use the answer against me endlessly through the rest of our long lives."

"You just gave me your answer!"

"I did not, I said nothing."

"It was implied."

"It was . . ." Darcy began to laugh. "Oh dearest, I love you."

"Not fair, sir." Elizabeth's eyes sparkled at him.

"Sir?"

"SIR!"

Darcy sighed and looked sadly down at their tightly clasped hands. "You do not love me."

"Now you are putting words in my mouth." She saw him peeking up at her. "You play dirty Mr. Darcy." His lips twitched. "Oh all right, I love you!"

"Was that so hard?"

Elizabeth stood and squeezed his hand. "I will not dignify your question with a response. Now if you will excuse me, I have letters to write."

"Sit here with me and write."

"I will accomplish nothing with those blue eyes looking at me."

"I will be quiet."

"I said your eyes, Mr. Darcy, not your voice."

"Please do not leave me alone." His voice was very low and soft.

She sank back down into the chair. "Now that request I cannot ignore." Elizabeth took a sheet of paper and picked up a pen. "Do not dare to smirk."

"I would not think of it." Darcy lifted the lid to the inkpot and smiled. *I won!*

"WHAT AN EXCITING DISPLAY!" Elizabeth looked around at the enormous crowd of Pemberley's tenants, rich and poor alike, as well as possibly the entire population of Lambton, as they spread over the grounds of the home farm and celebrated the successful end of the harvest on the bright mid-September day. She laughed while turning to beam up at Darcy. "I have never seen the like!"

"I wonder at your amazement, love. You planned it all." Darcy raised her hand to his lips and kissed it. "This is the most spectacular Harvest Home Pemberley has seen in my memory. Well done!"

She blushed with his praise and bit her lip, looking happily around at the animated faces of their tenants. "I hardly did this alone; in fact I hesitate to take any credit at all. All I did was look in awe at the plans your very capable staff presented to me. This is nothing new to them. I have always wanted to have a proper harvest celebration, and only requested that certain items be included. Longbourn has a small celebration every year, but . . . oh I wished to do so much more for the people who work so terribly hard." Elizabeth felt his hand squeeze hers tightly and looked up to see his warm gaze. "What is it, dear?"

"I hardly have words to explain my feelings. Never has this celebration been so jubilant, and your influence is everywhere, no matter what you say." He smiled happily and scanned the crowd. "I am glad that we chose to hold this now, before leaving for London. I like having this as a Pemberley affair alone."

"What would it be otherwise?" She laughed and he shrugged. "You did not wish to share this with our family and guests?"

"No. I suppose that is it. This is for us." He looked around and spotted Georgiana. "Do you realize that . . ." His eyes grew moist and he stopped. "Forgive me."

Elizabeth followed his gaze to see Georgiana laughing and dancing with the children. "These are probably Georgiana's last moments as a child." She saw him nod and leaned against his shoulder. "She will have dancing lessons now, and be taught the ways of society."

"She has been taught these things before but now they take on a far more serious connotation." He swallowed and sighed. "Soon she will be grown and gone." He looked down to see Elizabeth's soft smile. "I am a silly fool."

"No Fitzwilliam, you are behaving like a father." She touched his cheek and he kissed her fingertips. "That is a good thing, I think."

"I suppose." He smiled then pulled himself together to greet the tenants who came by in an unending stream to express their appreciation for his benevolence and care. Elizabeth stayed by his side, holding onto him tightly as he addressed and listened carefully to each man, acknowledged each farmer's wife, and solemnly greeted the silent children who surrounded them. She would bend far down to smile warmly at each child and compliment their mothers for how finely they were turned out, and after each family departed, Darcy would give her hand a squeeze. When at last the greetings were finished he turned to her and kissed her gently. A rousing cheer instantly spread through the crowd and both blushed. "I wanted to thank you for helping me through that. I forgot myself. Forgive me."

"I have never seen you so comfortable with greeting people before, you had nothing to endure at all." Elizabeth caressed his face and kissed him, which inspired another cheer. "Forgive me." She blushed and looked down. "Why do they cheer so?"

"They are happy to see the master married." He smiled as she blushed anew. "They are hoping for the future of Pemberley." Elizabeth raised her eyes to his. "Come, dance with me."

"In front of all of these people?" She teased as he led her to the line amidst the applause of the crowd. "What has come over you?"

He drew a deep breath and looked around. "These are our people, dearest, and you have made this our home. I would gladly never leave here again." He bent and kissed her before stepping back and taking his place. Elizabeth laughed and he smiled. "Now mistress of Pemberley, let us show these people how to dance."

WICKHAM SCOOPED UP HIS WINNINGS and gave his companions a slight bow. "I thank you for your generosity."

"If you want to thank us, you'd stay and give us a chance at winning it back." One man growled.

"No, not tonight, perhaps some other time, my lady awaits me." He gestured to a table where Mrs. Younge sat and watched him.

"Are you in love, Wickham?" The table erupted in laughter.

"I love what the lady is willing to provide." He smirked and the men's suggestions and commentary followed him across the room. Sinking into his chair he looked over the meal that was spread before them. "What is all this? No desire to cook tonight?"

"I got an advance in pay to buy supplies for my students." She shrugged. "Why not have a bit of meat for me as well?"

"hmm." Wickham tucked into the thick soup and looked up to see her hand out. "What?"

"Rent money, pay up now. I know you are flush, your friends gave that away."

Reluctantly he handed over the coins. "You are a hard woman, Dotty."

"I know to get it from you now before you spend it all." She regarded him carefully. "What are you going to do? You need an income."

"I know. I put some feelers out, my name remains one to avoid, but the gossip is dying down with most of society gone to the country. It's the mid-level gentry that I have to win over again, and they are still here in numbers."

"What do you plan to do in the meantime?"

"I have some ideas, of course, I have you." He grinned and she grimaced.

"I will be in the school next week. I saw the roster of names today."

"Oh? Anyone interesting?" He slurped his soup and reached to tear off a piece of bread from the loaf.

"Georgiana Darcy."

Wickham stopped his activity. "Is that right?" He said slowly. "So Darcy is sending his precious sister to school, probably so he can have his comely wife to himself, not that he knows what to do with her." He became lost in thought, remembering his visits to Darcy House when the son was away, and he acted as a playmate to the favourite child of his benefactor. The behaviour was effective in charming Mr. Darcy until he made that great mistake in suggesting that he would be an ideal choice as her husband. Wickham internally cringed when he remembered the jewels they were examining being slammed into a strongbox and saw that Mr. Darcy was working to control his anger when he stood to put it away. By the time he returned to his seat his face was a smooth mask, just the same as his son's, but Lord Matlock did not hide his disdain at all. "Idiot. You overplayed your hand. I bet I could have pulled it off if I was more subtle."

"What did you say?" Mrs. Younge asked curiously as she watched emotions crossing his face.

"Oh . . . Miss Darcy has a dowry of thirty thousand pounds."

Mrs. Young gasped. "And what were you going to do?"

"Marry her." Wickham shrugged when she laughed. "I know it was far-fetched, but the girl does like me."

"Thirteen-year-old girls like any handsome man who smiles at them."

"That is true." He said thoughtfully. "That is very true. Thirty-thousand pounds dowry. Darcy has entirely too much money."

"YOU BARELY ATE BREAKFAST, please dearest, have something now." Darcy pushed the bowl of soup closer and lifted the spoon in preparation to feed her. "Come, I do not like seeing you ill."

"You have never seen me ill, Fitzwilliam." She smiled weakly and gently pushed his hand away. "I am fine, I am just not hungry. When we arrive at Longbourn I am sure that Mama will have something prepared."

"But that will be at least two hours. Please, I cannot have you fainting there!"

"Because you would be left alone to take on my family?" She leaned on his shoulder and laughed softly.

"Well there is that, but I was thinking that your family would not think well of me appearing with their favourite daughter in less than pristine condition." He tilted his head and smiled a little, but the worry remained in his expression.

"Favourite?" She settled in closer. "Maybe to Papa."

"Oh your mother's last letter clearly stated how proud she is to be the mother-in-law of Mr. Darcy." His lips twitched a little, and he felt a pinch through his coat. "Please, Lizzy?"

"Do eat Elizabeth; Fitzwilliam is a nervous wreck when the people he cares for are ill. You have seen how upset he has been with Audrey and now Alicia's pregnancies." Georgiana looked to see her brother's expression change to reflect his fear. "I am sorry; I should not have mentioned it." He nodded and returned his intense gaze to Elizabeth.

"I am not ill, I am just not hungry." Elizabeth saw their scepticism. "Very well, give me some bread."

"And soup." Darcy pushed to bowl to her again. "Please?"

"A little." She sighed and took a mouthful, but did not miss the triumphant gleam in his eyes. "You sir, are a nuisance."

"And proud of the title." He smiled and watched her take a bite of bread and relaxed enough to eat his own meal. "We will stop at Longbourn long enough for greetings and loading Mary's trunks. I want you in our home with good reliable meals and a warm bed. If I was not hol . . ." Elizabeth's wide eyes stopped him before he blurted out to Georgiana that they shared a bed and that he held her freezing body all night. " . . .wholly convinced that we are already staying at the best inns, I would take our business elsewhere." He saw her eyes lift to the ceiling and smile at his quick recovery.

"I was comfortable." Georgiana shrugged. "But I will be glad to be in my bed tonight. I wonder what it will be like at school. Audrey and Alicia told me about it, but until I am there, I suppose it will remain a worry."

Elizabeth put down her spoon and Darcy immediately stopped eating to watch as she wrapped her arms around herself. "Are you worried?"

"Yes." Georgiana said softly. "But I . . . I have decided not to be afraid."

"Well that is good news. How has that come about?" Elizabeth startled when she felt a cup of tea being held to her lips. She saw the concern in Darcy's eyes and took a sip. He set it down and popped a piece of bread in her mouth. Elizabeth chewed and seeing Georgiana hiding her giggles behind her hand, at last closed her eyes and glared. "Fitzwilliam Darcy, stop this!" She said in a low angry tone. "I am not an invalid! I am simply not hungry!" She tore off a large piece of bread and pushed it between his frowning lips. "There! Do you see how it feels?"

"That will not stop him, you know." Georgiana advised.

Darcy chewed slowly and swallowed, then turned his eyes to his soup and began eating in silence. The two ladies exchanged glances as he steadily finished his soup and then drank his tankard of ale. When finished he excused himself and left the table.

"What happened?" Elizabeth asked worriedly.

"I think that his feelings are hurt." Georgiana said softly.

"Oh dear." They sat silently picking at their food and when he did not return for several minutes, Elizabeth stood to look out the window. She saw Darcy exiting the privy and glance up to see her watching. He nodded and turned away to speak with the coachmen and disappeared from view. Some ten minutes later the ladies finished their turns with the commode and returned to find Darcy waiting. He stood and left some coins on the table.

"Are you ready?" He asked quietly.

"Yes, Fitzwilliam." They both answered and he offered them each an arm and led them out to the coach. Georgiana entered first and Elizabeth stopped when he offered his hand to aid her. "Will, I am sorry. I did not mean to hurt you. I was just frustrated that you would not listen."

"I know." His lips lifted a little, and he caressed her cheek with the back of his hand. "I am sorry for upsetting you. *Are* you ill?"

"I think that I am just weary of travel." She smiled and he nodded, not quite believing her, but willing to accept her words for now.

"Well then let us finish this journey." He kissed her cheek and they boarded. When he sat down he saw Elizabeth looking at a basket on the seat next to Georgiana.

"What is that?"

"Buns." He smiled and his eyes twinkled when she sighed. "And cider. Just in case."

Chapter 4

"*I*t was awful, Aunt." Elizabeth took a little sip of tea then set down her cup. They were alone in the private room assigned to them while Georgiana and Mary were measured and fussed over by Madame Dupree's staff. "Lydia was dancing around, laughing at poor Mary, saying how she would be free to do whatever she wished since she was not going to that *horrid* school. Kitty seemed torn between joining her and wanting to imitate Georgiana's poise, and finally succumbed to Lydia's example. Well, then I mentioned that we would be coming here to purchase Mary's new gowns and began to talk to Georgiana about how wonderful it is to have a modiste dress you, and they were finally silenced." Elizabeth sighed. "Then Mama took note of the quality of Georgiana's dress and began fawning over her in such a honey sweet manner that poor Georgiana had no idea what to do. She kept sending me looks for rescue, which of course I did."

"Did your father step in at all?"

She nodded. "Eventually, so she turned her attention to Fitzwilliam and he stopped her with one look. Papa reminded Lydia and Kitty that next year they would be the ones to go. Jane told them how very fortunate they were to have this opportunity and that it should not be wasted. They need to develop as many skills as they can so they could not only attract a gentleman but keep his attention once they do since marriage is the only means they have of securing their futures."

Mrs. Gardiner's brows rose. "Really? I believe that Jane has learned some hard lessons. Has she done anything to improve herself?"

"She is taking on many of Mama's tasks, and has begun to read a little more. She sings in church now where before she remained silent. I intend to teach her my duties at Pemberley so she will have the knowledge I lacked when I married. If only we could help with her dowry, but Papa refuses to allow Fitzwilliam to do anything. Papa said that he would match the cost of the schooling that the other girls are receiving and add that to Jane's portion. He said that he is mindful that Fitzwilliam is already paying a great deal for Mary's education and dresses."

"That is foolish pride at work there! I thought that your father would gladly accept such generosity, perhaps fuss a bit and make noises of paying Mr. Darcy back, but in the end accept it without thought. It would make everything easier for him, and as you well know, he is not a man to put himself out."

"I know." Elizabeth sighed. "Fitzwilliam will speak to him again when we return for Jane. Next Season she can accompany us to affairs and hopefully our presence will help her." She wrapped her arms around herself and closed her eyes.

Mrs. Gardiner regarded her in silence for several moments. "Lizzy, are you well?"

"I . . . Of course I am." She looked worriedly at her Aunt. "Fitzwilliam is hovering over me constantly, I cannot be ill. It would frighten him so."

"What are you feeling, dear?"

"I have a headache." She sighed again. "I am not hungry and I . . . I am . . ." She looked down at her breasts and back up.

"Does it hurt when your husband touches you?"

"No, not pain, just tenderness. Oh Aunt what is wrong?" Elizabeth leaned forward. "Please tell me!"

"Have you had your courses recently?"

Elizabeth sat back and thought it over. "No . . . I have not even considered it, but no I have not since mid-July."

Mrs. Gardiner smiled. "I think you have not considered a great many things we discussed after your wedding. You my dear, may be with child."

"Oh!" Elizabeth's hand went to her mouth. "Oh no!"

Mrs. Gardiner moved to sit next to her. "Dear, it is a consequence of marriage; I thought that you looked forward to this?"

"But that was before Audrey and Alicia . . . oh Aunt; you cannot know how frightened Fitzwilliam is for his cousins! He even fears reading letters from his family should there be any mention of the pregnancies! He gives them all to me and only when I assure him that there is no bad news will he read. What will he do with me?"

"It seems to me that you should delay telling him this news until you are certain, although I doubt that you will be able to hide it for long. Your body will be changing and a passionate man like your husband will notice when he comes to visit with you." She noticed Elizabeth blushing and twisting her hands. "What is it? Has he noticed already?"

"Aunt, Mr. Darcy does not visit with me."

"He does not? But . . .I find that hard to believe Lizzy, he loves you deeply! Why would he stay away?"

"He does not." Elizabeth glanced up and bit her lip.

Mrs. Gardiner regarded her and tilted her head, then whispered, "He sleeps with you? Every night, even when your courses come?" She saw Elizabeth nod and a smile spread over her face. "Oh my. Well then, this is a secret I am afraid you will not be keeping for long at all. Perhaps you should think of a way to tell him, and I will speak to your uncle and have him sit down with Mr. Darcy when you do. Hopefully he can reassure him."

"Only my safe delivery will do that, I am afraid." Elizabeth sighed and looked down to her gown. "Should I order some larger things while I am here? Just in case?"

"I believe so. And I have no doubt of it." She smiled and turned to signal one of the girls. "Mrs. Darcy would like to speak to Madame, please."

"I wonder if Mama noticed, she started to speak of Mr. Darcy's heir and my duty to provide one and he gave her another of those quelling stares . . ." Elizabeth saw her aunt smile and held her hands. "If I am to be a mother, I hope that I can be like you."

"DARCY, I TELL YOU, she is a frustrating, infuriating, miserable . . ." Bingley spluttered. "I cannot say more with tact."

Darcy chuckled. "I understand, but I believe that you have said quite enough. In fact, I am amazed to hear what you have uttered. This is most unlike you Bingley; you are always seeing the positive side of things."

"Well, that was before I began playing matchmaker for my sister." He stared down into the glass in his hand. "It was so much easier with you." Hearing a cough, a crooked smile came to his lips, and he looked up. "But then, your lady *was* a lady."

"And what do you label your sister?"

Bingley snorted. "A shrew." A slight lift came to Darcy's mouth. "I notice that you do not disagree."

"No, I do not. In fact, I believe that your matchmaking rescued me from becoming the male equivalent of your sister. I was well on my way to being an insufferable social snob."

"Yes, that is true; however you have the pedigree to justify it." Bingley laughed to see Darcy's brows rise. "I am agreeing with you, not calling you names. Oh Darcy, what am I to do? She drives away the first circles, is laughed at by the second, and scares a perfectly acceptable wealthy tradesman away. Will I ever be rid of her?"

"Plenty of women do not marry, Bingley, women with much less."

"Yes, but how am I ever to marry if I do not have her out of my care?" He sighed and lifted his glass to his lips. "Who will ever want me?"

"A great many ladies will want you, you are quite the catch." Darcy assured him. "Just not yet. Perhaps next year at this time you might look into leasing an estate."

"So soon? You thought it would be another two or three."

"You are maturing more rapidly than I expected. Your sister's trials have aided you, I think."

"I was full of confidence that I could handle this situation on my own. I waved away Hurst, kissed Louisa goodbye, spoke with Mr. Gardiner, and convinced myself that by the middle of September I would be bidding my sister farewell on her honeymoon. I could stand up for myself, I thought. I was mistaken. I still need my advisor." Bingley sat forward and leaned his elbows on his knees. "I wished to escape your shadow, but I realize now that your aid was not hindering me, it was propping me up until I could be on my own. However did you take on Pemberley at two and twenty?"

"I had to. You do what you must. There was no choice."

"I have tried that, I am not you."

"You do not wish to be me, Bingley." Darcy smiled at his incredulous laugh. "I mean the responsibilities."

"Very well, I can accept that. You are rich beyond all imagining you know."

"Oh, I think there are many who surpass me."

"No, none of them have Mrs. Darcy." Darcy's brow creased and unseeing, Bingley took a sip of his drink and sighed. "Well, we will go to Scarborough in a few days. I will conduct my business and leave Caroline to spend a lonely winter contemplating her future, then I will come to join your house party. I hope that there will be an abundance of angels to distract me?"

"Several." Darcy laughed when he saw Bingley's eyes light up. "I thought you might be considering Miss Bennet."

"I might." Bingley winked. "As you say, not yet, but in the meantime, I will enjoy her smiles."

"Do you have someone else in mind?"

"Who? Oh no, I have no real intentions. My bride may be . . ." he looked out the window of their club to see a group of young girls peeking in a shop window, "still attending school and has no thought at all that an older man is just waiting for her to grow up." He turned back and grinned. "Perhaps I will rob the cradle as you did, Darcy!" Feeling the steely glare, Bingley cleared his throat.

Still glaring, Darcy asked, "Do you wish for me to try and identify a person willing to take on your sister, regardless of her personality deficiencies?"

"Yes, thank you." He replied quietly.

Darcy nodded and his lips twitched. "Well, I must go home to meet my child bride and sisters. You are welcome for dinner for as long as you are in town."

"Is tonight too soon?" Bingley perked up immediately and Darcy laughed at the instant cheer. "I will be glad to come and enjoy your home and your company."

ELIZABETH STOOD FROM HER CHAIR by the fire in the library when Bingley was announced. "Good evening Mr. Bingley, I am so happy that you could join us tonight! I am sorry to be receiving you here."

"Why leave a cosy chair for a cold drawing room?" He smiled and bowed. "Thank you for the invitation for dinner, I am eternally grateful."

"That sounds terribly serious." She smiled, then stopped her movement to rest her hand on the chair, gripping it tightly, but after a slight hesitation, continued. "Oh! My uncle had some papers for you to look over. I understand that you are investing in his business. I am glad that he has won your confidence. They are in my study, just give me a moment."

Bingley looked over her pale face with concern. "I will be happy to fetch them Mrs. Darcy, are they on the desk?"

"I . . .to be honest with you, I am not sure. I do not know where my mind has gone of late." Elizabeth laughed. "I feel as woolly as a grandmother."

Bingley chuckled and relaxed. "Well perhaps a second pair of eyes would help."

"Well come along then, Fitzwilliam is shut up in his study with his cousin, so who knows when they may appear."

"Ah, discussing secret military affairs, no doubt."

"Solving the world's problems over some port?" Elizabeth smiled back at him as he followed. "They need you in there."

"No, no Mrs. Darcy, I am not a man for military tactics, now finding a pleasant dancing partner in a sea of faces . . ."

"Oh, well I suppose that is a compliment to me." They arrived and she turned to see him smiling. "Thank you."

"You are very welcome." Bingley stood back and watched as Elizabeth bit her lip and rested her hands on her hips. In the background the sound of the pianoforte carried. "Is that Miss Darcy?"

She listened. "No, that is Mary, it is ponderous." She sighed dramatically. "I hope that Georgiana can discourage those tunes else we shall be preparing for a funeral soon."

"Heaven forbid." Bingley stepped over to the desk, "Are they here?"

"Hmm?" She looked up at him distractedly when her mouth formed an "O," her eyes closed and she began to crumple.

"Elizabeth!" Bingley reached for her and she fell into his arms. "Elizabeth . . ." He looked desperately around the room. She was leaning heavily against his chest with her face tilted upwards and her lips slightly parted. Hesitating for several heartbeats he gazed down at her, then moved, lifting and gently placing her on a sofa. Kneeling by her side, he took her hands and called out to the hallway. "Is anyone there?"

A footman appeared and startled to see the mistress' position. "Sir?"

"Please fetch Mr. Darcy, his wife needs him. And . . .and the housekeeper." He looked down to her face. "Elizabeth, please wake!" She opened her eyes and blinked. Bingley sighed with relief. "You had me quite frightened; do not ever do that again!"

Darcy flew in the doorway before she could answer. "Elizabeth! What . . . what happened?" He looked at Bingley who rose to his feet and moved out of the way. "Dearest!" Darcy sat beside her and held her hands.

"I . . . I am not sure. Mr. Bingley . . ." Darcy turned to him.

"We were looking for some papers from Mr. Gardiner and she fainted."

Darcy immediately spun around. "Fainted! You *are* ill! Enough of this, I will send for the physician immediately! You have not eaten for days dearest, you have no strength!"

Richard stood behind the sofa and looked down at her with an encouraging smile. "And that is why she faints. Do not send for the blood letter, feed her, she will be herself once she has a good meal."

Darcy's brow was deeply creased and he did not take his eyes off of hers. "Is that what you wish, Lizzy?"

"You are giving me a choice?" She smiled and extracted a hand to caress his cheek.

Richard laughed, and Bingley smiled and looked at the floor. "I would prefer that you be cooperative, my love." Darcy's hand lifted to hold hers against his face and he turned his head to kiss her palm. "I know enough of you that being a patient would not be something to your liking."

"Is it anyone's?" Richard asked, then noticed Mrs. Mercer hovering near the doorway. "Ah! A woman with sense. What do you recommend for our fainting mistress?"

"You fainted, madam?" Mrs. Mercer bustled in. "Have you eaten?"

"There!" Darcy said triumphantly.

"I think that was my conclusion as well, but do I get any thanks?" Richard sniffed.

"I caught her." Bingley offered.

"*I* should have caught you." Darcy said emphatically.

"Through a wall?" Elizabeth's brow rose and she laughed. "I am fine, truly."

Mrs. Mercer cleared her throat. "Perhaps you gentlemen would care to leave us for a moment?"

"Why?" Darcy demanded.

"So that I might speak to the mistress, sir." She said firmly but respectfully to her master.

"Go on, dear. I am well, truly."

"Come on man, nothing will be accomplished with you staring at her. Let the ladies have their discussion." Fitzwilliam put his hand on Darcy's shoulder. "Let us return to your study."

"How am I to concentrate on anything there? You wish for me to stay, do you not?" He clutched her hand tightly.

"I do, but clearly Mrs. Mercer has other ideas. I will be with you shortly."

"I will come to you." Darcy looked at his housekeeper. "I want to be back in five minutes."

"Yes sir."

Reluctantly Darcy stood and the other men guided him from the room. Mrs. Mercer shook her head then turned to Elizabeth. "Mrs. Darcy, I have had my suspicions since you arrived, but now I am convinced. Are you with child?"

"My aunt believes so." Elizabeth whispered. "I have said nothing to Mr. Darcy."

"He will have to be told, madam. This could be his heir."

"Yes, but you saw his behaviour."

Mrs. Mercer sighed. "Yes. His mother's death was devastating. He has been afraid of pregnancy ever since."

"I know; he has not been doing well with his cousins' news. My aunt tells me it will be some time before the child will make its presence felt."

"What is her prediction, madam?" Mrs. Mercer helped her to sit up.

"Late October."

"Hmm, some five weeks hence." She shook her head. "No, do not tell him yet. He will be a wreck and an enormous nuisance to you once he does know. We will just care for you quietly." She stood and nodded. "I will order you foods that will be more agreeable, however tonight you will have to make do with what we have."

"I will manage, I am sure." Elizabeth smiled. "I am glad that you know. I do not feel so alone now."

"We will take care of you, madam. We look forward to this house being filled with little Darcys." Mrs. Mercer smiled and turned her head at the sound of rapidly moving footsteps. "I leave you to care for this one." She winked at her and curtseyed to Darcy as she left the room. He took his place at Elizabeth's side and held her hands.

"You are well."

"That sounds more like a command then a question."

"It is a request." He kissed her hands. "Well?"

"I am fine, my love." She kissed his cheek. "And Mrs. Mercer will look after me."

"That is my position." He growled and hugged her. "No more fainting, do you hear me?"

"Yes dear." Elizabeth returned his fierce embrace and looked up to his worried eyes. "What are you and Richard conspiring over?"

He stared at her unblinkingly for several moments and she kissed him softly. Darcy closed his eyes and ran his tongue over his lips then relaxed his grip slightly. "He asks me of love."

"ooooh!"

"Elizabeth Darcy, I see that womanly glint of matchmaker coming into your eyes. Stop it now." He smiled and she giggled. "I will tell you about it tonight. We have guests to care for now, unless you wish to send them home?"

"Now that would be silly, we cannot send those two bachelors home to nothing." She rose to her feet with his help as the dinner bell rang. "There, they will have heard that and there is no ridding ourselves of them." Darcy laughed softly and she hooked her hand on his arm. "Is it Mrs. Carter he loves?

She will be at Pemberley! Oh, we can arrange for them to be partners for games, and I will place her seat with his at dinner, and . . ."

"Mrs. Darcy." He said sternly and stopped her excited conversation. "Put your energy to eating, not talking."

27 SEPTEMBER 1809

We have been in London nearly a fortnight, and it has been a whirlwind in this house. How three women can spend their every waking moment shopping is beyond me. I am exaggerating, I know, certainly Elizabeth has not felt up to being out much, and I know that she is putting on a happy face for my sake. If she thinks that I am fooled by her smiles she is vastly mistaken. I know how much she eats and I see how thin she has become, I am hesitant to touch her she seems so fragile. I know that she is ordering winter dresses for home while we are here, but I pray that they are not becoming smaller, she fits so perfectly to me, but I want all of her, not a waif. What plagues her? Is it worry over the girls starting school? I admit to my fears becoming quite insurmountable as the day approaches when we will part. Elizabeth knows this and comforts me so. Am I failing with my position as husband by not comforting her? Her misery seemed to begin when we travelled here. That must be it; she is worried for Mary fitting into this new environment. She wished this for herself, and yet, after spending time with my new sister, I see that she is nothing like my Elizabeth. But somehow, I think that the peace which seems to follow Mary will serve her well to deflect whatever criticisms may come amongst these new girls. I am proud of her stoicism; I have come to admire this young theologian in our midst. Although she is not quite confident enough to debate me, I am glad that she at least has become comfortable joining me and Elizabeth in the library as we read and, happily, has stopped staring when we hold hands as we sit side by side. I like Mary, and despite her father's refusal to accept my help with the girls' dowries, I plan to give them generous gifts when they marry. It is the least I can do, and I am afraid the most as well.

Darcy set his pen down and read over the rambling paragraph. "What will Elizabeth think of me when she reads this?" He chuckled and sighed. "I am worse than a mother hen sometimes."

Closing the journal he set it aside and pulled his correspondence forward. On top was a note from Bingley. He gave it concerted effort and giving up, set it on the edge of the desk with Elizabeth's letters. "I hope that you never write anything that a lady's eyes should not read, my friend."

Another letter was opened and he sat back to take in the news from Rosings. Anne had fallen ill with another fever but recovered fairly quickly this time, a testament to the new physician's skills. Mrs. Jenkinson reported that the delusions worsened with the illness and improved little as she did; Anne firmly believed that she was Mrs. Darcy, and the de Bourghs had determined that it did her no harm. Darcy rubbed his jaw with resigned acceptance, and picked up a missive from Claridge House, the home where his aunt now resided. Hesitating for a moment, he broke the seal and read, then crumpled it into a ball to toss on the coals. "No Aunt, I will not come to Rosings and speak to Anne about you returning to the mansion. I am married, your plans failed. You may live with the consequences."

His mood now dark he pushed aside his correspondence and picked up Elizabeth's journal. Opening it to a random page, he began to read, and a smile played around his lips.

21 May 1809
Tonight we attended the ball at Matlock House. I was dressed as well as any of them. I had Richard the pearl around my throat, my Fitzwilliam's locket in my reticule, his handkerchief tucked in my chemise, I rinsed my hair with rosewater made from a bouquet he gave me, read my favourite sonnet, and played his birthday song very badly before he at last arrived to take my breath away with his appearance in Uncle's drawing room. Oh what an impressive sight he was! All of my charms for good luck were unnecessary, how could I possibly fail when the man of my dreams was there looking at me with such devotion? Those beautiful searching eyes. And they were often staring right at Richard! I must have blushed a thousand times tonight. Much happened that I have no desire to remember so I will not write it down. What I will remember is the sound of Fitzwilliam's voice when he begged me to marry him, the caress of his breath and strength of his embrace as he held me tight, and the touch of his lips everywhere they roamed. I am in heaven and Fitzwilliam will be my husband. Dreams do come true.

Darcy picked up his pen and left her a little note on the page, then smiling, closed the book and returned to work. Before long he heard the ladies' arrival and he went to find them peeling off their coats. Georgiana and Mary were flushed with excitement over their school purchases and Elizabeth was standing behind them and rolling her eyes. The girls ran upstairs and he held out his hand to her.

"I suppose that we are worrying more than they?"

"Most likely." Elizabeth leaned against his shoulder and smiled up at him. "What did you do with yourself today?"

"Me?" He kissed her forehead and smiled while they walked into the study and he closed the door. "I was just dreaming."

"IT LOOKS BLEAK." Georgiana whispered nervously.

"I think it is rather handsome." Mary looked over the facade of their school.

"You are fond of gloomy things; just listen to the music you choose!" Georgiana watched their trunks coming down from the carriage. "Oh why must we come here?"

"To gain the education we both need to survive and advance." Mary said stoically. She took Georgiana's hand and squeezed it. "Remember what we promised each other last night."

"Together we will survive this and together we will succeed." Georgiana repeated their mantra.

"Are you ready?" Elizabeth smiled and joined them. "Fitzwilliam has gone ahead to check you in. Shall we find him?"

Both girls nodded silently and Elizabeth walked ahead, smiling confidently at the other parents with their girls, and noticing a fair number of the young ladies seemed to arrive with only servants as their company. *How sad.*

Darcy appeared, looking every bit the master, but Elizabeth could see the nervousness in his eyes. "You are all checked in ladies, the teacher in charge of your care is Mrs. Younge. She is waiting just inside for you." He smiled and drew himself up. "We should say our goodbyes here, your trunks are on their way up to your rooms, and Mrs. Younge will explain everything that you need to know. Remember, we will be in town for another week and . . . and the Gardiners will be here in a moment if you just send them a note, or . . . our staff will certainly be home if you want to go to Darcy House. You have a key, so you can get in since there will be no footman on duty when we leave. Do you have the purse I gave you? Keep it with you, these girls are wealthy but it does not mean they are honest. And, do your work and . . .and . . ."

"And have a wonderful time." Elizabeth took his hand and squeezed.

"And have a wonderful time." He repeated.

Elizabeth hugged Mary and whispered to her. "You are no different from these girls, Mary. You are every bit as beautiful and clever. Do not let them convince you otherwise!"

"They can say nothing to me that Mama has not already." Mary whispered. The sisters kissed each other, and Elizabeth was pleased to see Darcy holding open his arms to hug her, too, but was sad to see Mary shy away.

She turned to Georgiana to hold her. "You will do very well, I know it."

"I will." She squeezed her hard. "Thank you for being my sister."

"It was amongst the treasures I received for marrying your brother." She whispered. "Write to me."

Georgiana nodded, and letting go, she and Mary linked arms and disappeared inside of the building. Darcy gripped Elizabeth's hand and did not move. "Maybe, maybe we should just stay here for a few hours, just in case . . ."

"Fitzwilliam we are only a few miles away, if they need us, they know how to find us." She smiled up at his bright eyes. "Come dear." They turned and walked back out through the gate and climbed into the carriage.

Wickham moved from out of the shadows where he had been watching the arrivals. "So Darcy is sentimental about his little sister; and positively pathetic over his comely wife. You have far too much Darcy, I know what your father gave to the charities each year, you could have spared me much, much more. I deserved much more." He watched the magnificent carriage with matching chestnut horses slowly roll away, and thought of Dorothy's diatribe the night before. He had to find an income. She was living here now, and she was not going to support him anymore. Gambling was not dependable; and he was still not quite able to squirm his way back into society. It seemed that he had no choice but to implement the plan he had developed over the past months. He spat on the ground, startling the peer who stepped past with his daughter on his arm. Wickham eyed them speculatively. "If I am successful with Darcy, perhaps you will be next."

THE SUN WAS JUST PEEKING through the curtains when Elizabeth woke to the sound of a maid adding more coal to the fire. She opened her eyes to find Darcy curled around her and as always, immobile in his deep sleep. As the weather began to cool, the need for heat and night clothes made their appearance. In Elizabeth's mind it was a good thing. If a maid was entering their chambers to stoke the fire, she certainly did not want her stealing a glance at Darcy's unclothed form. "This is all mine." She whispered and reached out to caress his shoulder and study his face. She was feeling well this morning, a remarkable feat considering the previous weeks of nausea. Still unconvinced that she was with child, she had spared him the pain of speculation, keeping the secret to herself, making excuses for the absence of her courses, waiting for that little sign that her aunt said should come, willing it to happen now, even though she knew it was too soon.

And then, almost as the thought crossed her mind, she felt a flutter in her belly. Elizabeth's eyes grew wide and her hand moved to rest over her nightdress. She lay still holding her breath, waiting to see if it came again, but nothing happened. She bit her lip and willed Darcy to wake, but of course he did not. Whether it was real or not, she decided that the time had come to confess her secret. "Oh what a birthday gift I have for you today!"

Slipping from the bed, she hurried to use the water closet, opened a curtain to let in some light, brushed out her hair, looked herself over carefully, then danced across the cold floor and back under the covers. Darcy murmured something while reaching blindly to drag her against his chest, and buried his face against her throat. Elizabeth held him and thought of how he had been determined to abstain from lovemaking until he felt she was well. If she was with child, she was most certainly well! Debating her next move, she finally concluded that there was no other thing to do but wake him the only effective way she knew. Manoeuvring her way around, she managed to lift his head, and cupped his cheeks with her hands. She kissed his parted lips, first gently to hear his soft sigh; then with increasing passion until she felt his body come to life and saw his eyes fly open.

"Elizabeth!"

"Happy birthday, my love!" She giggled while he blinked himself awake. "I thought that I would start presenting your gifts."

Darcy laughed and rubbed the sleep from his eyes. "By all means, what do you have to . . ."

He stopped in midsentence when Elizabeth sat up and quickly pulled her nightdress off and tossed it across the bed, then remained there smiling at him and touching her breasts. "Are you hungry?"

Darcy's night shirt was off in a moment and she practically leapt on top of him, laughing and smiling down into his delighted eyes. She kissed his nose and rubbed herself over him. Darcy's hands rested over her bottom and he happily kneaded the soft skin while she ran her hands over his chest and began nibbling all over his face and shoulders. She paused to whisper wicked words of admiration for his form, then setting back to work, drove him to the edge of reason with her tongue's gentle strokes, and "Ohhhhh Lizzy," her nips and bites to his deliciously vulnerable throat. "What are you doing to me?" Darcy gasped. "Are you sure? Are you . . .ohhhhh."

She laughed, loving her way down over him, drinking in the scent of his body and revelling in the magnificence of his muscled form. "You are beautiful Fitzwilliam." She whispered from his naval. "I love having all of this to myself." Darcy groaned as she licked and kissed everywhere, everywhere but that turgid length that was pointing proudly in the air.

"Please dearest, please kiss . . ." She looked up and smiled, then shook her head. Darcy groaned, and she set back to work, running her tongue over his thighs, spreading his legs to kiss and then suckle gently his heavy balls and finally, as he begged again, her lips found their way up over his flaming length to taste the shining pearl that rested on its tip, before mercifully, her mouth encompassed and devoured him. Darcy gasped and clutched the bed clothes, watching in panting fascination, until he could bear no more and at last lifted her up and onto his chest for a searing kiss. They rolled in their embrace so he was now dominating and thrust inside of her welcoming, burning body. There was no stopping him, no time for anything but the piston-like delivery of his sword to her mound. Over and over in unending movement and groaned words he demonstrated his appreciation for her gift, ultimately lifting her legs to place on his shoulders and drive into her as deeply as he possibly could.

"Willllllllllll!" Elizabeth cried, closing her eyes with the rising tide and revelling in the sound of him gasping her name. Time, consciousness, everything stopped as they sank and shook together in the overwhelming abyss. When Darcy at last blinked open his eyes, he saw Elizabeth smiling up at him, her face and body were beautifully flushed. He laughed and let her legs down, then collapsed with a bouncing thud onto his stomach beside her. He grinned and kissed her happily.

"Could we start off every day like this?"

Elizabeth laughed and brushed away the damp hair clinging to his forehead. "I think that I could bear it nicely."

"I do not want you to bear anything. I want you to desire it as much as I."
He reached over to run his fingers through her hair and let them trail down to
rest over her waist, "This is how your birthday should have begun."

"Hush!" She admonished him and kissed his nose. "My birthday was
beautiful, although I am afraid that I cannot match your gift to me."

"No fireworks?" She shook her head. "No frenzied lovemaking in a hidden
glen?"

"I think that we have managed the frenzied lovemaking quite admirably, but
I do have a lovely dinner planned for you and our family."

Darcy propped his head on his hand and continued to trace his fingers over
her breasts and belly, following them with his eyes, then pausing briefly over her
stomach he looked back up to her. "Will you be able to enjoy this dinner?"

"I believe so. I feel well this morning, as you see." She smiled then kissed
the crease in his brow. "I am feeling hungry."

He was up before she could say another word. "Then let us eat!"

"Will!" Her nightdress was tossed and landed over her head. She pulled it
off to see him striding nude across the floor and entering his dressing room.
He stuck his head out and grinned.

"What are you waiting for? We need to feed you up! You are wasting away
to a feather, my love. I want my girl to be curvy and delicious." He ran back
across to the bed and ripped off the covers to her squeals of protest. "Up!"
Darcy lifted her to her feet, jammed the gown over her head, kissed her soundly
and giving her a solid slap on her behind, pushed her in the direction of her
chambers. "One-half hour, dearest. No more." With that he flashed another
happy smile and disappeared.

It was then that Elizabeth realized her gown was on backwards. "I have
married an insane man!" She laughed as she turned to leave. "Well, if you want
your wife curvy my love, you will be very happy soon."

The couple shared a pleasant meal. Darcy was delighted to see her consume
more than a mouthful of food and drink an entire cup of tea. His appetite had
been somewhat muted in her company, and he tore into his meal with
enthusiasm. He was meeting Richard and they were going together on an
appointment that morning, and she announced that she would visit her aunt.
They agreed to meet again at one o'clock and prepare for the few guests she had
invited to share his birthday dinner. Darcy departed first, feeling joy at the glow
that seemed to shine from Elizabeth's eyes and convinced that this would be a
birthday he would forever remember.

"DAMN YOU!" Wickham watched from his position leaning against the park
gate as the second Darcy carriage departed. "All the money in the world; and
you flaunt it. Well today I will even that out, today I take my share." He spat
on the ground and waited, watching. Slowly the routines that he had observed
over the past few months played out. Exactly on time the water man arrived,

and delivered his casks down the steps to the side door that led to the kitchen. Soon after his departure the milk peddler appeared with his daily supply. With the family in residence there was greater activity, and greater risk, but he had no choice, they brought with them the things he sought. The time to strike was finally at hand.

Wickham looked carefully and dodging the traffic in the street crossed at a point a few doors up from Darcy House. Dressed in his best, he blended in with the foot traffic of the neighbourhood, looking for all the world like a gentleman out for a leisurely stroll. When he came to his target, he stood briefly, seemingly admiring the facade, and when there was a lull in passersby he quickly ducked down the stairs. Even if he had not been watching the house so carefully he would know this path. He had explored this house many times when spending school holidays with the Darcys. Drawing an unsteady breath, he turned the handle of the solid door, knowing that every other entrance would be firmly locked, but this one, used constantly by servants and tradesmen, was vulnerable.

He slipped inside and moved immediately to the left and into the empty servants' dining room. He watched as the housekeeper ordered maids about and the cook sent her charges flying. "There must be a dinner tonight." Wickham observed, examining the great variety of meat lying on the table. "Flaunting your wealth again, Darcy?" He snorted. "With your mistress bride? Mistress, that was a rumour I knew was false from the start. Prig." Waiting for his moment, he saw the occupants of the room all congregate in a far corner, apparently to receive instructions from the housekeeper. With all backs turned he slipped out and into the kitchen then started up the steps to the ground floor. He paused near the top, peeking through the balustrade, then seeing no feet, slipped up and sidled down the hallway, his head in constant motion and eyes alert for discovery. The sound of maids coming up the kitchen stairs made him move like a shot into a room, and he waited behind the half-closed door. When the maids passed and he heard their footsteps on the main stairs he peeked out again. His heart was racing; he could see the open doorway to Darcy's study.

Stealthily he moved along, pausing in each doorway, slipping into the shadows, watching, listening, and finally he arrived to slide inside and close the door. When it clicked shut he heard a woman's gasp.

"Mr. Wickham!" Elizabeth cried.

Wickham was across the room almost before she could rise to her feet. "What are you doing here? I thought you left." He growled.

"You were told to never return!" She began to push past him to summon help by pulling the bell cord. Wickham grabbed her arm and twisted it, making her yelp with pain. "Let me go!" She opened her mouth to scream and Wickham's hand instantly clapped over it. Attempting to bite, she writhed in his grasp, and he responded by forcibly bending her arm backwards.

"Do you want me to break it, Mrs. Darcy? I will, do not doubt me!" Elizabeth's eyes welled with tears of pain and she shook her head. He relaxed the hold enough to give her relief, and swore again as his eyes darted around the room. Spotting the bookshelf where he knew the strongbox was hidden he looked back at his captive. "What should I do with you?"

Elizabeth tried to control her shaking as Wickham raked her with his gaze. She watched with growing horror as he looked to the door then back at her and licked his lips. "My first payment." He whispered, then removing his hand from her mouth grabbed her hair and jerking her head back kissed her roughly, forcing his tongue into her mouth while increasing his grip on her oddly twisted arm. Elizabeth tried to escape but no matter how she moved, the pain in her arm increased. His hand travelled from her hair to her hip, forcing her tight against his body. Backing her up to the bookshelves, he pushed her against the uneven surface, and knocked several volumes to the floor in the process. His mouth and tongue never stopped moving, and now with her effectively trapped, his hand moved up to fondle her breasts and then down to begin pulling up the fabric of her gown. Twisting and trying to kick, her free hand balled into a fist and beat on him, but her weakened state had left her in no condition to fight and her strength rapidly flagged. Remembering the books, she grabbed blindly, seeking a weapon, but only managed to knock more down to thud nearly silently on the thick carpet. She tried to pull his hair, but her fingers could not grab onto the slick pomade, so she scratched at his face, seeking his eyes. With that, Wickham dropped her skirt and grabbed her hand to hold in a vise-like grip above her head. Elizabeth sobbed, and his mouth continued to plunder hers. She was exhausted and he knew it. Wickham's eyes stared into Elizabeth's terrified gaze, his look and his aroused weapon pressed against her communicated clearly what was to come.

And then she fainted.

Elizabeth's eyes rolled back in her head and she slumped heavily onto his chest. Wickham startled, nearly dropping her as she began to sink to the floor. He watched her slide down into a crumpled heap and stood warily above her, watching to see if this was some attempt at escape. It did not take long for him to realize that she was truly unconscious. "Do you think this will put me off?" He demanded.

Nervously licking his lips, his eyes darted around the room and he rubbed his face, thinking hard. He had been with plenty of women, but he had certainly never raped one. The thought of taking Darcy's wife excited him nearly beyond reason; wild ideas flew through his mind. "If I had a carriage . . . Damn it, if that bastard had given me more . . . if I could get you to my rooms . . ." Wickham knelt by her side and ran his hands over her breasts and slipped one beneath her chemise to touch skin and feel her nipple harden under his fingertips. He looked at her with feral lust. "Oh yes I'd be on you every hour until he paid dearly to get you back. Thirty thousand pounds would do. I know he has it." Elizabeth moaned and began to move. "Why not? I deserve this." He considered her, talking himself into it. "Yes, yes, I can do this." Wickham started to lift her gown with one shaking hand and fumbled with the buttons on his breeches with the other, cursing when he could not get them open. He dropped her skirts and began twisting the buttons on the fall, then froze with the sound of servants in the hallway. Suddenly reminded of his dangerous position, he cursed again, and standing awkwardly, returned to his intent. "What am I doing? I should have been gone from here by now! Fool!" Stepping over her, he began tugging and pulling around the bookshelves, at last murmuring in triumph when they swung out and he rushed inside the recess to find the heavy, shackled strongbox. Grunting, he managed to lift it out and dropped it onto the desk.

Wickham shot a look at Elizabeth and then began pulling out drawers, scattering papers everywhere in search of the key. It was nowhere to be found, and he had no memory of where Mr. Darcy hid it. He thought of waking her to demand its location, but realized she probably had no idea, and would instead call for help. Spotting the silver letter opener he jabbed it into the lock, and tried to manipulate the mechanism. "Rat Bastard!" He muttered as he beat on the box. He lifted it, but realized it was far too awkward and heavy to carry quickly through the house; and impossible to carry out of a window alone and unnoticed. Spotting that Elizabeth was waking, he knew that time was running out. Again he grabbed the knife to open the lock, then sticking it into his waistcoat, seized a heavy marble bust and began to beat at the latch, heedless of the noise he was making, now only intent on his prize. He detected neither Elizabeth's eyes opening and closing, nor her careful movement backwards. He did not hear the raised voices in the hallway asking what was happening in the study. He did not hear the crash of the door flying open, but he certainly felt the hand that grabbed his neck cloth and the fist that struck his jaw. The last thing he saw as he crumpled to the floor was Darcy's furious face, and the glint of steel behind him.

"Lizzy!" Darcy ran to her side while Fitzwilliam slipped his sword back into its sheath.

"Will?" She moaned softly and cautiously blinked open her eyes to see him nose to nose with her. "Oh Will."

"Dearest!" He gathered her up and rocked her trembling body. "Are you well? Did he hurt you?"

"He . . . he frightened me more than anything." She whispered. "I was just trying to get to the door so I could run for help."

Darcy drew away to caress her dislodged hair and saw the evidence of the assault on her mouth. "My brave love. What else did he do?" He traced his fingertips over her lips. "Please tell me."

"He twisted my arm and forced me to kiss." She closed her eyes and laid her head on his chest. "He intimated more but I . . . I suppose that I fainted before he could act." Darcy looked over her dishevelled clothes and wondered what had happened when she was unaware, and clutched her, kissing her hair.

Fitzwilliam knelt beside them and he laid his hand on Darcy's shoulder. "Her fainting made him remember his purpose I would imagine. He was here to rob you, not assault Elizabeth. I think that his fate is sealed by that alone, there is no need to expose her story."

Darcy continued to hold her possessively and nodded. "Could you ask Foster to send for the magistrate? I will be upstairs with Elizabeth." He lifted her into his arms and stood, then glanced at Wickham who was beginning to revive. "Make sure that the magistrate knows that the silver knife in his waistcoat is mine, that he has attempted to steal it before; and it is worth . . ."

"More than the five shillings required to guarantee him the hangman's noose. I think the burglary is enough of a crime on its own." Fitzwilliam nodded and looked down at the man. "Of course it may mean transportation instead of death."

"As long as he is gone, I do not care." Darcy kissed Elizabeth's brow. "Come my love, we are going upstairs."

She burrowed against his neck. "Why are you here? I thought that you would be gone for hours."

"And I thought that you were going to your aunt." He blinked hard and hugged her tightly to him. "Dearest Elizabeth." He whispered.

"Sir, what has happened?" Foster arrived from the basement and stared in horror at his mistress's appearance and his master's distress.

Darcy's demeanour instantly sharpened and fixing his steely glare on his senior servant, spoke in a cold angry voice. "Wickham apparently easily entered this house. He attacked Mrs. Darcy and attempted to rob me. I want every door and window checked. I want to know how he was able to violate this home, I want to know why no member of the staff heard what was happening in my study, and I want to know who is responsible for disobeying my orders that the house be guarded at all times. This man is exactly the one I wished to keep out. It is by His grace that nothing tragic transpired."

"Yes sir." Foster said diffidently and bowed as Darcy swept by and began rapidly taking the steps. Mrs. Mercer followed closely behind.

"Is there anything that I may do for you or Mrs. Darcy, sir? Does she require a physician?"

Darcy stopped and looked at Elizabeth, his expression was that of the master, and he clearly would not brook opposition from anyone, even his wife. "Yes, please send for Mr. Gates." Mrs. Mercer hurried away and Darcy continued to look at her. "It is high time that someone determine what is wrong, Elizabeth. I will not bear this torture any longer. You are wasting away before my eyes."

"Fitzwilliam, I am well, truly. I felt better this morning."

"Shh, you would not have missed seeing your aunt if you felt well after breakfast. We never should have indulged our desires." His mask slipped and he pressed her head to his chest. Attempting to contain his emotion, he continued to their bedchamber. Gently he laid her on the bed, then sat down by her side. A maid appeared and relit the fire, another came in bearing a tea tray. Millie entered and offered to help Elizabeth change into a night dress and robe. All the while Darcy did not move; and after she was changed, he sat with her hands tightly in his grasp. When the commotion died he leaned forward and gently kissed her bruised mouth. "What did he do to you?"

"Fitzwilliam . . ."

"No Lizzy, I will not have you bury the memory of this incident. I want it completely exposed to the light of day, now, when it is vividly etched in your mind. If you talk about it now, it will not haunt your dreams or influence your behaviour. Tell me everything."

Elizabeth was struck by how calm and serious he was, and his manner gave her the strength to be the same. She felt his steady grip and staring straight into the blue of his eyes told him moment by moment the details of the assault. When she finished, his jaw was clenched and she could see it working, it was the only visible expression of his tightly controlled fury.

"May I see your arm, dear? Is it painful?"

"It is sore, but nothing more." He helped her to open the robe, then drew it down her left shoulder. It was red, and there was evidence of bruises forming, but it was not too ugly. Darcy closed his eyes in relief, then leaned forward and kissed over the marks and looking up to her bent head, gently kissed her mouth.

"So much better." She sighed and slipped her arms around his neck as he slipped his around her waist. Her jaw was tender, but she would never deny either of them this much needed assurance that all would be well. Darcy slowly kissed her then remembering that they would soon be interrupted, withdrew to hold her cheek in his palm and caress her lips with his thumb. "I love you." She whispered.

"Dear Elizabeth, I cannot express the depth of my love for you." He heard a knock at the door and Mrs. Mercer opened it. Instantly his master's voice returned. "Is the physician here?"

"Yes sir, shall I show him in?"

"No, I wish to speak to him first." He turned back to Elizabeth, smiled slightly and kissed her. "I will not be long."

Darcy stood and strode from the room, and left her alone. "This has changed you, Fitzwilliam." Elizabeth said softly. "I have a feeling that the master of Pemberley has fully assumed his role."

"TELL ME WICKHAM, what drove you to attempt something so foolish?" Fitzwilliam sat comfortably in a chair, his sword pointed in the vicinity of Wickham's heart, and sipped casually on a glass of port.

"Darcy owed me."

"He did nothing of the sort. You accepted his terms fair and square. If you are a poor negotiator, it is hardly his fault."

"His father said quite clearly what I was to receive."

"Indeed he did, and Darcy held up his end. Come on there is more to it than the living. Is this revenge for Darcy exposing your origins to Singleton? I did it at the club, why not rob me?" He chuckled. "Not brave enough to storm a barracks, are you? What drove you to lie to that Bingley woman? Of all the stories you could have told her to get that dowry, you had to claim a connection to Darcy? You should have known that one way or another that would get back to him and he would correct it. If I were you I would have moved on to another pigeon once I heard of the connection."

Shrugging, Wickham eyed the sword. "It was a risk, and it very nearly was successful. Women with that kind of dowry are rarely so unprotected; besides, he was so caught up with his mistress . . ."

"Watch it Wickham." The sword lifted and pushed in his waistcoat. "You do not ever insult Mrs. Darcy. Call him or me for that matter any name you wish, but that woman will not be maligned, not in my presence, let alone her husband's."

"I have tasted better." Wickham sneered then cried out when Fitzwilliam flicked the tip of the blade expertly along his throat, drawing blood. He clapped his hand to the wound. "What the hell are you doing?"

"I once thought that you were clever, but that statement proves me wrong. Consider your next words carefully. If we had caught you assaulting Mrs. Darcy, you would be dead now by my, if not Darcy's, hand. If you are fortunate, you may only be travelling to Australia."

"Why?" Wickham's eyes grew wide, and he watched the blade move and tap the silver knife on the desk. "I . . . I did not take it!"

"Yes you did, and look around you; the room is hardly in pristine condition. Robbery is a hanging offence, I believe." He smiled. "I wager that you could not find the key."

"Key?" Wickham swallowed hard.

"Key, Wickham." Darcy entered the room and removed a key from his pocket. "This one, as a matter of fact." He walked over to the strongbox and looking straight at Wickham, released the lock and lifted the lid. He glanced at the contents for a moment and then turned it towards his prisoner. "Which of Father's journals did you wish to read?"

"Journals?" He cried in dismay.

"Were you expecting gold or jewels?" Darcy laughed derisively and held up a worn book. "You gave up your life for this."

"But . . . that was full of jewels! I know it! I saw them!"

"Yes, I know." Darcy snarled. "My uncle told me. And when Richard noticed you hanging around the house one day, I sent him word to move that strongbox, and put this one in its place." He looked down at the books and back at Wickham. "My father gave you so much, and you have wasted it all." Leaning down he examined the blood trickling down his neck, and the bruises forming on his face. "You touched my wife." He said in a low voice. Wickham cringed. Never before had he seen Darcy so furious, but it was the control he exerted that terrified him. Suddenly Darcy grabbed his arm and twisted it behind his back. "How does it feel?" Wickham cried out in pain. Darcy ignored his begging, wrenching it further.

"Shall I hold him while you break it?" Fitzwilliam offered.

"Why not?" Darcy nodded.

"NO!" Wickham plead as Fitzwilliam stood and held him steady. The cousin's eyes met. Darcy let go of Wickham's arm and smashed his fist into the bastard's mouth. Blood dripped from his lips and teeth hung loosely from their sockets.

"Well done," Fitzwilliam smiled, "a payback from Elizabeth?"

"From both of us." Darcy flexed his fingers and stepped back to the desk, using his handkerchief to wipe off his hand while Wickham whimpered and held his face.

"Sir, the magistrate is here with his men." Foster announced.

The magistrate took in the scene, made note of the silver knife, made further note that Mrs. Darcy was injured and took the physician's name, but agreed that there was enough with the robbery that she likely would not be needed to prosecute. Soon Wickham was clapped in irons and led out to a closed wagon, cursing Darcy all the way. When he was gone Darcy stood in the middle of the study looking around at the mess that was left in his wake and at last let down his stance. Fitzwilliam approached with glasses and a bottle, and they sank into chairs. "Rather a shame that the magistrate appeared when he did, I think that you might have carried on for some time." He smiled to see his Darcy's eyes flick over him. "I know, you are no man of violence, and would prefer to have the law handle it, but it was sweet, and good for you to strike him yourself. I do not care to imagine what might have happened if you had not forgotten . . ."

Darcy held up his hand. "Please Richard; do not even let your thoughts drift in that direction. Mine are vivid enough. She was to be out this morning, but felt ill again after I departed." The weight of what had almost happened finally hit him. "I was going to surprise her with . . .and I might have returned to find . . . oh God!" He pounded his fists on his desk, and some of the scattered papers were pushed aside, revealing Elizabeth's open journal. Wiping his eyes with the back of his hand, he pulled it forward to read her unfinished thoughts.

2 October 1809

Today is my Fitzwilliam's twenty-fifth birthday, and I think that I may never surpass the gift I have for him. I felt something when I awakened; it was like a butterfly beating its wings rapidly inside of me. Aunt told me to expect this, but not for another month. It is probably my imagination, it likely is, but considering everything that I am feeling and Aunt's words, I think it is certain now, I am carrying our baby. I pray that Fitzwilliam will not be frightened and will instead rejoice in this miracle. He will be a wonderful loving father; just as he is a husband. I cannot wait to see him hold our child, our love in his arms. I can just imagine his eyes now, so overwhelmed with feeling. Do not fear my dear love, I will not leave you.

Looking up to Fitzwilliam, the raw emotion was evident. "What is it, Darcy?"

"Elizabeth is with child." He said numbly. "That is why she has been ill. That is why . . . Wickham might have taken them both from me!" Darcy jumped to his feet and looked wildly about the room.

"What are you doing?" Fitzwilliam was immediately at his side and gripping his arm.

"I will kill him!"

"Darcy, it is out of your hands, the courts will take care of him. Hire a solicitor to look after your interests . . . Stewart; he will certainly know how to handle this properly. The last thing that your wife needs is you going mad with worry and acting foolishly. You had your chance at him." He watched Darcy's fingers begin to twist his ring mercilessly. Fitzwilliam sighed and stepped away to find their glasses. "Come, you should return to her side to celebrate, but first let us toast this new heir!"

"Or heiress." Darcy whispered.

"Indeed!" Richard smiled. "To the newest member of the Darcy family, may this child enjoy a long and happy life, as his parents undoubtedly will!" Darcy met his eyes. Richard spoke urgently. "Come on man, all will be well."

"Mr. Darcy? Mr. Gates will see you." Foster stood aside as his master moved swiftly from the room and back up the stairs. Gates was just closing the door to the bedchamber when he arrived.

"How is she?" Darcy demanded. "Is she well, is the child well?"

"You know? Mrs. Darcy said that you were unaware."

"I just learned." He shot a look at the door. "Well?"

"She is fine sir. Her arm will likely be sore for a few days, but no lasting harm was done, and I suspect her mouth will be visibly fine in a matter of hours, although likely tender for some time, he held her in such a way that she could not close it while . . ." Seeing Darcy's fury rising, he moved on. "It is the fright that concerns me. Women have been known to miscarry after a fright, you know. As long as she remains at rest I think she will be fine. Of course we have treatments for her if the worst happens."

"Treatments?" He whispered.

"Bleeding of course; and ice baths amongst other things."

Darcy stared at him then drew himself up. "I am sure that those things will be unnecessary. My wife will be well."

"Of course, I only mention them so you are prepared." Mr. Gates looked him over. "She is far more concerned about you than herself. I suggest that you have your faculties intact before returning. Perhaps some port?"

"I am fine, sir." Darcy said quietly. "Is there anything else? Her general health, it was affected by the pregnancy?"

"Yes, but it should be recovering now that she is so far along. The baby will come in April." He waited for a response and not receiving one, cleared his throat. "I doubt that you will have further need of me unless . . ."

"They will be fine." Darcy said decisively. "Thank you, sir. I will see you out."

"I know my way. Should you need anything, please send for me."

Darcy nodded and watched him go, then taking a calming breath, opened the chamber door to see her sitting up on the bed and smiling softly with her arms open to receive him. "Elizabeth."

Chapter 5

arcy buried his face deeper into Elizabeth's hair and drank in her sweet familiar scent. He was sitting on the edge of the bed and had her small form encompassed in his embrace, but it was *her* arms that were giving the support, *her* hand gently stroking his head, and *her* soft whispers that were providing the comfort. "This is wrong; I should be wiping your tears, not the other way around."

"You wish that I cry?"

"Of course not, but you were the one who faced him."

"But fortunately our baby saved me from him continuing and gave you time to end it."

"Dearest, if I had not returned when I did, I cannot bear to think what may have happened." Darcy drew away and looked at her seriously. "I will not ever let another person harm you."

"And how exactly will you manage that?" She smiled and taking his hands in hers, examined the bruises that had formed. "Will you fight every man who looks at me?"

"If necessary." He said in a low voice. "I am ashamed that my wife was not safe in her own home. I am infuriated that he entered and violated these walls. I have failed you."

"Nonsense." Elizabeth said quietly. "Every door and window is shut up tightly. You anticipated this happening. You prepared as well you could."

"No, no, the staff did not take this as seriously . . ."

"Fitzwilliam, when was this house last burglarized?"

His brow creased. "Never."

"Then perhaps if the staff was negligent, it is because they had no expectation . . ."

"It does not matter dearest, they had their orders. How could they not have wondered what on earth was happening in the study?" He closed his eyes. "He was beating the box with a piece of marble! And it was no feather, I know, I purchased it on my tour . . ."

"You know that they will not enter a room if they know we are within." Darcy gave her a look of exasperation. "Very well, yes you are correct, I was alone in the room, and they could have knocked . . . but dearest, do you not see, you are looking to blame someone besides Mr. Wickham for this."

"No, I know who to blame, I blame myself!" Darcy's jaw set and he stared down at her hands. "How could I put you in such danger? Never, never again."

"And what do you intend to do? Never leave my side? Hire some ex-soldier to follow me around the house? Deny me my freedom to assuage your guilt? Guilt that you have no business carrying?" He looked up to her and she saw all manner of emotion playing in them. "Fitzwilliam?"

"Forgive me." He said softly. "I am terrified, and when I am this way, I say things without thinking of the impact upon those who are listening. I allow my feelings to rule and I . . ." He caressed her face. "I do not form my thoughts properly. I have trained myself to close off my feelings and not react at all. It has been a long time since I have felt so out of control. This is your doing, you know. It is because of you that I lost the power to hide all emotion."

"Oh?" She smiled and he nodded as he continued on to stroke her hair. "How have I bewitched you?"

"Countless ways." His eyes travelled over her face. "But most of all, you have become the voice in my mind. I need that voice. I am so proud of you, dear Elizabeth." She blushed and he smiled to see it. "How are you? How can you let me prattle on about my fears? You are far too generous, love. Please tell me what you are feeling."

"I . . .right now I feel relief. I am safe with you." She smiled and he held her hands, and fixed his gaze upon her. "You will not allow me to let it go at that?"

"Is that what you wish to do? Right now?" He squeezed and she felt his strength flowing through her. "I will do whatever you desire, love. But when you falter, when you need to let your guard down, know that I will care for you. You need not pretend with me."

"So I do not need to find your discarded mask?" Darcy smiled and she nodded. "Very well . . . I just do not care to speak of it anymore today."

Darcy wrapped her back up in his arms. "But you will think and dream about it."

"And that is when I will need you to hold me just as you are now." Elizabeth kissed his ear, and he nuzzled in closer. "I was terrified, Fitzwilliam. But he is gone forever. I . . . I would rather concentrate on this new person who has come between us."

"Who?" Darcy drew back and searched her eyes. "Who has come between us?"

"Well, I do not know, Will. Do you wish for a boy or a girl?" She smiled and caressed his face, and seeing his eyes close, took his hand and placed it on her belly. "Do you remember when you showed me my rooms? Do you remember standing in the doorway to the nursery and speaking softly about us having children someday?"

"Yes."

"What changed you from that sweet wistfulness to this tremendous fear that you display for your cousins and me?"

Darcy opened his eyes to find her loving steady gaze. "You were ill one night and . . . It was the first time I had seen you succumb to illness and it frightened me. It brought back all of the memories of my mother's death. Not so long afterwards we learned of Audrey and . . .all those fears just became overwhelming to me. I cannot lose you, Elizabeth. I cannot bear to stop loving you either, but that act has left you . . ."

"Pregnant with our child, the product of our love." She kissed his lips and he gratefully kissed her back.

"It does not hurt for me to kiss you?" He whispered.

"Not at all. See? I think it is better already, do you agree?" She took his hand to touch her mouth and he nodded. "Do you fear being like your father or Mr. Harwick?"

"Deeply."

"Well if I am like my mother and my grandmothers, I will be fine. When I was talking to Aunt about childbearing, Uncle came into the room and started telling a story about how his mother was up from her bed and giving orders to the maid a half-hour after Mama was born and he is without doubt that I have similar mettle." She smiled and wiped the tear that escaped his eye. "I am frightened too, but I promise that I will be strong for you if you are for me."

"I can be anything for you." He kissed her. "I cannot stop worrying, please do not ask me to try, I will fail."

"So how will this worry manifest itself?" She sat back and he wiped her tears, then took her hands safely in his. "Will you follow me about, carrying a cushion for my aching back?"

"I will carry you everywhere." He smiled a little.

"Oh so *your* back will ache instead?" She laughed. "That will not do, not at all." Darcy said nothing, only looking down at their clasped hands and running his thumb over her ring. "Will, I need you."

Darcy's head lifted and he nodded. "I love you."

"I love you." They kissed and Darcy pulled himself together while they both reached to wipe each other's eyes again. "Elizabeth . . . May I ask, why did your uncle know of your preg . . . our baby before I? Why did you tell him? Were you afraid I would be angry?"

"No, the last emotion I expected from you was anger." She saw his attention was fully focussed on her and sighed. "I did not tell my uncle, I imagine that Aunt must have said something to him. He brought up the story of my grandmother on his own. Aunt recognized the signs of my condition and we talked about it."

"You talked about me." Darcy's brow creased and he looked away. "I am a problem to be discussed."

She recognized his hurt. "Forgive me, but surely you understand that a woman would give me the advice I needed, especially my aunt who I trust so much."

"I thought that you could speak to me about anything." He looked back down to their hands.

"I thought so as well. I have been trying to deny the truth of this for weeks."

Darcy's head shot up. "Why? You want our child do you not?"

"Yes, but . . . Oh Fitzwilliam, you were not giving me the impression that you did. I was so afraid that to tell you my suspicions would, well I do not know exactly what you would do. I do not have enough experience with you to know all of your moods and behaviours, after all, see what you have confessed to me today? If I had come to you before we left Pemberley and told you my suspicions, what would you have done?"

Darcy remained silent, and his face was unreadable as he stared into her eyes. "I would have gone for a long ride."

She nodded and looked at him thoughtfully. "That makes perfect sense; I have twice found you in the park walking when you were upset."

Three times. Darcy nodded. "But that was before we were together." She smiled and he tilted his head. "You also walk when you are in need of relief, I know. We share these habits."

"We do." Elizabeth admitted. "So, you would have left me alone after telling you this momentous news and I would have been . . ."

"Devastated." He closed his eyes. "You do know me so well, Elizabeth. You knew that to tell me your suspicions was to invite misery, not joy. Forgive me for ever giving you the impression that I could not be your confidant." Darcy hugged her to him. "I never want you to feel alone like that again. I understand you wishing to speak with your aunt about such a subject. That makes perfect sense. I may have needed to walk but you know, I hope, that I would have returned to talk. You know that I might take time to find the words but that I will eventually."

She smiled then caressed his soft hair. "I suppose in a case such as this, I was unwilling to wait for eventually."

"So you avoided the discussion altogether." He smiled and stroked her cheek. "That is very unlike you."

Elizabeth groaned. "Well at least it did not spill out in a moment of vitriol! I have been working hard to control my tongue before my thoughts tumble out."

Darcy laughed softly and feeling better, sat up straight and squeezed her hands. "Every moment I find ways that we are similar! Tell me what you contemplated saying to me. Give me your worst."

"Oh, no." Her eyes grew wide.

"Come now, love. It was not in your journal, so you were holding it back. Were you cursing me for being unreasonably fearful? Were you furious because any other man would be thrilled to hear that his potential heir was coming?

Please do not tell me that you were afraid I would be angry? After all, I have been quite enthusiastic engaging in our marital duties."

"It is hardly a duty, Will."

"No, not at all." He kissed her and smiled. "Come woman, vent your spleen!" She shook her head. "Why not?"

"Because you enjoy seeing me angry too much."

"And you deny me my pleasure as your revenge." He smiled and saw a triumphant gleam come to her eyes. "Clever, dearest."

"I am glad that you recognize that." Elizabeth caressed his face with her fingers and he captured her hand to kiss. "Now, would you please call for Millie? I need to dress for your birthday dinner."

"What? Oh, Lizzy, no, no, we cannot possibly have a dinner, we cannot celebrate . . ."

"Not celebrate? The day of your birth? Are you addled? I intend to celebrate this day with great joy!" She pushed him a little and when he did not move she glared. "Fitzwilliam Darcy! George Wickham will not ruin this day for me! I refused to allow your cousin to ruin your name, and I will not let this, this jealous fool take my Fitzwilliam's birthday! Now, I am getting up and dressing. I suggest that you . . .go repair your attire." She gave him another shove. "Go on, then!"

Darcy smiled and then he chuckled, he was not being denied the allure of her anger after all. Her strength was nothing to his weight and she succeeded in little more than rocking him, but she was determined. When her feet began pushing his bottom he at last stood. "Are you sure? I can send word to the Gardiners . . ."

"You clearly are not listening, sir." She sighed.

"Sir?" He leaned down to look in her eyes.

"SIR!" She declared.

Darcy kissed her and nodded. "Very well."

"And Fitzwilliam, I know that you will want to investigate how he could have entered the house and discipline the staff, but that can wait for cooler heads, can it not?"

"You must allow me to do my duty as master, Elizabeth." He said slowly.

"But the house is my domain, as are the servants, are they not?" She tilted her head and observed him.

"I . . . we will discuss this tomorrow." He saw her smile. "Do not think that you have won yet."

"No, not yet." Her smile grew and he shook his head and pulled the bell cord before leaving the room with a loud sigh.

"SO THAT EXPLAINS IT." Mr. Gardiner mused while Fitzwilliam poured out his wine. "I knew there was some tension in the air that I have not noticed here before. The staff is on tenterhooks."

"They are waiting for dismissals, I suspect." Fitzwilliam held up the decanter to Darcy who shook his head. "When will you lower the boom?"

"Elizabeth will not let me." Darcy rested his chin on his folded hands. "At least, she demands that she make the decision with my advice."

"So she will decide." Mr. Gardiner smiled and Darcy's face was blank. "Perhaps you should demand the staff to investigate what may have happened."

"My butler already has, the only possible entry was through the kitchens. It was pure chance that nobody saw him. Wickham undoubtedly knew his way around."

"So it is an unfortunate accident."

"I would not characterize it so if Elizabeth had suffered more than a twisted arm and a memory that no amount of kissing will erase." Darcy said coldly.

"I did not mean to trivialize the incident Darcy. Clearly more happened here than you are willing to disclose, and I respect your decision to maintain your privacy. What is to be done?" Mr. Gardiner asked and was greeted by silence as Darcy worked to control his tongue. He cleared his throat and turned his attention to Fitzwilliam. "Tell me, what brought you back in time?"

"Oh, Darcy and I were on our way to look over an empty townhouse for a friend and then we were going to stop at the artist's studio and pick up the miniatures of their portraits. Darcy drew an absolute blank on the address when we left the townhouse so we were just going to drop in and confirm it before heading back out." Fitzwilliam settled in his chair and waved. "We returned to find Wickham at the desk and Elizabeth on the floor." The two men studied Darcy staring at the spot. "I was curious, why were your father's journals in the strongbox? I was wondering what was in there when I made the switch."

"They are precious." Darcy said quietly.

"I suppose that the jewels have been moved from where I hid them?" Fitzwilliam saw Darcy look up and back down again. "Not telling anyone? Well as long as somebody knows, else there will be a regular treasure hunt someday."

"Elizabeth knows everything. And she will outlive me." He said determinedly. "She will be strong and well for many years. I will *not* spend the rest of my life kneeling at her grave as my father did with my mother."

"She told you of the baby." Mr. Gardiner spoke softly.

"Yes, and apparently your wife informed you." Darcy said unhappily.

"Ah, I surmised the subject when I came upon my wife speaking to Lizzy about pregnancy, and seeing her unease with my presence told a story of my mother. Later that evening Marianne confirmed the news I suspected. Well, undoubtedly you will have the same problem I do, Marianne and I share nearly every worry with each other. You realize that you do Lizzy no favours by being so fearful. Stop it now."

"Good sense tells me that you are correct. But, do you not worry? I do not know about you, but I have experienced the death of my mother through childbirth, two of my siblings were stillborn, two more were lost to illness, I am acutely aware of the risks. Elizabeth, may God bless her, admits her fears, but blissfully believes that it could not possibly happen to her. It is not just surviving the birth, but also avoiding the fevers and disease that may come afterwards. That is what claimed my mother." Darcy ran his hand through his hair. "You have been through this many times, I know that you love your wife, how do you survive?"

Mr. Gardiner laughed. "I rejoice, Darcy. Now do not look at me with such disbelief! Granted, I know the risks and possibilities, but I choose not to dwell upon them. I honestly need Marianne to pull me down from the clouds I am so delighted! It is the most extraordinary miracle, do you not understand? Loving your wife creates . . . life!" He smiled and shook his head. "I understand your fears, Son, I do. But Lizzy is no more your mother than she is hers. She is a glorious and strong individual, she is desperate to express her joy, but is holding it back for fear of your reaction. She wants this for you."

"How do you know this?"

"I just told you, I have a wife who talks to me, just as yours wishes to do." He tilted his head, "At least my wife is not afraid to speak of any subject that concerns us."

"Elizabeth is not afraid of me!" Darcy growled.

"Is that so?" Mr. Gardiner raised his brows. "Prove it."

Fitzwilliam sat up and chuckled, then outright laughed. "Well done, sir! Well done! Come on Darcy, admit it, you are just dying to be excited about this. You just have to give yourself permission to do it! I am thrilled with the thought of being an uncle and corrupting these little ones!"

Darcy smiled and looked at his hands. "You will not corrupt my children, Richard."

"Ah, that's the spirit! You have just multiplied your brood, that bodes well, does it not?" Fitzwilliam laughed. "I cannot wait to take your boys riding! And to teach them how to fence and box!"

"I will teach my boys those things, Richard!" Darcy declared. "And you are not getting anywhere near my girls!"

"Would you care to bet on that? I look forward to bouncing them on my knee and telling them stories to make their eyes grow wide and squeal in horror before begging for more!"

"If anyone is to entertain my girls with . . ." Darcy stood and strode out of the room.

Mr. Gardiner laughed and Fitzwilliam stood. "Well that was entertaining." They walked down to the sitting room to find Darcy on the sofa with Elizabeth, holding her hands and complaining loudly about Fitzwilliam.

"There he is! There is the one who wishes to corrupt our children!" He pointed. "Trust me Lizzy, I grew up with him, he is evil."

"Oh that is just the red coat." Elizabeth laughed and squeezed his hands. "You are a sweet, gentle soul, are you not Richard?"

"I am." He lifted his chin. "And I will gladly entertain your children . . ." Darcy glared at him and Richard stopped. "Well at least let me tell them the story of my pearl." He pointed to the pendant hanging around Elizabeth's neck.

She raised her brow and pursed her lips while meeting Darcy's eye. "Perhaps Fitzwilliam would like to tell that story himself."

Darcy smiled. "I would. I would and I will." He reached out and hugged her tight. "I will try not to worry so much, my love."

"Thank you." Elizabeth rested her head against his chest. "Because I intend to be very happy."

12 OCTOBER 1809
At last we have arrived home. The journey back was far more pleasant than the one to town. Naturally knowing the reason behind Elizabeth's misery is a great part of that, and her health seems to have largely improved, her pallor is once again rosy, her appetite has returned, and above all, she is at last free to express the joy she feels for our child. Not only does she radiate happiness, but she has managed to make me feel it as well. I find myself drinking in her laughter and feeling that warmth chasing away my fears, or perhaps it is better to say the light is keeping the shadows of my fear at bay. The only darkness that falls upon us now are our dreams. We continue to comfort each other.

I found in my stack of correspondence a letter from Stewart. He has his contacts and through them will receive regular reports on Wickham and how he fares. Seemingly the inmates at Newgate have taken to him, so at last he is amongst his own. I am sure that before long he will cheat them as well, and find that they will grow fond of ruining the remains of his good looks with whatever means they have available. Stewart discovered that a woman regularly visits him, bringing baskets of food and funds to pay for his care and remove his shackles. She has not as yet been identified but he feels, and I agree, that it is best to be sure of her name. Wickham would not be beyond seeking revenge through an agent, although the chances of him escaping his gaol are unlikely. I cannot imagine him owning anything worthy of bribery, but one never knows, and Stewart told me that for a large enough sum, prisoners are given leave to exit the jail for a time. Why they would willingly return is beyond me. His trial is set for November, I have hired a solicitor recommended by Stewart to represent my interests and he will find a serjeant to serve as prosecutor. He expresses regret that as a barrister, he cannot appear for me, but will do all that he can to assure success. Of course, I realize that he is acting as much if not more for Elizabeth than I, and I will not fault him that at all. He will be at Pemberley in a week, and I look forward to his news.

Longbourn was different on our return trip to collect Jane. With Mary gone and Jane leaving, I believe that I saw something akin to panic in the eyes of Kitty. She took Elizabeth aside and asked if she might come to Pemberley as well. It seems that with her there alone with Lydia, she would become the preferred target of her mother's ire and she felt unable to rise to Elizabeth's level of strength and Mary or Jane's level of serenity. Elizabeth promised her that she would write to her weekly and she would ask their father to keep Mrs. Bennet in check. Miss Lucas and Miss Maria arrived to greet Elizabeth and farewell Jane, and were accompanied by their brother. We were introduced and he said that he remembered me from Cambridge, although I did not recall him. We spent some minutes discussing shared memories and then he begged my opinions on estate management, as I took advantage of his opinion on Netherfield. It was a satisfying and pleasantly unexpected conversation. When they took their leave, I resigned myself to visiting Mr. Bennet, while Elizabeth enjoyed her time with her sisters. I offered once again to aid him with the girls' dowries and he refused, stating that he will not take away from Elizabeth's children because he was negligent with his own. His recognition that Elizabeth was with child clearly struck him deeply. It was then that I realized something had changed in him. Perhaps this and news of Wickham's attack were the final events required for him to see his responsibilities. I noticed that he offered me ale, not port, and that his book was worn. He made no mention of it, but I believe that economizing was underway. We rejoined the ladies and I was pleased to see that he remained. Perhaps life at Longbourn is improving at last.

Elizabeth settled back into Darcy's chair, missing him since early that morning when he rode out with Nichols. "Your chair is no substitute for your arms, my love." She read over the passage again and considered the subjects that plagued him. He was telling her of his worry, but was trying to remain positive, that was good. He worried over her sisters, which truly amazed her. Perhaps when the baby came Kitty could come to stay. She smiled to see that little hint of jealousy that remained for Mr. Stewart. "You will never quite let that go will you? I suppose that he will have to be married and a father himself before you are satisfied!" She then thought of her father. He was different, it was hard to put her finger on it, but it was something that resembled pride. "Perhaps he is pleased with the efforts he is at last exerting to care for the family. Maybe by April Kitty will not wish to escape Longbourn."

She looked at the miniatures on the desk of his mother and sister, and then turned her eyes to see the newly placed painting of her face, and wondered how often he might be stopped in his work to gaze upon her. "That is not vanity. That is love. I know that I shall study your portrait constantly."

Remembering how he had stood behind her for those long hours of posing, she smiled. His thumb continuously teased her throat and shoulders, and if she just closed her eyes, she could imagine his touch and the scent of him surrounding her. What she did not realize was that when the artist had declared he no longer needed Darcy's presence and would focus on Elizabeth, he felt compelled to remain, and did not trust a maid to keep her company. He watched the man's eyes as they flicked continuously from his wife to the canvas.

He listened to the banter between the two, knowing that it would lend a sparkle to her eyes that he wished to have captured, but hating any man who could bring about that smile in her voice.

"Lizzy?" Jane called from outside in the hallway. "Are you here somewhere?"

"In here, Jane!"

Jane peeked around the corner and was about to leave when she spotted Elizabeth's small form buried within the great chair. "Does Fitzwilliam mind you in his chair?"

"Oh yes, he does." Elizabeth laughed. "But he loves it as well."

"That makes no sense." Jane entered further and looked around nervously at the intensely masculine room. "Should we be in here?"

"Of course, I answer my correspondence with him here. Are you uncomfortable? We can leave if you like." Elizabeth stood and she paused to put the ribbon in place before closing his journal.

"Should you bring that with you?"

"No, it is his. I read it daily." Elizabeth laughed to see Jane's astonishment. "My goodness Jane, will I do nothing today that does not shock you?"

"I am beginning to wonder." Jane clasped her hands and thought over her next words. "Lizzy, does Fitzwilliam like me?"

"Well, yes of course he does. Has he indicated otherwise?"

"No, he . . . He is just so quiet around me. I think that I make him uncomfortable. The trip here, he barely spoke."

Elizabeth tried to relieve her tension. "Oh. Surely you know how shy and restrained he is by now."

"Yes, I suppose . . . except when you are near."

"Well we know each other particularly well, would you not say?" She smiled. "Fitzwilliam will warm; you must realize that the two of you really have not spent a great deal of time together." They walked out into the hallway and Elizabeth led the way to a discreetly placed set of stairs near the dining room, and down to Mrs. Reynolds' office. "Are you ready to learn your mistress duties?"

"Your duties." Jane smiled. "I can only imagine what all is entailed with this home."

Elizabeth laughed as she knocked on the door. "Well whatever you imagine, quadruple it."

HARWICK WATCHED EVANGELINE fold her letter and then stare pensively outside at the leaves slowly swirling along the ground. When she failed to move after several minutes he cleared his throat. "Eva, do you wish to come to Pemberley with me? Would you rather not meet the colonel?"

"How did you know?"

"Know what? That you are receiving letters from him?" Harwick smiled. "He wrote to me with the news that he would be writing to you in August."

"He did?" Eva's hand fell over her heart and she looked back down to the letter in her hand. "He . . . He wished to be . . ."

"Unquestionably honest." He set down his paper and moved to sit beside her.

"What did he tell you?" She asked quietly.

"He said that you have his devotion, whether you accept it or not." Taking her hand in his, Harwick squeezed. "Eva, please do not feel obligated to stay with me. I will remarry, I must. I was a fool to think that I could do so without affection, and I was wrong to ever approach Miss Bennet."

"No, no you were not. She was a reasonable choice for what you felt you needed at the time. I was probably wrong to discourage you from her."

Harwick laughed. "As I recall you were quite determined to do just that. No Eva, I searched my soul while I tried to accept a fate that my heart would not allow. Ellen would have been so unhappy to see me lonely forever. I will do as she bids me to do every time I talk with her. I will find a woman who fills up my soul and makes me whole again. I think that I may have met her, and I think that she feels the same for me. And now . . . I am at last ready for her."

"Who is she?"

"Miss Laura Stewart. She will be at Pemberley and . . . if she is as she was when we last saw each other; I think that I will be ready to begin again with her."

"Oh Daniel!" Evangeline threw her arms around him tightly. "I cannot tell you how happy that makes me! Miss Stewart is a lovely woman, and she has so many interests in common with you! I know that she loves to ride, I have seen her in the park so many times with her brother, and she is so friendly. I know that Mrs. Darcy has taken to her, so that must be a good sign and . . ."

"Eva, Eva, slow down!" Harwick laughed. "I know all of these things and so many more. I do not require any convincing at all. I think that we could be . . ." His eyes welled up with emotion. "Very happy."

The two siblings hugged and Evangeline held him while his shoulders shook. "I have thought so long about this, and . . .talked to Ellen. I read her letters and her journals and I found a note where she even spoke of her love for me and her desire that should she leave me . . .that I should find love again." He sniffed and turned his head away to wipe his eyes. "I was not able to read her thoughts until we returned here in August. I just was not ready, but after I met Miss Stewart, I felt my heart beat again. That was when I felt that I could see what Ellen . . ." He sniffed and pulled himself together, and cleared his throat. Looking up he smiled and wiped his sister's tears. "So, you see my dear, I feel that my days as a widower may be coming to an end. What about your days as a widow? What do you fear?"

"I have control over my destiny now. I do not have to bend to the will of any man. I control my money; I have a home for life in town, I can do anything I wish. If your dreams come true, I will leave Meadowbrook and go to my townhouse."

"And do what, dear?" He whispered. "You need family around you. If you did not you would have been in that house years ago."

"You needed me."

"I did, but you were here for a year before Ellen died. You, for all your declarations of independence are not a woman who likes to be alone. You are strong because your husband forced you to become that way, but falling in love again, or for the first time," Harwick squeezed her hand and she looked up, "will not make you weak. I know Fitzwilliam; he is a strong, loyal, and honest man. I can imagine that there are layers of pain beneath his uniform that ache for relief. He assured me that his injuries, while no longer life-threatening, made him unfit for battle. He will not be leaving the country again. It is safe to care for him. And clearly Eva," Harwick took the crumpled letter she held in her grasp, "he cares for you."

"He does. He told me so."

"Ah." Harwick waited and he saw the longing raging in her eyes. "Give him a chance, dear. And perhaps by the time I have finished wooing Miss Stewart, you will be ready to find your home at last."

"Maybe." Evangeline whispered. "Will you be long, do you think?"

He laughed loudly and hugged her. "Oh dear, I have no idea!"

19 October 1809
Our guests begin to arrive today; I look forward to it, not just because these are our friends and family, but also because having more people here will give me more time with Fitzwilliam. With Jane as our only guest, we have felt obligated to remain with her, and we have had no opportunity to steal away for walks alone or even to simply sit together in his study and answer correspondence. It feels very much as it did when we were first engaged, and Jane is our chaperone once again. I suppose that we simply do not wish to inspire her disapproving words as we did before when we displayed our feelings. Without a doubt Fitzwilliam is growing impatient with the constrictions and I notice that he seems to urge me to retire earlier and earlier each night, for my health, of course. And naturally, he must accompany me. Perhaps with more guests in the house, they may entertain each other and we can return to enjoying some moments alone beyond the cloak of darkness.

Darcy's lips twitched and he placed the ribbon on the page then looked up to notice Elizabeth's eyes sparkling at him from across the room. He nodded emphatically, and delighted to hear warm laughter erupt from behind the hand she pressed to her mouth. Clearing his throat, he glanced at Jane's curious expression then back to Elizabeth. "What news does Mary's letter bring?"

"She is getting along fairly well. The other girls were impressed with her wardrobe, and Georgiana made it clear that Mary was her sister, so nobody has delved too deeply into the subject of Longbourn. She looks the part it seems, and she has decided that it is not deceitful to leave them to their conjectures so long as she does not proclaim herself to be something other than she is."

"It seems that Mary is learning how to work her way around society without even realizing it." Darcy observed.

"She seems to have found a way to reconcile it within her heart." Elizabeth smiled and his mouth lifted. "She is definitely enjoying her music lessons although she would rather not spend more time with the sewing mistress. Georgiana is undecided, but Mary feels that she seems overly friendly."

"How does she feel that Georgiana gets on?" He rose and settled beside her on the sofa, and peeked over her shoulder at the letter.

"She also enjoys her music lessons, and is paying earnest attention to everything that is presented. She is, as Mary puts it, a truly engaged student." Elizabeth put down her letter and leaned against Darcy's chest. Immediately his arms came around her and he pulled her close. They both looked up to see Jane blush with the display. "I am sorry to embarrass you, Jane. We will stop." She began to move away, but Darcy refused to let go.

Jane noticed his refusal with some relief. "No, actually I was wondering if something was wrong between you."

"Really?" Darcy broke his gaze with Elizabeth and looked to her. "Why is that?"

"Well, you have always been so affectionate with each other, I have certainly caught you enough times, and it seemed that you have barely held hands since we arrived here." Jane looked at her own clasped hands. "I hope that you have not withheld your affections because you fear my becoming jealous again. I am over that and very happy to see your love displayed so freely."

Elizabeth and Darcy looked at each other then back to Jane. "I am glad to hear that you feel this way now. I suppose that is what was keeping us . . . behaved."

Darcy chuckled. "And now we have license to misbehave?"

"Within reason, I suppose." Elizabeth laughed and he grinned. "Thank you, Jane. You are too good."

She smiled to see them settle into their embrace. "Why do I think that I have made a terrible mistake? Now I shall certainly be ignored as you two gaze at each other."

"Now you know that our guests begin arriving this afternoon, so you will surely have good company. I so look forward to seeing everyone and catching up on the news. Mr. Bingley undoubtedly will have stories of . . ." Elizabeth stopped and her eyes grew wide.

"Elizabeth?" Darcy turned to face her. "What is it?"

"Shh!" Elizabeth commanded.

"Lizzy?" Jane stared and watched as her sister's hands drifted to the slight bulge in her waist, and jumped when she gasped. "Lizzy!"

"Dearest!" Darcy cried. Elizabeth grabbed his hands and placed them over her belly. "What . . . The baby moved?" Elizabeth's head bobbed rapidly. The room became silent and they waited.

She jumped again and beamed at him. "Did you feel it?" Darcy's head shook. "Ohhhhh. He must be too small, yet. But, oh Will! It is real!" They threw their arms around each other. A footman appeared and seeing their occupation averted his eyes and spoke to Jane.

"Miss, a carriage has arrived. Should I disturb . . .?"

"No, I . . . I will go." She glanced at the embraced pair and smiled, they were oblivious to her departure. She walked to the front door to find Bingley entering. "Mr. Bingley, it is so good to see you safely arrived."

Bingley laughed and handing his things to the waiting maid walked forward and bowed. "It is good to have at last ended the journey! Where are our hosts? Do not tell me, my friend Darcy is somewhere about the grounds tracking down his wayward wife as she tests his nerves by walking briskly about the park?"

Jane smiled and took his offered arm. "No indeed, the happy couple is enjoying a moment of private celebration. Your arrival rescued me from acute embarrassment."

"Ah, Darcy. A man after my own heart." Bingley smiled as they walked back to the sitting room. "Tell me, what do you think of their humble home?"

Jane laughed at his description. "It is rather intimidating, beautiful, but far more than I can imagine ever wanting."

"I do not believe that your sister wanted it either, but she has adjusted." Bingley looked about and sighed. "I will never have the like either, but I will always be happy to visit." He smiled down at her and she nodded. "I surmise that I am the first arrival?"

"You are, Mr. Stewart and Miss Stewart will be here soon, and I believe that Colonel Fitzwilliam travels with them. Then Mr. Harwick and his sister will arrive together as well." Jane looked down to her feet.

"Does that bother you, Miss Bennet?" He asked quietly.

She looked back up to his warm green eyes and shook her head. "No, both of us deserve to find love in marriage if we can."

A slow smile spread over Bingley's face. "That is a notion that I do not believe I would have entertained quite so fervently had I not witnessed the bloom of the Darcys' joy. It is now something that I hope to experience myself one day."

"For both of our sakes, I hope that we are successful in our quests, sir." Their eyes met and both tilted their heads to smile and nod.

"Bingley!" Darcy called and strode forward to take his hand. "When did you arrive?"

"Hours ago, I have been waiting impatiently for my hosts to greet me but nobody heard me scratching at the door." He laughed and grinned. "I understand that celebration is underway? What is the occasion?"

"The joy of life, my friend." Darcy's eyes glowed with pride. "Come, Elizabeth is waiting for you."

"Ah yes." Bingley straightened and walked forward with Jane, then followed Darcy into the sitting room where Elizabeth was patting her hair. He happily took her hands as he bowed then kissed one when he straightened. "There is no need to fuss, Mrs. Darcy. You are glowing and lovely as ever."

"As are you, Mr. Bingley." She laughed.

"Flattery is always welcome, please do not stop now!"

"Bingley, may I remind you that Elizabeth is off the market?" Darcy said sternly.

"Why do you think that I feel free to flex my skills with her, Darcy?" Bingley laughed to see his glare. "I can see what is effective with a lady but be in no danger of leading her on!" He tapped his head. "I am a thinking man!"

Darcy let an exasperated breath escape before taking Elizabeth's hands firmly back into his. "There is no need to be quite so charming. You are not . . ."

"Ready to marry, I know, I know." Bingley turned back to Jane. "Have you noticed that your brother often sounds like a fearsome old aunt? I rather feel sorry for his children. They will have no fun at all."

"I believe that I can agree with that!" They turned to see Fitzwilliam enter with the Stewarts behind him. "Before you complain of your staff, Darcy. I waved them off and led the way." He kissed Elizabeth's cheek. "You, my dear, look beautiful."

"I think that I will like having guests if they insist on flattering me!" Elizabeth laughed.

"It seems that some rules need to be established." Darcy shifted his glare to his cousin who grinned and went to greet Jane. "Stewart, Miss Stewart, welcome."

"Thank you." Stewart smiled and turned to Elizabeth. "Shall I add to the chorus?"

"Consider it done, sir." She returned his smile and felt Darcy's hand slip around her waist and draw her to his side. She smiled to see the possessive glint in his eye. "Laura, I am so pleased that you could come."

"Oh, when I mentioned that we were coming to Pemberley, you would not believe the interest it raised!" She leaned forward and whispered. "It is a much-sought invitation."

"Why?" Elizabeth looked up to Darcy.

"Because nobody outside of family and Bingley have been asked for ages." He smiled at Stewart. "So you should be doubly honoured."

"Oh I can see where this house party is going already." Stewart sighed.

"Sir, another carriage has just entered the park." A footman announced.

"That will be Harwick." Darcy took Elizabeth's hand. "Perhaps this time we should greet our guests at the door?"

"I will wait with you." Fitzwilliam announced and cleared his throat when he caught Darcy's eye. "Quiet Cousin."

"I . . . I would like to come as well." Laura said softly. "I have not seen . . . Mrs. Carter for so long."

Fitzwilliam broke the startled silence and offered her his arm. "Well then Miss Stewart, we shall together greet brother and sister." He bent down as they followed the Darcys to the door. "I wish you luck in your quest."

Laura blushed and looked to her shoes. "And I wish you luck in yours."

"STOP RIGHT THERE." Darcy commanded Elizabeth.

"Why?"

"Now turn to your side."

"Fitzwilliam, what are you about?" She laughed and turned so that she faced the windows instead of the bed. "Anything else?"

"Yes, be still." He sat up on their bed and gazed upon her. The glow of the fire exposed her body through the fine fabric of her nightgown and there, finally visible, was the evidence of their baby. Elizabeth followed his gaze and biting her lip, smoothed the fabric over her stomach. "There he is." Darcy said softly.

"Or she."

"Or she." He held out his arms and she climbed up to curl under the covers and into his embrace. Darcy kissed her and she rested her head on his shoulder. "Do you still feel him?"

"I did after dinner when Richard was making me laugh so hard." She looked up to see his head shaking. "Although really watching all of you boys posturing was highly entertaining. I think that you have wonderful friends."

"I do." Darcy kissed her softly and laughed. "Although I would say that I heard a fair amount of cackling coming from the female side of things. You and Laura seem to be very well-suited."

"We are." She gave him a belated pinch and he jumped. "Cackling? So you compare me to a crone?"

He nipped her ear. "You are a temptress."

"mmm." Their mouths met for several moments of soft kisses. Elizabeth licked her lips and he growled before gathering her tighter to his chest. "Did you see how Mr. Harwick's eyes followed Laura everywhere she went?"

"Did you see how red she blushed when he exited the carriage and took her hand?"

"And how he nearly forgot to hand his sister down?"

"Did you hear him trip all over his tongue when he tried to talk?"

"And her nervous laughter?"

"And their inane conversation?"

"And how he kissed her hand when she left for the evening?"

"And how her brother had to guide her upstairs?" Darcy's eyes met Elizabeth's. "I am very happy for them."

"I am as well. I hope that over the time they are with us, they will relax and be able to talk comfortably. Perhaps we could walk out to the stables and go riding?"

"You are not riding, my love." He said sternly. "No risks."

"Now that is silly, Emma is the most gentle of ponies. I was not proposing that we leap fences!"

"No, but Miss Stewart is a very accomplished horsewoman, and she would, and you would feel obligated to keep up. Perhaps Richard and Mrs. Carter could ride with them. I am sure that Harwick's sister is every bit as fond of horseflesh as he is."

"Because they grew up together?" Elizabeth laughed and saw his brows rise. "Dear, how alike am I to my sister?"

"I stand corrected, then." He smiled and rested his forehead to hers. "Richard is lost."

"I know, and Mrs. Carter wants to be."

"He knows." Darcy smiled and shrugged. "He is willing to be whatever she wishes, as long as she does not send him away."

"I do not think that will happen. She was as blushing and nervous as Laura, and I have never seen Richard so . . . silly."

"I have, but that is another story." Darcy laughed to see her pursed lips and ran his fingers through her hair. "I have known him a little longer than you, my love."

"Hmm." She closed her eyes and sighed with his touch. "That feels so nice." He chuckled and her eyes opened to see his twinkling. "Will she say yes, do you think?"

"I hope so, for both of them. We looked at the townhouse she was given. It is modest but the location is very good. Of course we did not see the interior."

"Whose idea was that?"

Darcy shrugged. "She gave Richard the address and that is all. Of course he felt that she was asking for his approval."

"I think that all of these couples will do much better if they just say what is on their minds." She kissed his growing smile. "We did."

"After a fashion." He sighed. "And what of Bingley?"

"What of him? He is as sweet as ever and as you are fond of saying, he is not ready for marriage."

"Do you know why I say that?" Darcy asked and watched her face. "Besides the obvious answer that he is too young and has no estate and all the rest?"

"Why then?"

"He loves you." He watched Elizabeth's brow crease. "Well not love, perhaps it is a spectacular crush, but he cares for you."

"We are friends, Fitzwilliam, nothing more."

"I know." He hugged her tightly. "I know, but as long as that exists, he will not be ready to love, or at least care for another. And I think, if I am not mistaken, your sister likes him."

"I think that he likes her. So now what do we do?"

"We do nothing." Darcy said positively. "It is up to him. He has to marry off his sister, he has to establish himself in society, and he has to find himself an estate to purchase or if possible, lease. And all of this next spring when we will not be in town to mentor him."

"Why will we not . . .oh." Elizabeth giggled when Darcy's hand caressed over her belly. "How quickly I forget. By next spring you will be unable to hold me on your lap, I will roll off!"

"We will work something out." He kept his hand in place and they kissed. "Is it quiet in there?"

"At the moment." She laughed. "I cannot wait for you to feel it, too. Audrey says that it can be rather painful."

"Painful?" He looked down and spoke sternly to her belly. "See here young man or lady, you do not cause your mother any pain!"

"I am sure that he heard you, dear." They looked at each other and laughed. "Oh this is so nice." Elizabeth's eyes closed. "We must invite many ladies of the neighbourhood over for Mr. Stewart. He is the odd man out, it seems."

"I thought that we were not going to be matchmakers?" He tilted his head to see the little smile that played on her lips, and unable to resist any longer, he lifted her up onto his lap, and settled his back against the headboard. "mmm this is better." His lips began roaming her face as his hand did the same over her breasts. Untying the top of her gown, his hand slipped beneath the fabric to touch the warm soft skin, and tease her dark, hard nipples. "These are growing, my love." He whispered as he tasted her ear. "They beg to be suckled."

"Yes they do." Darcy nudged her cheek with his nose and she turned her face to meet his mouth, while her hand caressed his chest. "mmm." Elizabeth withdrew and his tongue peeked between his lips. She saw his eyes remained with her mouth and she returned to kiss him once again. Now his arms wrapped completely around her and they continued the caress. "Oh Will." She whispered shakily and kissed his throat.

"Kiss me there again."

"Here?" She suckled just below his ear.

"I love that so much." He rested his head on hers and sighed. "Do you think it is too cold to visit our little hideaway?"

"It probably is for lovemaking, but I would still like to visit my birthday present, and see how it has grown."

"mmm." Darcy agreed and sliding her gown up and over her head, settled her back down to the bed, and soon lay naked beside her. "You are shivering, that will not do." He whispered. "Come my love, let me warm you."

"Are you no longer frightened, Will?"

Darcy kissed over her face, down her throat, paused to suckle tenderly each breast, then kissed the growing baby before returning to lay over her and kiss her lips. He rested his forehead on hers and looked into her eyes. "I am still frightened, but I will not allow that to overtake my happiness. This is our precious time, and we will not waste it in fear. I would rather love you." Hearing her sigh as their bodies joined, he murmured to her lips. "Let me love you."

Chapter 6

The sound of pounding hoofs thundered in Darcy's ears then with an exhilarating *whoosh* he and his mount were airborne, over the fence and flying up the slope in a fruitless attempt to catch Fitzwilliam. The laughing man reigned in at the top of the hill and watched as the rest of the party reached his location. "Where have you been?"

"I have long ago acknowledged your superior horsemanship." Darcy grinned and caught his breath. "I am just thrilled to see you in action once again." He turned his head to greet Harwick, who was closely followed by Stewart. Bingley, the novice at riding the hunt, brought up the rear.

"I say, I was sure that one of you would be lying in my path with a broken neck!" He laughed and they joined him. "Is it like this when there is an actual fox involved?"

"It is far more exciting." Fitzwilliam declared and opened a flask to take a drink. "You have the hounds braying, the air is colder, and with luck, you have the company of some lovely ladies to observe as they . . .enjoy their mounts."

"Allowing one's imagination to wander to other subjects?" Bingley suggested.

"Unfortunately, that tends to slow the pace a bit." Stewart observed.

"There is nothing wrong with a steady pace." Harwick said to his hands and looked up to notice Darcy's barely perceptible nod.

Fitzwilliam put his flask away and sat up in the saddle. "Well we could entertain that particular subject all day, but as Darcy here is the only one able to enjoy the fruits of it, I say we should continue on." He turned his horse's head and without a warning, kicked her. "Catch me if you can!" He cried. Harwick took off after him and Bingley decided to try and keep up this time. Darcy and Stewart laughed and took a more leisurely pace to benefit their mounts.

"Onyx enjoys a good gallop, but I know when to let him breathe."

"Well, I appreciate the loan of Richard, and I realize that your hanging back is in recognition of *his* breathing, not that stallion of yours." The two rode companionably together and watched the others disappear. "I have not been able to pin down a court date for Wickham, but I asked to be kept informed and gave them this address. I should receive word very soon. I do want to plead it for you. I am honoured that you are allowing me the opportunity, but I have not had a great deal of experience with such cases. Marlowe Henderson may be the better choice."

"I want the best, and I want someone who has passion for the outcome." Darcy met his eye and acknowledged his nod. "Is it always this way? Not knowing what is coming?"

"Well, court is not in session, but yes, it is often a mystery when a case may come up, you can easily hang about the court for days or weeks not knowing. In any case, in November all courts begin again and of course I will have to return to London prior to that. I will depart the day after your ball."

"I should like to come with you."

"Darcy there is no need, you may be waiting for the whole month if it is scheduled later, you have done your part, you called the magistrate. You are the prosecutor, but they have your testimony. Now let your solicitor and me or Henderson take over. Would you really wish to be parted from Mrs. Darcy for so long?"

"Of course not, but I feel that I need to witness Wickham's trial and be assured of his disposition. I was unable to protect Elizabeth from his attack, but I'll be damned if I do not assure that he never touches her again." Darcy's jaw set. "My wife will not be forced to pretend strength when I know that she was terrified, some things are not so easily forgotten."

"I understand your fear, but you are a gentleman, that carries a great deal of weight. Do not leave her and let the courts handle it, the magistrate will testify. I will inform you of the result. I am nearly positive it will be transportation. As popular as hanging is, things are changing and for non-capital offenses, more often the prisoners are simply sent from our shores. Of course America is not an option anymore." He laughed but Darcy continued to frown. "So to Australia it will be, the ship sails again in the summer when the passage is safe from winter storms."

"Will he be able to return?"

"If he survives Newgate, the nearly four months at sea, and the years as a convict, yes. However by that time he will probably have established a liking for the land." Stewart saw Darcy's disgust. "He will be well and gone from you. Mrs. Darcy seems to be well; she has not let the event harm her humour?"

"She has put it behind her as much as she can, and is instead concentrating on our child; it is not in her nature to dwell on things that cannot be changed. I am the one who is holding on to the imagery and the what-ifs. I do want to be at the trial if it is at all possible. My testimony will guarantee his conviction, you know that. But most of all, it is my place as her husband, and I feel that I owe it to my father as well." He saw Stewart's nod and relaxed slightly. "In any case, I have been instructed to stop brooding. So, in that spirit, I ask you, what do you think of your sister and Harwick?"

"I am delighted." Stewart laughed. "She is very happy and it is good to see how she makes him smile."

"I am glad to see Miss Bennet tolerating the romance so well."

"Ah well, Harwick saw the same in Miss Bennet as I did when we were introduced in Meryton. She is lovely but . . .lacks intrigue."

"Bingley likes her, it seems."

"Good, then he will stop looking at your wife." Stewart watched Darcy's brow crease. "Why have you not corrected him?"

"I honestly believe that he feels only brotherly affection for her, we have talked about it in the past, and he was hurt by my query. I do not wish to hurt our friendship by accusing him of something that is not there."

"You had no such compassion for ours."

Darcy startled and regarded him carefully. "You outright stated your intentions, and Bingley does nothing more than smile and tease a bit. I had only suspicions of who you had abandoned last December, and I made it clear what my intentions were towards Elizabeth when we met at the ball. You are the one who mistrusted me." He paused then spoke seriously, "I thought this was behind us."

"It is, although you do clutch her tightly when I am near." He saw Darcy's expression freeze and sighed. "Ignore me, Darcy. You have what I do not."

"Well, leave it to my wife and she will happily play matchmaker for you." He smiled to see Stewart's brows rise. "We have invited the gentlemen of the neighbourhood to join us with our sport tomorrow, and they are bringing their wives and daughters along. The plan was for the ladies to ride, but with Elizabeth's condition they will instead enjoy tea and gossip, and wait for the gentlemen's return."

"Is that so?" Stewart smiled. "It seems to me that Bingley and I may be the only gentlemen available if my suspicions of Fitzwilliam and Mrs. Carter are correct?"

Darcy's eyes crinkled with amusement. "Ah, you have noticed his stares and her poor attempts at concealing interest?"

"It is not hard to discern, although she seems to be making an effort to avoid him." He laughed and gestured in the distance, "Perhaps this is the reason for his wild riding today?"

"From what I understand she is torn about what to do."

"You have heard the story of her husband, I suppose?" Stewart shook his head. "There are times that I admit to wishing I was the Viscount and had the freedom to do as I pleased, but I see so many unoccupied first sons become involved in dissolute activities that I am rather glad to be distracted with my position. You never had a chance to be distracted did you?"

"No." Darcy adjusted his seat and his gaze swept the land. "If my father had lived, I doubt that I would have gone too far astray before I was soundly corrected." He looked back to Stewart. "I imagine your father would have been the same?"

"Without a doubt." He sighed. "So, ladies will come tomorrow and . . ."

"There will be other bachelors in our party, but yes, the ladies will outnumber the gentlemen, and if you are inclined to be entertained, I am sure that the son of an Earl with the income you will eventually have is quite attractive. In fact, I remember that Mrs. Henley found you to be eminently suitable for her daughter."

Stewart's jaw dropped. "How on earth did that subject arise?"

"We were visiting, Elizabeth mentioned our guests, and she took it from there. Miss Henley was naturally embarrassed."

"I cannot blame her. My mother is the same with Laura." Both men smiled.

"Do you remember Miss Henley? You stayed with them last year for the hunt as I recall."

Stewart shot him a glance. "I was too miserable to really pay much attention to her last December. I recall that she is a very handsome woman."

Darcy cleared his throat. "Yes, I am sorry to have brought that up." Their eyes met and he saw Stewart's shrug. "She is handsome as are the rest of the ladies so; will you indulge my wife's desire to see you happy? She is determined, you know."

Stewart laughed. "She is a wonderful woman."

"She is indeed." Darcy laughed and they looked ahead as the sound of hoofs beating the ground reached their ears. "Ah, they have returned!"

Fitzwilliam arrived first, closely followed by Harwick and Bingley. "What happened?"

"Nothing. We needed to talk." Darcy nodded to Fitzwilliam's mount. "She needs to rest. I think that it is time to return."

"I know." He patted her neck. "Riding in town is nothing to riding here. I love this estate Darcy; it is so much more than Matlock."

"Your father said something similar once." Darcy smiled then kicking Onyx called out as they sped towards the stables, "Are you coming?"

"MRS. DARCY I think that I may speak for all of the ladies when I say that we are just so thrilled to be invited here today. I have wondered about Pemberley and how it has been faring for years, particularly after news of the recent fire travelled the area, but of course, we would not wish to act as common tourists and ask to walk through. It is the greatest estate in the county, and of course we all are interested in its welfare." The murmured agreement of the gathered women flowed from one nodding head to another.

Elizabeth set down her tea cup, and drew once again upon the careful preparation Lady Matlock had given her. "Thank you Mrs. Wilson, I am very pleased to have this opportunity to ask you all here, and hope that you have enjoyed the day. Has the estate proven to be as beautiful as you remember? I believe that the evidence of the fire has been removed. Mr. Darcy and our staff assure me that if anything the house is lovelier than ever, and I am delighted to invite our neighbours into our home." She smiled and glanced at Evangeline and Laura, who were nodding and smiling with approval across the room from her. Elizabeth breathed.

"Oh, it is just beautiful!" Mrs. Henley gushed. "Why, I remarked to my husband only last year, what a wonderful thing it would be for Mr. Darcy to marry and reopen Pemberley! I remember when Mrs. Darcy, your predecessor dear, was alive. Oh, the dinners and balls! She was a wonderful hostess! I was still light of foot then, and I danced and danced . . ."

"Yes, thank you Mrs. Henley." Mrs. Gregory interrupted. "Now tell us of your ball. Who is invited, besides us of course?"

"Well I believe that it is the entire neighbourhood of the local landowners and gentry, and of course we have some more guests arriving tomorrow who will be staying with us." She smiled to see the mothers clearly going over the list of families in their minds.

"May I ask . . . your guests, are they family?"

"Some are, the residents of Matlock will arrive, the Earl, the Viscount and their wives." She noted the disappointment, "And of course there will be the Earl of Moreland and his wife, Miss Stewart's parents." She nodded over to Laura.

"Oh, and have you many brothers Miss Stewart, Mr. Stewart seems to be amiable?" Miss Gregory asked.

"I do, my brother the Viscount and his wife are expecting their second child, and will not make the trip from home. My brother Daniel is unattached."

"Ooohhh," travelled around the room and Laura spotted Elizabeth's sparkling eyes and bit her lip. Evangeline sighed and joined in to help the matchmaking begin.

"He is a barrister is he not, Miss Stewart?"

"He is, and doing very well, Mrs. Carter."

"I believe that he . . ." Miss Henley paused when all eyes turned to her. "He is very gentlemanly."

"He is indeed." Elizabeth agreed.

Miss Wilson spoke up. "Mr. Bingley and Colonel Fitzwilliam are unmarried as well, is that correct?" Again the whispers rose and Elizabeth noted that Evangeline had reddened and Jane was staring at her hands.

"Yes they are, and both are very good men. I have been pleased to meet your brothers and husbands; it seems that Derbyshire is teeming with possibilities for you all."

A footman entered and bowed before speaking softly to Elizabeth. "Mrs. Darcy, the gentlemen will join you shortly."

"Thank you." She smiled knowing that Darcy would want to assure her that he was on his way. "Well, we will soon be entertaining the men; it seems that they have finished their port and conversation."

"So what shall we discuss before they arrive?" Mrs. Henley asked with bright eyes. "Mrs. Darcy, I have just been dying to ask all day, are you with child?"

"Margaret, will you never learn to hold your tongue?" Mrs. Wilson cried. "Do not answer Mrs. Darcy, she is impossible, believe me; I have tried for years to instruct her."

"I am not impossible!" She declared. "I am curious!"

"And if an announcement needs to be made, Mr. and Mrs. Darcy will in their own good time." Mrs. Gregory sighed. "Really Margaret, your country manners will be the death of me someday. How can you display such behaviour to Mrs. Darcy?"

"There is no shame in living in the country." Elizabeth spoke to the two ladies. "Derbyshire is a far cry from London, why would you look down your nose at your neighbour?" The older women and their daughters all looked at her with surprise. She glanced at Jane and saw her embarrassment, and the other women's fixed attention, and suddenly she felt the power of her position. "I appreciate the difference between genuine interest and posturing. Mrs. Henley was asking a reasonable question and yes, I am happy to confirm that our first child is on its way. Mr. Darcy and I are delighted, thank you."

"I thought so, my dear! You are simply glowing!" Mrs. Henley beamed. "Oh how wonderful!"

"MRS. CARTER, may I have a word with you?" Fitzwilliam approached the sofa where Evangeline sat alone. He took a seat beside her and noticed her eyes flick up to his face and back down. "What is wrong? Ever since you arrived you have avoided being alone with me. Have I angered you in some way? I have been searching my memory, and I can recall no incident that could cause your discomfort. Please if I have upset you, tell me so that I may correct it. I cannot bear to be left wondering like this. If I did not have the other gentlemen to occupy my mind I would be left to do nothing but worry."

"You seem to be bearing the interest of all of these ladies well enough." Her eyes swept the room, and stopped to watch Miss Gregory take her turn at the pianoforte. "You smile and laugh with them."

"I do, I will not be impolite to Elizabeth's guests." He looked to see who had caught her attention then back to her. "I would prefer to be standing with you clearly by my side, but you asked for time. I am waiting for you to give me a sign that you are ready, is this that moment? You seem to be a little possessive? That delights me, truly, but I honestly do not know what to do, I am as unschooled in courting as . . . Darcy was when he pined for Elizabeth all spring." He saw her look down and nod. "In the meantime, I will not stand like a tree and frown like . . ." He laughed. "Like your brother does as he sees Mr. Ryan talk up Miss Stewart." Evangeline looked to Harwick and a little smile appeared.

"He is waiting to speak to Lord Moreland before he declares himself to her."

"Ah, I see. Until then he will brood." Fitzwilliam cocked his brow at her. "You have not answered my question. You know full well that I would love to join Harwick in his state of jealousy, but you deny me that pleasure."

Evangeline's eyes darted around and she whispered in a low voice, "This is not the place for this conversation."

Fitzwilliam recognized her discomfort but refused to be dissuaded. "No, I will not accept that, you are well and truly trapped. Speak your mind, if you know it." He touched her hand. "Please."

"Richard . . ." She saw the relief and happiness appear in his eyes. "I . . . I continue to struggle."

"Eva." He whispered his disappointment.

"But I am closer to a resolution and when my brother is . . .settled, I think that I will feel free to make that decision."

Fitzwilliam's gaze travelled from Harwick to Laura and back again. He stood and strode over to the man, spoke in his ear, and gave him a shove. Harwick walked straight to Laura, bowed to her companions, took her hand and placed it on his arm, then led her away to a corner. Fitzwilliam returned to Evangeline and held out his hand to her. "Come my . . . Come."

"Where?" She placed her hand within his palm and rose to stand beside him. "What have you done?"

"I told your brother that I am not going to wait and watch while he mucks up this match."

"Richard, there is no possibility of Miss Stewart being lured away by another, she has told me of her feelings for him."

"I was not speaking of his match, I was speaking of ours." His eyes held hers. "I am a reasonably patient man, but if there is any possibility of moving things along, I will encourage them." Glancing out at the dusky garden he looked back to her. "Will you walk with me? It is not too cold outside."

"Alone?" She whispered and looked out of the window.

"We need to talk. No more avoidance." Fitzwilliam looked at her seriously. "Eva, I may seem to be pushing you to speak, and I apologize if you feel undue pressure, but nothing will be advanced if we continue this way, we must face the enemy, whatever it is. I may not be here much longer. If Darcy goes to London for Wickham's trial, I will accompany him and testify if needed. Our time is limited, and I have waited so long to be with you again. I do not want to waste it by dancing around the subject."

"Tomorrow then, we will talk tomorrow." She swallowed as his intense gaze burned into her. "In the daylight."

"You do not trust me in the dark?" He said softly.

"I do not trust myself." She began to move away but stopped and looked up to his eyes. "You promise to dance with me at the ball?"

He laughed with relief. "I promise to do anything you wish."

Stewart grinned and nudged Bingley. "I think that Fitzwilliam is finally making some headway."

Bingley laughed. "It is about time, he has been following her around like a sick calf, and she just walks faster!" He looked around the room and grinned. "It just leaves more ladies for us."

"Hmm." Stewart watched Bingley's eyes roaming over the room. "What are your thoughts on our friend Darcy's choice?"

Smiling, Bingley's gaze settled on Elizabeth as she laughed and leaned against Darcy's shoulder, and his hand supported her back. "She is an angel."

"What does that mean, in your mind?"

"It means that she is . . .everything that a man could wish for." He smiled at Stewart, but saw the serious expression in his eyes. "I mean no disrespect to Mrs. Darcy. I met her before Darcy did, well officially, and . . . well you were smitten with her, so you can hardly question my attraction, can you?"

"I do not question it happening, I only question to what extent it continues."

Bingley turned and faced him head on. "See here Stewart, the only man who has any business questioning my opinion of Mrs. Darcy is her husband. He is assured of my friendship and devotion to both of them. Mrs. Darcy is no more your property than she is mine, and I suspect that we both at one time wished that was different, however may I ask, if you were to have the opportunity to kiss her with no repercussions and no memory on her part, would you take it?"

Stewart stared at him for several long moments then spoke softly, "I take it that you had such an opportunity?"

"I did, and I called for her husband." Bingley said stiffly. "Now, he trusts me, she trusts me, and that is all that I want to hear of it."

"Very well, I stand corrected. Your feelings for both of them are familial." Stewart nodded and held out his hand. "Please accept my apology, I feel rather protective of them as well. Shall we form a pact, and stare more often at the unmarried ladies? Perhaps there is someone in this room for each of us."

Bingley relaxed and taking the hand; shook. "We could perhaps help each other? We do have a number of ladies to enjoy here tonight."

"And more to come at the ball. What do you think of them?"

"Oh, they are all lovely, I especially enjoyed meeting Miss Wilson, she is determined to please."

"Yes, a little too determined." Stewart grimaced. "She has her mother's ambition written all over her."

"I suppose that I was more interested in her smiles and her wit." Bingley shrugged. "Miss Henley is very handsome."

"Yes, she is." Stewart tilted his head and considered her. She was standing with Elizabeth and the two young women were laughing together. He noticed Darcy standing quietly by Elizabeth's side, and how a smile played on his lips as he listened. "Excuse me." He joined the group, and bowing slightly he smiled at Darcy. "You need some male reinforcements."

"Is that so? I think that I am doing very well." He took Elizabeth's hand in his and lifted it to his lips. "I have everything I need right here in my grasp."

Julia sighed. "I think that I made a grave error in not allowing my mother to chase after you, Mr. Darcy."

Elizabeth laughed and wound her hand around his arm. "Well I am grateful that he knew his mind." They looked at each other and smiled, then she turned to Stewart. "Are you taking note of this, sir?"

"I am." Stewart bowed to Miss Henley. "In that spirit, may I secure the first set of the ball with you?"

"Why . . .yes, I am flattered, sir! Thank you!" Julia laughed and smiled. "I thought that you might ask your sister for such an honour."

He laughed and looked across the room to Harwick and Laura. "No, I will dance with her, but I believe that it is safe to assume that her time will be otherwise occupied."

Laura smiled up at Harwick and he pursed his lips in a fruitless attempt to remain stern. "Well sir? You brought me here, in a highly noticeable manner. Is there a reason for your ungentlemanly conduct?"

"It was hardly ungentlemanly to remove a lady who was clearly feeling distress from an untenable situation." He smiled, then furrowed his brows back to looking stern. She laughed and he continued. "Mr. Ryan is a puppy, and he is better off flirting with maids of his ilk."

"His ilk, sir? He is the son of a gentleman, just as you are. His estate may not be so grand, but . . ."

"He is a boy, and belongs with girls. Let me meet him in five years and perhaps my opinion will be improved. You are a woman, and deserve far better." Harwick watched her brows rise and worked hard to contain his delight.

"Is there anyone in this room who would be good enough? Colonel Fitzwilliam is surely a man."

"He is but he has interests in another." Harwick looked to his sister and catching her eye stared at her then to Fitzwilliam and back. She hung her head and he sighed.

"She is hesitant, to begin anew is frightening." Laura said softly. "I have heard stories of her husband's death."

"They are nothing to his life, and Eva has said nothing of their home." Harwick sighed. "I wish for her to be happy."

"The colonel will undoubtedly be very persistent; he did not buy that rank as so many do. He earned it and is accomplished with battle." When she smiled, he relaxed and returned it.

"You are very likely correct." He paused and then taking her hand placed it decidedly on his arm, then covered it with his own. They both looked down and he laced his fingers with hers. Keeping his gaze down he spoke softly, "Miss Stewart, surely you know that I feel very strongly attracted to you. I . . . I thought when my mourning ended that I needed to remarry to produce an heir and that to do so I should choose one who did not touch my heart. I began a courtship with another . . ."

"Miss Bennet."

"Yes." He continued to look at their hands. "I went about it all so coldly, but in the process I discovered that I cannot marry without feeling, and that I require, that I need . . . I want to be happy. Miss Bennet, who is a very nice woman, inspired nothing in me, and I ended it. It would be wrong to subject her to such a heartless union, although it was wrong of me to raise her hopes."

"I do not think that she regrets you, sir." Laura looked over to Jane speaking to a young gentleman and smiling. "She is quite at ease with your presence."

"She served as a bridge between my mourning for Ellen and," he hesitated and looked up to her. "You."

"At last you speak." She smiled and her eyes sparkled. "I have been hoping you would say what your gaze expressed silently."

"I could say nothing with Miss Bennet on my arm, but my heart found its rhythm again the night I met you in the theatre and it frightened me, and is why I turned away to speak to Singleton when you and your brother visited the box. I did not know that I would be permitted such a pleasure again. That is why I did not go to the Derby; I knew you would be there. I . . . I owed it to Miss Bennet to be sure that she was not the one."

"That is what I admire about you so much; you are a gentleman in every sense of the word."

"Except when I drag you away from puppies." He smiled and she laughed. "Miss Stewart, will you accept my courtship?"

"Oh yes." She blushed and looked down to her shoes.

"Miss Stewart . . . Laura . . ." He whispered and she raised her head again. "I have never met anyone like you before; you are not a shadow of my Ellen. You are unique and I look forward to discovering so much more of you."

"Thank you for telling me that." She whispered.

"I hope that should our courtship go as far as I wish; that you will accept another woman's children."

"They are your children, are they not?"

"Of course." He said softly.

"Then they are part of you, and so I will . . ." She stopped, then saw the hope in his expression. "I will love them as you do."

"May I speak to your father when he comes?" Harwick asked with shining eyes.

"Please, yes, please do." She blinked and found a handkerchief pressed in her hand. "Why am I being so silly? It is not as if I have been proposed to, is it?" She sniffed and looked up to see him smiling with his head tilted and his brow raised.

"Not yet."

Bingley wandered over to Jane's side, and startled her from contemplation of Harwick and Laura. "You are turning quite a few heads this evening, Miss Bennet."

"I notice that you have received your share of attention." She smiled and he shrugged. "You do not agree or are you used to it?"

"I am not so vain as to ever be used to it. I simply realize that a smile is more attractive than a frown. During my first Season I have run across many personalities in the ladies, and I have determined that next Season, I will not waste my time with a woman who presents a haughty or unwelcoming air. It could be my background that she disapproves or my person, regardless, I will not try to fix someone who is inhospitable. I am learning from my mistakes." Bingley noticed her listening closely. "I imagine that you have long ago learned this? Ladies are thrust out so much sooner than gentlemen."

"I am feeling my way around much as you are, sir. We both come from places far removed from society." She looked to Elizabeth and noticed how Darcy's hand again rested on her back and how she was leaning into him. "I think that is what first drew you to my sister? At that dance where you met?"

"Hmm?" Bingley was watching the couple as well. "Yes, we were similar, and of course, she was approachable." He remained silent for some time thinking over his conversation with Stewart and watching Darcy's ease. "It is remarkable how different he is with her near." He returned to face Jane. "I attended a dance here at Pemberley for the tenants last year and he was as aloof and unreceptive as the coldest peer's daughter on her presentation day. But now, with the right woman he is, well he is comfortable." Bingley laughed. "Not transformed, but certainly easier in company."

"So he was won by a smile?" Jane asked.

"Oh, the smile is just the beginning Miss Bennet, you must have something behind it or you will be finished before you end the first dance. Of course, that goes for the gentleman as well. What lady wants to be bored all of her life?" He laughed and Jane's brow creased. "Well my sister would if the man was wealthy, but I have little hope of her finding anyone who will ever satisfy her."

"Mr. Wickham fooled her."

"Hmm, he fooled many people, and I regret it. I wonder if I should take some blame for your sister's experience. If he had been run off from Caroline, he may not have ever contemplated robbing Darcy, and Elizabeth would not have suffered the confrontation." He sighed and his shoulders fell.

"You cannot take on that burden, sir." Jane said softly. "My sister would not like that."

"I am glad to hear it." Bingley smiled at her. "I seem to have adopted Mrs. Darcy as another sister in my heart. As you said, we were beginning together in a strange new world. And next Season I will face it alone, it seems. My mentor will most certainly not leave Pemberley for town, not with his new baby being born in April. But then, they may travel as the rest of the fashionable set seems to do, once the lady is free of her confinement."

"I am not sure of their plans, but I cannot imagine my sister leaving her child behind. I imagine that Mr. Darcy will be required to travel for business, but when that may occur is unknown."

"That is true." Bingley mused. "And what of you, Miss Bennet, will you enjoy the Season again?"

"I will stay with the Gardiners, along with my sister Mary. I doubt that our paths will cross without the Darcys in town, your circle is far removed from the Gardiners now." She smiled and his brow furrowed.

"I think that we may manage to meet somewhere. However, I must rectify a grave error immediately. At the Matlock ball I failed to ask you for the first set. I hereby ask for your hand now, or am I too late once again?"

Jane laughed as he bowed and looked up to her. "No sir, you are not late at all. I will be glad to accept you."

Bingley nodded and straightened. "Very well then, we shall dance and the tongues will wag."

23 OCTOBER 1809

Richard has just left me, he is frustrated. At last he had a short private interview with Mrs. Carter and she stated again that she wishes to see her brother married before she would move to London, and made no absolute indication of her feelings for him. It is clear to every person in this house that she loves him as much as he loves her, but still she resists. I admit ignorance in understanding this, why would a woman not wish to live under the care and protection of a man who loves her? Surely that is better than loneliness? I hated my years alone in this house. I needed Elizabeth. Perhaps when Aunt Helen arrives today she may speak to Mrs. Carter, and help her to come to terms with her hesitation. They will be mother and daughter one day, I hope.

Stewart received word that Wickham's trial remains unscheduled, the best he can say is that it is definitely not to be in the first week, and he suspects it may not be in the second either. He is relying on our solicitor to find out some information and it was suggested that some sort of gift might ease the wheels of justice to turn far enough to assure us of a definite trial date. I have provided him with the funds and I trust him to take care of the matter, even if we must travel later in the month it should not be impaired too much by the weather, unless it rains excessively. Our ball is in two days and Stewart will leave for town on the 27th. Richard and I will depart as soon as we receive word. Elizabeth is no more pleased with our pending separation than I am, but I hope that she understands why I need to be present, even if it is only to bear witness to Wickham's inevitable sentence. I must be there. I will be there. She begged to come with me, but we have guests, and one of us must remain. I admit to being pleased with that fact. I do not care to risk anything with my love as she carries our child. I know that I am being overprotective, but she agrees that it is far better than my brooding over doom. I will remind her of that when I undoubtedly grow worse.

"You will grow worse, Mr. Darcy?" Elizabeth closed the book and he looked up from the letter he was scratching out. "What do you think you will do?"

"I could not say, love." He smiled and reached his arm around her waist then drew her down to his lap. "I only know that I will exert every method possible to assure your and our child's well-being."

"Where is your dictionary? I wish to add a word." Elizabeth's eyes danced and she curled up against his chest. "I need to put *mother hen* down with Fitzwilliam Darcy as the definition."

"I will be proud to see it." He kissed her and ran his fingers through her hair. "What will I do without you by my side?"

"Suffer, as you should." She declared. "You will make me sleep in that bed without you, how will I stay warm? *You* are endangering our child, not I. I might as well call to have Emma saddled and take a long ride over . . ." Her complaints were silenced by his kiss, and they melted into each other. "Please do not leave me." She whispered when they finally parted.

"I must. I know that you are frightened to be alone, love. But I must see him brought to justice. For both of us." Darcy looked down to her belly and caressed over the growing baby, then looked up to see her teary eyes. He gently caressed her cheek with the back of his fingers, and softly sang, *"From thee; Eliza, I must go, and from my native shore; the cruel fates between us throw a boundless ocean's roar. But boundless oceans, roaring wide between my love and me, they never, never can divide my heart and soul from thee."*[1]

"Fitzwilliam." She sighed and taking his face in her hands kissed him. Darcy remained still, and closed his eyes, letting her lips wander over his cheeks and back to his mouth where she suckled slowly. He shivered and drawing her closer, threw off his control to kiss her deeply.

"Do you know how much I love you kissing me?" He said hoarsely when he tore his mouth from hers, then lifted her chin. "I am lost when you reach for me." His hand skimmed up beneath her gown and between her thighs.

"Will . . . please."

"Now, love?" He asked shakily and burying his face against her shoulder, kissed her neck while playing lovingly in her curls, slipping two fingers within as his thumb caressed and circled her pearl. "Do you want me now?" Feeling her nod and clutching grasp, he removed his hand and lifted her up onto the desk. "Lie back." He urged. Elizabeth rested her head on the stack of letters and looked up to him as he quickly opened his breeches and stood between her parted legs. Leaning down he kissed her, and then lifting her hips, watched as he slid slowly inside. Elizabeth's legs wrapped around his waist, and Darcy

---

[1] Robert Burns, "Farewell to Eliza", 1786.

closed his eyes, standing still with his hands resting on either side of her. "It is so very warm, Lizzy. So warm."

Elizabeth reached up to caress his face and slipping her hand to the back of his neck, drew him down to kiss. "I love to keep you warm, Will."

Darcy groaned and began to move slowly, rising up from her mouth to push her skirt away so he could watch their union. He could not take his eyes from the sight. His hands gripped her hips and drew her closer. Elizabeth moaned and sighed as he filled her and thrilled as the fulfilment he brought slowly bloomed. Darcy looked to her eyes, they were open and watching him. His jaw set, the only sounds were their erratic breathing and the rhythmic wet slap of his body steadily thrusting into hers. They were desperately working not to cry out their pleasure, but at last Elizabeth gave in with a moan as her eyes closed. Darcy instantly let go of his tenuous control and gasped as the flood was released. He remained standing with his head down, quivering with the feeling. Her hands caressing his at last brought him back. Elizabeth smiled as he bent to kiss her.

"I have no desire to leave this place." He sighed. "Can we not remain this way?"

"I think that it might be noted." She laughed softly and touched his brow. "But I would like it as well, although, a pillow would be an improvement."

"But I will always remember the pleasure of loving you here, just as we are." Darcy kissed her once more, then reluctantly drew away and repaired his clothes. Elizabeth purposely remained sprawled upon his desk. He smiled at the sight of her still-parted legs and cream covered thighs, "Now this is vision to keep me warm." Lovingly he wiped her clean, then bent to kiss her thighs and breathe in the scent of their endeavours. "Have I told you how intoxicating your perfume is?"

Elizabeth laughed and sat up with his help, and stood leaning into his arms. His hands travelled up and down her back and she nestled her ear to his heart. "I love your scent, as well." He chuckled and they stood quietly swaying together, listening to the fire crackle and the clock steadily ticking. "I have come to depend on these embraces." She looked up to him, to see him smile and nod. "How did I ever manage to live before without them?"

"I have often thought the same, my love." He brushed a tendril of hair from her cheek then bent to kiss the rosy skin.

"You asked in your journal why a woman would not wish to be under the care of a man who loved her." Darcy's head nodded and he rested his cheek in her hair. "You forget that Mr. Carter was not a man like Richard. Mrs. Carter has not forgotten either." She looked up to him, "I have no desire to ever face such a decision as Mr. Harwick or Mrs. Carter have."

"I promise I will stay safe. I will be in your arms three days after the trial, without fail." He kissed her forehead.

"Very well, then." She sighed and hugged him tight. "Go."

"YOU REALLY HAVE TO BE more careful, Darcy." Fitzwilliam laughed. "I knew what was happening in here and I was halfway down the hall."

Darcy glared at him. "You likely had your ear pressed to the keyhole."

"Perhaps." He shrugged. "All right, it was not so loud, but I knew the telltale sounds, but your study, in the middle of the day? Lucky man! Where did you perform this act of love? I could not quite determine the location from the sounds . . ."

"I will not discuss this further." Darcy picked up some wrinkled papers and sorted through them. "Why are you not pursuing Mrs. Carter?"

"Because she is currently being interrogated. Apparently Mother took one look at me and another at Mrs. Carter, and as soon as her toilette was addressed, she accosted the poor woman and shut the door to the sitting room behind her." He sighed. "So either Mrs. Carter will run screaming for a carriage to take her away from here or . . ."

"Or?" Darcy paused in his work.

"Or she might come around." Fitzwilliam sat forward and rested his head in his hands. "Can you think of anything else I might do?"

"You have tried kissing her?" Darcy smiled and heard a loud groan. "Try it again. It always works on Elizabeth."

"Does it?" He lifted his head. "How?"

"If she is upset, I kiss her and . . ."

"No, do not tell me, she is transported to a fairyland of sunshine and flowers, and you the Adonis are bathed in a glow that entices her senses and makes her forget there ever was trouble on the earth."

"What exactly *did* you read during your recovery?" Darcy laughed. "You sound like a schoolgirl!"

"Speaking of which, I assume that we will be visiting our schoolgirl while we are in town?"

"Of course." Darcy smiled. "I cannot wait to see her."

"*Well!*" Lord Matlock and Lord Moreland wandered in and dropped into chairs simultaneously. Darcy and Fitzwilliam exchanged glances and held back their laughter. "Are you going to capture this woman or not? Your battle plans are a failure thus far, Son."

"Thank you for the reminder, Father." He said dryly and looked up to see Layton stroll in with Stewart and Bingley. "Wonderful, three more of you. Where is Harwick? Does he not wish to add his advice?"

"He is better occupied." Lord Moreland announced. "He was practically waiting at my chamber door wanting to talk courtship. I told him we might as well cut to the chase and talk engagement, but he said it was too soon. I would have been shocked at any other man acting so precipitously, but Stewart prepared me for the possibility, and I was glad that Matlock and Layton know him so well. It is a relief that Laura has found such a worthy suitor. He told me everything there ever was to know about him. Straight as an arrow. That man has it bad, and Laura is anxious as well, but I cannot fault his determination to do this properly. How did this come about, Stewart?"

"They met at the theatre." He shrugged. "It was instantaneous."

"Impossible notion." Lord Moreland growled.

"Not so sir, I can attest to it in my case." Darcy sat back and tossed his quill in the tray.

"Well, she certainly has done well for herself so I have no objections, the engagement is inevitable. Two little girls to raise; my wife is delighted."

"She does not mind? Mrs. Bennet did not like the idea for Miss Bennet."

"She suspected that Miss Bennet's children would be second to the first two." Fitzwilliam explained to the Earl.

"That is ridiculous, they are girls! If he had a son already, then certainly, he would take precedence. His girls have their dowries already set from their mother. Laura will bring her own money to the marriage, besides, when I heard that man confess his devotion to Laura well, it nigh brought tears to my eyes. A man like that will care for all of his children." He sniffed loudly and looked around. "Where is the port?"

Stewart jumped and poured a glass. "Here you are, Father." The Earl took it and fell into contemplative quiet.

Darcy looked at his uncle and his eyes travelled over the faces of the silenced men. He cleared his throat. "I appreciate you and Aunt Helen staying on while I am away, Uncle. I will feel better having so many to keep Elizabeth company."

"It is no trouble at all. I think that having Alicia here will be good for her as well, they can exchange information." He smiled to Layton. "It will not be long now."

"March Father, we have almost as long as Darcy to wait." Layton sighed. "This will be our last appearance until Spring. I was not too happy about taking the trip, but she insisted. I am surprised that Elizabeth did not try persuasion to allow her to accompany you, Darcy."

Darcy coloured and Fitzwilliam started to laugh. "She did Brother, but our cousin was . . . convincing."

As Darcy's blush deepened the rest of the men began to join Fitzwilliam's laughter.

"Good for you, Son! Show your wife who is master!" Lord Matlock cried.

Bingley grinned. "I hope that you will serve as my advisor in these matters as well someday."

The men roared with laughter and grew louder the angrier Darcy became. "I think that our lessons are at an end Bingley, you are hereby on your own."

"No, no, do not turn the boy out!" Lord Matlock wiped his eyes and chuckled again. "Oh you simply do not appreciate how good it is to laugh at you, Darcy. See the humour, do not take offense. I thought Elizabeth had cured you of that."

"I would feel more humour if the laughter was about any other subject, Uncle. Pick one, I beg you."

A quiet knock came to the door and Elizabeth appeared. Immediately they stood, the smiles were gone and the room was occupied with five men looking abashed and one looking very relieved. "Forgive me for interrupting, gentlemen. Richard, your mother requests that you come to the blue sitting room." Fitzwilliam was gone like a shot. She laughed and looked to Darcy. "And you Mr. Darcy, may I have a moment?"

"You may have more than that." He began to move towards her but the others exchanged glances and filed out.

She closed the door and locked it, then advanced towards him, stopping a few feet away to rest her hands on her hips. "What was that about?"

"They were laughing at my expense."

"Why?"

"Because I have a wonderful loving wife." He stepped closer.

"And that is amusing?"

"No, that is enviable." He slipped his hands around her waist and kissed her softly then hugged her tight. "Thank you for rescuing me. How did you know that I needed you?"

"I heard everyone's laughter but yours." She rested her ear to his chest and embraced his waist. "That is the sound I love, so I came to see what was wrong."

"Thank you." He kissed the top of her head and they stood quietly rocking together. "I love you, too."

"RICHARD, COME IN and close the door." Lady Matlock directed. Fitzwilliam did as he was told and took a seat on the sofa next to Evangeline.

He looked at her then to his mother. "Well, the atmosphere is as thick as London fog, which does not bode well."

"What it bodes is between you two. I have heard out all of Mrs. Carter's hopes and fears and have attempted to address them reasonably as a woman. What remains are issues that only you can answer." She stood and looked down at Richard whose concerned gaze was focussed on Evangeline. "I am not in the least concerned about propriety, take your time." She walked to the door and opened it, then closed it behind her.

Fitzwilliam waited for her to begin, but seeing nothing forthcoming spoke with what he hoped was a smiling voice. "She can be rather intimidating sometimes."

"Yes, I . . . understand that." She looked to her clasped hands.

After some silence Fitzwilliam tried again. "She was the one who meted out my punishment."

"Did that happen often?" Evangeline asked quietly.

"Oh yes, until I realized that misbehaving at home would not be tolerated." He laughed and warmed to the subject. "Of course I had to be careful that she did not hear about my behaviour at school either. I would bribe my brother to stay quiet."

Evangeline smiled and looked up to him. "What did you offer?"

"I offered not to beat him to a pulp." Seeing her wide eyes he laughed. "You are not man."

"I am very aware of that fact." She saw his smile fade and sighed. "Forgive me, Richard. You have been so kind and I have . . ."

"Been very dear." He said softly.

"I have not. I have vacillated with a decision, making you wonder and wait, letting you kiss me . . ."

"And frightening you in the process, I am sorry for that." He took her hand. "I could not resist."

"I was frightened, but . . . I have relived that kiss daily since we parted." Evangeline saw the smile slowly returning. "Richard, your letters have made me feel alive again. I was married when I was twenty. You were correct when you surmised that I was full of hope and dreams that day, but by the end of the wedding night, I . . ." She choked and began to cry.

"Dear Eva." Richard immediately let go of her hand and wrapped her up in his arms. "My love, you do not have to tell me." He held her while her shoulders shook. "I knew that he was dissolute but I had no idea that he mistreated you as well. Did your brother know?" He felt her head shake. "Nobody knew?" He kissed her hair and closed his eyes. "I love you; I have fallen so deeply in love with you. I have told you more in my letters than I have to any person except Darcy."

"I love your letters." She whispered and he hugged her. "I imagined you were holding me like this and telling me your stories."

"I imagined we were at home and you were sitting by my side. I imagined that the nightmares would end with your kiss on my brow."

"Oh Richard, I am so frightened to trust again, but I do not wish to be alone in that house in London until I die."

"What may I do to convince my Eva?" He withdrew and using his rough thumb caressed the tears from her cheeks. "Anything you wish, I will do." His gaze moved down to her lips and he leaned in to gently brush them with a slight kiss. Forcing himself from the temptation of kissing her tears away, he moved back and pushed her hair from her eyes. "Did Mother help you?"

"She told me all about Audrey and Alicia. She told me of her disappointment and guilt in the suffering they experienced and her joy with their reinvigorated marriages. She spoke to me of the women she knows who never married and now face their declining years with no children to look after them as their peers slowly die. She spoke of the loneliness. She spoke of your Aunt Catherine and how she is alone by her own hand. She spoke of the comfort of a good man by her side and the joy of holding a child created of their union in her arms. She listened to me. I have had no woman to share this with . . . you have a wonderful mother."

"She can seem hard at times but she is very fierce in her protection of those she cares about." He said softly.

"Just as you are." Evangeline looked up at him. "My good soldier."

Fitzwilliam smiled and caressed her cheek with his fingers. "I am yours you know, it is ingrained now, I am afraid. I will go to the ends of the earth for you. Please tell me what to do. Just please do not avoid me. One thing that I know from watching Darcy is that he and Elizabeth speak to each other and . . . I want that. Too much of my life I have been left to my lonely thoughts, I want to be able to turn to you."

"Oh Richard that sounds so good." She sighed.

"It does?" He smiled. "I thought of that all by myself." She laughed and touched his cheek. He took her hand and kissed the palm, then encased her hands within his own. "Will you tell me all of your worries? Do not hesitate, just tell me. I can bear anything but your silence."

Evangeline nodded and bent her head to kiss his hands. Fitzwilliam lifted her chin to kiss her lips, but the taste of her tears and the warmth of her skin was his undoing, and the strokes deepened, until his gently probing tongue was at last welcomed to taste all of her. Their arms wound around each other and they remained in the secure embrace for several moments of shared relief. Eventually Fitzwilliam stopped and kissed her once. He drew her head to rest on his shoulder and embraced her. "Now my love, talk to me."

Chapter 7

"*L*ovely." Darcy lowered the glittering diamond choker past Elizabeth's eyes and gently fastened it around her neck. He kissed below her ear and paused, barely tracing his lips across her skin, down her shoulders, and adding the delicate touch of his fingers up her arms. Feeling her draw a trembling breath and lean back against him, Darcy whispered, "So very lovely you are." Withdrawing, he looked at their reflection and smiled to see her watching him. He closed his arms around her and they studied the picture they presented, and slowly swayed to the tune playing on the music box.

"What is that?" She whispered and watched his lips caress her hair then down her temple to her ear. "A waltz?"

"Yes, love. Shall we dance?"

"I wish we could dance to this tonight." Elizabeth turned in his arms and faced him. "This dance is sensuous."

"Because we hold each other."

"Because you lead me. I move at your will." She saw the pride of possession appear in his intense gaze, then felt his hand take her waist as they began to sway and turn. "You cannot encompass my waist with your hands anymore."

"I am glad of it." He smiled as she looked at him doubtfully. "I am."

"Will you ever be able to do that again?"

Darcy chuckled, "Eventually the babe will be born, he will not remain forever inside of you."

"But will you still desire me after . . ." She was silenced with an ardent, insistent application of his lips. "Will . . ."

"mmm?" He sighed as they rested their heads together and continued to move.

"You know that I am capable of returning to a subject even after your admirable kisses."

"I do, but I also notice that you quickly take the hint that I feel you are being silly." Darcy's eyes opened to find hers inches away and staring at him. He kissed her nose. "Yes, love?"

"I am never silly."

"Oh. My mistake." His lips pursed and his eyes twinkled. "You are never obstinate either."

"No more so than you." She smiled to hear his chuckle as they twirled around the bed, when the music stopped.

"Ohh."

"Shall I reset it?" He offered and began to walk away.

"No, we need to go downstairs, our guests will arrive soon." She looked out of the window as she was again enfolded into his arms. "Help me tonight."

"Of course I will, as will Aunt Helen and Alicia, they are veterans of this sort of thing. I have never hosted a ball, only attended. I am nervous as well. Uncle Henry has given me strict instructions for my duties."

"Really, what are they?"

"To do whatever you tell me to do." He smiled at her and she laughed. "Ah, there is the sound I needed to hear." He kissed her and they hugged once more. "Are you ready?"

"No, but it seems we have no choice."

"Just remember, you my dearest wife, are the most powerful woman in Derbyshire."

"And the old guard will hate me."

"The old guard will court you." He said knowingly.

They let go and holding hands, exited their chambers to walk down the corridor. "Well it is about time!" Fitzwilliam pointed to an enormous clock ticking in the hallway. "Your guests are past the gate!"

"Who are you the watchman?" Darcy smiled and Elizabeth laughed. He came to a stop and looked his cousin up and down, taking in his polished boots and well-brushed coat. "You clean up very nicely, Richard." He saw Fitzwilliam's colour rising and letting go of Elizabeth took a slow turn around him, noted the gleam on his sword and then pausing, touched the pomade applied to his hair, then took a long sniff of the cologne that enveloped him. "Planning to impress, Cousin?"

"Quiet." He said through clenched teeth.

"Seductive scent, rather like a stallion after a hard run." Darcy noted, "And your hair is just as shiny as . . ."

"Hush Will!" Elizabeth admonished and taking Fitzwilliam's tightly clenched hands into hers, looked him in the eye. "You are more handsome tonight than I have ever seen you, and if I had met you before I was attached to your cousin, my head would assuredly have been turned." She saw a little lift come to his lips. "Your cologne is subtle and intriguing, your hair is luxurious, and I know that Evangeline will be hard-pressed to keep from abandoning all decorum and not running into your arms." She smiled and rose up on her toes to kiss his cheek.

"Well." Fitzwilliam's chest puffed and he bent to kiss Elizabeth's cheek in return. "Thank you." He glanced up to see Darcy's face redden. "You should know that my head *was* turned when I first saw you, and I was a gentleman and did not try to interfere, no matter how tempting it was." He winked at her and straightened. Elizabeth's eyes widened and then she giggled with her gloved hand raised to her lips.

"That is quite enough, Richard." Darcy took Elizabeth's hand and placed it decidedly back onto his arm then looked at her. "You, too."

She lifted her chin. "You started it."

"Hmmph." Darcy sniffed and leading her to the door, stood silently against the wall, and stared out at the drive.

Elizabeth and Fitzwilliam exchanged glances and noticing Evangeline descending the stairs, rushed to meet her. Elizabeth let go of Darcy's arm and stroked her hand over his shoulder, down the curve of his stiffened spine and then rested it firmly on his backside where she gently rubbed. Darcy's darkened eyes found hers sparkling up at him. He glanced down at his breeches. Elizabeth followed his gaze to the rapidly growing bulge.

"What are you doing to me?"

"Assuring you of my love. I am sorry if I hurt your feelings."

"I am an easy target for teasing when it comes to you, but then Richard is such an easy target when it comes to Mrs. Carter, I had no choice. I should not complain, but please spare me from those particular teases?"

"The ones that suggest I may have loved another? That is impossible; you had me from the very beginning."

"Elizabeth." He whispered and glanced around the hallway. Servants were everywhere, family and friends were descending the stairs and moving towards the ballroom where the musicians could be heard tuning their instruments. The fact that nobody had approached them yet was a miracle and he cared nothing of it. He wanted to act on his desire. "I would love to kiss you right now."

"And I would love to receive more than a kiss." She whispered. Darcy's hands clenched.

He looked desperately around the increasingly crowded room for a place of privacy. "You could not tempt me in our rooms?" Elizabeth smiled and leaned against his rigid body. Darcy's arm came around and he clutched her tightly when she embraced his waist. "We will follow through with this desire, will we not?" He looked down at her and attempted to regain control. "Will we?"

"Tonight?"

"During the ball." He demanded.

"In the ballroom?" She laughed.

"I do not care where!"

"Darcy! Really Son, your guests will be scandalized to walk in to find you grasping your wife like that!" Lord Matlock chuckled when they both startled and reddened. "Ah, you forgot where you were. I like that." He winked and moved away. "I like that."

The couple straightened and resumed standing side-by-side with Elizabeth's hand on his arm. The surprise of Lord Matlock's greeting had significantly reduced Darcy's situation and he was free to stand without pain again. Their eyes met. "I hold you to this promise, Mrs. Darcy."

"I do not recall making one."

He leaned down and seized her lips in a fervent kiss that left her breathless. Satisfied; he drew a deep breath and straightened when the door was opened when the first carriage arrived. "Ah, here are our guests!"

"WOULD YOU CARE FOR A SIP?" Darcy said softly to his sleepy wife. She was curled against him in a large leather chair in the library after the final guests had departed.

Elizabeth lifted her head from his chest and looked at the glass suspiciously. "What are you plying me with, Mr. Darcy?"

"It is only wine, love." He held the glass to her lips and tipped it forward, then taking it away, kissed her and tasted the vintage on her tongue. Setting the glass down on the table, he cupped her face and continued with soft, open kisses, then sliding his hands around her shoulders drew her into his arms. Elizabeth sighed and he kissed her cheek and her forehead, and cuddled her safely on his lap. She settled her head back onto his shoulder and closed her eyes. "Please retire, dearest."

"No. I want to witness this meeting of the gentleman's club." She said with a yawn.

"You are exhausted. Your first ball was a spectacular success, but I am afraid that you are going to be feeling the effects of it for some time."

"Then come to bed with me."

"I would like that above everything but this is tradition and I am . . ."

"A stickler for tradition, I know." She felt his chuckle and looked up to kiss his chin. "Your beard is growing."

"It is nearly dawn, my dear."

"mmm." She settled back into the warmth of his embrace and they listened to the fire crackle. "Why can you men not discuss whatever this is in the morning?"

"Because now is when it is fresh and the blood of the unrequited is boiling furiously." He laughed when one brown eye stared at him before she snuggled back to his shoulder. "I have not been much of a participant in the past, only an observer, and might I add, I have only attended three of these events. But I am the host . . ."

"Yes, yes."

Darcy brushed his lips across her temple. "Why do you not retire, love?"

"I have no desire to leave you." She closed her eyes and Darcy felt her settle further against him. "I am fine."

"You are barely awake." He said softly.

"I am resting my eyes."

"You are resting your entire body against me."

"Do you object?"

Darcy chuckled and kissed her cheek. "No my love, not at all." He laid his chin on her head and imagined their last dance of the evening. Hearing her hum the tune, he smiled to know her thoughts were his. "Would you care to lie on the sofa?"

"Again I ask, do you object to me in this position?"

"Dearest I am only thinking of your modesty, soon this room will be occupied with men."

"Are you embarrassed to have me here?"

"No, I am proud." He smiled to see a glimmer of satisfaction grace her lips. "Should we remove your slippers? Your poor feet are . . ."

"Fitzwilliam Darcy, please do not tell me how swollen and ugly they are."

"I would only like to rub them for you." He whispered against her cheek and felt her smile. "Did I at last say something acceptable?"

"mmmm."

Darcy chuckled and gave her a squeeze. "I did, then."

"I am hungry."

"I am not surprised; you have been starving yourself for three months."

"I want something sweet, something to just hold in my mouth." Elizabeth moved her hand from where it rested on his waistcoat and slipped it down his stomach to his hip.

"Lizzy?"

"Something to savour." She whispered as her fingers continued their exploration, now moving across the front of his breeches.

"Lizzy."

"Something that only you can share with me." She stroked slowly over the fabric and fingered the buttons of the fall. Darcy's hand came down to still hers.

"Lizzzzzy."

"mmmm?"

"You are cruel." He whispered warmly into her ear and pressed the arousal she inspired against her palm. "Why do you say things that I cannot possibly address?"

"Because we never had the opportunity to do so during the ball, and I know that when we wake sometime tomorrow, you most certainly will." Darcy's clasp tensed. "However it is I who will be doing the addressing, I am the one who hungers." She looked up and found his intense gaze fixed upon her. Moving her hands back up to entwine in his hair, she drew his face down and pleasured his lips. Darcy groaned as she whispered, "I want to swallow your pride." He muttered something under his breath and closed his eyes as she continued her seduction. "I want the satisfaction of gratifying you."

"I would dearly love to feed you." He growled against her ruby red lips, the vision of them wrapped around him further hardened his desire. "Ohhh my love." Darcy kissed her and looked into her eyes. She was not teasing anymore; she was simply expressing how much she wanted him. He nodded and with a sigh cuddled her back into his arms. He felt her embrace tighten around him and then relax. When he heard nothing further, Darcy tilted his head to see her peaceful face and soon he felt her soft steady breathing against the open collar of his shirt. Her body became heavier against him, and he held her, unconsciously stroking her back and kissing her hair, and allowing his thoughts to drift over the memory of their last encounter in that room.

Startling from his reverie, he was saved from the embarrassment of his tightened breeches by Elizabeth's warm presence on his lap when Fitzwilliam appeared. He bounced in and was about to drop into the leather chair opposite Darcy when he noticed his wife. "Darcy!"

"She is asleep." He smiled. "There was no putting her to bed. She will not hear a thing."

"Are you sure?" Fitzwilliam looked at her suspiciously. "It is quite disconcerting to see you in such a position, Cousin."

"I really do not care." Darcy chuckled. "Oh, and for obvious reasons, you can pour your own refreshment, if you have not had enough tonight."

"No, not by any means." He stood and poured out a glass of wine and returned to his chair. After studying Elizabeth's steady breathing for some time, he finally relaxed back into the cushions. "I want exactly what you have."

"Well, I think that you are on your way. Mrs. Car . . ."

"Do not call her that." He said gruffly. "Evangeline is her name, and soon I will give her a surname that is worthy of her."

"A proposal is necessary for that I believe, until then I will respect the name she has." Fitzwilliam sighed and Darcy smiled. "Are you any closer?"

"Yes." He sipped his wine and smiled at Elizabeth burrowing into Darcy, then standing, found a folded blanket and tucked it around her. The men's eyes met and he returned to his seat. "She is no longer hesitant with me. Surprisingly she has become shy though."

"Elizabeth did the same when we were first engaged and for a while after we married. It must be some sort of female oddity. Frustrating and endearing all at once." He peeked down at her face when he felt her pinch, then with a slight lift to his lips returned his gaze to Fitzwilliam. "So, tell me about the evening, I am afraid that being a host was rather time-consuming and I did not have the opportunity to observe."

"We danced." He shook his head. "Only twice. Ridiculous rules of behaviour. Why can a man only dance twice with the woman he intends to marry?"

"If you were engaged three might have been acceptable."

"Not with Mother lurking about." He took a good swallow of the wine. "No, follow decorum and all that. I did not like her being asked to dance by all these Derbyshire dandies you dug up for tonight. What was that all about?"

"There were a fair number of maidens as well, Cousin."

"Yes, and they were shooting arrows at your bride." He chuckled and Darcy smiled when Elizabeth squeezed him. "I have to tell you, Mother was immensely proud of Elizabeth tonight. She oversaw the battle without a flinch. You would think she had been attending balls from infancy. She handled all the petty squabbles and soothed the nerves of the mothers with aplomb and humour and I might add a fair amount of grace, you would never have guessed her age to see her." He lifted his glass. "Your wife is well and surely the mistress of Derbyshire."

"Your mother might disagree with that, Son." Lord Matlock entered and flopped into another chair, then cocked his head at Darcy. "Lap warmer?"

"A very welcome one."

"Hmm." He turned his head to his son. "So your mother is usurped by a country upstart?"

"If I am not mistaken Father, Matlock is in the country as well."

"Touché." Layton grinned as he came in with Harwick, followed closely by Stewart and Bingley. "I see that your little mother is in the same condition as mine."

"In more ways than one." Darcy chuckled. "Although you successfully convinced yours to retire."

"No convincing was necessary, after the last dance she practically led me up the stairs." Layton sighed and accepted his port from Stewart. "Well it was good to change from the formal wear. I see that you have simply decided to undress here?"

Darcy looked down at his rather unkempt appearance and shrugged. "I am much more casual about attire when we are alone."

"I imagine you will be putting on the layers soon enough." Lord Matlock shifted his chair closer to the fire.

"Lord Moreland chose not to join us, I see?"

"No, Father was done in. Giddy with Laura's success." He lifted his glass to Harwick who beamed. "Well, come on man; tell how my sister charmed you."

Harwick laughed happily. "No, I will not be the first, but I will say that . . ." He paused and looked at Elizabeth. "Tonight when I watched Mrs. Darcy, I saw her. I no longer saw a reminder of Ellen. I think that Ellen stayed with me until she knew I was safe and happy again, and now she is leaving me to move forward with Laura and not dwell on the memory of the past."

"She will never leave you." Lord Matlock said quietly.

"No, but instead of searching for her in the crowds, I will instead see her in the eyes of our daughters, and that is where she will live on." Harwick smiled and laughed. "Thank you for the loan of your wife, Darcy."

The other men joined in, relieving the seriousness of the conversation. "I will not address the implications of that statement, sir, but I am certain that Elizabeth will be glad to know that she helped." She squeezed him and he kissed her forehead. "So, will you propose?"

"Oh of course. I plan to do so before we depart Pemberley and invite her parents to Meadowbrook before they return home. I want them to see the estate and especially wish for her to meet the girls. I know that she has helped your brother's wife with her baby, Stewart." He nodded. "My concern now will not be so much the introduction of Laura into their lives, but the removal of Evangeline."

Richard nodded. "I think that it will be harder on her, as well. They have been very important to her over the last three years. Thank you for reminding me of that, in case she does not tell me her feelings of loss. I will understand any melancholy that comes about."

The men sipped their drinks and Bingley glanced at Elizabeth. "Um, is she truly asleep?"

Darcy tilted his head and watched as Elizabeth's lashes fluttered. "Yes, she is dreaming." He lifted his brows to Bingley and he cleared his throat.

"What is your opinion of Miss Bennet?" He looked around the room. "I know that she was not at all suited for you Harwick, and Stewart, you had the opportunity to court her in Hertfordshire but looked to Mrs. Darcy instead. Fitzwilliam?"

He sighed and stretched his legs out. "My first impression was that of a beautiful smile with nothing of substance behind it." He saw the other two men nodding. "All the proper behaviours were there, but I was not at all intrigued by her display of envy and dogged adherence to her mother's teachings even when they were clearly proven incorrect." Bingley nodded and met Darcy's eyes as he continued to listen to Fitzwilliam. "However, since meeting her again at Pemberley, I believe that some improvements have been wrought, and perhaps with time she might be worth more than a first look. What say you, Darcy? You have been living in close quarters with her?"

Darcy checked again to be sure that Elizabeth truly was asleep. He bit his lip and looked to Bingley. "Miss Bennet did little to encourage my good opinion, and for a time when we were here together, her presence was like a cold mist that dampened our desires to simply be ourselves as we had been this summer. Eventually it was Miss Bennet who addressed the situation and as you see, Elizabeth and I do not care at all if our close friends see us display our affection openly anymore. She has changed, she has grown. She spends time with Elizabeth learning how to manage Pemberley, she is reading, she takes walks and she is willing to sing in public. None of this would have been possible without Elizabeth's determined support. She is the miracle worker here, but it also required Jane's determination to improve. So to answer your question Bingley, I feel that Miss Bennet is making up for the absence of an education and the neglect of her personal fulfilment now, and with time she will hopefully be a woman who is admired for both beauty and accomplishment."

"I see." Bingley looked at his hands. "Of course you have the right to know why I broached the subject; she is your sister after all. Tonight I danced with . . . twelve women, eight of whom were unattached. Each had their charm. When I danced with Miss Bennet, we talked and were comfortable with each other. I pointed out to her that Captain Houghton was paying her particular attention. Of course she blushed and looked up to find him staring at her. When I suggested that I introduce them she . . . I saw her looking down to where her hand was clasped in mine." Bingley looked up to Darcy. "She . . .did not answer for a long time, but when she did, I heard the disappointment in her voice."

"I know nothing of her feelings, Bingley. Would you like me to speak to Elizabeth?"

"I am not ready to marry, am I? I need to spend at least another Season in town, and establish myself well." Darcy nodded, and he turned to Stewart. "Before you leave, could you sit down with me and, well all of you could help, and tell me of Netherfield? Perhaps if it is still available next August it might be a good enough place to start."

"I will be happy to tell you what I observed there." Stewart nodded.

"And I will be glad to look it over for you." Darcy said slowly. "But are you already committing yourself to Jane? Based on nothing more than a glance?"

"What did it take for you to commit to Mrs. Darcy?" Bingley said quietly. He saw Darcy's eyes drop to watch his sleeping wife. "I do not know what my feelings are, Darcy. I cannot define them, but I do recognize the effort that she has put forth in the past months and I feel that I have made changes to myself as well. Perhaps I am overly influenced by the evidence of love that is floating around this remarkable estate." He smiled and the others chuckled. "In any case, I am starting to look ahead. I hope that the title of puppy may be given to another man."

"I think Son, that you have with that statement become a man." Lord Matlock raised his glass to him. "Welcome to the club."

Bingley grinned and then flopped back in his chair. "I do not know if I can abide being so serious, how on earth do you pull it off all of the time, Darcy?"

The men roared with laughter and shouted insults at him. Darcy glared and shot looks down at Elizabeth and when she began to stir they were all silenced as they watched her eyes slowly open to see his face looking down into hers. She smiled sleepily and lifting her hand to his head, drew it down to bestow a tender kiss, then she sank down against his neck and sighed before falling back to sleep. Darcy closed his eyes for a moment then looked back up to the blushing men.

"Tell me, Darcy. This position you are maintaining appears to be very familiar."

"Do you mean that it is one you have enjoyed?" He said softly to his uncle.

"No I mean it is one that you enjoy regularly."

Darcy smiled. "I suppose that Aunt Helen told you of her disastrous advice to Elizabeth regarding our roles in the privacy of our chambers."

"Yes." He nodded. "She said that you were rather angry with her presumption. She felt terribly for it but she did mean well. She thought that Elizabeth would not know of the expected practice of our circle."

Darcy said nothing, he only smiled. "Hang on . . ." Layton looked between the couple and his father. "You sleep together? Nightly?" Again Darcy said nothing, only smiling.

"Darcy! Answer me!" Layton demanded.

Instead he turned his head to take in Stewart's thoughtful expression. "We have not heard from you yet. How did you find the ladies this evening?"

Stewart glanced around at the still fascinated men and cleared his throat. "I . . . I was wondering if I might pay a call before I depart for London." All of the eyes turned to look at him. "I, um . . . I rather enjoyed my dance with Miss Henley you see, and I would like to confirm her plans. She was unsure when her family would be returning to London, and since I will likely remain there for the winter . . ."

"Miss Henley?" Darcy smiled. "I thought that I noticed a rather spirited conversation between the two of you."

Stewart looked at his hands and was lost in the memory of their dance in an instant.

"You dance very well."

"You told me that before." She smiled and his brow creased. *"At my parent's home, we danced last year."*

"Oh, forgive me, but I . . ."

"Your heart was not in it." She laughed and they separated before joining hands again. *"You are far more pleasant this time around."*

"I should hope so." He grimaced then gave her a small smile. *"I am fully recovered."*

"Who was she?" Miss Henley tilted her head and his eyes widened. *"Oh never mind, it does not matter, I am certain that she is very happy where she is."*

"She is." He cleared his throat and unbidden his eyes travelled to see the Darcys trading conversation and smiles as they danced together.

"And what are your plans now, sir?" She stopped as the music did, and they faced each other. *"Are you ready to try anew?"*

Stewart laughed. "Are you playing matchmaker, Miss Henley? Surely you know the discomfort of that situation from your mother's efforts, why would you wish it upon me?"

"Perhaps I like others to share in my misery?" She smiled as the next song began and once again they advanced to hold hands and turn. "Oh, Mama has washed her hands of me."

"I understand that you have been quite particular." His brow lifted and hers matched it. "No?"

"Where did you hear this?"

"I will not reveal my sources, Miss Henley."

"But you cared enough to enquire, sir."

"Perhaps I overheard it in a crowded room?"

"Perhaps you do not wish to admit that you are interested?"

"Perhaps you would like to admit something of your own?" He smiled to see her blush. "I hit the mark, I see."

"That is unfair, you are used to prosecuting." She shook her head and he laughed as they hopped down the line. "You are sly."

"No more so than you." He turned her around and bowed as the set ended. "Will you be coming to town for the little Season or will you await the spring?"

"Why do you wish to know?"

"So that I may avoid you, of course." He laughed and she joined him. "I will be returning for court in a few days and will remain there. If you were to come this winter, I should like to call on you, if you were interested?"

"I am, and I thank you." Julia blushed and looked back up to his smiling eyes. "I will speak to my parents to learn their plans."

He nodded and then became serious. "I am only beginning my living, but it has great potential."

"There is no need to impress me with your occupation, sir. I am far more interested in your character." She spoke softly.

"I will remember that." He held her hand and waited for her to meet his gaze. "Thank you for the advice."

Richard's kick startled him from the memory and again the men laughed loudly. Stewart coloured but lifted his chin. "I like her and I wish that I had seen her clearly a year ago. I hope to see more of her in town and . . .we will see what comes of it."

"She likes you, too." All eyes turned to see Elizabeth's were open and she was smiling at Stewart.

"Pardon me?" He said softly.

"She likes you, too." Elizabeth repeated, then sitting up, she removed the blanket and stood. "I am going to retire now. Will you be long, Will?"

"No, in fact I will accompany you." He took the blanket from her hands and laid it on the chair. Elizabeth kissed Lord Matlock's, Layton's, and Richard's cheeks and smiled at the others, then taking Darcy's hand they began to exit the room.

"Wait! You cannot just leave it like that!" Stewart cried.

Darcy and Elizabeth looked at each other. "She is quite well-off." He offered. Stewart waved him off and stared at Elizabeth.

"You say that she likes . . . *me*?"

"She does." She laughed to see thoughts clearly flying through his mind. "She kept an eye on you this Season; she has rejected every man who approached."

"Because of *me*?" He said incredulously, and saw the couple's smiles and watched them depart the room. "She likes me." Stewart mused.

"Do you think that she was awake that whole time?" Bingley whispered when they were gone.

"If she was I think that she will have a great deal to impart to the subjects of our conversation." Harwick smiled. "Although I suspect she was not always with us."

Fitzwilliam stared at the empty chair then downed his wine and stood. "Good night, Gentlemen." Leaving the room he strode through the dark empty hallways until he arrived at the open doors to the ballroom. He stood staring at the mirrored walls that reflected the moonlight streaming in the windows. He could hear the music, and could see Evangeline as she took his hand.

"Richard." She whispered when he passed by her side. "You are in another world." He smiled and said nothing, only drifting by again then taking her hand, turned. "For a man who is never without conversation, I am puzzled by your silence."

"I wish to remember our first dance." He squeezed her hand and nodded to the Darcys. "Look at my model of behaviour. They are clearly enjoying a verbal joust, the likes of which I doubt I could accomplish, but they are secure, married, and happy. We have only just begun. I still am left to stare at you and keep my deepest thoughts buried."

"I thought that we have agreed to share our thoughts with each other." She smiled and he laughed, then as they came together to walk down the line he bent his lips to her ear and whispered. Instantly a becoming flush spread up her chest to her hairline and her eyes went to the floor. Fitzwilliam watched her and his lips twitched.

"You understand my reticence now?"

"Yes." She whispered.

"Do you find the thought objectionable?" He tilted his head and they let go to move around each other.

"No, I find it . . ." She stopped and fixed her eyes on his mouth and said nothing more.

"Ah, so we shall both bury our thoughts for the evening." Fitzwilliam laughed when he once again held her hands. "Who knew that the suggestion of a little kiss would be so disconcerting?"

"It is not the suggestion Richard, it is the anticipation." Evangeline looked back down to the floor and Richard squeezed her hand, and wordlessly continued the dance.

He nodded his head and whispered. "I anticipate so much with you, my Eva."

19 NOVEMBER 1809
We returned from church this morning to find an express waiting for us from Mr. Stewart. It seems that the trial has been scheduled for this Friday. Fitzwilliam and Richard will depart for London in the morning. No amount of cajoling or convincing has moved my husband; he will not permit me to accompany him. He claims it is because we have guests, although save for Mr. Bingley, they are all family and could certainly remain here alone. The Stewart family, Mr. Harwick and Mrs. Carter will depart for Meadowbrook. Laura's joy over Mr. Harwick's proposal yesterday was beautiful to behold; and I was so proud of Jane and the gracious way that she congratulated them.

Fitzwilliam is pleased that his dear friend and the Matlocks will remain behind to protect me, although from what I cannot imagine. I know that he hates to leave, I watched him tenderly wrap my likeness in his handkerchief to take with him, and I gave him letters, one for each of the eight days he expects to be away. He fears for me being exposed to whatever the publicity the trial may generate, and most of all he fears that our baby might be harmed by a long journey. He is haunted by his mother's death still. So as much as I hate this, I will accept his decision. I will trade my peace of mind of being together for his peace of mind for our separation.

"Do you understand?" Darcy asked when he looked up from the journal. Elizabeth nodded and he stood to embrace her. "I will be home before you know it. And you will likely wish me away again as soon as possible."

"Hush." She whispered. They stood near the window, looking out over the bare gardens. Layton and Alicia occupied a bench, and in the distance they watched two couples walking together. Darcy chuckled as Harwick led Laura behind a hedge. He looked down to see Elizabeth's eyes sparkling. She giggled at his grin. "What do you suppose is happening out there?"

"Hmm." He kissed her temple. "Well chaperoning duties are definitely being neglected."

Harwick looked down at Laura's hand on his arm and back up to see her smiling at him. "I cannot tell you how good this feels; I never hoped to experience this again."

"Well since this is my first time, I hope that I can live up to your expectations." She laughed.

He tilted his head and brought his other hand up to cover hers. "I have no preconceived ideas, my dear. You are a lovely woman, and so different from Ellen. I thought that to honour her memory I would not be permitted to feel anything again, and that to find happiness with another would be insulting her. I have realized that I need to feel again. If I brought home a wife who inspired indifference, then my daughters would not have the example of marriage I wish them to know."

"Jeffrey," She said softly. "Will you show me the example of marriage you wish to have?"

"Oh." He looked about to be sure of their privacy then smiling, slipped his arms securely around her before claiming her mouth. "With pleasure."

"Oh!" Evangeline cried and stopped dead as she and Fitzwilliam came around the hedge.

Quickly grasping her hand he hurried them away from the embraced couple, and when a respectable distance had been achieved, he stopped and grinned down at her. "We cannot interrupt such a tender interlude." She blushed and he laughed. "So how does it feel to catch your brother in such a position?"

"He is so private; he would be mortified if he knew." Her eyes widened when Fitzwilliam's lips pursed. "Oh you would not embarrass him, would you?"

"Me? Oh, no, I would not think of doing that to someone so wholly unrelated to me." He winked. "However, if we were brothers . . ."

Her expression changed instantly from surprise to teary as his softened and he raised her hand to his lips. "I must leave you tomorrow. If it were not for the love of my cousin, I could not possibly be moved from your side, but I must do as he, and leave the one I care for to remove a scourge from our lives. I cannot, will not, leave you though without saying this, I love you, Eva. I cannot possibly say anything more eloquent than that. I have never said those words to another. You are the only woman who I ever wish to love. Please trust me and be my wife."

Evangeline stared into the blue eyes of this gentleman soldier. He watched her wrestle with the words that were so clearly poised to be spoken. "I have revealed to you my soul, Eva. I have nothing else. You know that I have worked hard for what I have, you know that I have killed men, and you know that I suffer for the experiences that I have had. You know that I care for my boys deeply; you know that I am in pain nearly constantly. You know that I am lonely. And I at last know all of you. Perhaps . . ."

"Not perhaps, Richard." She pressed her fingers to his lips. "I love you, I trust you, and yes, I wish to marry you." Richard kissed her fingers and grinned, then squeezed her with a hug that made her squeal in protest. "Oh no, my dear, you are not escaping these arms anytime soon!" He kissed her soundly and she laughed. "You are very well mine!"

"And do you intend to suffocate me before we are wed?" She gasped.

"Oh no, I have wonderful plans for that night, and so many others!" He laughed and eased his grip. "I have been thinking of you most ardently."

"Perhaps I should change my mind?" She smiled and he shook his head. "You are a silly fool, Colonel Richard Fitzwilliam!"

"I am. And I believe that it is entirely possible that your silly fool of a brother will be glad to be rid of you. So do not even think of changing your mind." He kissed her softly and she gladly sank into his loving arms. "You would not do that would you?"

"No, that would be impossible."

"WELL I WILL BE DAMNED!" Lord Matlock laughed and shook Fitzwilliam's hand. "You did it!"

"Yes I did, and my breeches contain no dust on the knees." He winked at Evangeline.

"Oh he did not kneel?" Laura kissed her cheek. "Are you disappointed?"

"Not at all, he very happily displayed his admiration in other ways." She smiled up at him.

Fitzwilliam coloured and kissed her hand. "We will have to discuss acceptable subjects for public discourse my dear."

"Oh give that up now!" Harwick laughed. "My sister is quite happy to speak on any subject. Ask Darcy here if he can control his vivacious wife's tongue."

Darcy smiled and stood behind Elizabeth, and shocked no one in the room by slipping his arms around her waist and drawing her back to rest against his chest. He looked down to her upturned face. "I have long ago learned to revel in her thoughts, and would not think to ever try to silence her." He laughed and kissed her rising brow.

"You would not, would you? What about this afternoon when I was asking you to stay . . ." Elizabeth found her lips being caressed and the room filled with laughter as she was soundly muted. Darcy's eyes twinkled when he withdrew and they smiled at each other. "You know that I was hoping for a kiss."

"I do." He squeezed her, and rested his hands upon hers as they lay over the baby; and looking back up to his smiling friends and relatives ignored the catcalls of the gentlemen. "I hope that the four of you will be very happy."

"Thank you." The couples collectively proclaimed and laughed.

The newly attached couples settled on chairs adjacent to each other to begin forming what would eventually be their new family, and the earls and their wives leaned together to discuss the blending of their own. Stewart and Bingley found their own spot as the remaining bachelors, laughing and discussing how their mature friends had suddenly turned into cow-eyed youths, and the Darcys and Laytons drifted off to talk about their pending parenthood, leaving Jane alone for the moment. Elizabeth noticed her by herself and stood. Darcy began to follow her and she shook her head and smiled then walked over to Jane.

"Will you join us?" She asked and took Jane's hand. "Are you well?"

Jane smiled softly. "Oh yes, I am fine. I am very happy for them all." She noticed Elizabeth's relief. "It was never meant to be, Lizzy. I had my doubts as much as he. If I am destined for a marriage of convenience, it should not be with a man who knows what it is to love. He was trying to convince himself of something he knew was wrong, and I was too foolish to recognize that if I had tried, perhaps it could have been right." Jane smiled at her and shrugged her shoulders.

"You have grown in the past months, Jane." Elizabeth squeezed her hand. "I am proud of you."

She shook her head. "I have been dealt a hard lesson, I always knew that our parents were not perfect, but I refused to understand the effect that their negligence had upon all of us. I should have followed your example and educated myself. All I am is an empty shell." She smiled sadly.

"Then fill it, you have already begun, Fitzwilliam and I are both happy with the changes you have made." Elizabeth said quietly. "You are but twenty, Jane. Most girls do not marry for several more years. Perhaps you will find the right man for you, and should you not; you are very welcome to live here at Pemberley. You will always have a home with us."

"You and your ten children?" Jane laughed and patted Elizabeth's baby. "I would like that, I think."

"Well do not give up yet!" She laughed. "Come, join us in the corner, and listen to Alicia warn me of what is to come. Watch Fitzwilliam's eyes grow wide! He will surely dwell on every word when we are separated." They walked over to the trio and Jane sat with them. Darcy held open his arms for Elizabeth and she settled against his side and snuggled into his embrace. She smiled at her husband when he kissed her forehead and rested his cheek in her hair. "Now we are ready to hear anything."

"AND?" DARCY PRODDED Stewart as the carriage rumbled slowly through the streets of London after an afternoon spent at their club.

He laughed and sat back in the cushions. "And we will see. Miss Henley's mother confirmed that she has rejected every other man who has called."

"But she encouraged you. Besides, they were after that property she owns, not the woman."

Fitzwilliam chuckled and stretched out his long legs with a groan and no little pain. "What has become of us, three men in search of love, not money. Of course you do not need any Darcy. Call it second sons who defy convention!"

"But Mrs. Carter does have money." Darcy pointed out.

"I was serious, Darcy. Call her Evangeline." Fitzwilliam said sharply. "I intend to give her a respectable name very soon. That bastard deserved the bullet he got. If I knew his executioner, I would shake his hand."

Darcy and Stewart exchanged glances. "What is it, Richard?"

"Never mind." He said darkly. "Bloody long engagement! Whose foolish idea was that?"

"Yours, I believe." Darcy offered and received a glare. "I take it that you are impatient to claim your bride?"

"She will not leave Meadowbrook until Harwick does, and Miss Stewart will not marry without a proper engagement." He growled. "Eight weeks! I have to change her mind."

"But you have the time to begin the repairs to the townhouse, so it will be completed by the date of your wedding." Darcy pointed out.

"Yes, but in the meantime where is she? At Meadowbrook with Lord and Lady Moreland, and Miss Stewart. It is not fair, Darcy! Why does Harwick get to live under the same roof with his bride and play house?"

"Because they have not had the courtship you enjoyed with Mrs . . .. I am sorry Richard, but her name is Mrs. Carter." Fitzwilliam glared and Darcy raised his brow in return, and received a curt nod.

"We wrote letters, it is not the same as a flesh and blood woman in my arms." He gestured at his cousin. "And do not deny it! We practically had to pry your fingers from Elizabeth!"

"Do not remind me." Darcy looked out of the window and became silent, thinking of Elizabeth's tears dampening his cheek when they parted four days earlier.

Stewart cleared his throat. "Well my sister and parents will only be at Meadowbrook for a week if that is any consolation, then they will come to town to have her wedding clothes prepared. Mrs. Carter will be with you in a few weeks, and you Darcy, will be home within the next fortnight."

"Sooner than that." He said softly.

"And Miss Henley?" Fitzwilliam sat up and repaired his humour. "Will she be in town soon?"

Stewart looked at his hands and nodded. "Yes."

"And?"

"How should I know? It is early days yet." He looked up to see the cousins smiling knowingly at each other. "Do not start on me."

"Not yet." Fitzwilliam agreed.

"But given time . . ." Darcy's smile returned.

Stewart groaned. The coach at last stopped at the inn where he kept his rooms. The sight of the traditional quarters of barristers and judges silenced the banter. He turned to Darcy, "I will come by tomorrow with Smith. Henderson will not meet with you before the trial, Smith as your solicitor will speak for you to him. I know that you wished for me to handle this, but . . . I want to be absolutely sure that Wickham is convicted. You need a man of experience, not me." Darcy nodded but noted Stewart's disappointment with his own decision. "Although the magistrate could have testified alone, Henderson is relieved that you are appearing. The cases are quick, and well, he is presumed guilty. He has no funds to buy witnesses on his behalf and frankly a man of your status really will not be questioned. I will be with you; I have nothing on my schedule that day."

"I will gladly pay for your time, Stewart."

He smiled. "Now you know that we do not accept fees, Darcy! We only take gifts! We gentlemen of law are not in trade!" He snorted at the hypocrisy and climbed down from the coach. "I do this for my friends, Darcy, nothing more is needed." Touching his hat he smiled and entered the inn. Soon the coach was back in motion and Darcy and Fitzwilliam were left alone.

"I will testify if you wish." Fitzwilliam said quietly.

Darcy shook his head. "No. It will be a difficult experience but I can face the crowd for her. Seeing Wickham in the dock will be a pleasure." He looked down at the ring on his hand and touched it. "Besides, Elizabeth is with me."

"IT IS PURE LUCK you know, Mr. Darcy." Henderson sniffed as they entered the witness room. "It is a rare event when you know what case is coming up, but with a bit of persuasion I had it moved to today." He met Darcy's eye with a raised brow and he nodded.

"I appreciate that and I will be sure to augment your gift for the effort."

Henderson broke into a wide smile. "I thought you might!" He indicated two empty chairs in the noisy room. "Just wait your turn, it could be all day. Used to make you all sit in the pub, but now you have your own place."

Darcy sank into the chair and Fitzwilliam joined him. The room was filled with people from all walks of society, but for the most part, it was the working class. They appeared to be the only gentlemen present. Pressing his lips tightly together, Darcy clasped his hands and took in the scene.

"Quite an education we are receiving today." Fitzwilliam observed.

"It is worth it to see him convicted."

"Naturally. So how much bile is rising in your throat?"

"The smell . . ."

"Not rosewater, that is certain. Reminds me distinctly of the barracks."

The cousins exchanged glances and silently watched the people watching them. Stewart looked in the doorway and spotting them, entered and shook their hands when they stood. "I am sorry to be late, Smith has a few other cases today, but he is ready for you. I am sorry that the funds you gave me were not enough, seems there were a lot of hands asking for a piece of it to guarantee this date." He glanced at the door and waved. "Here is Smith!"

"Mr. Darcy, Colonel." Smith bowed. "You will be sworn, Mr. Darcy you are first, just answer the questions from Henderson as they are asked, Colonel you are next, then the magistrate, then Wickham. He will make it as straightforward as possible, Wickham has no representative."

A man came to the doorway, "Prosecutor for Elizabeth Hollingworth!" Darcy started with the name and a man stood from some seats behind them and the room silenced as he left. Smith watched them go and shook his head. "I'm betting on transportation for that one, servant girl stole a banknote from her employer's pocket book."

"Well you cannot be too careful when hiring servants." Fitzwilliam observed. "Mother only takes on relatives of our staff, or one recommended by a friend."

"I have not been involved in that, I have just left it to Mrs. Mercer and Mrs. Reynolds." Darcy mused.

"And now Elizabeth." Darcy met Fitzwilliam's raised brows and smiled.

"Yes." Darcy looked down and twisted his ring. Smith spoke to them some more and then another man appeared.

"Prosecutor for William Dean!" A man rose and Smith jumped.

"Ah one of mine, I will return shortly, this one stole a twenty-pound note from his employer, definitely transportation for him. Who knows, maybe William and Elizabeth will marry one day!" He laughed and departed the room.

Fitzwilliam chuckled. "Can you imagine if you and your Elizabeth committed some crimes and were sent off to Australia?"

"No, no I cannot." Darcy snarled.

"Relax, Cousin, our turn will come. I am glad that Smith convinced you to let me testify. I want my hand in this too." Seeing only a nod of assent, Fitzwilliam crossed his legs and took in the crowd, and gave up trying to relax Darcy. He was lost in his thoughts.

"Prosecutor for George Wickham!"

Darcy jumped up and Fitzwilliam was right behind him. They were met by Smith and were led into the courtroom. The solicitor took his place at a great mahogany table and Darcy and Fitzwilliam were showed their places in the witness box. Darcy's eyes wandered the room, and noted the looking glass positioned to catch sunlight from the windows to illuminate the accused. The jurors were seated and whispering amongst themselves while staring at them, and a crowd of noisy spectators was above. Wickham was led into the room and took a seat in the dock, opposite Darcy. He looked wan, his time in Newgate had not been easy, but the cockiness was unchanged. The men glared at each other.

"George Wickham, indicted for robbery, assault, and housebreaking."

Darcy was sworn in. Henderson took charge. "Your name?"

"I am Fitzwilliam Darcy."

"You are a gentleman?"

"I am; I live in Park Lane."

"Do you know the accused?"

"I do, he is the son of my father's deceased steward and was his ward."

"What took place?"

"His father left me a living, Darcy refused it to me and I demanded compensation."

"Did he give you nothing for the living?"

"A pittance of its worth."

Henderson held up a paper. "Is this your signature?"

"It appears to be."

"This document certifies that you received one thousand pounds inheritance and three thousand pounds in exchange for the living. Did you receive these funds?"

Wickham snarled. "Yes."

"You feel that this was not enough?"

"I do." The murmurs amongst the jury and the spectators increased. Darcy watched them talking and looked to Fitzwilliam. He shrugged and sat forward.

"You felt it necessary to threaten a pregnant woman to take this so-called compensation?"

"I did not know she was with child."

"Why did you not seek legal means to recover what you felt you were owed?"

"I could not afford representation."

"You had spent the four thousand pounds in a period of two years?"

Wickham was silent, then seeing Darcy's cold stare responded. "I did." More conversation broke out, and the judge struck his gavel and demanded silence. "I should have finished what I started, Darcy. That would have been acceptable compensation."

Darcy stood and slammed his fist on the table. "Then you never would have seen justice in this room."

"Enough!" The judge declared as the volume of the conversations rose. "Mr. Darcy please take you seat. Jury, you have heard enough. Render your verdict."

Darcy sat down but kept his eyes boring into Wickham's identical cold gaze. Fitzwilliam kept a hand near Darcy's elbow, ready to drag him down if necessary. The jury leaned together and after several minutes of whispered conversation signalled they were ready. The foreman stood.

"We find the defendant guilty."

"Fourteen years transportation." The gavel was struck and Wickham was hustled out, but his eyes remained with Darcy's until the end.

"I will be back to collect!"

Fitzwilliam grabbed Darcy and held him fast then hustled him from the courtroom. In the background he heard a loud voice call, "Prosecutor for John Bridge!"

Stewart was down from the spectator's seats and joined them along with Henderson and Smith. "How do you feel Darcy? I was waiting for you leap across the courtroom and strangle him. In a few months he will be gone."

"On the morning of October 2nd, Wickham entered my home through kitchen door, evaded detection by the staff and gained entry to my priv study. He was surprised to find my wife at home and in the room."

"Why is your wife not here to bear witness?"

"My wife is with child and unable to travel. She was with child wh Wickham attacked her."

"You were not present?"

"No."

"What does Mrs. Darcy claim occurred?"

"She rose to her feet and reached for the bell pull to summon he Wickham grabbed her arm and twisted it, threatening to break it if s screamed." The conversation in the courtroom increased. Darcy met Smith eyes and he nodded. The kiss would not be mentioned. Raising his voice so would be heard, Darcy continued, "My wife then fainted and fell to the floc Wickham left her there and proceeded to open a secreted space and remove t strongbox kept there."

"How would he know of this place and the strongbox?"

"He observed my father removing it on many occasions."

"And then?"

"He attempted to open it using a silver knife kept on the desk for openi letters."

Smith held it up to show the jury. "Is this the knife?"

"It is. If you observe it is engraved with the initials GD, that was my father.

"And then?"

"He failed at picking the lock, picked up a marble statue and attempted break the lock with it. It was at this point that I and my cousin Colon Fitzwilliam returned to the house and entered the room. I struck him and we to my wife's aid."

"And the knife?"

"Was in his waistcoat."

"What is it worth?"

"I would estimate no less than five pounds."

"And then?"

"Colonel Fitzwilliam stood guard over him until the magistrate arrived. took my wife to her chambers and awaited the physician."

"Thank you. You may step down."

Fitzwilliam was sworn in and gave his testimony. The physician was una to appear but the magistrate did and had his record. At last it was Wickha turn.

"Did you enter uninvited the Darcy home, threaten and assault his wife, attempt to steal the contents of his strongbox?"

"No, I was trying to recover monies that were owed to me."

"And what is that?"

"But he will be back." Darcy spat. "You heard him. He is not through with me. He will nurse this."

"He will never be back." Henderson assured him. "I would not waste a moment of worry over that."

Darcy glared back at the courtroom silently then finally looked up to the barrister. "I hope that you are correct. Thank you for your efforts today." He shook off Fitzwilliam's clutching hand and straightened.

Henderson shook his hand and gripped his elbow. Darcy passed a packet to Smith; he extracted an envelope and handed that to Henderson. Both men bowed, and Henderson left to take his next case. Smith paused. "Oh, the woman who visits Wickham in prison is a Mrs. Dorothy Younge. I understand that she teaches sewing at a girls' school." He bowed again and disappeared back inside of the Old Bailey.

Whatever relief Darcy had felt was replaced now with fear. "Georgiana!" He took off to find his coach and Fitzwilliam was right behind him.

"What is it?" He demanded.

Darcy turned and glared. "Mrs. Younge works in the school where Georgiana and Mary are enrolled! Mary mentioned her; she said she was overly friendly!"

"Good Lord." Fitzwilliam muttered and when they finally located the coach they immediately were on their way to Mrs. Banks' School for Girls.

Chapter 8

lizabeth rubbed her hands up and down her arms and finally moved away from the window. The cold radiating from the glass did not help the feeling of loss that settled over her within hours of Darcy's departure five days earlier. Jane approached and placing a shawl around her shoulders, gave her a hug. "It will not be long now."

"No, the trial was today." She smiled a little and they walked together to sit by the fire. "I can only hope that it was worth his effort to be there."

"Without a doubt it was, Elizabeth." Lady Matlock smiled. "I know that separation from your husband is difficult, especially this first time and when you are so newly married, but it is something that will happen many times. He will need to attend to his business, just as he did when he had to address the fire, and you may often find yourself unable to join him, whether it is because wives are not welcome or because you are again carrying a babe."

She caressed over the bulge in her gown. "It seems to have grown in the past week."

"I noticed that as well, once the quickening was felt, my waist began to expand at a greater rate." Alicia touched her rounded belly. "March seems a lifetime away." She looked up to Elizabeth who nodded and then left the room. "Did I say something wrong?" Alicia asked Lady Matlock and Jane.

"No dear, she is simply missing Darcy." She smiled and looked back at her work. "She is so young. Sometimes I forget that."

When Elizabeth did not return, Jane stood to look out of the window. "She is walking."

"Alone?"

Smiling, Jane resumed her seat and picked up her sewing. "Elizabeth has been walking alone since she was eight, and there is certainly nothing to fear here, is there? I imagine that she knows these paths very well by now, and she certainly will not take any risks."

Lady Matlock studied Jane as she steadily plied her needle through the fabric. "What are your plans?"

"Mine?" She looked up with surprise. "I do not know. I will return to Longbourn, I suppose. I would like to be here for Lizzy when the baby comes, but I know that the Gardiners expect me to come to them for the Season. I have come to the realization that my future is my own. I know that I am welcome at Pemberley for my lifetime, if I choose. I know that the survival of my family does not rest on my shoulders by whatever marriage I might make. I was such a fool for being jealous of Lizzy's love for Mr. Darcy. I should have rejoiced in the freedom it gave me."

"I am very happy to hear you say that. I suppose that you are aware of the pain your behaviour brought upon your sister?"

Jane stopped her work. "I am. I was blind to so many things, and we are only now beginning to talk again as we once did. I know that Mr. Darcy regards me with caution and is not comfortable with me. I know." She sighed and clasped her hands. "And I know that it is not fair for him to have the sole burden of caring for me, let alone my family should Papa die. I must marry so that my family can contribute someday. But . . . I can marry with my heart now, I think."

Alicia looked at Lady Matlock then to Jane. "I did not marry with my heart, Miss Bennet. And I know that Lady Helen did not either. We were both comfortable with our chosen husbands and I can honestly say that I do love him with all my heart today. I do not know about the Earl, but my husband, being thirty when we wed, was quite set in his ways, and it took him time to adjust to his new role. It was painful at times, but I would say that we have at last arrived at a happy marriage."

"As happy as my sister's?" Jane smiled and cocked her head.

"Nobody can live up to that example." Alicia laughed. "But what I am saying is that you do not necessarily have to fall head over heels in love to find an acceptable mate. He just might grow on you."

Nodding, Jane stood to look back out at the retreating form of her sister. "Mr. Darcy's passion for Lizzy is overwhelming. Her feelings for him are beyond my understanding, as is my confusion over how they came to be together at all. I . . . I do not know that I would care to be caught up in such a marriage. I suppose that was one reason why I did not feel entirely uncomfortable with Mr. Harwick's proposal of courtship. I want to care for my husband and love my children, but somehow I do not see myself sitting with a locket containing his hair in my grasp or . . ."

"Slipping into his study to sit in his chair?" Alicia smiled and Jane turned back to her. "Every one of us is different Jane, if what makes your sister happy is not yours, that does not make it incorrect."

Lady Matlock listened and made a decision. "Miss Bennet, I have observed you for some time, and I think that it is going to be my undertaking this Season to introduce you to society. Your sister has obviously taken you under her wing to teach you household duties, as Mrs. Reynolds has clearly taught her. I have no fear of her doing very well when she returns to London after the child is born, however that may not be this year. We will not waste this time for you simply because you are not located at Darcy House."

"Lady Matlock, you are very kind, but I cannot impose myself . . ."

"Nonsense! Alicia requires nothing from me, and neither does Audrey. I know already that Georgiana will be returning to her brother until the next school term begins. They will function as a family and will take her to venues suitable for a girl of her age. I do not envision them exploring the parties and balls unless they are with close friends. That leaves you, Miss Bennet, without a proper chaperone for much of the Season."

"My Aunt Gardiner . . ."

"Is a wonderful woman and one I am proud to call a friend, however she and her husband cannot provide entré into the higher levels."

"Perhaps I am not meant for them." Jane said softly.

"Perhaps you should stop denying that you are attracted to Mr. Bingley." Lady Matlock said directly and Jane looked up to see her piercing eyes boring into her. "He looks at you as well, Miss Bennet. Now, are you going to let him slip away? He is interested, but not focussed; there remains work to be done if you are to secure him."

"Secure him, I . . . I like him, but, what can I do? I have nothing to offer him, my dowry, my education . . ."

"I will give you the education. You are giving him a wife who is a gentlewoman. He is a gentle soul, and I notice he is easily captivated by a pretty face. I have noticed though that he shines in your sister's company. Why is that?"

Jane sighed. "I do not know. I do not have her wit."

"Perhaps not, but it is not wit that draws a man like Mr. Bingley. He is attracted to her because she is honest and open as he is. She does not hide her emotions, and she is not afraid to engage in conversation. Mr. Bingley appreciates being heard, that talent is in short supply amongst the ladies of his circles who are more concerned with the match than the marriage. I have heard that his parents did little other than push him to become a gentleman and to reject his roots. A man like that craves attention. Both of you have an excellent example before you of marriage. If you are already attracted to each other, why not spend this time cementing the attachment? Surely you can be an attentive and interested partner."

"You mean that I should pursue him?" Jane said with her eyes growing wide and looked to see Alicia laughing and nodding her head. "But . . . how?"

"Leave that to me." Lady Matlock nodded. "We know he will not marry this coming year. We have time."

ELIZABETH WALKED STEADILY along the damp path into the trees and finally up into the special glade where she and Darcy often escaped to find time alone. She saw that the gifts he had planted were safe. The rose bush had given up its blooms months ago, but the leaves, yellow and green, remained. Tucked safely amongst the thorny branches was the true treasure, Elizabeth's tree. Darcy chose an Elm for her, one that had begun, he said, all on its own. No gardener started it in a nursery or babied it along. That was why he felt the tree was hers. He thought they were the same.

Darcy was so proud of his gift and spoke of how they would spend their lives loving each other under the shade of this tree. *Fitzwilliam.* Elizabeth touched the bare branches and wiped her eyes, then moved back out to the path, and eventually into a meadow. She stood looking at the long grass, now fallen with the weight of rain on its blades and was just going to turn and begin the long walk home when she heard galloping hooves, a man's voice, and then saw a horse leap over a hedge with no rider on its back. "Oh no!"

She ran as fast as she could to the spot where the horse landed. "Hello?" She cried, trying to see through the greenery. "Is anyone there?" The horse came up and nudged her. "Richard." She sighed and looked at the saddle. "Who was riding you?" She took the bridle in her hand and held on to the animal. There was no stile or nearby break in the solid mass, and it was a long walk to get around to the other side. Eyeing the horse and hearing nothing else she bit her lip and led him to a fallen log. "Stay still, Richard." She ordered, and with some difficulty, managed to hoist herself onto the tall animal. Sitting like a man, she grimaced when she imagined Darcy's wide eyes to see her on horseback and alone. "Forgive me, Fitzwilliam." Her feet were hopelessly short for the stirrups, but she was afraid to get down and readjust them in case she could not remount. Instead she nudged him and they walked to the hedge. "Are you well?" She called.

"ohhhh."

"Mr Bingley?"

Silence. She nudged the horse again and they made the long slow walk around the hedge and then back up the opposite side, and approached the bundle of blue sprawled on the ground. "Mr. Bingley!"

Elizabeth eased herself down, and tied the horse to a branch, then rushed to Bingley's side. "Mr. Bingley? Are you in pain? Are you awake? Please, say something!" Elizabeth knelt and touched his face, then lifting his head rested it on her knees. "Mr. Bingley? Charles?"

"ohhhh." He moaned. "I hurt everywhere."

"Does anything seem broken?"

"I do not believe so." He sighed, then opening his eyes; he tried to focus on Elizabeth staring down at him. "An angel. I always thought that you were an angel."

"You think every woman is an angel." She laughed with relief, and he smiled at her as his vision gradually cleared. "Now tell me what hurts."

Bingley continued smiling and said nothing for a while as he slowly came around. "I am afraid that is impossible to tell you."

"Why?"

"Because you are a lady." He touched the hand that was holding his cheek. "And I am aspiring to be a gentleman."

"May I assume that you will not be comfortable in your seat for some time, sir?" Her eyes danced and he groaned. "I see."

"You would." Bingley sighed and closed his eyes. "Well if someone had to find me this way, I prefer that it be you."

"What happened?"

"The horse leapt but I . . . I am not good at this at all." He glanced over at Richard. "How did you two arrive here?"

"I mounted and we rode over." Elizabeth blushed when his eyes widened.

"Ohhhhh, Darcy will *NOT* be pleased with you."

"Please do not tell him!"

Bingley started to shake his head, then rubbed his temple with a groan. "I am going to hold this secret and use it to my advantage."

"You are no gentleman." Elizabeth admonished. "Can you sit up?"

"This is a bit wrong, is it not? I am sorry." Elizabeth put her hands under his shoulders to push and very slowly he moved to a sitting position. "Oh that hurts." Bingley's eyes closed and he held his face in his hands. "Why did I have to fall off of a horse to speak to you privately?"

"Have you wished to?" She brushed off the grass that clung to his coat. "You can speak to me anytime, you know."

"No, I cannot Mrs. Darcy." He sighed then looked up to see her concern. "Now, while I still can, please tell me, were you awake in the library after the ball?"

"I was and not. Did I miss anything?"

"Did you hear me?" He searched her face and saw her head shake. "I asked everyone's opinion about Miss Bennet, and if I should . . . tell me what to do. Does she have feelings for me?"

"She likes you, and she feels comfortable with you." Elizabeth bit her lip and looked into his wide green eyes.

"Is it my imagination that she looks at me?"

Elizabeth laughed. "You have a wonderful imagination Mr. Bingley; however I do believe that it is not deceiving you with this question." His eyes lit and she laughed again. "You are only one and twenty, why are you in such a hurry to marry?"

"That is the pot calling the kettle black, Mrs. Darcy. Are you but moments over the age of eighteen?" He smiled down to his boots. "Very well, your husband, your cousins, your friends have all told me the same. Do not marry just because everyone else seems to be settling down."

"And I have told the same to my sister. What is wrong, Mr. Bingley? Are you lonely?" She smiled softly when he looked up to her. "Are you not anticipating the next Season without Fitzwilliam as your anchor?"

"You really got to the crux of the matter. You are definitely not meant for me."

"My husband will be delighted to hear that." Bingley blushed and she laughed. "Come on sir, let us try and get you on your feet." She stood and held out her hands. "Come now."

"I cannot allow a woman in your condition to lift me. Your husband would kill me, if he does not call me out for this entire conversation to begin with." They heard the sound of horses approaching and looked to see Lord Matlock and Layton approaching. "Bloody hell." He muttered then saw Elizabeth's raised brow. "I am sorry!" She shook her head and he struggled up to his feet.

The men arrived and took in the scene. "What happened?" Lord Matlock noted Bingley's muddy coat and breeches, and then saw Elizabeth's dress was muddy as well. "Bingley?"

"My horse leapt but I did not." He looked to Elizabeth. "And I was rescued by the fair Mrs. Darcy."

She laughed and brushed the grass from her gown. "Hardly. I am certain you would have managed on your own. Now gentlemen, I will continue my walk."

"No, no, you are a muddy mess." Lord Matlock leapt down. "Here, let me give you a ride back to the house."

Elizabeth smiled and shook her head. "No thank you. I was having a lovely talk with my husband when Mr. Bingley's cry drew me away. I would like to continue it on my own." Turning she walked off, leaving the three alone.

"Well?" Lord Matlock said sternly. "Did she answer your questions?"

Bingley stared at him with his mouth agape. "How did you know?"

"Son, you have been dying to talk to her since the ball."

Layton grinned as Bingley cautiously climbed onto Richard and groaned. "So what is the verdict?"

"I may proceed with caution, but she suspects my true intent. I wonder what it is myself." Bingley murmured.

"So, what is your plan?" Lord Matlock demanded as he remounted.

"Plan?" Bingley said blankly.

Layton put his hand to his ear. "Father . . .am I mistaken or did I just hear a puppy yap?"

"No Son, I do believe that you did. Shame, I had hopes . . ." The two men turned their mounts and began to gallop away.

"Hey!" Bingley cried and kicked Richard forward. With the first bump he groaned but was determined not to let them see him as weak. "Wait for me!"

"SO YOU UNDERSTAND our justifiable concern, Mrs. Banks." Darcy said to the headmistress as she nodded vigorously. "It would be a poor reflection upon you to employ a woman known for visiting a convicted burglar who preys upon the families of your clientele."

"Yes indeed sir! I will dismiss her immediately!"

"I believe that such a step would be premature, I would like to interview her, if I may. It is possible that she is merely a pawn of his and nothing more. I would not like to send a woman into poverty without cause." He fixed his steely eyes upon the woman. "Do you agree?"

"Certainly sir." She stood and departed the room to search for Mrs. Younge.

"You could have been a mighty King's Counsel or judge, Darcy." Richard observed. "I think that you would have enjoyed it."

"Uncle Roger liked the life, as I recall." Darcy said softly. "I remember his visits to Pemberley when I was a boy. It was one of the few times I saw Father's melancholy lift after Mother died. He was just a boy with his brother, no first son, second son animosity." He looked up to notice Fitzwilliam smiling. "You and Stephen seem to be improving your relations."

"We are." He laughed. "I would not mind a good fist fight with him once more."

"Oh, that would be cruel." Darcy smiled. "He would rout you."

"What?"

"He cheats." Darcy's brows rose when Fitzwilliam rolled his eyes, then his smooth mask reappeared as the door opened and Mrs. Banks entered with Mrs. Younge. When the ladies were seated he began his questions. "What is your relationship to George Wickham? You are known to visit Newgate with gifts of food and funds."

"We are friends, sir, that is all. I gave him a place to stay when he was down on his luck." She studied Darcy as she spoke. "He spoke of you often."

"I have no doubt of that. Did you know of his desire to rob me?"

"No sir, I truly did not. He spoke of being cheated of his inheritance but I always knew that was a load of . . . it was incorrect. You gave him four thousand, after all."

"So you knew he was a liar, why did you remain with him? Why did you visit him?"

"He wasn't bad company, sir. He kept my bed warm, helped with the rent, was good for a laugh. I did not expect more and he didn't ask for it." Darcy's piercing gaze was met straight on. "It was a matter of survival, sir. It is difficult to be a woman alone."

"He was found guilty and will be transported for fourteen years." He watched her eyes widen and heard a sharp intake of breath, but could not read her face. "You do not seem surprised?"

"No sir." She said quickly.

"Are you aware of any threats posed to me or my family by him? Or of any future plans for vengeance?"

"No sir, not one. He did not speak of his plans to me. When I saw him at Newgate, he would not let on his feelings about his situation. We spoke of surviving inside. Besides, I was there for more pressing matters, if you understand my meaning." Fitzwilliam coughed and her gaze went to him. "He was wary of you."

"Well that is comforting." Fitzwilliam smiled. "Why is that?"

"He said Mr. Darcy might be full of words that can damage but you know blood, of course that was before you stuck him." She looked back to Darcy and openly studied him. "He is very jealous of you, Mr. Darcy. He wanted your life and was unhappy when you interfered with his." She shrugged. "I suppose that is why he felt that robbing you was the thing to do. I never asked."

"Do you bear any animosity towards my family, Mrs. Younge?" Darcy stared at her and she flinched. "As you said about Wickham, your answer is a matter of survival."

"I have been nothing but friendly and kind to Miss Darcy and Miss Bennet, sir. I do not wish to jeopardize my livelihood." She drew herself up. "I hope that you believe me."

"I hope that you believe me that I will not tolerate anything less." He delivered his words slowly and she shrank under his gaze. "Do we understand each other, Mrs. Younge?"

"We do, sir." She whispered, then glancing at the headmistress she stood. "I have students waiting for me."

When she escaped the room Darcy turned to Mrs. Banks. "I trust you to enforce this with her? My sister Miss Mary has reported to us that Mrs. Younge was unusually friendly. My wife and I thought that this was simply a young girl unused to such kindness from an adult, however now that I know Mrs. Younge's connection to Mr. Wickham, I am suspicious of everything. I will hold you responsible should Mrs. Younge attempt to hurt my sisters in any way. I would like to see them now, please."

"Of course sir, of course." Mrs. Banks was gone again and Darcy eyed Fitzwilliam.

"What do you think?"

"I think that this woman knows on which side her bread is buttered and will not jeopardize her situation. Especially with Wickham convicted. He is of no use to her now. However, the girls should be warned. I do not trust her, but I do not see that we have enough to demand that she be dismissed."

"Should we remove them from here?" Darcy murmured. "They both have been doing so well, and are comfortable."

"I believe that Mrs. Banks will put the fear of God into Mrs. Younge. She might look like an easy woman, but she is fighting for the survival of her livelihood as well. A bad report from you would be sent through society in a heartbeat and this school would be closed. You have power, Cousin, and you are subtly exercising it, Mrs. Banks feels it radiating from you." Fitzwilliam cocked his head and saw Darcy's mouth set in a tight line.

"Well then . . . I will speak to both girls, but particularly to Mary." Darcy lifted his chin and twisted his neck, then his fingers found their way into his waistcoat pocket. Drawing out the little box he opened it, gazed at Elizabeth's ebony tress for a moment then closing it, returned the treasure to its place.

"Better?"

"Not until I am home." He said softly. "Where is your token?"

Fitzwilliam smiled and reached into his coat pocket to remove a handkerchief and opened it to show off the curl of hair Evangeline had given him. "You will have to direct me to your jeweller." The door burst open and Georgiana appeared, beaming, with a far more sedate Mary in her wake.

"Brother!" She cried and flew into his arms. "Oh I could not believe it when Mrs. Banks said you had come! I miss you so much! Is Elizabeth here? May we go home? I have so much to tell you!" She gave him no opportunity to answer when she turned to her cousin. "Richard!" She hugged him and kissed his cheek while he laughed. "You look different!"

"Is that good?" He grinned. "I say, schooling agrees with you, my dear. What do you say to several extra years of it Darcy?"

"An excellent idea." He laughed when Georgiana protested and turned to Mary. "How are you, Sister?"

"Oh, I am well, sir." Mary smiled. "It is very good to see you.

"Mary, you may call me Fitzwilliam, or Brother, but please not sir."

"Yes, sir." She blushed and he gave her hand a squeeze. "Brother."

"Elizabeth sends her love to you both, as does Jane." He noticed the disappointment right away. "I am sorry that they did not come, we had some business to attend and we had guests at home. Elizabeth had to stay behind."

"Is Mr. Bingley still at Pemberley?" Georgiana asked shyly.

Darcy's brow creased and Fitzwilliam's lips pursed. "Yes he is, dear. Along with the Matlocks."

"Oh."

Fitzwilliam snorted then pinched his nose and looked away before he started to laugh. Darcy shot a look at him then turned back to Georgiana. "We were hoping to share dinner with you tonight before I return to Pemberley. Richard will remain in town; he awaits his love's arrival."

"His love?" Georgiana spun to face him. "You have a love?"

"I do." He smiled. "I do my dear, I am to be married. Mrs. Carter has accepted me."

"OH!" She hugged him again. "When?"

"In February, dear. At Mr. Harwick's estate."

"Mr. Harwick?" Mary looked to Darcy, "The man who left Jane?"

"Yes, he is to marry Mr. Stewart's sister, and Richard will marry Mr. Harwick's sister."

"*Oh what a tangled web.*"[2] She whispered and saw Darcy's smile. "Sir?"

"Brother. I see that you are expanding your reading beyond sermons." He nodded with approval. "I am very happy to know that, especially something so recent, although no lies were involved with this."

"No, the only lie would have been if Jane and Mr. Harwick married." She said thoughtfully. Darcy and Fitzwilliam exchanged glances and nodded.

"May we go home for the night, Fitzwilliam? I would love to take a long bath at home!" Georgiana pled.

Darcy laughed and Richard joined in. "Of course dear, go and pack up whatever you need and you may come to the house for the evening. You will have me all to yourself. Will that make you happy?"

Georgiana stopped at the door and looked back at him and tilted her head. "No, you look lost without Elizabeth standing beside you. But we will make do, Brother." The girls left and Darcy turned to face Fitzwilliam.

"She is an excellent observer, is she not?" Fitzwilliam smiled. "I like how she is developing."

"I do as well." Darcy smiled and looked down at the ring on his finger. "I do as well."

24 NOVEMBER 1809

It is odd sitting here in my study in Darcy House once again. I am alone and yet I am not. If I were to suspend reality, I could well imagine that this was eight months ago and the sound of Georgiana playing and Richard's voice would be all I could ever expect to hear in this vast home, but my mind plays with me. Through the tinkling of the keys I can imagine my Elizabeth's laughter as she prods me with her foot, determined to force me up from my chair and off to join the others. She is not here and yet she is. I hear you love, I do. I will stop hiding and join the family soon.

I have read my allotted letter for today. Adams keeps them safely hidden; else I would be tempted to rip them all open at once to read her words of love and suggestions of passion and play. My valet has become quite adept at hiding my wife's treasures from me.

Tomorrow I begin the long journey home alone. It is a wonder but I have never done that before. Of course I will not really be alone as Adams will ride with me. I am half-tempted to steal Georgiana from school. She begged me after dinner to take her home to Elizabeth. It tore at me, it did, and if I had not managed a private conversation with Mary earlier, I may have been swayed to believe how desperately Georgiana hates her days at school, but clearly Mary is not one to be fooled. She describes my sister as shy and reserved, but when with a few of the girls, she lights up, just as she did when she hugged me in Mrs. Bank's office. It is Mary's opinion that my sister is benefitting from the experience. We will see how things stand at the end of the spring term, and then I will consider sending her for a second year or

---

[2] Sir Walter Scott, <u>Marmion</u>, "Canto vi. Stanza 1", 1808

perhaps finding her a companion and hiring masters for her. She wants so much to be with Elizabeth, their constant correspondence has given her a cherished sister even though they are separated by so many miles. I know how good it would be for them to be together, but I also must not neglect this opportunity for her education that Elizabeth and I value so highly. In truth, Georgiana's place is in London, making friends, taking advantage of the educational opportunities, and growing as a proper young woman should. It is what Father expected for her.

Mary expresses a hope that she might come to Pemberley and confided that Elizabeth was her favourite sister and she misses her deeply. Such opposites they are but Mary seemed to consider herself and Elizabeth equals in that household, both seeking attention by improving their minds and skills, but my wife being a truly outgoing woman succeeded where Mary, more naturally inclined for introspection remains, she feels, an outcast. She asked if I would mind if she never married and came to live with us. Of course I reassured her. She is young and insecure; I look at her and realize, she is older than Elizabeth's age when I first spied my love. I never would have mistaken Mary for a woman. No she is still a girl.

Darcy looked up when Foster knocked. "Sir, a courier has just arrived and asks to see you personally. He is from Rosings."

"Rosings?" Darcy sat up and nodded. A young man appeared and stood with his hat in his hands. "You have come from Rosings?"

"Yes sir, Captain de Bourgh has a letter for you and Lord Matlock. He said to stop in London and make sure nobody from the family was here before I continued to Derbyshire." He handed him his letter. "Is Lord Matlock in town, sir?"

"No, he is at Pemberley." Darcy looked up. "I will read this and have a letter to include with Lord Matlock's. Foster, please take him down to the kitchens and find something for him to eat. I will send the letter to you when I am finished." They departed and Darcy began to read.

24 November 1809
Rosings

Dear Darcy,
There is no other way to say this but to simply report the news that our cousin Anne lies at death's door. She was found by Mrs. Jenkinson in the morning, barely clinging to life, her breathing is shallow. It is a blessing that it will come, her delusions are generally managed by the laudanum but her physical strength wanes by the day. Lady Catherine is stoic in her response. I expect that you are at Pemberley, but took the chance that you might be in town with the trial date approaching. There is nothing to be done. I do not request your presence. I am only delivering this news, and will of course inform you when the inevitable occurs.
Sincerely,
Captain Peter de Bourgh

Darcy held the letter in his hand and stared at it for several long minutes, then stood and walked down the hallway to the music room. Georgiana finished her piece and he applauded along with Richard and Mary.

"Brother, where have you been?" She demanded.

"Forgive me for stealing away, dear. I will join you again shortly, but I am afraid I must borrow Richard for a moment." Darcy caught Fitzwilliam's eye and he saw the serious expression.

"Well then I should go immediately, so that this bee in your brother's bonnet can be addressed." He rose and bowed gallantly to the girls. "Excuse me, ladies." The two men left and Darcy led him to the study, closing the door. Picking up the letter from his desk, he handed it to Fitzwilliam.

"So it is nearly over." He said softly.

"At last." Darcy agreed and watched the emotions passing over his face. "Richard . . ."

"No, I do not regret my decision not to marry her, Darcy." He looked up and smiled. "I have my Eva, what is an estate to love?"

"Well, for you it is nothing." The men stood silently and stared at the letter. "We should go and pay our respects."

"Are you sure, Darcy? I can go alone and represent the family. You are leaving for Pemberley in the morning."

"No, I stayed away because I could not trust Anne's behaviour in my presence, and I feared for Elizabeth. Our cousin cannot harm anyone now. She may very well have died since this was written."

"What of Aunt Catherine? Does she want you there?"

Darcy looked up to his mother's portrait to see her watching him. "I do this for Anne; her behaviour was encouraged by her mother. If I can ease her passing by fulfilling her vision . . ."

"You are a good man, Darcy." Richard clasped his shoulder.

"I must write to Elizabeth, she will worry when I do not return as expected. Perhaps you could write a note for your father?"

ELIZABETH WOKE and automatically her hand reached to her right, feeling the empty mattress by her side. Slowly her hand withdrew and rested over the baby, feeling a little kick, she stroked over him. "Papa will be home soon, sweetheart." She sighed and sat up. Sleep had been difficult in coming and she only seemed to manage short periods of rest. "I even miss you snoring on my shoulder." She laughed and rubbed her tired eyes then spoke in an imitation of his deep voice, "No, a Darcy does not snore, a Darcy breathes heavily."

Drawing back the bed curtains she stepped out onto the cold floor. Taking a match, she lit the candles by her bed and walked with the candelabra into his dressing room. She hunted around and opening a drawer found a handkerchief, then turned to see the neat line of bottles on a table. Running her fingers over them, she chose her favourite scent and tipped a little cologne onto the fabric.

Taking her treasure back to the bed, she tucked the handkerchief into her gown and let his scent surround her. "There you are, Fitzwilliam."

DARCY STARED UP at the canopy, already regretting his decision to go to Rosings and delay his return home *for how many days?* He had lost sleep over the travel and pending trial, and knew that all would have been so much better if Elizabeth had come with him. "Never again will I leave you behind. You could have dealt with this trip, you are strong. How many women travel to London their last month to give birth, after all?" His hand reached over to touch the cold empty mattress on his left. "I miss you kicking me in the night." He smiled and rubbed his eyes, and spoke in his imitation of her lilting voice. "I do not!" He chuckled again to imagine the argument that would inevitably ensue and the wonderful resolution it would always bring. With a groan he rolled over and jumped from the bed, lighting a candle and wandering to the mistress's chambers and into her dressing room. "Surely there is something of her here?" He hunted around; all of her gowns had been packed for Pemberley. Biting his lip he opened drawers and searched then cried with triumph to find a sachet filled with lavender in her dressing table. "There you are my love!" Happily clutching his treasure he returned to the master's chamber and back into the bed, where he placed the silk sachet under his pillow and let the scent permeate through the feathers and fabric. "Now you are with me." He sighed and closed his eyes, "Now I may dream of you."

FITZWILLIAM GLANCED at Darcy as they neared Hunsford and watched him twist the ring around and around. "You are going to sever your finger if you keep that up."

Darcy glanced down and back out of the window. "Serves me right."

"What, for visiting Anne or torturing Elizabeth with my parents' company for a few more days?" He smiled and was rewarded with a glare. "A combination?"

"I hope that she understands." He said quietly. "I hope that she does not think that . . .never mind."

"That you harboured some romantic feeling for our cousin? Surely that is unlikely."

"No, no, that I feel guilty for not . . . following . . ."

"Duty?" Fitzwilliam suggested. "Well I could be blamed for the same, you know. I could have married her and saved Rosings, but is it not in the hands of the man who should be its heir? Anne was to die, she was not meant to bear children, that was determined years ago. No, this estate has never been meant to go to anyone other than a de Bourgh, so it went from Lewis, to Anne, and now to Peter. It is well."

"When did you become so philosophical?" Darcy smiled and relaxed a little. "I thought that you only read novels during your recovery?"

Fitzwilliam chuckled. "So I did, I had enough histories at Cambridge."

"Days long past." Darcy sighed and smiled. "I cannot say that I remember them fondly."

"Why not? Well I suppose that you were not the most jovial student. All those prizes you won . . ."

Darcy shrugged. "I am not given to carousing." The carriage at last turned into the gate and rolled up to the house. "I never thought I would return here." A footman opened the door and he climbed down to look up at the windows, then to the door. No black crepe was hung, Anne still lived. The men straightened their coats and walked up to the landing. An unfamiliar butler received them and escorted them to a drawing room that was remarkable in its simple decoration. It seemed that Lady Catherine's imprint had been erased.

"Darcy, Colonel, welcome. I hardly expected to see anyone from the family, this is a great surprise!" De Bourgh shook their hands and brought them over to greet an older woman. "Mother, this is Fitzwilliam Darcy and Colonel Richard Fitzwilliam."

"It is a pleasure to meet you, madam." Darcy bowed. "May I ask how our cousin fares?"

"The pleasure is mine, sir. Anne is conscious but failing." She studied the subject of Anne's delusion carefully. "Her mother is with her."

Darcy nodded and glanced at Fitzwilliam. "I would suspect as much. I came . . . We were not sure what we would find but the note we received indicated that my cousin suffers still with her thoughts of . . .a union with me. I . . . I thought that perhaps . . .my presence might give her comfort. If I would be a distraction or burden then I will naturally not approach her. I leave it to you."

"You think well of yourself, coming to offer comfort to the dying girl who you rejected!" An angry voice spoke from behind him. "YOU could have saved her from this fate!"

Everyone turned to see Lady Catherine entering the room. Darcy maintained an even tone. "Aunt, I did not come to start an argument with you, I came for Anne. Her condition is not her fault."

"So you blame me?" Lady Catherine glared. "Is it not enough that I am thrown from my home to accommodate Anne's delusion? She did not improve when I left and she assumed the title of mistress, you know. Her delusion only grew!" She spun to point at de Bourgh. "This cousin and his family, squatting in her parlour, waiting like spiders on their web for the weak one to die so they could pounce, how dare you bring this upon me!"

"Upon you?" Darcy said through gritted teeth. "You created this situation, Aunt, not I."

"Darcy." Fitzwilliam spoke softly and touched his shoulder. "Let us go and visit Anne. As you said, we are here for her."

"You are no better, Fitzwilliam!" Lady Catherine spat.

"Aunt, I will disregard your manner in light of the pain you are likely feeling with the pending death of your only child; however you should have been prepared for this day years ago. We will not carry the burden of your anger." He spoke very softly and steadily. "Now, let us visit Anne." He looked at Darcy and the men followed Mrs. de Bourgh out of the room and up the stairs.

"You did that very well, sir." She spoke quietly as their boots rang out on the marble. "I have observed her carefully over the past months. I wondered if her distress originated from pain over her daughter's fate or her own." She stopped at the chamber door and placed her hand upon the knob. "I have come to the conclusion that her concern was selfishly motivated." Turning to look up at Darcy's expressionless features she nodded. "I hope that you listen to your cousin."

He nodded and followed her into the darkened room. It was chillingly familiar. He closed his eyes against the rush of memories that flooded his mind; the atmosphere of pending death was nearly suffocating. First he thought of his father, then opening his eyes, he saw a vision of Anne Darcy in the still form lying on the bed. "Mother." He whispered, and began flexing his hands, needing to clutch onto something. Fitzwilliam noticed the nervous gesture and he nudged Darcy's arm to rouse him from the memory, then stepped forward to bend over Anne.

"Anne, it is Richard." He said softly with a smile and held her hand. She blinked slowly and looked up at him. "I have come to see you."

"Where is Fitzwilliam? I have waited for him." She faintly whispered.

Darcy drew a deep breath and saw Mrs. Jenkinson in a corner nodding and urging him forward. He stepped up and took Richard's place, holding her frail hand in his. "I am here, Anne."

"Husband." She smiled and sighed. "At last."

He did not know how to reply, so he wrapped both of his hands around hers, and watched as she closed her eyes and sank back into the pillows. They remained that way as the others looked on for endless moments, until gradually, her wasted body relaxed, and he felt the hand in his grasp become limp. He knew what had happened. "Be at peace, Anne." He leaned down and kissed her cheek, then placing her hands together over her chest, he stepped away and walked to the window to hide the unbidden tears. Mrs. Jenkinson stepped to his side.

"Thank you sir, thank you for giving her this." He nodded, not looking at her. "She never really believed that you were not married."

"Please, do not tell me more." Darcy wiped his eye with his thumb. "I cannot know."

"But you should know, sir. She was the happiest I have ever known her these past months. Her mother was gone from her daily life, she believed herself to be married, and she occupied her time redecorating her home. She was full of happiness for the life she thought she was leading. It was not difficult to convince her that you were away for good reasons. It gave her happiness." She looked back at the still figure as Mrs. de Bourgh kissed her and left to find Lady Catherine. "You gave her life."

Darcy met her eyes, but could not speak of Anne. "If you need a situation . . ."

"I will be fine sir; the Captain's sisters need a companion." She smiled. "It will be well."

The chamber door opened and Lady Catherine entered. Darcy bowed to her. Richard caught his eye as they slipped from the room to the hallway where de Bourgh waited. ""She asks that you not stay for the funeral. I am sorry. I do not agree with it."

"No, it is not your fault. We came to see her in life; she knew that we were here. You are the master now; we will stay if you wish. We are here for Anne; and Anne alone." Darcy glanced back at the room where Lady Catherine stood looking down at her daughter. "Your mother seemed to believe that our aunt was unaffected by this."

"I do not know." He shrugged. "She lets nobody in. We will look out for her Darcy. Perhaps she will soften now."

Richard shook his head. "No, she will remain as you see, defiant to the end."

"ARE YOU WELL, ELIZABETH?" Lady Matlock placed her hand on Elizabeth's waist and embraced her lightly. "Do you mind Darcy's decision to go to Anne?"

Elizabeth wiped the tears rolling down her cheeks and glanced down to the letter in her hand. "No, not at all. I have never been prouder of him." She smiled and looked up. "He is the best of men."

Chapter 9

"Well." Fitzwilliam dropped into a chair by the fire glowing in the library at Matlock House. "I suppose that Father will have a great deal to say when he comes down." He propped up his feet and stared at his boots. "He seemed rather impatient to hear the news."

"I am amazed at their speed; they left almost as soon as the messenger arrived, if it had not been for the weather, they might have been here in three days rather than four." Darcy accepted the glass of port a silent footman offered, and watched de Bourgh lean into the fireplace, poking at the coals and saying very little. "I will be happy to go with you to visit the solicitors tomorrow. I use them for Pemberley."

He looked up and smiled. "The Earl is here, Darcy. I know that you are anxious to return home. You have answered all of my questions. I am sure that the he will look after me." Setting down the poker, he found a chair and sat back. "Sorry for being so pensive. I am just now feeling the weight of what I have inherited."

"It hits you hard when the funeral is over, and the people are gone." Darcy said quietly.

"I . . . This will probably sound unlikely, but I am sorry to have lost Anne." De Bourgh noticed Fitzwilliam's incredulous stare and continued. "Yes I know that it would mean that I would still not be master of my fate. Also, I am well aware of her behaviour of the past. Mrs. Jenkinson informed my mother and me, and I realize that had she seen you it would have been ugly. But she was, well for the time that I knew her, a wistful, and determined young woman. Of course I know that is entirely because she was living in a fantasy with you, Darcy." He saw him close his eyes. "Forgive me, but she did. What struck me though is what sort of a woman she might have been without her mother's interference."

Fitzwilliam spoke when clearly Darcy would not. "Sadly we will never know that, but your care and appreciation for a relative you were essentially forced to attend for an unknown period is appreciated by all of us."

"It was no trouble; I feel that I in some way earned the honour of being Master of Rosings by this. And of course, I will always have Lady Catherine in my ear." He smiled and the others relaxed and joined him.

Fitzwilliam glanced at Darcy. "How long will you stay?"

"I just wish to speak to your father about our decisions regarding Mrs. Younge, and I want to visit the girls once more." He stared at his feet. "I hope that it will not be a long wait."

The Earl cleared his throat and the men all looked to the doorway. "I changed as quickly as I could, Darcy."

"Forgive me, sir." Darcy said as he hurriedly stood. "How is Elizabeth?"

Standing aside, he waved towards his study. "Your aunt and I are well, thank you." Darcy sighed as Fitzwilliam and de Bourgh chuckled. "Come along, Son. Let us get you squared away." He walked on to the study and took his chair behind the desk, and watched Darcy close the door behind him. When he was settled, the Earl drew a letter from his coat and handed it over. "Elizabeth is well, although she misses you deeply and is incapable of hiding it. There is something missing in her laughter, and her eyes are not as bright without you by her side." He watched Darcy caress the envelope and how his fingers twitched over the wax seal. "She is also extremely proud of you for going to Anne."

Darcy looked up to him quickly. "She is?"

"I do not know what she says in your letter, we left within an hour of receiving the news of Anne's imminent death, so she did not have time to expound. I imagine it is more words of love than anything." Darcy blushed and placed the letter in his coat. "So, I will hear enough of Rosings from the boys, tell me of the trial."

"There is not much to add, it was over very quickly. I am afraid that I let my emotion get away from me at the end, when he made references to Elizabeth and threats to return and finish what he began." Darcy stood and began pacing. "That is impossible, is it not? He cannot escape, can he?"

"I have heard Newgate described as a filthy rabbit's warren of passages, and treatment is really dependent on how much kindness the prisoner can buy." He shrugged. "As is normal out here in the light of day, he who has funds lives a more comfortable existence. Gaolers are well-known to demand bribes for food, clothing, freedom from chains or work, women, whatever a free man would desire can be had." He chuckled, "After all, they like their inmates, why else would they demand payment to let them out when the sentence is served? Then again, he might be farmed out to one of the privately run prisons around town."

"But then could Wickham . . ." Darcy stopped by the window and stared out at the darkened street. "We learned that a woman friend of his was visiting and bringing him food and money."

"Not surprising. Gaolers are under no obligation to feed their prisoners. That is for the charities and the bribes to handle."

"She teaches at Georgiana's school." Lord Matlock sat up. "I warned her to stay away from him, and to leave the girls alone. I told Mrs. Banks to watch her and told Mrs. Younge that I would keep tabs on her." Turning to his uncle he watched for his reaction. "I feel that she was likely duped to appreciate Wickham's charms, much as my father was. I do not care to be the means for sending a woman to poverty."

"You are trading on her gratitude for saving her employment by your compassion to appease her anger for losing her lover? Perhaps knowing her location and watching her behaviour is good as well?" Lord Matlock settled back in his chair, and steepled his fingers. Tapping them on his lips he considered his nephew. "You are either naive or brilliant."

"What would you have done?"

"I would have had her tossed out on her ear; I am surprised that her employer has not already." Darcy said nothing and looked back out of the window. "Do you believe that she knew of Wickham's plans?"

"No, I think that he was simply using her. He complained of me, but well, when has he not?" He sighed. "I spoke to Georgiana and Mary briefly before we left for Rosings. More Mary though. She is older and in some ways wise beyond her years."

"All those sermons." The Earl smiled. "Elizabeth was speaking of her one day."

"Ah." Darcy smiled fondly. "Well both she and Mary are the well-read girls of that household, they are similar in some ways, but where Elizabeth was the subject of her mother's unending criticism, Mary was simply ignored. They both worked to distinguish themselves. I like her."

"Well then, if she has half the good sense your dear wife does, I am certain she will not be taken in by any foolish attempts by Mrs. Younge. And you are of course, quite correct. Good jobs are hard enough to find, and undoubtedly this one pays room and board as well. She would be daft to jeopardize it for a man who will be on a ship to Australia in a few months. No, go ahead; continue with your compassion, Darcy. But I would certainly speak to both girls again before you depart. When is that, by the way?" He glanced at the dark street. "Too late to leave today."

"Unfortunately." Darcy smiled and at last took a seat. "I will visit the girls tomorrow and take care of some business while I am here. Then I will return home where I belong."

"She will be glad of that." Lord Matlock considered him for a moment. "Are you nervous?" He watched Darcy's head tilt and smiled. "Stupid question, I know. I am anxious to hear how Audrey fares. Their current plan is to travel from Ashcroft to his father's townhouse. After we have everything settled with Rosings we will return to town to await the birth and Parliament opening, then we have Richard's wedding and Alicia's confinement . . . It is more activity than we have had in years, and I for one will be happy for the peace of the Season." The two men laughed at that thought and Lord Matlock said softly, "From listening to my wife, I know that Elizabeth and Alicia are quite anxious to hear every detail of Audrey's laying-in. They are in desperate need of reassurance."

Their eyes met and Darcy noted the unspoken concern that mirrored his own. "I suppose that Aunt Helen's accounts of her children did nothing to help?"

"No, they want to hear it from someone not so far removed from the experience." Lord Matlock laughed, "You know, someone familiar with all the modern techniques."

"I have been doing some reading on the subject, myself." Darcy coloured when his uncle's brows rose. "I have to know. I have done my best to remain calm and optimistic, but after seeing Anne's death, I am afraid that I was haunted once again with visions of Mother's deathbed, and with no Elizabeth there to persuade me against my dark thoughts, my only option was to seek information. The library at Rosings did not yield much, but I found some books at home, and plan to visit a few bookshops before my return."

"Cold hard fact, then?"

"Indeed."

"And are you reassured yet?"

"No." Darcy laughed and rubbed his face. "But I will try."

"YOU NEED NOT WEAR MOURNING, dear." Darcy said softly when Georgiana and Mary entered Mrs. Banks' office. "You barely knew her."

"But she was my cousin." She looked at the dress. "It is only for another month, and the dresses are not too tight from Papa, just a little short." She sniffed and fell into Darcy's open arms. "I miss him."

"I do, too." He kissed her hair and stroked her back. "How are you, Mary?"

"I am well, Mr. Darcy." Mary said softly from the open door.

"Now what did I tell you about my name?" He smiled when Georgiana withdrew from his arms.

"Habits are difficult to break." She smiled. "I will endeavour to improve."

"Excellent." He smiled and realized he was staring when she blushed. "Forgive me; your features are reminiscent of Elizabeth."

"You miss her."

"Deeply." He admitted. "I will be home within five days, four if the weather is good."

"I have a letter for her." She held it out. "You said that you might stop before you returned."

"I will gladly give it to her." He placed the letter in his coat and saw Georgiana standing with her hands on her hips. "What is it, dear?"

"Mary, will you not kiss your brother?" Mary's blush grew even deeper in colour, and Darcy's lips twitched.

"No, thank you. No offence sir, Brother." She glanced at him and back down to her hands. "Your face belongs to Lizzy, and . . . I will shake hands with you, sir." She held hers out and he took it.

"Has nobody ever embraced you, Mary?" He said softly. "Besides your sisters?"

"My aunt and uncle do sometimes." She whispered and felt Darcy's arms close around her. "oh." He let go quickly and saw the embarrassment in her face, but he also saw the appreciation in her eyes.

Georgiana clapped. "Is that not so very nice? He is not as round as Papa was, but he reminds me of him when we hug."

Darcy looked to her with a grin. "I am glad not to be so round as Father." He chuckled. "But I am glad that I remind you of him, thank you." Georgiana giggled and he asked them to sit down. When they were all settled, he launched into his speech. "We spoke about Mrs. Younge before I left for Rosings."

Mary nodded. "Yes, and I have paid close attention to her since then. She is not any different than before, perhaps a little less . . ." She searched for the word, "attentive?"

"Does it affect your education at all?"

"No, sir . . .Brother. I could sew competently before I came here. That is one lesson that mother taught us, that and providing a fine table." She sighed. "We all had to remake our clothes, so needle skills are important."

"Oh, I hate sewing!" Georgiana wrinkled her nose.

"Then it is fortunate that you do not need to remake your things." Darcy said sternly. "Count your blessings."

"Yes, Brother." She glanced at Mary who looked at him with approval.

"Now then, I am trying to determine if I have made a wise decision. Are you both truly happy here?" He looked between them. "Are you learning new things? Are you making friends? Do you dread your lessons? Are you treated well? Is anyone bothering you?"

"Is this about our schooling or Mrs. Younge?" Georgiana asked.

A small smile played on his lips. "You are definitely growing to be a very clever young lady."

She blushed, but lifted her chin. "I am a Darcy."

"Hmm. Remember, pride in position is not our goal." He said seriously. "Although I have no doubt that just such an attitude is necessary amongst your peers. If that is what you must do to survive in this mix of girls, I will allow it. However, it is what resides in your heart that counts." He tapped her shoulder. "Do you understand? Remember the family history I had you read."

"Yes, Brother." She sighed. "Elizabeth would be so disappointed if I left here."

"She would. She is grateful for Mary's opportunity that she never had." He looked to see Mary nodding.

"I have learned much already, I understand very well what a gift this is." She was rewarded with a brilliant smile from her brother.

Georgiana's brow creased and she spoke up. "Mary told me to be wary of Mrs. Younge's friendliness ages ago, and now you have twice. What did she do? You have not explained that. Should we not know?"

He turned his smile to her as he realized she was trying to shine before him. "As I said when we last spoke, she is a friend of Wickham's." He frowned when he noticed her consternation. "And I know that he was kind to you, dear, but you have to remember that some people are kind on the outside because they want something from you in return. He robbed us and tried to hurt Elizabeth, and now that he is found guilty, he will pay for his crime."

"So Mrs. Younge is kind because she wants something?"

"I do not know, I only ask that you remain wary. You know by now when a servant is overstepping their place, do you not?"

"Yes, I think so." She turned to her sister. "Maybe I should just ask you if I am not sure."

"Absolutely." He smiled with relief. "I rely on your older sister to look after you, and Mary, do not hesitate to contact Mrs. Banks, the Gardiners or the Fitzwilliams if you have the slightest apprehension regarding Mrs. Younge or any other's behaviour. Until Wickham is on his way to his fate, I do not trust anyone who ever regarded him as a friend. May I rely on you with this charge?"

Mary smiled and straightened her shoulders. "I am glad to take on the challenge, Brother."

"Excellent." He smiled. "Your resemblance to Elizabeth is remarkable when you sit so confidently."

"oh." She blushed and lifted her chin. "Thank you."

Turning back to Georgiana, he took her hand in his grasp. "So do you truly wish to stay here?"

"I want you and Elizabeth to be proud of me." She glanced at Mary and said determinedly. "Yes."

"Good. Now you know that the Christmas school break is coming, and since I am here now, I will not be returning then. I will not leave Elizabeth again, and I will not make her travel in her condition. You will spend the holiday at Matlock House."

"And what of Mary?" She asked with concern.

Darcy smiled and nodded at her. "You will travel with the Gardiners to Longbourn. You should see your family as well."

"Well she should but I do not know how happy she will be about it." Georgiana giggled.

"Georgie!" Mary hissed.

"Oh you have told me enough stories . . ."

"Well then they are private and you should not speak of them before anyone else." Darcy said quietly. "Mary trusts you."

"Yes, Brother." Georgiana blushed.

"Now, I have some work to do before I leave for Pemberley. I imagine that you have lessons to attend, so we should probably say our farewells now." He stood up and wrapped his arms around her, then kissed her forehead. "I love you."

"I love you too, Fitzwilliam." Georgiana kissed one cheek then the other. "That one is for my sister."

"I will give it to her." He turned to Mary. "One more hug? I will understand if you do not wish for it?" He smiled when Mary's arms tentatively circled his waist. "Thank you, Sister. I will tell Elizabeth this is from you." He drew back and she instantly pulled away. "I love you, too. Thank you for looking after my little sister."

"You are welcome . . . Fitzwilliam." She glanced up at him and pecked his cheek. "That is for Lizzy, too."

"She will love it, I am sure." He watched the girls leave and paused for a moment to dab at his eyes, then drawing himself up, asked for Mrs. Banks. He wished to give one last warning before he felt it was safe to go home.

CLOSING HIS EYES for a moment he let the rocking of the carriage soothe his weary body. "Two more days." He said softly.

"Pardon me, sir?" Adams roused himself from his position in the corner of the cabin, opposite his master.

"It was nothing, go back to sleep. We will not be stopping for another hour or so." Darcy watched the man nod and wrap the blanket back around his shoulders, and soon he was softly snoring. Beside him were several medical books, all describing childbirth in horrifying and unbelievable ways. *Which do you believe? Either it is an experience that goes on for days and the woman is left to suffer because she deserves it, or she is medicated with opium and the process slows to a standstill, or she is laughing through the entire easy event, surrounded by visitors wandering through the room as she occasionally writhes in agony.* He sighed, not believing any of it was likely true. *Who is better to deliver her? A mid-wife, and accoucher? A surgeon? I do not know! Do we stay at Pemberley, do we go to London? Do we deliver at home or at the hospital?* His head swam with the possibilities, and the curse of an intelligent mind and a vivid imagination. Once more his hand darted into his coat to pull out Elizabeth's letter.

28 November 1809

Dearest Fitzwilliam,
Do what you must and I will be waiting, as patiently as I am able, to welcome you home and into my arms where you belong. Your compassion and kindness overwhelm me, but they do not surprise. I would expect nothing less from my husband.

There is so much that I wish to tell you, love. But it will wait for your return. Until that wonderful day, I shall leave you with this: The lake, the glade, the meadow, the library, the study, our bed, our home, our future, your lips, your throat, your chest, your heartbeat, your moan, your taste, your touch, your whisper, your kiss, your gift, your power, our embrace. Our love. For now I will live with the memory of your love, and every night, I will dream of you.

Be safe, my Fitzwilliam. I wait for you alone.

I love you,

Elizabeth

Folding the letter and closing his eyes, under the cover of the blanket covering his lap; his hand touched the heat she had generated, and lost himself in their memories. *You know just what to say, love.*

TWO MORE DAYS OF TRAVEL PASSED, and at last, early in the afternoon, Darcy entered Pemberley House. Immediately he was surrounded by servants who gathered his coat, hat, the valise full of his work . . . He scanned the great hallway and confused, turned to find Mrs. Reynolds beaming at him. "Welcome home, sir! I trust your journey was comfortable?"

"It was fine, Mrs. Reynolds." His brow knit. "Where is Mrs. Darcy? Is she ill?" After nearly three weeks of separation, illness was the only explanation he could fathom that would keep Elizabeth from greeting his return.

"No sir, she is out."

"*Out?*" He stared at her. "Where?"

"Visiting tenants, sir."

"Is Viscount Layton or Mr. Bingley with her?" He demanded.

"No sir, your cousin and Lady Layton returned to Matlock two days ago when he received word from his steward of a problem, and Mr. Bingley has been gone five days since he received a letter from his sister." She saw Darcy's incredulous stare and spoke quickly. "Mrs. Darcy assured Viscount Layton that she would be just fine waiting for your return on her own."

"And tell me, Mrs. Reynolds, is my wife *alone* on these tenant visits?" He fumed.

"Mr. Nichols accompanied her, sir." Mrs. Reynolds whispered. "He said it should not take too long. We were not expecting you, sir, and Mrs. Darcy wished to be useful in your absence . . ."

Darcy nodded curtly and looked up when the front door opened. "Mr. Darcy, I saw the carriage at the stables, welcome home, sir." Nichols smiled and greeted him. "I have a great deal to discuss when you are at your leisure . . ."

"Where is my wife, Nichols?" Darcy said quietly.

"Mrs. Darcy is walking, sir. She thought to take a turn before returning to the house." His smile faltered when Darcy's eyes went to the window. "She was excellent with the tenants sir, soothed a great many worried families with her delivery of food and medications."

"She visited homes that contained illness?"

Nichols looked at Mrs. Reynolds nervously. "Nothing catching, sir. And we did not stay long."

"You endangered my wife and child?" Darcy glared at him. Pointing to a maid he commanded. "My coat. Now."

"Sir, she is . . ." He saw Darcy shrugging into his coat and snatching his hat from the maid. "She was walking towards the lake . . ."

"The lake." Darcy's eyes closed. "Of course. Could she not pick a more dangerous path?" He stalked to the front door and pulled it open, then was off.

Nichols puffed out his cheeks and looked at Mrs. Reynolds. "Well, if we had known he was coming, she would have been here. That woman misses him terribly."

"You do not have to tell me." She walked to the open door and closed it. "He misses her just as much, why else would he lash out at us; he will be fine once he finds her. I suspect that he was hoping to surprise her by coming unannounced." She shook her head and smiled. "It is good to see such a love match."

"Not for anyone who stands in the way of it." Nichols laughed and they headed down to the kitchens. "I think you should order some bath water for their return." The two elder servants eyed each other and smiled.

"And dinner suitable for eating in their chambers, as well."

Outside, Darcy continued his rapid pace, stamping through the snow and muttering to himself about family abandoning his wife and servants abandoning their orders to care for her, then turned his mind to muttering about his obstinate wife who likely shooed everyone away in her annoying display of independence. "What do you expect, Darcy? You left her. You know that she will not sit still if left to her own devices. How many times have you come home to find her off in the woods somewhere? Without you?" He snorted and growled. "Someday my love, you will be harmed and . . ." He shuddered and banished the thought. "Do not even think it."

Approaching the lake he went directly into the trees, following the small footprints in the fresh snow. He could hear a voice amongst the trunks, softly singing, and he just caught the end of the song as he turned around a bend to see Elizabeth standing alone on a little bridge set over a stream. She was staring down at the rushing water, and he saw her gloved hand brush what had to be tears from her cheeks.

"Take away those rosy lips, rich with balmy treasure. Turn away thine eyes of love, lest I die with pleasure! What is life when wanting love? Night without a

morning. Love's the cloudless summer sun, nature gay adorning.[3] Her voice cracked as her hands went up to her face and she began to sob.

Darcy's relief was instantly dashed to find her so heartbroken, and hurrying to her side, had her in his embrace before she knew what had happened. Elizabeth looked up to him in utter surprise. "Oh!" Her cry was swallowed by his kiss, and there he tasted the tears that lay upon her rosy pink cheeks. Pulling her tight to his chest, he kissed her eyes, her jaw, and loved deeply her lips. She wrapped her arms around him and they held each other tight. "I love you," was whispered over and over until the frenzied reunion slowed and they stood still, firmly together once more.

Darcy lifted his face from Elizabeth's hair and caressed her cheek with the back of his fingers. "*Now* I am home."

"I did not like this experience at all, sir." She said softly.

"Sir?" He whispered as his mouth hovered over hers.

"S . . ." Once again, her voice was instantly silenced with his kiss.

When at last he released her mouth, he demanded gently, "What are you doing out here alone? What are you doing visiting the sick?"

"I wished to do my duty, just as you were, and then I wished to cry where nobody would see me." She whispered.

"Oh my love. What am I to do with you?" She smiled as he kissed her again. "You have one duty, to stay well. I will not have you risking your health walking into homes that contain . . . Lord knows what disease!"

"Do you think me so foolish as to go somewhere that might risk my or our baby's health?" She demanded from his shoulder.

"Oh Lizzy, please!" He murmured against her ear and increased his nearly suffocating embrace. "I came home and you were not there. For the last three days, I have been anticipating holding you like this, and when I walked in the door; my heart was nearly bursting with joy, expecting to find you waiting for me. When you were missing . . .it stopped beating."

She closed her eyes and held him as tightly as she could. "If I had known you were coming I never would have ventured farther than the first step, where I would have been waiting for you."

"I wished to surprise you." He kissed her forehead, then down her cheeks. "Why were you crying?"

"I cry all of the time, it seems." He wiped her cheeks and she smiled at him. "But today it was because I wanted my love to come home."

"Elizabeth." Darcy said quietly as he kissed below her ear, "Please say my name."

"Fitzwilliam." She closed her eyes and wrapping her arms around his neck, stood on her toes to whisper, "Fitzwilliam, my Fitzwilliam."

"Who am I?" He said hoarsely, "Please love, say who I am to you."

---

[3] Robert Burns, "Thine Am I, My Faithful Fair," 1793.

Taking his face in her hands she searched his brightened eyes. "Husband. You are *MY* husband." She felt his breath let out in a shaky rush. "Husband, my Fitzwilliam, my husband, my love, *mine.*"

"Thank you." Darcy rested his cheek on her head and hugged her. "It has been a very long wait for that."

"I do not even have to imagine why you needed to hear it." Elizabeth stroked his cheek and he kissed her hand.

He looked up to see snowflakes were beginning to fall around them. "Come love, we should go inside. I do not want you to catch cold." They leaned into each other, his arm wrapped around her waist, and they walked back to the house in silence. When they approached the door he stopped and kissed her upturned face. "Never again will I leave you behind."

She smiled and brushed the snow from his shoulders. "Do not make promises you cannot keep, Fitzwilliam."

"I will endeavour to keep this one as much as possible." They entered the house and the staff took their coats. Darcy looked over his smiling wife carefully. "You have changed, my love." His warm hands held her face, and he smiled at her. "Your cheeks are full." His hands caressed down her shoulders to stroke over her ripening belly. "Our child is growing. I am so sorry to have missed this time with you." The baby kicked and he looked up to her with wide eyes. "Did you feel that?"

Elizabeth laughed and held his hands to the spot. "I cannot avoid it, Will."

"He was not doing this when I left!"

"He was, but you did not feel it." She raised her hands back up to hold his face as his eyes grew sad. "You are here now."

Swallowing back his disappointment, he changed the subject. "Everyone abandoned you. I was dismayed to find you were alone. I thought that only my aunt and uncle had gone."

"They left after your letter arrived, and agreed to drop Jane off at Longbourn."

He nodded when he remembered Jane. "Yes, that was kind of them to take her; I saw Uncle Henry and Aunt Helen in London before I departed. He wishes to be of aid to de Bourgh and was meeting with the solicitors, making sure that the transfer of Rosings went smoothly."

"And Aunt Helen thought that Lady Catherine might wish for a peer to help her." Elizabeth saw his shaking head. "She was not happy that you decided to remain for the funeral, was she?"

"No, she thought it was an act to rub her nose in her loss, her loss of Rosings, not Anne. I felt that I needed to stay. I . . . Elizabeth do you understand why I remained? I . . . I did not regret . . ."

"I know, Fitzwilliam, she was your cousin, and someone needed to attend the funeral besides Captain de Bourgh."

"I just want you to be assured of that, I want you to be absolutely clear that I was not mourning a woman I wished I had married." He stopped as they reached the top of the stairs and again held her face in his hands. "Do you understand? I felt that it was my duty . . ."

"Hush. I know." She sighed and kissed him. "You should not bear the responsibility for her death, and I will not allow you to torture yourself over it any longer. You explained it all in your letters, there is nothing to apologize for." Darcy took her up in his arms and held her as closely as he could.

"You do know me well." He smiled a little and they walked on. "I will not do this again, leave you like this again. It was a nightmare."

"You slept? Lucky you!" She poked his side and he rubbed it ruefully.

"I take it that your sleep was as nonexistent as mine?" He touched her weary face. "Never again, love."

"Now you have repeated that enough times that I am forced to believe you." They embraced and paused in the hallway.

"I doubt very much that you could be forced to do anything." He took her hand and squeezed. "I need to greet you properly."

"And what does that entail?" She laughed and his eyes lit up with the beloved sound. "Mmm, perhaps we should send word that we will have dinner in our rooms?"

Darcy nodded and bent down to kiss her as they walked. "Perhaps breakfast as well?"

"Fitzwilliam!"

"Yes." He laughed, relaxing at last, and opened the door to the master's chambers. "Definitely breakfast in bed. I intend to take full advantage of this guest-free home." Pulling her inside he soundly shut the door, and pressed her back against it, then stood looking down at her. "I intend to ravish my lovely bride."

"Oh, now that sounds promising." She reached up to deftly untie his cravat. Darcy quickly unwound the fabric and smiled as her fingers caressed the skin. "Have I ever mentioned how I adore your neck?"

"I believe so." He whispered and bent to kiss her. "Once or twice."

She set to work on the buttons of his coat, and slipped her hands inside. "mmmmm, warm." Darcy's hands were hardly still, he was busy unbuttoning her gown, and their mouths were in perpetual motion, kissing everywhere as their fingers dragged, pulled, attacked. Darcy's coat was on the floor along with his waistcoat. Elizabeth's gown was pulled down to her waist and the stays were released and thrown across the room. While lifting her chemise up and over her head, Darcy stopped dead, and stared at her breasts.

"What has happened here?" He said hoarsely. "Elizabeth!" His hands slipped up and over the enormous swollen orbs. "Oh my love!" He bent and began suckling hungrily.

"Will!" She cried and laughed, and he looked up to her with a blissful smile. Taking his head in her hands, she kissed him. "You are mad!"

Caressing over the soft, beautiful skin he kissed her. "I have dreamed of these, and here you have . . . oh love." He smiled stupidly and then scooped her up in his arms.

She squealed and laughed when he bit her throat. "Fitzwilliam!"

Adams appeared and was about to announce the availability of bath water when he saw his master drop the mistress on the bed, and rip off his shirt to her cheer of approval. Wide-eyed, he hurriedly shut the dressing room door, and directed the housemaids to start carrying the buckets of water back downstairs.

Darcy removed Elizabeth's half-boots and stockings and kneeled above her, staring down at her nude body, "Look at you." His warm hands caressed over her shoulders and breasts, then surrounded their baby. He leaned and kissed her round belly. "I am home, my child." Looking up to her he had tears in his eyes. "How could I leave my family?"

"Fitzwilliam." Elizabeth sat up and reached for his breeches, unbuttoning them and sliding them down his hips. "Come to bed."

"Of course." He turned and sitting on the edge, tugged and pulled, then hung his head in frustration. "My boots will not budge. I have too many pairs of socks on." Elizabeth moved behind him and wrapped her arms around his shoulders. She kissed his ear and watched him try again. "I will have to call for Adams."

"Nonsense." She climbed off of the bed and straddling his leg, bent down and lifted the boot, then looked back at him. "Come on then, you know what to do."

Darcy sat motionless, staring at the sight of his nude wife, her bottom lifted high in the air, her glistening mound open and waiting for him, and her face, surrounded by tumbled down hair, looking back at him expectantly. He caught his breath and bunched the counterpane in his hands to stop from grabbing her and burying his shaft into the welcoming sight that second. "Lizzy . . ."

"Fitzwilliam, as often as I have imagined my naked husband striding around our chambers wearing nothing but his Hessians and a salute, I would rather feel his toes on my legs than leather." She laughed and he woke from the journey into his imagination, and blushed. "What were you thinking?"

Placing one boot on her bottom, he smiled. "Pull these bloody things off and you will find out." With a few tugs, Elizabeth ripped the boot from his foot and toppled onto the floor. "Elizabeth!" Darcy stood and started to come after her."

"No, no!" She laughed and tossed it aside. "One more!" She again assumed the position of his valet and laughing, he placed his sock-covered foot on her bottom, and this time the second boot slid off without too much trouble. Elizabeth straightened and dropped it. "Now then. I am cold."

He grabbed her waist and drew her between his legs, and happily began kissing her throat. "I see that, love." His lips wandered down her breasts to find the tight, erect nipples waiting for his tongue. He suckled and nibbled, and ran his hands up and over her body. She moaned and he looked down to see the series of strawberries all over her skin. "Look dear." He kissed her lips.

"I have a feeling that I am going to be covered with love bites very soon." Elizabeth wrapped her arms around his neck and they kissed. Darcy fell backwards on the bed, taking her with him, and they lay together, kissing softly. "Nobody will see us for months."

"I feel free to decorate you most liberally." He smiled and ran his hands over her. "You feel so different."

"I have a feeling that positions like this will become a thing of memory before too long." She caressed his hair from his eyes. Darcy ran his fingers through her dark tresses and studied her face, then in one swift movement rolled them over so he lay above her, still maintaining the contact, but mindful of the baby. "It seems that you have some ideas." She laughed.

"You certainly gave plenty of inspiration in your letters." He quickly slipped the rest of his clothing off, then returned to kiss her slowly. Feeling her hand gliding over him, he watched as she guided his length back into its home. "Ohhhhhhhhhh, yesssss."

"You wrote to me how much you missed our lovemaking, Will." Elizabeth suckled his lips, then held his face in her hands and stared into his eyes. "I wish that you could know the joy it brings to me."

"Oh sweet Elizabeth, I am so lost without you." Darcy began moving steadily. Elizabeth raised her hips, meeting him stroke for stroke, building their motion. Their heartbeats in unison, their breath rasping, their mouths devoured each other, and the loving couple easily found their rhythm once again, and very quickly found bliss. Afterwards they lay spooned together under the blankets, kissing and touching, whispering together. Darcy laid his hands over the baby, and jumped when he felt the movement. Elizabeth placed her hands over his and turned to see his face. Their eyes met and he nuzzled her ear, drinking in her scent. "I have no words for this."

Elizabeth kissed the bare skin of his chest, "This is what I missed so much, being surrounded by you." They closed their eyes and dozed together, and eventually fell soundly asleep for the first time in weeks. When Darcy blinked awake, he took in her peaceful face and hugging her, let his gaze travel over the familiar room. He noticed a handkerchief with his initials peeking out from beneath a pillow, and wondered if Elizabeth had slept with the token while he was away. Carefully manoeuvring his hands, he managed to snag it. But not before her eyes fluttered open. "oh."

He smiled and peeked at her. "What is this, love?"

She blushed then lifted her chin. "Smell it."

Lifting it up to his nose he bit his lip and blushed with her. "Sandalwood. Lizzy . . . You truly missed me."

Her eyes grew wide. "I thought that I made that clear already."

Hurriedly, he gave her a squeeze. "You did, love, you did . . . It is just so wonderful to have it confirmed so . . . Dearest, I slept with your lavender sachets under my pillow."

"You did? Oh Will!" Elizabeth squeezed his hands, then began to giggle.

Darcy kissed her shoulder. "What is it?"

"I had contemplated our reunion and for some reason I imagined a trail of clothes leading from the front door, up the steps, and us not even making the bedchamber before we succumbed to some ferocious expression of desire against a wall in a hallway."

"Well that certainly would have drawn the attention of the staff." He chuckled and hugging her waist, rubbed his burgeoning erection against her bottom. "Do you know what I imagined?"

"Tell me."

"I thought that you would be waiting for me." He pinched her nipple and she pushed her hips back. "And I thought that we would fall into each other's arms, then I would carry you up the stairs, drop you on the bed and ravish you the first time . . ."

"The first time?"

"Yes." He kissed her ear. "The first time, before we even undressed. Then the second time as we bathed together, the third as we returned to our bed, the fourth as we fed each other, the fifth when I woke you in the night, the sixth when you woke me . . ."

Elizabeth laughed and turning in his arms, pressed her fingers to his lips. "You are full of glorious ideas. Shall we take them in order?"

"No, I have a new idea." Darcy kissed her then licked his lips. "Mmm."

"Does it involve a pair of recalcitrant boots?" She giggled as his eyes lit up.

"We can forgo the boots, if you will just . . . bend over for me?" He asked hopefully.

"Whatever you want, love." Elizabeth laughed when he whipped off the covers and jumped to his feet, then reached to pull her up. She resisted his tug and he stopped to see what was wrong. "I will gladly be your valet if you will be my mount."

A brilliant grin appeared and he lifted her up and off of the bed. Standing behind her, he stroked his hands down her shoulders and murmured in her ear as he covetously caressed her bottom. "I will take you on the ride of your life."

DARCY TURNED THE PAGE of Elizabeth's journal, placed the ribbons to mark that he had read the daily descriptions of her life without him and closed the book, passing his hand over the cover. "If there was ever a doubt about your feelings for me it would have been banished with this reading." He said tenderly, and thought of her last entry.

I miss you my Fitzwilliam. I miss the safety of your embrace. I miss your touch, your eyes, your beautiful voice, oh and your taste. I miss drinking the wine from your tongue and the sugar from your loins. I miss the scent of one man. I miss your cries of passion, I miss feeling your body tremble under my fingertips and I miss the feel of you coming into me. You speak of the warmth of entering me, but it can be nothing compared to the heat of receiving you. I am empty without you, love. Come as soon as you are able, I ache to be filled once again.

"We are too shy to speak these things out loud." He smiled then chuckled. "The safety of our private thoughts first spoken only to ourselves, but now I have no doubt that we will be discussing them in depth."

Setting the book aside, he glanced at the work piled on his desk. "There is so much to do here." He began looking through the letters then let them drop, instead drifting back into the memory of that morning, when he spied her lying in bed when he woke, already in possession of his journal and catching up on his entries. Hearing her laugh, Darcy looked up when he noticed Elizabeth entering the room with the book in hand.

"What were you reminiscing about?"

"How happy I am to be here." He smiled and stood.

"I marked an entry that I liked very much." She blushed and watched as he opened the book and moved the ribbon aside.

To be without her is to be without my heart. To spend a day without once hearing her laughter is to be without the sun. To spend an evening without her voice is to be bereft of music. To spend a night without her touch is to be so very cold. I want you to hold me, dear Elizabeth. I want to come home and feel you hold me.

Elizabeth leaned against his chest to listen to his heart beating steadily, while she wrapped her arms around him. "I was feeling so low then." He whispered, and kissed her hair.

"Do you feel better now? I do." She looked up to see him smile. "I could use some sleep, though."

Darcy laughed and kissed her. "I imagine that we both could." Hugging her tightly he kissed her again. "Shall we begin? We have many subjects to discuss, and not all are matters of the heart, it was a busy time for you."

She smiled and kissed his nose. "I will take such pleasure in the peace of being alone with you. I enjoyed our family being here, but I was not sorry to see them go."

"I am grateful that they kept you company, dearest." He said seriously. "Keeping guests happy was a distraction, it seems."

"It was, and it was good to know Alicia and Stephen better, and Mr. Bingley as well for as long as he stayed."

"He left when Jane did?" Darcy kissed her hair and they swayed gently together.

"No, he left when he received a letter from Miss Bingley." She looked up to smile at him. "But we suspected you would return before long, so he felt that I no longer needed his exuberant cheer."

"Hmm." They remained embraced in companionable silence until Darcy continued the conversation. "Bingley told me before I left that he had appointed himself your protector in my stead." He added softly, "He is very fond of his role as your big brother." Feeling her laugh he looked down to see her smile.

"Well then my brother has his hands full with his other sister. Miss Bingley is difficult, I gather."

"What has she done now?"

"Nothing new, I just feel for the poor man. She is ready to return to town and try again, and does not wish to wait for spring. I imagine the gossip over her faux pas with Wickham has died, she can only be seen as a victim now that he is convicted and to be sent away. Mr. Bingley left for Scarborough and will retrieve her before returning to his brother's home. She says that she has learned her lesson and will be sure of her suitor's credentials, and will not set her sights quite so high in the future."

"Ah." Darcy smiled. "Her attitude has been adjusted, I see. Good for her. I hope that she finds a suitable mate, however, I am eternally grateful that I am married to you and will not be the subject of her interest."

"I think that you know my opinion on that topic." She laughed and he chuckled.

Tilting his head, he brushed a curl away from her eyes. "Tell me, does Bingley's unending happiness ever grate your nerves?"

"No!" Elizabeth squeezed his bottom. "What a thing to say! I thought that you were grateful for his good humour!"

Darcy kissed her and squeezed her bottom in return. "I am love; I am, though I sometimes wish that he would be more serious."

She sighed, "He is capable of it. We had a serious talk about Jane."

"Yes, I saw that and was glad of it, why he would fear my reaction to him seeking your opinion . . . well I suppose that I have threatened him a few times." He chuckled. "I read your story about his falling off of the horse; I look forward to teasing him about that." He noted her silence. "What are you not telling me?"

Elizabeth glanced up to see his raised brows. "What do you mean?"

"Lizzy."

"Oh all right, I mounted Richard and rode around the hedge to locate him."

"Elizabeth!" He cried and stared at her. "No!"

"I am clearly well," she said stubbornly, "and he needed me." Darcy stared at her and she stared back. The contest of wills continued as they fought silently, then ended when he drew her in for a passionate kiss. Elizabeth caught her breath and lay her head back against his pounding heart and felt his arms tighten around her. "I will not ride again."

"Thank you." Darcy closed his eyes and kissed her forehead, then clearing his throat, continued where they had left off. "Bingley expressed his interest for Jane?"

"ummmhmm." Elizabeth snuggled into his embrace and he resumed stroking her back. "What do you think of the match?"

"Is it a match?" He asked softly.

"You do not like Jane, do you? You are still uncomfortable around her."

"It is difficult for me to reverse my opinion once formed, but I recognize her efforts and appreciate the changes she has made." Hearing her sigh he whispered, "You will allow me that hesitation?" She nodded and he kissed her temple.

"You do not wish her for your friend, though?"

"You are as close to Bingley as I, my love, he is your friend, too. What are your thoughts?"

"I want them both to be happy in their choices. I want my sister to find who she needs and not try to imitate us or any other couple. I want her to be safe and cared for, but I will not try to do more. It is between them."

"Do you feel that Bingley is serious in his thoughts of her?"

"I think that Mr. Bingley wishes for love and attention because he is not yet comfortable in his own skin." She felt Darcy's laugh rumble through his chest. "What did I say?"

"So because Bingley would rather spend his time dancing than in solitude with a book it means that he is not ready to settle down?"

"Is that what I said?"

"I think so." Darcy kissed her tenderly and stroked his fingers over her cheek. "Not everyone is like us, love."

"I like to dance."

"But you like to be left alone as well."

"So do you."

"Hence my example." He hugged her tightly. "If they can fulfil each other's needs then I will be happy for them, but I think that in a case such as this, I will step away and watch."

"No matchmaking by us." Elizabeth whispered. "That will not stop your aunt and uncle, you know. They have plans."

"Then we will offer our friendship to their victims, whatever the outcome."

"LYDIA, PAY ATTENTION." Jane said quietly. "This is very important."

"Why?" She sighed and looked wistfully outside while her mother climbed out of the carriage. "I wanted to go to Meryton!"

"You have lessons."

"This is all Lizzy's fault! She is the one who made Papa think of school! I do not want to go to school, and I do not want to read! Why is that so important?" She slammed the book shut.

Kitty looked up from the drawing she was working on and whispered. "Do not let Papa hear you slam a book like that! He gets so mad if they are mishandled!"

"He loves them more than us." Lydia's bottom lip stuck out.

"Papa wants you to have as good of a life as you can, and that means that you must improve yourself." Jane said patiently. "We all need to improve ourselves, and hopefully we will marry well."

"Oh that is simple, all I need to do is smile, Mama said . . ."

"Lydia." Jane said sternly. "Mama is wrong." At last the girl's attention was caught by the unprecedented tone in her sister's voice. "You must have more than a smile."

"Mama said that Mr. Harwick is marrying soon." She said slyly. "You must be angry."

"No, I am grateful. He is very much in love with Miss Stewart, he will be happy as he deserves to be." She sighed. "I will find my future elsewhere, and you sister, should stop trying to provoke me and attend to your reading." She pointed to the book. "Go ahead."

Lydia wrinkled her nose. "You hate it as much as I do."

"But I do it just the same." Jane smiled. "Do you not wish to catch a man like Mr. Darcy?"

"No." Lydia opened the book and started reading. "I just want a man in a red coat."

Jane thought of Fitzwilliam and nodded. "Well, they can be quite appealing as well."

"Do you know any?" Lydia asked eagerly.

"I do, and he is to be married very soon as well." She tapped the book. "Read."

"What are you girls doing?" Mrs. Bennet hurried into the room with Mrs. Gardiner following at a more sedate pace. "You know the Lucas' are coming for dinner! Mary, where is she?"

"She is playing Mama, can you not hear her?" Kitty asked.

Mrs. Bennet paused. "*That* is Mary?"

"She is much-improved, is she not?" Jane smiled. "Lizzy would be so pleased to hear her."

"She would, I will tell her how well Mary is getting on with her music." Mrs. Gardiner nodded. "I wish that Georgiana would play for us sometime, but

Mary says that she only plays for her master, and when they go to spend time with Colonel Fitzwilliam at Darcy House."

"I wish that she could have come to Longbourn with you. She is a sweet girl." Jane smiled.

"She is but . . ." Mrs. Gardiner glanced at the other occupants of the room and caught Jane's eye. "She could not leave her cousin alone."

"I imagine that he would have been quite happy to entertain Mrs. Carter alone." Mr. Gardiner chuckled and entered with Mr. Bennet. "Well, where are these neighbours of yours? I am hungry." He rubbed his stomach and Mrs. Gardiner shook her head. "Our sister always sets a fine table, my dear."

"Any more of her table and you will soon resemble your niece."

Mr. Bennet said nothing, but settled in a chair and looked at the book Jane was attempting to read. "Are you enjoying Mr. Shakespeare, Daughter?"

Jane smiled a little. "Honestly Papa, I am afraid that the words stare back at me. I do not really understand it."

"Do you wish to?"

"Should I? I will never be Lizzy."

"Lady Matlock will take you in hand this spring dear, and you will learn everything that you need to move in society." Mrs. Gardiner smiled. "She will surely introduce you to special men." Jane nodded and looked back at the book, then closed it with relief when the Lucas and Philips families at last arrived.

The familiar families easily blended to share the Christmas dinner, Mr. Bennet regularly reminded his wife to stop bragging about Mrs. Darcy. Lady Lucas spent her time keeping her husband from telling the same stories of St. James's and how he expected to see the Darcys there this Season. When the meal was over Jane helped to pour the coffee and tea, and was surprised to find Robert Lucas standing by her side.

"Would you like some more?" She offered.

"No, I am just escaping our mothers." He smiled and appreciated her blush. "They try to top each other in their bragging. I am afraid that your sister's success has quite surpassed my mother's hopes for Charlotte and it does not sit well with her."

"I suppose that she will not rest until you are married well." Jane smiled back at him and he shrugged.

"I suppose. I hear that you are to be the toast of London under the care of an earl's wife." He saw her eyes cast down. "I hope that your mother's disappointment over your courtship . . ."

"I would rather not speak of it, sir. I am very happy for his engagement."

Lucas's brow creased. "I did not realize that he has become engaged, forgive me. I . . . It rather shows that he was not all that serious about you, does it not?"

"Mr. Harwick was serious, I will not allow anyone to speak ill of him."

Lucas saw her flushed face and touched her arm. "I always admired that about you, Jane." She looked up and he smiled. "You cannot help but see the good in everyone, no matter the situation."

"I strayed from that this summer, to my detriment." She set down the coffee pot and clasped her hands. "What are your plans, sir?"

He studied her quietly. "I am to find a bride. Father is under the mistaken impression that his knighthood and Lucas Lodge will grant me access to the crème of London society, but I am not so foolish as to try. I know that I must supplement the income of the estate and have spent some time speaking to your uncle about investing in his business, as your new brother has apparently done." Jane nodded and looked at him in fascination. "I do not want a grand estate; I honestly do not care to wander the halls of St. James's. I merely wish to marry a lovely girl, care for my family, have a small brood of children, and live my days right here in Hertfordshire." Lucas' head tilted. "Now I just have to find the girl."

"I . . . I wish you luck in that." She said softly and then looked down to her hands.

"When your courtship ended, I believe that luck smiled at me." He said quietly. "Unless your attention is drawn to a life such as your sister has. That I cannot, nor do I desire to, match."

"Oh."

"I am Mr. Darcy's age, but I will never approach a tenth of what he has."

"It is nice to visit Pemberley, but I do not feel comfortable there." She looked back up at him and he smiled and touched her hand.

"I am not going anywhere, Jane. Think it over, and perhaps I will at last be allowed to display the admiration I have felt for you for many years." He bowed and walked away.

Jane stared after him until Mrs. Gardiner approached. "What happened just now? Did Mr. Lucas make his intentions known?"

"You were expecting this?" She turned and saw her aunt's smile. "Why did you not tell me?"

"Mr. Lucas spoke to your father, who brought your uncle into the conversation. Mr. Bingley's interest was discussed." She smiled and looked back to the young man talking easily with his younger brother and teasing his little sister. "You have much to consider, dear. Take your time."

Chapter 10

"Eva." Fitzwilliam called when he entered the drawing room of Harwick's home, and reached for her to hold tight to his chest. "I could not wait to see you at the Morelands'. When I received the note that you had arrived last night, it killed me that I could not come to you that instant!" He kissed her forehead and squeezed harder. "Damn duty!"

"Richard!"

"Why did I have to play nursemaid to the General? Why last night?" He complained and looked down at her. "And why did I have to be at work again all morning? My mind was with you, not the boys!"

"My mind was with you, but I understood the delay." Evangeline laughed when he began kissing all over her face. "You *are* impatient!"

"You know full well I am!"

"And how does that serve you when facing an enemy?" She squealed when suddenly she was lifted off of the floor and into his arms. "Richard what are you doing?"

"I intend to anticipate our vows, my love." He growled and kissed her.

"Richard!"

"I am a desperate man!" He whined.

"Put me down!" Evangeline demanded. "I will not be . . .manhandled by you!"

"I would love to manhandle you, my lovely girl." He whispered warmly in her ear.

"Do I need to call my brother?" She said a little less convincingly. "He will kill you if he sees us in this position!"

Fitzwilliam settled them onto a sofa and happily began kissing her throat. He lifted his head to smile at her. "Do you truly believe that your brother would support you? I am certain that he would be on my side. I saw how he could hardly contain his desire for Miss Stewart when he met me at the door and spoke of her."

"Richard how can you speak so plainly?"

"Very easily my dear." He laughed and kissed her soundly. "I will hold back nothing of myself from you, and that will have to include my soldier's persona."

"Crude? I do not think that I like that."

"No, honest, love. Unendingly honest." He smiled to see hers appear. "I am honest when I confess that I love you and want you. And I am honest when I say I will wait for our vows, but that I am very, very impatient."

"And I am honest when I confess that I am as well." She whispered. Fitzwilliam laughed and she kissed him. "Now, manhandle me until my brother appears!"

They heard Harwick in the hallway and groaning, Fitzwilliam reluctantly let her go, then rose to his feet. "I cannot remain in the same room with Harwick."

"Why?" She laughed and he looked down at his breeches. "Oh." Evangeline tilted her head and studied the evidence of his declarations.

"Say what is on your mind, woman."

Reaching forward she gave him a little pat and he groaned. "Very nice."

"Good Lord." He kissed her and flew out of the room. Evangeline laughed, knowing full well what he was going to do, and walked across the hallway to her brother's study. He was standing near his desk and looking through the pile of letters that had just arrived, and cocked his head at her. "Fitzwilliam just ran past the door on his way upstairs."

"Did he? Well he did say something about freshening himself before we leave." She smiled and looked at her hands.

"Yes." He cleared his throat and took a seat at his desk after she chose a sofa near the fire.

"I see that you are ready to go." Evangeline inspected his careful attire. "You are quite handsome tonight."

"I have been ready for hours, I think. I missed her the moment I stepped into my carriage after I visited last night. I think that Fitzwilliam would have felt the same way about you if he had been here." He smiled at his sister and shrugged. "Why did we agree to this interminable engagement?"

"So that your new bride will be properly outfitted."

"And what of you?"

"I do not need so many things, I can order them now and they will be ready for when we return, besides I have been married before. I was happier to spend the time with the girls." Evangeline smiled sadly.

"You will always be welcome to visit." Harwick reassured her. "You are not disappearing from their lives."

"It will be a long time, though." She sighed. "Well, at least I will see them at the wedding."

"And they will have a mother again, and perhaps someday they will have siblings. Just as you might have your own children." He coughed when he felt his emotion rising and reached for the letters. Brother and sister became quiet as they were lost in their thoughts, then he began to chuckle.

"What is it Jeffrey?" Evangeline smiled to see Harwick wiping his eyes. "You laugh so easily now, what has tickled you this time?"

"Darcy." He smiled and held up a letter. "He seeks advice from an experienced man for managing a very emotional wife."

"Poor Elizabeth." She settled back and saw his raised brows. "*She* is bearing the child."

"*He* is bearing with her." He laughed to see her pursed lips, then watched her expression change to worry.

"She is so young."

"She will be well, Eva." Harwick reassured her.

"She will be magnificent." Fitzwilliam proclaimed as he returned.

"Richard!" Evangeline stood and was soon resting in his arms. "Where have you been?"

He cleared his throat to speak when he sensed her need for reassurance. Hugging her tightly, he whispered a promise, then kissed her hair. "Have you not noted my impressive new uniform? I had it made in honour of your arrival. I have to keep you interested, my dear." He stood back and let her admire him. Harwick snorted to see his sister blush, and Fitzwilliam smiled at him then sobered. "Besides, mourning for Anne ended today, so I felt that it was not right to wear anything quite so . . . bright, before the black was off of my arm. I can honestly say that I only mourned her life, not her passing. I was happy for her release."

"Knowing so much of her story now, I can only agree with you." Evangeline squeezed his hand and they settled on the sofa.

"Have you heard from de Bourgh? How has your Aunt dealt with the past six weeks?" Harwick asked sombrely.

"She remains in the dower's house, seeing and speaking to nobody but her servants. Mother said that an odd sense of peace has fallen over her. I am not sure that is the correct term for it. I wonder what she is thinking."

"Perhaps it is the release after years of vigilance and uncertainty." Harwick said thoughtfully. The three contemplated the theory in silence, and then Evangeline noticed Fitzwilliam's expression. She recognized it as a sign that he was drifting into a dark place, and nudged him, startling him from his thoughts.

She smiled and brushed his coat. "You are very handsome, sir."

"Hmm." He took her hand and kissed it. "Well, this is purely for you. I was afraid that when you saw me again, you would be disappointed that your memory was better than the real man." His gaze fell down to her hand in his and stayed there.

"Richard, do I look or act even remotely disappointed?" She asked softly.

"No." He said quietly, then looking up at her, he shrugged and smiled. "Do not mind me."

"I love your ring." She touched the band containing her hair.

"I had to have one. Darcy was hanging on to his like a lifeline." Their eyes met and hearing Harwick turning over a letter, remembered that he was still in the room. Fitzwilliam resumed his normal cheer. "Speaking of Darcy, did I hear you mention my stodgy cousin when I entered?"

"I did." Harwick looked up from his work and smiled. "He is suffering as all husbands do."

"He has a volatile woman in his home." Fitzwilliam laughed and smiled at Evangeline. "You spent some time with Elizabeth, what is your opinion of her?"

"You know full well that I like her very much, just as you do. I admire how she has taken on Pemberley and Darcy."

The men laughed and Harwick held up the letter. "Darcy should be admired for taking her on. I knew that she was like Ellen when I first met her. I believe that I can give him some excellent advice."

"I do not think that I like the way you speak of her, as if she is a problem to be handled." Evangeline glared at them both and sat up. "I am going to speak to Laura about you Jeffrey, and give her advice on handling you!"

"Eva." He sighed when she stood and left the room. "Sorry about that, Fitzwilliam."

"No, I do not mind at all. I like seeing this fire blazing from her. She is not afraid to speak her mind. I have a feeling that she suppressed it for a long time." He raised his brows and Harwick nodded. "Well, two weeks to our weddings, are you prepared?"

"I was prepared when I proposed." Harwick sighed. "This engagement only confirms that Laura is absolutely suited for me, we share so many interests, she has given me a smile, the girls loved her when they met . . . I could hardly fathom my life taking such a turn, or even consider anticipating the future with such elation again."

"And what of Ellen?" Fitzwilliam asked softly.

Harwick smiled and looked down at the ring on his finger. "I will never forget her, but on my wedding day, I will let her go and love the living woman whose hand will be in my grasp."

"Love?"

"Darcy once told me that I should love or not marry at all. He was correct."

"He is annoying with that." Fitzwilliam laughed and turned his head when he heard Evangeline in the foyer, asking for her coat. "It seems that my love is ready to depart."

"I cannot wait to see my Laura." Harwick jumped to his feet.

"It has only been a few weeks for you."

"You say that as an accusation!" The future brothers walked out to join Evangeline, and soon they departed for the townhouse occupied by Lord and Lady Moreland, to greet the gathering of family.

LORD MATLOCK gave his son a nudge and winked. "Harwick is hopeless, trying to maintain his proper behaviour. Look at how his hands keep clenching! He is itching to hold Miss Stewart."

"Then hand the man a glass!" Fitzwilliam laughed. As if on cue, Stewart approached his future brother and gave him some wine. "Good job, man!"

"How is that little love affair going?" Lord Matlock nodded over to a sofa where Julia Henley was sitting with Evangeline and Laura.

"Difficult to say. He absolutely refuses to call it a courtship. I suppose that he is a bit gun shy of the process after behaving so poorly over Elizabeth." He laughed. "Can you imagine Darcy without her? What would he be today if he had let her go? Where would we all be now?"

Lord Matlock considered the question. "You would not have met Mrs. Carter, would you?"

"No, perhaps Stewart and Miss Henley may have met since she was eyeing him already, and the families are friends. Harwick and Miss Stewart though," he shook his head, "I do not know if that would have occurred. He had his mind set on marrying quickly and for different reasons. If it was not Miss Bennet it would have been some other girl who caught his eye at a ball. No, I would say that Darcy's love affair has certainly been the reason for several others."

Lord Moreland approached and gestured to Harwick. "What do you say, put these two boys out of their misery and marry them off tomorrow?"

Fitzwilliam's eyes lit up. "I second that notion!"

"Now, now, Son, restrain yourself!"

"Why?" He demanded. "The house is almost finished; we can step around a few drop clothes for a week or so!"

"No, you fought the Carters too hard to get them to agree to the repairs."

"It is their property; they should have been keeping it up. They tried to take it away from her when they learned she was remarrying, we had to get the attorneys to read that settlement. For her lifetime the house is hers. She earned it." Fitzwilliam glared. "They should be grateful that such a woman as Evangeline ever agreed to marry that bastard."

"Richard." Lord Matlock warned. "I did not mean to raise your ire. Calm yourself."

"Yes sir." He caught Evangeline sending him a worried look and attempted a smile.

"She is becoming adept at reading you."

"And I am doing the same with her. Something was bothering her at Harwick's home, but it was not the moment for discussion. I believe that it was about Elizabeth's pregnancy. I have not heard of any troubles, have you? I imagine that the women might share things amongst themselves that they would not say to us?" Fitzwilliam looked at his father worriedly.

"Your mother would tell me if there was a problem." Lord Matlock smiled. "Of course Audrey is due any moment now, so that might be on her mind as well."

"Yes." He sighed. "I ran into Singleton and his father the other day at the club. What a bastard he is."

"Singleton, Senior?" Lord Moreland sniffed. "Short fuse on that one. Control is his game; you do not want to cross him. Gave up playing cards with him long ago."

"Yes, the things you learn when it is too late." Lord Matlock mused.

"I am sorry that Audrey must live in their home. At least her husband is a new man now, and someday that home will be his." He looked down at his feet then back up to Evangeline. "I wish . . ." He stopped and walked away.

Lord Moreland watched him go. "When will you tell him, Matlock?"

"After the wedding."

"A damned fine wedding gift. Gets them away from the Carters forever." Lord Moreland smiled, "Smart of you to wait and approach with the offer after they had agreed to foot the cost of the repairs." He laughed to see Lord Matlock's smirk. "Well, it is not an estate, but their own townhouse, something to pass on to his son. That will make him feel like a man."

"He could have had an estate." Lord Matlock looked after Fitzwilliam, standing next to Evangeline and laughing as she smiled and held out her hand to be kissed. "He chose love instead."

10 JANUARY 1810
We received word today that Audrey safely delivered a beautiful daughter. Her name is Grace Alene Singleton, she has her father's blonde curls and the blue eyes that all of the Fitzwilliams seem to own. Audrey did as she promised and wrote a very detailed letter describing everything that she endured, including the sound of her husband collapsing in a dead faint when she cried out in pain. He was carried from the sitting room outside of her chambers and left to recover while she continued. Aunt Helen and Mrs. Singleton remained by her side for the entire ordeal, while Mr. Singleton and Uncle Henry attempted to distract Robert from his worry.

Unfortunately Fitzwilliam saw Audrey's letter to me, and I saw the colour drain from his face as he read her description of the experience. My poor dear husband looked at me with what can only be described as panic. He clutched me so tightly! I appreciated Audrey's candour even if Fitzwilliam did not. I compare it to the three presentations I received concerning the marriage bed. Aunt Marianne's was by far the most explicit and at the same time the most reassuring, however Aunt Helen and even Mama said things that were true and proved to be useful. And even with all of that preparation, I still was surprised that first night in my husband's embrace. I am certain that my childbirth experience will be unique, but I now have the knowledge to face it courageously.

"I am glad that you are feeling courageous, my love." Darcy sighed and set down the journal, and resumed his vigil by the study window on this cold February day. He had reread that particular passage countless times since Grace's birth weeks ago, and unwittingly found the place where Elizabeth thought she had hidden Audrey's letter. The calm that had reigned for several months had again given way to fear. His worry grew with her increasing belly, and now he must leave to attend the double wedding at Meadowbrook. *How can I leave her? How can I not take her with me? How many times did I promise her never to do that again?*

"She is fine, sir."

Darcy startled from his preoccupation of watching Elizabeth walk out in the snow-covered garden. "I see that." He glanced again at his wife then clearing his throat walked deliberately back to his desk and took a seat. "Do you need anything, Mrs. Reynolds?"

"Yes, sir. Mrs. Darcy is approaching her confinement. I thought that she should meet the local midwife so she will be reassured that a good woman will be with her when her time comes." She watched as his face lost expression. "It might reassure you as well, sir."

"Do I seem wary?" He said quietly.

"Sir . . .it is not my business." She cast her eyes down and he stared at her for several silent moments.

"Speak your mind, Mrs. Reynolds; you have never failed to do so in the past."

"I am aware of your daily walk to visit your parents, sir." She saw Darcy close his eyes. "She is very young, but I have grown to respect Mrs. Darcy enormously. She has taken on her duties at Pemberley much as you did when your father died. She is very strong in spirit."

"But so small in figure." He murmured. "And as you say, she is so very young." Shaking his head he stood again. "She will not like this, she does not approve of me dwelling on her possible loss. What do you think?" He swung around to face his housekeeper. "You have far more experience than I."

"Sir, I have never been married." She smiled and seeing his obvious fear was reminded of the little boy who used to follow her around the house after his mother died. "I have been present at many births, sir. She will be quite well, I know it. She is not like your mother at all. If you remember, she was very delicate."

"Mrs. Darcy cannot be described as indelicate." He glared at his housekeeper.

"Forgive me sir, I did not mean to imply . . ."

"Finish your thought, Mrs. Reynolds." He said tersely.

"She is a good strong country girl, sir." She said emphatically. "The staff is very pleased that you chose a such a woman for our mistress instead of one of those creatures who inhabit society." She sniffed. "Like those women who were here for your ball."

"I thought that you were pleased with the ball."

"I was pleased that none of those fortune hunters were after you, sir." Mrs. Reynolds declared. "They are nothing to our mistress." Darcy's lips twitched and she looked down. "Forgive me, sir. I have stepped beyond my place."

"No, no, forgive me. I am worried for her. She is my life." He picked up the miniature from his desk and studied her face.

Mrs. Reynolds smiled and nodded. "Shall I ask the midwife to visit?"

"Yes, please, although it is not decided yet who will deliver our child." Darcy smiled slightly. "Why did you ask me instead of Mrs. Darcy?"

"So that you could express your worry, sir." She nodded and left the room.

Darcy watched her go and laughed softly, then returning to his post by the window, started when he saw Elizabeth walking from the garden onto the path that led to the lake. "Oh no, my girl." He strode out of his study and called for his coat. Properly attired he set off after her. Moving much faster than his ungainly wife, he caught up to her just as she was about to begin wandering down the path to their little hideaway, and saw her slip on a patch of ice. "What are you about, Mrs. Darcy?" He demanded when he captured her hand and pulled her up.

"Fitzwilliam!" She beamed and taking his face in her hands, kissed him soundly and declared, "I am visiting my tree!"

"In the snow?" He said in exasperation. "Dearest there is nothing there but a bare trunk and some twigs! You should not be risking your health . . ."

"I will visit my tree!" She glared at him. "IF you are so concerned about the cold, then you may return to the house. I did not invite you." She spun and set off down the path. Darcy stood staring after her in stunned silence, then seeing her slip again and her arms fly out, he rushed forward just in time to catch her.

"Elizabeth. You do not have the balance you once did."

"Because I am huge and ugly." She turned and looked up at him. "I am hideous."

Darcy swallowed and looked into her tear-filled eyes; in an instant she had changed personalities again. "You are beautiful, and I have never wanted you more." He held out his arms and she fell into them and began to sob. He kissed her forehead and rubbed her back. "I love you, Elizabeth." *My dear, irrational, Elizabeth.* He felt her arms tighten around his waist and they stood on the quiet path while the brisk winter wind swirled around them. Her behaviour of late reminded him uncomfortably of Anne, but Harwick, Singleton, Layton and Gardiner all assured him that they had experienced the exact same thing. "Dearest?"

"Hmm?" She looked up to him and smiled softly. "I am acting oddly again."

"Ummm."

"You may say it, Fitzwilliam. If I become offended I will likely want to kiss you again a few minutes later." She laughed and he visibly relaxed. "I do not know what possesses me sometimes."

"Neither do I." He whispered and kissed her. "You frighten me."

"Because I wanted to visit my tree?" She cocked her head and he nodded.

"Amongst other things. Please do not scare me like this anymore. I have enough things scaring me."

"Such as?"

"Leaving you to go to the weddings. Who will keep you safe from your whims with me gone?"

"Then take me with you." She said positively.

"I dare not risk it." He held her to him. "Please, please promise to stay safe. Do not leave the house. Wander the halls, please darling." Drawing back he studied her carefully. "Yes?"

She did not hide her disappointment, but nodded. "Yes, I do not wish your hair to turn gray." Darcy sighed and she rested her head on his chest. "Besides I believe that your coach is not well-sprung enough. Every jostle and I would undoubtedly be begging you to stop at the next inn."

"Undoubtedly." He clutched her to him, still struggling with his decision, "I will remain here."

She pulled back and spoke seriously. "No. Richard is your best friend; he deserves to have you at his wedding. If Stephen can attend, so can you." They kissed and Darcy sighed, resting his head against her bonnet. "Fitzwilliam?"

"Hmm?"

"Will you please be careful?" She said against his coat. Darcy's embrace tightened.

"I will, love." He closed his eyes, unsure of what to do, then after several minutes in each other's arms, made a decision. "Come; let us visit your tree."

"HAVE YOU SEEN the bedchambers, Jane?" Lady Lucas asked.

"Oh, I have been to Charlotte and Maria's room, Lady Lucas." She blushed and bit her lip. "I remember that it is lovely. As is the rest of Lucas Lodge." She added quickly.

"It is a fine home." Lady Lucas lifted her chin and cast her eyes over the large drawing room where the neighbourhood was gathered. "My husband was delighted when he first found it. It was just the place, he said, for a knighted gentleman to live out his days. I have certainly never felt confined in any way, and that is quite something considering our many children." She smiled fondly at her boys, and then grimaced slightly at her girls. "Of course they will be gone before long, and the house will be empty again. We do look forward to seeing Robert's little ones come along one day. When he marries." Her gaze returned to her subject.

"Yes madam, as you should." Jane murmured. She was not entirely sure how Lady Lucas felt about her, but the words *disappointed* and *resigned* crossed her mind.

"Lady Lucas! Did you know that Lady Matlock, she is Mr. Darcy's aunt, has decided to take my dear Jane under her wing and show her society? Oh I am not at all surprised! Of course she could not help but see such potential in her!

After all, if Lizzy could capture a rich man like Mr. Darcy, why my Jane will surely find a titled man, a peer I mean. Jane cannot help but do well, she is so beautiful!"

"Mama, please." Jane said quietly. "I have no aspirations to surpass Lizzy."

"Of course you do not, but I am sure that if Lady Matlock, did I mention that she is an Earl's wife, Lady Lucas? That Lady Matlock would certainly not expect you to settle for less than Mr. Darcy if she is taking her time with you." Mrs. Bennet nodded and took a healthy sip of wine. "Do you not agree, Lady Lucas?"

"I cannot fathom Lady Matlock's purpose as she has not spoken it to me." Lady Lucas said stiffly.

"Well is it not wonderful that Lizzy's husband has given my girls the opportunity to be put in the way of rich men? Yes, yes, they will all do very well, one day." She beamed out over the room and watched Lydia giggling with a group of the neighbour boys and Kitty standing silently nearby. "They are going to an exclusive school next year. I do not like the thought of losing my Lydia, but I suppose that it has made a difference in Mary. At least she can play a bit better now."

"She plays very well now, Mama." Jane sighed. "I am sure that all of my sisters will find someone who makes them happy one day, just as Charlotte and Maria will." She smiled at Lady Lucas. "Excuse me."

Lady Lucas looked after her and turned to Mrs. Bennet. "My son is interested in Jane."

"And so is a man with five thousand a year." Mrs. Bennet's voice lost its silly tone.

The two women eyed each other. "I believe that a man with seven thousand already rejected her."

"He was a fool." Mrs. Bennet countered. "And when she is finished being instructed by Lady Matlock, she will be fit for any man."

"Or ruined." Lady Lucas sniffed.

"My daughter will marry very well." Mrs. Bennet declared and then smiled. "And what are your girls' prospects?" She glanced around the room. "Oh, my brother Philips has a new clerk. Perhaps he will do for one of them." Lady Lucas glared at her and Mrs. Bennet walked away.

Lucas saw Jane's embarrassment and approached her. "I am sorry about my mother. She has enormous expectations for me, she is as blind as my father about our true circumstances, I think."

"I am sorry about my mother. I think that she is similar to yours. I suppose that they had to find out about..your interest."

"Well, once your mother knew, it was inevitable." He sighed and looked down at his hands. "I am afraid that my family is just as willing to gossip as yours."

"My family does not . . ." Jane blushed when he raised his brow. "Well, yes I suppose some members do enjoy the news."

"It is entertainment in such a small community. Four and twenty families, I believe."

"That is a great many!"

"Miss Bennet, you have lived in London, surely you know better?" Lucas smiled. "But it is good to see you defend your home neighbourhood from being slighted, even from one of its own."

Jane smiled and sighed. "London hardly needs anyone to jump to her defence."

"Do you like it there?" He indicated a sofa.

"Parts of it." She admitted and took a seat. "I do enjoy Cheapside, where my relatives live. People flock there to shop, you can entertain yourself for hours just wandering the streets and ducking through a door to find a courtyard and even more shops, and never spend a shilling."

"Do you ever wish to buy?" He asked softly and sat down.

"Oh, I suppose. There are so many things to catch your eye." Jane smiled. "But then you wonder whatever will you do with the item once it is home."

Lucas laughed. "Yes, I think that is quite true. I had some friends who had the opportunity to take a grand tour after their days in Cambridge were over. I received letters reporting on the knickknacks they acquired, meant for their future homes and solid proof that they had taken the journey, just something else for the maids to dust." He looked around the room. "I am afraid that anyone who enters here will fully appreciate that well-travelled does not define this family."

"Pemberley is full of artwork." Jane mused. "As is Darcy House and Matlock House. Everywhere you look there is some sort of statue or painting."

"Gaudy? Darcy did not impress me as one to decorate to show off his wealth."

"Oh, oh no, neither of his homes are covered in gilt or decorated for show. They have been in England for hundreds of years; they are bound to accumulate things after so long. It is . . . Lizzy describes it as understated elegance." She laughed. "My sister has seemingly blended seamlessly into her new world, it amazes me. She is so different, I hardly recognize her sometimes." Jane added pensively.

"Is that so?" Lucas asked softly. "Why do I like the sound of that?" Jane blushed and they heard the sound of the pianoforte. Rising to his feet, he extended his hand. "Will you dance with me, Miss Bennet?"

"Of course." She gave him her hand and he held it for a moment. "Mr. Lucas?"

He shook his head and smiled. "You will be here a few more weeks before you leave to be dazzled by your sister's world. I refuse to press you during this time. All I can do is be myself in the surroundings that I will have for my lifetime." Leading her to the spot where the couples were forming lines to dance he looked around the room and back to meet her eyes. "This is all I have."

"You should be very proud of it, sir." She said sincerely.

He drew a deep breath and stepped forward to take her hand as the dance began. "I am."

"OOOOH *LOOK AT YOU!!*" Elizabeth squealed and ran, or rather walked quickly, to awkwardly embrace Alicia.

"You are *enormous!*" Alicia cried and kissed her cheek, then pulled away from the hug to place her hands on Elizabeth's swollen belly.

"I know, I grow bigger every day, it seems!" She happily laid her hands on Alicia's belly and smiled up at her.

"You are beautiful, Elizabeth!" Laura cried and Evangeline stood back and wiped the tears streaming down her face. Lady Matlock gave her a hug and soon the group of chattering women were gone from the foyer and the sound of laughter drifted from a distant drawing room in Meadowbrook.

Darcy stood in stunned disbelief and stared after them. Layton grinned and walking up to him, clapped his hand on his shoulder. "Let me guess, if you had dared to say that your wife was enormous you would have found the air inside of Pemberley to be so cold that a thousand fireplaces could not hope to warm the house."

"Either that or she would be sobbing and calling for the mirrors to be covered." He closed his slack jaw and turned to his cousin. "She was just complaining of her sore back and the carriage hitting every rut, and how tired she was!"

Lord Matlock grinned and was joined by Fitzwilliam and Harwick. "Do not feel bad, Son. Alicia did something rather similar when we arrived. I think that the ladies simply needed to see other ladies, and commiserate together."

"Well, if that is the case, then it is worth the worry of making this trip." Darcy said quietly. "I just could not bear to leave her again."

"We will be continuing on to London from here." Layton observed. "We have decided that she will have her confinement at Matlock House, I am anxious to be on our way as soon as possible tomorrow, we think that we have a few weeks, but . . . well, I will be glad to arrive."

"I can certainly appreciate that. We have decided to remain at Pemberley."

"I am surprised at that." Harwick led the way into his study where Lord Moreland sat and Stewart was manning the port. "I would have sworn you would opt for the best hospital or the surgeon with the greatest reputation, and they are to be had in town."

"I have opted for the mid-wife with the greatest reputation." Darcy accepted a glass and sank into a chair. "I have hired Mrs. Griffiths to be Elizabeth's monthly nurse."

"Oh, I have heard of her!" Layton took a chair and smiled. "She will do well for you, I am sure. We will have a male mid-wife, we hope anyway, I have made the arrangements. I received a letter from a friend, Jacob McMasters, you know him? Well, his wife went into labour and the accoucher was too late for the delivery. The housekeeper did the job. McMasters sued him and won a pretty rich amount, took his wife on an extended holiday when she was up and around again with the proceeds."

The men laughed and Fitzwilliam grinned. "Well, if your business is delivering babies, it is good to be there on time."

"You never know how long it might take. Unpredictable little devils." Lord Moreland raised his glass to point at Stewart. "You were a troublesome one for your poor mother."

"So I have heard every year on my birthday for as long as I can remember." He smiled sheepishly and shrugged. "I do make sure that she receives a gift that day."

"Instead of you?" Harwick chuckled. "Your mother is brilliant!"

"OH YES, MY DANIEL *ALWAYS* REMEMBERS ME on his birthday!" Lady Moreland nodded and lifted her chin triumphantly.

"My mother is excellent at laying on guilt, but I never had her expect recompense for having me." Elizabeth laughed and the ladies joined her. "Oh this is so nice to be with you all again!"

"Is Fitzwilliam a nervous wreck, Elizabeth?" Alicia tried to reach the sugar and Evangeline moved to fix her tea for her. "Thank you, I look forward to bending again."

"Or seeing my toes." Elizabeth looked at her feet ruefully and shook her head. "Two more months, I cannot imagine myself any larger; and yes poor Fitzwilliam is such a dear. I know that I am nonsensical much of the day. That cannot help but add to his worry."

"I remember eating nothing but marmalade and muffins for days and days, and then when Henry had ordered our poor cook to make endless batches of it, I suddenly could not stand the sight of it!" Lady Matlock laughed. "That was with Audrey."

"How is she?" Elizabeth asked. "I received her letter about the birth, but have not heard from her since."

"She is well, it is difficult for her to write, her hands are still a bit sore from all the swelling she had. You two girls look svelte compared to her, poor thing." Lady Matlock said sadly. "I was quite concerned for her and the baby, but thankfully they both came through it well."

"It is a blessing." Evangeline agreed quietly. The ladies exchanged glances and Elizabeth spoke up.

"Now, tell me all of your wedding plans!"

"It is very simple, Elizabeth. Neither of us wanted anything too much." Laura took Evangeline's hand and squeezed. "Our concerns are calming our nerves for the ceremony."

"You are nervous?" Elizabeth smiled. "I remember being so frightened of disappointing Fitzwilliam."

"That would have been impossible, my dear." Lady Matlock assured her. "And I say the same to you ladies. My Richard is the happiest I have ever seen him, Eva. I can only imagine his joy will be bursting from him tomorrow morning."

Evangeline smiled. "Thank you, I look forward to making him happy."

Laura nodded, "I am not so worried for Jeffrey's happiness, he tells me so often of his joy, and I already love the girls."

"I had my talk with Laura about what to expect tomorrow night." Lady Moreland announced to her daughter's embarrassment. "I did my best."

"Oh I hope that it was better than what I did for Elizabeth." Lady Matlock sighed.

"What did you say?" Lady Moreland asked and Lady Matlock shook her head.

"No, I will not presume to give another talk like that again. When Georgiana's time comes, I leave it to you, Elizabeth."

"I imagine that it will depend on the man she chooses." Elizabeth smiled at Laura. "I have a feeling that you have nothing at all to fear. Mr. Harwick reminds me of Fitzwilliam."

"Oh."

"And Richard does as well." Elizabeth addressed Evangeline. "They are both gentle and loving men."

"I have an inkling that the other men have planned a bit of a send-off for the grooms this evening." Lady Matlock sighed. "So what shall we do to entertain ourselves, ladies? Will it be whist or gossip?"

ELIZABETH AWOKE to the sound of stumbling footsteps across the floor of the bedchamber. "Elizabeth?" She heard a soft, almost frightened, voice call. The bed curtains began to move and were suddenly thrown wide apart. She faced in the glow of the firelight the searching eyes of her very dishevelled and obviously worried husband. "LIZZY!" He fell upon her and she gasped.

"Will!" He held her possessively and showered her face in kisses. Elizabeth managed to put her hands on his shoulders and push him away, then held his head in her hands. "What has come over you?"

"I . . . I, oh Elizabeth, I must have had a nightmare, I dreamed . . ." He sighed and sat beside her on the bed, drawing her against him. "It does not matter, I awoke and you were not beside me."

"You must have been so confused to wake in a strange room." She stroked the hair from his brow and smiled at him.

"I was, and it never would have happened if I was in the bed where I belong. We never sleep apart, why . . .why was I banished to my own chambers?" He searched her eyes.

"Mr. Darcy, look at yourself." He furrowed his brow. "Go ahead, what are you wearing?"

Darcy looked down. He was dressed in breeches and a shirt. "Where are my night clothes?"

"Do you have any memory of last evening?" She tilted her head. "Perhaps of a strange servant leading you to bed? He certainly would not have expected you to be sharing mine."

"I . . . We were celebrating, after you retired, and Richard suggested that we toast . . ." A look of comprehension came over his face. "Richard! He got me drunk!" He stared at her incredulously. "I never drink to excess! What did that fool do to me?"

"I imagine that you must have cooperated in some manner, my love." Elizabeth smiled.

Shaking his head he stared at her. "No, you do not know how he operates, he has done this before, believe me, the man knows how to do it." He held his hands up to his head. "No wonder my mind feels like it is spinning and my tongue feels like it is covered in wool. Oh, and I kissed you with that mouth, I am so sorry, dearest."

"Hmm, the woolly tongue was not quite as bad as the fragrance. I definitely prefer you bathed, and wearing sandalwood." She rubbed his throbbing temples. "Perhaps you would like to wash and come to bed with me?"

"You will allow your sottish husband room in your bed?" He leaned gratefully into her touch.

"As it is the first; and hopefully the last time I have seen you this way, I will grant you dispensation for celebrating your friends' last night of bachelorhood." She smiled and he frowned.

"I am not sure if that is why I drank." He looked at her then lay his hands over her belly. "I remember now, Harwick showed me a portrait of his Ellen. You truly do resemble her."

"Oh Will." She wrapped her arms around him and they rocked quietly.

"I am trying so hard, love." He whispered.

"I am glad that we came here together."

"Why?" He rested his head on her shoulder while she gently stroked his hair.

"I think that you needed to be amongst some men for a little while and . . . just relax with them, and I think that it has done me some good to be amongst the women." She kissed his brow. "I am trying very hard too, Fitzwilliam."

He squeezed her, "I know. It helped to talk to everyone in person.. You confuse me."

"I confuse myself." She laughed and squeezed him back. "But it felt good to hear that I am not so silly."

"Your tears . . ."

"Are normal." She whispered.

"Are you sure?" He kissed her and sat up. "I have not read of them . . ."

"I think that you have read enough. Those books are doing you no good, only worrying you more. You read and imagine." She drew herself up. "When we go home, I want you to put them away, unless you intend to give up Pemberley and become a surgeon."

Darcy smiled. "That is what Uncle Henry told me, he said I had read enough to frighten me for a dozen children."

"Well, let us just have one for now." She laughed and smiling at his nodding head, climbed out of the bed and held her hands out for him. "Come, let me take you to your dressing room and prepare you for a good night of sleep. We have weddings to attend very soon."

He sighed and let her help him up. Wrapping his arms around her he kissed her hair. "I love you, my dear Elizabeth."

"And I love you, my inebriated Fitzwilliam."

He chuckled and gave her a squeeze. "Get back into bed. I will join you shortly." The tinkling sound of freezing rain against the window drew his eyes to the closed curtains. "We may not be able to travel home today."

She listened and saw his consternation. "I am sure that Mr. Harwick and Laura would be thrilled to have more guests for their honeymoon."

"He has no intention of leaving his chambers. I do not think that he really cares about who is here." Elizabeth gasped and started giggling. Darcy caressed the fallen hair from her face. "I hope that you were kind in your advice to the brides?"

"That depends on the advice that you offered the grooms, does it not?" She raised her brow and he smiled. "What did you tell them?"

"I told them to love their wives." He kissed her and was pleased to see her smile. Dropping his eyes to her belly, he caressed the baby and felt a little kick. "If you ever catch me over-indulging in drink again, please discourage me. In any way you feel will garner my attention."

Elizabeth wrinkled her forehead and nodded. "I will promise to do just that." She watched him leave the room and climbing back under the warm covers, listened to the rain. "Such a man I have married."

LAYTON PACED THE BEDCHAMBER and pulled out his pocket watch, glanced at the time and jammed it back in place. "What is the delay?" He demanded.

"It seems to me that I should be the one issuing the commands for time to fly, Brother." Fitzwilliam stood still while his batman adjusted his uniform and gave his sword a final brush with his cloth. "What is your worry?"

"I want to leave for London before the day is done! The weather is turning and I do not want to risk Alicia having to wait to travel, it is already too close to her time to be moving there as it is." He said tightly. "Who marries in February?"

"Men who do not wish to wait until March." Fitzwilliam declared. "Calm yourself! Darcy's worry is rubbing off on you. The weather is fine. You will be off for London in three hours."

Harwick entered the room and grinned at them. "Well, I am ready."

"And handsome." Fitzwilliam grinned back. "Laura will be delighted, I am sure."

"Well let us not keep her waiting!" Layton demanded.

"Brother, if you push me one more time . . ."

"Boys, enough." Lord Matlock entered the room and looking them over, nodded at them in approval.

Lord Moreland was right behind him and folded his arms. "Here is a sorry lot." He smiled at the men. "If I am not mistaken, the grooms are far happier than the groomsman . . . Where is Darcy by the way?"

"I believe he is making use of a chamber pot." Richard smirked. "His stomach is not at peace."

"He did indulge rather heavily in that fine illegal wine of yours, Harwick." Lord Matlock noted and laughed when Darcy appeared with Stewart grinning behind him. "Good Lord man, you are green!"

Darcy wiped his lips with his handkerchief. "I am perfectly fine, now why are we not on our way to the church? We would like to make Pemberley before the weather turns."

"YES!" Layton pointed at him and nodded vigorously. "Come on, the time is nigh!"

"I am of a mind to wait until noon, what say you, Harwick?" Fitzwilliam grinned.

"It is an idea." He rubbed his chin.

"Your brides would not be best pleased, and on this day of all days, you want your wife to like you." Lord Matlock winked and the men, except Darcy and Layton, laughed.

"I assure you that my sister would have your head, Harwick." Stewart proclaimed. "She has been anticipating this hour since the day she first laid eyes on you."

"Really?" Harwick's face lit with a delighted smile. "I felt the same." A knock sounded and a footman appeared.

"The coaches are ready, sir."

"Ah, at last." Fitzwilliam cocked his head at Darcy. "Well, Cousin?"

Darcy smiled and let down a little. "Come on." The group made their way downstairs and donned their coats. Stewart took his place as Harwick's best man in one coach, and Darcy walked with Fitzwilliam to board theirs. He saw a glimpse of fear in his cousin's eyes. "Are you well?"

"I am going into battle." Fitzwilliam said softly.

"Nonsense, you are returning from it." Darcy assured him. "How many nights have we spent over a glass of port talking of our dreams for home and family? I have not forgotten them, have you?"

"Of course not, but I never believed mine would come true."

"It certainly surprised me that any woman would ever want you." Darcy sighed and Fitzwilliam startled. "Well look at you! She could do so much better. Poor woman, when she sees those scars tonight she will be running away."

"Darcy!" Fitzwilliam growled.

"And wait until she hears that snore of yours."

"What do you mean?"

"I mean that you rattle the roof. But then she will not wish to sleep with you every night anyway." Fitzwilliam's brow creased and he stared down at his hands.

"Richard." Darcy said with a smile. "I am joking with you. Your wife will think you the most handsome man that ever walked the earth and if she is like my Elizabeth, she will prefer to sleep by your side, even if you do snore."

"It is not kind to torture me today, Darcy. I have told you before that humour does not sit well with you." He watched the church looming closer. "Is this real?"

"Shall I strike you and find out?" Darcy offered and Fitzwilliam at last relaxed and chuckled. "I am quite willing, you know."

"No doubt, I wait for the day when I am paid back for last night. I think that I was just the recipient of a taste of what is to come." He took a shaking breath. "Why am I behaving like such a fool? I slept not a wink; my hands . . . look at my hands!" He held them out and they watched them tremble.

Darcy smiled. "To paraphrase a wise man, let me say, *how fortunate you are to be sleep deprived and nervous on your wedding day.* You, Cousin are a man in love."

"Who was that wise man?" He smiled. "Thank you. It will not take long, and do not feel obligated to stay. I know that you want to return home."

"Elizabeth wants a piece of cake." Darcy winked.

"But of course!" Fitzwilliam tilted his head. "How did she feel about your appearance last night, or should I say this morning?"

Darcy shook his head then closed his eyes against the dull headache that remained. "She decided that it did neither of us any harm, but strongly suggested that I not do it again."

"You know Cousin, I am looking forward to being married." Fitzwilliam said wistfully.

"Well, it appears that we are here. You made it at last." Darcy nodded to the church outside their window. He held out his hand and clasped Fitzwilliam's shoulder. "Congratulations, Richard."

He drew a deep breath and smiled. "Thank you, thank you for falling in love so that I could, too."

The ceremony was the identical one spoken to every couple marrying in the church, but of course it was unique to the individuals involved. Darcy stood by his rock solid cousin, no steady hand was needed on his forearm. This man knew war, once at his post, the business of watching a woman strolling down an aisle was simple to endure, particularly this woman. Harwick's eyes were bright with joy, and he stepped forward first to take Laura's trembling hand from her father, and they gladly turned to face the vicar and awaited Evangeline and Fitzwilliam to join them. Harwick and Laura exchanged smiles and squeezed their hands. Fitzwilliam winked at Evangeline and she rolled her eyes. Darcy stood facing the couples and remembered his day, and found that in his hand he grasped the box containing Elizabeth's lock of hair, remembered the love radiating from her entire being, and found himself repeating his vows as Fitzwilliam took his. Stewart nudged him and smiled, and told him to turn around to look at Elizabeth. She smiled at him through her tears while Darcy wiped his own and blushed.

Back at Meadowbrook, the wedding breakfast was well underway when Darcy noticed Richard taking Evangeline by the hand and slipping out into the hallway with a devilish grin on his face. He laughed to see her so willingly following him and imagined that they were not going to wait for nightfall to officially begin their marriage. His gaze moved away to take in Harwick and Laura, and how he was darting envious looks at the doorway where Richard had gone. *Go ahead, do it.* Darcy urged, and smiled when he recognized Harwick sighing at his own reticence, and settling for a fervent kiss to his Laura's hand.

Layton joined Darcy to watch and chuckle at their friend's predicament. "So, you are happy for them, but you are thinking that there is no possibility that their match can ever approach your own."

Darcy laughed to see Layton grinning. "How did you know?"

He shrugged and clapped his back, and smiled over to where Alicia was seated with the ladies. "Because I was thinking the same about my dear wife."

Seeing Elizabeth walking towards him, he held out his hands for her and spoke over his shoulder as he waited for her to arrive, "Come on Cousin, let us feed our wives some cake and return home." He smiled down to her when she slipped her hands into his. "I am ready to go home."

Chapter 11

arcy nodded at the tenant and Nichols ushered him from the study. Quarter day was approaching and two tenants were unable to make their rent payment on time, and were asking for leniency. Darcy worried that he had not allowed them enough income from their work, but discovered that both tenants had illness in their families that robbed them of their excess funds, and had been too proud to approach Mr. Nichols and even less willing to ask Darcy for the help he would have readily provided. The men left with a new understanding of his expectations and trust for the young man who had become their master not so long ago. Rubbing his face, Darcy studied the papers before him, then looking to the doorway, waited for the next man to arrive, this one wishing to discuss the crops he would plant that year. His brow knit at the delay and he was about to call for Nichols when Elizabeth appeared.

"May I interrupt you for a moment, dear?"

"Of course." He stood and walked over to her. "I welcome the intrusion."

"Well if I am intruding . . ." She laughed when he smiled and stood behind her to deliver a hug. "Oh, I look forward to facing you again!"

"I do, too." He whispered in her ear. "Although loving you has become a very creative exercise."

"Will, please . . ."

"I love how our baby has made you want me constantly." His lips nibbled beneath her ear. "Now you know how I have felt for so long."

"Fitzwilliam . . ."

"Hmmm?" He gently caressed over her hips and she moaned. "Shall I close the door?"

"Oh, no, no there are too many men waiting and, and you know how noisy we are . . . and . . ."

"But you do want me, don't you?"

"Oh Lord yes, I do!" Elizabeth's eyes grew wide and she clapped her hand to her mouth. "Did I say that?"

Darcy chuckled and squeezed her. "You certainly did; my good wife. Thank you." Turning her around he kissed her lips. "Well, we shall continue this particular topic later. What brings you to me?" He stroked her cheek while she stared up at him in fascination. "Dearest?"

"Hmm?"

"Do you wish to show me the letter you are crushing?" He tapped the paper in her hand.

"Oh!" She looked down. "Oh yes, it is a girl!"

"A girl?" His brow creased. "Alicia?" Elizabeth nodded and beamed. "She is healthy, they both are?"

Elizabeth saw the fear and anxiety appear, and smoothed the wrinkles in his brow. "Yes, she is well. She had an easier time than Audrey, according to Aunt Helen. Margaret Helen Fitzwilliam; named for her grandmothers." Tears began to slip down her face just as Darcy's eyes welled up. "She said that she is bald with enormous blue eyes, and so beautiful!" They held each other as tightly as they could.

"Our baby will be beautiful, too." He whispered and kissed her cheek. "It will not be long dearest; soon we will join our cousins' joy." They swayed together until they both were again calm, then Darcy kissed her softly. "I will write a note for Layton to include with your letter to Alicia."

She nodded and smiled. "I will leave you to your work." Caressing his cheek she wiped away his tears. "I love you."

"I love you." He kissed her hand then walked her to the door, and nodded to Nichols to bring the next man in. He drew a deep breath and sank down onto his chair and looked at the miniature of her face. "One more month."

"TELL US OF LONGBOURN JANE." Mrs. Gardiner handed her a cup of tea and settled back against the sofa. "How is everyone?"

"Well." She smiled when she saw Mary's eyebrows rise expectantly. "Papa has not quite given up his attempts to improve our minds, but I think that he will be most pleased when Kitty and Lydia are away at school in the autumn. Book learning is not something that either of them enjoys; and I count myself in that same group. I have tried, but the words do not strike me the way they do Papa. Lizzy has suggested less challenging authors, and I have enjoyed some of their work, but Lydia and Kitty . . . Well, they can read and write, and do the simple accounting for a household, so I imagine that will have to do for now. Perhaps proper teachers will inspire more, but I have my doubts, for Lydia at least."

"Kitty shows some hope, then?" Mr. Gardiner took a biscuit and bit in. "I thought she had more to her than Lydia."

"She does, she needs to escape her influence." Mary said quietly. "She is too easily led."

"Perhaps separate schools?" Mr. Gardiner suggested. "They will not be attending Mrs. Banks' school, will they?"

"No." Mary sighed. "I am ready to go as well."

"But Georgiana will return?"

"Yes. Fitzwilliam wishes her to be fifteen before she departs, and then they will interview companions for her. She will benefit from the masters in London until she is out. Mrs. Younge has not been any trouble at all, so he is confident that all will be well for Georgiana to attend alone next year, she knows to be wary."

"And you will be going to Pemberley with her this summer." Mrs. Gardiner said gently. "Do you look forward to that?"

Mary looked up and smiled. "Oh, so very much! I miss Lizzy terribly and Fitzwilliam is so kind. I cannot wait to care for their baby!" She glanced at Jane. "I have not heard from Mama or Papa for some time."

"I think that they leave the correspondence to me, Mary. It is not a slight. You know how they are."

Mary nodded and shrugged. "I will be happy to live at Pemberley or wherever Lizzy is. Fitzwilliam said that I was welcome to stay with them forever if I wished."

"Mr. Darcy is very kind." Jane smiled a little and glanced up to see her uncle studying her. "Mr. Lucas sends his greetings. I have a letter for you upstairs."

"Ah, and how does the young man get on?"

"Very well, we have seen a great deal of each other, and have danced together several times." She blushed and saw the speculation in the raised brows. "I . . . have enjoyed his company."

"That is obvious." Mr. Gardiner saw his wife's pointed look and he shook his head with a smile.

"Mama . . ." Jane started and dropped the subject, and looked back down at her hands. Mrs. Bennet had been very clear on her expectations of a match with Bingley, and told Jane not to let Lizzy ruin the attachment as she had with Mr. Harwick. The subject of Robert Lucas was ignored entirely.

Mrs. Gardiner realized that a need for a private conversation with her niece would be necessary to learn what havoc her sister had created, and moved on. "I understand that the Matlocks had hoped to join the viscount and his wife on a holiday to Bath when Lady Layton's confinement ends, but that the timing just is not quite right for Parliament's Easter recess. Instead I believe that they will visit Rosings. Lady Matlock regrets not being able to stay with Lizzy for her confinement, but Mrs. Singleton will be with her. I am surprised that they are not coming to London for the birth, as Lady Layton did. This is where the best care is, after all. In any case, you know that we will be glad to take you around to any balls or dinners that come about in our circle until Lady Matlock begins with you." Jane nodded and she added, "Mr. Bingley visited last week, and inquired after your health. He has been in town since December."

"Yes, so Lizzy tells me." Jane twisted her hands and bit her lip. "I think . . . Lizzy said that I need to experience what Lady Matlock has to offer so I can decide where I feel I belong."

"So no decisions have been made yet." Mrs. Gardiner smiled. "That is wise, dear."

"Decisions about what?" Mary asked and looked between them. "Has Mr. Bingley offered for you?"

"No." They all said. "He has expressed admiration, dear." Mrs. Gardiner smiled.

"He is terribly handsome," Mary said thoughtfully, "but not anyone I would want."

"Why ever not?" Jane asked curiously. "Is he wanting in some way?"

"No . . .well I only really saw him at Lizzy and Fitzwilliam's wedding. I rather liked . . ." She bit her lip and blushed.

"Who?" Mrs. Gardiner prodded. "Come now Mary, you have never expressed admiration for any man, who caught your eye?"

"Nobody." She whispered.

Mr. Gardiner tilted his head and studied her. "Well of the unattached gentlemen present at the wedding breakfast I would say it was one in uniform, and further, one who was wearing blue, rather than red?" He smiled and Mary looked at her hands. "Ah, a navy man for you." He chuckled. "Well, well."

"I did not say that I liked anyone at the wedding."

"Oh . . ." Mrs. Gardiner smiled. "Well I am pleased to hear that dear, Captain de Bourgh is ten years your senior."

"Oh."

"Perhaps another older gentleman has attracted you?" Mr. Gardiner smiled. "Come dear, you cannot know that many."

Mortified, Mary stammered, "I did not say that, I . . ." She rose up and ran upstairs.

"We hurt her." Mrs. Gardiner sighed. "Mary is so sensitive."

"She is not used to being teased in a friendly manner." Mr. Gardiner agreed. "She is also not given to flights of fancy regarding young men. But it is nice to see that she is thinking about them."

"That is a change." Jane smiled. "I had not thought of that."

"So what about you, dear?"

"I . . . I will see what Lady Matlock does with me when she arrives in a few weeks, and if Mr. Bingley approaches me, I will . . . see what he has to say." She closed her eyes. "Why do I wish I had gone to Pemberley instead?"

"Your life is the one that you must consider, dear. You cannot hide behind your sister's." Mrs. Gardiner smiled. "It is time to find your way." She stood and walked to the door. "I think that I will go and apologize to Mary for our teasing. I want her to be sure that she can count on us, just as you can, Jane."

DARCY GROANED then smiled to see Elizabeth open her eyes. She was napping in the chair next to his desk. "Forgive me."

"What is it?" She yawned and rubbed her eyes. "Why is it so hot in here?" She glared at the coals glowing in the grate. "Is that fire really necessary?"

"It is for those of us who are not with child, love." He chuckled and held out a letter. "I have no desire to ruin my eyes trying to decipher this."

"Mr. Bingley?" She laughed to see the tell-tale splotches. "What are we to do with him?"

"Perhaps if he wrote in crayon it would be better?" Darcy stretched his legs out and rested his head on the back of his chair. "Read on!"

"Oh my." Elizabeth giggled. "Miss Bingley has a nibble."

"I heard that before and it was Wickham." He leaned forward on the desk and rested his chin in his hands. "Who is it now?"

"An acquaintance of Mr. Hurst's." Elizabeth tilted her head and bit her lip. "I think . . . yes, he is a newly minted gentleman and a continuing tradesman . . .His estate earns two thousand a year!" Looking up she saw Darcy's smile. "Imagine that!"

"Indeed." He chuckled. "And?"

"Mr. Bingley is assured of his credentials and worth, has had him thoroughly vetted, and if the two of them are interested, he will gladly encourage the match." She smiled. "And happily wave goodbye at the church door!"

"Hide your feelings, Bingley, there's a good man." Darcy smiled and reached his hand out to grasp hers. "Well if it should come to pass, then he will be able to concentrate on his future. He will be speaking with the owner of Netherfield sometime this summer, I believe."

"But what of the problems you perceive?"

"Ah, Stewart will accompany him on the meeting, but really, he is just renting a place to live so that he can entertain in the country. He is not responsible for the estate unless he purchases."

"I would hope that he could find something near us." Elizabeth smiled at Darcy's warm gaze and he squeezed her hand. "I know that is unlikely."

"We will have to watch the market, dearest." He nodded at the letter. "What else does he say?"

"Hmm?" She refocused her attention and returned to the letter. "OH!" She blushed and her free hand went to her mouth. "OH!!"

"What is it?" He let go of her hand and came around the desk to lean over the chair and read. "What . . ." Darcy squinted and stared at the blotch where Elizabeth's finger lay. "It says . . . he . . . Harris' list . . ." He blushed.

"Fitzwilliam, what is *Harris' List of Covent Garden Ladies*?" Elizabeth whispered.

"It is . . .dearest . . . It is a list that is nearly a dozen years outdated . . . It gives the names of . . .courtesans and their . . . attributes and specialties." He watched her eyes widen and sighed. "It seems that someone might be starting a new list and Bingley was shown a copy."

"This was something that men used to . . ."

"Find relief." He said cautiously. "Elizabeth?"

"That is disgusting."

"Indeed." He nodded vehemently. "It does not appear that Bingley actually used this information." He added gently.

"No, it says right here that he enjoyed the favours of one Miss Clarissa at Madame Hofner's establishment on Bond Street. Oh Fitzwilliam! Do men truly speak of their experiences to each other?" She glared at him.

"Dearest, I . . . I am not the one to ask and no, I am not suggesting speaking to Bingley either . . . I knew that I should learn how to read his letters." He took the crushed note from her hand and set it on the desk. "He is not married, love, nor is he attached to any woman, even to Jane."

"But he expresses interest in her." She said angrily.

"But he is not committed to her, they are not courting, they are only friends." He sighed and took her hands. "Come."

"Where?" She said as he helped her to rise.

"Upstairs. I need to soothe you as only a husband can do for his wife."

"I do not wish to be soothed." She protested. "I do not understand this . . . habit of men."

"Do you not?" He said softly as they walked slowly up the stairs. "Do you not after nearly a year of marriage to me?"

"But you love me." She explained. "You wish to express your love to me."

"A man wishes to express his love to his wife, but if he has no wife, he still has desires." He sighed and she stared at him. "It was a long wait for you, trust me." Their eyes met and he opened the door to their bedchamber, ushered her in and closed the door, locking it. "Now, you look very tired, shall we retire for the night?"

"It is early." Elizabeth yawned.

"A nap then?" He whispered and started unbuttoning her gown. Elizabeth let his fingers do the work of her maid and before long she was undressed. Darcy caught up her nightdress and slipped it over her head. "I would prefer to leave you unclothed but you seem too sleepy for anything else."

"I am not sleepy." She cuddled onto his chest. "I am just . . ."

"On the verge of motherhood." He whispered. Peeking down at her closed eyes, he smiled and lifted her up and onto the bed. While she curled up with a pillow, he went to his dressing room and changed into his nightshirt, then returned to settle beside her. With her journal in hand, he wandered through the entries until he stopped on one from only a week earlier.

22 March 1810

We received word from Matlock that Alicia delivered her baby girl Margaret Helen yesterday. I think that I cried for a full half hour when I learned the news, then I waited outside of Fitzwilliam's study to tell him, and there I was faced with my tearful husband. Oh, and I cried again! I am sure that our tears were for entirely different reasons, well perhaps not. We both carry our fears of the unknown and wishes for an easy birth and healthy child. I am so emotional now, I looked outside to see the spring bulbs pushing through the earth, and I cried. Millie delivered a love letter from Fitzwilliam this afternoon and I cried. I wrote him a letter in return and cried all over that! I think that if Mrs. Reynolds were to tell me that my household accounts were correct I would cry again! Oh I have never been so emotional. I do not have any memory of this at all! But then I do not have the capacity to remember either, or pay attention, or do anything with my addled brain. My poor dear husband, how he bears me in this state is a mystery. I pray for a houseful of children but I pity this man who must endure me to get them. What did I just write here? Oh I cannot bear to look, I know that you are reading this sweetheart, whatever I have said, know that I love you.

Darcy chuckled, closed up Elizabeth's journal and placed it on the table next to the bed, then began rubbing her swollen feet. "What has you so amused?" She asked, opening one eye to spot his warm smile. "What were you reading?"

"It was the entry announcing Margaret's birth."

"Oh?" She gasped with a sharp kick, and before she had a chance, his hands were reaching to rub the sore spot on her ever-expanding belly. "Thank you." She sighed.

"Are you still feeling courageous about the pending arrival of your tormentor?"

"Are you still feeling panicked?"

He kissed her toes. "mmmhmmm." She looked up to see him smiling, then laughed when he dropped her feet and ran his hands up her nightdress to hold her hips. "What are your intentions, Husband?"

"I believe that I will assert my desires."

"What of mine?" She watched him grab a pillow to place beneath her bottom, and lifted his nightshirt off.

"You do not desire me?" He kissed her, then traced his tongue over her lips and down her throat to her breasts, and mouthed the sensitive and responsive nipples through the fabric. His hands caressed her thighs. "You are so wet Elizabeth, you must desire me."

"I must?" Her voice hitched.

"Please?"

"Oh yes, please." She moaned. Darcy chuckled. "I am afraid that our offspring is getting in the way of this method of loving." He kissed her belly and ran his hands over her.

"I need to look in your eyes." Elizabeth touched his face and he smiled, rolling onto his back and holding up his arms for her.

"Come, love."

She climbed over him and slowly lowered down to envelope his waiting length. "Oh, Will." She moaned. "I do not know what it is but I crave you constantly."

"I have no objection to that, not at all." Darcy moaned with the pleasure of her warmth. His hands travelled upwards and he removed her gown, then caressed her swelling breasts, sitting up to suckle them while she embraced his head and sighed. "Oh, my love!" Darcy pulled away with a startled look on his face. Elizabeth looked down to see him licking his lips then returning his mouth to suckle her again. "Oh Lizzy." He sighed and she felt his tongue and jaw working, then move to encapsulate her other nipple. He beamed up at her. "You have fed me!"

"What are you saying?" She laughed and he drew her down to suckle happily again, the rocking of their hips and the touch of his tongue quickly relieved her desire, and she slid off to settle back against his chest so he could thrust with the vigour that brought his shuddering release. They lay spooned in their embrace while both of them felt the response of their baby. "He seems to enjoy it." Elizabeth whispered as they both stroked over her belly.

Darcy chuckled and cuddled her closer. "So we are indulgent parents?"

"Mmmm, you may indulge me anytime, Husband."

"You will tell me when you cannot bear my attentions any longer. I know that time is coming." He said softly. "I do not wish you to feel obligated to this duty."

"When has it ever been a duty?" Elizabeth turned her head to see his worried eyes. "Stop."

"Yes, love." He sighed and settled his face back into her hair. "Elizabeth?"

"Hmm?" She sighed and was asleep in his arms.

Darcy held her tightly and kissed her shoulder. "Please, please darling, do not leave me."

"THE DECISION IS YOURS, LAURA." Harwick reined his mount and they stopped on top of a rise, looking out over the grounds surrounding Meadowbrook. "I am sure that you wish to see your friends and dance."

Laura laughed. "As sure as I am that you want to remain here?"

"My dear, I do not expect you to spend your life solely at this estate, you are meant to be out in the world, how can I deprive society of your company?" He smiled and she laughed. "Was I convincing?"

"Not at all. I do not wish to separate you from the girls, and going to town would surely do that."

"They are old enough to endure the trip, I think." He said softly. "But I wish to make you happy."

She studied him and nodded. "Very well then, we will remain here, then perhaps we might visit Elizabeth and Mr. Darcy sometime this summer." A smile spread over his face. "I see that you like the solution?"

"Very much. Darcy's company will be welcome and I have no doubt that he will be remaining close to home for quite some time." He reached out to hold her hand. "Are you sure of this, dear? You are still a new bride; you would receive all of the privileges and recognition that comes with it, in fact should you not be newly presented at court as my wife?"

"Are you trying to tell me that you *want* to go to town?" She asked incredulously. "Please speak your mind, sir!"

"I . . . It occurs to me that perhaps it would be . . . pleasant to show you off a bit." He chuckled to see her mouth drop open. "I am not without my pride, my dear. I am very pleased with my bride."

"I hardly know you!" She cried. "What happened to the man who wished to remain at home?"

"I do . . . I just . . . I have reason to live as well." He kissed her hand. "So, a month in town and then come home?"

"We will go dancing?" Laura asked hopefully.

"We will." Harwick said positively. "And then we will return home and . . . work on other matters."

Laura blushed then kicking her horse, galloped away. "You will have to catch me first!"

10 APRIL 1810

My wife is a wonder. For weeks now she has been sleepy, moving more slowly with each passing day, unable to summon the energy for more than a kiss. She has cried enough tears to fill the lake, and exasperated me with her swings of temperament, but through it all she has made me feel her confidence and determination that all will be well. I have never laughed so much as I have with Elizabeth as she contemplates her advance into motherhood. But today, after a very welcome night of lovemaking that seemed gloriously endless in its quantity and diversity, my suddenly insatiable wife is up, running about the house with a level of energy I have not witnessed in ages. Can it be that she needed my loving to achieve this vigour? I would be dishonest if I did not admit that the thought makes me quite proud!

It should be very soon, we think. I will forego the spring activities and leave them in Mr. Nichols' capable hands. I wish to remain close, just in case she needs me. The monthly nurse, Mrs. Griffiths, will arrive tomorrow to complete the preparations for the birth and she will remain with Elizabeth until she is recovered. The wet nurse, Mrs. Robbins, will come to us in another week. Elizabeth is unhappy with the arrangement, but Aunt Helen has written to her steadily about this subject as have Audrey and Alicia. It is another of those differences in our backgrounds appearing again. This child shall have every advantage, I am determined in that.

I have read and reread the letters from every father I know, giving me advice for coping with her moods and her fears, and thankfully they have all spoken of how I should manage my own. I want to be nearby when her time comes, I wish to be brave enough to stay by her side, but fear that I will fail when she cries in pain. And they all assure me that she will cry and it will be difficult to bear. Audrey and

Singleton will join us in a few days. I am not terribly close to him, but Audrey can give Elizabeth the comfort that she will need. I pray again that all will be well.

Darcy set down his pen and caressed the lover's knot of ribbon before closing the book, then hearing a melodious voice he looked out into the hallway. There he found his bright-eyed wife, singing and merrily dusting the frames of his ancestor's portraits. "Elizabeth." His lips twitched. "What are you about?"

"I am cleaning." She gave him a look as if he was daft and continued on. When she moved to stand on a chair to reach the top of the frame he rushed forward and carefully lifted her down. "Fitzwilliam! I need to finish this!"

"It is perfectly well, love. I saw . . . Mrs. Reynolds dusting there just yesterday." He nodded and she stared him in the eye.

"You sir, cannot tell a lie." She said seriously.

"Perhaps it was another day." He countered.

"Hmmm." Elizabeth looked out at the bright and warm spring day. "Let us visit my tree."

"Lizzy." He said softly. "It is too far to walk."

"I need to see my tree!" She insisted. "Please?"

Darcy held her hands and looked down at her. "Are you sure?"

"I have been confined to this house for too long, I just wish to feel the sun warming my face." Tilting her head she smiled softly. "Please?"

How am I to resist you? "On one condition." He caressed her warm rosy cheek and kissed her. "We will drive a gig as close as possible so that you will not need to walk so far. Agreed?"

"Yes." Elizabeth hugged him. "Thank you for bearing my fancies, Will. I know that I am nonsensical."

"I do my best, love." Kissing her hair he let go and went to order a gig and call for their coats. Elizabeth watched him walk away and rubbed her back, it had been aching dully since she awoke. She passed it off as the result of their lovemaking and ignored it, along with all of the other endless aches and pains she seemed to have been feeling of late. When Darcy returned he caught her stretching. "Are you well?" He asked softly, "Perhaps we should remain?"

"No, I need to see my tree." She insisted. "We had a busy night, that is all."

Nodding, he smiled and kissed her. "I am afraid that I am feeling the effects as well."

"I am sorry that we have not loved each other for so many weeks . . ."

"Hush." Darcy hugged her and kissed her ear as he whispered, "It made last night so special." A maid arrived with their coats and the gig pulled up outside. Carefully, Darcy helped her up and seeing her settled with a shawl over her knees, took the reins and urged the horse on. Glancing at her he laughed to see her eyes sparkling and happy. "I am glad to see you enjoying this warm day."

"I am glad to see they still exist! This winter was harsh, certainly nothing that I have experienced before. I wish that we could have played more." She looked ruefully down at their baby and spoke to her belly. "You prevented your parents from having fun!"

"I think that we managed quite nicely." He patted the baby. "Do not mind your mama." Darcy moved the gig off of the drive and into the grass. The cart jostled a little and Elizabeth gasped when the movement seemed to make her back ache sharply. Darcy stopped the horse. "Dearest?"

"I am well. I am unbalanced even when seated, it seems." She smiled and looked ahead. "Drive on!"

Sighing he flicked the reins and said nothing. *Drive on; drive on to see a tree! You my love are driving me to drink with your whims and fancies!* He shot her a glance and watched as she bit her lip with narrowed eyes. He started to open his mouth to ask again if she felt well, but decided that her humour was good, and toying with that would be a mistake. Instead he enjoyed the feel of her leaning against him and kissed her forehead. "Here we are." Stopping the horse at the entrance to the woods he smiled at her. "Are you certain you wish to walk in? We could simply continue to drive?"

"No, I need to be in our special place." She sat up wiped her eyes. "I need to see this place."

Helplessly he wiped her cheeks against a new assault of tears. It was useless to question her, so he jumped down and holding out his arms, lifted her to the ground and slowly they began to walk down the familiar path. That she leaned heavily on him was nothing unusual, that she gripped his arm almost painfully tight was, but she gave no indication of wishing to stop. At last they reached the path to their little glade, and found their way to the sunny spot. "There it is." Elizabeth sighed and he was pleased to see her obvious relief. "It survived the winter." They approached and saw tiny leaves forming on the tree and the rose bush. "New life."

"I love the spring because of that." Darcy whispered and she nodded. "Do you feel better now, seeing this?"

"I needed to know that I would always be here." Elizabeth said softly and reaching up to hold his face confessed, "I love you."

She said it so simply that his heart nearly stopped beating. "Elizabeth . . ."

"Know that I love you, and know that I want you to always be loved." She continued earnestly.

"You are frightening me." Darcy said worriedly. "Please let us return to the house, we should not have left."

Elizabeth nodded and gasped. "Oh!" Looking down at her boots they saw that the hem of her dress was wet. She looked back up at him then nearly doubled in pain. "OH!!"

"Elizabeth!" Darcy cried as she sank to the ground. "What is happening? Let me take you home, here, I will carry you . . ."

"No . . . no it, oh!!" She swallowed and tears began flowing freely. "Oh Will, I feel something . . . Ohhhhhhh!"

"Lizzy?" Darcy knelt beside her and stroked back the hair from her face. "The baby is coming now?"

"Right now, ohhhh!" She clutched his hands and screamed in agony.

Darcy felt a rush of panic and fear flow over him, but when her terrified eyes opened and stared into his, he nodded and felt his courage rise. "We can do this, love. We can do this together." Taking off his gloves, he tore off his coat, and laying it on the ground helped her onto it. In his mind, everything he had read, studied, heard about, went flying through. *The baby is coming fast, the baby cannot be stopped. I must be strong for her.*

The air was rent with another bloodcurdling scream and her tears poured down her face. Darcy held her tightly as the pain of another merciless contraction seized her small body. When it relented, she tried to sit up a little and catch her breath. "Do you want to lie on your side? No? We need something to support your back . . ." Desperately he scanned the grove and spotting a massive oak, grabbed a hold of his coat and dragged her over, grasped under her arms and lifted her so she was settled against the trunk. The ancient roots surrounded her like the arms of a chair. Both of them were panting with the exertion. "Is that better?" He begged her to answer.

Elizabeth whimpered and nodded then reached for his hand, gripping it hard and crying as the next contraction came and went. "Oh, it hurts!" She sobbed, "So much!"

"I am so sorry, Elizabeth!" Darcy whispered as he held her shaking body.

She gasped and her hands clutched him. "Will . . . I . . . oh I think, oh . . . I need to . . ." She looked in his anxious eyes and clamped her mouth shut.

"Scream dearest, scream. Do not hold back!" He held her hands tight while she cried again. As she panted against his shoulder, he tried to calm and ran through the stages of birth, and knew that there would be no help forthcoming. "I am going to look and see . . .what is happening, Elizabeth. I will have to let go of you. Do you understand?"

"Yes." She gasped and he nodded. "I will try not to . . ."

"You do whatever you feel is necessary." He commanded. Then lifting her skirt up over her bent knees, he was greeted with the extraordinary sight of a baby's curls crowning between her legs. "My Lord, Elizabeth, he is coming!" He looked up at her in amazement. "How you are not screaming constantly is a miracle!" Darcy saw the flicker of a smile appear on her face just before she cried out and pushed. Darcy's eyes widened and instinctively, his hands reached forward as the baby's head delivered. A sudden gush of blood and fluid followed as with two more excruciating pushes, the entire child appeared, sliding right into his hands. Darcy stared down at the unmoving blue baby while Elizabeth gasped.

"Help him, oh help him to breathe!" She choked out.

Turning the baby over he remembered witnessing mares licking their foals, and the books giving directions to bring the new babe to life. Vigorously he rubbed, concentrating hard on his task. He dipped his bloodied hand into his pocket to find a handkerchief, and wiped the baby's nose and mouth, then continued the rubbing, speaking softly, encouraging that first breath and at last was rewarded with a sudden squall; and the miracle of a pink and angry infant in his hands. Darcy lifted his head to be greeted with a mirror of his face in Elizabeth. They both had tears flooding down their cheeks. "Oh Elizabeth! She is beautiful!"

"A girl?" She laughed. "We have a little girl?"

Darcy swallowed and kissed his baby. "We have a beautiful, beautiful girl!" The elation in his voice and joy in his smile brought more tears to her. "I love you my darling Elizabeth!"

She began to respond then gasped, "Oh . . .something else is coming!"

"There is more, yes . . . I must cut the baby free from you." He looked around for a place to set her and then smiled shyly to see Elizabeth holding out her hands. "Of course, the safest place." Carefully he rested his daughter in her mother's hands then reached into his pocket to find a knife. Meeting Elizabeth's eyes, he separated her from their baby, then taking a ribbon from her hair, tied off the stub. Within moments the rest of the delivery was completed. Darcy sat back on his heels and watched Elizabeth take the shawl that she had worn over her pelisse to swaddle their daughter and kiss her tenderly.

Her face radiated joy. "What were you so worried about? See, we did it all on our own!"

Darcy laughed, looking around at the evidence of the birth all over their clothes and the ground, his blood soaked coat, her crimson dress, the extraordinary smile on her face . . . "If we ever have another baby love, you are not going anywhere from the house from your eighth month on. My heart cannot bear this again!"

"I will not bear another child unless you are my midwife." She declared as the baby squirmed.

"How do you feel, dearest?" He moved to sit beside her, and she leaned into his arms.

They looked down at the baby and she whispered, "I ache, but I do not feel it." Looking up to him they kissed. "Thank you."

"You have given me a family, Elizabeth. Thank you." They rested their heads together and listened to their baby gurgle and then startled when suddenly she began to cry. Without thought, Elizabeth drew down the front of her gown and placed the baby at her breast. Darcy stared in wonder to see Elizabeth help her to find and latch onto the nipple.

She looked up and beamed. "All of your practice taught me what to do, Fitzwilliam."

Fascinated, they watched and listened to their daughter humming as she fed, then when she fell asleep, Darcy drew Elizabeth into his arms to hold her tight and gaze at the marvel in hers. Eventually, he caressed her cheek and lifted Elizabeth's chin to kiss her. "Are you well?" He asked her seriously. "You have to be exhausted."

She laughed quietly. "I am not prepared to go dancing." He chuckled and they kissed again. "I think that I am well enough to return to the house."

"I think that is an excellent idea." He moved away from the tree, and removing his topcoat, fashioned an undergarment for her from his waistcoat. Carefully lifting his family into his arms, he slowly carried them through the woods to the gig where he placed them in the seat. Darcy stood next to them and smiled at his sleeping daughter. "She looks like you."

"She looks like you." Elizabeth caressed his face. "I love you, Fitzwilliam."

Darcy kissed her softly and wrapped his topcoat around her legs, "I love you, Elizabeth." He climbed up onto the seat and kissed her again. "Let us bring the Darcy family home."

Slowly the gig moved as the horse walked back across the grass. Both of them were staring at the bundle in Elizabeth's arms and barely noticed the group of riders coming towards them. "Mr. Darcy!" Nichols called and stopped. "We had a report of a woman scream . . ." His voice was halted by the sight of the bedraggled family in the cart. "Sir, Mrs. Darcy . . . the baby . . . are you well, madam?"

Elizabeth smiled and nodded, and Darcy wrapped one arm around her shoulders. "She is well, as is our daughter." He kissed Elizabeth's cheek. "Will you ride ahead and alert Mrs. Reynolds?" Darcy smiled wearily.

Nichols nodded to one of the men who immediately galloped towards the house. The steward pulled the reins from his master's grasp and moved ahead, guiding the gig so that Darcy could wrap both arms around Elizabeth. "How do you feel, love?"

"So tired." She admitted at last. "I am so tired."

"We will get you home and cleansed, and then I want you in our bed with no arguments." He said sternly. "Where you should have given birth."

"Would it not be wonderful if our next baby is conceived next to my tree?" She murmured and settled against his chest. Darcy stared at her peaceful face. *You are thinking of the next? Now?*

As Elizabeth relaxed, he placed his hands under hers to help support their daughter. "A new Darcy. Open your eyes sweetheart, look at your home." He urged and laughed to see her yawn instead. Elizabeth opened her eyes to find him smiling.

"How are you, Fitzwilliam?"

"I have no words." He admitted and kissed her when they at last arrived at Pemberley's door and were surrounded by servants. "Grateful and hopeful. Be well, my love."

Chapter 12

"Damn!" Fitzwilliam proclaimed and eagerly read the letter again. "I will be damned!"

"Richard what on earth has . . ."

Grabbing his squealing wife, he spun her around. "Darcy, *my* cousin, the stoic, stick-in-the-mud, scared-to-death-of-his-wife's-pregnancy-fool, delivered his own child, alone in the woods of Pemberley!" He chortled and setting her down kissed her soundly. "Damn!"

"Oh, poor Elizabeth!" Evangeline cried and held her hands to her face. "How did that happen?"

"Apparently she had a whim and he indulged it, and nature took its course unexpectedly." He grinned and sighed. "Miss Rosalie Elizabeth Darcy has joined the crowd of first daughters. Oh I can just see their fathers commiserating together the spring that they come out!" Chuckling, he kissed her. "Elizabeth is very well. I knew she would be fine; she was five days along when he wrote this. I imagine that he was so worried about her that he could not tear himself away to write a few letters." He smiled at Evangeline then read some more and snorted. "She absolutely rejected the notion of lying in a darkened room. She insists that if she is forced to stay in bed that the curtains and windows be opened. The monthly nurse he engaged is at her wit's end." He looked back up. "I always knew that she was wonderful! Darcy praises her to the moon."

"As he should." Taking the letter from him she read the ecstatic report herself. "His joy leaps from the page."

"It does. I wonder if he has written to my parents." Fitzwilliam smiled, at last calming down. "I would love to be at Pemberley now."

"More so than with your brother or sister?" She tilted her head.

"Darcy and I are very close, my dear. I would love to share in his joy." He shrugged and she caressed his cheek.

"You are soft-hearted."

"Only you know that." He kissed her palm as she shook her head at his delusion and his face coloured. "Well we shall see Mother and Father in a few days, so I will contain my excitement until then." He raised his brows, "Perhaps we should take advantage of the fecund state of the Fitzwilliam women?"

"None of these women are with child any longer, Richard." Evangeline smiled as he scooped her up in his arms and kissed her. "I need to dress for the theatre!"

"Well then I am going to be of aid by ridding you of your current attire." Richard kissed her soundly. "I feel rather inspired, my love."

"You are perpetually inspired." Evangeline sighed as they made their way up the stairs. "I think that I should move to my own chambers so I might find sleep again."

"Oh, you will find sleep." Fitzwilliam growled. "I will assure you of that."

DARCY STARTED AND SAT UP IN BED, then hurried to the nursery door. Sitting in a rocking chair, he found Elizabeth cuddling their daughter to her breast. He leaned on the doorframe and watched his sleepy wife feed her, then slipped in to kiss her hair and sit by her side. "You woke." Elizabeth whispered. "You never wake."

"I am awake more often than you know. I missed you. I am acutely aware of when you are gone. You, my love, should not be out of bed." He caressed the bundle and smiled when a tiny hand gripped his finger.

"I know I must accustom myself to not rising." She looked up to him. "Since you insist that we have a wet nurse and she has arrived."

"I will not relent in this, love." He said softly. "I want you to sleep; we are defying enough of convention with your recovery. I will not risk your health any more than we must, and you need to rest. All that I have read tells me that infants wake frequently to be fed."

"By their mothers." She said stubbornly.

"You are not just any mother." He whispered.

"I am no different than any other."

"You are a Darcy; this is not something that women of our society do." Their eyes met and she glared at him, and he met her stare head on. "Mrs. Robbins was engaged for a reason. She should be performing this duty. I am sorry that she was not here for the past week and you were forced to serve. I can only imagine what task you have her performing now to get her out of your way. Mrs. Griffiths has been practically apoplectic about you since she arrived. You promised." Darcy reminded her and watched her eyes cast down.

"That was before she was born. I was being berated by my mother and Aunt Helen to follow the dictates of society. It will probably be the only time that they ever agree." They both looked down as Rosalie let go and Elizabeth moved her up to her shoulder. Darcy's gaze drifted from the sight of his baby to that of his wife's uncovered chest. He closed his eyes and reached over to gently arrange her gown, then met Elizabeth's gaze as she spoke again. "Would you not prefer that your daughter be fed by her mother, and not some stranger? Is that not healthier?"

"Georgiana had a wet nurse." Darcy said softly. "She was fine."

"But I am here, Fitzwilliam. And willing."

"Neither Alicia nor Audrey feed their babies." He continued. "This is what I was taught was right. Audrey did not bring Grace with her . . ." His voice trailed off as he touched Rosalie.

She saw his sadness, and knew there was more. "What really worries you? You know that I am healthy and able to feed our child. You know that if I need to rest, I will. Something else is behind this. Please tell me."

Darcy remained silent for several minutes, watching Rosalie sucking on Elizabeth's shoulder. "I have heard of husbands losing their wives once the children come." He touched Elizabeth's face. "It is horribly selfish, I know, but I could not bear to lose you."

"Where would I go?" She smiled and clasped his hand. "I am right here. Surely you will not be jealous of a baby? Do you think that I would love you less? I would be angry that you doubt my devotion, but I know very well that you do not any more than I doubt your love for me."

"No dearest I know there is no doubt between us." He said softly, and gently caressing Rosalie's mop of black curls, kissed her. "I love her so much. I am warring with all that I know, all that I have been taught, Elizabeth." He looked up to her.

"What is it really, Fitzwilliam?" She asked and he said nothing. Elizabeth felt his old habit of keeping difficult subjects to himself being reasserted and knew that she must wait him out, and further, keep him from running off. "Here." Elizabeth placed Rosalie into his arms. "Sit with her while she falls asleep."

Darcy cradled her and looked down at the bright blue eyes of his daughter blinking at him in the soft candlelight. Elizabeth stood and kissed his cheek. "Where are you going?" He asked with a little hitch in his voice.

"I will not be long. Talk it over with her." She left the room and Darcy returned his gaze to the baby, who yawned.

"Well, it seems that your mother is determined to have you play on my heart strings." He said softly. "I am not jealous, dear one. Not of you. I just depend on your mother so very much." Rosalie made a soft mewing sound and he laughed. "Are you arguing with me? Do you take after her already?" He kissed her then wrapped the blanket around her a little tighter. "I was so frightened for so long, waiting for you to come, I feared losing your mother. And now that you are here and all is well, I want to hold her all of the time, but I want to hold you, too. I love her so very much Rosalie, and I want her to be well. Can you understand that?" Rosalie's eyes drifted shut and he kissed her again. "And I want you to be well, my dearest little girl. I do not know of any parents who care for their children so closely. My father doted on your aunt Georgiana, but he was not . . ." Darcy sighed and made his confession. "If she feeds you . . . I may not love her, and I need to . . . I have no examples to follow. Your mama grew up in a different world, and I know that even with that she was neglected in so many ways." Elizabeth appeared and he looked up to her with brightened eyes. "I am a fool."

"No Will, you are a man in love with two women." She kissed him and taking the baby from his arms, settled her in the cradle. The nursery door opened and Mrs. Robbins gasped to find the couple standing hand in hand over their daughter.

"Forgive me . . ."

"We were just leaving." Elizabeth smiled and still holding Darcy's hand, led him from the room and closed the door behind her. They walked back to their bed and climbed in. He enveloped her in his arms. "I might need to nap for a little while until she sleeps through the night, but I think that we managed to survive my napping when I was carrying her."

"Yes." He said softly.

"And if I am feeding her, I will not become with child again. That would be less of a worry for you. We can find Mrs. Robbins a new position and just use the maids we engaged for the nursery."

"Yes." He nestled his face against her hair and sighed.

"And in a few more weeks when I am healed, we can love each other again." Elizabeth caressed the arms that were embracing her tightly. "I look forward to that so much."

She heard a quick intake of breath by her ear. "You . . . you would be willing to let me . . . but I thought that lovemaking spoils the milk." He whispered. "I thought that if you feed Rosalie, we . . . we could not be intimate again until she is weaned."

"oh." Elizabeth whispered and finally understood. "Is that what worries you?"

"It is one of the things, yes." He admitted and hugged her. "I need you. I confess it. I could not bear a year or more of not loving you. A month is enough torture for me."

"Fitzwilliam, I could not bear it, either." She attempted to turn in his arms but could not move from his iron grip. "I am a reasonably intelligent woman and I have found that you seem to be a reasonably intelligent man, at least in some areas." Darcy gave a hollow laugh. "I cannot believe that from the dawn of time that all women have given up feeding their own children to a surrogate, and further, that all men have given up their marriage bed while those children were fed. Somehow through all of this humanity survived."

"Something has happened, dearest, your wit has returned with a vengeance." He chuckled and sniffed while hugging her. "Do you remember when we first married and we declared that we would forge our own path?"

"Yes." She kissed his hand and he kissed her ear. "Is that what we shall do again as parents?"

"I think so." He wrapped his body around hers. "Bear with me; I am a very new father." Darcy kissed her hair and paused before speaking again. "It also occurred to me that you are trying to love our daughter the way that you did not receive at Longbourn. I just now understood that. Forgive me for thinking that I might lose my place in your heart."

"Fitzwilliam, I . . . I did not expect to feel so strongly about this, about so many things that have happened this week. It has grown every day since her birth. I want to care for her . . ."

"So do I!"

"I know, dear." Elizabeth sighed and he clutched her. "I do not question that."

"I know." Darcy kissed her softly. "We have to be different in everything do we not?"

"Mrs. Griffiths is very unhappy with us." Elizabeth laughed softly. "I daresay she has never run across a couple like us before. I look forward to her being finished with her duties so she will stop being scandalized by our sharing a bed. I felt terribly when she came in to attend me and panicked when she could not find me in the mistress' chambers. Supposedly tomorrow I may officially sit on the sofa. But heaven forbid I step over the threshold to the hallway."

"She is here to care for you, love. She simply wishes you to heal. So many women are lost to the childbed, you know that." Darcy kissed her gently. "She is the best monthly nurse in the country." He chuckled, "And she was denied so many of her duties, she was so unhappy about me delivering Rosalie."

"She was unhappy that Rosalie was born the day before she arrived! Out of doors! And that I was not lying prone in the dark, and that I sat up before a week was over, and . . . I believe that she was even disappointed that I have not become feverish." Elizabeth giggled and he kissed her. "She worries that you will wish to assert your husbandly rights if I sleep with you."

"I am not without restraint, love." He sighed. "As long as I may hold you."

"May I feed our baby?" She was met by silence. "Fitzwilliam?"

"If you will allow Mrs. Robbins to remain until you are healed, and allow her to perform her duties while you are so tired, and if you will please consider letting her remain after that to perform her duty at night. Please." He kissed her and smiled when she turned to face him, a position they had not managed for so long. "Agreed?"

"Yes." Elizabeth stroked the hair from his brow and kissed him, knowing any other man would lay down his decision and she would have no choice but to agree. "I listened to your talk with Rosalie."

"Oh."

"I need you just as deeply as you need me." She tenderly kissed his lips and he sighed. "I want to hold you all of the time, too. I was so frightened for the past months and I survived it because of you." Darcy's eyes opened wide in surprise. "You never guessed how terrified I was? Were not my unending tears enough evidence for you?" They kissed passionately until Darcy forced himself to stop and closing his eyes, rested their foreheads together. "You needed me."

"You dear man." She whispered while raising the hem of his nightshirt and gently took his arousal in her hand. His eyes opened to look into hers. She caressed him while they slowly kissed, allowing her hand to give him the pleasure and reassurance that he deeply needed. When he arrived at the blissful end, he clutched her tightly while he gasped and then took her face in his hands to kiss her fervently. "The moment, the second you are well, you tell me and I will love you the way you deserve." Elizabeth laughed, and taking up a towel that she kept nearby, gently wiped him off while he watched, then looked up to see his eyes were warm and happy. "I love that laugh."

"I am just fulfilling my vow to laugh every day." She kissed him and put the towel away. "I will tell you when the time comes. I love you."

He turned her back around to spoon their bodies together, nestled his face on her shoulder and sighed. "I love you, dearest. I do."

18 APRIL 1810

Dear Papa,
Forgive me for being so slow to give you our news, but I am very happy to tell you that you are a grandfather. Rosalie Elizabeth was born on the tenth. I will not tell you the circumstances because it will only send Mama racing for her salts, but I am so proud to tell you that my dear husband delivered her singlehandedly. I cannot imagine ever wishing to endure childbirth without him by my side again.
Rosalie is strong and beautiful. She has black hair like mine, and beautiful blue eyes like Fitzwilliam's. She has him wrapped around her little finger already, and he is full of joy. Please tell everyone that I am well, as is our dear little girl. I will write more soon. Give the family my love.
Your daughter,
Elizabeth Darcy

Mr. Bennet closed his eyes and said a silent prayer of gratitude. He had been expecting a missive from Pemberley and was most happy to see that it came in his daughter's hand. That alone told him that at least she had survived. Now he could rejoice over the healthy baby. Rising from his desk he walked out to the sitting room where Mrs. Bennet sat alone.

"Good news, Mrs. Bennet. You are a grandmother."

"She had the baby!" Mrs. Bennet cried. "And?"

"Rosalie Elizabeth Darcy is very well, as is her mother."

"A girl!" Mrs. Bennet said and sighed. "She has failed Mr. Darcy."

"She describes him as smitten and joyful; I would doubt that he would consider Elizabeth to be a failure." He said sternly.

"Of course she is! He requires an heir. Well, she is young, he will get her with child again soon, I am sure." She looked down at her needlework.

"So you are not grateful for her safe delivery, or does it not matter because it is a girl?" Mr. Bennet sat down next to her. "Mr. Darcy is very happy with his daughter; it is his opinion that matters, not yours. I hope that when you next write to Elizabeth that you not berate her for failing him."

"You were happy with Jane." Mrs. Bennet said.

"I was, and I was happy with all of them."

"No, Mr. Bennet, you were disappointed after Mary came." She met his eye. "I remember."

"Perhaps I was, but I was grateful for your health and hers, as well as Kitty and Lydia. I have never regretted my daughters' lives, Mrs. Bennet." He said quietly. "I am sorry if you felt that I have, and I am trying to make up for their neglected education now."

"I wondered if you would have been different with them if there had been a son amongst them." She said quietly. "I hope that Mr. Darcy is a good husband to Elizabeth and her daughter."

"I have no doubt that Mr. Darcy will be a good husband to Elizabeth, and an excellent father to his daughter." He stood and left the room. "It is I who seem to have failed."

"IT IS A COURT PRESENTATION, JANE. It is not Almack's. You are a gentleman's daughter; you may curtsey to the Queen." Lady Matlock informed her. "I want you to be able to go anywhere that Mr. Bingley may wish to take you, and undoubtedly that will include St. James'."

"But Lizzy has not been presented yet!" Jane protested. "How can I go before her?"

"If she was in town I would be doing the exact same thing with her. She is very happily married and a mother now. You have yet to find your husband. It is your duty to be married, and St. James' is an excellent place to expose you to potential suitors, but particularly Mr. Bingley." She stopped and looked to Mrs. Gardiner. "Will you try to talk some sense into the girl?"

"She is correct, Jane. Even if Mr. Bingley is not your ultimate choice, you should not miss this opportunity to gain access to these affairs. I will never be permitted to attend, but you may. I am sure that Lizzy will be presented some other year, but undoubtedly she and Mr. Darcy do not care or they would be here now."

"She just had the baby three weeks ago!" Jane gasped.

"When her recovery is complete, they will certainly travel. Alicia and Stephen are in Brighton for a nice long holiday." Lady Matlock smiled. "Audrey and Singleton will be going to Bath before returning to London."

"I doubt that Lizzy and Mr. Darcy leave Pemberley for anything other than Georgiana." Mrs. Gardiner laughed and looked over towards where she and Mary sat at the pianoforte. "They are not a couple that cares for social standing."

"No, but they should make an appearance when they come to collect the girls in June." Lady Matlock sighed. "Social standing is very important, whether they like it or not. They still have Georgiana's future to worry about and now they have a daughter. Do not allow me to begin again on the circumstances of her birth or I will be unable to address Jane's disposition." Her mouth set in an unhappy line.

"Lady Matlock, I appreciate that you wish to do well by me, but I beg that you not force me to go through this exercise before my sister." Jane said softly. "I have not earned the right to be above her in anything. She is a married woman, she has endured the pain of childbirth, and she is of the first circles. I will not usurp her position. I tried to do that once and I regret my behaviour, it has cost me more than a suitor."

"What do you mean, Jane?" Mrs. Gardiner asked and took her hand.

"I fear that Elizabeth and I will never be as close as we once were. No, no. I will not risk the relationship I have with her or Mr. Darcy by doing anything that might jeopardize it." She looked up to Lady Matlock. "If I marry a man who is able to visit court, I will gladly be presented, but only as his wife, just as Lizzy will someday do."

"My goodness. I realize that you feel your relationship with your sister has changed, but that was inevitable when she married Darcy and moved away. Letters are not the same as conversation, but I am certain that Elizabeth is not the least concerned about who is presented first." Lady Matlock looked at Mrs. Gardiner and she shrugged helplessly. "Is this about Darcy? Are you concerned about his opinion? My nephew is a very kind man, and very protective. If he displays any unwelcoming behaviour . . ."

"He does not; Lizzy assures me that he is very shy." Jane sniffed. "Oh please let this be! Teach me what you will and let us go through this Season. Satisfy Lizzy's desire that I see all that I might have and let us be done with it!"

"I cannot begin to understand your wishes but if this is how you feel, of course we will not force you to go through this presentation." Lady Matlock studied her and shook her head in exasperation. "You would not have attended alone in any case, you would have come with the Earl and myself, and you may still attend as our guests." She then looked directly into Jane's eyes. "And you will."

"Yes, madam." Jane looked down at her hands.

Evangeline had been listening quietly and finally spoke up. "My brother is very happy, Miss Bennet. I am grateful for his marriage to Laura. If you had married him, I do not believe I would see my brother feeling joy, and he deserves it. You do as well, and would not have found it with him. I believe that your loyalty to your sister is admirable, but I also believe that you are confused about which circle you wish to join, and that is what is behind your hesitation." She looked up as Bingley entered the room in the company of

Fitzwilliam, Mr. Gardiner, and Lord Matlock. "I hesitated for a long time before I found my way, and now I am grateful for my husband."

Fitzwilliam spotted Evangeline's smile and walked over to the ladies. "Well, have we interrupted anything particularly interesting?"

"Were you bored with the gentlemen's talk, Richard? Your father was undoubtedly full of stories tonight. Likely of his granddaughters."

He chuckled and stood behind his wife and rubbed her shoulders. "Ah yes, bragging mightily. I think, my dear, that we will have to have a boy."

"Do you now?" Evangeline said softly. "And how do you propose we do that?"

"Hmmm. I am not sure, but I am determined to best all of the men in this family." He kissed her cheek and winked. "Show all these first sons a thing or two!"

"And if it is a girl?" Lady Matlock smiled at her son. "What will you do, be ashamed?"

"Of course not!" He puffed out his chest and tapped his sword, "I will be proud; and woe to the man who tries to take her away from her Papa."

Tugging his hand Evangeline drew him down to whisper in his ear, "One detail dear, I am not in the family way."

"Yet." He kissed her cheek and grinned at the ladies then bounced away to join Bingley at the writing desk.

"He is coming back to his old self." Lady Matlock smiled to her daughter-in-law. "Thank you for that, dear. I look forward to seeing him with children."

"Yes." Evangeline said quietly. "His enthusiasm is contagious."

"To all but you, it seems." Mrs. Gardiner observed, and leaned forward. "I understand that you fear your brother's first wife's fate. It is something that we accept as possible when we marry."

"Yes, I know." She looked down at her hands. "We also must face the loss of a child."

Lady Matlock's brow creased and she moved to sit next to her. "Did you lose a child with Mr. Carter?" Evangeline nodded. "Oh my dear, I did not know."

"It was a boy, he was stillborn three months after Mr. Carter died, I was about six months along. Ellen helped me through it, and then she died giving birth to Ella." She looked back up to see the women watching her and Lady Matlock took her hand. "I have not told Richard this. I do not want him to fear losing our child should one come. He is so joyful for the success of his siblings and cousin."

"Of course, dear. I am sure that we all understand." Mrs. Gardiner looked around at the women and ended her gaze with Jane, whose hand was at her mouth. "I have miscarried, but was not as far along as you."

"Mr. Carter's family was devastated when they learned the heir had died."

"Were you?" Lady Matlock asked delicately. "I imagine that you regretted the child but not the tie to your husband." Evangeline nodded and she squeezed her hand. "I understand, dear. I was impressed with you before, but now my respect for you has only grown for your willingness to take on my son as husband."

Richard's happy laughter floated across the room and Evangeline lifted her head and smiled. "How could I pass up the chance to live with such a wonderful man? He makes every day a pleasure."

Bingley's answering laughter made Jane look up to see him grinning at her, and without hesitation she smiled back, then looked to Evangeline. "You have given me much to consider, Mrs. Fitzwilliam."

Mary nudged Georgiana who was staring at the men and biting her lip. "What shall we play next?"

"Oh." She blushed and looked at the sheets. "I do not know, you choose."

"Maybe we should wait for a request." Mary held her hand and smiled. "I have missed you over our holiday. I am glad that your aunt and uncle let you come to dinner tonight, I would have been very disappointed not to see you."

"I think that Elizabeth was behind that. Aunt Helen still believes that I should not eat anything except mutton and porridge until I am seventeen." She smiled and Mary made a face.

"Do you look forward to returning to school tomorrow?"

"I want to go home." Georgiana said softly and looked back over to the gentlemen.

"Go on write it down." Lord Matlock pointed at Bingley. "I do not want you coming back tomorrow claiming that you forgot everything."

"Yes sir." Bingley sharpened a pen and set to his task. "I appreciate your assistance, Stewart was kind enough to tell me all that he remembered of Netherfield, and I wrote to Darcy asking his advice . . ."

"What about Fitzwilliam?" Georgiana appeared suddenly. "Did you hear from him? What did he say? Is Elizabeth well?"

"Nothing my dear, Bingley only wrote to him." Lord Matlock smiled to see her disappointment. "I am sure that all remains well with your sister and niece. You will be back to school tomorrow and home before you know it."

"It has just been so long, and letters are not the same." She glanced down at the page that Bingley was writing and wrinkled her brow. "Forgive me Mr. Bingley, but your handwriting is atrocious."

Bingley looked up in surprise while the men all joined in laughter. "It is?"

"Surely my brother has commented on it! He never hesitated to tell me that mine was terrible and I remember the day we sat in the schoolroom when I was a little girl, and we wrote out the alphabet over and over." She pointed at the blotches pretending to be letters. "There is no excuse for that!"

"You are worse than my governess!" He cried. "And it occurs to me that you are still a little girl."

"I am fourteen!" She glared.

"I win my argument." Bingley returned to his work and his lips twitched as he watched her expression set. "Tell me, did Darcy give you lessons on staring at people menacingly as well?"

"No, Elizabeth did!" She spun and walked away. Bingley grinned and caught Fitzwilliam laughing. "She is growing up. It was not so long ago that she would hide at the top of the stairs to smile at me."

"She has a steady diet of letters from Elizabeth, I understand. I can see why she is very anxious to return to Pemberley." Fitzwilliam grinned. "Poor Darcy, alone in a household of women!"

"I doubt that he minds. I was overwhelmed with his letter announcing his daughter's birth." Bingley saw his companions smile. "I was also warned to repair my handwriting or not speak of my forays onto Bond Street."

"Let me guess, Elizabeth read your letter."

"So it seems." Bingley shrugged. "How was I to know?"

"It seems that my cousin was correct, then." He tapped the letter. "Hmm?"

"Miss Darcy!" Bingley called and winked at Fitzwilliam. Georgiana turned from where she was talking to the rest of the ladies. "Perhaps you might give me a handwriting lesson after all?"

"Really?" She lit up and looked to Lady Matlock. "May I?"

"Yes." She laughed and looked to Mary who walked over to stand nearby with her uncle. Lady Matlock watched as Georgiana sat down at the writing desk and set Bingley to work. Turning to Jane, she smiled. "He is very kind to tolerate her." Jane watched him slowly writing out his letters, then caught him looking up to smile at her and roll his eyes. She blushed and looked down. "Perhaps he is trying to win your attention."

"Perhaps." She peeked back up to see him still looking at her then laughed when Georgiana cleared her throat, and tapped the paper. He apologized and returned to his lesson. "He is very sweet."

"He certainly is." Evangeline studied the student and teacher and listened to their innocent banter, then looking away, noticed Mary paying them close attention as well with a small smile on her face. She pursed her lips and nodded, realizing a secret was shared between the girls, and then looked back to Jane. "It seems that Mr. Bingley may be a neighbour of yours soon. Mr. Lucas will have some competition." She raised her brows to see Jane's face flush. "I see your dilemma now."

Mr. Gardiner came over and took a seat with the ladies and smiled over at the writing desk. "Bingley has so many things occupying his attention; he cannot keep them all straight. Once his sister is married off next week, he can at least concentrate on this estate business. He desperately needs Darcy back, definitely a man in need of direction."

"Is not the attention of you and Lord Matlock enough?" Mrs. Gardiner laughed. "You both seem to have taken him in hand."

"Ah, but we are not young." He sat back and rested his hands over his stomach. "We forget the turbulence of youth. And Fitzwilliam cannot offer advice with the estate as Darcy can. No, he needs his friend." He smiled and caught Jane's eye. "He only recently celebrated his birthday."

"He is the age that Darcy was when his father died." Lady Matlock observed.

The collective group watched the laughing young man writing out his letters, and Jane's thoughts turned to an older man who knew exactly what he wanted. She found her uncle's eyes upon her, "They are both good men, Jane." He smiled. "And neither is in a hurry. Take your time."

"I CANNOT THANK YOU ENOUGH for this, Darcy." Singleton smiled over to him as they rode along with Nichols and his assistants. "I have learned more during three weeks at Pemberley than I daresay my father has taught me of Ashcroft in a lifetime, and that is with you entirely distracted by your wife and baby."

"I am glad to help you." Darcy's mouth lifted in a small smile. "You are eager to learn, and I have nothing but respect for that. Surely your father sees the difference in you?"

"I hope so. He has not had much to say to me of late, he . . .is difficult." He sighed and watched the other men move ahead. "Father is a rough man to please. I think that most of my conversations with him involved time with a lash more often than instruction. Perhaps he thought that was instructive." He caught Darcy's furrowed brow. "Marriage to me was freedom in a way I had never experienced before. I did not dare put a toe out of line at home or school, but suddenly to have Audrey in my bed and her dowry in my pocket, I . . . I look at that man now and wonder what I was thinking."

"What were you thinking?"

"I had no idea how to love her." He looked up and back down. "Lord knows I wanted to. We had such great fun together, courting. But the rules are so strict then, and I am used to rules, and consequences. But then there we were, married, and our wedding night, I could not behave with her as I wanted, instead I followed the rules and disappointed her. After that I did not know how to make it better, so I took all of the passion I felt for her and gave it to courtesans, and all the anger I had for my father I gave to the taverns and gambling dens. Thank God my brothers kicked some sense into me, and thank Audrey for letting me win her back."

Darcy stared straight ahead and thought over what he said. "And now you live your marriage by a different set of rules."

"Yes. I will follow propriety to the letter. I am afraid that if I stray, I will fall back into the abyss I occupied before, and Audrey does not deserve that, and neither do our children. The only small concession, well, not small, is that I am at last free to give her the passion she deserves."

"That is not small at all." Darcy turned his head to give Singleton a genuine smile. "And I will tell you that she is very happy with you." Singleton's eyes widened. "She spoke to Elizabeth, and my wife is not a woman to be fooled. You have succeeded in your reformation."

"Thank you for sharing that." He drew a deep breath and smiled, looking ahead at the fields where Darcy's tenants were working.

"Why have you shared your tale with me?"

He tilted his head. "I am not sure; I have not ever spoken of it to anyone before. I guess . . . I would like to earn your good opinion, and I hope, one day, your friendship."

Darcy laughed. "You have kept me sane during these first terrifying days of fatherhood, if I did not count you as a friend after this then I would be a mean man indeed." Holding out his hand, the men shook. "I respect the changes you have made to your life and marriage, and I respect the choices you follow to keep yourself on the right path. As long as my cousin is happy with you, I will be as well."

"Was that a threat hidden amongst the compliments?" Singleton laughed to see Darcy's brow rise. "Ah another formidable family member to watch over me, so be it. I thank you." He bowed his head and his eyes twinkled. "So, I suppose that you are looking forward to the churching ceremony?" Darcy glared at him and Singleton backed off. "I will not mention the marriage bed again, Darcy. But by the way you are gripping your reins; I would say I have my answer."

"OH I CANNOT WAIT to leave these walls!" Elizabeth groaned while she watched Darcy and Singleton ride towards the stables. "I need to walk and feel the sun again. Why must my first outing be to church? Can it not be in the garden? This is Mrs. Griffiths' doing. She did not have her way with any other part of my confinement, but she must have said something to Fitzwilliam and he has steadfastly supported her."

"I know exactly how you feel, but at least it was winter when I went through it, so the attraction of the outdoors was not as strong as a good fire." Audrey laughed and patted the sofa. "Come on, we leave in a few days so let us take advantage of this time without our husbands hovering nearby and you feeding Rosalie. You know that is what is at work here; Darcy simply does not want you to suddenly become ill or out of someone's sight."

"Mother hen." She said with frustration and she heard Audrey's amusement. "I do love him."

"How could you not? I wondered how I would have done with him." She said thoughtfully. The silence from her companion was deafening and the glare was scorching. "This was years ago . . . Elizabeth! I only thought it because Aunt Catherine was so adamant about Anne marrying him and I thought, well, what about me? I never . . ." She sighed. "Elizabeth. Stop it. I am very happy with Robert."

"Forgive me. I am rather possessive of my husband." She said quietly, and settled beside her. Audrey held her hand. "I think of how he worried about losing me and it breaks my heart." She wiped her eyes. "I spent so many nights watching him sleep, and thinking of Mr. Harwick, and wondering if he would find someone to love him the way he needs so badly." She burst into sobs and Audrey held her tight. "What is wrong with me?"

"Nothing dear, nothing. As you say, you love him deeply." She kissed her cheek. "There now, you do not want him to see you like this."

Elizabeth sniffed and sat up. "I do not seem to be crying as much anymore, and my mind is not as cloudy as it was."

"No that improves rapidly. Do you feel sad? Alicia did, that is why they went to the sea. Her last letter seemed to have her back in good spirits again."

"No, I am not sad." She took a deep breath and smiled. "I am well, just tired. But please do not tell Fitzwilliam that!" Audrey laughed with her and they held hands. "Now, you must write to me. I want to hear everything of Bath."

"I promise that I will write to you." Audrey smiled and stroked her hair. "I am most looking forward to seeing Grace again. She will be waiting for us in the house that Robert's parents have taken."

"How are you getting along with them?" Elizabeth asked delicately. "Are things improving somewhat?"

"Oh, well, his father has never given me any trouble; it was always Robert who could never measure up. I am sure that he will be a good father to our children to spite his own. But we are both glad that we will be alone in Bath." Seeing Elizabeth's understanding smile, she laughed. "Oh, Elizabeth, I watch you with Rosalie and wish that I could have been so brave to feed Grace, but Robert would not hear of it. Well neither would my mother or Mrs. Singleton, so that settled it. You are fortunate to have no interfering relatives!"

"That is because we live so far away, another reason not to give birth in London."

"London! You did not even give birth indoors!"

The two women laughed and Elizabeth sighed. "Tell me about the churching ceremony."

"Surely you have seen it done? It is just a blessing to you, a celebration of your recovery, and some say, it wipes away the sin of you becoming with child to begin with." Both of them shook their heads with the foolishness of the notion. "It is most important to your husband."

"Yes, he is eager." The women exchanged glances. "I am as well." Seeing Audrey's raised brows, Elizabeth looked down at her swollen breasts, her still rounded belly, and thought of every other part of her that had changed, and said softly, "I think I am."

DARCY WALKED INTO HIS DRESSING ROOM to change from his muddy riding clothes and found Adams at work. His valet removed his boots and poured out water for him to wash, and when Darcy stood from the ewer and reached for a towel, he noticed a letter tucked into the bundle of his soiled shirt and breeches. "What have you there?"

"Your clothes, sir." The man flushed and cast his eyes down. "I will just set these in the stairwell and we will have you dressed in a moment, sir."

"Adams." He touched the pile in his arms. "There is a letter under here. What is it?"

"It is nothing . . ." Taking possession of the pile, Darcy found a letter with his name written in Elizabeth's hand. "What is the meaning of this?" He demanded.

"Sir . . . I was given that by Mrs. Darcy to hold. I am returning it to her now that she is clearly well." He continued to look at his feet and spoke very quietly.

"Why would you wish to return it, why did you not give it to me?" He looked at the envelope and back to Adams. "Why does her health make a diff . . ." Darcy stopped and stared at his name; and his heart began to pound. "I was to be given this if she died." Adams said nothing, which confirmed the fact. "Leave me."

In a flash the man was gone. Darcy stood still and stared at the unopened letter in his hand and wondered if he dared to read what he knew were to be Elizabeth's last words to him. Sinking down into the shaving chair he continually passed his hand over it, and tears began to trace down his cheeks as he considered the situation where he might have had to read the letter. *Would our daughter have survived? Would I have faced two deaths? Would Elizabeth have died in my arms in the woods? How could I have left her all alone to summon help? Would I have had to accompany them both home, walking with their bodies back to the house, covered in their blood? Would she have lived only to die days later? What would I be doing now? Would I be drunk, refusing all offers of sympathy? How would I go on?*

Darcy did not hear the dressing room door open, but he did feel the touch of Elizabeth's lips upon his and her hands taking the letter away. "Fitzwilliam." She whispered, "Look at me."

He lifted his head and grasped her hands. "I cannot bear to think of the world without you in it."

"Then do not, because I am very much alive." She smiled and kissed his cheeks. "Stop mourning me."

"This letter . . ."

"Was never to be read. I asked Adams to return it to me. You were unfortunate in catching him." Darcy drew her into his arms and she stood between his legs while he rested his face on her shoulder. She whispered in his ear. "Shall I burn it?"

"No dearest. I will never read it, but I cannot burn any letter of yours. I know it contains your love, and that should never be destroyed."

"Then I shall keep it for you. Together we can lock it up in the strongbox in my dressing room, and you will not be tempted to read it."

"I never wish to read it." His embrace tightened. "I was just beginning to relax. You are well. You are exhausted, but you amaze me with your care of Rosalie and me, as well as our guests and home. You should still be in bed, and you are walking about this house . . ." He swallowed hard. "You are well. Rosalie is thriving . . ." He sighed and kissed her hair. Elizabeth kissed his bare shoulder and ran her hands over his back. He sighed again and she looked up to kiss his lips, and then gently probing his mouth with her tongue, found his to suckle. Darcy groaned and melted into her. "Lizzy, you cannot kiss me this way."

"I can if I mean to love you." She said softly and kissed his neck. "Come to bed with me."

"Elizabeth, we cannot . . ." He looked at her and his eyes were full of his longing and need. "Can we?"

"You told me that the moment I was ready . . ." She looked down, and Darcy lifted her chin and kissed her, then cupping her face in his hands kissed her lips slowly. Moving around her face, he kissed her eyes, her jaw, then down to stroke over and over beneath her ear, drawing her body closer into his arms as her sighs and moans made his desire grow.

"Elizabeth!" He gasped and unbuttoning her gown drew down the front, and helped her to pull her arms from the sleeves. She wore no stays over her chemise, and her breasts, swollen and heavy, were there before him. "ohhhh." He sighed and she blushed, embarrassed by their appearance. Darcy saw nothing at all wrong and lifted his hand to touch with the barest caress, and milk began to leak, then flow over his hand. Elizabeth cried her dismay and turned away. "I am sorry!" She sobbed and held her face in her hands.

"Elizabeth." Darcy immediately slipped his arms around her waist and drew her back against his chest. "Why are you apologizing? You are not ashamed of your milk, are you?" He kissed her shoulder and her throat. "I marvel at you feeding our baby. Why would I care about a little spilled milk?" He whispered and kissed her ear. "Would it help if I drank from you?" He felt her nod and he smiled, and turned her around to find that his mouth was just at the perfect height to suckle. Elizabeth rested her cheek in his hair as he moved from one nipple to the other, and when he finished, rested his face between them. "Whenever you need this service, my love . . ." Elizabeth laughed softly, and he looked up to see her smiling shyly.

"Now, what of the rest of these things?" He started to draw down her skirt and her hands immediately clutched it. "What frightens you, love?"

"I do not look as I did before." She confessed. "I fear that you will be disappointed."

"I loved you how many times the day that you gave birth, and I found you more enticing than ever, how could I not love you now that you are not great with child?" He tugged at the gown and it fell to the floor. Darcy ran his hands up over her legs and felt the new curves that she had been given. "Ohhhhh, Elizabeth!" He moaned. "You were a beautiful woman before but now, oh I am a fortunate man!" Darcy stroked over her hips, then up her slightly rounded belly, "And look at this!" He sighed and kissed her naval. "Your body is beautiful!"

"It is misshapen and soft." She said unhappily. "Oh how can you look at me without disappointment? Now I understand why men turn to courtesans, if their wives are stretched and ugly . . ."

"Stop." He looked up and commanded her. "Stop." Darcy drew her chemise over her head then standing, lifted her into his arms, and carried her to the bed. He looked over her, taking in her figure, then lay down and without preamble, Darcy lifted her so that she lay on his chest. Elizabeth gasped then laughed, and he smiled before kissing her again. "I love you. I love every inch of you. I love your shape, your scent, your beauty, your laugh, your eyes, everything, everything about you. I am lost entirely without you. I do not ever want to know what it is to not wake with you in my arms, or hear your voice when I enter the house. Your body is different because you carried the second greatest gift you ever gave me, and I will treasure her and every child we ever have. If I were to reject you because your body changed, I would be the most ungrateful fool that was ever born and would be undeserving of your love."

"That is true." She smiled and he laughed softly. "Forgive my insecurities; I am supposed to be comforting you."

"I prefer us comforting each other." He ran his hand down her back and cupped her bottom.

She caressed away the hair from his brow, "Rosalie was the second greatest gift?"

Darcy smiled and caught her hand, then kissed her ring. "This is the greatest gift, by far. I love you above everything." He kissed her lips then rolled so that she was beneath him. "Are you sure that you are ready?"

"Yes." She tugged at his drawers and he had them off before she could blink, and started to laugh. "You are eager!"

Darcy settled over her and chuckled. "I cannot tell you how good it feels to lie like this once again; I hardly know what to do without a baby in the way!" He kissed her and laughed when she wrapped her arms and legs around him. "Taking possession, my love?"

"You are all mine, and I have missed you." They lay together kissing and exploring each other's bodies with their hands and mouths as if it were their wedding night once again, until Darcy stopped and looked down at her with that familiar and very welcome silent question in his eyes. Elizabeth slid her hand around from where she was caressing his bottom to take his arousal into her hand, and stroked him, then wordlessly answered his question by guiding him to her entrance. They kissed, their mouths sliding together, their tongues entwining, their arms wound tightly around each other, and he at last lifted his hips to slide inside of her once again.

"Ohhhhhhh, I have missed you!" He gasped. They began to move, a little awkwardly at first, learning how to make love once again and finding the rhythm that they had lost. It did not take long for him and Elizabeth's rapture was marked by another shower of milk. They lay gasping and laughing, covered with the liquid and kissing each other. "Everything is an adventure with you, Elizabeth!"

She sighed as he took up a towel and wiped her off. "I do not know whether to laugh or cry."

"You know my opinion." He smiled as she took the towel from him and performed the same service. He lay down again and pulled her to his chest so that they faced each other. "You felt no pain?"

"No, only bliss." She smiled and he grinned proudly. "Did it feel differently?"

"If anything it was better, we have lived through a terrifying experience, and it only makes me love you more." She wrapped her leg around his hip and tucked her head under his chin. Darcy relished the feeling of them holding each other so closely again. "Being inside of you Elizabeth, is like coming home."

Elizabeth laughed and looked up at him with dancing eyes. "Well, it seems that the knocker is back on the door. Welcome home, Fitzwilliam."

Chapter 13

"Good Morning, Mr. Bennet." Robert Lucas called.

Mr. Bennet turned and smiled, then dismissing his steward waited while the young man dismounted. "Good morning, Lucas. What brings you to Longbourn?"

"I heard from my sister that Miss Bennet has a suitor."

"Well you certainly do not hesitate do you? No dancing around the subject?" He laughed and saw that Lucas was in no humour to play along. He reminded him of another young man. "You knew of Mr. Bingley months ago."

"I did, and I knew that he was in town. I do not know the extent of his attentions towards Miss Bennet, nor how she is receiving them. My sister was unable to give me the answers I require."

Mr. Bennet cleared his throat. "I am unsure if I will be able to, either. My understanding is that Mr. Bingley has called frequently upon Jane at my brother's home, and has met them at a few dinners, but that he seems to be awaiting the Darcys' arrival before pressing his suit, if indeed he does."

"He is not serious? He is playing with her affections?" Lucas asked with concern while rubbing his horse's head, then readjusted his grip on the reins.

"He has only just married off his difficult sister; I believe that he has not been able to focus on much else until that was accomplished. He has called as a friend at the Gardiner home, and has been in attendance at a few dances where the Matlocks were also present. I do know that he is speaking with the owner of Netherfield about leasing the property."

"Then it is settled." He said softly. "I thank you . . ."

"Just a moment, sir. Mr. Bingley is a young man wishing to fulfil his father's wish that he purchase an estate. My son Darcy has urged him to get his feet wet by leasing. Their friend Stewart, you know him, recommended that he investigate a convenient and affordable estate. It is pure coincidence that it is near Jane."

"I see." Lucas considered the problem. "I have spoken to Mr. Darcy about Netherfield. I did not know that it was in regards to Mr. Bingley, but then, I had not spoken to Miss Bennet yet, either. He was kind enough to offer me advice on Lucas Lodge." He fell into thoughts about the quiet man he had observed while attending Cambridge.

"I hear that the King's illness has suspended the court presentations until further notice." Mr. Bennet offered. "Anybody may attend St. James' for now."

"Yes, Father is rather appalled, as you can imagine." Lucas smiled. "He is claiming that he will not attend this year for his annual visit because the exclusivity is eliminated. Why do you mention this?"

"Lizzy said that they will go to one large social event while they are in town to retrieve her sisters. Lady Matlock insists that it be at St. James' to give the Darcys maximum exposure to as many peers as possible. Jane will accompany them." He looked at Lucas meaningfully. "Perhaps the date could be coordinated and you could accompany your father, should he go?"

"I imagine that Mr. Bingley will be present." He said thoughtfully.

"I have no doubt." Mr. Bennet smiled. "I will not push my daughter in either direction sir, but I have my opinions. Perhaps a side-by-side comparison would aid her. Shall I write to Lizzy?"

Lucas smiled. "If you write to her, please send my congratulations for her safe delivery, and my regards to Miss Bennet. I will, however, not be attending St. James'. Miss Bennet has seen enough of me to know my character. I will not play a game." He paused before mounting his horse. "Your opinion does not rest on the suitor's wealth?"

"No, on my daughter's potential for happiness, she would be cared for in either situation." He watched the young man ride away and walked towards the house to go and write to Elizabeth. "I just had my opinion confirmed."

"BRRRRR." Adams said dramatically when he took his place back in the servant's coach.

"It is terribly quiet between them." Millie said softly and looked at Mrs. Robbins. "Mrs. Darcy was in tears when I tried to clean her gown."

"Miss Rosalie finally fell asleep when I held her. I tried to convince Mrs. Darcy to let me take her in here for a while, but she would not agree. She is determined to . . . Well I do not know what she is doing. How was Mr. Darcy?"

"Silent as the grave." Adams said grimly. "The man's coat is covered with all manner of baby. He clearly tried to give relief, good man. I talked to John, he said the child was crying nearly constantly, and finally Mr. Darcy was banging on the roof, yelling for him to stay clear of the ruts. For him to raise his voice in the presence of his wife, he must be frustrated indeed."

"Mrs. Darcy said every time the baby seemed to drift off they would hit a bump and she would be crying again." Millie said worriedly. "I have never seen them so silent with each other."

"Mr. Darcy wished for her to leave Miss Darcy at home." Adams said in defence of his master. "I heard Mrs. Darcy say that she would stay home herself before she left her child behind. Then I heard him saying that he would never leave home again without Mrs. Darcy."

"I heard that argument, too. They were not listening to each other." Mrs. Robbins sighed.

"But why would Mrs. Darcy insist on caring for Miss Rosalie by herself?" Millie asked. "That is what you are for, Mrs. Robbins."

"I have a feeling that Mr. Darcy is wondering the same thing. I do not know, but Mrs. Darcy can be stubborn as a mule about things when she gets an idea in her head." Mrs. Robbins sighed.

Adams rolled his eyes. "So can the master. I suggested that we simply stay here for the night and the look I received from Mr. Darcy was scorching. He said he had no intention of extending this journey any further than the three days they were scheduled to travel. I offered to open the luggage and get him a new coat and breeches and he looked at himself and asked what the point of that would be. The man is frustrated. You saw him walking alone outside of the inn." They looked out of the window and saw the Darcy's coach ahead of them as they began the next leg of the journey to London. "Two more hours and we will stop for the night."

"I will be ready to take the baby as soon as we arrive." Mrs. Robbins murmured.

"We will have some serious work to do as well." Adams nodded at Millie. "Be prepared for anything."

"THERE YOU GO." Stewart brought Julia a cup of lemonade and taking a small sip, she made a face.

"Tart?" He laughed and she joined him.

"Just a little." She smiled and they stood comfortably together, watching the crowd milling around the theatre lobby. "Mother is lurking."

"I see her." He shrugged. "I think that I have grown used to her vigilance. I am relieved to have my sister and Harwick as our chaperones for a while. That is if you would like to keep seeing me."

"I have not stopped seeing you for the past four months, Mr. Stewart; I think that I can bear to continue the habit." She looked down when his fingers grazed her hand and she gently touched his in return. "If you feel that you should explore more options . . ."

"More?" He tilted his head. "Are you tiring of me?"

"No, I . . . I just have seemed to be taking up all of your time."

"Is that not the purpose of courtship?" He said softly.

"Are we courting? You never officially asked." She whispered back.

"You did not want me to, remember? You wanted no expectations. You were afraid of the stories you heard about my behaviour."

"Was that wrong?" Julia looked up to see his warm smile. "I could not bear a broken heart. Not when I have been so careful with it."

"Nobody has touched me as you have, Miss Henley." He took the glass away from her and wrapped her hand around his arm. "What worries you about my behaviour?"

"It is very loyal."

"And that is worrisome?" He laughed and laid his other hand over hers.

"No." She laughed. "No it is very admirable."

"Well then?" He stroked her hand and watched her fingers beneath his. "I cared, but never loved, I needed to learn the difference. I have yet to give my heart away, and you are the only woman who I truly have courted, even if we have not called it that."

"We have been dancing and to the theatre . . ."

"And to dinner at our parents' homes . . ."

"And taken walks in the gardens. And talked so much."

"We have not gone to church together . . . I would like very much to see you in church." Stewart said quietly. A gong sounded and the crowd began to wend their way back to their seats. Julia looked up to him and he whispered, "I would like to see you in a bridal gown."

"You would?"

"Will you marry me, Julia? My love?"

"Your love?"

"You are the one who has captured my heart. Do you doubt my feelings?"

"No." She sighed and smiled into his warm eyes. "Yes."

"Explain that please." He laughed.

"No, I do not doubt, and yes, I will marry you." She laughed and he kissed her hand.

"I thought so." He sighed and wrapped her arm back around his and led them to the box.

Harwick nudged Laura and she looked closely at her beaming brother and quickly to his blushing companion."Finally!" She whispered to him.

"Patience, my dear. You were with me." Harwick said quietly, but took her hand to squeeze. "But it is about time!" They laughed at the oblivious pair.

"Shall we tell your mother?" Stewart asked.

"No, let her speculate a little longer." Julia leaned on his shoulder and he closed his eyes. "I do not care to provide the entertainment for the crowd, and her reaction would not be silent."

"No indeed." He led her to her seat.

She whispered when he sat beside her. "I love you, Daniel."

"I love you." He saw Mr. and Mrs. Henley watching them intently, caught his sister and brother laughing, then smiling down at Julia, bent his head to kiss her lips. Mrs. Henley gasped and clapped her hand over her mouth. "I could not resist." He smiled when Julia blushed. "But I promise to behave now."

"Must you?"

Stewart chuckled, and raised her hand to his mouth. "Well, at least until the theatre is dark."

"SHHHHH, DEAR, SHHHHH." Elizabeth rubbed Rosalie's back while she screamed. Nothing seemed to comfort her. Elizabeth was near tears herself, but she closed her eyes and held the wailing exhausted baby to her breast and softly sang. When Darcy again pounded on the ceiling in frustration, calling to the coachman to keep to a smoother path, then muttered about paying tolls to drive on such impassable roads, Elizabeth cringed. Hearing his irritation and seeing him sitting stiffly and staring at them with his jaw set made her defensive. "I am doing my best, Fitzwilliam. Your unending stares of disapproval are not helping me. I know that you are angry." She continued in a strained voice, "You made it very clear that you did not want our daughter on this trip. I insisted that she come. I will settle her." Before he could answer she said bitterly, "I refuse to abandon my child for months at a time in the care of servants like Audrey and Alicia do. I will not ignore and despise my child as my mother did me." She choked out the last words and looked back to Rosalie. "Please Rosa, please." She plead; and finally after a very long day, she gave in to the pressure and the tension, and started to cry. "Please." She sobbed and dropped her head onto the blanket.

"Elizabeth." Darcy said softly, and she felt him kiss her cheek. She looked up at him through blurry eyes and watched as he removed the baby from her arms. "Come here, dear girl." He murmured and held Rosalie tight and securely, and stared into her eyes. "Now, what is this all about?" Rosalie hiccoughed and stared at him, then screwed up her face up to cry again and he shook his head. "No, no, love. Enough of this. You have made Mama cry, and that will not do. You have had your time to express yourself and we all know your opinion. Now then, enough." He bound her tighter to his chest. She cried out and stopped, and at last the contest of wills had a winner. She blinked, and he sang, *"Bye baby bunting, Papa's gone a'hunting, gone to get a rabbit skin to wrap his baby bunting in."[4]* Rosalie stared in fascination as he repeated the verse. In the corner of his eye, he saw Elizabeth shakily wipe her face and hug herself. He lessened his grip on the baby slightly then willing himself to maintain his calm voice, began speaking to his daughter seriously.

"What is your advice?" Darcy asked. "I have hurt your mother, and I know not what to do. She said many worrisome things. I pray that it was more frustration from the trip than anger with me. I love you dearly, but you are a challenge to your poor parents. Especially to your beleaguered mother who has taken on the duties of caring for you in ways I never imagined my wife doing. What am I saying? I never imagined anything of the care involved for a baby." A hand escaped and reached for his mouth, and he kissed it. "Your Aunt Georgiana spent her first year in the nursery. Father visited with her and she brought him happiness, but it certainly was not his position to care for her or feed her constantly. What example have I other than his? My cousins do the same with their own. They describe their encounters with their daughters, and I

---

[4] "Bye Baby Bunting", English nursery rhyme, circa 1784.

am hesitant to describe mine with you. We are so unlike everyone and your mother is so unlike every other woman I know."

Darcy spied Elizabeth wiping her eyes and leaning against the side of the carriage to listen. Rosalie reached for his nose and he bent his head to let her touch it and laughed gently. "It is large, dear, I know. But I will tell you, I love it when your mama kisses me there." She cooed and he kissed her, then darted another look to Elizabeth and was relieved to see a small smile. "How can we make her happy again? I think that you are as much in her bad graces as I, you know. After all you are the one who chose to cry all day! And how a person as small as you can be so wet all of the time! And nurse so much! My dear, you will be a millstone to carry if you keep growing as you are!" He chuckled as she gurgled and patted his face, then suddenly smiled. "Ahhhh so your plan is to win her back with your charm, is it? I have no charm, what may I do?" He lifted Rosalie to his shoulder and closed his eyes. "I did not mean to hurt her. I hope that she understands that." Elizabeth touched his face and caressed the hair from his brow. His eyes opened and their gazes met. "What is she doing?"

"Her eyes are closed." She said softly. "Forgive me, Fitzwilliam."

"Your opinion is harsh." He said quietly. "I am sorry that my behaviour inspired it."

"No, I was feeling so helpless . . ."

"No love, you were upset before we left, and it is my fault for not explaining myself then, and it was my fault for not intervening more today when you clearly needed me." He looked at her clasped hands sadly. "I was not staring at you to find fault, Elizabeth. I was marvelling at your self-control. How you have remained so calm and positive during the journey amazes me."

"It does?" She said softly. "You seemed so disappointed in me."

"No." He sighed. "I was very frustrated, and I withdrew into myself." Darcy knew that she was waiting for more of an explanation. "I was unhappy. I had been looking forward so much to being alone with you. I remembered our honeymoon journey and thought of how I wished to repeat the experience, alone together in the carriage, watching the world go by; and . . ." Elizabeth's eyes filled with tears, and he drew a sharp breath when he saw her handkerchief rise to her mouth, and rushed through the rest of his confession. "I was unhappy that you absolutely refused to let the servants perform their duties. You are Elizabeth Darcy. You are not some shopkeeper's wife travelling by stagecoach. You have people who are employed to make your . . . our life easier. I was unhappy that you seemed to be trying to make a point about yourself that was unnecessary to do." He heard her sniff and stared out of the window so that he could finish. "And lastly, I . . . I was afraid that you were rejecting me. It was so lonely sitting next to you but feeling that I was unwelcome. I think that I welcomed you pouring out all of your feelings in a barrage of angry words more than being treated to your silence."

"So I did." Elizabeth whispered and reached to turn his face back to hers and saw the tears pricking at his eyes. "Fitzwilliam, am I a horrible mother for wishing we had more time alone before we had children?"

"If you are than I am a horrible father." Carefully slipping one hand off of Rosalie, he reached out for Elizabeth's and entwined their fingers. "That is why I wished for her to stay at Pemberley. You have had no chance to rest since her birth. Most new mothers of our station travel and enjoy their recovery. With your feeding duties, you are always at work. I was not wishing to abandon our daughter; I wanted to . . . be with you. I wanted to see you relax. Sometimes I am not very talented at understanding other people's emotions. I did not consider your feelings from your childhood. I simply wished to give you time away."

"But you would have missed her terribly, and been so frightened if something happened and we could not get to her immediately."

"I know, and I would have regretted you losing the closeness you share by feeding her. And I would have missed her as well." He raised her hand to his lips. "I am so sorry. What should I have done? What were you wishing for under that calm façade?"

She shook her head at his description. "Before we left and we were disagreeing about taking Rosalie, you should have told me to stop acting less like a child and more like the mistress of Pemberley. And I should have reassured you that I love you more than any person in the world and need you deeply." Elizabeth kissed his hand and was relieved to see his little smile. "I did not understand your desire to be alone with me until you pointed it out. I am afraid that spending so much time caring for Rosalie has made me blind to many things. And one is that I need not be so independent."

"No. I am here, as is all of our staff."

"Fitzwilliam, it is not your position to care for our child. No man does such things."

He looked at the baby sleeping on his shoulder and raised his brow. "I am not suggesting that I do the work of Mrs. Robbins or the nursery maids, Elizabeth. And I do not want you to do them either." He looked at her seriously. "We are privileged to live as we do. Do you know what this reminds me of now? When you first came to Pemberley and felt that you had to prove to Mrs. Reynolds and the staff that you were good enough to be mistress. You worked so hard when you really did not have to. I think that this new position of mother has roused you the same way." Elizabeth watched him and thought over his observation, then carefully rising, she moved to sit on his other side, and leaning against his chest, wrapped her arms around his waist. Darcy sighed and placed his arm around her shoulder.

"I think that you are correct." She finally whispered. "Although learning my position as mistress was very important and has earned me the respect of the staff, in this case, I was trying to prove that I could cope with everything since I insisted that she come with us. I feel like such a fool."

"I am just as foolish. I should have spoken." He drew a breath and plunged on. "Dearest, would you be willing to let Mrs. Robbins look after her in the other coach when we continue our travel? We stop often enough you could still feed her . . ." He looked into her eyes. "We need our time alone. We are no good to anyone if we are so tense with each other. Perhaps Rosalie sensed that somehow."

"She certainly responded differently to you." Elizabeth said sadly. "She only screamed for me."

"Dearest she screamed for me most of the journey, too." He kissed her forehead. "I think that she was just ready to give in, and a new voice gained her attention long enough to let her quiet and calm."

"Thank you." She closed her eyes and he tightened his embrace. "It is very close in here. That probably did not help her disposition. It is warm . . ."

"And . . . unpleasant." He said delicately.

"Perhaps we can purchase a great supply of napkins for her, and . . . leave the soiled ones behind when we travel?" She suggested tentatively.

"We could take the cost out of her dowry, perhaps?" He said with a little smile.

"Perhaps." She finally relaxed and smiled. "Aunt and Uncle Gardiner never come to Longbourn with the children."

"And why is that?" Darcy drew her closer and she settled her face on his shoulder.

"She always said that the trip was to preserve her sanity." Elizabeth sniffed and laughed. "I never understood that until now, Longbourn was hardly a calm location."

"But perhaps it was calmer than a home full of small demanding children." He gently kissed her lips when she looked up. "I am so sorry, Elizabeth. I never meant to hurt you."

"No Fitzwilliam, I am sorry for not turning to you or anyone else for help." She caressed his face and kissed him. "Perhaps your suggestion for the rest of the trip will make it pleasant for all of us."

"Too bad we will have Mary and Georgiana with us for the ride home." He smiled and she sighed. "The carriage was not so confining when it was the two of us alone."

"No, not at all, it was very cosy. We have two more days; we should make the most of them." They stared at each other sorrowfully. "I had a terrible vision of you becoming like Papa when you walked away from us at the last inn."

"I will not become your father Elizabeth, not anymore than you will become your mother. I just needed to . . .regroup." He smiled to hear her laugh again. Hugging her tightly to him, they both drew deep breaths.

She watched Rosalie wiggle and they heard her sigh in her sleep. "One reason that I did not wish to leave Rosa at home was because I was afraid that if I did not feed her for a few weeks, my milk would dry up, and I would never have that opportunity again."

Darcy started to chuckle. Elizabeth pinched him. "Forgive me love, but when have I failed to drink from you since she was born?" He smiled and laughed. "Dearest I would gladly feed from you, any chance I am given."

"Fitzwilliam!" She cried.

"Say the word and I will right now." He looked at her with his head cocked and she shook hers, but was smiling at his expression. "Anytime, love." He said warmly in her ear.

"What would I do without you? Please be assured that you will never lose me. I should not have kept my concerns to myself, it just breeds misunderstanding. I have learned a great deal today."

"So have I." He kissed her softly and she melted into him. "Rosalie seems to be comfortable now."

"Naturally." Came her muffled reply.

"I think that she prefers her bed not to be moving, or should I say, not jostling over the ruts in the road." He kissed her throat and hugged her.

"I think that she prefers your shoulder. I know that I do." She laughed and he chuckled. "Perhaps the rest of the journey will be better?"

"Hopefully you and I might rest a little." He smiled. "And we should talk with the Gardiners about travel. We already know what my relations would do, let us hear from yours."

"Very well." She sighed.

"We should arrive at the inn soon. Would you like to be left alone?" He asked quietly. "For a little while?"

"No, I have spent enough time unnecessarily alone today. I would like a bath and a bed." She smiled at him. "I would like to sleep with you."

"How did you know what I wished your answer would be?"

Elizabeth kissed his nose, and he laughed softly. "Because I know you, and I should have known better."

"I think that we both could say that, my love."

"I AM LOOKING FORWARD to seeing the Darcys." Bingley smiled at Jane. "I can imagine that you are very excited."

"Yes, I cannot wait to meet my niece." She smiled at him as they strolled through the park in Gracechurch Street, a maid trailed behind them. "My sister's letters have been ecstatic, she says that she loves being a mother and that Mr. Darcy is a wonderful father."

"He was very nervous during the long wait, though." Bingley chuckled. "I still am amazed that he actually delivered the child."

"I believe that neither of them wish to dwell on what may have happened." Jane looked down at her feet. "How is Mrs. Robinson getting along?"

Charles smiled. "I have no idea. My sister's honeymoon trip is likely to last another week or so, I know that she wished to be back in town for the end of the Season, to display her triumph, such as it is."

"She is unhappy with her choice?" Jane said worriedly

"No, no, it is not what she expected for herself, but Mr. Robinson does have an estate, even if it is small, and of course, she is disappointed that he remains in trade. Her ambitions were far greater than what she could achieve."

"So she settled."

Bingley looked at her thoughtfully. "I do not know if I would say that. Certainly she at last realized what sort of man would be willing to marry her, she did herself no favours last Season with her behaviour, even though Wickham has proven himself to be a blackguard. No, her dowry could not buy her the favour of the society she craved, so she accepted a man who did not mind her history."

"Does she love him?"

"Love?" Bingley smiled. "No, my sister has never considered love to be an important component in her marriage prospects. She wished to be greater than our mother. By marrying a man with an estate, she has achieved her goal."

"Is he kind?" Jane whispered.

"I do not fear for her well-being, Miss Bennet. He is ambitious, as she is. He is also not one to suffer foolishness. Success came to him through hard work, he is not weak. I think that they are well-suited."

"I understand that Mr. Robinson's estate is the same size as Longbourn."

"Yes, about two-thousand a year. His true income is from his business." Bingley tilted his head when she stared down at her hands. "Is something wrong?"

"Do you consider a small estate to be a disappointment?"

"I have no estate at all, Miss Bennet; I am not one to judge."

"But you have ambitions for something far greater, just as your sister did." She said steadily. "You also enjoy the attractions of London."

"I do, very much." He laughed and looked around him. "I suppose that my roots are more in this neighbourhood than in the one that I occupy at my brother's tolerance, but over the last year or so, I admit that I am becoming increasingly comfortable in Mayfair."

"Instead of Cheapside."

"I am not insulting your family, Miss Bennet." He creased his brow. "Trade is very much a part of my blood and unlike some who are leaving it to become gentlemen; I will not deny my roots. I do, however, wish to honour my father's desires."

"And live as my brother and sister do."

"Hardly." He laughed. "I have not, nor can I imagine ever achieving their income, or their property. But I do wish for a substantial estate, and I dearly love the pleasures of town. So in that light, I suppose that I have come to prefer the life that Darcy enjoys." Seeing her pensive expression, he asked, "Is that wrong?"

"No." She smiled and shrugged. "Of course not. What are your feelings about family?"

"The one I have or the one I hope for someday?" He sighed. "Well, my sister is settled so I can now relax. My eldest sister's husband is saved from drowning his sorrows in a bottle so he can relax, and I . . . I hope for a lovely angel of my own one day." He smiled at her and she met his smile with her own. "May I ask, what concerns you?"

She looked into his green eyes and let the warmth she always felt in his company to scatter the nagging doubts that were in her mind. "I have none; the life you describe is precisely one that any sensible woman would enjoy. My sister has certainly taken to hers."

"Ah, but Mr. and Mrs. Darcy will not be the social beings that I and my wife will be." He looked down at the hand on his arm and back up to her face. "I am no recluse. I envision enjoying the whirl of the Season, then hosting friends in my home. I look forward to parties and balls, hunting and dinners. I look forward to it all."

Jane nodded, and then turned her gaze ahead. "It sounds as if you plan a wonderful life."

DARCY TOOK ROSALIE from Elizabeth, then held out his hand to help her from the carriage. Exchanging weary glances, they walked up to the front door. Foster and Mrs. Mercer were waiting for them and other staff members looked on as the little family entered. "Oh Mr. and Mrs. Darcy!" Mrs. Mercer whispered and peeked at the sleeping baby in his arms. "She is precious!"

"Yes, she is." Elizabeth smiled.

"Congratulations sir, madam." Foster peeked as well. "It is good to see the next generation arrive, sir."

"Indeed." He looked at Elizabeth and she nodded, holding out her arms. "I will be up in a few minutes, love."

"There is no rush."

He kissed her cheek and watched her walk up the stairs alone. Foster and Mrs. Mercer exchanged glances.

"Sir, may I get you anything?" Foster asked.

"No, thank you." He smiled slightly and walked down the hallway to the library and closed the door.

"What is wrong?" Mrs. Mercer asked, and spotting Adams entering behind the footmen with their trunks, accosted him. "Adams! Millie!" He joined them, and introduced Mrs. Robbins. "Is anything wrong? They have always been so happy! Why have they separated?"

"They are fine, now anyway. That first day though . . ." He looked at Mrs. Robbins and Millie, "Well, let us say that the trip began with no little tension. But the last two days have been better, even if we were enlisted to take turns with the child."

"That is what we are paid to do, Mr. Adams." Mrs. Robbins said sternly.

"*You* are paid for child care."

"And *You* are paid for Mr. Darcy's care." She reminded him. "Giving him some peace is part of that."

"I am glad to be in a house again." Millie squeaked. "And I am going up to care for Mrs. Darcy. Excuse me." She went up the stairs and the four older servants looked at each other. Mrs. Mercer raised her brows at Adams. "*And a child shall lead us.*"[5]

"It is good to be home." He smiled and started to climb the stairs, then stopped. "I would start some bath water warming, for both of them."

"One bath?" Mrs. Mercer asked.

Adams laughed. "Prepare for two, and I will be prepared for one." He turned. "Mrs. Robbins, your duty?"

"Very amusing, Adams." She retorted and followed him.

Mrs. Mercer and Foster watched them go. "Well, it seems to have been a challenging journey, but our honeymoon continues." Foster said thoughtfully. "I wonder if they will leave the baby at Pemberley next time."

"I hope that the trip back will not be so difficult." Mrs. Mercer fretted.

"I have a feeling that they will be remaining in town longer than expected," he chuckled, "to avoid the trip home. We will hear the entire story tonight."

Darcy sat in the leather chair next to the unlit fireplace and closed his eyes. He could hear the creaking of the floorboards above him as their things were put away. In the hallway he heard muffled voices, but here in his room, his sanctuary, there was blessed silence. He drew a long deep breath and relaxed, and tried to think of nothing for a half hour. A quiet knock roused him and a maid appeared.

"A bath is prepared for you, sir." She curtsied and disappeared quickly.

"Ah, that will feel good." He sighed. "Good man, Adams." He looked down at his coat; it was not as bad as it had been that first day, but here in this room that smelled of leather and parchment, he stank of urine and milk. "I am tired if I did not rip this all off immediately." He sighed and looked back at the ceiling, and wondered what Elizabeth was doing, and felt guilty for not going up sooner. She had it far worse than he. Opening the door, he nodded to the servants he passed, and made his way upstairs and into the nursery. Mrs. Robbins and the nursemaids were there, but no Elizabeth. He saw that Rosalie

---

[5] Isaiah 11:6, "And a child shall lead them."

was in her cradle and he touched her before leaving. Elizabeth was not in the mistress's chambers, not in the master's chambers, not anywhere. "Where are you?"

He entered their sitting room and there she was scratching away in her journal. Darcy took a seat and watched as her pen flew across the page. He knew it was something that she must have needed to express for some time; they had no opportunities to record their thoughts during the trip. His mind wandered over the possibilities until at last her pen ceased its movement. She read the passage over and her shoulders slumped. Darcy rose to stand behind her and rub the tension away. "Should I read that?"

"If you wish." She said softly.

"You know that I do." He bent and kissed her throat.

"Mrs. Darcy, your bath is prepared." Millie announced and disappeared.

"Excuse me." She stood and wiped her eyes. "I need to bathe; her napkin was very wet when we arrived." She drew a shaking breath, and smiled at him.

"Elizabeth . . ."

"Please Fitzwilliam, just leave me be for a while. I know that you understand." She left the room and he watched her go, then turning back to her journal, opened the book to the last entry.

6 *June 1810*

After three long days our journey has at last ended. While it would be perhaps theatrical to compare it to Homer's Odyssey, the overwhelming exhaustion that has settled over me since at last gaining the quiet peace of our bedchambers can, I think, be comparable to Odysseus' feelings when at last finding home.

This journey was not so much one of moving from one home to another, as one that I believe will define our marriage. We began at odds, each wanting to satisfy our individual desires, but not taking the time to listen to each other, and understand the reasons behind our vehement stances. We each stubbornly held onto our views, and it took a day of anger and hurt feelings between us, and a daughter who sensed our discord and made it clear that she did not like it, to force us to speak coherently, and at last understand. What fools we were!

I love you, Fitzwilliam. I love your patience and unending desire to care for everyone who is within your reach. I promise to listen to what you are trying to tell me, even when you do not quite know the proper words to make your desires clear. I thank you for understanding me when I become defensive, and I thank you for loving me despite my faults.

Darcy closed his eyes and sat down. "So this is what you think of me? I am a stubborn man who loves deeply and will do anything to care for you." He wiped a tear that appeared in his eye. "You know me so well."

Adams appeared. "Sir? Your bath?"

He stood and walked towards his dressing room, pausing to look through the mistress's chambers to her closed dressing room door, then silently turned and went to bathe and change. When he emerged, he learned that Elizabeth was lying down, and he wondered what to do, her tears were impressed on his memory, and the entire time that he soaked in his bath he wondered over the words of her journal. *She asked for some peace.* "Adams." He turned to the valet. "Please inform Millie and Mrs. Robbins that Mrs. Darcy is to be undisturbed. Rosalie is not to be brought to her, and I will speak to Mrs. Mercer about sending her a tray."

"Yes sir." He watched his master walk downstairs, and went to locate the other servants and pass on the news.

Elizabeth watched Millie carry in a tray and set it down on the table near the window. "What is this?"

"Mr. Darcy thought that you would prefer to enjoy your solitude this evening, madam." She lifted the cover to reveal a meal and Elizabeth rose from the bed and looked it over, and raising her hand to her mouth, laughed. Millie curtseyed and noting her mistress' response, disappeared to report to Adams, who in turn discretely told his master who was alone in his study reading letters. Darcy closed his eyes and sighed with relief, then glanced up at his parents' portrait. "I am trying, Mother. Women are a mystery."

Elizabeth shook her head as she inspected the tray, and saw that his journal had been placed prominently in the centre. She picked up the toast spread with her favourite marmalade, took a sip of the chocolate she adored, and laughed softly to see nearly every confection and morsel she had craved during her pregnancy. "You know my weaknesses and are plying me with them, Fitzwilliam Darcy." Elizabeth whispered, then opening up his journal to the page marked by her lover's knot, she read his assessment of their trip.

6 June 1810
My dearest Elizabeth has compared our journey to one worthy of the Greek gods. I laugh to think of it in such a way. It was certainly a test of endurance and patience, as well as an opportunity to discover the parts of our individual personalities that lie dormant in the ease of the everyday. Ah yes my love, we are stubborn and caring partners. But that is the key word. We are partners, and because of that, because we choose not to waste time feeling insulted or misunderstood, and because we wish to live our lives together, our love will endure, and can only grow as we do. We may be fools, but I love being your fool, yours alone.

She closed his journal and smiled. "We have grown, I think." Looking around her empty room, she appreciated the gift of solitude he had offered her, but it was time to be partners again. Writing a little invitation, she rang the bell to have it delivered, and smiling, sat down to watch the clock and see how long it would take for him to arrive.

"YOU LET ME SLEEP!" Elizabeth hurried into the breakfast room the next morning. He raised the cup of coffee to his lips and took a sip, then leaned over to kiss her. "You never let me sleep!"

"Now that is a misstatement. Both of us are early risers." His eyes twinkled. "Besides we hardly slept all night."

"I feel as I did the morning after we wed." She whispered in his ear. "I waddle."

"And I ache." Their foreheads touched and she lovingly kissed him. Darcy sighed. "We should fight more often."

"Fitzwilliam! We have not fought for days."

"But we did not have the opportunity to make up properly until we were home, so we were still fighting until it was resolved." He winked at her when she rolled her eyes. "Perhaps we should . . ."

"What?"

"Hmmm, if I say it we will begin to fight and I do not think that we have time to fall into bed again before we are visited by the residents of Matlock House." He kissed her again. "But I will hold my thoughts for later."

"Be sure that you do." Elizabeth stroked his cheek and popped a bit of a bun into his mouth. "Eat."

"Hmm." He looked down at her barely contained bosom. "I know what I would like to drink."

"Leave some for our daughter, dear." She sat back and they laughed. "I am glad that we have worked out our plans for travel."

"I look forward to improving on them, I have some ideas." Darcy caught her eye. "But not for a few weeks."

"No, I am in no hurry, I assure you."

Foster entered the room and quickly hid the smile that appeared when he spotted the still besotted couple. "Sir, Miss Darcy's luggage has just arrived."

They exchanged glances. "If her luggage is here, then the family will not be far behind." Darcy smiled and Elizabeth sighed and turned to the butler.

"Foster, please notify Mrs. Mercer, and have . . . Well whatever is available brought up for refreshments, we will be in the yellow drawing room. Please ask Mrs. Robbins to bring Rosalie."

"Yes, madam." He bowed and left to speak the orders to a footman.

"Well so much for our quiet breakfast." Darcy sighed and putting down his napkin rose as she did. "The Gardiners are coming for dinner, along with the Matlock group, and I invited Bingley to join us."

"You did?" Elizabeth took his offered hand and they walked towards the door. "When did this happen?"

"When you were luxuriating in your bath and I was trying not to burst in on you last night, love." He raised her hand to his lips. "Four days without you are four days too long."

"You make it sound as if we are like rabbits every night." Darcy chuckled and she smiled at him. "But I agree that the reunion makes the wait worthwhile." She leaned against him and they went into the drawing room. The sound of voices downstairs alerted them that the family had arrived. Georgiana led the way inside and hearing where they were, flew up the stairs.

"Georgiana!" Lady Matlock admonished.

"Leave her be, dear." Lord Matlock grinned. "It has been a very long wait for her and the moment she stepped over that threshold she returned to Darcy's care."

Chuckling, Fitzwilliam took Evangeline's hand and they were the first to follow Georgiana. He called over his shoulder to the rest of the laughing family, "We have been abandoned."

"I think that you need to rescue them from their sister." Layton said and smiled at Alicia. "I do believe that our cousin is ready to be home again."

"I cannot say that I blame her." Alicia whispered and nodded at his mother.

He cleared his throat and hid a smirk. "I will not address that statement."

"I am surprised that you are not running yourself." Evangeline smiled and Fitzwilliam squeezed her hand. "You have spoken of nothing but seeing Darcy for days."

"You make me sound lovesick." He laughed. "I want to meet this amazing child they have brought into the world. She is a prodigy, you know."

"At the tender age of two months?" She smiled at him when he shrugged.

"Fitzwilliam!" Georgiana squealed. "Elizabeth!" She threw her arms around her brother and they hugged tight. "Oh it is wonderful to see you!"

"I missed you as well, dear." He kissed her and she was gone and accosting Elizabeth. "Gently dear!" He admonished. "Do not crush your sister!"

"I can bear a hug." Elizabeth smiled. "I missed you. I cannot wait to have you back at Pemberley."

"I cannot wait to go! Mary is so excited! She and Jane will be here for dinner, did you know? The Gardiners are anxious to see Rosalie. Can we go and meet her now? Do we have to wait until everyone is here? Oh it feels so good to be home again! You look wonderful!"

"Breathe, Georgiana!" Elizabeth laughed and squeezed her hand.

Georgiana nodded happily and looked eagerly around. "Where is Rosalie?"

"Here she comes." Darcy looked up when he heard his daughter's voice, and held out his arms to accept her from Mrs. Robbins.

"Ah the Darcy family, reunited." Fitzwilliam stepped forward and grinned. "You are stunning, Elizabeth! I am so proud of you." He whispered hoarsely as he hugged her. "Everything is well?" Elizabeth saw Evangeline smiling and shaking her head, and when Darcy cleared his throat, Fitzwilliam let go, grinning unrepentantly.

"Richard, I am well, truly!" She squeezed his arm and kissed his cheek. "Come and meet our little girl."

"Ah the miracle child." He sniffed and leaned over his cousin to see her. "You are beautiful, my dear."

Elizabeth embraced Evangeline and whispered, "What has come over him?"

"He was overwhelmed with the story of her birth, as were we all. He admitted to me that he would not have done well. He witnessed a woman give birth and die along with the babe when he was in Spain, and it affected him deeply. You must have been so frightened."

Elizabeth caught Darcy's eye and he took her hand. "We were both terrified, but had no time to feel anything until it was long over."

Fitzwilliam turned to Darcy, who handed Rosalie to Elizabeth, then the two cousins embraced and laughed. "I think that they need some time alone." Evangeline suggested.

"I think that you are correct." Elizabeth smiled and laughed at Georgiana. "I have never seen such a smile on your face!" She nodded happily and peeked at the baby. Elizabeth drew back the blanket. "Meet your niece, Rosalie."

"Ohhhhh." Georgiana was enchanted. "May I hold her?"

"Of course, but I think that we should finish greeting everyone first." Elizabeth took her hand. "You are happy to be home, I think."

"I am." She sighed. "I am so happy. I am happy to be with you and Fitzwilliam again, I am happy to be returning to Pemberley with you. I am happy to leave London."

"Was school so terrible?" She looked over to where Darcy and Fitzwilliam stood talking by the window. "I thought that you enjoyed it."

"Yes. Not like Mary did, though."

"Well, Mary had an entirely different upbringing. This was a whole new world for her."

"She is dying to see you, and so is Jane. Aunt Helen is anxious to get you to the modiste for your new ball gown." Elizabeth glanced at Alicia who rolled her eyes.

"I am sure that she is, and we will see them tonight along with Mr. Bingley." She looked over to Darcy and caught his eye. He grinned and clapping Fitzwilliam's shoulder, the cousins returned to the family.

"You are beautiful, Elizabeth." Layton kissed her cheek and touched Rosalie's hair. "As is your daughter. I think that Margaret would be jealous of these curls."

"Is she still bald?" Elizabeth laughed.

"I understand that a few wisps have appeared." He said softly. "We will be returning to Matlock soon."

Everyone found seats and Lady Matlock held out her arms. Elizabeth looked apologetically at Georgiana and carefully placed Rosalie in her great-aunt's embrace. "She is the image of you, Darcy." Lady Matlock said softly as she cradled her.

"No, she is her mother." Darcy took Elizabeth's hand and kissed it.

"My eyes are brown."

"Your eyes are fine, as are our daughter's." He smiled into them. "Are you sporting for an argument?"

"Oh ho!" Fitzwilliam laughed. "The Darcys argue? Now that would be a treat. You two could not so much as argue as I could . . .deliver a baby alone in the woods."

The family laughed and Darcy and Elizabeth looked at their clasped hands. "Believe whatever you wish, Cousin."

"Lady Helen, may I?" Alicia held out her arms. The baby was traded to her. Layton sat by her side and placed his arm around her shoulder. "It is nice to see a baby with so much hair." She said tearfully.

"How was the journey with her?" Layton asked without looking away. "We thought it would be too difficult so we decided Margaret was best left at home."

"It was a challenge." Elizabeth agreed. "And we will certainly do things differently on the return journey."

"And avoid the argument that began this one." Darcy added with a wink to Fitzwilliam.

"Aha." Lord Matlock chuckled. "I thought as much. You two are going to be like Helen and me, I think."

"And what is that, Uncle?" Darcy smiled. "I have never seen you two disagree."

Laughter travelled the room and Rosalie began to fuss. Elizabeth stood and walked over to her. "She is ready to be fed, excuse me." She picked her up and left the room. The women watched her go, wondering over her actions and the men regarded Darcy with sympathy.

"How are you holding up, Son?" Lord Matlock leaned to him and said quietly. "She is sure to have this out of her system before long; she cannot keep you waiting a year. No wonder you argue, you must put your foot down."

Darcy met his eye and smiled, then turned to Evangeline. "I understand that congratulations are in order."

"Richard!" She cried.

"I am sorry, dear. I had to tell him." He stood and placed his hands on her shoulders, and faced the room. "My lovely bride is in the family way."

"Eva!" Lady Matlock hugged her. "Oh my dear! When?"

"Early December, we think." She looked up at her beaming husband. "We were going to wait a little longer to announce, but it seems that my husband is unstoppable."

"I am overwhelmed." Fitzwilliam gladly received hugs and wiped his eyes. "Look at me! I cry as much as my wife!"

Darcy chuckled and walked from the room in search of Elizabeth. He found her across the hallway on a sofa. "What happened? I heard cheering."

"Eva is with child." He kissed her and watched Rosalie feed. "He is overjoyed but a nervous mess, he was desperate to hear me tell him all would be well."

"She is likely terrified." Elizabeth said softly.

"We could invite them to Pemberley for her confinement." He laughed when she sighed. "I think that he would wish to participate in a more traditional manner, though." He stood when there was a knock at the door and Lady Matlock entered. "Your sister misses you." She announced and gave Darcy a look.

He squeezed Elizabeth's hand. "I will go and reassure her that you will soon return."

Lady Matlock took his place and watched mother and daughter. "You know that I strongly disagree with this behaviour."

"I do." She smiled and stroked Rosalie's cheek. "But it is not your concern, is it?" Lady Matlock's brows rose and she started to speak, but Elizabeth was first. "We told you the week of our marriage that we would follow our own path, Aunt. We know that you disapprove and that you have made your feelings clear to your daughters. I am only concerned with my husband's feelings, and he is content."

"Be careful Elizabeth. Darcy has needs that a wife must fulfil."

"And who says that I am not caring for them?" Elizabeth met her eye and Lady Matlock's widened. "Do not question the way that we choose to raise our children, Aunt Helen, or the way that we conduct our marriage. It may not be what you would expect for yourself or your children, and it may not be what society considers proper, but we are very happy, and that is what matters to us, and is our concern alone."

"How old are you now?"

"I will be nineteen in August."

"What will you be when you come of age?" Lady Matlock smiled slightly. "Very well, I will stay out of your business and only offer my opinion if asked. I do not agree with your choices, but I will not say anything more. Clearly it will fall on deaf ears."

"I appreciate that, Aunt Helen." Elizabeth rubbed Rosalie's back. "Are you taking the place of my mother-in-law?"

"I have a feeling that Lady Anne Darcy would be on your side of the argument." She stood and Elizabeth joined her at the door. "You have matured a great deal since I last saw you."

Elizabeth kissed Rosalie's hair, and smiled. "I am a mother now."

Chapter 14

"Elizabeth!" Bingley's mouth dropped open when he entered the drawing room. Darcy coughed loudly and Bingley blinked and blushed. "Forgive me, Mrs. Darcy, I . . . I had forgotten how . . . I am . . . You look lovely." He sputtered and met Darcy's raised brow. He knew full well why Bingley reacted as he did. Bearing a child had done extraordinary things to Elizabeth's already lovely figure, and deep down, the possessive little boy in him was jumping up and down with glee at his friend's response.

She looked between the red-faced man and her husband, noted the pleasure in Darcy's expression, and took Bingley's hands in hers. "Thank you, you are looking exceptionally handsome yourself."

"Well that is laying it on rather thick, but I thank you." He laughed and recovered his composure. "Forgive me. How is your little girl? Will I meet her this evening?"

"If you like, I have no doubt that my family will demand to see her. Fitzwilliam's family met her this morning when they brought Georgiana home." She titled her head. "Do you like children?"

"Well as much as any man." He shrugged. Just then Georgiana entered the room and he beamed at her. "Of course some children should be left in the nursery."

"To practice their letters?" Georgiana sniffed, then curtseyed. "Good evening, Mr. Bingley."

"Good evening Miss Darcy." His eyes twinkled. "Shall I receive another lesson, tonight?"

"If you have not taken the time to practice then it is a waste of mine to teach you. Perhaps some schoolbooks would be more useful." She looked up to him sternly then blushed and became shy. "Forgive me. That was rude."

"Not at all, it was well-deserved." Bingley bowed. "I provoked you."

"What are these lessons?" Darcy said quietly, and looked up to Elizabeth who was watching the pair with great interest.

"Oh, I recommended that Mr. Bingley practice his letters." Georgiana darted across the room to watch for the Gardiner's carriage before her brother could comment.

"A worthy enterprise." Darcy said to his friend, who was still smiling after Georgiana.

"It was." He laughed and turned back to Elizabeth. "I do not wish to run afoul of Mrs. Darcy again."

"So you heard. Mr. Bingley you are an unmarried man and what you do with your time is your business, however, I think that it could be spent far more productively, particularly if you intend to marry a good woman someday." She glared at him and went to join her sister at the window.

"Well. I am in trouble with two women and the entire party has not arrived." He grimaced and caught Darcy tilting his head and considering him. "What is it?"

"I have never seen Georgiana tease anyone outside of family before. Why you, I wonder."

"She only sees me in the company of family, perhaps in her eyes I am accepted as such?" Bingley shrugged. "She is growing into a lovely young lady, Darcy. You will be beating them off with a stick before long." He smiled at her as she whispered to Elizabeth. "She will be wonderful, I am sure. She will know all of the social necessities from Lady Matlock and school, but she will benefit most from that indescribable extra that Mrs. Darcy will provide. Some young man will be very fortunate one day."

"Indeed." Darcy said softly and caught Elizabeth's eye. She had clearly remembered his story of Georgiana asking after Bingley last autumn, and had formed an identical thought now.

"Oh, they are here!" Georgiana called.

The Gardiners, Mary, and Jane came upstairs and when the exclamations of joy and reunion settled, Bingley found himself seated next to Jane. He cleared his throat. "You look very well, Miss Bennet."

"Thank you sir, as do you." She said to her clasped hands.

"Darcy tells me that you will be accompanying him and Mrs. Darcy to St. James's on the anniversary of their wedding."

Jane looked up and spoke slowly, "Yes, Lady Matlock has been most insistent that I attend some event there, but I thought to wait until my sister arrived. Will you attend as well, sir?"

"Yes." He smiled softly. "I hope that I might beat the crowd of men by asking for your first set now?"

"Oh, I would like that very much." She smiled and blushed.

"Very good." He cleared his throat again and noticed that they were being watched, and found that the most disconcerting gazes came from the members of the Darcy family.

Elizabeth broke the silence. "Who would like to meet Rosalie?" All of the ladies departed and the men were left alone.

Darcy poured out some wine to enjoy while they awaited the party from Matlock House. "Well?" He handed Bingley his glass then took a seat. "What are you doing?"

"With regards to what?" He laughed and took a sip. "Choose a topic and I may just have an answer!"

Darcy smiled and heard Mr. Gardiner's chuckle. "Well, your sister, she is out of your way?"

"Indeed! She is Mrs. Robinson now. Her husband purchased a small estate two years ago, just to say that he has one, but lives mostly here to keep up with his business. He could care less about sport, but wants to fit in with the crowd." Bingley shrugged. "I do not particularly like him, a little too calculating for me, but Caroline likes his ambition to be at the top of society one day. He treats her well enough according to Louisa's observations. It is no love match, but they get along. She has her baubles, he has whatever charm she displays, they go about to the fashionable places. Who knows, maybe they will be in your circle one day and all of her dreams will be fulfilled."

"Remind me to be well away from town then." Darcy said dryly. "Fascinating that Mrs. Robinson wound up with a man who is both tradesman and landowner. What is his product? He does not happen to have a useful connection to contraband brandy does he?"

Bingley laughed. "If he does I dare not speak of it. No, he imports oranges, the sour kind that they use for marmalade, as well as other exotic fruits."

"We have a few trees at Pemberley in the hot houses, along with peaches and lemons. I think that my gardener started a few pineapples, as well." Darcy mused.

"Not everyone is you, Darcy." Bingley winked.

"Well if you ever purchase an estate, you too can enjoy these things." He jabbed back.

Placing his hand over his heart he gasped in horror. "And put my brother out of business?"

"Perhaps not. Forget that. So, speaking of estates, where do you stand? I ask this for several reasons." Seeing he had both Bingley's and Mr. Gardiner's attention he began, "First, we know that Netherfield has been largely neglected by its owner and have learned that the land is not yielding as it could due to the steward's refusal to embrace modern farming practices. Second, have you looked at other properties? And third, there is Jane Bennet."

Bingley shifted uncomfortably and looked down at his glass. "I was wondering when Miss Bennet would come up."

"Well?"

"Stewart and I rode out to see the estate last month. I know that you took a look at it last autumn and spoke to a neighbour." Darcy nodded, remembering his conversation with Robert Lucas and saw Mr. Gardiner's interest. "I think that it is the owner's problem to address."

"That is true, but he has not. By not fixing the problems now, he avoids the cost, and you would lose the time waiting for the fields to improve after you take possession should you buy. You will need that income right away, you cannot afford to wait. This should be made clear to this owner. I cannot understand his neglect."

"He does not care about it much. I am dealing with his solicitor." Bingley shrugged. "Your concern about my looking at other properties . . . I have, but I want to be near London, my life is here. I am more accepted, Caroline is married off, I love all that there is to see and do . . . The other estates that my solicitor has identified are too far away. If I was married and settled, then a lovely estate near Pemberley would be ideal." He smiled at his friend. "I would like that more than anything."

"Thank you." Darcy smiled. "But that leaves us with the next question. How goes it with Jane? If you are courting her . . ."

"I am not, not officially. We have met at a few balls and dinners; I come to visit the Gardiners. I have escorted her to the theatre . . ."

"Have you escorted any other ladies?"

"No." He said softly. "But I have danced a great deal."

"And you continue to visit courtesans. That tells me that your heart is not engaged, Bingley." He saw his friend stare down at his glass and continued. "If you take Netherfield, it will be a signal to Miss Bennet that you are more serious than you seem to be."

"You sound like Mr. Gardiner." He looked up to see the older man raise his brows.

"Well, I have been silent enough. I was waiting for Darcy to arrive before I said anything. You sir, are confusing my niece." He said pointedly. "You smile, you laugh, you visit, but make no move to telling her precisely your intentions. You have spoken of liking her, you have asked the advice of every man of your shared acquaintance, what exactly are you waiting to determine?"

"I am not sure." He noticed the expectant stares of his companions and tried to explain. "She smiles at me, and I believe that she makes an effort to display her accomplishments. My sisters wish for me to marry an heiress, naturally, but Caroline cannot discount the attraction that me married to Miss Bennet would give her a solid connection to you." Darcy grimaced. "Not that it would lead to an invitation, but still there is no denying family."

"All that is well and good Bingley, but do you feel anything for her? Do you feel love? Do you want to be with her?"

"What does love feel like?" He asked quietly.

"You know. I know that you loved one woman, or at least thought that you did once." Darcy said just as quietly. "I believe though, that what you felt in that case was deeply caring for another person's happiness, and a wish to contribute to that in some way. You have never felt what it is to want to give yourself to another person for the rest of your life; you may not have met that person yet. Do you feel anything that resembles that level of care, or are your attentions to Miss Bennet done out of some feeling of obligation? You felt her admiration and knew of her disappointment with Harwick, and you did not wish to be the subject of another heartbreak for her?" Bingley looked up to Darcy and he tried to read the truth in his friend's eyes. "Whatever you do Bingley, do not marry because you feel an obligation to spare her feelings. This is a lifetime commitment, not a dance with an angel for half an hour. Regret will come fast and never be relieved."

"I do not know what I feel." He heard Darcy release a frustrated breath and tried to put his mixed emotions into words. "I like her. She likes me. I know that she is not after my money, after all if that was her motivation she would have secured Harwick in a heartbeat." Seeing Darcy nod his head thoughtfully he went on. "She is beautiful, which is no small thing." He smiled to see the other men exchange glances. "Last autumn when I spoke to Elizabeth, Mrs. Darcy, about this, she asked me if I was lonely, and if that was my motivation. I am." He sighed. "Everyone around me, my closest friends are married and happy."

"We are also older, and settled in our respective lives." Darcy said seriously. "Are you considering Jane because you think that you will achieve the contentment that we have found?"

"She is part of a wonderful family." Bingley said quietly. "I speak of the Darcys, Fitzwilliams, and Gardiners."

Mr. Gardiner placed his hand on Bingley's shoulder. "I consider you to be a great friend of my family, and I have enjoyed acting as a sort of father for you these past few months. I will not relinquish that relationship if you do not offer for Jane."

"You are also well aware that my friendship is unshakable, and that Elizabeth loves you as a brother, as does Georgiana, it seems. However, I will not lightly tolerate Jane being hurt should you play with her affections then choose against her. She is my sister."

"What should I do?" He looked between the men.

"Have you shown Jane precisely the life you hope to achieve?" Mr. Gardiner asked seriously. "If you are undecided, it may be because you do not know if she will fit into the life you imagine. Now that Darcy and Lizzy are here, perhaps the four of you can go out together."

"Show her your world. If she rejects it on her own, she will not feel regret should you both decide against this possible alliance." Darcy agreed. "I know that Pemberley is not to her liking."

"Yes, she mentioned that to me once." Bingley said softly. "I could never afford it, but I love the estate."

Darcy tried again. "Perhaps you are lost in her beauty but have not looked at the woman beneath the face. I do not know, but in my experience, when I first saw Elizabeth, I knew that she was the one, even though I thought that she could never be mine. I suppose not every love match happens at first sight." He sighed when he saw Bingley's creased brow. "Tell me, what do you want out of your wife? Someone to run your household and be pleasant, to be pretty to look at and compliant to your desires? Someone who never bothers you with the details of children and servants? Someone who does not question your activity during the day, but is there to serve you when you return? Someone to ornament your arm when you go out together?"

Bingley's mouth opened and closed. "I . . . well, is that not . . . from your description it seems that wishing for those things is wrong? I was not raised in a gentleman's household, but certainly . . ." He looked at Mr. Gardiner. "Does not Mrs. Gardiner work to make your home as pleasant as possible for you when you return from work?"

"Of course, but I also married her to be a companion of my mind as well. Just as Darcy has chosen Lizzy." Darcy smiled and looked down, and Mr. Gardiner chuckled. "Well I suspect that Darcy's choice of my niece is rather more complicated than that."

"It is." He met Mr. Gardiner's gaze then looked back to Bingley. "So you need to decide not only if you wish to marry, but what sort of a life you wish to lead. If you are seeking a woman to please you, I have no doubt that Jane is ideal. If you are seeking a woman to stimulate more than your libido . . ." He grew silent for a moment. "I do not have an answer. Jane must decide what sort of a life she wishes to have, and as the wife of a man like you, she could lose herself in the social whirlwind or take the path that I suspect Elizabeth will, dedicating herself to good works and becoming a formidable woman in the society she chooses to inhabit. We will be glad to go enjoy some evenings with you both, and then there is the ball at St. James's. Be yourself, completely yourself, and then she can decide. I will ask Elizabeth to give Jane the same advice, and you can decide as well. But only *you* can decide. And my friend, it is time that you do."

"Very well then." Bingley lifted his glass in a toast to the air. "To honesty."

"So?" Elizabeth looked over to the corner where Mary and Georgiana were delighting in the baby then back to Jane. "How are things with Mr. Bingley?"

"He is a very kind man." She said softly. "He comes and visits; and we have been dance partners many times; and . . . Oh Lizzy! I do not know what to think!" Her hands twisted and she looked at Mrs. Gardiner for help.

"He is a good man, of that I have no doubt at all. Edward has spent a great many hours with him over the past months; I would say they have almost a father-son relationship. When Mr. Bingley was working so hard to assure his sister's suitor was right and then to accomplish the wedding, he was a nervous wreck. It was good that Jane was with us in the end, to provide him a warm smile when he would emerge from the study."

"Are you courting?" Elizabeth asked.

"No." Jane sighed. "He has not asked, he . . . He has so much on his mind."

Again Mrs. Gardiner stepped in and spoke to Elizabeth. "You know that he is considering leasing Netherfield?" Elizabeth nodded. "We believe that he is hoping to conclude that transaction before he settles into any other commitments. With him right there, Jane could return home and they could court easily. Of course after marriage they would split their time between Netherfield and London. He seems to slowly be making inroads into society; at least he is receiving invitations on his own now."

"He seems to be very interested in enjoying all that London offers." Jane added.

"Does that appeal to you?" Elizabeth grasped her hand. "I know that you are more of a homebody."

"I am, but so are you and Mr. Darcy, and you seem to manage quite well."

"Yes, but Fitzwilliam has no need to establish his name. He is already a powerful man, but he chooses not to exercise it, and does not wish to deal with the *ton* any more than necessary. I am enjoying caring for him, our child, and our home, but I am also taking on duties related to our tenants, and eventually I hope to follow Aunt Helen in her work with the many charities that can use our attention."

Mrs. Gardiner returned to the subject. "Do you like him, Jane?"

"Very much." She smiled. "How can I not? He can make the lowliest maid feel good."

Elizabeth glanced at her aunt then back to her sister. "Your letters have not spoken of deeper feelings."

"No."

"From either of you."

"No."

"I know that you feel that you should not display your preference for a gentleman first . . ."

"I used to feel that way, Lizzy."

"So if you felt something for Mr. Bingley . . ."

"We were both in town on May Day." She smiled a little. "But I did not take advantage of it and express feelings of love for him." Elizabeth looked at her seriously. "As I said Lizzy, he is kind and lovely to everyone."

"But he does not pay you particular attention?"

"He is not at my side every moment."

"Do not compare him to Fitzwilliam." Elizabeth said seriously. "He is the exception to the rule."

"No, I know that." Jane sighed. "I do not know what it is precisely. It is almost as if he is fulfilling an obligation by coming around."

"Fitzwilliam has mentioned that Mr. Bingley has an appreciation for lovely women." Elizabeth said carefully and met Mrs. Gardiner's eye.

Jane did not catch the silent communication between the married women and continued musing, "I wonder if his appreciation is short-lived and I have given him nothing to particularly desire for a lifetime, but he continues with me . . .”

“Because he sees your desire for him?”

“I thought that I desired him.” She said softly.

“But now?” Mrs. Gardiner prodded.

“Perhaps I am the one that feels an obligation to continue. Lady Matlock is quite determined to succeed with this match. She is difficult to resist.” She looked up to see Elizabeth roll her eyes. “You agree?”

“I had a discussion with her this morning about my choices for caring for my daughter and husband. The trick to managing Lady Matlock is to stand up to her. She respects that.”

Mrs. Gardiner nodded. “I agree, Jane. She is a forceful woman, but she appreciates anyone who has an opinion and states it. However, she has put a great deal of effort into your improvement, and I understand her desire to see you achieve what she perceives as an ideal match for you.”

“I think that it would be an ideal match except . . . Well you already said it, Lizzy. I am a homebody. I see your life and it overwhelms me. Pemberley, Darcy House, the responsibility, the duties, the prestige, the social obligations, and you and Fitzwilliam do not even participate as you could. Mr. Bingley wants an estate, a townhouse, and the social whirlwind as well. He says outright that he intends to enjoy all that London has to offer and what comes with his position. I . . . I comprehend the security and the advantage I would feel with him, as well as for my children, but I just cannot see myself spending the rest of my life in this social fray that Lady Matlock has demanded I experience.”

“My goodness Jane!” Elizabeth exclaimed. “That is the most fervent declaration I have ever heard from you about your desires! Lady Matlock is rubbing off on you!” The three women laughed and the tension eased a little. “Now, tell me of Mr. Lucas. How does he figure into this?”

Jane looked at her hands. “He takes my breath away.”

“He reminds me of Fitzwilliam.” Elizabeth smiled. “Fitzwilliam with a small estate. He is hardworking and determined.”

“Yes.” Jane blushed. “I like how strong he is.”

“He is a man.” Elizabeth smiled. “I appreciate that of Fitzwilliam so much.”

“Mr. Bingley is sweet.”

“He is, and I care for him, but do you want someone sweet or do you want a man?”

“In a few years . . .”

“Mr. Bingley will be a man, too.” Mrs. Gardiner said softly. “Do you want to wait, or return to the man who is ready for you now? Would you regret not adapting your feelings about the social life Mr. Bingley desires and losing him? With marriage and children that activity may decrease significantly if he is the man I believe he will be. I wonder how much of that desire to be a part of society is really him attempting to fulfil his father's wishes that he become a gentleman? It would be an entirely different life with Mr. Lucas, perhaps even less than what you know at Longbourn." Mrs. Gardiner held her hand. "You have to choose between two homes that are not just miles, but worlds apart."

"DARCY, CONGRATULATIONS!" Peter de Bourgh smiled and shook his hand. "How is your lovely bride?"

Darcy smiled. "My wife is showing off our daughter to the ladies and is radiant. How are your ladies? I understand that your sisters are both engaged?"

"Yes." He chuckled and accepted the glass of wine that Bingley poured for him. "Mother hoped that they might change their minds, now that they are gentlewomen, and quite young, but their hearts are set on marrying navy men." His chest puffed. "I cannot help but be proud of them."

"I suppose that you hope for something of that dedication in a lady one day." Bingley smiled.

"I can only hope. Well, at least my sisters are safe now. I will always have a home for my mother and I am proud that I can assure her and my sisters security should something befall their husbands."

"That is a sad reality." Mr. Gardiner murmured.

"One I am fortunate to escape." De Bourgh agreed without emotion.

Darcy broke the silence that fell between the men. "George Wickham sets sail to Australia next month." He said grimly. "What do you know of the passage south?"

"It is not trouble-free, but the winter storms should be subsided by the time they arrive. It takes about four months; I have made the trip myself a few times over the years. It is not comfortable for crew or cargo, but it is in the captain's interest to keep them alive. He earns a bonus for live bodies to sell."

"I wonder what would be preferable, to die on board the ship or be sent to a colony for my sentence." Bingley mused. "Neither is appealing."

"Then do not commit a crime." De Bourgh grinned and looked up when the ladies appeared. Elizabeth was arm and arm with Mary. "Who is that?" He said softly.

Darcy looked between de Bourgh and the ladies. "My wife and her sister."

"She is lovely."

"My *wife* or my *sister*?" Darcy asked pointedly.

Mr. Gardiner chuckled when de Bourgh startled. "Answer quickly sir, Darcy is not patient with gawkers."

"Seriously man, would I openly comment on your enchanting wife? In your presence? I gave up my sword with my uniform. That is Miss Mary, correct? Well she is different from a year ago, cannot a man notice?"

"I suppose." Darcy growled.

"She attended school with Miss Darcy this year, as I recall." He tilted his head and smiled at her. Mary's brow creased and she whispered to Elizabeth. De Bourgh looked to Darcy. "Seventeen?"

"Almost. In August." He said quietly and darted a look at Elizabeth who was watching de Bourgh.

"Ah." De Bourgh grinned and decided to fluster Darcy some more. "Well then, I will have to refrain from paying a call for another month."

"See that you do."

"What is all this?" Fitzwilliam's voice boomed. "Darcy, your hackles are raised. Do not tell me you are going to call out our cousin?" He entered with Evangeline and turned to de Bourgh. "What have you done to our host?"

"Not a thing." He smiled. "I only enquired after his sister. In fact, perhaps I should leave him and go greet Mrs. Darcy." He winked at Fitzwilliam and bowed over Evangeline's hand before departing.

"Which sister?" Fitzwilliam said under his breath. "Georgiana?"

"No, Mary."

Evangeline rolled her eyes. "Richard." He turned to her. "Behave."

"Of course, my dear!" They watched her walk over to greet Elizabeth and put their heads back together. "Well?"

"He noticed that she was . . . improved in looks." Darcy said delicately. "She is a bit."

"She is no Elizabeth or Jane." Fitzwilliam said softly. "But . . ."

"I like Mary very much; I do not wish her to be hurt by an ex-navy man who undoubtedly knows his way around the world." They looked at each other and Fitzwilliam grinned. "You have exchanged stories, I suppose."

"We have." He shrugged. "What do you expect? Neither of us likes to discuss military battles, but battles female, that is something we can share without difficulty, at least when my lovely wife is not present." He smiled and Darcy let down a little. "Come on, if he pays her a little attention it will do her some good, do you not think so? Boost her morale and all that?"

"I suppose." Darcy said cautiously. "She is my responsibility for the foreseeable future, and I have a feeling it will be until she marries. If she does."

"The man has two sisters, Darcy. He knows what he is doing, neither of those girls are goddesses, he got all the looks in that family. I think that he just might be bestowing some brotherly attention to a plain girl." Darcy sighed and Fitzwilliam grinned. "Besides, Elizabeth is there. She would throttle him."

"So true." Darcy shrugged and smiled at Elizabeth. She raised her brows at him and her lips twitched when she saw him relax, then turned back to the conversation.

De Bourgh continued with his story. "So you see; I am in a quandary. My pastor has given notice that he wishes to retire, and my brother Michael has not taken Holy Orders yet. It will be another month or so."

"But is there not a curate at Hunsford?" Mary asked. "He could take over the duties until your brother is there. Certainly the reverend at my home church has his curate give the sermons often enough. I believe that he has several livings. It is quite unfair if you think of it. All of these young men searching for positions and one man going about, glad-handing the different estate owners and collecting the livings, and becoming quite rich in the process." She huffed. "I do not like the system at all! After all, if you had not inherited Rosings, what fate would your brother have suffered?"

"He would likely be a curate." De Bourgh smiled. "You take a great interest in the affairs of the church."

"Well, I care that the concepts of it be followed, and somehow power has become more attractive than the commandments."

"That is true in any field, Miss Mary. Whether it is politics, military, or even in a shop. I imagine that you care more for the well-being of the people who look up to the leaders."

"Is that incorrect?"

"No, not at all. As a ship's captain I knew that to be productive I needed a healthy and relatively content crew. The same applies to my tenants now." He smiled at her. "Where did you learn your opinions? Did you serve on board one of my ships and I failed to notice?"

Mary blushed. "Captain de Bourgh, you are being silly." She peeked up to see his brows were still raised. "I learned everything that I needed to know from Lizzy."

De Bourgh grinned. "Mrs. Darcy?" Mary nodded and he turned to her. "Well done! Your daughter will be wonderful!"

"Well she already is, sir, but I cannot help but thank you for the compliment. Both of you." Elizabeth hugged her sister. "What will become of Mr. Collins?"

"Honestly, I do not particularly care, but he did mention that he has applied for a church near Meryton." Elizabeth's eyes grew wide. "He said he would one day inherit an estate . . . oh, Longbourn, that is your family's estate, is it not? Well, the little weasel!"

"He is planning to come and sit like a spider to watch his inheritance?" Elizabeth gasped. "No!"

"I am afraid so, Mrs. Darcy. I believe that he has already received his call to take the post. He said the current curate will receive a living in the north somewhere."

"Oh Mama will have a fit!" Elizabeth murmured. "Excuse me." She swept over to Darcy and whispered the news to him.

"You know what Mama will do; she will demand that one of my sisters marry him!" She darted looks at Mary and Jane. "And as Mary will truly be out in another month . . ."

"Mary will be safe at Pemberley for the rest of her life if she chooses." Darcy said determinedly. "Jane?"

"Oh no, she will be married to one man or another." Elizabeth bit her lip and was thinking of Kitty and Lydia when she felt her husband's hand on her arm.

"What did that mean?" He said quietly. "I need to speak to you about Bingley."

"I need to speak to you about Jane." She whispered.

"Sir." Foster appeared and bowed. "This was delivered from Matlock House."

Darcy opened the note and read, then nodded. "Arthur Singleton has died." He looked up to Elizabeth and the conversation in the room stopped. "Uncle Henry apologizes that they will not be coming for dinner tonight. Audrey sent word to Matlock House with the news. They will all be making the journey to Ashcroft, and accompany the body there." He saw Fitzwilliam looking to him. "Your father asks that you come to the house this evening before they depart in the morning." He nodded and looked to Evangeline who came to his side.

"We will leave immediately. I am sorry Elizabeth." Fitzwilliam kissed her cheek. "I cannot leave town, so we will certainly be with you another evening soon."

"Of course, I understand." Elizabeth kissed Evangeline. "Come over whenever you can, and tell Aunt Helen we will miss their company."

"I will." Goodbyes were said all around and Fitzwilliam leaned next to Darcy and was handed the note. "Does it say what got the bastard?"

"There are no details but your father mentions apoplexy as a result of a heated argument with Singleton."

"I wonder if Robert finally had his chance to stand up to him and his father died of shock." Fitzwilliam handed the note back. "Well, I will let you know if there is more to report."

"Please tell your father to send our . . . offer of support should they need it, particularly with becoming master."

Fitzwilliam nodded grimly and taking Evangeline's arm, they departed. "What happened?" Elizabeth came over to hug him.

"We will talk of it later, love." He kissed her hair and hugged her tightly. "It seems that we will have a long night of talk tonight."

7 JUNE 1810

We were exhausted when we finally fell into our bed last night, and only managed a kiss before Fitzwilliam's eyes were closed and he was asleep on my shoulder. I must remember never to invite family over the day of our return to town again! Even a seriously depleted guest list did not help the fact that we were essentially entertaining from breakfast to bedtime.

There are entirely too many topics to wonder about this morning, and until I have Fitzwilliam's opinion and observations, I dare not speculate any more upon them lest I draw some markedly wrong conclusions. Oh, I should not even pretend that I can adhere to such a ridiculous notion! I must record these thoughts or burst! Was it my imagination or did I see my intensely shy sister Georgiana become almost flirtatious with Mr. Bingley? Aunt Helen would have banished her to the nursery if she had seen it! And did he respond in kind? What was that about? Georgiana has always had a little crush on the man, but my goodness, she is but fourteen! He would have years to wait for her! Does he even realize how he smiled at her? I am sure that he thinks of her as a sister, but I saw Fitzwilliam's surprise, oh what was he thinking?

Jane is another subject entirely. That she feels enormous pressure by Aunt Helen to be wooed by Mr. Bingley is understandable. The woman has put a great deal of effort into grooming Jane. I certainly sympathize, having experienced a similar process myself. Undoubtedly she feels an obligation to offer herself to him. But she speaks of Mr. Lucas with a light in her eyes. I have no idea what advice to give her. I would love to have Mr. Bingley as my brother, and I have no doubt at all that once he decided he was in love, he would be a devoted husband and father. But is he in love with Jane? Is she foolish to let him go? I want her to be happy, but is Mr. Lucas truly the means to that? Has she really considered what she would have as his wife? It would not even be what we had at Longbourn.

Oh, and Mary! What on earth was Captain de Bourgh up to? I hope he realizes that my poor sister walked around with stars in her eyes after his attention. I surely hope that he was simply being friendly, but I know full well that he has a bit of the rake in him, just as Richard does.

This is all too complicated, and to add Mr. Singleton's death on top of it! I need you Fitzwilliam! Please wake! I hear Rosalie, so I will stop my wild speculation and wait for my husband's calm reassurances before I jump to any more conclusions. My power to understand characters seems vastly depleted this morning.

Darcy closed the journal and blew out the breath he had been holding as he read, then rubbed his face. "You are not alone in this confusion, love." He closed his eyes and went over her questions. "Yes, I noticed Bingley, no; I do not think that he realizes how he responded to Georgiana. I do think that it was genuine care, but of a brotherly nature." He shook his head and stood to go lean on the window. "Georgiana was entirely too flirty with him, and I should have said something then to her, but she ran off to the window and withdrew from conversation with him, perhaps she realized her error. But . . .if it was just sisterly teasing, it would have been fine. Was it?" He began to pace up and down the small sitting room. "And Jane may be in love with Lucas? I cannot question who anyone loves, certainly not on material grounds, but for a woman with nothing to consider Lucas Lodge as her future . . . is it love or not? Why on earth am I caught up in matchmaking? I just wished to come to town and retrieve my sisters!" He came to a halt and placing his hands on the desk he closed his eyes and tried to relax. Hearing Elizabeth's voice drifting in from the nursery, he felt his tension ease and went to seek her out.

"Twinkle twinkle little star, how I wonder what you are. Up above the world so high, like a diamond in the sky. Twinkle twinkle little star, how I wonder what you are."[6]

Darcy leaned against the nursery door to watch Elizabeth rocking Rosalie and singing to her softly. "I know that tune, but the words I know have nothing to do with stars." He laughed when she looked up with a contented smile.

"What a difference a day outside of the carriage makes to all of our dispositions."

Darcy chuckled and kissed the baby. "So true, I could not agree more."

"She had a busy day yesterday. She slept through the night, which is a wonderful accomplishment." Elizabeth leaned down to bestow a kiss and found her hair caught up in Rosalie's little fists. "No, no, dear. Papa likes my hair."

"I certainly do." He helped her untangle the locks and was faced with his smiling girl. He knelt next to the rocker and sang to her softly the same tune. "Ah! vous dirai-je, Maman, ce qui cause mon tourment. Papa veut que je raisonne, Comme une grande personne. Moi, je dis que les bonbons, valent mieux que la raison."[7]

"hmmmm. I like my lyrics better." Elizabeth whispered as Rosalie's eyes closed. He carefully picked her up and walked around the room, cooing at her as Elizabeth fixed her gown. He sang the tune to her again then placed her into the cradle. Elizabeth pulled the bell for the maid to return then they stood looking down at her as they waited.

"My lyrics are about Papa."

"Papa liking thinking better than candy." She giggled and leaned into his embrace. "Well Papa, what will we talk about this morning?"

Darcy kissed the top of her head. "Bingley is unsure of Jane."

"Jane is unsure of him, and thinks she cares for Mr. Lucas."

"Yes, I read your journal." He sighed. "Bingley could give her so much more."

"I know." Elizabeth snuggled into his chest. "What should we do?"

"I would prefer to remain out of it." Darcy said quietly. "Is that possible?"

"I do not know that they will let us." She looked up to see his frown. "What of Georgiana?"

---

[6] Jane Taylor, Rhymes for the Nursery, "The Star," 1806.

[7] Translation: Ah! Vous dirai-je Maman! Mozart, 1785,

Ah! I shall tell you, mum, That which causes my torment. Papa wants me to reason like an adult. I say that sweets are better than reason.

"I do not think that he realizes what he does, he is a big brother." He met her eyes. "And she is still feeling a crush, I think, that is all."

"I was not too much older when I fell in love with you." Elizabeth reminded him.

"A year when you are that young is a very long time."

"I know, although it was closer to two years." She said softly and embraced his waist. "And even then I waited yet another two for you."

"Our anniversary of our first sight is approaching, love. I would like to celebrate it with you." He smiled when she beamed at him. "A picnic by that particular bench?"

Elizabeth squeezed him tightly. "Oh yes! And a walk through Kensington Gardens? I could show you where I spied on you, and saw Miss Bingley try to latch onto your arm."

Darcy chuckled and kissed her. "Mrs. Robinson."

"Thankfully *not* Mrs. Darcy."

"No, no. That position was yours, even then." They hugged, and did not hear the door open when the nursemaid arrived. Her embarrassed "oh" roused them, and they left the room. "Well?"

"Well." Elizabeth put her hands on her hips and looked at him. "Stay out of it unless we are asked?"

"Fate was our friend, love. Let us see what it has in store for them." He held out his arm for her and grinned. "Care for a stroll in the park before breakfast? We can talk about our friends' tangled lives."

"We will walk alone?" She asked hopefully.

He opened the door to the hallway. "I have a feeling that moments alone will soon become precious commodities."

"And we will take full advantage of every one."

"MRS. DARCY, may we offer our congratulations?" Mrs. Gannon smiled stiffly as they met in the lobby of the theatre the following evening. "You have a daughter?"

"Yes, we do." Elizabeth smiled up to Darcy who was smiling warmly at her. "We could not be more pleased."

"Of course, of course." Mrs. Gannon glanced at Victoria standing silently by her side and looking unhappily at Darcy.

Elizabeth turned to her and inclined her head. "How are you enjoying your Season, Miss Gannon?"

"Oh, it is quite agreeable, Mrs. Darcy." She looked at Elizabeth's hands wrapped around Darcy's arm and turned to her mother. "I believe that Mr. Walker has arrived, we should greet him." She smiled at Darcy. "You know him, do you not? He is the heir of Oakland, in Devon?"

Darcy nodded. "Yes, we have met." Seeing that he was not going to add to the conversation, the ladies curtsied and moved off. "I thought that she would do well, she is too young to settle, and of course she might just be chasing him."

"What do you mean?" Elizabeth whispered.

"Mr. Walker is a man who is waiting impatiently for his father to pass on." He smiled. "And he is also renowned for being a goat." Elizabeth pinched him. "Forgive me love, but it is the truth, although, he is not unlike her uncle, Lord Creary, or her father for that matter." Shrugging, he looked after her. "I suspect that she is not concerned with that since she grew up with the behaviour."

"I am so grateful that you would never consider such a thing."

Hearing her serious tone, he smiled back at her. "Never."

"There you are, Darcy." Bingley approached with Jane on his arm. "We have been greeting friends. Do you know Frederick Hamilton? He was in my year at Cambridge, he is here with Mellie." He blushed at Elizabeth's pointed look. "Forgive me, his sister, Miss Melissa Hamilton. Our families grew up more or less together. His father is in textiles, as mine was. They are putting in the automated looms, really revolutionizing the business. Mr. Hamilton is determined that his son be a gentleman, too." He laughed. "But he is not about to give up his bread and butter, either."

"Perhaps you should consider the same." Darcy suggested. "Times are changing, and that is certainly on the cutting edge."

"Hmm, there is something in that." Bingley rubbed his chin. "Well, in any case, it was good to catch up with them. I have not seen Hamilton or Mellie in ages." He smiled at Jane. "You seemed to enjoy your conversation with her?"

"Oh yes, she is a lovely young woman, she seemed very lively. She seemed to be a combination of Elizabeth's personality and Miss Darcys' colouring."

"I wonder if we will ever produce a daughter like that." Elizabeth laughed. "How did Georgiana manage to escape the dark Darcy blood?"

Darcy shrugged. "You have seen Mother's portrait, love. Who am I to question what heaven presents us with when a baby is born. Do you know that I was blonde, once?"

"No!" Elizabeth considered him. "Oh, I do not think that would suit you, at all!"

"So you would not have fallen in love with my friend if he was fair?" Bingley laughed. "Ah, you see, it is physical attributes that matter."

"They draw the eye, sir, but what is it that holds one's attention?" Elizabeth smiled up at Darcy who smiled in return.

"That depends on the individual."

"What do you think, Jane?" Bingley prodded her.

She studied Bingley's smiling eyes. "I think that the physical beauty is important, but that . . . knowing your goals are important as well, confidence is attractive."

"I cannot argue with that."

"Nor I." Darcy agreed. "Well, we should probably move back towards our seats." They heard a gong. "Aha, I knew intermission was ending."

"Darcy." An imposing man and his bejewelled wife stepped before them. "I was pleased to spot you, I did not know that you were in town, is this your bride?"

Darcy became very formal and serious, "Indeed it is, Your Grace. Sir, may I present my wife, Elizabeth Darcy. Mrs. Darcy, this is the Duke of Devonshire, Sir William Cavendish, and his wife, the Duchess, Lady Elizabeth Cavendish."

Elizabeth took the cue from his behaviour and curtseyed. "It is a very great pleasure to meet you, sir."

Cavendish looked her over with an appreciative eye and nodded. "Well chosen, sir." He turned back to Darcy. "Pemberley continues to prosper?"

"It does, sir. My father's instruction was excellent." Darcy met his gaze steadily. "Thank you for asking."

"I was fond of the name he chose for your sister, although I suspect it was after your parents rather than for my first wife."

"I suspect that you are correct, sir." He said respectfully.

"Good man, Darcy was." He nodded and looked Elizabeth over once more. "Well done."

The Duke and Duchess walked away and it was impossible to miss the flurry of whispers that followed them. Darcy's wife being acknowledged by such people was significant. Darcy stiffly led the party back to their box and after holding the chair for Elizabeth, took his seat. "We are being closely observed." He said softly. Elizabeth saw the flash of opera glasses as they were trained their way. "That was unexpected."

"That was terrifying." She whispered and grasped his hand. "Is he a friend of the family?"

"Our estates rival each other in size, love, and as they are both in Derbyshire, our families naturally are acquainted." He smiled slightly. "You did very well."

"I smiled, Fitzwilliam."

"You held your own and did not flinch. I am very proud." He kissed her hand and she squeezed back. They looked over to Bingley and Jane. He was staring in wonder at the attention they were receiving, and could feel his value rising simply by association with Darcy. Jane was staring at her hands. "I am sorry not to have introduced you."

"Darcy, I hardly expected such a thing, the man was there to greet the son of George Darcy, not to meet a man of my origins." Bingley laughed. "That was extraordinary." He smiled at Jane. "What say you, Miss Bennet?"

"I am glad that we were not introduced." She met Elizabeth's gaze. "Does this happen often?"

"Meeting a Duke?" She laughed and relaxed, which relieved her husband. "We met one last year, did we not?"

"We did, but he was just a little Duke." Darcy smiled to see her eyes roll. "We may meet royalty at some point."

"Wonderful." She shook her head. "Do you have any other surprises?"

"I suspect that you will be the one with surprises in the morning." Nodding to the crowd, he squeezed her hand. "The invitations and calls will be greater than I expected before."

"I thought that we were just slipping into town to retrieve our sisters?"

"I did not plan this, love."

"I did not, either." Elizabeth sighed. "I could politely decline."

"You could."

"But I should not?"

"It is your decision."

"Some direction would be nice."

"You know my opinion."

"I do, but that does not answer the question of what we should do."

"I would say that the acknowledgement of the Duke is far more memorable and important than appearing at a ball or dance." His eyes twinkled.

"Ah, so in one moment, we are relieved of social obligation?"

"I would say so. But I will not suspend your pleasure."

"No, but you would make your displeasure clear." Elizabeth's eyes danced and as the lights dimmed they leaned towards each other and kissed. "We will continue as planned?"

"Whatever you wish, Elizabeth, I am your pawn."

"Pawns can be just as powerful as a queen." She felt his lips caress her ear. "Although I rather think of you as king." His lips moved to her throat. "Will."

"We will continue this later, love." He whispered, and raised her hand to his mouth. "My queen."

Bingley smiled to himself and looked over to Jane. He could barely make out her expression. "Quite a fascinating world the Darcys inhabit."

"It certainly is." Jane whispered.

Chapter 15

"Now then Georgiana, we have to talk." Elizabeth said seriously. She sat down in the rocking chair and with a practiced hand, released the button at her shoulder and dropped the front of her gown to begin nursing Rosalie. "Sit down."

Georgiana watched in fascination as the baby hummed and drank. "Does that hurt?"

"No." Elizabeth looked down and stroked Rosalie's cheek. "But it is not something to be discussed outside of this house." She met her eyes and raised her brows. "It is our choice to care for our children this way, but it is not smiled upon by many in our society, particularly the older generation."

"Yes, Aunt Helen has spoken to me about it."

"What else has she told you about children?" Elizabeth asked quietly. "Has she told you how they are formed?"

"No." She whispered. "But I heard tales at school. Girls talked about all sorts of things there. It was embarrassing, but difficult to ignore. Mary was good at getting them to leave her alone, but I am afraid that I . . . I was curious."

"Mary knows full well what happens because I told her." Elizabeth said steadily. "She is older than you and I wanted her to be aware of the facts. What have you heard?"

"Nothing." She stared at her hands then looked up to see her sister's unrelenting stare; it was unnervingly similar to her brother's and she felt compelled to answer. "I . . . I saw a copy of *Aristotle's Compleat Masterpiece*."

"Your brother has a copy."

"Oh."

"Do you have any questions?"

She focussed on Rosalie. "I do not have the . . .desire for the *embrace*, I think. It sounds terrible."

Elizabeth studied her for a few moments. "I want you to know that it is not terrible, and it is one of the greatest expressions of love for a married couple, particularly when the couple cares for each other, however, you do know that the desired result from the embrace between a husband and wife is to form a child?" Georgiana nodded. "Do you know that to smile and flirt with a man is to encourage him to desire you for such an embrace?"

"Is that when his *yard* becomes swollen?" She twisted her hands, and Elizabeth thought quickly.

"You made a study of this book, Georgiana." She watched her sister's face redden. "Very well, yes that is when his yard becomes swollen. It is not acceptable for you to flirt openly with a man to encourage this disposition. You are only fourteen, and you must not engage in such behaviour until you are married."

"You kissed Fitzwilliam; I remember seeing him holding you in his study."

"A kiss is not procreation." Elizabeth said sharply. "And we were engaged. Your behaviour with Mr. Bingley was not appropriate."

"What behaviour?" Her head came up and she encountered her sister's gaze. "Oh."

"Oh, indeed. Your aunt would have dragged you from the room and sent you to the nursery. I chose to give you the benefit of the doubt and assumed that you were simply teasing a man who you like very much but look at as a brother. Am I correct or do you have a crush on him?"

"I . . . I have always liked him." Her eyes expressed a world of torment. "Am I not to like him?"

"Yes, but he is a grown man, not a boy. And he cares for you as a brother. That is all. It is fine to smile and tease, but I believe that you knew full well that you were crossing a line when you behaved so impertinently towards him. Would you ever act that way with Fitzwilliam?"

"Oh no!" She gasped.

"Why?"

"Because . . . because . . . well you speak to him that way!"

"I do, because I am his wife." She said steadily. "And any feelings of ardour that are inspired may be freely expressed to me. You are still a girl, who does not know what she is doing. Do not behave that way before Mr. Bingley or any other man again before you are at least out and preferably courting. It is too easy to fall under a man's spell, one who only seems kind, one who will not stop, one who may leave you with a baby in your arms." Both of them looked at Rosalie. "It is not a fate that you want outside of marriage, and will bring great shame upon our family."

"I . . . I was just . . . having some fun."

"I know." Elizabeth smiled. "And you still could have done so, and teased him. Think of every man as your brother, and then you will know how to behave, until you are much older. Agreed?"

"Yes, Elizabeth." She watched as Rosalie let go and she was lifted to Elizabeth's shoulder. "I thought it would be easier living with you."

She laughed and fixed her gown. "Oh, I think that you will find that it is. We just want to be sure of your happiness. You are not a little girl anymore, but you are not quite a woman. It is a difficult time."

"Does Mr. Bingley love Jane?" Georgiana asked her shoes. "He seems reluctant."

"How do you feel about his attentions to her?" Elizabeth rubbed Rosalie's back. "Are you jealous?"

"No . . .maybe a little. Mad perhaps." She saw Elizabeth's brow lift and then spoke angrily. "He is a wonderful man, why does she not see that?"

"I cannot answer that. Only they will." Studying her sister, she asked, "Why are you upset with Jane?"

"I do not believe that she is encouraging him. I know that Aunt Helen has been working with her. Why does she not see how kind he is?"

"I think that she does, Georgiana."

"Then why does she not tell him?"

"What makes you think that she has not?"

"They are not engaged." Georgiana looked back to her hands. "She must not tell him enough."

Elizabeth thought over her statement. "Are you judging Jane based on the relationship you see between me and your brother? I do not think that you have seen them together enough to form any such opinions. And most important, you cannot expect every couple to be the same as we are, not everyone is as open as we are. You are spoiled perhaps by watching us. Certainly the example of Audrey and Alicia's marriages should tell you that. You also have to keep in mind that a proper woman does not throw herself at a gentleman she likes. I certainly never did such a thing with your brother, and if you would ever to do that with a man you liked, you might appeal to his baser instincts, but you will not impress him as a woman he would want to be his wife. A gentleman does not wish to marry a wanton woman."

"So a girl must wait for the man to tell her he likes her. She might wait forever if she gives him no sign of her affection."

"Unfortunately that is true, but a girl can encourage a man without doing anything more than smile." Elizabeth laughed. "It depends on the man. When his eyes light up, you will know what makes him feel pleased."

"Oh."

"But you are too young to be concerned about these things. Do you understand that? When you are out, then we will delve into this more. Until then, leave Jane and Mr. Bingley to find their own way."

"Yes, Elizabeth."

They sat quietly and listened to Rosalie talk, then Elizabeth pulled the bell for the nursemaid to return. "Now, what shall we do? It is just the two of us for a few weeks, and Fitzwilliam has business to attend this afternoon. I am all yours." She smiled to see Georgiana returning to herself.

"May we . . . may we go to the pastry shop and get some ice cream?"

Elizabeth laughed. "Absolutely! And we must be sure to tell your brother so he will be jealous!"

DARCY WAVED AWAY the servant bearing the snuff box and instead accepted the proffered glass of brandy. Taking a sip he nodded to some passing acquaintances and smiled at Bingley. "Nothing changes, does it?"

"What do you mean?"

"Same faces, same vices, all is the same." He sighed. "I missed nothing in the past months."

"Except for the camaraderie perhaps? Or even just the opportunity to exercise with men? How is your fencing?"

"Quite adequate." Darcy laughed to see Bingley's eyes roll. "You do not believe me? Care to take me on?"

"No, no. I will be happy to watch, though. I suppose you found someone to practice with at Pemberley?"

"Of course! Elizabeth . . . "

"Good Lord!"

"Bingley." Darcy glared. "I was going to say, Elizabeth mentioned to our new pastor that I had no worthy opponents and he admitted that he became quite accomplished with the art in seminary." He shrugged and grinned. "So naturally I had to try him out. Mr. Evans is as he said, a talented man."

"Too talented?" Bingley asked then chuckled to see Darcy's eyes twinkle. "I see. Well, this man owes his livelihood to you, perhaps it is gratitude?"

"I hope not." Darcy shook his head. "I was glad to give it to him. He is the nephew of our former pastor. When the living came open recently, Mr. Repair was eager to recommend him. I am pleased with the choice."

"The variety of duties you face overwhelm me." Bingley sighed. "I have missed your company these past months." He smiled when Darcy nodded and looked away. "We will have to get you to London more often! Our evening at the theatre was extraordinary." He laughed to see Darcy's grimace.

"It was a pleasure to enjoy the evening with you and Jane, however, a short stay is quite adequate. With the knocker going up tomorrow, Elizabeth will be inundated with visitors." He paused to smile softly to himself, then noticing Bingley's curious look, he cleared his throat. "Then she will have calls to make and we are to socialize a bit. Speaking of which . . ."

"Yes." Bingley's smile fell away. "You said that Mrs. Darcy was unhappy when she read my letter, and it was clear in her greeting to me the other night. If I had known she would I . . . well I would not have mentioned my activity. I felt lower than a snail crawling across the ground to feel her remonstration."

Darcy studied him silently for a few moments, then setting down his glass clasped his hands together. "You know the story of my cousins."

"Layton and Singleton? Yes." Bingley looked down. "I am not married."

"I am not speaking of betraying your wife; I am speaking of exposure to disease. I do not want to see the day when your face is destroyed from inhaling mercury fumes, or you begin to drool black phlegm from the treatments for the French Disease. It is avoidable."

"You spent your time in the brothels before marriage." Bingley said defensively.

"Not really, not much. I was exceptionally uncomfortable. How do you enter a room and . . . well, perform with a woman to whom you have no affection let alone connection? No. My experience was limited to a few times at school and on my tour. I am too self-conscious for more. I suppose if I were to be a bachelor all my life I might have contracted with an exclusive courtesan, but honestly, I may have just as easily remained celibate. The momentary release was not worth the risk or embarrassment." Darcy watched Bingley thinking. "When I married, I was glad that I had enough knowledge to not be inept, but not so much as to be weary." He laughed at Bingley's creased brow. "Discovery was and continues to be mutual."

"Oh."

"And . . . I felt Elizabeth's hurt when I told her of my past."

"Why would you tell her?"

"I tell her everything." He asked quietly, "Would you feel comfortable telling Jane everything of yourself?"

Bingley smiled. "Ah, you are not staying out of it."

"You are avoiding the question." Darcy said pointedly.

"I feel that she does as well." Bingley shrugged. "Something is happening with her, it is so hard to read her. She is friendly and smiles, but . . . Maybe it is just my inexperience showing again. I cannot quite put my finger on it. I wonder sometimes if she is feeling pressured by others to want me?"

Darcy smiled, knowing that was indeed the case. "Are you feeling pressured to want her?"

"I really have no business doing so; after all, I am the one that created the situation by asking about her. I do not know, Darcy. I am just trying to live up to my father's dreams; that is all. He envisioned his son the gentleman going to all of the places that were denied to him, taking advantage of society, and living in a home that he did not live to purchase himself. Maybe that is the problem, maybe I need to determine what my dreams are and live them instead."

"Damn Bingley, you are impressing me today!" Darcy laughed and Bingley beamed. "Well said!"

"Well where is a pen? Let me write down this wisdom before I forget!"

"You will never be able to read it."

"So your sister tells me." Bingley chuckled and saw Darcy's brow crease. "Forgive me for responding to her as I did. I did not mean to imply . . ."

"No, no, your behaviour was that of a charmed friend. Elizabeth is speaking to her today of hers, which is part of the reason why I am out of the house." He sighed and shook his head. "I do not like her growing up."

"She will be a delight when she does, I am sure. I quite look at her as the sister I wish I had." The men laughed in shared understanding, then looked up when they heard a familiar voice.

"Darcy!" Stewart grinned and hurried over to their chairs. Darcy and Bingley stood and they clasped hands all around. "I heard you were back! How is your wife? And daughter? My God man, you are a father!"

Darcy chuckled and they all sat together. "Indeed, I am. My ladies are both lovely and well. How is Mrs. Harwick?"

"Oh, quite well, she and Harwick recently arrived to enjoy a month of the Season. She has transformed the man, why I would say that he resembles your happy mien." Darcy smiled with the compliment. "I imagine he would not mind a visit from you."

"I will be glad to come by. I am sure that Elizabeth would love to visit your sister. I will send a note over when I get home." He lifted his chin. "And how is Miss Henley?"

"You mean my betrothed?" He puffed his chest and grinned as both men laughed. "Thank you. I can hardly believe that Julia has agreed to be mine. I am overjoyed." Shaking his head he looked at his boots then met Darcy's eye. "I was such a fool over Mrs. Darcy."

"No, I think that many men envisioned a future with her." He smiled at Bingley who caught Stewart's eye.

"Well I have found the woman I adore." Stewart turned to Bingley. "And you? I have seen you with Miss Bennet. Is that your future?"

"I . . . Nothing is decided." Bingley said uncomfortably.

"Oh. Well. I hear that Netherfield was leased. I ran into George Shaw, the judge from King's Bench who handled Wickham? He decided he would like a little hunting this year and did not want the travel to Scotland. He knows the owner, did him a good turn once. So I suppose you will have to look elsewhere for your leasing possibilities, for the next quarter at least. Bad luck, that was so convenient to Longbourn. But I am sure it will be available again in the spring."

Bingley stared at him in surprise then turned to Darcy. "What . . . Now what?"

"I do not know." Darcy looked to Stewart. "Are you certain of this?"

"Oh yes, I was interrogated about the sport. Of course he will only be there until the Michaelmas session begins in November, but he does not mind, and maybe he will get in some fox hunting during the winter."

"I am not sure how I feel about this." Bingley said slowly.

"What do you mean?" Darcy watched him. "You are delayed until spring at the most; you can spend the winter at Pemberley and then take the lease on the first quarter day. It is not so long."

"Oh, I say Bingley; do not let this put you off of Miss Bennet!" Stewart looked between the two worriedly. "This is simply a business transaction of a very short duration."

"Right." Bingley said tightly. The men fell silent for a few moments and Darcy watched him closely.

Stewart felt a need to break the tension. "Um. Wickham sails around the 18th of July."

"Good." Darcy looked back to Stewart. "Is there any way to confirm his departure?"

"Well, the prison will keep a record of it, he was moved from Newgate you know, he is on one of the prison hulks, the HMS Savage, working hard labour on the river during the day. Do you wish to actually see him board?"

Darcy let a long breath escape. "I suppose that would be too much? Following a cart to . . . Portsmouth?"

"No they will take a ship from here." He tilted his head to a window and the Thames. "The hulk is located near Woolwich." Stewart grinned. "He is certainly getting a taste for his life on the sea now. He will be taken out to the transport ship a day or so before, then they will be gone with the tide one fine day."

"Let me know what you can," Darcy said grimly, "so that I can tell Elizabeth. We will not be truly assured until we know that he is gone."

"Of course. I have kept tabs on him in prison. He has done rather well there, I am sorry to say." Seeing Darcy's concern he shrugged. "Either someone is funding him or he is very adept with his begging. Regardless, before he was moved, he had the coin to keep the shackles off, his belly full, and his baser needs satisfied. He even got some poor bugger to sell him some teeth, I understand."

"So my fist did not leave any lasting damage." Darcy sighed.

"No, but the scar on his neck from Fitzwilliam's sword remains." Stewart smiled. "Too bad the neck cloth covers that."

"That woman from Georgiana's school said that she would stop visiting him."

"My people have made no report of her, of course, she may be using someone else, but what does it matter? He is gone soon. Relax, Darcy." Stewart watched him stand. "Where are you off to?"

"I have a surprise to purchase for my wife." He smiled and bowed. "If you care to come along, you are welcome."

"I have court, but I wish you well." Stewart smiled and stood along with Bingley. "I think that Julia will call on Mrs. Darcy. Perhaps we could all meet for an evening?"

"I will let you know." Darcy shook his hand and smiled at Bingley. "Can you come?"

Bingley picked up his walking stick and downed the rest of his brandy. "Absolutely. Give me a lesson in pleasing a wife. Someday it may be useful to me. For some woman." He walked ahead of Darcy and his smile fell away. Darcy watched him from behind and wondered what was going through his mind.

12 JUNE 1810

We returned from church this morning to find that a note had been delivered from Matlock House. The warm weather demanded that the funeral for Mr. Singleton be accomplished quickly and he was buried the morning after they arrived at Ashcroft. Uncle could not remain away from Parliament for long, so he and Aunt Helen returned yesterday evening, and they came here for dinner tonight. Layton will help Singleton to address the countless requirements of taking over the estate, then he and Alicia will forego the rest of the Season and return to Matlock. They are anxious to see their daughter again. Perhaps seeing us with Rosalie and the Singletons with Grace influenced them. Whatever the reason, I am happy for them.

Uncle reports that Mr. Singleton had become quite drunk at his club, and when he returned home, found Audrey sitting with Grace in a drawing room. Apparently he became enraged at the sight of his granddaughter, and swore unspeakable words at her, then raised his cane to beat Audrey for having the temerity to birth a girl instead of an heir. It seems that he had been welcoming of her as his daughter-in-law until she had this child, and since then his rage had only barely been in check. Singleton heard Audrey's cries and wrestled the cane from his father, and struck his face with his fist. When his father attempted to retaliate, he clutched his chest in mid-stride and dropped to the floor, never to breathe again.

No neighbours came to pay respects; the undertaker had to hire mutes to stand about the grave. I compare this man's passing to my father's and the contrast is spectacular. I am hardly a man with a great number of friends, but I believe that when my time comes, I will not be sent to eternity alone. Examples such as this move me to live as good a life as possible, be fair to my tenants, and attentive to my relations, and deeply love my wife and child. "And as ye would that men should do to you, do ye also to them likewise.[8]"

Elizabeth put the ribbon in place and sat at the desk in their sitting room unmoving, and stared through the doorway into the bedchamber they shared. Darcy appeared and smiled, and then saw tears in her eyes. "What is it?" He asked and knelt next to her chair. "Elizabeth?"

"I do not like reading of your passing." She met his gaze. "Please . . ."

"I will not write of it again." He said softly. "I understand."

"I cannot bear the thought of . . ."

"Shhhh." He closed his eyes and hugged her. "I understand." Letting go, he kissed her cheek. "I was thinking of Singleton's father, not of reminding you of . . . There I have done it again. When will I learn to think before I speak?"

"I could not say, but I certainly hope it is soon." Elizabeth sighed. "I am sorry; I suppose that I am a little pensive today. I received a letter from Audrey describing Robert's confrontation with his father. If they had any idea how angry he was with Grace's birth, they never would have come to his father's

---

[8] Luke 6:31

townhouse after they left Bath. She was terrified, not just for herself and Grace, but to see in person the abuse that Robert suffered under his father's hand. She said that he had told her some of it, but I believe that he was far more open with you." Darcy nodded and caressed her hair. "That Robert was capable of such violence frightened her. She said there were times when, before he reformed, he would come home and she would walk on eggshells around him, afraid that anything she might say would inspire a barrage of bitter words." She looked up to see his concern. "They were never directed at her and he never touched her."

"Thank God. I suppose that his words were inspired from the drink, perhaps it loosened the memories of his father's behaviour. I imagine that the strike she witnessed, however, was that of a man determined to protect his family from the abuse he suffered for most of his life." Darcy said softly. "I have no doubt that I would do the same."

"You have already." They kissed and Elizabeth leaned onto his shoulder. "Audrey described Mr. Singleton, and she said that she understood now that voice that Robert once had. She has no fear of him becoming that way again, but it helped her to understand more of his past behaviour. It seems that your thoughts match hers." Darcy continued to caress her hair, as she spoke against his chest. "How can a father hate his son so much? Can you imagine hating any child of yours?"

"No, but I was raised by George and Anne Darcy. I could never understand that feeling of not being wanted." He kissed her forehead. "You are thinking of your mother."

"How did you know?"

"I know you, love." He smiled at her. "Do you wish to talk about it?" When she did not respond he took her hand and squeezed. "I cannot see you treating your daughters as your mother did you."

Looking at him with surprise, she shook her head. "You know me too well."

"Oh that will take a lifetime, a very long lifetime." He kissed her gently then stood and holding out his hands, helped her to rise. "Now, we must repair this damage. We have friends coming."

Elizabeth wiped her cheek. "It would not do to see the Harwicks with red eyes."

"No, not at all, especially with Evangeline coming as well. The poor woman will have enough tears for all of us." He chuckled when she glared. "No, no dear. I do not deserve that look! You cried rivers when you were with child."

"I did not."

"Oh no, I remember it well, I would swear the roof was leaking, the house was so awash with tears." Darcy's eyes twinkled.

Hands on hips, eyes flashing, Elizabeth glared. "Are you through?"

"And add to that the time I found you polishing the silver . . ."

"It was tarnished." She sniffed. "If we had a proper butler . . ."

"As soon as Bernard is finished with his training, we will." Darcy laughed. "Of course the nightly presentation of feet in my lap to rub was charming."

"If *your* feet were swollen *I* would rub them." She walked away then spun to face him. "And I would not complain. I would be grateful that my husband asks for my aid. Furthermore . . ." Elizabeth stared at him. "Why am I arguing with you?"

"I do not know; why are you?" He tilted his head.

"You are distracting me."

"Me?" He gave her a hug, nuzzling her throat before nipping at the skin, then soothing it gently with his tongue. "Come, love, we have friends visiting."

"You sir, are too smug for your own good." Elizabeth settled into his arms, and Darcy kissed her hair. "What would I do without you?"

"Do not start this again, Lizzy. I am trying to keep my own dark thoughts at bay." He wrapped her up tighter and they stood together, silently swaying.

Georgiana, hearing their voices raised, had snuck into the bedchamber and peeked around the corner into the sitting room. "Is everything well? What is wrong?" She asked nervously.

They startled and glanced at each other, agreeing wordlessly that she had invaded their privacy. "Nothing." Elizabeth said quietly, and wiped Darcy's cheek. "Nothing at all."

"No, nothing." He kissed Elizabeth and hugged her to him. "All is well."

"Please tell me." Georgiana plead. "I want to know. I do not like hearing you fight."

"We were not fighting Georgiana, and you should not have been listening to us." Darcy looked at her sternly then to Elizabeth. "I am no good with explaining this."

Elizabeth smiled with his mild remonstration and turned to her sister. "First of all Georgiana, your brother is absolutely right, eavesdropping is rude and entering the room where a private conversation is occurring is inexcusable unless there is some urgent matter to be addressed. I know that it is uncomfortable to hear people you care for seemingly disagreeing, but what you just did was incorrect and it should not be repeated. A proper young lady would not do that."

Darcy smiled to himself to hear Elizabeth chastise her, but maintained his stern expression when he furthered Elizabeth's censure. "I have no doubt that your aunt would not have allowed such a thing; and if you wish to remain out of the nursery and allowed to join us for meals and when our family and closest friends visit, you will have to maintain proper behaviour. Do you understand?"

"Yes, Brother." Georgiana clasped her hands and cast her eyes down. "I am sorry."

Elizabeth exchanged a look with Darcy and he lifted his lips in a small smile. She turned back to her sister, "Now, since we seemed to have worried you, I want you to think about when we spoke of how to behave with a man. How too much flirting might encourage him to act inappropriately?" Georgiana nodded and Darcy's brow creased as he looked worriedly between them. "And that his actions might move him to behave in such a way that might leave you with child?"

"Elizabeth!" Darcy cried. She looked at him sympathetically.

"That is a man who does not love or care for the girl in question. That is an example of a man who only seeks his pleasure. Your brother and I love each other deeply, and the reason we are speaking somewhat emotionally to each is because we just reaffirmed our commitment."

"How?" Georgiana breathed.

"By admitting that we cannot imagine life without each other." She smiled and turned to him. "Or wish to be reminded of the possibility ever occurring. We were *not* fighting."

"oh." She saw that Darcy's gaze had softened, and blushed. Darcy and Elizabeth recognized that she understood their discussion was playful.

Elizabeth looked back to her. "Such conversation or behaviour is acceptable between a married couple, or an engaged couple. Do you understand the difference? The tone of a conversation that you may hear can be misinterpreted."

"I guess that this is another example of how every couple is different. I guess that this year when I go back to school, I will be more like Mary and not listen to the girls so much."

"I think that would please her very much, I know that it pleases me."

"I think that I will be interested to hear what you were told." Darcy directed his gaze to Elizabeth. "Perhaps a school in a new location would be preferable."

"I have no doubt that the same conversations are held no matter where groups of girls are gathered, dear." Elizabeth squeezed his hand. "And I am sure the same applies to schools for young men, as well." Darcy's eyes grew in alarm with the memory of his school days.

"Mrs. Darcy . . ." The maid saw the master and mistress holding hands and looked away. "Forgive me madam; there are some visitors here for you. Mr. and Miss Lucas."

"Charlotte!" Elizabeth cried. Darcy laughed to see her mixture of excitement and distress. "Oh I must look terrible!" She rubbed her face and patted her hair.

"You are beautiful, love." Darcy tucked a curl behind her ear and kissed her hand. "Did you expect this visit?"

"Yes, well no, well . . . Charlotte said that she might visit if her father decided to come to town, and I said that she could stay with us." She smiled when he raised his brows. "It is for one night, dear."

"She is your friend, and most welcome." He kissed her cheek. "Let us greet our guest, or is it guests?"

"Oh." She laughed. "I think that her father was to stay at a hotel."

"Umhmm." He held out his arm. "Come, love."

"Are you coming, Georgiana?" Elizabeth asked when she noticed her not following.

"You will let me greet guests?" She said quietly. Darcy and Elizabeth stopped and turned. "Aunt Helen said that I was too young for such things."

"This is our home. I just told you that if you maintain the proper behaviour, you will be welcome. Besides, you have met Miss Lucas." She smiled when Georgiana perked up. "I know that Lady Matlock is determined to teach you the proper ways of being a lady, but I cannot imagine keeping you from greeting our friends."

They made their way to the drawing room designed for receiving guests and were surprised to find Charlotte and her brother Robert waiting to greet them. "Oh Mrs. Darcy! Your home is breathtaking! I am afraid to touch anything." The ladies hugged and laughed.

Elizabeth drew away and smiled. "If I hear you call me Mrs. Darcy again I will be most unhappy with you."

"I was just giving you your due, you *are* married and a mother, and well, look at where you live, it is such a change from Longbourn." She looked around again. "Mr. Darcy, you must be so proud."

"I am very proud of my wife and child." He bowed to her and turned to Lucas. "This is a surprise; we were expecting your father. I should have realized it was you when Mr. Lucas was announced instead of Sir William Lucas."

"Father is still affronted with the lack of exclusivity at court, and refuses to come. But business still must be conducted, so it fell to me." He smiled to see the ladies lost in conversation already. "Charlotte begged for a chance to visit with Mrs. Darcy. I apologize for the lack of notice, our departure was rather sudden."

"As was my knowledge of the entire plot." Darcy nodded to the women. "Your sister is staying with us; you are certainly welcome as well. We are expecting guests for dinner tonight, but I am sure that you will enjoy meeting them, we all attended Cambridge at one time or another. Stewart will be among them."

"I would appreciate that, thank you. Your tolerance is remarkable." Lucas smiled. "We took a cab from the stagecoach stop, and I have not been to the hotel as yet." He looked around at the room. "This home is more than I imagined. Pemberley . . ."

"Would you care to see a painting?" Darcy offered. "There is one in my study, we could speak privately."

"Is there a need for that?" Lucas caught the serious tone of his voice.

"I believe so." Darcy stepped over to Elizabeth. "Dear, I will take Mr. Lucas downstairs to the study."

"I can imagine the subject of your conversation."

"I imagine yours will be of a similar bent?" He smiled slightly. "So much for staying out of it." He kissed her cheek then bowed to Charlotte. "Lucas?" He indicated the door. "Shall we?"

WICKHAM PICKED UP a stone and hefted it into the cart at the edge of the river. His eyes darted left and right, taking note of the guards and the other prisoners. Slowly he walked back down the rocky bank, bent and swirled his hands through the filthy water of the Thames, found another stone, and delivered it to the cart. Once again he studied his guards, as he had every day since beginning to labour from the prison hulks. He saw their disinterest in their jobs, and noted their habits. Unshackled while he worked, he knew this was his one chance . . . He walked back to the water, watched the guard turn his head, bent as if to retrieve a stone, then continued forward, slipping beneath the lapping water, his mouth and eyes tightly shut, and swam below the surface, allowing the current to move him along.

When his bursting lungs demanded a breath, he poked his head up, and saw that he was some fifty yards away, and had not been noticed. Striking for the shore, he clambered up, ignored the destitute waifs there picking coal, and hurried up to the street. A head count would find him missing soon, and his distinctive prison uniform had to be discarded. Looking around the crowded street, he saw that his wet appearance was drawing attention. He needed to act quickly. A man lying between two buildings, passed out with drink, was perfect for his plans. Wickham approached, glanced around, grabbed the man beneath his arms and dragged him into the dark alley.

Two hours later, the body of George Wickham was discovered in the alley, and guards searching for him from the prison were relieved that they would not be held responsible for his escape. His face had been badly beaten, and the neck cloth used to strangle him obliterated the known scars that he possessed, but the wet uniform, and items found on his person were good enough to identify him. With that, his body was immediately dispatched to a surgeon for anatomy practice.

A tall man with dark hair stepped from a nearby bath house after a good cleansing and shave, noted the excitement across the street, and checking his pockets was delighted to find a purse filled with cash. "Well, look at this; I did do well, did I not?" He took a deep breath of the fetid London air. "Now, who shall I visit first?"

"WHAT CAN I OFFER YOU?" Darcy indicated the bottles of port, brandy and wine. Lucas had no answer. "Port, then."

"Thank you." He took a sip of the fine wine. "This is the best I have ever tasted. The port my father drinks is often spoiled."

"Yes. Well if the war ever ends, we can go back to French wines." He walked over to the Pemberley landscape. "This is my estate."

"So it is." Lucas stared at it and said quietly. "What are you trying to tell me, sir? That I should give up my hopes for Miss Bennet because she is now accustomed to your home?"

"No." Darcy indicated the chairs before his desk and sat down. "I know that you approached her at Christmas and you quietly courted her . . .or at least called on her and danced a number of times, and that your families regularly meet for social events in the neighbourhood."

"I wished for her to be sure of her choice. I knew that she was going to be educated by Lady Matlock."

Darcy saw his grimace and looked at him thoughtfully. "Yes, my aunt is determined to be successful with the match to my friend Bingley."

"Sir, there is no need to be subtle or attempt to intimidate me. Just be honest. You think of me as below Miss Bennet and as my wife she would not be living up to her potential." He looked down at the glass in his hand. "I cannot compete with a man of your wealth."

"You are not competing with a man of my wealth, but you are correct that Mr. Bingley is a wealthy man. However, he is hesitant, and I believe that Jane has determined she does not like," he waved his hand at Pemberley and around the room, "all of this."

Lucas sat up and studied him. "She is seriously considering me?"

"I believe so." Darcy smiled to see his eyes light up. "I realize that it has been impossible for you to court her, and you were left to the tidbits of information that Miss Lucas could relate to you in Elizabeth or Jane's letters, but I believe that you need to show your hand to both Jane and Mr. Bingley. Now."

"But what of your friend?"

"I think that he would be relieved to see that she would not be left abandoned if he were to bow out." Darcy's lips lifted in a small smile. "He is a man of honour."

Lucas regarded him carefully. "You are not saying this because you feel that Miss Bennet is not good enough for Mr. Bingley?"

"Would I not be more concerned with my sister's future than my friend's?" He smiled to see Lucas considering the question. "I take the care of my sisters very seriously. You know that she comes to you with very little?"

"Yes; and my parents will be disappointed in that, but I have been given a bequest by my grandfather, and Mr. Gardiner has helped me to invest it. That unexpected gift is what drove me to finally, after years of quiet admiration, approach Miss Bennet at Christmas; I felt that I could afford to take a wife now.

Of course, I also have my allowance from my father, and I will inherit Lucas Lodge one day."

"And there is Miss Bennet's dowry."

"It is more than enough." He said seriously. "I honestly did not expect a great deal from any woman. It is not as if Lucas Lodge is . . .well, Longbourn, to use an example we both know."

Darcy smiled to hear the determination in his voice. "I like your forthright and honest attitude."

"Sir, my grandfather felt that my father made a grave error, giving up his trade when he was knighted. Father felt that he was meant to be a man in a manor house and would spend his life being the genial host. That is a fine ambition if you can afford it . . ."

"Yes. But I gather he did not prepare for his children's disposition before quitting his business?"

"Yes. I am afraid that my sisters have only as much as the Bennet girls do. For that reason my parents can hardly object to Miss Bennet's dowry."

"What of the boys?"

"My younger brothers are considering apprenticeships or the navy. I wish that I could do more for them, but I have my sisters to consider." He sighed heavily. "My grandparents have left them each smaller bequests than mine, so they are not entirely helpless. But Miss Bennet . . .she knows me, she knows our neighbourhood . . . She would not be disappointed."

"No, I believe that she would be very happy at home, caring for her husband and children, being able to keep an eye on her aging parents, participating in the events of the community. I believe that Jane belongs in Hertfordshire. Furthermore, I believe that she belongs where her heart wishes to live."

Lucas looked him in the eye. "What do I need to do?"

"Well, you are here. At dinner tonight, you will meet Bingley."

"Miss Bennet . . ."

"Will not be here this evening." Darcy lifted his brow. "But perhaps you might stay another day and we will make sure that you see each other."

Taking a deep breath Lucas finally relaxed. "I would like that very much."

Darcy chuckled and took a sip of his port. "I have no doubt of that at all."

"OH ELIZA, I am so sorry, we would never have come if we knew you were entertaining." Charlotte looked around the beautiful bedchamber and sighed. "I can just stay in here. It would be a pleasure."

"Do not be ridiculous." Elizabeth watched the maid unpacking her small trunk. "These are some of our dearest friends, and we have not seen them for months. It is a very small party."

"But they are your friends . . ."

"So are you."

"I have nothing to wear." Charlotte looked at her gown and then to Elizabeth's. "I am sorry. Perhaps Miss Darcy would enjoy the company tonight. I will gladly spend time with her; she seems to be a sweet girl."

"She is, and because this is practically family coming tonight, she will be permitted to remain." Elizabeth touched a dress that just came out of the trunk. "I am sorry that you are taller than me, or I would lend you one of my gowns, but this is lovely. Did Mrs. Jones make it for you? I miss her shop; she was so easy to work with, and did not challenge my taste in fashion." She held up a simple blue dress. "I always had to battle Mama with the whole lace issue." She laughed. "I see you do not have to fight your mother."

"No." Charlotte smiled. "At least in that we are in agreement."

"My maid will do your hair, and I have a lovely necklace you may borrow; and some earrings as well." Elizabeth squeezed her hand. "You will look just fine. Please do not feel intimidated; Mrs. Fitzwilliam and Mrs. Harwick are very kind." She went to the door and paused. "I sent a note to Gracechurch Street and hopefully Jane and Mary can join us tomorrow. They are attending a dinner with our aunt and uncle tonight."

"And Mr. Bingley is coming, tonight? Without Jane being here? She wrote to me about dancing with him." Charlotte closely watched Elizabeth. "I cannot say that her letters seemed . . .settled."

"Mr. Bingley is coming simply as our friend." Elizabeth smiled to see Charlotte trying to read her face. "He is a dear man."

"Oh." Charlotte startled when another maid appeared. "How many servants do you have?" She whispered as Elizabeth led her out of the room and into the mistress's chambers. She watched her friend's eyes widen when she saw the decoration, and just kept moving on to the dressing room. Charlotte gasped when she saw Millie inside and opening a closet to expose countless gowns hanging on rods and pegs within. "Oh my!"

Elizabeth dismissed Millie and closed the door, then clasped her hands. "It is just a closet, Charlotte. I was overwhelmed when I began purchasing my wedding clothes. With my pregnancy, I doubt that I have worn half of them, but I know that they are necessary to be Mrs. Darcy. I have grown to understand that the longer we have been married, and the more people we have met." She sighed and looked around. "Fitzwilliam's aunt has made sure that I am properly turned out. She is determined that I do well. She has been a tenacious, but very important teacher to me, and now to Jane."

"Yes, she mentioned her lessons with Lady Matlock. She seems to be a pet project, not that Jane would ever say something like that. It is just my impression."

Nodding and lifting her eyes to the ceiling, Elizabeth explained, "She has married off her girls, so now she wishes for Jane to do well."

"With Mr. Bingley." Charlotte said sadly and sinking down onto the chair at the dressing table, attempted not to be dazzled by understated display of wealth that was arrayed before her in Elizabeth's brushes and perfumes. "She wants your sister to be a worthy companion to you."

"I do not think that is her plan, she truly cares for Jane's welfare." Elizabeth went to a cabinet, and unlocking it retrieved a velvet bag, fished out a necklace and earrings, and carefully returned the bag to its place without embarrassing Charlotte with the spectacular collection of jewels within.

"And what do you tell Jane?" Charlotte asked as she looked down at the fine gold chain that held Richard the pearl. "This is the most beautiful necklace I have ever seen."

Elizabeth smiled and touched it. "I wore this on my wedding day; it is extremely special to me and my husband." Their eyes met then Charlotte's went back down to the necklace. "I want Jane to make up her own mind. She already had the experience of feeling pressured to accept Mr. Harwick purely for security, and it made her a person none of us recognized. Whatever her choice, Mr. Bingley, Mr. Lucas, or someone unknown, she must be comfortable with it. Now that I am married almost a year, I understand that lesson so very well."

"You would not marry for security?" Charlotte sighed. "Even if it was your only chance?"

"Have you met someone?" Elizabeth took a chair by her side.

"There is a new curate in Meryton. A Mr. Collins . . ."

"Ah, the heir of Longbourn."

"What?" Charlotte looked up with wide eyes.

"Well, he will be when his father dies." Elizabeth shook her head. "He is a miserable little man, Charlotte."

"But . . . He is new; he does not know me as all the other men in Meryton do. But I imagine that your mother might wish him to marry one of your sisters."

"True, but I hope with all my heart she does not accomplish it. And I pray that you can do better." Elizabeth held her hands. "I want your happiness as well."

"Well then Eliza, please, put me in the way of some rich men!" Charlotte laughed and looked at the diamonds sparkling in her hand. "Or just a man with pleasant breath?"

"SHE IS BEAUTIFUL, ELIZABETH." Laura leaned down to smile at Rosalie. "I hope that we will be so blessed before long, but in the meantime, I am enjoying our two girls."

"How have they adjusted to gaining you and losing Evangeline?" Elizabeth saw Charlotte looking down, and added, "Mrs. Fitzwilliam is Mr. Harwick's sister, and the two couples were married in a double wedding in February."

"What a wonderful event to share with your sibling." Charlotte smiled a little, and looked back down when she felt Laura's eyes pass over her again.

Self-consciously, she stood straighter and tugged at her sleeves then touched the pearl before clasping her hands.

"It was wonderful." Laura agreed. "My brother mentioned meeting you and your brother when he stayed at Netherfield. He described your father as a most genial host."

"My father is quite pleased with his position in the neighbourhood." Charlotte blushed.

"I had hoped to join my brother at Netherfield when he visited our cousin, but Mother had other ideas." She smiled and turned back to Elizabeth. "The girls were mostly upset when Eva departed, but I think they are quite fine now. Margaret is almost five, so she is certainly aware of who I am. Ella was a little clingy with her governess for awhile before she began reaching for me."

"She is just a baby." Evangeline said wistfully, then stroked over her belly. "I miss them both."

"So do I." Laura smiled. "Poor Jeffrey is suffering through this trip solely for me. Well, perhaps not solely, he does seem to take a great deal of pleasure in dancing, and we have enjoyed seeing the sights together." She laughed and held up her hand. "Forgive me, but I was thinking of how silly he was when we visited Vauxhall last week. It is a favourite haunt of his."

"I see where he has much in common with Fitzwilliam, although, if we were not here for my sisters and visiting with our family, we would not hesitate to stay at home. London's attractions are wonderful, but I suppose that I am as much a country girl as my husband is a man of the land, we would rather be at Pemberley."

"Dearest, may I steal our daughter?" Darcy appeared with a smile. "I want her to meet Harwick."

Elizabeth handed her off, and Darcy happily cuddled Rosalie, bending to kiss her chubby cheeks and whispering as he carried her off across the room. "He is a man in love. I will have to watch carefully and make sure that she is not spoiled. They have frequent secret conversations." She smiled after him affectionately. "When I take a nap, I have awakened to find them settled in the rocker in the nursery."

"He is a man transformed. I remember how frightened he was. Jeffrey told me of the nearly constant letters they exchanged during your pregnancy." Laura observed Darcy with open amazement. "Jeffrey loves Ella and Margaret deeply, but to appear in a roomful of our friends, showing them off for more than a few minutes . . ." They watched Darcy engaged in conversation with the other gentlemen and Elizabeth laughed to see him unconsciously swaying as Rosalie wriggled up his shoulder, peeking over the top at Fitzwilliam as he made silly faces at her. "My brother is smitten."

"Richard is so excited to be an expectant father." Elizabeth observed.

"He is, but I know that he is every bit as nervous as Fitzwilliam was with you." Evangeline looked at him fondly. "For all of his bluster, he is a very tender-hearted man."

"I think that I always saw through him." Elizabeth smiled. "His mask was different from my husband's but he wore it just the same."

"This is a foreign world." Charlotte murmured and the other women turned to look at her. "My father never came anywhere near us when we were that small. I do not think that he paid much attention to any of us until we were old enough to be of use."

"You were put to work?" Evangeline asked.

"Not for long, but yes, I helped a little around the shop. I was the eldest and it was my position to do the sweeping. My brother Robert was working when he was very small, I believe he began when he was five, at least until Papa was knighted, then everything changed." She looked back down at her hands.

Laura and Evangeline exchanged looks, knighting was not as glamorous as it sounded, a meaningless honour bestowed for a favour to the crown. Elizabeth stood next to Charlotte and wound her arm onto hers. "I am very fond of Lucas Lodge. I have spent so many wonderful hours there."

"Thank you, Eliza."

Recognizing that Elizabeth was supporting her friend, Laura changed the subject. "Well, I can tell you, my father certainly never cuddled a baby to his chest. He was much more likely to hold us out at arm's length and pray that the napkin would remain dry!" She laughed. "I do not think that he had much use for us until we were old enough to sit on a pony. Then at least he had something in common with us."

"Ordering you to ride properly?" Evangeline smiled. "Yes, I remember father's lessons well. He was a stern teacher, but I treasure those moments with him. He died just as I was old enough to be able to talk to him. Jeffrey felt his loss keenly then."

"That sounds like Fitzwilliam's experience with his father. I would have liked to have known Mr. Darcy. Fitzwilliam has described his behaviour with you, Georgiana." Elizabeth smiled at her silent sister. "I think there must be something in the Darcy blood about cuddling little girls."

"I think that I was very fortunate to have the time I did with Papa." Georgiana said softly. "I hope that whoever I marry will be like Fitzwilliam."

"hmm, well that is something that you do not really find out until you have a baby of your own in your arms." Laura looked at Harwick leaning over Rosalie. "Someday I will find out, although I suspect I already know the answer."

"She is quite the handsome young lady, Darcy." Harwick smiled and touched her little bonnet. "I had forgotten how tiny they are."

"Tiny? I can barely lift her now." Darcy let her down from his shoulder and smiled at her. "We have discussed her great weight. Soon my back will be bowed with the effort to hold her." He was rewarded with a waving fist in the jaw, which Fitzwilliam applauded.

"I think that boxing will have to be taught to this little lady, Darcy."

"Richard . . . Do not test me, you will soon be in my position."

"Perhaps I will be the father of a son?" He nodded at the surrounding men. "It is about time that one of us produces one."

"And I shall be sure to teach him how to be a gentleman." Darcy glared.

"You know how?"

"Far better than you." Darcy was about to continue when he spotted Bingley coming up the stairs. "Ah, here is Bingley." Catching Elizabeth's eye, he handed Rosalie back to her, and she signalled a footman to send for Mrs. Robbins.

Lucas had been standing off to the side, listening to the good-natured conversation, but feeling very uncomfortable amongst these very wealthy men. Darcy, understanding his discomfort had left him alone, but now he stepped to his side. "What am I to say to him?" Lucas asked.

"Good Evening is a fine place to start." Fitzwilliam offered before Darcy could speak. "Bingley!" He strode forward and clapped his back. "How are you old man?"

"I am well." Bingley gave him a bemused look and turned to Darcy. "Is he in his cups already?"

"Perhaps, but he does not handle his liquor well. You should be sure to stand upwind of him."

Fitzwilliam snorted, and Bingley grinned. "Harwick it is a great pleasure . . . ah there are the ladies." He bowed to Laura and Evangeline across the room, then smiled at Georgiana, who promptly blushed and looked away. He looked to Elizabeth who raised her brow at him and containing his desire to laugh, focussed on Charlotte. "I do not believe that I know the other lady, do I?"

"That is Miss Charlotte Lucas." Darcy said quietly, "She is a childhood friend of Elizabeth's, and lives in the estate that borders Longbourn and Netherfield." He introduced them then they walked over to Lucas. "And this is Mr. Robert Lucas, her brother. They are spending a few nights here. Miss Lucas is visiting with Elizabeth while Mr. Lucas conducts business. Hopefully Miss Bennet and Miss Mary will get to see their neighbours as well while they are in town."

"Of course." He bowed. "Mr. Lucas." Bingley faced the older man and felt the uncomfortable sensation that he was being examined closely. "I have heard much of your . . . neighbourhood."

Lucas' sharp eyes took in Bingley's fine clothes, handsome features, and confused expression. "Yes, I understand that you are interested in Netherfield."

"I am, or I was, but it seems that my uncharacteristic deliberation has at the least delayed my leasing it."

"Oh?" Lucas looked to Darcy. "I was not aware of this?"

Darcy nodded. "I did not wish to presume that Bingley would continue to entertain the notion of taking the property when we learned it was let for the hunting season. Our mutual friend Stewart gave us the news."

"oh." Lucas said softly, the ramifications of Bingley not taking the lease were swirling in his mind.

"By a judge." Darcy added.

"I see." He turned back to Bingley. "So your plans are . . .delayed?"

"Does it make a difference?" Bingley asked quietly, almost to himself. "Would anyone care if I were to take up residence or not?"

Lucas nodded and could almost read his thoughts. "It would depend upon what your intentions were once you arrived, sir. The sport around Netherfield is very fine."

Fitzwilliam looked between the men, one who fully understood that he was facing his opponent, and the other who was only battling with himself. He looked up to Darcy who was watching just as closely and catching his eye, shook his head. Darcy nodded, staying out of it, and offered no enlightenment to Bingley. Harwick tilted his head, listening. He knew enough of Bingley's involvement with Jane to guess that Lucas was a third suitor for her hand, and it seemed, from the intense way he regarded Bingley, the most serious.

"My intentions are dependent on what would be best for all parties." Bingley said and looked to Darcy with a shrug, thinking that of the men present, Lucas would not know what he was really talking about. "It seems that I will have plenty of time to consider my options, although clearly my hesitancy has cost me already."

Harwick felt most qualified to enter the conversation. "That is admirable, Bingley, and I appreciate your careful consideration after having been in your position once, however; I can only support the notion that while disappointment is momentarily painful, it is sometimes the most important step to make." He looked quickly to Laura and met Bingley's widened eyes. "Do you understand?"

"I think that I do." Bingley smiled. "I appreciate all of my mentors."

"Well Lord knows you need a roomful of them!" Fitzwilliam laughed and turned to Lucas who was still studying Bingley. "Mr. Lucas, my cousin mentioned that your brothers are considering the navy, might I plead the case of the army?" He grinned and nudged him, holding out a glass of wine.

Lucas startled and stared down at the glass in Fitzwilliam's hand. "Oh, I would be happy to hear you out, sir."

Taking advantage of the change in topic, Bingley indicated that Darcy follow him across the room to pour some wine for themselves. "What is Lucas about, Darcy? He was staring at me as if he was expecting something to sprout out of my ears!"

"Mr. Lucas is a potential neighbour of yours; I suspect that he was interested in your plans." Darcy sipped and looked down, then across the room. Bingley tilted his head and watched him carefully.

"Your cousin once told me that you cannot lie."

"What did I say that was untrue?"

"Nothing, I am sure, but I suspect there is more to this than you say." He looked back at the three men and saw Lucas again watching him. "The Lucas family is close to the Bennets, you say?

"Some members more than others." Darcy noted. "Miss Lucas is very close to Elizabeth."

"And Mr. Lucas?" Bingley asked softly. "How close is he to Miss Bennet?" Bingley's eyes met Darcy's. "He is interested."

"He is." Darcy said simply.

"Did you invite him here?"

"No, his appearance was an absolute surprise, Bingley. We thought that his father would come and Miss Lucas would stay for a short visit. He is aware of your . . .calls."

"What should I do?" Bingley murmured.

"I will not direct you in this. Only you can answer this question." Darcy placed his hand on his shoulder and spoke seriously. "Whoever you marry deserves a man who is focussed on the marriage more so than his pleasures, and one who knows himself and his goals. Perhaps you should present her with the possibility of waiting for you or moving on. If she does decide not to wait for you, I hope that she will take some time to freely look around London and determine if she wishes to continue here or return to Longbourn."

"To him." Bingley murmured.

Darcy smiled and gave his shoulder a squeeze. "Of course, pistols at dawn might do just as well."

Bingley laughed, "Then leave it to her to reject both of us and we were bloodied for nothing!"

"Well, that is certainly a possibility. A woman's mind is a mystery." Darcy's eyes twinkled as he watched Elizabeth approach. "Particularly my dear wife's."

"Was I just insulted?" Elizabeth smiled.

"I leave you to determine that, my love." He took her hand and bestowed a kiss before tucking it onto his arm. "What news have you?"

"Foster just informed me that the Captain and the Reverend de Bourgh are on their way up." She smiled at the doorway. "Here they are."

"Darcy, Mrs. Darcy!" De Bourgh grinned and bowed. "What a pleasure to see you! I do not believe that you have met Michael?" He nodded to his brother.

"It is a pleasure." The soft-spoken young man bowed. "Forgive our intrusion."

"It is no trouble at all; you are certainly welcome to stay for dinner." Elizabeth smiled. "We are very happy to have your company."

"No, no, we are merely dropping off a letter for you, Darcy." De Bourgh drew an envelope from his coat. "Lady Catherine demanded we play pigeon."

"She would. And what does she wish now, any hints?" He looked at the well-sealed envelope and sighed.

"Not a one. She sits and fumes in her house, mother regularly visits to be assured that she has not strangled any of the servants, and merrily tortures her with observations of the decoration."

"I wonder if those two have become fond of each other." Fitzwilliam smiled and joined them. "Rather alike in some ways."

"Do *not* let my mother hear you say that." De Bourgh chuckled and nudged his brother. "Eh, Michael?"

Michael startled from his observation of Charlotte and blinked. "Oh, yes, Mother would be most unhappy." He tilted his head and looked back over to Charlotte. Elizabeth's eyes danced and she smiled at Darcy. He sighed and let her arm go.

"If you will not stay for dinner tonight, perhaps you might come tomorrow? My sisters will be visiting, and our houseguests will remain." She smiled. "Shall I introduce you both now?" Hooking her hand over their arms she led the way across the room. "Reverend Michael de Bourgh, and Captain Peter de Bourgh, this is Miss Charlotte Lucas of Lucas Lodge in Hertfordshire. Miss Lucas, Mr. de Bourgh has the living at Hunsford, at his brother's estate of Rosings in Kent." She nodded at each man in turn.

Fitzwilliam leaned over to Lucas. "She is matchmaking, you know."

"Is she good at it?" He asked quietly while the rest of the room watched Elizabeth clearly at work.

"Well," Fitzwilliam smiled and catching Lucas's eye glanced over to Bingley. "I think that she only has one failure." He raised his brows and gave him a wink, then nodded at Evangeline. "Patience is rewarded in the end."

Chapter 16

Darcy thoughtfully read the letter in his hand and picking up his pen; began to write a response when he heard some hesitant footsteps outside of the study door. He paused and listened. It was a man, from the sound of the boots, and it surely was not a servant since they would be about their well-practiced duties. "Mr. Lucas?" He called.

Lucas looked in the doorway. "Forgive me, I did not wish to interrupt . . ."

"Not at all, please come in." Darcy had risen to his feet and indicated a chair before his desk. They sat down and immediately a maid appeared. "Coffee?" Seeing his nod, Darcy looked to the girl. "Please."

"Yes, sir." She bobbed and disappeared.

Lucas watched her go. "Do you have people poised to serve?"

Darcy regarded him, and saw that the question was asked more in wonder than in disdain. "My staff is trained to perform their duties. My mother set them years ago, and my housekeeper has continued the practices. My wife has learned them as she took over the house, and modified their behaviour to suit her preferences."

"I do not mean to criticize." Lucas said hurriedly. "I am simply unaccustomed to so much. A footman in the hallway at night, maids and men, a butler . . ." He sighed. "My sisters must help my mother with the cooking."

"It is not unheard of." Darcy said diplomatically.

Lucas laughed. "Perhaps not for your tenants."

"Some of my tenants do very well." He smiled slightly. "Some farm lands in excess of the size of Longbourn or even Netherfield for me."

"Perhaps I should become a tenant of yours." Lucas rubbed his jaw. "Although I suspect those particular spots are coveted. You have been described to me as an exceptionally liberal master."

"Really?" Darcy looked up when the maid entered bearing a tray of coffee and biscuits, then poured out two cups. "Thank you, Maggie." She bobbed and disappeared.

"Mr. Bennet speaks of you."

"That is surprising, although he has been asking more often for advice regarding his estate." Darcy stirred cream into his cup and took a sip. "What are your appointments for the day? I should tell you that Mr. Gardiner responded to our note; he said that he will come this afternoon with his wife and my sisters."

"Oh." Lucas drew a deep breath and let it go. "Well, I do need to speak with him regarding my investment. I wish to increase it."

"I have had some excellent returns from him." Darcy sat back comfortably. "I am certainly pleased."

"Yes." Lucas took a sip then set down his cup. "This coffee is very good."

Darcy saw through him. "You know, you need to stop comparing the life you can offer Jane to the one her sister leads. You must be proud of what you have or else she will never be able to be proud of it as well." He smiled when Lucas startled. "It is one thing to be ambitious to improve your situation, but it is another thing entirely to covet another's property and sink into self-pity as a result. Which man would a woman prefer as her husband?" He glanced back and indicated the portrait behind him. "My father taught me to be proud of our heritage, our people, and our land. Pride in our position was not the most important factor."

"That is precisely what my father values the most, his knighting is his pride." Lucas said tiredly. "It defines his every move. It has elevated his self-importance and as a result, has left his family poorer."

"Then you shall right the ship." Darcy tapped a letter on his desk. "I received a letter last night from my aunt, her position was her pride, and she attached all of her self-worth to it. She attempted to keep her status by manipulating her daughter cruelly and by attempting to arrange my destiny. Now she finds herself alone, reduced to the role of widow in an adequate home. hardly the position of exalted mother-in-law and honoured grandmother that she expected. She wrote to me humbling herself; asking to be part of my life. But in her words I see the avarice and desire to be what she never was to her own child. I will forgive her, but deny her request. I have no room for such a person in my life, just as I suspect you have no room for envy in yours." He tilted his head. "What do you fear seeing when Jane comes here today?"

"Disappointment." He said without hesitation. "She has seen so much now. What I was able to show her of myself this winter is surely superseded by Mr. Bingley, and your aunt, and you." He looked around then met his eyes.

"You have such little faith in her."

"What do you mean?" He said sharply.

"You are still valuing the material. If I did that, I would not have fallen in love with Elizabeth the moment I first saw her. After all, the fifteen-year-old girl I saw that day was not dressed in silk, was not a refined woman, but was a sweet girl from an insignificant estate in Hertfordshire. It was the girl, now the woman, that I valued. Tell me, do you really think that Jane Bennet values the number of carriages you own, or is it the man who makes her smile?" Darcy sat back and steepled his hands.

"Why did I not meet you in Cambridge?" Lucas smiled. "I could have used a brother like you."

Darcy laughed. "I was not the man I am now. I doubt that I would have been of much use. However, if things work out in your favour, perhaps we will be brothers one day."

"Perhaps." Lucas looked at his hands then back up. "I love her."

"I know." Darcy met his gaze. "You love her so much that you want only the best for her, and you are willing to let her go if it will make her happy." He studied him and spoke softly. "I let Elizabeth go once, and I regretted it deeply. Tell me something, this business you have in town that you simply had to rush here to address, is it truly so pressing or were you leaping on any excuse to come here and perhaps see her?" Lucas' face turned pink as he blushed. "I see. I wish that I had been so impulsive."

"I am not used to speaking of my feelings to anyone."

Darcy watched him slowly twisting his hands together. "I understand, and I understand the torture of waiting."

Lucas nodded and clasping his hands, searched for a better way to occupy himself. "Well. I have some appointments to keep. It seems that the ladies are slow to leave their beds."

"No, no. We do not keep town hours. My wife is with our baby, and usually we go for a walk before breakfast. Of course with your sister here, our plans will be curtailed for the day. Would you care for a ride in the park? That is a favourite way of mine to release my preoccupation with difficult subjects."

"I would very much; however, I really do need to take care of business, and I wish to be back in good time for Miss Bennet this afternoon." He stood and Darcy did with him. "Your cousins will be visiting as well?"

"Yes." Darcy chuckled. "Did I see a spark or two flying between your sister and the reverend?"

"I hope so." Lucas laughed and relaxed.

"I do as well." Darcy bowed and Lucas went to the door and turned.

"Thank you. For . . .the reassurance."

"I am glad to have provided it." Hearing the front door closing, Darcy settled back into his chair and smiled as he returned to work. "Well Bingley, I wish you well on your assignment today."

"THANK YOU FOR THIS OPPORTUNITY, Miss Bennet." Bingley said softly. "It was kind of your aunt to allow it."

"She has no reason to fear you, sir." Jane looked at her hands clasped in her lap.

Leaning towards her from his chair, he waited for her chin to lift. "Miss Bennet. I have come to regard you as not only one of the most beautiful women of my acquaintance, but also one of the kindest."

"Oh."

"Your care for your family is obvious, and that is something that I admire deeply."

"Thank you."

Bingley took a deep breath and looking her in the eye, drew on the conversation he had with Darcy the day before. "I feel that for me to continue as I have, giving you no true indication of my intentions is unfair, and today I wish to make them perfectly clear."

"Yes, Mr. Bingley?" She whispered and looked back down.

He paused and tried to read her body language and face. She was nervous, even frightened, but her smiles when he arrived gave him no signal of her feelings. "Miss Bennet. I have learned that Netherfield has been leased to another man for at least the next quarter. I had intended to take the estate and begin my journey to landownership there. I have not found another property that I felt was suitable to my needs. With this delay in mind, I have thought long and hard about my desires." He waited for her to look up, and gathered his resolve. "I have decided that I have not attained the experience or the credibility to be a landowner or husband as yet. For this reason, I have decided that I will speak to Mr. Darcy, and discover what is necessary for me to embark on a grand tour. I wish to round out my education properly as all gentlemen should, then when I return to England in a year or so, I will be prepared to settle down, find my estate, and marry."

Jane stared at him. "You . . . you are leaving?"

Bingley swallowed, clenched his fists to stay focussed, and nodded. "That is my decision, yes." He searched her eyes and saw, for a moment, relief. All of his questions were answered in that sudden flash of honesty, and at once he felt sure. "It would be unfair to propose anything to you with such a plan in my mind. I know that Lady Matlock has been working to make you into a lady of society, and I know that she hoped for an alliance between us. I realize that is in no small part due to my queries to her husband and sons, and . . . If it raised your hopes, I beg your forgiveness. I am at last hearing clearly the advice of so many; I am too young to marry."

"I . . . I do not know what to say, sir." Jane twisted her hands. "Are you telling me that I should wait for you?"

"No. I am telling you that if when I return we both are unattached, then perhaps I will be at last ready to be a good husband, but that if during my absence you find someone who makes you happy, do not hesitate to take that opportunity."

"You do not love me."

"No more than you love me, I suspect." Bingley said kindly. Jane looked back to him and nodded. "Well then, this is the proper move. I do not wish for a marriage of convenience, although that was what I was raised to expect. I want love. I dare not hope for the example of the Darcys, but I do hope for more than my sisters' unions. I fear that we have both felt pressured by others to make something out of nothing."

"I felt we had at least a good friendship, sir."

"I agree wholeheartedly with that, and I do hope that it continues. Perhaps in the future . . ."

"No, sir." Jane looked up. "As you say, if I find love, in whatever form I can, I will claim it."

"Very well." He smiled and reached out to squeeze her hand. "*Are* you well?"

She smiled. "Yes. I feel as if an enormous weight of expectation has been lifted from me. I do not want the life you do. I do not want the whirl of society or the spectacular residence. I simply want a home, a husband who cares for me, and children to love. That is all."

"I hope that is what I will give my wife someday." Bingley laughed with obvious relief. "With a bit of dancing to boot."

Jane laughed. "And an estate."

"Yes." He sighed. "It is my lot in life to be as grand as my father's dreams allow."

"I wish you joy in your future, Mr. Bingley." Jane stood and he rose with her.

"And I wish you happiness in yours, wherever it leads you." Bingley kissed her hand and bowed. "Goodbye." He walked from the room, stopping to say goodbye to the confused Mrs. Gardiner, and taking his hat from the maid by the door, stepped out of the home. He stood out on the step for several moments, looking down the street towards the park where he had walked with Jane so many times. Snippets of conversations played in his head, and he slowly descended to the street. Turning, he looked back up at the house. This had been the most difficult conversation he had ever had. He did not like it at all, but somehow, having performed it, he felt good about himself. "I needed to do this alone." He climbed into his carriage and settled back into the seat. "Thank you, Darcy, for making me come alone."

Jane watched the fine carriage pull away and turned from the window. "Jane?" Mrs. Gardiner came in the room. "Are you well? What happened?"

"He was not here to propose, Aunt." Jane smiled and then wiped her eyes. "He . . .came to release me."

"Release you? But you were not engaged, were you?"

"No." She sank down onto a chair. "No, nobody wishes to be engaged to me, it seems." She wiped her eyes. "I do not know why I am crying. He was correct, I do not love him."

"Did he love you?" Mrs. Gardiner asked softly and held her hand.

"No." Jane smiled and looked up. "We were just friends, and I have known that for some time. I kept thinking about Alicia telling me that she was not in love with her husband when she wed, but that now she loves him deeply. I thought that I should probably be the same as she, that my care would grow with time."

"He did not share that sentiment."

"No, he outright said that he wants to love his wife from the beginning."
Jane laughed. "I suspect that Lizzy and Mr. Darcy have had an effect on
everyone who they know."

"So you are telling me that if your sister was not so clearly in love with Mr.
Darcy, you would never have hoped for that yourself? Your mother's desire
that you marry any man to save the family was yours as well?" Jane looked up
as Mrs. Gardiner continued. "Would not marriage to Mr. Bingley have been a
marriage of convenience, an undoubtedly very pleasant one, but convenience
nonetheless?"

"Have I made a terrible mistake? Should I have pretended more? I know
that Lady Matlock will be very disappointed in me. Are you? Did you want me
to marry him?"

"I want you to be happy, dear. This is your life and your decision, only your
feelings matter. Stop trying to please others." She smiled. "Now, what is this
about nobody wanting to be engaged to you? Is there not a young man in
Hertfordshire who would undoubtedly be overjoyed with the conversation you
just had, and the decision you made?" A smile appeared on Jane's lips and her
eyes took on a lustre of happiness as she imagined Lucas's face. "Is not that
young man the reason you answered as you did?"

"Yes." She whispered. "But does he still want me? I have been gone so
long, and I do not know when I will see him again."

Mrs. Gardiner handed her a handkerchief. "Well, I suppose that you will
find out soon enough. Now wipe your eyes. It is time that we leave for Darcy
House."

DOROTHY YOUNGE heard a quiet knock on the door to her rooms in the
small boarding house adjacent to the girls' school. Wiping her hands onto her
apron, she walked forward and opened it, then gasped. "George!"

She threw her arms around him and he kissed her hard. "Hello, Dotty!" He
growled and with a backwards kick, pushed the door shut. He pulled back and
looked her over. "You look so good."

"You look terrible." She held his gaunt face in her hands. "Did you ever
eat?"

"Not often." He sank down onto a chair and looked at his beaten hands.
"It was hell in there. Not fit for the vermin we caught and roasted for dinner."

"What happened?" She brought him bread and cheese, and poured out
some ale. She sat beside him and looked over the bruises. "Did you have to
fight with the guards? How were you able to slip away? Did anyone give you
trouble?"

"No, not too much." He continued to stare at his hands.

"I am sorry that I could not come to see you. Darcy . . ."

"Yes, I know you were being watched. I got your notes; I paid the ransom
for them." He laughed hollowly. "I might have been able to bribe my way out

months ago, but for that. Instead I was sent to that floating dungeon." He looked up at her. "You had to watch yourself around the girls, I gather."

"If I put a toe out of line that Mary Bennet would have had me dismissed in a heartbeat. She is quiet, but she watched me. No, I needed the job, it is a good one." She stood to get him some meat and he grabbed her hand.

"Do you have the money for the ship?"

"Yes, I stole what I could from the little heiresses; they had so much that they never noticed it disappearing. It was risky, but I was alert. I even got some from Miss Darcy; she was careless with her purse." She saw him smile at that. "Darcy contributed to your comfort."

"Well, how gentlemanly of him." He sneered. "I want to be on the way to Portsmouth within the week, before anyone gets the bright idea that I am not dead."

She stopped her movement and turned to him. "Dead? Do they think that you drowned? I thought that you were going to exchange clothes with some beggar, and let the guards follow after him while you disappeared. Are you afraid that he will say something when they speak to him?"

"No, he'll keep quiet, I'm sure. Don't mind me, Dotty; it is just the relief of being out of that hellhole making me wary." Picking up a knife, he sliced off a piece of cheese. "I am anxious to be well away from here. I just need to settle a score before we go." Taking a bite, he closed his eyes. "And start over."

"MISS LUCAS, tell me about growing up with Elizabeth." Georgiana looked at her sister and back to Charlotte. "I want to know if she ever misbehaved."

"Georgiana, what are you about?" Elizabeth asked with narrowed eyes.

"I am just curious." She said innocently.

"*You* are trying to see a way around the rules that your brother and I have made, and are trying to use my childhood against me. Well, I was not a perfect angel, but without delving into specifics, I believe that I was justified in whatever indiscretions I did manage to commit."

"Oh Eliza, I can only agree with that." Charlotte laughed then looked to Georgiana. "I am six years older than Eliza, so you could hardly call me a contemporary playmate of hers, but I certainly knew her from being neighbours and of course from her regular walks from Longbourn to Lucas Lodge. I always thought of her then as a very curious and pleasant girl. I suppose that we became friends when she was fifteen and Mrs. Bennet put her out. That was when we were frequently in company, and were able to commiserate with each other about the desires of our mothers to see us married off."

Elizabeth laughed. "Oh, and we did that often. How many assemblies did we spend sitting without partners and watching Jane smiling and dancing the evening away?"

"Well, I would say at least ten, and then there were all the evenings we spent partnering each other until your Mr. Darcy took you away permanently."

Charlotte smiled when Elizabeth squeezed her hand. "Your father is not the only one who misses his most sensible daughters."

"Maria will be out this year."

"Yes, she will keep me company at the assemblies now."

Georgiana looked from one woman to the other. "I suppose that not every girl is asked to dance all of the time."

Elizabeth turned back to her and shook her head sadly. "No. At least not in a place where all of her is known, and if that information is not encouraging. Besides, there were a great many ladies and not so many men to go around."

"But you said that Jane always danced." Georgiana pointed out. "Were you not equal?"

"She is beautiful." Charlotte said softly. "Beauty wins dances when circumstances deny marriages."

"Oh." She bit her lip and looked at Elizabeth. "So . . . Forgive me, you were considered . . ."

"Good fun but not handsome enough to tempt any man who knew of my family to marry me, at least, no gentleman, until your brother spied me."

"But you are lovely." Georgiana argued.

"Thank you, but I am older now." She smiled.

"And I am just old." Charlotte sighed and laughed. "Poor Robert, he may be stuck with me forever."

"Pardon me, Mrs. Darcy. Captain de Bourgh and Reverend de Bourgh are here?" Mr. Foster announced.

"Please show them up and tell Mr. Darcy." She looked at Charlotte and bit her lip to hold back her grin. "Now what was the advice that you always gave us about securing a husband?"

"Hush Eliza!" Charlotte said in a low voice. Georgiana's brow creased and they rose to their feet as the men were shown into the room.

"Good afternoon, ladies!" Peter grinned and bowed. "You are lovely to behold, do you not agree, Michael?"

"Of course." He bowed. "Good afternoon." He turned to smile at Charlotte, then addressed Elizabeth. "I hope that you are all quite well?"

"Quite." Elizabeth laughed when she saw Charlotte blush. "My husband and Mr. Lucas will be upstairs soon, I am sure."

"Excellent!" Peter took a chair near Elizabeth and looked pointedly at his brother then to Charlotte. When Michael said nothing, he sighed and caught the sparkle in Elizabeth's eye. "Well, Miss Lucas, are you enjoying your visit with the Darcys?"

"Oh yes, I love seeing them. It has become a rarity, I am afraid." The ladies squeezed hands and she looked up to him. "I suppose it is just as rare for you to see them?"

"For me? Yes, because not only do they rarely come to London, but they also choose to live so far away in Derbyshire. Tell me Mrs. Darcy, how did your parents feel about your removal to such a distant estate upon marriage?"

She tilted her head and regarded him with a smile. "It is my opinion, sir, that sometimes a letter does just as well as a visit when certain relatives are involved."

Peter laughed. "Ah, I seem to recall some discussion of family relations at your wedding."

Gently clearing her throat, she ignored the smile that played on his lips. "And how goes your family? Your sisters are engaged?" Elizabeth noted how his gaze softened. "That is joyous news."

"Yes, I am very happy for them, although they are a little young, perhaps, I could not deny the men who love them. There will be a double wedding at Rosings. Michael will have the pleasure of performing the ceremony." He looked to Charlotte. "He will have the living at Hunsford Parish."

"How ironic that the former candidate is now the curate in Meryton." Charlotte at last smiled at him. "He is certainly attempting to ingratiate himself with every family. Some more than others." She exchanged a glance with Elizabeth.

"Yes, my future congregation has expressed relief that he has moved on." Michael smiled when Charlotte's eyes widened. "I have heard enough that I cannot blame them, though I am afraid that the garden has suffered for his absence. It seems that Reverend Mousely frequently sent him outside to work. For his health, of course."

"What a brilliant idea." Charlotte laughed softly. "I wonder if I could have conceived such a thought."

"If pressed to relieve stress, Miss Lucas, I am sure that you would." Michael laughed and relaxed a little, and the two tilted their heads and studied each other. "How long will you remain in town, Miss Lucas?"

"Oh. Well my brother has business to accomplish, so when he is through we . . ."

Peter interrupted, and turned to Elizabeth. "Speaking of which, perhaps I might go and join your husband?"

"Certainly, let me show you the way." Elizabeth started to rise, but Georgiana was first.

"Oh, I will do that, Elizabeth." She smiled warmly at the handsome man and stood posing prettily by the door. "Follow me please, sir."

Peter saw Elizabeth's frown and caught her eye. Facing Georgiana he bowed formerly. "Thank you, Miss Darcy. When you are a woman, you will certainly be a wonderful hostess." Noting Elizabeth's approving nod, he flashed her a smile and turned to Georgiana who was looking at her slippers. "Shall we?" He waved his hand at the door.

Georgiana curtseyed and nodded. "Yes, sir."

13 JUNE 1810

I cannot believe my eyes. I am at the writing desk in the yellow sitting room, and not ten feet away are Reverend de Bourgh and Charlotte Lucas, sitting side by side and having an animated conversation about the proper role of a pastor in the life of his parishioners. The arguments they are putting forth are eminently sensible, and they are in agreement of nearly every subject. The most amazing aspect to me is that neither one of them is attempting to hide their opinions, there is no show being put on here. All of Charlotte's pronouncements that a woman must secure the man first and find out about his personality after marriage are clearly being ignored when it comes to her personal interests! I have to refrain from laughing, they seem to be so deeply involved in their conversation, I swear they are married years rather than acquaintances of not even two hours! Oh dear, if Charlotte has her way, she will have Reverend de Bourgh proposing by dinner time! This is a woman on a mission, and her quarry does not seem to mind!

Elizabeth heard a chuckle and looking up to the doorway, received a wink from Peter de Bourgh. Standing behind him were Darcy and Lucas, who were equally amused. Darcy walked in and bent to kiss her cheek, then casually read her entry. He bit his lip to stop the laugh that was threatening to spill out, and instead whispered to her. "I have never seen the like."

"It makes me wonder why she never caught anyone at home." Elizabeth whispered in awe.

"Perhaps at home there was nobody suitable?" He asked with his brows raised. They watched as Lucas joined the conversation, giving Michael a stern stare before assuming his place as guardian to his elder sister. "Too late, old man." Darcy whispered. "Just let nature take its course."

"Fitzwilliam! He is a man of God!"

"His children will be conceived the same way that our daughter was, love." Darcy's eyes twinkled at her. "He is a good man, his brother assured Lucas of that." They saw Peter take a chair with the group. "Well, perhaps we see a new family being formed." Taking the pen from her fingers and placing the ribbon back in the cover, he closed the book. "Shall we join them?"

"Where is Georgiana?" Elizabeth asked as she stood.

"I passed her out in the hallway, she is watching for Mary." He smiled and kissed her hand. "She misses her sister."

"She wants someone to complain to about our rules." Elizabeth laughed. "We need to watch her; she was trying to flirt with Captain de Bourgh."

"She was?" Darcy looked back out at the landing. "Even after your warning?"

"I am afraid so. She is discovering men. The pull of a handsome face is difficult to ignore."

"I do not like this at all." He said worriedly. "What should we do?"

"I will speak to my aunt while she is here. Perhaps a companion should be hired? I cannot be with her all of the time."

"If we do that we may as well keep her from school. That is where she got all of these ideas." He huffed. "You were not this way at that age."

"How do you know?" Elizabeth smiled at him.

"I . . . I just do." Darcy said positively. "You never desired any man before me." His grasp tightened on her hand. "Of that I am certain." Looking down at her sparkling eyes he furrowed his brow. "Lizzy?"

"Mrs. Darcy, the Gardiners have arrived." A footman announced.

"Oh, we should go meet them." She started to walk away but found her progress was stopped when Darcy remained stationary.

"Lizzy?"

"Yes, dear?"

"Did you ever desire another before me?"

"Did you?"

"That is not the question to be answered."

"I think that it is a perfectly reasonable one."

"No, it is a tactic of avoidance. You are swerving to dodge my fire."

"You compare me to a battleship now? That is hardly complimentary. I believe that I am quite offended." She tried to retrieve her hand but was unsuccessful. "Mr. Darcy, unhand me."

"No."

Elizabeth whispered furiously, "Mr. Darcy, our family is on its way up the steps as we speak!"

"Answer me."

"Would not my answer be suspect at this point? If I say no, you will think I am lying to appease your pride. If I say yes, you will think that I replied positively because my ire is raised."

"I still demand an answer."

"No."

"Why?"

"Because I do not respond well to demands." She shook his hand and looked to the door. "Fitzwilliam!"

"Answer me, Mrs. Darcy."

"No, sir."

"Sir?" He smiled, and relaxed his grip.

"Sir." She said under her breath as their family entered the room. "Are you satisfied?"

"Oh, I will be love." He moved behind her, passing his hand over her bottom as he walked, and bent to her ear. "And so will you." Straightening, he smiled and bowed. "Mr. Gardiner, Mrs. Gardiner, how good to see you!"

Her soft voice filled his ear. "You have not answered my question. Sir." She walked away and Darcy stared after her.

"What happened, Son?" Mr. Gardiner laughed as he watched Elizabeth hug her Aunt and Mary. "Lose an argument?"

"I am not sure." His head tilted. "I thought I had won."

"From the smug expression on Lizzy's face, I would say you should rethink that supposition." Mr. Gardiner smiled and clapped his back. "As well as your next move."

"I will lose no matter what I say." He mused. "Yes will bring her indignation. No will bring her disbelief."

"Which is true?"

Darcy chuckled. "The wrong one, I am afraid." He sighed. "But I will do my best. Either reaction will be a pleasure to soothe."

"I have no doubt." Mr. Gardiner saw Elizabeth shooting a glance at Darcy and smiled, then turned to him. "Bingley stopped by."

"Ah."

"You knew he would?"

"It was time, do you not agree?"

"Absolutely, it was time that some sort of a decision was made." He smiled. "And the decision was no."

Darcy glanced out of the doorway to see Jane still at the bottom of the stairs. "Is she well?"

Mr. Gardiner looked at her and shrugged. "She cried when he left, but I think that it was relief. I wonder though if there will ever be regret."

"Not if she is choosing for herself instead of pleasing others." Darcy nodded over to Lucas. "If she would just come up here, there is a man who wishes to make her happy waiting for his chance. You did not tell her he was here?"

"No, not knowing the situation, we felt it was better to let him do the talking instead of leaving her to speculate." He glanced at the stairs. "Marianne is convinced that she loves him, I have always had a difficult time reading her."

"You and I share that." He looked over to Lucas who was staring at the doorway, and catching his attention, signalled him to join them. "Well? There she is." He smiled and placed his hand on his shoulder. "Just so you know, her answer to Bingley was no."

Lucas let go a stale breath. "She will not wait for him. She does not want him." The three men looked down the stairs to where she remained standing alone, then exchanging glances with Mr. Gardiner, Darcy gave Lucas a little shove and stepped away to go join their family and friends.

Jane listened to the greetings as the family met, and hearing the front door close behind her, startled and slowly walked up the beautiful staircase, and took in the understated elegance. Twice now she had been offered the opportunity to live like this, and twice she had not exerted herself to take it. Why, she wondered, was it that that despite the deceptive simplicity, she had never felt comfortable in this atmosphere? No, it was something more, it was not only her discomfort with the trappings of the life she would have with either Mr. Bingley or Mr. Harwick that she was rejecting, the men who offered it were lacking in something else she was seeking, something she had yet to define.

Hearing her sister's laughter, Jane thought about her position. Elizabeth had taken to it so quickly, seemingly accepting and blending into the world she had been given. She was different now, assured, no longer the shy girl, insecure of her beauty or worth, she was becoming every day the woman who would undoubtedly be a force in London society, in whatever capacity she chose to excel. The pride that Darcy felt for her was evident no matter how it was displayed. He had chosen well. He knew he had found his future the moment he first saw her, and she knew the same. *How did they know?*

Jane remembered that fateful day in Hyde Park, seeing the handsome, well-dressed man, and wondering over his status: bachelor, rich, gentleman . . . all of the qualities she had been taught by her mother to seek for her husband, and now she realized that Elizabeth had seen only the sorrowful man in need, and Darcy had looked to see only a girl and a smile. Jane's hand came to her mouth as she finally understood; all of the riches in the world did not matter to them at all, and never had. They would have loved each other no matter where they had met.

Arriving at the sitting room door, she saw a mixture of people from nearly all levels of society, comfortably talking with each other in the midst of the decoration of an affluent life, and her eyes fell upon the man in the simply-tailored suit who stood staring at her; and her alone. "Robert." She whispered as his eyes lit up with hope.

He watched her face transform as she exposed her heart. "Oh, Jane." Lucas stepped across the room and took her hands in his. "My Jane?"

Tears began to pour down her cheeks. "Why did I not see you months ago?" She demanded as he produced a handkerchief to wipe her face. "Why did I leave you? Why did you not stop me?"

Laughing, he lifted her hands to his lips. "Because my Jane, I knew in my heart that you needed to forget before you could see clearly what was before you."

"What on earth does that mean?" She sighed. Hearing laughter around them they both blushed and looked down at their clasped hands. "I forgot that we were not alone."

"Shall I ask for permission to speak to you alone?" He said softly. "I think that you know what I would like to ask you."

"Yes. My answer is yes."

Lucas chuckled and smiled into her teary eyes. "Should I not propose first? Perhaps declare my heart and explain my feelings?"

"Oh." She blushed again. "What is wrong with me? I am never so impulsive!"

"I like it." He whispered. "I like that I manage to bring it out in you." She looked up and he leaned to her ear. "I love you, and it has been such torture waiting to find out if . . . if you would finally see good sense and love me back."

"Mr. Lucas!" Jane whispered. "I have known that I loved you for quite some time."

"But you did nothing about it. You kept following through with others and their plans for your future." He squeezed her hands and his eyes glowed with joy. "Because you needed to forget."

"What was I forgetting?" She asked desperately. "I do not understand."

"You were forgetting a lifetime of expectations that were heaped upon you." He lifted her hands to his lips again. "I understand that all too well."

"I think that I understood that as I walked up the stairs."

"I watched you." Lucas looked down at her hands in his. "I cannot offer you a home like this, Jane. I cannot even offer you a home of your own until my Father is gone. But I am working very hard to make it better than it was when he bought it, and I promise to do my best to see that we are comfortable always. I want more than anything to make you happy. It is not much, but . . ."

"Robert . . .you are the only man who has ever spoken of my happiness." She lifted her hand to touch his cheek. "You are not seeking a conduit for producing an heir, nor an adornment to accompany you, you just want me." He nodded. "That is why you take my breath away."

"Jane . . ."

"Well are you going to kiss her or not?" Peter called out across the room. "Come on, I have a bet riding on this!"

The room erupted in laughter and Lucas and Jane turned sheepishly to face them, still holding hands. Darcy was sitting on a sofa, Elizabeth beside him and clasped in his arms. Charlotte was beaming at them and wiping the tears rolling down her face. Georgiana and Mary were standing together and giggling, while the de Bourgh brothers stood a little away from the family gathering and looked expectantly at the couple, each holding up a guinea. Mr. Gardiner smiled at his wife and approached the couple. "Well, Mr. Lucas, as the duly appointed guardian of the unmarried Bennet daughters in London, I believe that a conversation is necessary between us, if our assumptions of your behaviour are correct? Or does Darcy need to dust off his duelling pistols?"

Lucas laughed and smiled down at Jane. "I have not formally asked the question sir, although I believe I have been accepted." He then turned and knelt down on the floor. "Miss Jane Bennet, will you please do me the honour of accepting my hand?"

"Yes, Mr. Lucas." She laughed as he kissed her fingers and rose to his feet. "I will be honoured to make you happy."

Lucas smiled and leaned forward to softly kiss her lips. Jane gasped and melted into him for a second, longer kiss. In the background, Peter groaned and handed his brother the coin, and while the attention was directed to the men, Lucas whispered in Jane's ear. "Now, do you see why I wanted to be alone?"

"I do." She was blushing furiously.

"But at least everyone knows that you are mine." He stepped back a little and smiled as the family began to advance to offer their congratulations. Wiping the tears that were flowing down her cheek he leaned forward as she wiped his. "And the next time I kiss you, we will be."

13 JUNE 1810

Last October, my uncle took me aside at Pemberley and asked what is in the air because clearly it inspires a desire for connubial bliss. I admit that I found the notion laughable, after all how could the mere air of our beloved home inspire three couples to form, four if you include the early beginnings of Bingley and Jane. But now, when my uncle hears the news that not only has Jane become engaged to Robert Lucas, but that her future sister Miss Lucas has discovered previously unknown abilities to charm a gentleman under my roof, I am afraid that he will instead take great delight in telling all who we know to steer clear of our homes, unless they have a distinct desire to fall madly in love with someone unexpected. Perhaps it is true; the tendrils of love from Darcy House followed me into the park each time that I encountered my Elizabeth there. I am being fanciful, I know. I blame it on the air.

Bingley's talk with Jane was well-timed, it seems. It was precisely what she needed to hear, and finding Lucas here waiting for her seemed to be the answer she had been seeking. I wonder now if she would have been so quick to realize her heart had she come to Darcy House and not found him here. I wonder if she would have instead endured the remainder of the Season, searching, perhaps successfully, for a man of higher worth. To witness the warmth in her eyes when she looked upon Lucas, and the unhidden elation in his, confirms all of my suspicions. Jane belongs in Hertfordshire. I sincerely believe that her time in London with her aunt and mine, and her time spent with us at Pemberley were beneficial to her, not only so she could see what she did not want, but also to help her see who she was. I have no doubt that one day she will be quite content to be Mistress of Lucas Lodge, and no more. I am happy for my sister.

"I am as well." Elizabeth said as she closed the journal. She turned to see Darcy laying on his stomach on the bed, propped up on his arms and blowing kisses on Rosalie's belly while she giggled and clutched his hair. "What a picture you present!"

Darcy lifted his head and grinned. "I cannot resist. Her laughter is as contagious as yours, love." Hearing a squeal he returned to his duty, blowing again to the delight of his daughter.

"You will have her excited and then she will never sleep." Elizabeth lay down next to him and started nibbling toes. Darcy gave her a sidelong glance and she shrugged. "She is irresistible."

"Just like her mama." He kissed her and smiled when his nose received a kiss in return. "Are you truly happy for Jane?"

"Of course." Elizabeth played with Rosalie's curly hair and watched her giggle. "I never thought she would be happy with Mr. Bingley, well perhaps she would, but they are both so . . .nice." Darcy's chuckle made her look to him and smile. "You know what I mean."

"They would dare not ever argue with each other for fear of giving offence?" He kissed her. "But Jane had no problem offending when it came to us."

"That was because she was jealous and felt threatened; it was not her true nature." Elizabeth studied him. "You never took to her, even before she veered from herself."

"No. I was never attracted before she veered, as you say, but then when she did, I . . . I like her now."

"Always honest." Elizabeth caressed his hair.

"My opinion has improved." He said softly.

"There is no need to explain. After all, you clearly were making amends for it by encouraging both Mr. Lucas and Mr. Bingley to act." She kissed his cheek. "I thank you for that."

"I do not want your gratitude, dearest." He rested his head on his arms and they watched Rosalie's eyes close. "She will do well with Lucas, I think. He is not a man to always agree. I think that will be good for her."

"Jane will have to learn to defend her opinions then." She rested her face on her arms and they looked at each other nose to nose. "Mama will be angry she let Mr. Bingley get away."

"But she will remain close to home. That must count for something."

"Papa will be happy." Elizabeth said softly. "We will not see each other very often will we?"

"We will stop at Longbourn whenever we go to and from town." He reached out to caress her hair.

"But they will not be able to afford the journey to Derbyshire. Not often." She buried her face in her arms and he drew her close and kissed her. She lifted her head and smiled a little. "That would not have happened if she had married Mr. Bingley. I had hoped that Mr. Bingley would be our brother, even though I knew they did not belong together."

"Why?" Darcy asked quietly.

"Why did they not belong together?"

"No. Why did you want him as our brother?"

"Because I feel his need to be part of a family." She smiled and curled up next to him and kissed his lips. "We have a wonderful family."

Darcy looked at Rosalie and smiled. "Let me put her to bed, and when I return, you and I can discuss family."

Elizabeth watched him carry their sleeping girl away. When he returned, he closed the door to the mistress' chambers and pulling off his nightshirt, walked around the room, blowing out the candles. He climbed into the bed and sat up against the headboard, and held out his arms. "Come."

"What do you have in mind?" She laughed as she crawled over to him and kissed his mouth. Darcy tugged at her night dress and she lifted it off then straddling him, slid down his length. They both sighed and kissed slowly, allowing their tongues to explore each other's mouths, and their lips, warm and soft, slid as they savoured each other. Darcy drew away first and rested his forehead to hers, then cuddled her head against his neck while holding her body. Elizabeth wrapped her arms around him.

"Are you comfortable?" He whispered and kissed her ear.

"Very." She squeezed his hard shaft buried deep inside of her, and she felt his answering twitch. "Very, comfortable."

"What shall we talk about first?"

"Well, we did have a disagreement before we were distracted by an engagement." She murmured against his neck. "What frightened you today? What made you so demanding on such an inconsequential subject?"

"So if I told you that I felt desire for another once in my past you would deem it inconsequential?"

"You are not answering me."

Darcy sighed. "Do you realize that our anniversary is approaching?"

"Of course. We will be married one year on the twenty-first."

"Not that anniversary, while unquestionably important, it is not the one I refer to. I mean that extraordinary day when I first saw you." He kissed her softly. "That day."

"Yes." Elizabeth stroked back his hair. "I feel it is more important than the wedding day as well."

"When you spoke of Georgiana being attracted to men, and she is just fourteen, it suddenly struck me that you were just fifteen when we saw each other, and I was ready to marry you there and then."

"I was nearly sixteen."

"Dearest you were nonetheless close to her age, and the thought of you smiling at anyone else as you did to me that day . . ." He rested his head in her hair. "I do not like sharing your smiles with anyone."

Elizabeth hugged him with her arms and her body, and he moaned softly in her ear. "I understand, and the answer is still no, although I admit to experimenting, just as Georgiana is doing now."

"Please do not tell me more."

"And you?"

"I may have looked with lust, but there was no desire for love behind it." He added quietly. "I was a boy."

"When did you become a man?" Elizabeth looked up to him and kissed his temple and his chin. "And do not tell me when we met."

"It is true."

"It is not." She laughed. "You were a man before you left to tour the continent."

"No." He stroked his hands over her shoulders then lifted her to thrust a few times, and she slowly rode him while they engaged in open kisses, exploring each other's mouths. Darcy's breath became ragged, and stilled her movement, closing his eyes while he regained control. "I became a man the day my father told me he was to die. I remember it settling over me, an uncomfortable mantle of responsibility relieved only by the gift of your laughter and concern."

"Oh Will."

"So, today when I was struck by the thought, once again, that had we not met . . . I became my possessive self. Forgive me for making you angry." His lips lifted in his little smile. "Although I do love to see your ire raised."

"That I know." Elizabeth ran her fingers through his hair and kissed him. "Lay down."

He tipped over and with a great deal of laughter; he was on his back with his hands on her bottom and Elizabeth lying on his chest. "Better?"

"Hmm." She sat up and dangled her breasts before him. Laughing, he happily suckled her, then licking the milk from his lips, groaned when she began mastering her mount once again.

"Oh Elizzzzzzzzzabeth." He panted and moaned. "Slow, slow, dearest, I . . . I want to last." Reaching up he dragged her face back down for more kisses. "Oh love, this feels so good."

She lay back onto his chest and he held her to him. "I am so close."

"Hold on, love. Think of something else."

"What?" She moaned and squeezed the throbbing rock inside of her. "Ohhhhh, Will."

"Shhhhhhhh. Not yet, please." Darcy searched for a subject. "Mary."

"Mary?"

"De Bourgh was . . .ohhhh . . .laughing at her."

"With good reason." Elizabeth began suckling his neck below his ear and he responded by biting her shoulder. "Bite me again!" She nipped his lobe.

"No . . .oh sweetheart, no, not yet." He panted and held her face up to keep her lips from driving him insane. "Please. This is exquisite torture."

"It certainly is." She stared into the dark pools of his eyes. "Mary."

"yes, yes." He grabbed onto the subject again. "What happened?"

Elizabeth thought desperately to remember. "She was . . . Fordyce . . . ohhhhhhhh . . . he had never . . . heard . . . laughable."

"Must . . . burn . . . all . . . copies." Darcy declared as he drove upwards.

"Ohhh . . . he was . . . oh, Will." Elizabeth whimpered.

"You . . . did not . . . read . . . Fordyce."

"No."

Darcy bit her throat, and she moaned. "I am . . . so . . . grateful."

"As am I."

"You are wanton." He growled.

"You are a rake." She cried.

"Elizabeth?" Darcy panted as his voice rose an octave. "Now." He rolled her over and looked down for a moment, then began thrusting as deep and fast as he could. It took only moments before they both felt their bodies dissolving into the all-encompassing pleasure. "Ohhhhhhh." Darcy moaned and kept moving as he felt her relaxing. When his moment came, he collapsed and pressed his face to her shoulder to keep the oaths he wished to swear from his tongue. He desperately wanted to shout out his pleasure so all of London knew what he was feeling.

"Will!" Elizabeth cried. They held each other and sighed. "ohhh."

"Dearest." Darcy breathed in deeply. "My sweet Lizzy." He kissed her and bathed her shoulder gently with his tongue. "My dear Lizzy." Kissing her gently he at last withdrew and immediately pulled her to him. "Dear sweet Elizabeth."

She giggled as he incoherently mumbled endearments and fell asleep. "I suppose that we will finish this conversation in the morning." She reached for the counterpane and drew it over them, then cuddled into his arms. "Good night, my love."

"WHERE ARE YOU GOING?" Mrs. Younge sat up and asked when Wickham rose from the bed they had been sharing vigorously all evening. She watched him relieve himself in the chamber pot and then pull clothes over his wasted body.

"I need some things." He said softly. "I need some clothes."

"I have the clothes that you left behind when you were sent to . . ." She stood and went to a corner, and opened a trunk.

"You do take care of me, Dotty." He murmured, and looked through his belongings, fingering the fine lawn of a shirt from his former life. "I will save these for our journey." Buttoning his breeches, he tucked his shirt in. "I need to pick up a few other things."

"Maybe I have them?"

"I doubt that you have a pistol." He gave her a crooked grin and reached out to tweak her breast. "I am an escaped prisoner. I need to be ready."

"You wouldn't kill anyone, would you?" She said worriedly.

"Of course not, lovey. Of course not." Wickham pinched her bottom and kissed her. "Don't dress, I'll be back soon." He slipped out of the door and looking around, went down the steps to the quiet street, then started walking towards Hyde Park. He passed a watchman and nodding to him, kept walking.

The man touched his hat and moved on. "Eleven o'clock and all is well!"

Chapter 17

"All alone?" Bingley asked Hurst when he wandered into the breakfast room.

"Blessed silence." He said wearily.

"This does not sound like it is about Louisa." Bingley poured a cup of coffee and settled into a chair. His gaze roamed the table and he looked back to Hurst. "Two extra places?" Hurst said nothing as Charles again scanned the room, and then saw the telltale evidence of Caroline. "Oranges."

"The Robinsons are here."

"It is not anywhere close to orange season." Bingley stared at the bowl, then plucked one out. "It is petrified!"

"My mother hangs them about with cloves over them." Hurst examined one and returned it. "Caroline thinks they are more decorative this way."

"Then let her decorate her own home." Dropping the shrivelled fruit into the bowl, he looked to Hurst. "Well?"

"Their house is under renovation, and they have come to keep us company while it is completed." He laughed mirthlessly. "If you had come home last night, you would have been entertained with a litany of Caroline's complaints of the society who have yet to recognize the wonders of her company. And her husband's complaints that none of the higher society that I inhabit," He coughed, "care to participate in his dinner parties."

"They are well-matched, without a doubt." Bingley murmured. "Actually I was here, I came home rather early. I simply decided to keep my own company in my rooms."

"You spoke to Miss Bennet?" Hurst sat back and folded his arms.

"Yes." He shrugged. "I never should have tried. How many men told me not to pursue her? Even Mrs. Darcy questioned my desire. I fought it even as I moved forward. I suppose that I was trying to live up to the challenge presented by Lord Matlock to be a man. It was Darcy who put forth the question that I finally heard. He asked if I were to marry her today, full of passion and excitement, would I have anything to say to her by the date of the first anniversary?" Bingley smiled. "Passion. Waking up this morning, I realized that Miss Bennet is a woman incapable of passion, at least for me, and that my feelings can hardly be described as burning."

Hurst shook his fork at him. "You want what Darcy has. You cannot compare your prospects to anyone else. How many marriages start without regard, let alone passion?"

"I refuse to settle for a mediocre life, Hurst." Bingley said decisively. "My parents had that; ambition was the only common ground that they held. No, Darcy got me to thinking and I envisioned us smiling at each other and going our separate ways. We really have nothing to say to each other. We were pleasant companions, friends, and we always got along . . . Do I sound as miserable as I think I do? I sound like I am trying to make her sound like a, well like a person she is not. She is very sweet and kind; she simply is not the girl for me."

"This is the closest you have ever come to marriage; it is not surprising that you would feel a bit emotional about it." Hurst smiled understandingly.

Bingley sighed and picked up his cup to take a sip. "Darcy assured me that conversation and friendship is almost the entire relationship, but that mutual goals and support are crucial, and lovemaking is the bonus. He told me about something Harwick said to him once, that there are many hours to the day in a marriage, and one cannot always be at sport or business; you must have something to share with your wife. Of course in Darcy's case that is not a problem in the slightest, but for normal men . . ." Bingley smiled to see Hurst rolling his eyes. "Well, he did not want to see me turning to a courtesan to provide the companionship that I might not receive at home."

"It sounds as if Darcy is not impressed with his sister."

"It is not that he does not like her . . . He is spoiled by his wife, just as she is spoiled by him." Bingley stood and perused the dishes on the sideboard, then filled his plate. "But he makes excellent points, do you agree?"

"I find no fault in them." Hearing the sounds of women's voices, he sighed. "Brace yourself."

"Charles!" Caroline breezed in with her husband and sister, and waited for someone to pull out her chair. When it was clear that nobody would, she covered her hesitation by turning to the sideboard. "We missed you last night. Louisa told me that you were visiting the Darcys?"

"Yes, and they are very well." He took his seat. "I will be speaking to Darcy again this afternoon."

"Really?" She looked at Louisa and smiled. "Perhaps we could join you and pay a call on Mrs. Darcy?"

"Mrs. Darcy is hosting some friends for several days, I do not know if she has time for visitors."

Caroline brushed him off. "Why of course she does! You were there!"

"I was visiting Darcy, not his wife." Bingley said pointedly.

"Of course you were." She smiled brilliantly.

"Caroline, you are not going to bother Mrs. Darcy. There is no point to it. You are not going to Pemberley. Darcy has made that quite clear any number of times."

"Oh, but when you marry Miss Bennet . . ."

"No, Caroline, I will not marry her." He glanced at Hurst who smiled and caught Louisa's eye. She looked at her brother and back at her husband with her mouth open.

"What did you say?" Caroline slowly turned. "You have been courting her."

"I have ended our relationship. I realized that it is time to move on."

Robinson had been sitting at the table studying him. "Bored?" Bingley's brow creased. "Well the woman is beautiful, but it is well known she brought nothing to the table, at least nothing significant beyond the connection to Darcy." He glanced at his wife and smirked. "Unlike you, my dear. So much for your plans."

"What plans?" She darted a look at Bingley who folded his arms and stared at her.

Robinson laughed shortly. "Caroline, I am not a fool. And I will not be a cuckolded husband, no matter how hard you try. I'll get to the first circles some other way." He watched her colour rise and turned back to Bingley. "It is a disappointment, but Bingley here is still friends with the Darcys, I presume. We will undoubtedly meet at some function or other and I will make use of the connection then."

"No, you will not." Bingley glared. "I will not have my friendship used for your purposes."

"Is it not in your best interests to see your family well-off? If my business fails, we might very well appear on your doorstep, baggage in hand." He chuckled.

"Then I suggest that you attend your business and stay well away from mine. Go to your estate and live off the land." Standing, he threw his napkin on the table. "I have lost my appetite."

"Come now, Bingley, I was just getting a rise out of you." Robinson laughed. "You are always so easy; it is good to see that you are capable of affront."

"I do not need, nor desire, to be treated as a mouse by a cat." He said angrily.

"You have said enough, Robinson." Hurst cut in before his brother could retort. "If you wish to remain here while your home is repaired, I suggest that we attempt to live in harmony." He looked to Caroline. "That goes for you, as well."

"You are not my husband." She sniffed.

"No, but I am master of this house, and my welcome is crucial. I could care less if you must live with workers and paint for the duration of your renovations, Caroline."

"Please, this is most unseemly." Louisa shot a look to the door. "The staff does not need to hear any of this."

"Forgive me Bingley; I am merely a tradesman on my way up the social ladder." Robinson nodded. "Caroline. No more talk of Darcy, Pemberley or any other such nonsense. We will arrive on our own."

She glared. "You certainly did not mind talking of your plans for meeting him before, Mr. Robinson."

"I will meet him. But it seems that he has no desire to meet you." He smirked. "What is his club, Bingley?"

"You would go to his club? Without me?" Caroline screeched.

"It is a gentleman's club, my dear. No proper ladies allowed." He winked at Bingley.

Bingley felt the heat rising in his face. "Darcy does not participate . . ."

"Oh calm down, man. You know that nobody is offering me a membership there." He sighed. "How did you ever get in?"

"A friend of Father's sponsored me. He died almost immediately after I was accepted." Bingley said quietly, as silence calmed the heated atmosphere of the room.

Robinson picked up a banana and examined it. "So? You are doing what now if you are not courting Miss Bennet?"

Bingley remained silent for several moments, and resumed his seat. "I have decided to take a tour for the next year." He turned to Hurst. "I thought that you and Louisa might like to come along."

"Ohhh, really?" Louisa gasped and turned to her husband. "You never got to travel when you graduated, could we, Gerald?"

"You would waste our father's money on travel?" Caroline demanded.

"It is my money, Caroline, to do with as I please. You have yours. And may I remind you, our father wished for me to be a gentleman. Part of that education is seeing the continent." He noticed Robinson looking at him and addressed Hurst. "What do you think? I was going to ask Darcy for advice on where to go. There are plenty of guides to take us along, and keep us safe."

"A year?" He said thoughtfully.

"Well, it does not have to be, but enough time to do it properly. I need to fill some time before considering Netherfield for next year or hopefully something more suitable will become available. I would rather do it improving my mind than hanging around the clubs."

Hurst smiled then stared at the bowl of rotten oranges. "How long will your renovation work take, Caroline?"

Robinson eyed him. "I would say at least six months."

Hurst drew himself up and nodded. "Yes Bingley, I think that a little tour would do us a world of good."

"WHAT ON EARTH is she thinking?" Lady Matlock demanded. "All of that work, the dresses, the lessons, taking her around, introducing her . . . I am appalled!"

"I would not have told you of the engagement before Mr. Lucas spoke to my father, but with a roomful of family witnessing its formation, I felt that of all people, you should know before any embarrassing statements were uttered when you see her and meet Mr. Lucas this afternoon. Do not think that Jane is ungrateful, Aunt Helen. I know that she is anxious to thank you for all of your efforts." Elizabeth said patiently. "What you have done for her has surely made her into a far better woman than she was. You have opened her eyes to the greater world."

"Yes, and now she closes them against all that she has been shown! She is returning to . . .forgive me, my dear, but she will be so much less than she is now!"

Elizabeth became defensive. "Both Mr. Bingley and Mr. Lucas are the sons of tradesmen."

"Yes, and there is a spectacular difference in their prospects!" She stood and glared out of the window. "Lucas Lodge, indeed."

"If you had not pushed her so hard towards Mr. Bingley, she might have found someone you felt was more suitable, but in the end, it is she and she alone who will choose." Elizabeth's eyes flashed. "I will not allow you to criticize her decision. She is happy, as is he. They know each other, they are comfortable with their expectations, he is a hardworking and kind man, and undoubtedly they will do quite well together."

"My reputation is at risk here, as well, Mrs. Darcy." Lady Matlock reminded her.

"She is not your child to direct. And since it is highly unlikely that you will spend time with them in a social situation outside of our home again, I suggest that the damage to your reputation is insignificant."

"What did you say?" She glared. "I put my effort into rescuing her from that upbringing you both suffered. My friends were anticipating a brilliant match as a result."

"And so she has found one. For her. Is not that the point? Was she a pet project of yours or did you care about her? Or would you prefer that she suffers an unhappy marriage like your daughter did for the sake of being rich?"

"Audrey is very happy now!"

"And how miniscule was the chance of that happening?" Elizabeth asked steadily. "Jane and Mr. Lucas are from the same world, neither of them want what we have, they have identified precisely what they desire. Please stop projecting your ideals onto them. They are pleased with each other."

"Does she love him?" Lady Matlock sighed and sank into a chair. "I realize that she did not love Mr. Bingley, but that was not something that I considered important. I saw compatibility."

"I believe that they do love each other." She relaxed her stance. "He will give her the strength that she lacks, and she will give him the compassion that he craves."

"This is no passionate affair, then."

"I cannot compare it to my marriage, but it is not a calculated union, either. They are entirely different people from us, but all that matters to me is that Jane is very happy."

"Forgive my frustration dear, but frankly, your sister is not the easiest woman to improve." She saw understanding in Elizabeth's gaze and continued. "She is not without intelligence, but something is decidedly lacking in that girl. It must be an incredible absence of ambition. I truly did wish to do well by her."

"She was taught that it would come to her if she smiled." Elizabeth agreed. "I suppose that a lifetime of misdirection is difficult to overcome. But she did learn that it was important to display her feelings once she was sure of them."

Lady Matlock considered that and tilted her head. "She displayed them clearly to Mr. Lucas."

Nodding her head, Elizabeth smiled. "So she did. And seeing her with Mr. Lucas now tells me that she has always been capable of ambition and determination, but it took falling in love with the right man to bring out her strength. That is something that I can understand very well."

"Well." Lady Matlock sniffed and adjusted her gown. "No doubt her daughters will benefit from my efforts when Jane teaches them."

"I am sure of that. I know my Rosalie will benefit from them." She noted the pleasure that statement gave her and glanced at the clock.

"She will be awake soon and wish to be fed. Would you like to join me in the nursery? Our guests will not be home until this afternoon, they are taking in the sights with Jane and Reverend de Bourgh. Mary and Georgiana will be at their music lessons for some time, and you know that Fitzwilliam and Uncle Henry will be at work until we call them for luncheon."

"Oh." Lady Matlock frowned. "Well . . ."

"You could hold her and talk to her about some important subjects, just as her father does." Elizabeth stood and was immediately joined by the elder woman. "Last night he was explaining to her the importance of sheep manure to producing a viable crop."

She gasped then laughed. "He did not!"

"Oh yes, he did." Elizabeth laughed and led the way upstairs. "He would have waxed on for hours if she had not fallen asleep. She is a brilliant child."

"I hope that you were spared the subject."

"Hmm, yes." She paused at the door to the nursery and began to turn the handle. "I was treated to a speech on animal husbandry. Now *that* I was able to turn into something far more productive." She smiled and opened the door.

"Elizabeth, you make an old woman blush." Lady Matlock smiled and laughed. "Animal husbandry!"

"HOW DID YOU KNOW she was engaged?" Darcy asked his uncle.

Laughing, he gestured towards the doorway. "We walked in and I asked Mrs. Mercer if cupid was still flitting about and she commented that cupid does very well here." He saw Darcy's frown. "Come Son, she was not telling tales of you. She did not even confirm an engagement, let alone who Miss Bennet had accepted. You did that yourself."

"I know, but Lucas should speak to Mr. Bennet before the general word goes around."

"He is speaking to Gardiner today, is he not? And Bennet gave him full power to approve all engagements?"

"Yes." Darcy relented. "I suppose that is true. The only reason I told you is because, well I did not want you to say anything before Bingley when he arrives, about Jane." He met his eye. Lord Matlock chuckled again and they both looked up when Foster appeared.

"Mr. Bingley, sir." He bowed backed out.

"Good Morning!" Bingley declared and dropped into the chair beside Lord Matlock. "It is a fine day!"

"It is." Darcy smiled and lifted his brow. "You look the best I have seen you in a long time."

"Making decisions suits me, I think."

"Ah, good man, letting the idea go." Lord Matlock nodded.

"Oh . . . Darcy told you I gave up my . . . well whatever it was for Miss Bennet? But you were pushing me, sir!" Bingley reminded him.

"I was, and I regret making you feel so obliged to continue when you were battling yourself. Part of being a man is learning when to tell other ones to back off." He smiled to catch Bingley's open mouth. "You did not catch that lesson did you?"

"Obviously not." Darcy smiled. "It was a subtle one; I admit that I only realized it recently."

"I . . . You were actually hoping I would tell you to . . ."

"Tell me to go to hell." Lord Matlock smiled. "Never take the advice of a stranger against your heart, Son." He tapped his chest. "Ask for an opinion, weigh it carefully, but listen to your heart. Then you are free to make terrible errors on your own, and you cannot be angry with your friends who advised against it." Chuckling, he crossed his legs. "Well, all's well that ends well, it seems, now that she is engaged."

Darcy's face reddened and he shouted, "*Uncle!*"

"What?" Bingley stopped smiling at his feet and his head snapped up. "Who?"

"Miss Bennet." Lord Matlock watched his face fall. "Darcy . . ."

"She is *engaged?*" Bingley demanded of Darcy.

"I am afraid so. I did not mean to have you learn this way." He glared at his shrugging uncle, "But yes, Lucas proposed almost as soon as she arrived yesterday and she accepted."

Staring in silence, Bingley finally found his voice. "Not that I mind her . . . Could she have waited until the sun set on ONE day before she . . ." He sat in stunned disbelief.

"Bingley?" Darcy said softly. "Are you well?"

Lord Matlock pressed a glass of port in his hand and automatically Bingley gulped it down and coughed. "Every moment, I am happier to be away from her."

Darcy and Lord Matlock exchanged glances. "Why is that?"

"Caroline wanted her because it would bring the connection to you," He pointed to Lord Matlock, "You wanted her because it would make a man of me. Your wife wanted me to . . . I suppose because I am a catch. I am sure that her mother wanted me for the same reasons. Undoubtedly the dustman had an interest in it as well, everyone but the principal parties. I kept it up to satisfy everyone but myself, as I am sure that she did." He sighed. "No, I kept it up because . . . Am I still welcome here?"

Darcy smiled and relaxed. "Elizabeth spoke of that last night. What is a family without a younger brother? You are always welcome wherever we are, for as long as you wish, and we both would be terribly hurt if you thought otherwise."

Bingley smiled with clear relief. "Thank you. In all honesty, as kind and lovely as Miss Bennet is, and as unlike my sister as she is," The men chuckled, "I honestly feel that her greatest attraction for me has always been all of you." He coloured and looked at his hands. "This morning's conversation at breakfast only cements that idea in my mind. My sister and Robinson only look at my marriage as a means to their own ends. That leaves me with the Hursts. He has his own family. I suppose that I feel rather adrift."

"Bingley, you are family." Darcy said quietly. "Please stop thinking that you are not."

"I add my sentiments to that pronouncement, Son. I have grown rather fond of you." Lord Matlock smiled. "But I will continue to try to teach you lessons." He nodded to Darcy. "Both of you."

"Yes, sir." The men said in unison.

"Well what brings you here today? I understand from Darcy that you are making plans for the coming year?"

Bingley at last relaxed and sat forward, leaning on his knees and looked between his mentors. "Hurst and Louisa have agreed to the tour idea. So, what must I do?"

"Ah, excellent plan! What was that outfit you used, Darcy?"

"Mssrs. Tate, Longwood, and Jones." He smiled. "They will gladly educate or placate you, whichever you prefer. They will even do your shopping so you need not ever leave your bed."

"I want to see the sights, Darcy, not read about what is outside of my window."

"Well, if your languages are not up to snuff, it will not matter, since you will likely be around Englishmen the whole time anyway." He wrote out the address and handed Bingley a letter of introduction he had prepared. "Pay them a call, they will be happy to oblige."

Looking it over, he tucked the letter into his coat. "Thank you." He sat back and grinned. "Now, what shall we discuss? I am in no doubt that you both can fill my imagination with tales of your tours." Lord Matlock began to launch into his well-worn story of falling from a gondola in Venice when they were interrupted.

"Sir? Mr. Stewart." Foster bowed and the men turned to see Stewart stride rapidly into the room, then back to the door, which he closed.

Frowning, Darcy watched his friend begin pacing the floor. "What is it?"

"I had to bring you the news as soon as I heard." He stopped his movement and beamed, "Dead! Wickham is dead! He escaped the prison hulk, and was found dead!"

"He *what*? How is this possible? How did he escape?" Darcy demanded.

Stewart waved his arm. "Who knows, it is not as if they are admitting anything. Likely it was bored guards not paying attention when they were working on the river, you know, finding stones for ballast on the ships? They are not chained so he probably swam away."

"I thought that guards were held accountable for their prisoners, or did he manage to bribe one to look the other way?" Lord Matlock frowned. "This must be investigated and the prisoners better controlled."

"Well I leave that to you and Parliament." Stewart finally landed in a chair. "Bribes are certainly used to gain all sorts of privileges. I have heard of debtors being able to get their freedom for a few days, or even live outside of the walls. I have never heard of anyone convicted of a capital offence being able to buy his way out, of course they are hung fairly quickly. In any case, Wickham was convicted of breaking into a house and getting away with nothing."

"He attacked Elizabeth!" Darcy bellowed.

"According to the court records, he twisted her arm and she fainted." Stewart reminded him when he was met with his furious glare. "I am sorry, Darcy. But the salient point here is that he is dead!"

"I want to see the body."

"Impossible."

"I know that it is June, but surely it is still available?"

"No, he was found in an alley, still dressed in his prison rags. A letter was found on him, which identified him. His body was happily accepted by a

surgeon. Lord knows what they do with it when they are done carving him up."
Stewart shuddered. "Disgusting."

Ignoring the image, Darcy demanded more information. "What about the guard who was supposedly watching him work, what is his explanation?"

"He said he was distracted breaking up a fight.

"Likely betting on one; is more like it." Bingley said quietly.

Lord Matlock disagreed. "No, no, if there was one, it would have been quashed quickly, they were in a public area. Now a fight within the hulk, now that I can see being allowed to continue."

"Do you know what happened?" Darcy demanded impatiently.

"Well I am guessing that Wickham swam through the river, and went up onto the shore when he was far enough away. There was a bathhouse nearby, and he surely must have wanted to wash off the river stench, and change his clothes and appearance. There he might have got into a fight. Or maybe he never made it to the bathhouse and he was simply robbed." Stewart mused and rubbed his chin. "Who knows, the area abounds with thugs. The river is right there after all, and there is usually a corpse or two floating about."

"Or not." Darcy said darkly. "I would have liked to have seen his body. Can we speak to the men who found him?"

"He is gone, Darcy. Rejoice." Stewart smiled. "One less to feed to the sharks on the way to Australia."

"Now that would have been a fitting end for him." Lord Matlock muttered. "I do not like this, something seems dodgy."

"It does." Bingley agreed. "Do you know of any friends he might contact?"

"There was Mrs. Younge, but she has not been anywhere near the prison since we warned her off." Darcy looked at Stewart for confirmation. "I cannot see her letting him in the door, not when she is still living at the school. Perhaps we should just check with her?"

"He is dead, Darcy." Stewart said with frustration. "Why can you not be delighted? Instead of waiting another month for the ship to leave, you are rid of him now and forever! I thought that I would be hearing cries of joy, not muttering and teeth gnashing!"

"Forgive me, Stewart." Darcy looked at his uncle. "I am noted for pessimism. But I will feel better sending a man to interview her."

Lord Matlock smiled. "Go ahead, Son, confirm that at least in your mind and in the meantime, we will not look this gift horse in the mouth. Wickham is dead. Let us have a toast to the man who accomplished that feat, whoever he is."

18 JUNE 1810
This morning I said goodbye to our guests, and my sister. Mr. Lucas simply could not stay away from Hertfordshire any longer. We tried to convince them to remain and attend the ball at St. James's with us on our anniversary, but he flat out

refused. I never appreciated how much he disliked his father's display of pomposity with his knighthood before, but it seems that he finds it embarrassing to pretend to be more than he is, and attending St. James's for him would, I think, be even more uncomfortable than it will be for my Fitzwilliam, who is equally unhappy with the prospect. If it was not to appease Lord and Lady Matlock, I would not wish to go either, but they demand that we make one appearance in society during our time in London, so this, I am afraid, is the chosen venue. We received an invitation from the Crearys to attend their annual ball, and I returned it with our regrets before Fitzwilliam had a chance to burn it.

Charlotte and Reverend de Bourgh managed almost an entire week spent in each other's company. They dined here every evening, and we enjoyed frequent strolls through the park. Charlotte is not at all hesitant in showing her admiration for the Reverend; and it seems to please him to no end. He already has plans to visit Hertfordshire and meet the family within the next week, with the generous help of his brother, before he officially begins the duties involved in taking over the parish, and serving his new congregation. I think that the trip to Lucas Lodge will end with a courtship beginning. Captain de Bourgh made some reference to Charlotte's determination to Fitzwilliam and he nearly spat out his tea and certainly blushed spectacularly. What was said remains a mystery, since my dear husband absolutely will not speak of it. I will pry it out of him one day when he least expects it, but it seems that the military can never be blotted away from this gentleman's memory.

I am avoiding writing of the news that burdens my heart. Jane is gone back to Hertfordshire. She said there was no reason to remain in London. Mr. Lucas needs to speak to Papa and begin to prepare a space for her in Lucas Lodge. Her wedding clothes will be from the dress shop in Meryton. I can only imagine the fighting that will ensue between Mama and Lady Lucas for the wedding plans. Despite the anticipation of upheaval at Longbourn, Jane seemed as eager as Mr. Lucas to retreat as far as possible from Mayfair, and almost seemed defiant in her preparation to face Mama's disappointed hopes when she learns that Mr. Bingley is lost forever. I wonder when she visits London again as a married woman if they will stay with us or if they will prefer Cheapside.

Fitzwilliam insisted that they use his carriage to return home. Of course it was a battle of wills between the men, but in the end, Mr. Lucas could not turn down the offer. The savings to him is significant. He also attempted to refuse the wedding gift that Fitzwilliam offered, one-thousand pounds, to match Jane's dowry. Mr. Lucas said that he will only accept it on the condition that it be immediately invested for her should he die. He is a proud man and wishes to earn everything that is used to support his wife and family. I wonder if my dear husband would have been similar had their situations been reversed. I think that he would. I know that I will rarely see my sister again. It grieves me to accept that fact, but she seems with her engagement to have returned to her peaceful self, and that is the woman who caught Mr. Lucas's eye long ago. I will miss her, but I think that she is exactly where she belongs.

Darcy contemplatively put the ribbon in place and setting her journal aside, watched as she finished reading his thoughts of the day.

18 June 1810

Today I said goodbye to my sister Jane, and my future brother. I could feel the sadness between Elizabeth and Jane as they parted, but on both sides there also seemed to be an essence of acceptance and joy. Both sisters have found their places in the world, and with the right men. I know that we will see them only briefly in the future, but we will remain in their lives as much as we are able.

I now turn my attention to the other women in my life, my sister Mary, literally on the cusp of womanhood and not at all eager to embrace it, and Georgiana, who seems to have rediscovered proper manners around men. When Bingley recently visited, you would hardly have known she was in the room, so quiet was she. It confused him as much as us until Elizabeth recalled how de Bourgh had gently but firmly reminded her of her age. Perhaps having a gentleman, practically a stranger, inform her that she was inappropriate was just the voice she needed. She is withdrawn, but not shy. I realize that is a contradiction but it is the truth. My love believes that it is the security Georgiana feels in our home that gives her the confidence to display some of her self. I believe that is correct, but I cannot discount the fact that she is a very attentive observer of my wife. Both she and Mary watch her as she confidently cares for our home and daughter. I have caught Georgiana listening outside of the drawing room when Elizabeth is receiving callers, even mimicking her gestures. I asked her what she was about, if she behaved this way at Matlock House, and Georgiana blanched at the thought of doing such a thing there. I wonder at the difference and which is correct. My dear Elizabeth does not mind, she would be glad to provide Georgiana with an example, and said that she prefers being watched for education rather than to find fault!

Elizabeth laughed and closed his journal. "Do not forget dear, I once did the same. I used to try and imitate the women I observed."

"Yes, I do remember that. And I also remember trying to discourage you from trying to be like anyone other than yourself."

"I was merely learning the rules, Fitzwilliam, not changing my personality." She smiled at his gentle disagreement. "No?"

"I was afraid of you becoming one of them."

"Well, clearly that did not happen." She laughed and looked back at the journal. "I wonder if we will remember these times when Rosa is this age? Or will we be starting all over again?"

"We can always come back and read our thoughts." He smiled and wrapped his arms around her waist. "But seventeen years is a long time from now."

"1827." Elizabeth rested her head against his heart. "I cannot imagine what the world will be like."

He rested his cheek in her hair. "Hmmm. Napoleon will at last be defeated."

"I certainly hope so!"

He chuckled and squeezed her tight. "Railroads will cross the land." She looked up at him and he smiled. "I am certain of it. We will travel like lightening one day."

"We could visit Jane."

"And she could visit us." He kissed her forehead. "And you will have given birth to our fourteenth child." Elizabeth pinched his bottom and he yelped.

"I would have long past pushed you from the bed, sir, or better yet taken up residence in my own!" She glared at him.

"No, no, never relegate me to sleeping alone." He begged. "Promise me that."

"Why you would still want to touch me after the thirteenth child is beyond me." She sniffed, and felt his embrace tighten. "I promise."

"Thank you." He kissed her softly. "I love you, dearest."

"I love you." She looked up to his twinkling eyes and smiled. "And no, you will not miss the ball."

"Did I ask?"

"You were beginning to sweet-talk me." She tapped his nose. "An admirable attempt, but we must go."

"Why?" He said unhappily. "A private ball would be bad enough, but this public exhibition disgusts me."

"Because it is not so exclusive anymore?" Elizabeth let go of him. "Surely that is not it. You have attended St. James's how many times in the past?"

Darcy closed his eyes. "Perhaps six?"

"And?"

"Dearest . . ."

"Fitzwilliam, we cannot be entirely invisible. We have not accepted any invitations to anything at all since our arrival. My desk is overflowing with requests to attend balls, routs, breakfasts . . . I could go on and on, and you know that I am not going to push you, but the plain truth is that Mary will be seventeen in weeks! Why if she were so inclined, we both would have been presented this summer, and would have begun taking her to private balls! We must think of her future. And it will not be long before we have Georgiana to consider. We must think of them with our behaviour, so they have the best opportunities!"

"You sound frighteningly like your mother and my aunt." He said worriedly.

"I do?" Elizabeth blanched.

"I am afraid so." He walked away and ran his hand through his hair. "Mary does not want to come out until next year."

"But she needs the experience." Elizabeth sighed. "I am not saying public events. I only wish her to . . . polish her skills for someday. She knows so little."

"She has had a year of dance lessons." He pointed out. "And etiquette, and so many other things. She is far more prepared than . . ."

"Than I was?" Elizabeth said coldly.

"I did not say that."

"Did I embarrass you with my naiveté, sir?"

He shook his head in frustration. "You are not jumping to conclusions, you are leaping to them. Do not put words in my mouth or presume to discount my feelings."

"Oh, so I am presuming now?" Elizabeth paced to the opposite end of their private sitting room and turned. "And what, pray tell, have I said that treads upon your delicate feelings? I always thought that I was rather the guardian of them, but apparently I presumed incorrectly there as well?"

Darcy stared at her. "I thought that you understood." Turning on his heel, he left the room. Elizabeth watched him go in disbelief and her arms, which had been protectively embracing her chest dropped to the side.

"What did I not understand?" She said angrily. "I just wished for him to go to a ball! Willingly! For our sisters, not for us! We are settled, we do not need to put on a show, but they . . ." Horrified, her hand went to her mouth when she realized his feelings. "Oh, Fitzwilliam!"

She ran from the room and out into the hallway. Spotting a footman, she inquired after the master and was told that Darcy had gone downstairs. Elizabeth reached the foyer in time to see him reaching for the door. "What will I do with you?" Darcy looked at her and said nothing, but she could read the distress in his eyes, then watched as his gaze shifted over her shoulder. "Georgiana?" He nodded curtly and opened the door. She asked for her bonnet and went after him. It did not take long to catch up; he was waiting at the end of the walkway, staring into the park. Together, they walked without touching to that one particular bench and sat down. Darcy rested his elbows on his knees and stared at his clasped hands. When he did not look up after several moments, Elizabeth broke the silence. "I understand."

"Do you?"

"Yes." She drew a breath and did not touch him. "You were forced by your well-meaning relatives to attend endless functions, meeting people who neither interested you, nor who appreciated anything of you other than your possessions. You despised it. You fought it, and if you had acquiesced to it . . . you would be forever lost in an unfeeling marriage to some proper heiress right now, or perhaps be living in the eighth month of mourning for your wife, Anne." She wiped the tear that fell down her cheek. "Instead you waited and hoped for the unspoiled, unformed, unlikely possibility of me."

"Yes."

"Can you understand my feelings?"

Darcy looked up at her and watched her eyes well up with tears. "You see, I spent that time feeling every moment how unworthy I was, how uneducated and how I could never, ever allow my hopes to come true. I thought that all of my dreams were to remain that way because even had we met, once we did, you would see me for what I was and reject me out of hand."

"Never." He said fervently and moved beside her to wipe her cheek. "Never."

"Never is a strong word." She whispered, "But even so, I did not know that those years I waited." She sniffed and took his hand. "I am not pushing for our sisters to be on the marriage mart, I . . . I just want Mary to have confidence that I know she does not have naturally. She has the benefit of lessons, yes, but a group of girls is not the same as mixing with real people. I . . . I want her to know what she wants so that when the day comes that a special gentleman asks her to dance, she will recognize him." Elizabeth caressed his cheek. "I was not rejecting your feelings by asking that we prepare ourselves for this inevitable and fast-approaching time in their lives. I was simply saying that even if they are not ready, we need to be. We need to know what to expect when we take them out there. It will not be we dancing alone and shutting out the world. It will be we, watching and evaluating every man who approaches."

"I never meant to imply that you are uneducated or unworthy in any way."

"I never meant to imply that I did not understand your struggles."

Drawing her into his arms, Darcy kissed her. "I am so sorry, love. You are so confident now that I forgot how insecure you once were." He looked into her eyes and kissed her again. "And still are. When I saw you becoming defensive, I knew that I had to leave before I made it worse."

"Forgive me for not realizing what you were saying, and for overreacting." Elizabeth leaned her head on his shoulder, and they sat embraced, ignoring the scandalized looks of any who passed, and stared out at the sunlight glinting on the Serpentine. Eventually they both took deep breaths and let them out. "Is everything well?"

"It always was. You know that I would have been back to talk to you, do you not?"

"Yes, Will." She smiled softly. "I know you as you know me, and was not upset with that; I just chose to come after you instead of waiting. How many times have I become silent with you?"

"I think that it gives us time to form coherent thoughts." He saw her eyes roll and shrugged. "I know that it helps me. I do not have your tongue, my love."

"Yes you do." She let it peek between her lips and he groaned.

"Dearest Elizabeth, how can you speak to me of your tongue here? What I would give right now to feel it upon my person." He closed his eyes against the enticing sound of her laughter, then opened them to see her warm gaze, and shook his head. "But it seems that we need to seriously plan for Mary. I understand your desire to do well by her."

"Perhaps we should include her in the conversation." She smiled and caressed his cheek. Darcy kissed her hand and nodded. "And . . . Since she is adamant about not coming out until next year, I suggest that we celebrate our wedding day with a trip to Vauxhall with our sisters, and skip the ball at St. James's."

Darcy smiled and hugged her. "Oh? So you replace one bit of torture with another?"

"I seem to recall that you enjoyed our visit there." She laughed. "Especially dinner."

"mmm. Perhaps we can ask Richard and Eva to join us. He knows something about the dark paths where a gentleman can take advantage of his lady." He kissed her gently. "I like this idea of yours."

"Then on the anniversary of our meeting, we may return right here." She looked over her shoulder. "There is a lovely bit of grass. We can picnic there."

"And walk at Kensington afterwards." He reminded her.

Elizabeth smiled and kissed him. "Alone."

"Together."

21 JUNE 1810
Today is the anniversary of my becoming husband to Elizabeth Bennet Darcy. No other words are necessary to express my absolute joy.

What do I remember of that glorious event one year ago today? Exhaustion, exhilaration, laughter and at last, completion. What do I remember of this past year? To list the emotions I have enjoyed and suffered would be impossible. To imagine experiencing them with anyone other than Elizabeth is unthinkable. You have given me a life that I know would never have come with any other. Thank you, my love.

21 June 1810
Where my husband is unable to express his joy in words, I shall take up the charge to express mine. One year ago today I ran down the aisle and embraced my future by grasping my Fitzwilliam's waiting hands. And now I find myself not only a wife, but a mother. We both have grown so much, but now the joy is that the memories we have created are shared. It is not our hopeful imaginations that fill the voids in our lives anymore, but the family we have created together. Every day is not perfect; we range from teases to arguments, play to work, silent contemplation to breathless lovemaking. In it we discover who we are and who we wish to become. I will forever be grateful for this life you have given me, Fitzwilliam.

Darcy smiled and looked up from the journal to see Elizabeth smiling at his. "We are a silly pair."

"Philosophical." She nodded and closed the book. "So you became husband to Elizabeth Darcy?"

"Do you disagree?" He closed her journal and took her hand. "There is a bit of gold here that indicates it is so."

"Hmm. So there is." She lifted her hand and smiled at the simple band. Darcy took her hand and kissed the ring. "Ah that was very nice."

He chuckled and hooked her hand over his arm. "To the pleasure gardens, my wife?"

"Well we could argue that the pleasure gardens are in this suite of rooms." She smiled wickedly.

"No, no, I have no argument with you there." He grinned and nipped her lip with his teeth. "But I do believe that our sisters would not understand the sentiment."

"Elizabeth! Fitzwilliam!! Are you coming?" Georgiana's voice was heard floating in from the hallway.

"Off we go." He gestured to the doorway. "The commander has spoken."

"Darcy, do I need to unsheathe my sword?" Fitzwilliam called.

"You know, if I were a woman who read novels, I could find some interesting comments to make about their choice of words." Elizabeth's eyes danced as Darcy's grew wide. "But of course, I am an innocent."

"Maybe a year ago, love." He smacked her bottom and she squealed as they headed out the door. "No more!"

"Do you know, I think that my cousin has at last learned to enjoy life. He had a grand time ferrying around his wife and sisters at Vauxhall. Why the man smiled! Almost as often as his lovely wife laughed." Fitzwilliam grinned.

"Really?" Lord Matlock stretched out his legs and snatching a tart from the tray before him, popped it in his mouth before his wife could move them away. He snorted in triumph and began looking over the remaining morsels. "Well, I cannot doubt that he enjoyed missing the ball, although, it was remarked upon."

"In what way?" Eva caught Lady Matlock's eye and drew the tray to the other side of the table. Her father-in-law glared at her and she smiled. "Perhaps one of us would like one too, Father."

"Well . . ." He shrugged and gave in to her smile. "Very well."

"How generous of you, Henry." Lady Matlock opened her parasol and shaded herself from the sun in the garden behind Matlock House. Addressing Evangeline, she explained, "Darcy and Elizabeth were expected, when they did not appear, speculation was if there was trouble in paradise."

"Fools." Fitzwilliam snorted. "Those two will never float down from that cloud they inhabit."

"Richard, they are hardly doe-eyed youths, they are well-grounded in reality." Evangeline chastised him. "I think that they appreciate what they have together and simply will not let anyone or anything ruin that for them."

"I know, I know." He took her hand and kissed it. "I endeavour to emulate them." She smiled and he turned to his mother. "So the crowd missed gawking at them, is that the gist of the gossip?"

"That and their noted non-acceptance of the Creary's invitation." Lord Matlock smirked. "Well done, Darcy."

"He does *not* let go of offences easily." Fitzwilliam reminded him. "He was after me yesterday, asking if I knew any ex-soldier friends who could confirm that Wickham was really dead. He wanted them to seek out the surgeon who got his body for anatomy practice and see if they observed any marks before they hacked it up."

"Oh, this is pleasant." Lady Matlock said coldly.

"Forgive me, Mother." He cast his eyes down.

Lord Matlock's lips twitched. "And were you able to accommodate him?"

"I know a few and put them on the case." He shrugged. "He will not rest until the news is confirmed. He did send someone to interview Mrs. Younge and she swore on her mother's grave that she had seen nothing of Wickham. I think he is satisfied on that count, at least."

"Well, I suppose that I can understand his worry." Lord Matlock smiled. "So what happened at Vauxhall?"

"Oh, well, a married Darcy is a rogue." Fitzwilliam grinned. "I showed him just which path to visit while we distracted the girls with the jugglers." He winked at Evangeline. "He was quite grateful for my advice, and they were rather flushed upon their return."

"Hush Richard." Evangeline poked him. "It was their wedding anniversary!"

"Why do you think that I made the offer?" He looked offended. "Any other day and I would have disappeared with you and left him to chaperone!" Evangeline sighed while his father laughed.

"One year. It seems much longer than that." Lady Matlock smiled. "I can only imagine what the next year will bring."

"FITZWILLIAM!" Elizabeth cried. "What are you doing?" He laughed, and keeping his hand over her eyes, guided her into the study.

"It is a surprise!" He said proudly. "To mark the day we met, three years ago, today."

"Fitzwilliam Darcy! I demand that you unhand me this instant!"

"Wait, wait . . ." He positioned his body behind hers and leaned down to kiss her ear. "Ready?"

"Yes!"

"Look."

Darcy lifted his hand away and slid his arms around her waist. Elizabeth blinked and looked at the canvas displayed on the easel before her. "It is lovely." She smiled and looked back up at him. Seeing that he was clearly waiting for something more, her gaze returned to the landscape. Carefully examining it, she began to feel the stirrings of a memory. "I have seen this before . . ."

He nuzzled his lips to her ear and kissed it gently. "Yes."

"Where . . .Will how can I think when you kiss me like that?" She whispered while his mouth nibbled her throat. "It was not recent . . ."

"Mmmm, no." He traced his tongue to her shoulder and began his nibbling again. Trailing his fingertips up over her breasts to tenderly circle the nipples, he felt the dampness of her milk letting down and stopped his movement. Instead, he firmly stroked his hands down her waist to caress her hips, while his mouth continued its slow torture of her skin.

"The art . . ." She moaned. "oh, the Royal Art Exhibition?"

"I was standing right behind you, love, almost as close as this. If I could have peeked around your bonnet, I would have pulled you into my arms then and there, before your uncle, before my sister, and made you mine." He whispered heatedly. "I heard your laughter, I knew it was you." He turned her around to look down into her eyes. "I heard your voice, I knew it was you. It had to be you."

"Oh Fitzwilliam." Elizabeth stood on her toes and met his ardent, insistent kisses. Darcy's hands ran down her back to her bottom, and lifted her up to rub his erection against her centre. "If I had but torn that damnable bonnet from you then, we would have found each other . . . Oh my love!" He kissed her hard, then dropping her back to her feet, unbuttoned the front of her gown to expose her ripe breasts. Hungrily he fell upon them, sucking them, feeding upon one, then the other, emptying her so he could now feast slowly, and enjoy her as he wished. "I love you." Darcy dropped to his knees and lifted her gown up to her waist and pressed his lips to her thighs.

"What, oh . . . Will!" She sighed as he licked and savoured the wetness that nearly dripped from her mound. She parted her legs for him and he found her nub, sucking it and drinking in her flavour while she held his shoulders, writhing and moaning above him. When she cried out and trembled, he tugged her hands, pulling her to the floor to kneel with him. Darcy stared at her, eyes dark, nostrils flaring, breath ragged. "Will?" She whispered and closed her eyes when one hand wrapped around her waist and the other was buried in her hair. Elizabeth's arms embraced his neck and they were instantly lost in the fervour of their kiss.

Slipping one hand down to open his breeches, she drew out his erection, caressing it as she suckled his tongue. Darcy groaned in her mouth and let go of all control, letting her pleasure him with her loving touch. His body shivered and he clutched her while their kisses continued with the slow passion he adored. "My love." He breathed as she kissed along his jaw to find his throat, and savoured the place that drove him mad. "Oh Lizzy." He breathed and tilted his head back. "Yes, love, yes." His hands traced over her back as she continued to stroke his burning flesh. Darcy's eyes opened and he looked deeply into hers, then licked her warm, glistening lips. Resting their foreheads together, they watched her steady hand, and when her thumb circled the tip, spreading his essence, he shuddered, and covering her hand with his own, together they brought him to heaven.

Their hands remained clasped over him as he shuddered, until at last he swallowed and took a long, unsteady breath. She smiled and laughed softly, caressing back the hair that fell across his sleepy eyes, then finding the handkerchief he kept in his coat, wiped their hands. Instantly she was in his arms. "My lovely Lizzy." He sighed, and held her to his chest. "My own."

Eventually they rose to their feet and held each other. "Will?"

"Mmmmmmmmmmmmmm."

She laughed and looked up to his warm gaze. "Will you ravish me tonight?"

"Be prepared to be quite occupied." They kissed and remained embraced, slowly rocking together.

Outside of the study window, hidden by a manicured bush, Wickham lifted his pistol and drew back the hammer to full-cock. "Well Darcy, I hope that you enjoyed your sweet wife one last time. What a waste she will be." Taking aim he waited for them to separate, and watched impatiently as they kissed again. "That's it, kiss her goodbye. She's going to sleep now." Darcy smiled and caressed a curl behind Elizabeth's ear, and Wickham saw them draw apart. "There you go . . . One last smile for him to remember, Mrs. Darcy." His finger twitched against the trigger.

A knock on the study door made the couple jump apart. Wickham swore at their sudden movement. Darcy laughed. "You would think we were not married!"

"We are undressed." Elizabeth blushed and fixed her gown while he adjusted his breeches and asked who was there.

"It is Mrs. Robbins, sir; Miss Rosalie is ready for her walk."

"Oh!" Elizabeth cried. "I forgot that we were walking!"

Darcy chuckled. "I am pleased to have accomplished that." Elizabeth sighed as he moved to open the door. He held out his arms and took the squealing baby, then walked to Elizabeth with her. "Hello my sweet girl." He kissed her.

"Damn it!" Wickham dropped the gun to his side as the family drew together.

"Are you ready my Rosa?" Elizabeth laughed and kissed her. Looking up she saw Darcy's happy face. "You look ready to burst."

"My heart is full." He kissed Rosalie, then leaned to bestow a lingering kiss to Elizabeth and was firmly smacked in the cheek by a waving hand. "Ow!" He rubbed it and laughed. "She does not like to share!"

"Well she will have to grow used to that." Elizabeth kissed her and said seriously. "Papa is mine, too."

Darcy wrapped his arm around her shoulder and they strolled from the room. "I will meet you in the garden; I have another surprise for you. For both of my ladies."

"Oooohh, what is it?"

"You will see." He paused in the doorway. "Happy anniversary, love. The third of so many to come."

"Happy anniversary, Husband." They kissed once more and separated.

Wickham stared at the empty room, and looked down at the gun hanging in his grip. "What is it Wickham, did you lose your nerve when a baby came in? It's HIS baby!" He spat. Hearing the sound of a wagon stopping in front of the house, he ducked behind the bush. The water casks were right on time. When the man rolling the barrel passed, Wickham moved away from the house and headed down the street to the corner, ran around the last townhouse and to the alleyway for the mews. He had heard Darcy tell her to go to the garden, and he was determined to get there first. Skidding to a stop, he came to the stables for Darcy House. All of the stable workers were gathered around a baby carriage, and were laughing at the tiny Shetland pony that Darcy had purchased to pull it. With them all occupied, he easily slipped into the empty, well-tended garden. He moved behind the necessary house, and watched the home. The garden door opened and out stepped Elizabeth with the baby cuddled in her arms.

Wickham licked his lips, studying her. "What would hurt him more, losing his wife or his baby? Maybe both with one shot?"

Elizabeth moved closer, pausing to show Rosalie a peach. He heard the baby squeal and Elizabeth's laughter. "That's it Mrs. Darcy, come to papa." He glanced around to see that the staff was still occupied. "I want him to see this." An idea hit him. "No, I want him to sweat it out! That's it!" Looking over his shoulder, he knew it was then or never.

Bending to kiss Rosalie, Elizabeth whispered to her, "What is Papa doing, do you think? We will have a picnic after your walk. You do not mind sharing him with me today, do you?" Hearing rapid footsteps across the gravelled path, she looked up with a smile, expecting to see her husband, and instead saw Wickham, his eyes focussed, his teeth bared, and flying towards her. "NOOOOO!" She screamed as he snatched Rosalie from her grasp. "Let her go!" Elizabeth reached, trying to take her bawling baby back. She kicked at him and clawed at his arm as he pulled the gun from his breeches.

"Do you want to die, too, Mrs. Darcy?" He snarled.

"No, NO!! Let her go! Please! Please do not hurt her! You let her go!!" Elizabeth grabbed at her daughter and disregarded the pistol. "Take me . . . Please do not hurt my baby!"

Darcy was just coming to the garden door, the bracelet he was giving Elizabeth in his hand, when he heard her scream. "Elizabeth!" He ran outside to be greeted with the scene of Elizabeth struggling with an unknown man; and

Rosalie under his arm. Without hesitation, he ran hard across the garden and tackled the man from behind. The force and surprise of his attack made Wickham loosen his grip on Rosalie, enough for Elizabeth to pull her free and safely into her arms. "GO Elizabeth! Get Away! Take Rosa away!" Darcy bellowed and held the man's waist as his other hand closed around his throat. Gripping tight, Darcy saw the scar. "WICKHAM!!" He felt Wickham choke and grab at his fingers, then felt the cold barrel of the pistol against his other hand as Wickham struggled to lift it and fire.

"Fitzwilliam!" Elizabeth screamed, unable to move, and clutched Rosalie to her breast.

"You BASTARD!" Darcy shouted and struggled, grabbing at the gun. Suddenly the weapon's hammer was knocked back, fully-cocked, and fired. The deafening blast threw both men violently backwards, Elizabeth cried out, and Darcy fell, his head striking a stone planter. Wickham lay stunned in his arms.

Staff poured in from every direction. Men arrived from the stables, footmen and Foster from the house. Darcy felt Wickham being pulled away from him and blinked his eyes, struggling to stay conscious, "Elizabeth?" He croaked and tried to escape from the swirling light and buzzing noise in his ears. Slowly he turned his eyes towards the distant sound of Rosalie's hysterical cries. "Lizzy?" He swallowed and finally focussed on the bundle of yellow that was his wife's gown, and then spotted the bright red stain that was slowly spreading across her chest. He reached his fingers to touch her limp outstretched hand as he finally succumbed to the blow. "My love."

Chapter 18

"Lord Matlock?" The harried servant asked the doorman at the entry to the House of Lords.

"Matlock?" He turned slowly and scanned the room, groups of men were in small gatherings, arguing, laughing, glad-handing. "No, I don't think he's here."

"Well where is he?"

Raising his brow the doorman stared. *"Not Here."*

"Fat lot of good you are! You didn't even look!" He started to push past and was given a shove. "I need to locate him!"

"Jones, what is all this?" Lord Moreland glared at the two men.

Jones snapped to attention. "Sir, this . . . servant was looking for Lord Matlock. I told him he was not present."

"Matlock?" Lord Moreland turned. "He is right in that corner there. Use your eyes, man."

The footman did not wait for more; he was through the door and flying straight for his master. "Lord Matlock, sir!"

Lord Matlock turned from where he was laughing with his friends and his smile instantly changed to a deep frown. "What are you doing here, Robbie?"

"Sir!" He began and lowered his voice. "Sir, you are needed at Darcy House immediately."

"Darcy?" He looked to the men listening in and nodded, raising his voice. "Gentlemen, if you will excuse me." Rapidly they left the room and Lord Moreland caught his arm. "Not now, I need to be off. I will contact you later."

"Right." Lord Moreland saw that something clearly was amiss, and heard the voice of Lord Creary behind him.

"Darcy in trouble?" He sniffed. "What a shame."

"He is a finer man than you ever were, Creary." Lord Moreland glared. "You do not know what is wrong, so keep your mouth shut, or do you enjoy gossiping like a woman?"

"Watch your mouth Moreland!"

"Or what, you will not ask me to your ball?" Lord Moreland growled and walked away, casting a concerned look to the doors.

"WHEN DID THIS HAPPEN?" Lord Matlock demanded as the carriage crawled through the heavy traffic.

"It has been hours, sir. The butler at Darcy House sent word to Matlock, but you and Lady Matlock were out. I was sent to find you, nobody knows where her ladyship is, and she has Miss Darcy and Miss Bennet with her. I think that someone was sent to Cheapside from Darcy House for Mrs. Darcy's relatives, but it takes hours to get there and back. I . . . I am sure that the surgeon has been called."

"Yes." Lord Matlock closed his eyes and thought. "Richard, was anyone sent for Colonel Fitzwilliam?"

"Sir, I do not know, I was off with the carriage the moment it was brought around." He looked at him anxiously. "I . . . I was in the war, sir. I pray that Mrs. Darcy . . ."

"Well if she was alive when you got the word . . ." His voice trailed off and he clutched his walking stick. "Darcy was alive?"

"He was unconscious, sir."

"The baby?"

"I do not know."

"Wickham?"

"He was injured, but the staff had him trussed up and ready for the magistrate when the man from Darcy House left. I gather that the staff was taking turns at him for hurting the Darcys. If he is still alive, it is only because they want to see him swing."

"They are not alone."

"HAVE YOU SEEN LIZZY?" Darcy asked with a smile. "Beautiful Lizzy. Lizzy, Longbourn, Gracechurch Street, London." He sighed and looked up. "Have you seen Lizzy?"

"Yes, sir." Adams murmured and seeing his master's face grow white, helped him to turn over to his side so that he could vomit again into the chamber pot. Darcy shook, and his voice was weak. "Have you seen Lizzy?"

"Yes, sir."

"Beautiful Lizzy."

"Yes, sir."

"I cannot see." Darcy moaned. "Adams?" He reached out blindly and then held his head and closed his eyes. "Oh . . ." He turned and vomited again. "Ohhh." Laying back in the bed he opened his eyes to pant and touched his aching head. He felt the bloody bandage and tried to remove it. "What . . . Ohhhhh Stop the noise! Why can I not see?" He cried out and started to panic.

"Sir?" Adams grabbed his hands and held him down, a footman joined him. "Sir you must lay quiet now, the doctor will be along right away."

"Oh." Darcy blinked, trying to clear the lights from his eyes. "Have you seen Lizzy? Beautiful Lizzy. Lizzy, Longbourn, Gracechurch Street, London."

"Yes, sir."

Adams and the footman exchanged glances and stayed by their master's side.

"SHOT?" Mr. Gardiner's mouth dropped open as he read the note. "What happened?" He stared without comprehension at the footman twisting his hat in his study.

"Sir, as near as we can tell Mr. Wickham came upon Mrs. Darcy in the back garden and tried to snatch the baby away. Mr. Darcy went after him and in the struggle the gun fired."

"And Lizzy was shot." Mr. Gardiner tried to calm the queasiness in his stomach and reached out to grip the back of his chair. "She was alive . . ."

"I . . . I believe when I left, she was, but the blood, sir . . ." He looked to his hands. "Mr. Darcy will die if he loses her."

"And Darcy . . ."

"Sir, I . . . I was in the war with Colonel Fitzwilliam. I saw my share of wounds. Mr. Darcy had a good knock on the head, but . . .Mrs. Darcy . . ."

"The baby was uninjured?"

"I heard from Mrs. Mercer that she was safe in her mama's arms." The young man gulped. "Sorry, sir. We have the best master and mistress, sir. We failed them once before."

"I understand." Mr. Gardiner drew a deep breath and nodded. "I will be on my way as soon as I am able. I must call for the coach."

"Yes, sir. If you don't mind, I'd like to get back, see if I can be of use to them, sir."

"Yes, of course." Mr. Gardiner pulled himself together, asked for the carriage to be prepared, then stopped to say a prayer before leaving his study to go upstairs to the nursery. "Marianne."

The tone of his voice made her instantly come to his side. He glanced at the children then led her to their rooms and gave her the news. "Do you wish to come with me?"

Mrs. Gardiner took her hand from her mouth and nodded. "Of course. I will not be a moment." She went to give orders for the staff and was downstairs and joining him at the door as fast as she could. Grimly he took her hand and they climbed into the coach. "Fitzwilliam is alive?"

"He was." Mr. Gardiner said numbly.

"And Lizzy?"

Saying nothing, he shook his head and drew her into his embrace, and remained that way for the long drive through London's congested streets.

"NOW THEN MARY, I want to hear this new song you have learned." Lady Matlock smiled. "Georgiana has been singing your praises and I want to hear what an accomplished performer you have become!"

"Georgiana is far too willing to have me display my talents." Mary blushed. "I think it is so she can avoid doing so herself!"

"Mary!" Georgiana cried. "You are the one who is coming out!"

"Not yet, Lizzy and Fitzwilliam promised that it can wait until next year." She stared out of the carriage window. "I am in no hurry to marry. I cannot wait to go to Pemberley and be with Lizzy."

"I cannot wait either." Georgiana said wistfully. "You will love it there, I promise. And watching Elizabeth and Fitzwilliam play is very entertaining!"

"Georgiana!"

"Oh Aunt, they just love each other so much." She sighed. "Fitzwilliam has such a lovely day planned for them today. Right now they should be at Kensington Gardens."

"She spied him there once, I believe?" Lady Matlock smiled. "Such a sweet love story."

"He showed me the bracelet he found for her." Georgiana said with a giggle. "All diamonds with three rubies, one for each year that they have known each other. He said that each year he will replace a stone with another ruby until it is all red."

"Where on earth does he form these impossible ideas?" Lady Matlock laughed. "Rubies."

"Red is the colour of love." Mary smiled.

"I CANNOT BEAR TO LOOK at that gown any longer." Millie whispered and pointed to the gown soaked with Elizabeth's blood sitting in the corner of the dressing room. "Can we not burn it?"

"The magistrate said to keep it for now." Mrs. Mercer glanced at the yellow, now red silk, then went to wring the blood from the cloth she had been using to press on Elizabeth's wounds. "Come, we are needed back inside." They heard Rosalie crying inconsolably. "She wants her mama and papa."

"I pray that she will have them."

"CLARKE." Lord Matlock said in a low voice when he arrived upstairs and saw the physician exit Darcy's chamber. "What is the news?"

"I am treating Mr. Darcy; the surgeon is in with Mrs. Darcy."

"They both live, then?" He asked urgently.

"For now, yes." He glanced at the door to Darcy's chambers and motioned him to the door of the sitting room that served the master and mistress. They entered and Lord Matlock began pacing the room. "Tell me!"

"Darcy received a very sharp blow to the back of his head when he fell. He had his arms around the intruder, Wickham, the pistol he was holding discharged, and at that range, the force was . . . well you can imagine. They were tossed backwards. The concussion of the blast was deafening. Wickham suffered burns to his hand and arm, or so it seems."

"What do you mean?"

"There is not much left of the man." Clarke said grimly. "From what I could see of the marks on his neck, if the gun had not discharged when it did, Darcy would have strangled him with the grip from his one hand. He is an exceptionally strong man." Both of them glanced towards the door to his chambers. "After he fell, Darcy's men apparently took over for their master, and displayed their loyalty for him and Mrs. Darcy rather effectively upon Wickham. I doubt that he will be able to stand up for the noose he is destined to sport soon. I will be surprised if he lives through the night."

"Oh no, I want this bastard to swing." Lord Matlock growled. "He was trying to kidnap the baby?"

Clarke shrugged. "I am not sure. They were alone in the garden, Mrs. Darcy screamed, Mr. Darcy came to her aid, and by the time the staff arrived it was over."

"What does Darcy say?"

"He is nonsensical, asking the same question over and over. It is common enough with a blow to the head. He is ill, very ill. The good news is that I saw no sign of blood in his ears, and his face is not bruised. I hope with time he will be well again."

"Not if his wife dies." Lord Matlock could hear the activity in the mistress' chambers and then looked to Darcy's door. "Can I see him?"

"He finally stopped vomiting, but we will not give him laudanum for the pain until we are sure. He is, we think, sleeping."

"Not alone?"

"No, his man is by his side."

Lord Matlock rubbed his face and sighed. "I will stay right here, then."

"I will go look in on Doctor Brandon." He paused. "He has a great deal of experience with gunshot wounds."

"Yes, he treated my son." Lord Matlock's eyes filled with tears and he turned to the window. Standing there he stared out over the trees of Hyde Park at the beautiful, cloudless day. He drew out a handkerchief and wiped his face then trying to distract his mind, saw two books sitting on the writing desk. He picked one up and it fell open to the page marked by a beautifully tied ribbon. Without thinking, he moved it aside and began to read.

25 June 1810

Today, today three years ago, I fell in love. My dearest, loveliest, Elizabeth appeared before me, and laughed. Oh how I needed that sound at that moment. Since I have known of you, my love, that laugh has rescued me from despair, and highlighted the happiest moments of my life. I have spent many hours contemplating my years before knowing you. Of course there were times of happiness and laughter with my family and friends, but joy was not a word that I could possibly comprehend until your musical voice wended its way through the atmosphere to my ear. You live inside of my heart. You keep me safe and warm. I treasured and nursed every memory I had of you before we met at last in truth. You make me whole, dearest.

Bless you for loving me. Bless you for giving me our dear Rosa. I love you darling Elizabeth.

Lord Matlock wiped the tears that slipped down his face, and closed the book, not wishing to tread any further on the private thoughts of his wounded nephew, who may never be whole again. Quickly he picked up the other book, hoping to change his thoughts, and instead opened it to find a horribly misshapen knot of colourful ribbon, and an entry written in Elizabeth's hand.

25 June 1810
Oh what a child I was three years ago today! What a silly little girl! How different I am now, and how much better I am for loving you, my dear husband! When I look back at that day, I remember so clearly wondering just who was this handsome gentleman, staring at me so intently! Why how dare he do such a thing! I was of a mind to stamp up to you and correct your impertinence, sir! Yes, SIR. You see at the time that is who you were, a man, an unknown man who had shot the arrow of his admiration straight into my soul. Oh you wicked man, stealing a young girl's heart even before she knew that she had one to give! If we had never met again, I would have remained lost to you, my love. If I had been left to find my path some other way, it would have been you holding my hand in my mind. So many laugh at our love, dear, I know. But I think that is envy and ignorance. Envy for what they will never know, and ignorance for what they could not possibly understand. How could I have lived a complete life without you? I do not know, and my love, I am forever grateful that I will never have to discover such a horribly bleak place. You are the blood and the fire that course through my veins. You are my heart. You have given me love, you have given me a home I never could have imagined, one where I am safe and wanted. You have given me our baby, your little cherub who has you so tightly wound around her finger it makes me laugh each time I see you hold her. I love you my dear husband, my dearest friend, bless you for loving a silly little girl.

Reverently, he closed the book and set it down carefully next to Darcy's. "Which am I; I wonder, one of the envious or the ignorant?" Walking to the door that led into Darcy's chamber, he steeled himself, and pushed it open. There on the bed lay his nephew, pale and drawn, his eyes closed and his lip caught in his teeth as he grimaced with pain. Adams stood from the chair by his side and Lord Matlock moved to take over. "How is he?"

"Sleeping, sir." Adams looked at him worriedly. "He has nothing left in his stomach, it seems. We will give him the laudanum when he is conscious again."

"The questions . . ."

"The same, over and over. The doctor is sure that should stop after he sleeps."

"Will he remember what happened?" Lord Matlock mused.

"I think it is best if he does not, sir." Adams met his eye. "It was a horrific scene. Mrs. Darcy crumpled on the earth, bleeding . . ." Adams wiped his eyes. "Mr. Darcy was still conscious then, he . . .sir, his heart was breaking."

"I can well imagine."

Hearing a knock at the door they looked up to see Mr. and Mrs. Gardiner entering cautiously. "Matlock." They looked at Darcy. "How is he?"

"Very ill." He sighed. "But hanging on for now. The physician is hopeful."

"Lizzy?"

"I do not know, yet." He glanced at Mrs. Gardiner. "The surgeon and physician are with her."

"I will go to her." Mrs. Gardiner began to leave and her husband caught her arm. She just gave him a look and he dropped it. She turned and left the room. "A little blood is meaningless to a woman, I have noticed." Mr. Gardiner tried to smile.

"Yes, the notion that they are the weaker sex is laughable." Lord Matlock murmured and squeezing Darcy's shoulder, indicated that they go to the sitting room. Taking a chair, he watched Mr. Gardiner stare out at the park. "Would you care to read something?"

Turning to face him, Mr. Gardiner was handed the journals. When he finished, he set them down and wiped his eyes. "I always suspected they were quite beyond anything I could comprehend."

"So you are one of the ignorant or envious?" Lord Matlock asked with a slight smile.

"Perhaps I am a different category, of men who are striving to meet their standard." He smiled a little then looked down at his hands. "She has lost a great deal of blood, I take it."

"Yes. Shot in the shoulder, I do not know if it passed through, but she is so tiny, it had to hit bone." Jumping up, he began to pace. "Why do they not tell us anything?" He demanded.

"Marianne will come." Mr. Gardiner said softly.

The sound of boots rapidly crossing the floorboards and a raised voice startled them. The sitting room door burst open and Fitzwilliam appeared; a murderous look in his eye. "Bastard! Where is he? I should have killed him when my sword was at his throat!"

Lord Matlock glared at him. "Calm yourself! He is gone, the magistrate has him."

"The bloody magistrate had him before and he got away! Darcy was right to suspect he was not dead. I will never laugh at his worrying again." Fitzwilliam stormed around the room, and spun. "Well?"

"Darcy sleeps with a blow to the head, Elizabeth was shot in the shoulder. We do not know."

"Shot?" His face drained of colour. "She bled?"

"Yes, as did he." Fitzwilliam moved towards the door to the mistress' chambers. "Richard! Brandon is with her."

He stopped and nodded, then without a word disappeared into Darcy's chambers. "Word got around." Mr. Gardiner observed.

"The staff did admirably on their own." Lord Matlock agreed. The two men lapsed into silence until another voice was heard and the door opened to reveal Lady Matlock.

"Well?"

"We are waiting for word on Elizabeth." Lord Matlock said softly. "Darcy sleeps."

She nodded and looked at Mr. Gardiner. "Marianne is with her." Immediately she entered the bedchamber. "I do feel rather useless compared to the women." He said quietly.

"They give birth, we only inflict pain." Lord Matlock returned to the window and clasped his hands behind his back. Fitzwilliam reappeared and stared at Elizabeth's door, then took a seat. "He will have a devil of a headache for a few weeks. I felt that knot he has grown."

"You hit your head once, I recall."

"Yes." He laughed without humour. "Wickham pushed me down the stairs at Pemberley, said it was an accident. If I had my faculties I would have beat the bastard to death then." He growled then grimaced. "Any word?"

"Your mother is with her now."

"What of the girls?"

"I did not ask, but as they are not here, I imagine that she left them at home."

"Good." Fitzwilliam noticed the open books and stood up to go stare at them, read the passages and turned away. "They met today."

"Yes, it seems so."

"This was the day he returned from his tour, the day he learned his father was to die."

Lord Matlock startled. "I did not realize that."

"I pray that it is not the day he learns that Elizabeth . . ." Fitzwilliam left the thought and went to stare out of the window.

"WELL, THAT SHOULD take care of it. Now we wait." Dr. Brandon wiped his hands and looked down at Elizabeth's pale face. "At least we found the ball."

"So it did not pass through?" Clarke looked at her with interest.

"Well, yes and no. The way she was shielding the child, it seems to have passed through the back of her arm before it lodged near the socket of her shoulder. Exceptional luck that, no bone was harmed, and the babe was not struck. My only guess is that the bullet passed through something first that slowed its delivery enough to be . . .well, less than it could have been. Look around out in the garden, there should be a clean shot through something."

"Perhaps it passed through Darcy?" Lady Matlock asked as she stood by Elizabeth and stroked her damp hair.

"No, I examined him, the only blood he lost was from his scalp, and that was profuse enough. Wickham perhaps. He was beaten to such a bloody pulp it is difficult to say."

"I am not concerned with the hows and whys, I only care for my niece." Mrs. Gardiner said angrily. "You have her drugged with laudanum?"

"Yes, madam." Dr. Barton nodded to Millie. "The girl knows the dose to give her. She will have pain and of course will feel the effects of the drug; no doubt she will be confused upon waking. And . . . be prepared for fever." He looked down at his hands. "It is not over yet."

They heard Rosalie cry and Lady Matlock exchanged glances with Mrs. Gardiner. "It is good that they have Mrs. Robbins."

"I hope that Rosalie accepts her, for a long time." Stroking Elizabeth's hair she leaned to kiss her clammy skin. "Be well, my child."

DARCY'S HAND WENT UP to his face and travelled on to hold his throbbing head. "What happened?" He murmured, and rubbing his other hand over his aching stomach, slowly blinked open his eyes. The room was dark, save for a few candles. Slowly his eyes adjusted to the low light and he took in the view. "Elizabeth?" He said softly and reaching for her, felt nothing. Creasing his brow, he wondered where she was, then heard the sound of Rosalie's cry. "She must be tending to her." He sighed and closed his eyes, waiting for his baby to settle and his wife to return to bed and tell him why he ached so much. But the cries did not cease. Blinking his eyes open again, he listened. "Maybe she needs my help." He started to sit up and the dull throbbing became blinding pain, and instantly his hand went to his head, finding the bandage. "What?" He tore it off and saw the dried blood, then ran his hand through his matted hair, finding the large, tender lump. "What happened to me?"

Looking around the room he noticed Adams, snoring quietly in a chair. "Adams?" Darcy said with confusion. "What is . . . Where is Elizabeth?" Ignoring the intense pain and the suddenly spinning room, he struggled to his feet and began walking haltingly towards the sound of his wailing daughter. He passed through the sitting room and seeing the light around the frame, pushed open the door to the mistress's chambers. It was a mirror of his room, dark, lit softly by candles, Millie slept in a chair, and there . . . his heart stopped. Tucked neatly on the bed lay Elizabeth, her white face was peaceful, her hands were folded over her stomach, and in her fingers he saw the locket. Suddenly the scent of a doctor's work filled his nostrils and the memory of his mother, father, cousin, lying in the repose of death overwhelmed his weakened mind. "NO!" He stumbled in and fell upon her body, wrapped her in his arms and dragged her up into his embrace. "Darling no, no, please! Please Elizabeth, do not leave me!" He kissed all over her face, willing her to breathe again.

Millie woke with a start and stared helplessly at the mourning man. Adams had heard his cry and came running in, and placed his hand on his master's shoulder. "Sir!" He shook him, but Darcy heard nothing through his grief. "Sir, please!"

Darcy kissed Elizabeth's face and found her mouth, it was only then that he felt warmth in her skin. His frenzied movement stopped and he cradled her in his arms. "Dearest?" He whispered, and stroked back the hair from her eyes. "Dearest Elizabeth?" His fingers traced her cheeks and down to her throat, and rested over her steadily beating pulse. "Thank you, Lord." His lips caressed the gently throbbing skin, and he remained there, letting the assurance of her life flutter against his mouth. He whispered in her ear. "I love you darling, please wake, please."

"Sir, she has been given laudanum to sleep." Darcy did not move, he only caressed his wife lovingly and continued to whisper in her ear. "Sir, she needs to rest, as do you . . ." Adams said fruitlessly. Glancing at Millie, he tilted his head, and they exited the room to give their master some privacy.

"Lizzy love." Darcy kissed her. "Wake darling, just for a moment." Hearing a soft sigh he kissed her lips, then her eyes. "Darling?"

"Will?" She breathed.

"Oh, love!" He climbed further into the bed and lay beside her, wrapping his body around hers. "Here I am."

"I . . ." At last her heavy eyelids slowly opened to find his nose touching hers, and tears streaming down his face. She reached up to stroke him. "You are beautiful." She smiled a little.

"No love, that is you." He gently kissed her hand. "What has happened?"

"I do not know, exactly." Seeing his confusion she continued to caress his brow, and tried to explain what she knew. "You had almost strangled Wickham."

"Wickham!" He cried, and stared at her as comprehension slowly began to appear in his eyes. He listened to her as intently as he could, fighting to understand while his head throbbed with increasing pain as his heart began to pound again.

She nodded and continued as his look urged her on. "Yes, he was purple and gasping for air . . . I think that . . . He was . . . Going to shoot you . . ." Tears were slipping down her cheeks, and when he gathered her closer, his hand touched the bandage and she cried out.

"I am so sorry, love!" He jumped and examined her. "A gun? I . . . I remember . . . you screamed . . . Oh dearest what happened to you?"

Elizabeth focussed on his searching blue eyes, and willed herself to waken from the laudanum haze. "The gun fired and I felt burning in my arm; that is all I remember." She kissed him and caressed his face. "Rosalie?"

"I heard her crying, I think that it is the sweetest sound in the world."
Darcy kissed her. "I . . . I do not know what happened to me. My head aches, I
am sore and dizzy, and there is a knot on top." Elizabeth's fingers wandered
through his hair and found the spot, making him jump.

"Oh Will! What has he done to you?" She hugged him as hard as she could
and began to sob.

"You were shot." He gulped back his emotion and kissed her forehead.

"But we are both alive." She said fiercely. "You fought him so bravely,
Fitzwilliam. I am so proud of you."

"I . . . I remember seeing a man holding Rosa and you were beating him.
My brave love!" He kissed her. "I . . ." He closed his eyes and struggled to
remember more. "I . . . tackled him?"

Elizabeth's face reflected her own struggle to remember. "Yes . . . yes, and
that is when I took our daughter back. And when you fought him." She smiled
a little. "My knight."

"Your knight has no memory . . .ohhhhhhh, oh Lizzy, I . . . I remember
seeing you . . . Oh, on the ground . . .your gown . . . oh darling!" He held her
tightly to him. "Oh my love!"

"Shhhhh, shhhh. I am well, as you see." She said weakly and he looked at
her carefully.

"You are so pale." Darcy kissed her. "You bled, I remember it now."
Looking her over carefully, he examined the bandages around her shoulder and
arm, and decided that now was not the time to discuss her wounds. Instead he
wiped her tears and kissed her cheeks. "You must be so tired, love, and here I
am waking you."

"I am grateful that you did. Nobody told me how you were when I was
awake before. Aunt Gardiner gave me my locket to hold . . . Where is it?" She
asked as fear crept into her voice. Feeling around the covers, Darcy found it
and placed it around her neck. "There." He kissed her. "I am with you."
Elizabeth rested heavily upon him and he gathered her tightly in his arms.
"Rest dear, I will not leave your side. Sleep."

"I need to care for you. I am well."

Darcy looked down at her in disbelief and suddenly the forgotten rage
reappeared. "You were shot, Elizabeth! In our home! ON OUR DAY!!" He
bellowed. "Where is that bastard! I will kill him!" Adams and Millie appeared
and Darcy sat up with a groan, and clutched Elizabeth protectively to his chest.
"What happened? Where is Wickham? Did I kill him? Did anyone finish it for
me?" He demanded.

Adams told them everything that he knew, and Darcy tried hard to sort
through it all as his head pounded harder than before. Elizabeth rested in his
arms and saw Millie standing by the bed. "Please bring us Rosalie."

"Madam, you are too weak!"

"Bring us our daughter, clearly she needs her parents." She looked up to Darcy and he nodded, seeing her would force him to calm. Rosalie was carried in and the moment she was in Elizabeth's lap, she relaxed and began rooting for her breast.

Darcy willed himself to concentrate on his family, and watched Elizabeth fumble with her nightgown. He laid his hand over hers. "Dearest, are you sure? I can feel your exhaustion."

"It . . .it will comfort all of us, I think. Just for a little while. If you help me, I think that I can manage. Please help me." She met his eye and he saw her need to do this reflected in them, and he nodded.

"Just for a little while." He whispered.

Darcy helped to open her gown and Adams, blushing, hurried from the room while Millie positioned the baby at her breast. Darcy wrapped Elizabeth in his arms and supported Rosalie. Millie made sure that all was well, and slipped back out of the room to leave the family in peace. When she returned a quarter hour later, she found all three in the same position, and all three were asleep. Taking the baby from her mother, she carefully handed her over to the nursery maid, covered her mistress, and with Adams helping, eased the sleeping couple down into the bed. They tucked the blankets around them then stopped to watch as Darcy turned to spoon his body to Elizabeth, his hand protectively around her waist.

"I think they will be fine alone." She whispered. "They are both so tired."

"As long as she does not turn onto her shoulder."

"How many times have we found them asleep?" Millie sighed as she looked at them. "They won't be moving."

He nodded at the young girl. "I was scared to death today."

"So was I." She startled when she felt Adams take her hand and squeeze.

"You did very well." He smiled.

"Oh."

"Go to sleep in your bed, I will watch over them." He watched Darcy's head settle into a position on Elizabeth's pillow he had observed countless times over the past year. "I pray that all will be well."

"I WILL BE RIGHT BACK." Fitzwilliam murmured to Evangeline.

"They are fine, you need to sleep." She took his hand when he sat up and he shook his head. "Someone would call us if we were needed."

"No dear, Darcy is my brother. I just need to see him." He stood and pulled on his robe. "I just need to know."

"Then I will check on Elizabeth." She sat up and he stopped her.

"I know how very tired you are, dear. Sleep, she may need you in the morning."

"Richard, you are not the sole obstinate one in this marriage." Evangeline stood and found her robe. "She is my sister, and it *is* morning."

"Barely." Fitzwilliam smiled and held his hand out for her. "You would have made a fine soldier."

They walked down the hallway together. "Marrying one is enough for me."

They came upon a sleeping footman and Fitzwilliam was of half a mind to wake him, but thought better of it. Darcy's staff had fought valiantly for their master that day. Opening the door to the master's chambers, they were surprised to see the empty bed. Adams appeared from the dressing room. "Colonel, may I do anything for you?"

"Yes, explain my cousin's disappearance!" He demanded.

"This way, sir." He led the way to the mistress's chambers and stood away from the doorway. Fitzwilliam and Evangeline looked in to see the Darcys entwined and asleep. Adams spoke. "He woke and went looking for her a few hours ago."

"How is he?" Fitzwilliam asked in amazement.

"I believe that he was in terrible pain, but it was nothing to his fear for his wife; or his anger over the incident."

"He remembered?" Fitzwilliam said with no little surprise, then stared at Elizabeth. "And Mrs. Darcy?"

"Determined to care for him and the child."

Evangeline smiled and looked up to her husband. "I think that they will be well."

"It is too early, dear. I did not become desperately ill until I was on the ship." Fitzwilliam looked at the bandages on Elizabeth's arm and shoulder. "I pray that she does not face what I nearly did."

"Losing a limb?"

"Yes." He whispered. "If it was not for Brandon . . ."

"Then she will be well." Evangeline said positively. "Come, back to bed." Taking his hand she led him from the room.

"SHOT?" MARY GASPED.

"Please keep your voice down, we are not telling Georgiana." Lady Matlock said angrily.

"Why not? Her brother was just as severely injured!"

"She is a child." Lord Matlock said steadily.

"And how exactly do you intend to keep it from her? I will not lie to her." Mary turned and started to leave the room.

"Where are you going?" Lady Matlock demanded.

"I am going to my sister!" Mary said determinedly.

"We will visit in a few hours; you will remain here with Georgiana."

"Lady Matlock, where you can order my sister Georgiana about, you have no such control over me. I will go to Lizzy!"

"And how do you propose that you get there?" Lord Matlock asked.

"I am used to walking into Meryton, sir. It is a mile each way. I do believe that I can survive a trek of half that distance to Darcy House."

"You will do no such thing." Lady Matlock stood. "If you insist, you may join us. We have had no word of any urgent need to be there at the crack of dawn."

Mary was trying her best to stand up for herself in front of the formidable couple, and balling her hands into fists, drew on her last reserves, and thought of Elizabeth. What would she do? "Elizabeth and Fitzwilliam are my family. They have offered me a home for the rest of my days. They have opened their hearts to me without condition. They love me. I *will* go to them." She spun around and walked straight into Peter de Bourgh's chest. "oh!" She cried and looked up to him as tears began to pour from her eyes. She kept her back to the Matlocks and bowed her head. De Bourgh took her hand and squeezed it, then looked up to the Lord and Lady.

"I will take her over. My carriage is just outside." He looked down at her and smiled. "Go and get your bonnet and I will meet you at the door." She nodded and left without a word or a backward glance, and he entered the room. "You cannot keep a loyal woman like that from her family. You should know that."

"I only wished to spare her. It was horrific there yesterday." Lady Matlock sighed and sank back down. "How did you get the news?"

"I do not know what the news is. I ran into Lord Moreland last night and he asked if there was any word on Darcy. I decided to see you before going there."

"Well." Lord Matlock told him the tale. De Bourgh's jaw set and he stood upon the story's end. "Richard is there with Evangeline, and he would have told us if anything happened in the night. We will be over after we speak to Georgiana, and I am waiting for news on Wickham."

"Tell her the truth." De Bourgh said seriously. "Do not pretend that all is roses; do not delude her that this is not serious. The girl has lost her parents already, and she will be frightened for her brother, but if he is not gone now, he will likely survive. I know men who have died from a blow on the head. It would have been clear by now that he would die." He stepped to the doorway. "Bring her along."

Walking to the foyer he found Mary staring out at his carriage. He offered his arm and led her up and onboard. Giving the orders to the coachman, he took his seat opposite and watched her staring at her hands. "How did that feel?"

"Pardon me?" She whispered.

"To stand up for yourself?" He asked with a smile. "I imagine it was a rare event?"

"I . . . I only wish to see my sister. She would . . . walk across broken glass to get to me."

"I am sure that she would, as would Darcy." She nodded to her hands and then bursting into tears, found de Bourgh by her side with his arm around her. He offered her his handkerchief and said softly, "Cry now, but you must be strong for them when you arrive." Mary nodded and sniffed, and did not draw away. When they arrived, he gave her arm a squeeze and stepped down from the coach. "Wipe your eyes, Miss Mary."

"Yes, sir." She wiped and drew a deep breath, then took his hand to step down. "Thank you."

"It is no trouble to help a true lady." He smiled and again offering his arm, led her into the house. They were directed to the dining room where Fitzwilliam sat with Evangeline.

"Well, this is unexpected." Fitzwilliam shook his hand and bowed to Mary. The men's eyes met and de Bourgh smiled at his cousin's raised brow. "Mother and Father?"

"Will be along, with Miss Darcy."

"How are they?" Mary asked Evangeline urgently.

"They are sleeping." She smiled and took her hand. "They are improved."

"Fever?" De Bourgh asked Fitzwilliam.

"Not yet." He sighed and sank into his chair. "I pray it will not come."

"Yes." Watching the women leave the room, he folded his arms and studied Fitzwilliam. "You and I know too much, do we not?"

"Far too much." He smiled ruefully. "I have managed to bury most of the memories, but . . ."

"Yes, I well remember the screams of the men as we brought them back from Spain." De Bourgh rubbed his hand over his face.

"Perhaps you captained my ship of death."

"I may have." The men's eyes met and they fell silent, lost in their thoughts.

Evangeline put her arm around Mary and paused before she opened the door. "What have you been taught about married couples and their sleeping arrangements?"

"Oh . . ." She blushed. "That they always sleep separately."

Nodding her head, she said softly. "Your brother and sister do not follow that practice. Do not be shocked." She quietly opened the door to reveal Darcy still firmly wrapped around Elizabeth. Mary gasped, and blushed deeply. Evangeline quickly pulled her from the room. "There, they are well. Now when they wake, we will return." She nodded and taking Mary's hand, led her back down the stairs.

"That did not take long." Fitzwilliam said and pulled out a chair for his wife.

De Bourgh settled Mary and studying her, fixed her a cup of tea. "Sugar?"

"Oh . . . yes." She startled as the cup was placed before her. The cream was set by her side, as well as a plate of buns. She looked up to see his smile.

"My sisters like sweets when they are unhappy."

She smiled a little and nodded. "Then we have something in common."

Taking his seat again, he raised his brows to Evangeline. "News?"

"Sleeping."

"Excellent." He drew a deep breath and blew it out. "Wickham is where?"

"Newgate, I imagine." Fitzwilliam mused. "Father was going to see what he could learn. That is why he was not rushing to come over here; he is awaiting word from his men." He glanced at Mary who blushed and picked at her bun. "You stood up to Mother, I understand."

"I am so embarrassed." Mary whispered.

"No, no. She will fume, but she will like you better for it." He assured her. "I cannot tell you how many times Elizabeth has done it to her, and Mother likes her enormously." Fitzwilliam smiled and glanced at his wife. "What are you thinking?"

"I think that your mother likes anyone who fights for family."

"I think, my dear, that you are correct." He reached out and took her hand, and they remained that way for quite some time.

ELIZABETH AWOKE and felt intense burning pain in her arm, and the heavy reassuring warmth of her husband's embrace. With the laudanum worn off, she was fully aware for the first time since the attack. She turned her head a little and saw his bearded face resting on her pillow, and his blue eyes watching her. "Good morning." He said hoarsely.

"Good morning." She whispered. "We have not moved in some time."

"Are you sore?"

"That is a silly question. Should I ask it of you?"

"Well my mind was addled." He smiled a little and winced. "It still is."

"So my fearsome husband's legendary mind is suspect?"

"Love, my mind is not prepared for witty banter." He sighed and snuggled against her. "How do you feel?"

"Weak." She admitted.

"Hungry?" He whispered. "I am starving."

"Me, too." Elizabeth glanced at the bell pull.

Darcy watched her gaze and chuckled. "It is too far away."

"I suppose that we can just wait for someone to visit and have mercy on us."

"So far we have had Richard, Eva, and Mary, along with a constant parade of servants."

"How do you know?"

"My mind is addled, not my ears." He whispered and she laughed softly. "Ahhhhhhhhh, that is the balm to my soul, the sweet laughter of my love."

"Do you know what would comfort me?"

"Tell me, dearest."

"Going home to Pemberley." She felt his lips on her ear. "Please?"

"As soon as we are able, love. I will drive the coach myself."

Chapter 19

"Mr. Bennet, I beg you, do not do this!" Mrs. Bennet fretted and waved her handkerchief.

He continued on with his steady writing, then sanding the ink, sealed the envelope and pulled the bell to summon Hill. "Yes sir?"

"I want this posted immediately." He handed the letter over and watched as Mrs. Bennet moved to snatch it away. "I would just write another one." He said frankly. "It is done, Mrs. Bennet. Jane will marry Robert Lucas. That announcement will soon be in the papers. I will speak to our pastor about purchasing the license. I will not have the banns read. I will not risk you standing up and objecting to them. I suggest that you and Lady Lucas find a way to live with this decision."

"How can you do this?" She cried. "How can you condemn us in this way?"

"Condemn?" He stared at her in disbelief. "How exactly does Jane accepting the fine son of our neighbour condemn us?"

"Robert Lucas will care for his family first, and you know that he has no money! And you know that Mr. Darcy dislikes us." She said angrily. "I see his disdain, and he only stays as long as necessary to rest his horses. He does not let me speak freely in my own home!" Mrs. Bennet glared at her husband. "You will die and he will do nothing for us. He will sit in his mansion and laugh. We will be tossed out with nowhere to go."

"How do you form these ridiculous notions? Have you not spent the last year bragging about Mrs. Darcy to the disgust of all in our circle? I thought that you were happy with her triumphant marriage! Lizzy will be sure that you are cared for."

"Lizzy! Ungrateful girl! I am sure that she is why Jane lost Mr. Bingley! She surely ruined her chances with Mr. Harwick, and I am certain that it was her impertinence that drove Mr. Stewart away."

"So that is what is behind this? You were pleased with her success as long as you thought it would get Jane the same or better?" Mr. Bennet looked at her with new eyes. "You continue to be wilfully blind to everything that has happened around us, Mrs. Bennet. Stewart rejected our family, not Lizzy. Harwick rejected Jane and our family. Mr. Bingley . . . From what I understand he determined that he wishes to mature and be a success on his own before marriage. A normal and might I add, an admirable inclination for any young man, would that I had done such a thing!   He was kind to let Jane be free to accept Mr. Lucas."

"She deserves better!"

"She deserves happiness."   He shook his head.   "As for Mr. Darcy, he is kind enough to help with the girls' schooling and has informed me that he will supplement Jane's dowry substantially.   If he has a difficult time spending time with us, it is not through any fault of his.   I appreciate whatever tolerance he does afford."

"He keeps Lizzy and the baby from us."   She sniffed.

"Well as I recall, you think that she failed her husband with a girl, and when did you ever wish to spend time with her?   You just want to show off the baby as some sign of your success.   You are angry that the Darcys have never made themselves available to be displayed to the neighbourhood."   Mr. Bennet watched her face redden and looked at her seriously.   "It is Elizabeth who will save you, Mrs. Bennet.   She is the one who will be sure to provide you with a home when I die.   It is she who will convince her husband to set you up somewhere and keep you fed.   It may not be at Pemberley, in fact, I sincerely doubt that it will be far from Longbourn, but it will be a home.   I suggest that you start grovelling to both of them."   He glanced out of the window when he saw a rider appear and leap from his horse.

"Sir?"   Hill appeared with a letter.   "This express just arrived.   The messenger is waiting for a reply."

Ripping it open he read the letter through three times and let it drop to the desk.   "My Lord."   He whispered.

"What is it, Mr. Bennet?"   Mrs. Bennet demanded.

"Our daughter Lizzy was attacked during an attempted kidnapping of our granddaughter.   Mr. Darcy fought the man and in the process was thrown to the ground and struck his head.   Lizzy was shot."

"Shot?"   She cried.   "Is she dead?"

"No . . . no, Gardiner says that she lost blood and is in great pain, they pray that the surgeon's skill will prevent any further consequences."   He picked up the letter.   "Mr. Darcy suffers from terrible headaches and is disoriented, but the baby is well, thankfully.   This occurred three days ago, Gardiner wished to be sure of their road to recovery before alarming us with the news.   She suffers with a fever, but it seems to not be worsening.   Darcy must be frantic over her."   He closed his eyes and imagined his fearsome son-in-law and how gently he treated his daughter.   Mr. Bennet was snapped out of his thoughts with his wife's voice.

"She must not die!"   Mrs. Bennet declared.

"I am sure that she will have the best of care, my dear.   I am sure that she will recover.   Do not fret."   He said reassuringly.

"If she dies, then Mr. Darcy will feel no obligation to care for us at all!"   She said piteously.

Mr. Bennet rose to his feet and bellowed. "Is THAT all that matters to you? Not her health? Not her husband's health? Only YOUR comfort? You disgust me madam! If I had a hunting cabin in Scotland I would banish you there for the rest of your days!"

"Mr. Bennet!"

"I realize that you fear for your future should I die. I know that I did not save as I should or prepare our children for life. I understand my failings and I am trying to make up for it. You should be grateful that Elizabeth found a man such as Mr. Darcy, but it is not her obligation to marry off our daughters. Jane WILL marry Mr. Lucas, and if she had never met any of these men who did not offer for her, you would have been overjoyed with such a fine match! Lizzy's success has made you avaricious; you crave her circumstances and disdain her happiness. I will go to London to see our daughter because I care for her and respect our son. When I am there, if he is able to hear me, I will beg him to ignore this family when I die. It is not for him to repair what I created." He stood and began to leave the room and stopped. "The curate in Meryton is named Collins. He will be the heir of Longbourn one day. If you wish to court some man's favour to help you survive, I suggest that you ingratiate yourself to him."

"Mr. Collins is the heir?" She whispered.

"His father is, but eventually this will be his home." He looked at her in disbelief. "Do you even care how Lizzy fares?"

She looked at her husband and lifted her chin. "Of course I do. She is Mrs. Darcy. I only feel that she should show her gratitude for all I have done for her."

"If you ever realized what she has done for you, you would be on your knees begging for her forgiveness." Mr. Bennet left the room to go find Jane.

ROBERT LUCAS SMILED at Jane and looked down at her hand on his arm. "I cannot quite believe this is real."

"That we are engaged?" She smiled softly and blushed.

"Yes." He fought his urge to kiss her, and drawing a deep breath, turned his eyes forward as they strolled the lanes. "Do you know when I first noticed you?"

"I have a feeling that it was during one of our family dinners." She said ruefully.

"It was not; it was at the assembly, about three years ago, as a matter of fact." Seeing her apprehension, he laughed. "No, it was not so bad. We danced, do you remember?"

"Yes." She smiled. "I think that was the first time that we did."

"Yes." He stopped their walk to take both of her hands in his, then began to move through the familiar pattern of a simple dance. Jane laughed as he hummed a tune. When he stopped, he smiled into her clear blue eyes. "I was lost then."

"Why did you not say something?"

"Oh . . .no, no. I was but two and twenty, fresh from Cambridge. What did I have to offer a woman? All I could do is watch as the most beautiful girl in the county danced with every man who approached. I cursed every one of them."

She gasped. "Robert!"

"I did." Slipping his arms around her waist, he drew her against his chest. "I was sure that some lucky man would take you away, put you on a pedestal and worship you for all of your days for the angel you are."

Jane blushed when she felt his lips caress her cheek. "I am no angel; please do not call me that."

"Goddess?"

"Such words do not suit me and sound odd coming from you." She closed her eyes and trembled when his mouth wandered to her jaw. "I . . . I . . . I am just . . . Jane."

Lucas moved away, and untying the ribbons of her bonnet, pulled it off so that her hair was free to shine in the sunlight. He ran his fingers through it and then lifted her chin up to meet his lips in a tender kiss. "My Jane."

"Yes." She whispered against his mouth and wrapped her arms around him. "Yours."

"Sweet Jane?" He asked and kissed her again. "Will you allow me to call you my dear, sweet Jane?"

"If I may call you my dear, handsome, Robert."

He laughed softly and kissed her cheek. "I can bear to be handsome if you can bear to be lovely."

"Only if you promise to never make me beautiful or . . .anything meant for heaven." She said seriously. "Please."

"Done." He agreed and kissed her again. "My dear, sweet, lovely, Jane." He rested his forehead on hers and spoke seriously. "Our mothers are not so happy. They both wished for more in our mates, I am afraid. Will you let them ruin this for us? I think that my mother will come around and will rather enjoy taking on your mother for the wedding plans."

"I . . . I suppose that I will someday wish that we lived farther away from Mama, but . . . I know that she will not feel free to burst in upon us to visit as it is still your parents' home. I believe that as long as I get along with Lady Lucas, all will be well."

"That is an excellent point, my dear." He hugged her tight.

"This is very nice." Jane sighed.

Robert kissed her and smiled as she snuggled into his arms. "I certainly enjoy it."

"Now I understand why Lizzy and Mr. Darcy are always this way." She looked up to his soft brown eyes. "We will do this often?"

"I think that I can manage that." He laughed and saw her smile grow. "I can think of a great many things that I look forward to doing with you often."

"Oh!" Jane startled. "You mean . . ."

"yes." He whispered into her ear and clasped her tightly to his body. "Do you feel me, my Jane?"

"I . . . I yes, I have felt this before with you."

"Do you wonder what it is?" He kissed her throat. "It is my desire for you."

"Oh."

"We will have to learn to be quiet, I am afraid that the walls are thin, but . . . I hope to love you often . . .my dear Jane." His breathing hitched and wrapping her up in his arms, one hand in her hair, the other on her bottom, he kissed her, seeking and gaining entry into her mouth and letting her feel the heat raging in his loins. Jane nearly fainted from the kiss but as he did not relent, she began to respond, kissing him back and touching his tongue, even moving her hips against his. She heard him groan in her mouth then felt his tongue in her ear, and his lips on her throat. "Yes, Jane, that is it, move with me, enjoy this." He urged her. "Do not be afraid." He looked into her eyes. "I want you to welcome your husband into your embrace."

"I . . . I will. But . . . oh Robert, we will be seen . . ." His mouth fell upon hers and they kissed more deeply with each passing moment, until at last he stopped and held her to his chest. "Why . . ."

"Did I stop?" He panted.

"Yes."

"Do you wish to go on, my Jane?" He looked into her eyes. "If we continue, we will anticipate our vows. My control is at its edge."

"Oh."

He saw the conflict in her eyes and he smiled. "Do I speak too plainly?"

"I . . . I am not sure." She looked down and blushed. "Lizzy has spoken to me of . . .marriage; and my aunt as well. I understand . . ."

"But you wish to wait?" He smiled and laughed. "I never intended to continue, dear. I respect you too much, and I can feel your discomfort being out in the open like this. I am a private man as well, but how can I resist you in my arms? Besides, I was curious what you would say."

"You are unkind!" Jane said furiously.

"No. I am myself. And you, my dear, will have to grow used to that. I am not above teasing, as my siblings can attest."

"Lizzy teases." She said pensively. "Did you ever like her?"

"Hmm." He looked thoughtfully up to the sky.

"Robert!" She demanded, but he could hear the note of worry in her voice.

"No, Jane, I honestly was never drawn to her. She is sweet and kind as are you, and her wit and talent for conversation are admirable, but . . . she just was not the one for me. Remember, I was caught up in thoughts of you, and she was a young girl when I last really saw her. I wished for a woman." He could see the relief in her eyes. "I answered properly, I see."

"I am tired of competing with her."

"I have a feeling that she was tired of competing with you." Lucas said seriously. "She did all of her life, compete for your mother's attention and that of every man in Hertfordshire? I watched."

"I never encouraged it!"

"You did not have to, you exuded beauty which attracted the attention, wanted or not."

"Do you truly believe that Lizzy wished to be like me?" Jane stared at him in wonder.

Brushing back the hair that blew into her eyes, he tilted his head. "I thought that you were close."

"We were." She whispered. "I ruined it."

"What happened? I saw her behaviour with you. She loves you." He kissed her softly. "Tell me what happened. She married Darcy, and . . ."

Glancing up at him, she felt his love and felt safe enough to be honest. "I became jealous."

"And now?"

Jane did not answer. Lucas watched her face and then saw her eyes close for a moment before meeting his. "Why do you want me? Why were you attracted to me?"

"You are beautiful." He said with a twinkle in his eye.

"Oh I am so tired of being told that I am beautiful!" She cried. "Is there nothing else of me that . . . Why, why do you want to tie yourself to me for the rest of your days?"

"Why do you feel it would be a torture to do so?" Lucas smiled as she was forced to think. "Jane, you were always a calm centre in the world of your rather chaotic family. I enjoyed watching you attempt to soothe everyone and make all disgruntlement disappear." He chuckled. "And sometimes it was a success, at least with your mother, and you did handle your younger sisters well. That tells me that you would prefer a harmonious home life, which is appealing to me. However, I do know all of your behaviour towards your sister when she found love."

"That was not me." She said with a blush.

"Of course it was." Robert laughed at her shock. "Jane, something inside of you felt desire for love and excitement, perhaps passion. You watched your sister attract one man after another; men of means, men with great strength of character? I believe, dear Jane, that you wanted a man who would allow you to at last be yourself, but one who did not force you to become someone you did not wish to be at the same time."

"What do you mean?" She stared at him in fascination.

"I mean, you had no desire to live in the society where Mrs. Darcy resides, it does not interest you in the slightest, but you would dearly love to have the freedom to . . .not be perfect. It must be terribly hard work to always smile and see the good in everyone, to be admired and praised for your beauty?"

"It is exhausting." She admitted and then lifted her hand to her mouth.

Lucas smiled and kissed her. "Well, hearing of your lapse with your sister told me that deep inside of you there is a woman just itching to discover who she is. And I hope to spend my days coaxing her out."

"What if you do not like who you find?"

"Oh, I am sure that I will. You cannot drift too far from your sweet persona, but I do expect to meet the side of you with the sharp tongue, and I will not be in the least afraid to take you on. I may even provoke you to use it." He laughed as her eyes widened. "Dear Jane, how could you be your mother's daughter and not possess such a skill?"

Jane's mouth dropped open. "You . . .you think that I am as . . . outspoken as Mama?"

"I said that you have the potential." His eyes laughed as her face grew red. "Shall we discuss your sisters?"

"No!" She drew herself up. "Perhaps we should discuss *your* family?"

Lucas laughed. "I would be delighted, my dear! Have at them!"

She stopped just as she was about to speak. "Robert, is this what you meant? That . . . I will be free to be . . ."

"Yourself." He kissed her softly and smiled to see her eyes light up. "I cannot wait to meet the true Jane you have kept hidden away while you tried to please everyone but yourself."

"Lizzy always tried to make me be myself." Hugging her to him, he heard her sigh. "We will not see her often will we?"

"Probably not. We might go to Pemberley once every few years, perhaps to London more often when they are visiting. Do you mind?"

"No." She sighed and rested her head on his shoulder. "I am home right here, where I can just be Jane for you." The sound of an approaching horse forced them apart quickly, and to see that it was Mr. Bennet brought blushes to both of their faces.

"Lucas . . . I am in no doubt that I caught you behaving questionably with my daughter, and am surprised that you have no chaperone, Jane . . ."

"Mr. Bennet . . ."

"Papa . . . I . . ."

He held up his hand and shook his head. "No, I will not say anything else, I have far more pressing business than a stolen embrace between an engaged couple." Dismounting, he handed the letter from Mr. Gardiner to Jane. "Prepare yourself for some terrible news."

"SO WHAT WAS IT, his lover's husband come to call him out?" The men gathered in the card room of the gentleman's club laughed loudly.

"Darcy with a lover? A married one? That dull stick wouldn't know where to put his pole, let alone how to use it!" Creary laughed. "Now I could give the boy a lesson or two."

"We all know to lock up our daughters when you are on the premises, Creary."

Gannon poked him. "I imagine that Darcy's wife would beg to differ with your opinion, he is a new father."

Red faced, Creary snorted. "Ha! I suspect that the man was *her* lover. He is the one that got her with child, and now Darcy has found out about him! Cuckolded no doubt! If she had agreed to accept my favour, it would be a male child. Imagine that, Creary blood in Pemberley. Well, perhaps I will offer my services again . . . I saw her the other day, pregnancy did a great deal for her already delectable figure. I do enjoy taking small women." Creary smacked his lips and the others laughed.

Stewart looked up from his table when the conversation mentioned Darcy's name, and when they began debating his and Elizabeth's commitment, he put down his cards and went to stand nearby. Feeling a presence at his elbow, he noticed that his father had quietly joined him.

"Well, whoever the man is, it seems that Darcy got the best of him. I hear he is in Newgate."

"For a duel? They don't prosecute gentlemen for that!"

"What's the name?"

"Let me see." One man rattled his paper and searched the columns. "Ah here it is, Wickham."

"Wickham!" Stewart startled and moved forward to grab the paper. "But he is dead!"

"Moreland, you really should teach your boy some manners." Lord Creary sniffed. "Oh, but then he fancies himself a friend to Darcy, so he has none at all."

"If anyone is going to learn manners it is you, Creary. I thought that I told you not to spread wild gossip, and here you are with your cackling hens doing it just the same. Extraordinary how desperate you are to knock down a man who did nothing more than tell you to leave his wife alone, and not to invite him to your parties. Or are you jealous of Devonshire publicly acknowledging him and his wife?"

Creary ignored the last comment. "Seems to me his wife wants to be with somebody, why else would she be bedding this Wickham?"

"You bastard! How dare you suggest such a thing of Mrs. Darcy!" Stewart growled and the men laughed at him.

"What's this? A soft spot for the lady? My, my, poor Darcy, how many lovers does she have?"

"If you knew them you would choke on your words." Stewart spat and shook the paper. "What happened? This says nothing, only that there was an attack!"

"I told you, boy. He was facing his wife's lover down." Creary sneered.

Stewart spun around. "Do you know anything more, Father?"

"No Son, I am sorry, I only know that Matlock was summoned to Darcy House four days ago, I have heard nothing since. I thought that to inquire would be an intrusion. Matlock will contact me if there is anything I need to know. He pointed the paper. "I had not read that news."

"I am going to Darcy House and learn the truth of this." Stewart started to leave and returned to the table. "I will also present your theories to Lord and Lady Matlock. I am certain that they will be interested to hear of them, and to add some theories of their own to your fantasies." Stewart stormed out and Lord Moreland smiled at his son's back.

"You had better do something about your boy, Moreland. He won't ever get his silks if he keeps crossing his betters."

"His betters? Moreland growled. "Watch your tongue, Creary. You are not talking to a servant. Your importance is falling as your age increases. How many ladies sneer at your approach now? And . . ." he laughed, "How many can you keep properly entertained?" Creary's companions joined in the joke until they felt his gaze upon them, and returned to their game. Lord Moreland looked over the room and seeing the interest of the crowd waning, left to see what he could learn on his own.

"I AM SORRY SIR; the Darcys are not accepting visitors." Foster said diffidently at the door.

"Is there . . . I am hearing terrible rumours can you confirm that they are well? I would like to protect their good names." Stewart argued with the gatekeeper. "Is Lord Matlock present?" Foster hesitated and Stewart jumped on it. "I would like to speak to him, please."

"Stewart!" Bingley called from the walkway. "I have heard the most outrageous rumours about Darcy! Caroline was full of it this morning. What has happened?"

Stewart spun and faced Foster. "Well?" The butler's smooth expression wavered, and then nodding, stepped back.

"Please wait in Mr. Darcy's study, sir." He opened the door and they entered the empty room.

Bingley turned to Stewart. "I heard Wickham's name mentioned."

"I did as well."

"I thought he was dead." Bingley watched him pacing the room. "I heard something of a duel? Who on earth would Darcy want to duel? I do not visit for a few days and the world turns upside down!"

"I do not know what has happened, but Foster's behaviour is worrying." They looked up when they heard boots on the wood and deflated to find that instead of Darcy, it was Lord Matlock entering. His face was grim. "Sir, I have heard horrifying news, please, tell us what has happened?"

"Your information of Wickham's death was faulty." He said in a cool voice. "Darcy's suspicion and desire to view his body was not as laughable as we surmised."

"Sir . . .please, where is Darcy?"

"Darcy lies in his bed, he is sleeping. He continues to suffer excruciating headaches after rescuing his . . .wife." Lord Matlock pulled himself together. "My niece was shot . . . She is suffering now with fever. We pray that she will recover. Darcy is terrified of losing her."

"SHOT! When did this happen? What happened? Why is Darcy in pain?" Stewart and Bingley stepped closer, demanding news.

"Wickham attempted to take the baby, Darcy fought him, a pistol fired, Darcy fell and struck his head, Elizabeth received the bullet." He spoke tonelessly. "Wickham is in Newgate, chained to the wall. He will be allowed to heal, and then . . . We will by God hang that bastard as he should have been to begin with!" Lord Matlock paced the room and turned to see Stewart's stricken face. He pointed at him. "I charge *you* to find out how he managed this!"

Stunned, Stewart spoke numbly, "Sir, we already know that he slipped away from the work crew on the river."

"Well then, something must be done to prevent this from happening again. Keep them in irons; assign a guard to every man!" Lord Matlock growled and seeing Stewart's suffering, relented. "It is not your fault. I have enough people looking into this already. Something must be done. Corruption in the courts, corruption in the prisons . . ." He fell silent as he fumed.

"I agree." Stewart whispered. "Mrs. Darcy . . . will she . . ."

"Live?" Bingley finished.

"We believe that she will, but Darcy was frantic." Closing his eyes, he wiped his hand over his face. "Her fever appears to be abating. She was doing well, it seemed, and then it just . . ." He turned away to wipe his eyes.

"Darcy will recover?" Stewart asked cautiously.

"Yes, however his pain will remain for some weeks, we believe, and we are unsure of any lingering effects from the blow." Lord Matlock sighed and finally took a seat. "We have decided to keep him asleep until she improves; she is dosed with laudanum as well, but not as much."

"Would she not benefit from hearing his voice?" Bingley asked. Seeing the others looking at him, he dropped into a chair and leaned his elbows on his knees. "Forgive me, but I know very well the connection between them. I witnessed her despair when she learned he would not return as planned last autumn. I witnessed his despair when he thought they could not marry. Sir, you must allow him to care for her. If she dies . . . Please sir, do not wake him to find her gone. He would have no chance of surviving for his baby. He would die."

"I agree with Mr. Bingley." The men startled to find Jane and Mr. Bennet at the doorway and rose to their feet. Jane spoke quietly. "Mr. Darcy loves my sister deeply; do not keep him from caring for her however he feels he must. I think that all he wishes is to hold her. We have all witnessed it enough times."

Bingley met her eyes and nodded. "Yes, we have."

"I would like to see my daughter, please." Mr. Bennet asked as his voice cracked.

"Of course." Lord Matlock glanced at Stewart and Bingley then moved to lead the Bennets upstairs.

Jane paused and looked to Bingley. "Thank you, sir. I . . . I appreciate your care for my brother and sister."

"It is no trouble Miss Bennet; please give them my . . .hopes."

She smiled a little and left the room. Stewart watched Bingley's expression. "Are you well?"

"Yes." He blew out a breath and sank into a chair. "I was not prepared for that."

"Do you regret her?"

"No." He smiled a little. "I have had time to reflect upon her, and I think that where I once thought that I would like a beautiful woman to adore, I realize that I want even more a woman who wants to enjoy the life my father has given me, who wants to learn with me, and be my partner and my friend. I believe that I was drawn to Miss Bennet because she is so opposite of my mother, who was an aggressive and social climbing woman. Miss Bennet clearly is not, but it took me some time to realize that she also was not interested in anything I could offer her, other than safety with a genial companion." He laughed hollowly and looked at his hands. "My angel awaits me somewhere, but she has not presented herself as yet. It was a shock though to have Miss Bennet become engaged the day that I gave her up! I mean; what a blow to my ego!" Closing his eyes he sighed. "I wish that we could see them."

"I do, too. But we are not blood." Stewart said quietly. Both men returned from their momentary distraction to dwell on their true concern. "You were correct; Darcy must be allowed to care for Mrs. Darcy."

"Well with Miss Bennet and her father here now, perhaps that will happen." Bingley's gaze moved to the ceiling as he willed his friends to be well. "I wonder how Miss Darcy is feeling, or if they have even told her. She must frightened to death, the girl is already orphaned, and Darcy is her father now." He stared back down at his hands. "They *must* be well."

JANE SAT BY ELIZABETH'S SIDE and wiped her face with a cool cloth. "oh Lizzy." She whispered. Elizabeth's eyes opened slightly and she looked at her sister. Seeing that she was trying to speak, Jane leaned close and heard the whispered words. Moving back, she stood and leaned over the bed to take Elizabeth's hand, and place it in Darcy's open palm as he lay sleeping on his back beside her. She watched as both of them curled their fingers together in a weak grip. "oh." She kissed Elizabeth's brow and walked into the sitting room where Lord Matlock was speaking to Mr. Bennet. "She is conscious; she wants her husband's touch. Please allow him to wake for her."

"Yes, I . . . We were frightened for him, he was beside himself when she became feverish, and then my son Richard was so upset that Evangeline forced him to return home. Mary decided that she was better off looking after Georgiana at Matlock House. She . . . I am grateful for your daughter, sir. We . . . had thought to keep the entirety of the news from Georgiana, but Mary and de Bourgh both insisted that she be treated as an adult in this. She lay over her brother's chest and sobbed, and he was too drugged to notice her. She begged to stay and care for him and Elizabeth, but she was far too distraught to do either of them any good. That is when Mary agreed to take her home, although it was clear that she wished to remain." He sighed. "Georgiana calmed then, and was grateful that she had been permitted to see them, so she could comprehend our agitation, but she also knew that she was not strong enough to remain. My wife will join me here soon. She has been working on the rumours." He glanced at Mr. Bennet's angry face. "You were not here when Elizabeth and Darcy were first together, but it seems that old gossip is difficult to squelch, even when it is proven wrong time and again."

"I understand; I live with a woman who thrives upon it." He turned to Jane. "I would like to see Lizzy."

"It is not frightening, Papa." She smiled and took his hand to lead him into the bedchamber. They stopped just inside the doorway when they saw that Elizabeth had managed to roll over to lie next to Darcy, her head was over his heart, and even more remarkable was seeing that he had risen from the morphine-induced haze to wrap his arms around her. Both were asleep. Father and daughter quickly retreated, leaving the couple to Millie's care.

"What is it?" Lord Matlock went to the doorway and looked in then returned to them. "You know, one of these days, we will learn to listen to them and stop trying to impose our will. We tried to keep them apart after the attack, and Darcy came to her. We tried to send him away after she became feverish and he nearly broke the door down. We tried to drug him to keep him calm and . . .well, from this point on I will tell the staff to leave them be, and treat the pain, not the behaviour."

"If I were in the throes of death my wife would be beating on me to live, but it certainly would not be out of affection." Mr. Bennet mused. "Well, just that entirely improper sight of them lying together warms my heart and relieves my soul. I am certain that they will be well." He said determinedly. "I will take the carriage to my brother's home."

"I am sure that Darcy would wish for you to stay here, sir." Lord Matlock offered and saw Mr. Bennet's resigned smile.

"Perhaps, but I would never presume to invite myself. I will await the master's invitation. Jane, you will remain?"

"Yes, Papa."

"Fine, I will leave your luggage here. I expect that I will return this evening with the Gardiners." He kissed her forehead. "I will write a note home for your mother and, I suppose that you will prepare one for Lucas?" She blushed and he laughed softly. "Very good, dear."

"I will show you out, sir." Lord Matlock left the room and after seeing Mr. Bennet on his way and speaking to Mrs. Mercer about Jane, he returned to the study. "Well Bingley, your wish is fulfilled, I think that Darcy is coming around as is Elizabeth, we will just let them make the decisions from this point on, and give them enough laudanum for the pain, but not to keep them unconscious."

Bingley smiled with relief. "Good then, I will be happy to see them recovered."

Stewart closed his eyes then drew himself up. "What shall we do with the gossip, sir? Creary was saying in the club that it was likely Elizabeth's lover that Darcy fought, and intimated that the baby was not a Darcy."

"Now what?" Lord Matlock groaned. "Creary was it?"

"Yes, sir. He also suggested that he would gladly father her next." Stewart's face grew red with anger. "My father was there and set him down, and I am afraid that I suggested to Creary that I would speak to you of this."

"I thank you." Lord Matlock rubbed his chin. "What a child he is. Darcy will not come to his party so he has to whine. I suppose that his friends were enjoying his posturing?"

"Yes, sir."

"Hmm." He sat down and folded his hands over his waist and thought. "You are still engaged to the Henley girl?"

"Yes, sir, we are to marry in two weeks." Stewart could not help but smile.

"Good, well, Mrs. Henley is one who is always poised on the very cusp of London's gossip, I suggest that you go and give her something to spread about. Knowing that woman she will be calling for her carriage five minutes after you finish." He glanced at the clock. "Too late for her to make calls today, but I have no doubt that she will get the word around nicely in the morning. Perhaps if they are to attend something . . ."

"They are, sir, there is a ball tonight . . ." Lord Matlock raised his brows and Stewart stood. "Off you go, lad."

Bingley was left with Lord Matlock, and awaited his orders. "Sir? Miss Darcy, is she well? And Miss Mary?"

Lord Matlock considered him for a moment and nodded. "Both are well, and are supporting each other at Matlock. Georgiana is frightened, naturally. Mary is surprising." He smiled. "She gave me and my wife a tongue lashing and has not said a peep since." He chuckled and saw Bingley's concern. "I gather that it was a novelty, she is a student of Elizabeth's I think, and undoubtedly Georgiana will be as well before long. Something to keep in mind for whatever young man falls for either of them, just look to their sister!"

Bingley nodded and smiled. "Yes sir, I am glad to know that they are safe. So sir, what may we do to help?"

"What say you to some whist, Bingley?" Lord Matlock rose to his feet. "How is your play?"

"Terrible, sir."

"How is your purse?" Lord Matlock's lips twitched.

"Too heavy, sir." He grunted when Lord Matlock's hand clapped on his shoulder. "Are we going rumour mongering?"

"Rumour killing Son, and perhaps starting a few of our own." Arriving at the front door, he looked up at the stairs then turned to Foster. "My wife will be here before long, if you have need of us, we are at the club fighting a war of words."

"Yes, sir." Foster handed them their hats and bowed. "I wish you great success, sir."

"OH MY, CAN YOU *IMAGINE*! That horrid Lord Creary, claiming such things of Mrs. Darcy!" Mrs. Henley fanned herself rapidly. "She is the dearest young woman, why, well I should not say such things, but . . ."

"Come now, Mrs. Henley, you know that you are just dying to." Lady Grafton's lips twitched and she saw Lady Monroe step closer to listen.

"Well . . ." Mrs. Henley glanced around and leaned in closer. "At the ball the Darcys held at Pemberley, I saw the two of them steal away from the ballroom. I just happened to be on my way to . . . To the card rooms, yes, and . . . I saw the two of them engaged in a rather passionate exchange!" She blushed and nodded. "And when they ended their . . .conversation, Mr. Darcy held her to him and they danced alone in the moonlight." She sighed. "It was so scandalous! I think it was the waltz!"

"The waltz!" Lady Monroe said with her mouth open. "Well, I have heard of that dance and I can assure you it will not be performed at Almack's anytime soon!"

"Tell me that you have never swayed in the arms of your husband?" Lady Grafton asked. "Alone in your home?"

"Well . . ." Lady Monroe coloured, and turned her attention back to Mrs. Henley. "Mrs. Darcy was known to be with child then, I understand."

"Oh yes, I asked her myself!" Mrs. Henley said proudly.

"When was the girl born?" Mrs. Smythe asked.

"Just this April. Of course we were so sorry to miss the christening." Mrs. Henley smiled. "But I did call on Mrs. Darcy last week and met her. Such a dear little one. She reminds me so much of Julia, why when she was but a month old . . ."

"Yes, yes." Mrs. Kendall waved her hand. "It seems to me that Mrs. Darcy became with child after she left London. I distinctly remember when they departed, as I wrote of the news to Lady Catherine de Bourgh. No it seems that once again, Creary is behaving as the child he is. Mrs. Darcy refused his advances, and her husband set him down. Nothing he says has any credence."

"I agree. He chased after me in my younger days." Lady Monroe rolled her eyes and the ladies laughed. "He was quite the specimen then, and I certainly know enough women who succumbed to his charms. Now though, he is an old fool."

"But what of this man who attacked them?" Mrs. Smythe asked and ignored Mrs. Henley bouncing with excitement. "I am not in the least pleased that he escaped and that the Darcys had to suffer his intrusion. Something must be done!"

Lady Grafton nodded vehemently. "An intrusion is hardly the word for it. If the papers have it correct, he violated their home, and attempted to harm them! Thankfully Mr. Darcy is a man who will go to the ends of the earth to protect his family. Does anyone know if they are well?"

Lady Monroe turned to Mrs. Smythe. "I understand that this Wickham broke into their home last autumn. We were gone back to the country then, but my husband heard about it all at his club. There was a great cry to reform the way prisoners are watched, but who knows if anything will come of it. In any case, it makes perfect sense that he would wish to wreak his revenge upon Darcy somehow if he escaped. He was sentenced to Australia."

"It makes sense for a fool." Mrs. Kendall sniffed and tapped her fan against her hands. "Leave it to a man to escape prison and instead of continuing out of town to a safe location and new life, what does he do? He returns to the scene of the crime to be caught again! It just proves that men do not think with their brains."

"Ah, I agree, all of their thinking seems to be centred on that one particular organ." Mrs. Smythe smirked as her eyes drifted down and all of the women laughed. "Well then, I am certain that the story presented by your daughter's betrothed is the one to be believed, and, might I add, the one to be spread. I understand that Lady Matlock has been making calls today."

"She has. I have never seen her in such a fury." Lady Grafton nodded. "She is a mother protecting her defenceless young."

"Well ladies, I suggest that we help our friend." Lady Monroe sniffed. "Fan out, you know what to do."

MRS. YOUNGE SAT by a window in the tavern near the boarding house, and ate her solitary meal. She kept her eyes on the street, watching for Wickham. As the days passed, her hope that he would return was waning. The fact that he did not take anything with him told her that his absence was unplanned. She had almost come to accept that he would probably not escape the prison, and that he would in time be sent to Australia, but then he succeeded, and returned to her, and seemed so sure, so ready to embrace their new life in America. Sighing, she looked down at the newssheet that another patron had left behind, and began to read. "Oh no."

Attack at Darcy House

An intruder with nefarious plans came upon Mrs. Fitzwilliam Darcy in her garden Wednesday, and apparently attempted to kidnap her infant daughter. Mr. Darcy himself heard his wife's cry and came to her defence. After a great struggle, in which all but the child were gravely injured, the staff subdued the actor, Mr. George Wickham, a recently escaped convict who was awaiting transportation following an earlier robbery attempt at the same address.

"Why did you have to return there!" She cried and ignored the curious stares of the people around her. "You stupid fool!"

DARCY CAUTIOUSLY OPENED his eyes and was relieved that this time the room was not spinning. From the shadows on the wall; he suspected it was early morning. Another blink and the decoration came into sharp focus. "Well, that is an improvement." He stayed still, assessing his condition. His head ached dully, but he no longer felt as if an ice pick was jammed in his brains. His stomach ached uncomfortably, but that seemed to be from hunger. His mouth was dry and his muscles were stiff, but the strange feeling of heaviness combined with euphoria and fear was gone. Raising his hand to his face, he was surprised with the beard he seemed to possess. Absentmindedly, he scratched at it. "Elizabeth will not like this." Then his eyes widened and he turned his head quickly to find her face resting on his shoulder. Letting out a relieved breath, he gently kissed her forehead, letting his lips linger to gauge her temperature. She was cool. "Thank you, Lord." Darcy kissed her lips and her eyes opened. "Hello, my love."

"Hello." She smiled and reached up to caress his face. "What have you done to yourself?"

"Do you like it?" He laughed softly when her nose wrinkled, then leaned down to kiss her again.

"I do *not* like your whiskers!"

"Shall I begin a new fashion, love? Be a bearded gentleman?" He rubbed his cheek against hers.

Elizabeth batted him away. "If you do, you shall not be kissed by *this* lady."

"Oh, well then, could you suggest one who would enjoy my kisses? Miss Gannon is still available . . ."

"Fitzwilliam!"

Darcy smiled and then laughed to see her eyes sparkling with indignation. "You feel better."

"So do you to be teasing me so cruelly." Elizabeth frowned, but quickly softened her expression in the presence of his twinkling eyes. "You *are* better?"

"My head throbs, but it is tolerable. Of course I have not moved yet. Your pain? How is it?"

"The same as yours, throbbing but not intolerable." She sighed. "I am hungry."

"So am I. And I feel a deep desire to bathe." Darcy and Elizabeth gazed at each other for a long time. They both looked ill and certainly felt unclean, but their eyes were alive once again, and both knew instinctively that the worst was past them. Rolling over, he carefully embraced her then lowered his lips to hers for a very tender kiss. When he drew away, they both sighed. "You are so beautiful." Elizabeth caressed his matted hair and shook her head in disbelief. "We are going to be well." He whispered. "I love you, dear Elizabeth."

"I love you, my Fitzwilliam." They fell back into their gaze, and held each other quietly, just letting the truth of their survival wash over them. Finally Elizabeth kissed his nose and he smiled. "A safe spot for your lips?"

"Until you rid yourself of that . . . carpet on your chin." She laughed.

"There is my laugh. I dreamed of your laugh." His smile fell away and he caressed her tangled hair. "You had me so frightened."

"I know dear, Jane told me. She told me you would recover, so that I could relax and not worry."

"Jane?"

"She was here most of the night, pouring out her heart when she thought I was asleep."

"Is she well?" His brow creased.

"Yes, love. She is very happy, and wants to be happy in her marriage as we are. She told me all about Robert." Elizabeth traced her fingers over his brow. "Papa told me about Mr. Stewart going to the Henleys and telling them the truth of what happened. I remember thinking that Mrs. Henley was a refined version of Mama. Papa met her last evening when she tried to visit, and he said as much to me when he sat with us. Mama . . ."

Darcy watched her eyes well up. "No, do not say it if it is painful."

"Papa would not have told me if he knew I could hear." She swallowed. "She was worried what her future would be if I had died."

"Oh, love."

"I suppose that is all I will ever be to her."

"I am sorry." He hugged her.

She wiped her eyes and pushed away the hurt. "Mr. Bingley and Uncle Henry went to the club and gossiped like schoolgirls. Aunt Helen told me all about it. They had the whole club laughing at Lord Creary. I guess that his prowess is diminishing."

"Lizzy!"

"Aunt Helen was practically gleeful to talk about it. I have never heard her so pleased."

"She thought we were asleep as well, I take it." Darcy played with her hair and she nodded. "Any other visitors?"

"Aunt Gardiner brought in Mary and Georgiana; she hugged you for a long time." He smiled a little and raised his shoulders, admitting he knew nothing of it. "She apologized for being scared, and Mary kissed us both and whispered to me that she was looking after Georgiana and not to worry. And Eva sat with us for a little while but had to leave to care for Richard. He was so angry and worried, she said. He wants to destroy Wickham and anyone associated with his escape." Elizabeth saw his eyes close. "It is the fear talking, I think. He is your brother."

"Now he knows the worry I have felt so many times for him." His eyes reopened.

"I understand that the Harwicks visited the house, as well as Captain de Bourgh." She smiled a little. "Mrs. Mercer whispered that there is a stack of cards from the curious who wished to pay a call, something was in the paper, it seems."

"I imagine that she enjoyed turning them away." Darcy took her hand and kissed it. "I seem to remember them having removed me to the other room again and waking up alone." He looked down and confessed, "I think that I lost my mind when you became feverish. I was so afraid that if I left your side you would leave me forever."

"You must have made that clear to them since you are here now." Darcy swallowed back his emotion only to look up to see her eyes just as bright. They leaned together and kissed again. "I gathered that they kept you asleep to keep you calm. Mr. Bingley told Uncle Henry that they needed to let you wake and care for me."

"Bingley." Darcy smiled. "So many friends were fighting for us." His hand caressed over her face and down over her bandages. Elizabeth flinched. "Does it hurt a great deal?"

"Not more than I can bear." She saw his head shake and laughed. "I have had a child, Fitzwilliam; I can bear a great deal."

"So you can, but it does not mean that you should." His hand drifted over her breasts and his brow furrowed a little. "You are not . . .as large as you were."

"I am not?" She felt herself and her eyes widened, becoming aware of the aching. "Oh Will! Have I lost my milk?"

"I do not know how long we have laid here. Here, let me see." Opening her gown he first paused to smile at the sight of her breasts and then bent to kiss them. Running his warm hand over the mounds, he took a nipple into his mouth and began to suckle. Elizabeth closed her eyes, half-worried that her ability to feed their baby was gone, and half-enjoying the reassuring presence of her husband's touch. It took some determined work, but at last Darcy's efforts were rewarded with a mouthful. He moved to the second nipple and did the same. "There." He smiled and kissed each one. "We will have to repeat this often before Rosalie can return to you."

"Somehow I do not think you will mind." She smiled with relief and relaxed into his arms again.

"No love, that is one duty I will gladly perform." He laughed and kissed her. "Besides, I am very thirsty!"

"So am I."

"I do not think that you are up to suckling me, dearest." Their eyes met and she raised her brow. "Lizzy . . . no, let me bathe first!"

"If you must." She pursed her lips and hugged him.

"You are teasing me." He whispered.

"Maybe." They remained embraced and listened to the sounds of the household coming awake, then heard Rosalie's first cry of the morning. Elizabeth let go of him. "Help me, please."

Darcy slowly sat up and placing one hand behind her back and grasping her uninjured arm, helped her to sit up. Without thought he got out of the bed and walked around to the other side to help her to stand. "There you go." He smiled and they walked, unsteadily, to the nursery door. Darcy opened it in time to see Rosalie's napkin string retied. "Good morning, my girl." He called. The nursemaid jumped and then broke into a wide smile when she turned.

"Mr. and Mrs. Darcy! Oh what a wonderful sight you are!" Mrs. Robbins cried and rose from the rocker where she was waiting for Rosalie.

Rosalie's eyes grew wide at the sound of her father's voice and they watched her head turn. Darcy's heart nearly burst with happiness to witness her searching for him. Elizabeth laughed to see him beam. "Good morning, Rosa." She said softly.

Immediately she began wiggling and making noises. The nursemaid picked her up and handed her to Darcy. Elizabeth kissed her face. "I am sorry that I cannot hold you, sweetheart, but as soon as I can, I will." She reached out and touched her hair, as tears began to track down her face. "Did he hurt her?"

"No madam, she was well, not a mark on her." Mrs. Robbins wiped her eyes to see the family together again.

"We will find a way for you to hold her, dear." Darcy smiled as his eyes brightened, and he leaned down to nuzzle Rosalie's cheek. "I love the smell of my little baby girl."

Elizabeth wiped her eyes and he kissed her. "You sound like a woman wishing for a newborn." Smiling up at him, she caressed his gaunt face. "Well, perhaps we should tend to our needs, then we can take care of our daughter."

"I suppose." He kissed Rosalie and handed her to Mrs. Robbins. "Thank you for looking after her for us. How long have we been away?"

Mrs. Robbins smiled to see Darcy immediately seek Elizabeth's hand. "It has been six days since the incident, sir."

"Six days." Elizabeth whispered. "We *were* ill."

"Yes madam, the staff has been so worried."

"Well . . . I think that we need to thank them for their hard work in our absence." Darcy turned to Elizabeth and without care, kissed her before the servants. He caressed her pale face and smiled. "Which would you prefer first, a bath or breakfast?"

"Oh a bath! And some tooth powder!" She laughed when he led her back to the bedchamber and pulled the bell. "I want you to sniff me and wear that silly smile you had for Rosalie."

Darcy chuckled and they walked over to the window to look out over the trees of Hyde Park. He stood behind her and carefully wrapped her in his embrace. "Dearest, I believe that I can summon a silly smile for you no matter the reason. I love you, my dear Elizabeth."

"I love you, my woolly, Fitzwilliam." She reached up to rub his face and he leaned into her hand, and groaned.

"That is it, love, scratch there, oh, please!"

Chapter 20

8 July 1810

A week has passed since Elizabeth and I were brought back from the Land of Nod. Slowly we have regained our strength, but I fear that my wife will take some time to regain her confidence. She clings to me, as I do with her. We nearly fight to hold our daughter! I had the advantage at first, but my resourceful wife has adapted and with the aid of her fashionable silk sling, she is somehow able to support both her arm and our child. We have agreed to terms, my love has her for feedings; I have her for kisses afterwards. Rosa and I have had many talks about her mother over the past days, and we have come to agree that she is the most extraordinary woman, and that Rosa will do very well to grow up to be just like her. She will soon be three months old. It is difficult to imagine the world without her in it. I am eternally grateful that she was spared.

The rumours surrounding the incident have been effectively quashed by our friends and family.

Darcy stopped his writing when Lord Matlock entered the study. "Uncle Henry . . ."

"Stay seated, Son." He smiled and sat down, then looked out to the hallway. De Bourgh and Fitzwilliam strode in and the colonel plopped into a chair. "Watch that sword, Richard."

"Father, I am an expert with the blade, I will harm nothing that does not deserve it." He grinned at Darcy. "You look better."

"So do you." Darcy noted an affectionate glare coming over his features. "I feel better. If cook has her way I will soon be required to visit a tailor for new clothes."

"Self-control, Cousin."

"I am acquainted with the concept." He smiled and said determinedly, "No, I am not concerned; I will soon be fencing again."

"How are your headaches?" De Bourgh asked as he settled gracefully into a chair near Lord Matlock.

"Not so bad, after exertion they come on." He shrugged and looked down. "Maybe no fencing for a while longer. I am resolved not to take any more laudanum. I did not like how it made me feel."

"Now you understand why I stopped taking it." Fitzwilliam said thoughtfully as he easily read the lie his cousin spoke, and letting it pass for now, stretched out his leg. "It is addicting. I saw too many of my comrades return from battle only to be fighting a new demon. I would rather live with the pain."

"I remember Father drank down more and more towards the end, and it did not seem to help." Darcy studied the pen in his hands. "Elizabeth refuses to take any more, either."

"But she does feel pain?"

"Yes . . .but she . . .she wishes to feed Rosalie." He kept staring at the pen and thought of when he noticed that her milk tasted odd, and how she immediately concluded that it was the morphine. "I hate knowing that she is suffering, she will not admit to more than a twinge though."

"It will get better, Darcy. I swear." At last Darcy looked up to see Fitzwilliam's gentle smile. "By the time your head stops aching, I wager she will be feeling better, too."

He startled when he realized that his claims of being well did not fool him. "Thank you." He smiled a little. "I owe Elizabeth a picnic. Perhaps that will be a pleasant distraction."

"That was a special day, I am sorry that Wickham has ruined it for you." Lord Matlock said quietly.

"No, he is not permitted to ruin it. If you recall, his first attack fell on my birthday, and Elizabeth refused to let him take that day from us. She will not tolerate us losing this far more important date." He opened a drawer and took out the diamond and ruby bracelet that had been recovered by Mrs. Mercer. "She may not be receiving this on the day I intended to present it, but now it will be a symbol of another reason to celebrate. We lived."

"So likewise I should celebrate the day I was shot?" Fitzwilliam chuckled and his father looked at his hands. "Why not?"

"I see no humour in the subject so I will move on. I have news of Wickham." Lord Matlock announced. "He is alive at the moment. He was not shot, it seems. Whatever that bullet hit before striking Elizabeth, well, be thankful it was there. In any case, Wickham's wounds are no mere scratches. The prison surgeon will not be surprised to see him succumb to disease before long, and expects him to die in prison if he does not reach the gallows soon."

"Oddly enough, the ship he was to take to Australia is due to depart in the next week or so." Fitzwilliam noted.

"Will he be on it?" Darcy asked.

"No, no, he will hang this time, for certain. We cannot prove that he murdered that man in the alley, but he certainly did attack you, Elizabeth, and Rosalie. That should be more than enough." Lord Matlock said angrily.

"Why do I doubt that?"

"You doubted he was dead, too." De Bourgh said thoughtfully.

"And I was correct."

"So you were."

"What do you want to happen to him, Darcy?" Fitzwilliam asked and watched his cousin staring at the diamonds as he ran the bracelet over his fingers again and again. "Darcy?"

"Would he live long on the ship, do you think?" He looked between Fitzwilliam and de Bourgh.

"He will be packed tight in a hold with hundreds of others. They will not have a breath of fresh air often, if at all. Disease is rampant; the privateers who sail the vessels are only interested in profit . . . I can see him being food for the sharks, before long." De Bourgh studied him carefully. "You would prefer to see him die that way?"

"I wish for him to suffer." Darcy looked up from Elizabeth's diamonds. "I want him to lay and listen to men dying around him. I want him to become more ill, and not have anyone there to look after him. I have no desire to see him to health only to hang him. I want him to be alone, utterly without a friend, and let him realize the life he might have had compared to the one he chose."

"I doubt that Wickham is capable of such reflection." Fitzwilliam murmured.

"No, that is where you are incorrect. He is greatly capable of imagining all sorts of horror. What he did to us was no impulse; it was a long considered plan. I want him to feel the relief of escaping the hangman's noose only to have him experience hell on earth on that ship. I hope that he suffers for a very long time before he meets his end. My memory of that day is gradually being restored, and I will likely dwell on it the rest of my life. I want him to do the same."

Lord Matlock studied his nephew's expressionless face. "I will speak to the magistrate, Darcy. But I think that this may be out of your hands."

"I will accept whatever fate the law delivers; these are simply my feelings, if they matter at all. He will die regardless of the method chosen." He placed the bracelet in his pocket and smiled slightly at the silenced men. "I suppose that I should be more forgiving."

"I think not." Fitzwilliam declared. "I am kicking myself daily for not killing him when I had the opportunity."

"I agree with you." De Bourgh nodded. "Had I been near with my sword I would have . . ."

"If the pistol had not gone off, I would have had the pleasure." Darcy said softly.

"No Darcy, it is not pleasurable to kill." Fitzwilliam said quietly. "It may be necessary, but never speak of it as sport."

"Forgive me."

"I prefer that you remain ignorant."

Darcy and Fitzwilliam read each other's eyes and Lord Matlock broke the silence that descended over the room. "Darcy, I will not patronize you and claim that I know what you feel, but . . . Well I think that common sense tells us that the privateers are not going to accept a prisoner who is already at death's door when his bed can be given to an able-bodied man who will earn them a profit. This ship is the last of the year; it will be a very long time before the next sails, probably not until January."

"So he will hang." Darcy murmured.

"Most likely."

"Another trial." His anger flared. "And likely this time there will be plenty of interested onlookers."

"No doubt." Lord Matlock said sympathetically. "Although, perhaps he will simply be automatically condemned to death for the escape and attack. He received mercy the first time with the sentence of transportation. I have friends at the King's Bench; perhaps this can be handled quickly."

"I would appreciate it, Uncle Henry. I am afraid that if I were to face him in court again, I would be hard pressed to remain seated and civil." Darcy's fingers began twisting his ring. "I would look at him and see that stain of blood spreading over Elizabeth's gown." He let go and pounded his fist on the desk. "Damn him!!"

"Darcy . . ."

"Do not tell me to calm, Uncle." He growled. "He tried to kill my family."

"And he will swing for it." De Bourgh said steadily. "You do not help your family with your fury. He will not escape this trip, Darcy. Focus on something else."

Fitzwilliam stood and began to pace. "What I want to know is what happened between the escape and him appearing in your garden. Who was this dead man identified as Wickham? Obviously he was murdered and his features obliterated, but time passed between the escape and him turning up here. Who harboured him? Who fed and clothed him? I doubt that he had a shilling on him, so it had to be a friend."

"I cannot imagine who would be his friend." Lord Matlock said as he watched Fitzwilliam pass again.

"Mrs. Younge." Darcy looked up to Fitzwilliam. "She cared for him. Perhaps she lied to the man who made inquiries for me."

"Is she still at that school?" He straightened his uniform. "I'll be off, then."

"What are you doing?" Lord Matlock demanded.

"I am going to see what she knows, and see her in irons and hanging beside him if she is complicit." He growled. "At the least I will see her dismissed."

"Richard . . ." Darcy bit his lip. "I will come with you."

"You will do no such thing." Lord Matlock ordered. "There is a room full of women down the hall who will have my head if I let you leave this house. Richard, you go, de Bourgh . . . Keep his temper under control."

"Yes, sir." De Bourgh stood and glanced at Fitzwilliam. "I believe that I can do that."

Laughter filtered down the hallway and the men's activity ceased. Darcy looked to the door and visibly deflated. "Perhaps . . . I think that the ladies would be very displeased if you were to leave now." Fitzwilliam's fiery expression died. "It has been so good for Elizabeth, having all of her sisters around her. Jane is fiercely protective of her, I hardly recognize her from the woman I knew before. Georgiana and Mary are never far away. I almost have to fight to be by her side."

"Why do I think that they will gladly give up their seats for you?" Lord Matlock smiled and relaxed a little.

"Fitzwilliam!" Elizabeth's voice called. "Fitzwilliam, hurry!"

Alarmed, Darcy was up and out the door, closely followed by the other men. He arrived at the music room; and worriedly searching, spotted Elizabeth on the floor. "Lizzy!" Rushing to her side, he stopped, confused, as she turned to beam at him. "Lizzy?"

"Look, Will!" Excitedly she grabbed his hand and pulled him to kneel beside her. "Go ahead Mary, put her in position." They watched as Mary carefully picked up Rosalie and placed her on her belly. "Watch." Elizabeth whispered and squeezed his hand.

"What . . ."

"Shhh!"

Rosalie pushed up shakily and looked around with wide eyes, blew a succession of bubbles, then dropping to lie down again, very slowly rolled over to her back. Cheers erupted and she squealed in response. Darcy laughed and scooped her up in his arms.

"What a brilliant girl you are!" He kissed her and she laughed. "Well done, my girl! You amaze me!" He kissed and hugged her, then turned to kiss Elizabeth. "Is this what all the laughter was about?"

"Well the laughter was from watching her trying to tip over, I called when she finally managed it." She rubbed the baby's back. "You witnessed her second success." They kissed again, and rested their foreheads together.

"Ahem." Lord Matlock cleared his throat. "Do you two have any sense of decorum?"

"What a silly question." Elizabeth smiled and looked into Darcy's eyes. "Does he know us at all?"

"Obviously not." Rosalie squealed and he let her down from his shoulder, standing her on her feet while holding on. "There you go dear, a new perspective." She bounced, and the family laughed.

Fitzwilliam sat down next to Evangeline and slid his arm around her waist. She rested her head on his shoulder and together they touched her growing belly. "Darcy on the floor with his baby." He chuckled. "What a sight he is."

"I was just imagining you doing the same." Eva smiled up at him and he blushed. "So no ribbing him."

"Oh dear, I am sorry but I cannot possibly stop." He kissed her cheek. "Darcy! What wonder will this child perform next?"

"I could not say." He laughed when she squealed again. "Aunt Helen, you should know."

Smiling sadly she shook her head. "No Darcy, I would not. My children were left to the care of the staff at Matlock at that age. We were here." She looked up when Lord Matlock sat down beside her. "We missed moments such as these."

"We were told of them, though, and were invited to the nursery to observe when we were home." He sighed. "Well, we did what was expected." They watched Darcy put Rosalie back on her belly and immediately she rolled over again. "Look out, Son. Soon she will be crawling."

"I look forward to it." He laughed to see her staring in fascination at her hands. "All of it."

"Do you need help rising, Miss Mary?" De Bourgh offered her his hand.

"I am afraid that my leg is sleeping." She grimaced when he pulled her up, then stumbled into him as she felt the pins and needles of her renewed circulation. "Oh! I am sorry!"

He laughed and looked down at her. "It is quite all right." Their gazes held for several moments and the sound of the family's happy conversation seemingly disappeared. "You are returning to Longbourn?"

The spell was broken and Mary startled. "No . . . I mean yes, to pick up my things, and then I will go to Pemberley."

"Well, I might have accompanied my brother on his visit to Miss Lucas, but now I will stay at home." De Bourgh helped her to take a seat.

"Oh." Mary turned to look at him. "Why?"

He laughed and sat back in his chair. "Because the prettiest rose in Hertfordshire will be missing."

Mary's eyes widened as a blush travelled up her neck to the roots of her hair. "Teasing is rude."

"I agree. Do you think of me as rude?"

"No."

"Then it was a compliment, Miss Mary." He patted her hand and noticed Jane was watching them. "Miss Bennet, have you settled your wedding date?"

"No sir, my coming here interrupted our planning." She looked to the sofa where Darcy sat with Rosalie in his lap and Elizabeth leaning on his shoulder. Georgiana sat on her other side. "Lizzy, do you know your travel plans yet?"

"No, but I suppose that we could leave at any time. I will feel the same whether I am in a carriage or on a sofa. What do you think, Fitzwilliam?"

"I . . .we have some business to address before we depart." He watched as her brow creased and he kissed the wrinkles. "Perhaps in a week or two."

"So long?"

He nodded and before he could say more, Foster appeared. "Mr. Bennet and the Gardiners, sir."

"This has become a party." Lord Matlock laughed as they stood to greet the guests.

"Well, it is good to see everyone smiling so." Mrs. Gardiner took a seat and looked to Rosalie. "I believe that we know the source."

"Endless entertainment." Mr. Gardiner bent to chuck Rosalie's chin before sitting. Mr. Bennet stood quietly near the doorway.

"Will you not come in, Papa?" Elizabeth asked.

"Yes, of course, but I would like to speak with you and Mr. Darcy privately if I may." His eyes were on his granddaughter.

"Of course." Elizabeth turned to Georgiana. "Will you take Rosa for us?"

"Oh yes!" She beamed and happily accepted her.

Darcy helped Elizabeth up and they led the way down the hallway to his study. Mr. Bennet took a chair and Darcy closed the door, then went to stand behind Elizabeth's chair. "What can we do for you, sir?"

He looked at his hands then back up to see how Darcy's were protectively resting on Elizabeth's shoulders, and how she had lifted her free hand to hold his. "Jane and I will depart for Longbourn in the morning."

"Yes, she told me that. I am sorry to see her go, we . . .we have seemingly found our friendship again this past week." She looked up to see Darcy nod. "It is as if her finding love has made her understand us at last."

Mr. Bennet smiled at that. "I agree, she and Lucas are in love. I was hoping that she would accept him. And I want to thank you both for giving her the opportunity to love whoever she wished."

"Sir, Mr. Lucas always would have been a fine choice for her and would have undoubtedly made his interest known to her eventually."

"Very well, Mr. Darcy, I will not give you any more credit than you desire." He chuckled then became serious. "Sir, I understand that your sister, Miss Darcy, will return for another year of schooling."

"Yes." Darcy felt Elizabeth squeeze his hand.

"I was . . . Would it be possible to send Kitty to this school with her? I know that she needs to be separated from Lydia if she is to derive any benefit from the experience. I would like to see her improve as Mary clearly has." He sighed and looked back at his hands. "And . . .when the year is over, if you wish and she desires it, she may go to Pemberley to live with you."

The Darcys exchanged glances. "Papa, I know that Kitty once expressed a desire to come to live at Pemberley, but that was because she was afraid Mama would centre her ire on her with Mary gone."

"Well I have not allowed that to happen, however, I believe that she is in some danger from your mother's machinations. I lost my temper with her when she learned of your condition."

"You told me." Elizabeth said softly.

"I did?" He said with a surprise.

"You thought that I was asleep." His eyes opened wide and she smiled.

"Mr. Bennet, if I had been there, I would have had a difficult time remaining civil." Darcy said quietly. "But despite my opinion of my mother-in-law, I hope that you know I would never shirk my responsibilities to my wife's family. It would dishonour my Elizabeth to do anything else."

"Thank you, Fitzwilliam." She whispered and he kissed her hand. "What happened that you did not tell me before, Papa?"

"That fool Collins has come to Meryton, and I made the mistake of telling your mother that he will eventually be Longbourn's heir. And that she should start grovelling to him." Darcy groaned. "I know, it was a tactical error. Well, she is going to be matchmaking in earnest, and I am grateful that Mary is with you. I simply wish to protect Kitty, as well."

"What of Lydia?" Elizabeth asked.

He laughed softly. "I think that it might do her some good to be married to a preacher."

"Papa!"

"I am sorry, Lizzy, but I do not think that any amount of schooling will change Lydia. If she does not find her man in a red coat, I think she could do far worse than to marry the heir of Longbourn. And your mother would have her favourite by her side until she dies."

"May I point out that none of your girls can marry without your consent?"

"Yes, Mr. Darcy, I realize that. But I also know that I can only resist the sound of my wife's voice for so long. Lydia is too young to marry, that is in her favour, and I will send her to school this autumn. I simply see more potential in Kitty and . . .well perhaps Miss Darcy would like the companionship."

"It would make me happier to have Georgiana there with a sister." Darcy mused.

"And she would be the experienced one; she would be teaching Kitty and looking after her." Elizabeth added.

"So you think that it could be a good experience in responsibility for her?"

"I do." They looked at each other and Darcy smiled. "I will speak to Georgiana."

"Thank you." Mr. Bennet sighed and sat back. "I know that my efforts at schooling have been poor, I am glad to give her this opportunity. Miss Darcy is a credit to your family, sir."

"Well, hopefully you will say the same of all of your daughters, one day." Darcy straightened. "And sir, perhaps when you next visit London, you will stay here."

Mr. Bennet's eyes widened and he looked to Elizabeth who was smiling up at her husband. "Thank you, sir. Please know that you are certainly welcome to stay at Longbourn."

"I . . .thank you, sir, however . . ."

"No, no. I will not suggest it again." He smiled. "I assume this is not a universal invitation."

"No sir, it is not."

"Will you be attending Jane's wedding?"

Silence ruled the room. "That decision is yet to be made, sir."

"ROBERT!" Maria Lucas said urgently.

Lucas handed the reins of his horse to the groom and turned to face his little sister. "My goodness, what has you ladies in such a flutter?"

Lydia giggled and pointed to the house. "Mama and Lady Lucas are arguing. We can hear them from the window."

"I said that we should not be listening." Kitty announced.

"Oh you never want to have fun!" Lydia stuck her tongue out at her.

"Miss Kitty is correct, it is rude to eavesdrop." Robert said sternly. "Surely there is some occupation that is more worthy of your time? Where is Charlotte?"

"She is helping in the kitchen." Maria said guiltily. "She said that I could entertain Lydia and Kitty."

"Then go find something else to do."

"They are arguing about your wedding." Lydia said in a sly voice. "And all of the parties they will have to celebrate your engagement."

Lucas's eyes closed and he spoke tonelessly. "Are they."

"Perhaps you should . . ."

"Miss Lydia, my and your sister's affairs are none of your business. Maria, see to your guests." Lucas strode into the house and paused, he could hear the nerve rattling tones of Mrs. Bennet against the lower, less strident notes of his mother coming from the drawing room. He turned to his father's study, where he found him sleeping in his chair. "Father."

Snorting and coughing, Sir William startled awake and sat up. "Really Son, you should not sneak up on a man in that way!"

"Forgive me sir, I wished for your aid."

Sir William's brow furrowed. "What is it?"

"Mother and Mrs. Bennet are arguing over my wedding."

Laughing, he removed his glasses and started to polish them. "Surely that is no surprise?"

"Would you please do something about it?" Lucas demanded. "Jane is not here to voice her opinion, but I do not wish to be dragged through endless parties to satisfy our mothers."

"Mrs. Bennet was denied this with Eliza's wedding. I am sure that she will not relinquish the opportunity for Jane." He placed the glasses back on his nose. "What is wrong with a little celebration?"

"Little is not a word that either woman understands." Lucas paced the room and stopped to stare out of the window, and caught sight of Lydia creeping to stand outside of the drawing room window and signalling Maria and Kitty to join her. They were not moving. He sighed. "Father they will listen to you."

"No they will not. They are going to try and outdo each other in every way, and why not? This is joyous event! Why Meryton is abuzz with the news of your engagement. Such happy news! And more than one long face on the ladies of the neighbourhood who lost their opportunity with you." He winked at him knowingly. "Ah Son, you could have had any lady of London, but here you chose Miss Jane Bennet."

Lucas ignored his delusion and focussed on the problem. "Father, we want a simple wedding."

"Well Son, I think that you will have to resign yourselves to the wedding of the century." He stood and clapped his back. "All you have to do is smile. Jane can teach you to do that!"

"NOW THIS IS FOR YOU." Elizabeth nodded to Millie and she carried in a large blue box to set beside the ladies seated on Jane's bed, and then left the room. "Do not fight me. Just accept it."

"What have you done, Lizzy?" Jane smiled and lifting the lid, set it down on the floor. "oh."

"I thought that the blue was just the shade of your eyes. I am so glad that I got to give it to you in person before you left, instead of sending it to Longbourn." Elizabeth smiled a little and Jane leaned over to kiss her cheek. "Perhaps not under these circumstances."

"No." Jane's eyes grew bright and Elizabeth shook her head.

"Do not get me started." She pushed the box to her. "Come on, look!" Jane pulled out the beautiful silk gown and held it up against her body. "And there are matching slippers, too." She held up the shoes. "Try it on!"

"Oh Lizzy, I cannot . . ."

"What did I say? Let me give you this before you are married and claim that you must live within your budget. I know that Mr. Lucas will love to see you in this."

"He will." Jane sighed and sat on the bed. "Oh Lizzy, he is such a good man."

"I know." She took her hand. "You love him."

"I do." Jane sniffed and wiped the tears that sprang to her eyes. "I do. I can hardly describe it, Lizzy. I watched you fall in love with Mr. Darcy, well, when you were actually together. I had no idea that you loved him for years before."

"How could I admit to a love that would never come to life? It would have broken my heart to say it out loud, and I am sure that anyone who heard of it would call me a foolish girl for entertaining such a ridiculous fantasy."

"So you kept it a secret until you finally met." Jane whispered as Elizabeth nodded. "Oh to see you both love so deeply and so fast was overwhelming to me. I wished so much for even the slightest taste of it for myself." She looked down at her hands and smiled. "And here it came creeping up on me instead."

"So it was no lightning bolt of instant recognition with him?"

"No." Jane laughed. "No, not at all. It was . . . It was warmth and comfort; it was steadiness, surety that he knows precisely what he wants and hopes for. Oh Lizzy, who would think that silly Sir William could have such a wonderful son?"

Elizabeth laughed. "Well who could think that our mother could have produced us?"

"Robert said something of that to me!" Jane said in a low voice. "Lizzy, he as much told me that he means to provoke me to react to him!"

"Good for him! I have been trying for years!" She clapped. "Oh Jane, if you could see how you glow with happiness!"

"I am happy." She sighed. "Mr. Bingley is a very good man, too. But Lizzy, I . . ."

"You liked him but did not love him?"

"Yes, but it was . . . Oh Lizzy, you know the house that Longbourn is. I was afraid that Mr. Bingley is so unsettled that . . . I would be moving from one chaotic life to another one, except there would be better furniture and much more money." Elizabeth laughed. "I crave . . ." Jane fell silent. "Robert sees beyond my looks. No other man has ever looked at me the way he does or cared to hear what I thought." She looked at her sister. "You told me once that you wished to feel respect for and from your husband."

"I did." Elizabeth agreed. "You understand that now. Respect is so important for love."

"Yes. I do understand. I do not wish to speak against Papa, but . . . Robert is the opposite of him, and that is very attractive. He knows what he wants and . . . how to care for his loved ones. I imagine that was a quality you saw in Mr. Darcy and admired as well?" She saw Elizabeth nodding and sighed. "I am so sorry that we have lost so much time, Lizzy. I wish that you did not live so far away."

"We will have letters, and when we come here, you can come and stay with us." Jane hugged her and Elizabeth wrapped her one arm around her waist, as they both started to cry. "We can send a carriage to bring you to Pemberley."

"You know that Robert would not accept that."

"Oh Jane, you must learn how to work around your husband's obstinacy." Elizabeth laughed and they hugged tighter. "I have so much to teach you!"

The two sisters drew apart and wiped each other's eyes. "I love you, Jane."

"I love you, Lizzy." They both looked up when there was a knock on the door. It opened slowly and Georgiana and Mary entered.

"May we join you?" Georgiana asked.

"Of course." Elizabeth moved back on the bed and made room for the other girls. "I cannot remember the last time that I spent an evening with a bed full of sisters!"

"I never have, this is exciting!" Georgiana jumped onto the bed and drew her knees to her chest. "We heard you talking and Mary said that you and Jane used to do that every night, and that it would not be rude to interrupt. What do you talk about? May we do this at Pemberley? It is so nice to have Mary staying with us now! I feel like our family is really complete now!"

Laughing, the other girls all picked up pillows and whacked Georgiana on the head. "There, now you know what we do to girls who are silly!" Jane reached and fixed Georgiana's mussed hair, then turned her around to rebraid her plait. "We talk about whatever concerns us. Do you have any worries?"

"No." She said and bit her lip.

"Yes, you do." Mary nudged her. "Come on, you can trust Lizzy and Jane."

"Is something wrong?" Elizabeth took her hand. "Please tell us."

"I . . . I have not slept well since . . .since it happened." She glanced at Elizabeth's shoulder. "I am afraid that he will come back."

"I do not think that is possible, Georgiana," Elizabeth whispered, "but you should know that I have the same fear."

"You do?" Her eyes opened wide. "But you are so brave!"

"I rise to the occasion." She smiled.

"I have not slept well, either." Mary admitted. "I cannot understand how this happened at all. I have had a difficult time accepting that such evil exists in the world."

"How sheltered we were at Longbourn." Elizabeth sighed and squeezed Georgiana's hand. "And at Pemberley."

"I cannot wait to go home. When will we?"

"I am not sure."

"I imagine that once you are there, you will not return for the wedding." Jane said quietly. "You would not wish to be near Mama that long anyway. Certainly Mr . . .Fitzwilliam would not wish to be there."

"No, he would not, but I have not had the opportunity to speak to him yet. Something is on his mind and he does not say when we will depart, let alone speaking of the wedding plans since you have not fixed a date. I am certain that it has to do with . . . him." She said quietly. "I do not know if we must go to court."

"Oh Lizzy!" Mary cried. "You would have to face him?"

"I doubt that Brother would allow that." Georgiana whispered.

"I do, too. But I do not wish for him to have to go either." Elizabeth sighed. Hearing the creak of floorboards outside of the chamber door, she looked up and listened, then heard the quiet snap of a door closing down the hallway. She smiled and glanced at the clock. "I think that it is getting quite late, and I should retire. You ladies should carry on."

"Oh no, please stay!" Georgiana begged.

Elizabeth kissed her cheek and carefully scooted off of the bed to the floor. "No, I need to rest. I will see you in the morning." She kissed Jane and Mary, and with their calls of goodnight following her, she left the room and walked down the hallway. She smiled at the footman and opened the door to the master's chambers. In the glow of the moonlight, she saw Darcy lying on his side under the covers, his back to the door. Quietly closing it behind her, she stood still and looked over his imposing form at rest. All she could really see was his fine black hair just touching the bare skin of his shoulder, and his one arm, lying along his side, the muscles highlighted and shadowed with the gentle light, and his long fingers . . . *ah!* Elizabeth smiled. His fingers were moving; his thumb was caressing the gold of his ring. Biting her lip, she reached up and carefully slipped the sling from around her neck, letting her arm fall free for the first time in weeks. She winced a little, but the pain was not terrible. Carefully, she removed her nightdress, and had just draped it over a chair when she heard the soft rumble of his voice.

"Will you *please* come to bed?"

Elizabeth smiled to hear the hint of a whine in his voice. "I am coming, Will." Lifting the counterpane, she slid in behind him and spooned her body to his, her head resting against his back, his tight bottom firmly in her lap, and her arm around his waist. She heard the sharp intake of his breath when he felt her bare skin against his. They had not loved each other since that day. Darcy's hand moved to clasp hers. "I do not think we have ever slept this way."

"No." He whispered. "I . . . I . . ." His voice was halted when she moved their hands down to his groin, and she began to slowly caress up and down his burgeoning arousal. "Lizzzy."

"Shhhh." She kissed his shoulder and pressed her breasts against him. "Relax."

"I miss you." Came his muffled reply.

"I miss you, too." She felt him pressing back against her and smiled, kissing his shoulder again. "Is that why you were listening outside of Jane's door?" She laughed when his head jerked up, and she gave his now hardened shaft a firm squeeze. "What were you about, Mr. Darcy?"

"You were taking so long." He sighed then moaned as her hand continued its caress. "And from the sound of the laughter, you might have stayed all night."

"I might have. It will probably be the last time I am ever alone with Jane like that." Her movement stopped. Darcy's hand rested on hers and he traced over her fingers. "It was as if we had never come to London, we were just sisters again, on our bed at Longbourn. She is back to be being Jane again."

Darcy felt her tears on his back, and entwined their fingers. "You will see her again. We will host her here or at Pemberley, you know we will." He closed his eyes tight. "And if you wish, we will . . .perhaps attend the wedding."

"Perhaps?"

"Oh Lizzy, once I have you home . . ."

"I know, I never want to leave Pemberley, either. Not for a very long time, anyway." She sighed. "But how can we not attend? And Mary, what of her? Two of Jane's sisters not attending?"

"You know as well as I do that distant relatives do not travel for weddings."

"We are not distant."

"I meant where we live." He sighed. "Dearest, I do not know when we will leave here. I must . . . I must know Wickham's fate."

"I suspected as much." She kissed his shoulder and began caressing him again. "I do not wish to go to Longbourn, either, but I do not wish to hurt Jane or Robert."

"I was thinking; do they have a wedding trip planned?" Darcy's hand moved with hers as she slowly stroked. "Wedding journeys to visit relatives are common are they not? And journeys to the Peaks are as well, could they not combine the two? We could invite them to Pemberley, and then they could go on to the Lake District for some time, and then return to us before journeying home?"

"They could never afford it." Elizabeth whispered, but Darcy heard the excitement in her voice and pounced.

"It would be our gift, I could send a coach, or hire one in Meryton for them to use to Pemberley, then take one of ours to the Lake District, and rent another for the trip back to Hertfordshire." He turned and faced her. "What do you think?"

She laughed to see his hopeful expression. "You truly do not want to go near Longbourn."

"No Elizabeth, not after hearing of your mother's pronouncements against you. No. I would rather not, nor do I wish to be a subject of interest to the neighbourhood." He kissed her. "We will propose it in the morning?"

"Very well." She whispered. "But Will, if we are to journey home and it happens to be near their wedding day, perhaps . . ."

"Yes, then we will attend." He hugged her. "And move on, not to stay overnight. Agreed?"

"Agreed." They kissed and he opened his eyes to smile at her, then creased his brow. "Elizabeth, your arm." He touched her shoulder, then got up on his elbow to tip her forward, and saw the exposed stitches of her wounds. "Dearest, should . . . Is this safe?"

"I am healing, am I not? It feels better." She said determinedly.

"Does it hurt?" He looked at her seriously.

"A little, but not enough to stop me from wanting you." She lifted her arms to hold his face, and he drew in a sharp breath when she bit her lip and winced.

"Are you sure?" Darcy's voice dropped to a deep whisper and he searched her expression, even as he was moving to hover over her. "It will not hurt?"

She ran her fingers through his hair and felt the slowly receding lump on his head. "Does this hurt?"

"No." He said firmly and pressed his lips together. Elizabeth drew his head down and they kissed softly. "I need you so badly." He said against her ear. "I have missed you so much." Pushing up on his arms he looked down at her teary eyes. "I have missed you more these past weeks than I . . . I have wanted to love you so badly."

"And I need you, just as much." She kissed his lips and guided him forward. When her warmth and wetness touched his sensitive skin, he was lost, and slid into his home, settling his full weight upon her.

"Thank you." He said fervently. "Thank you." They clung together tightly, and both audibly sighed in relief. Darcy heard her laugh softly and lifted his head to look into her sparkling eyes. "Everything is well."

"Now it is." She smiled up at him and he kissed her. "So, Husband, love me."

Darcy smiled and kissed her. "Gladly." He buried himself in her as far as he could then as she wrapped her legs around his waist; he wrapped his arms beneath her shoulders. The stitches were pressed against his forearm and he was careful not to rub there, but every other part of her body was subjected to the massage of his skin on hers. Elizabeth's hands wound into his hair and they kissed deeply as they rocked together. It was steady and loving and over too soon. "Oh, I needed that." He rested his forehead on hers as they regained their breath. "I need more of that."

"I do, too." She laughed and kissed his nose, making him chuckle and nip her throat. "And we were quiet!"

"Give me a moment love, and I will make sure that you sing." He growled. "I hope that you were not planning to sleep tonight."

"Fitzwilliam!"

"No, love. I need you." Darcy stopped his kisses and caressing her face, lifted her chin before kissing her tenderly. "I need this, deeply. Please."

"I did not say no, did I?" Elizabeth smiled and hugged him, and whispered in his ear. "I need you, too. Please do not stop."

"Just give me a moment." He chuckled when her hand caressed over his bottom to urge him forward again. "And I will take care of you." Darcy moved off of her and they rested together. "I love you."

"I love you." Elizabeth traced her fingers over his long sideburns and he tried to hide. "Are you ticklish here?"

"No." He smiled when she raised her brow. Her fingers travelled to his mouth and paused over his lip. "What do you see?"

"How did you get this scar? I have always wondered." He blushed, and she laughed. "Tell me."

"Richard."

"Oh come now, is everything that has ever happened to you related to your wayward cousin?"

"Yes." Darcy sucked on the finger playing around his mouth. "He decided to play valet."

Elizabeth gasped. "Oh no, did you let him shave you?" He nodded. "Your father must have wished to strangle you!"

"I think that I was fortunate that Richard did not slice my throat when I jumped." He smiled ruefully.

"Is your scar named Richard?" She giggled then squealed when he rolled back on top of her. "Will!"

"If you continue to laugh at me love, I will most assuredly make you scream."

They heard the sound of girls giggling in the hallway as Mary and Georgiana left Jane's room and moved off to their own. Darcy paused and they stared at each other. "I forgot about them!" Elizabeth whispered. "We must be quiet!" He shook his head. "Fitzwilliam!"

"Too many sisters are here." He growled and began nibbling below her ear. "Too many virginal sisters."

"Oh Will . . ." She moaned.

"Shhhhhh." He suckled as she writhed below him then kissed his way down her body. "Just lie back and enjoy."

Chapter 21

"Now then, the Gouldings have a dinner planned for Tuesday, and my dinner will be Friday." Lady Lucas said.

"Well that is ridiculous; my sister Philips will be hosting an evening for them on Friday." Mrs. Bennet pronounced.

Rolling her eyes, Lady Lucas ignored her. "I am the groom's mother, so my choice takes precedence. I will also be planning another dinner with dancing the next week."

"Well, I am the bride's mother, and my desires take precedence over yours! My sister's tea is Friday, and WE are hosting a ball . . . on Tuesday!" Mrs Bennet fluttered her handkerchief. "You have no say in this! Jane does not belong to your son yet! She is still a Bennet until that day, and I forbid her to do . . ."

"Mrs. Bennet!" Mr. Bennet spoke up. "Enough!"

"Mr. Bennet, you are surely aware that we will be losing Jane forever to the Lucas's, whatever we want we shall have." Mrs. Bennet sniffed. "It is bad enough that she is marrying . . ."

"That she is marrying me, Mrs. Bennet?" Lucas said coldly. "I know of your objections, madam, and I do not appreciate them."

"I am sure that is not what she meant, Mr. Lucas." Jane touched his hand and he broke his gaze with her flushed mother to look at her. "Is it, Mama? You and Lady Lucas are just concerned about fitting in all of these events before the wedding date, correct?"

With the eyes of the room upon her, Mrs. Bennet clasped her hands and nodded. "Of course. Why you wish to marry so quickly, I do not understand."

"It will be five weeks from our engagement, Mama. And I want Lizzy and Mr. Darcy to be present, if possible." She said patiently. "They will be leaving for Pemberley as soon as they can."

Glancing at Lady Lucas, Mrs. Bennet preened, "Describe Pemberley to me again, it is a very large estate? Mrs. Darcy made a very fine match with such a rich man! Why she can have anything she desires! Do you know, Lady Lucas, that Mr. Darcy has promised to care for us when Mr. Bennet dies? Is that not so very good of him?"

"Are you implying that my son would ignore his wife's family if they were in need?" Lady Lucas said tersely.

"Do not look a gift horse in the mouth, my dear." Sir William chuckled. "If Darcy wants the responsibility, I say give it to him."

"I rather would prefer that you refrain from discussing my pending demise when I am in the room, and preferably not until I am actually at death's door." Mr. Bennet raised his brow to see Lucas's eyes closed and his hand gripping Jane's tightly. "And I suspect that my future son would appreciate a change in topic as well before he lets his tongue loose."

Lucas looked over to Mr. Bennet. "I hope that you know I would do right by your family, sir."

"I have no doubt of that, but it is not your or my son Darcy's responsibility. I will do my best to provide for my remaining family." Hearing Lydia and Kitty in the background, he looked at his wife. "Soon it will be just we two living here, Mrs. Bennet, imagine the savings we will incur without constant visits to the ribbon shop."

"Oh what will I do without my dear Lydia?" Mrs. Bennet cried. "How can you send her away to school?"

"I will still be near, Mama." Jane said soothingly.

"Dear Jane." She sighed sadly. "You are so beautiful."

And I have wasted my beauty on Robert, yes, I know your feelings, Mama. Jane felt Lucas's eyes upon her and felt his support as he continued to hold her hand. "Mama, Lady Lucas, it seems that with time so short before the wedding and with so much to do, I think that the Goulding's dinner and Aunt Philips' evening will be quite enough celebrating for all of us. Instead of wasting time having all of these extra dinners, you both should work together for a grand wedding breakfast that all of our guests can enjoy." Seeing the surprise on everyone's faces except Lucas's she sat up a little straighter when he smiled at her with approval. "And, I think that my time will be better spent preparing my wedding clothes and . . ." She faltered.

"And making sure that your betrothed remains interested and does not jilt you." Lucas lifted her hand and kissed it. "I think that you have made some excellent suggestions, my dear."

"I agree." Mr. Bennet smiled. "You are not leaving the neighbourhood forever. There is no need for some tearful farewell."

"But . . .but the parties!" Mrs. Bennet whined.

"You have three more daughters, Mrs. Bennet; surely you will have your fill of engagement parties before you are through." Mr. Bennet said sternly.

"*Will* Mr. and Mrs. Darcy be coming to the wedding?" Lady Lucas asked. "I hope that we will not be planning around their schedule."

"Their schedule is dependent on others, Lady Lucas. All I can say for certain is that they are feeling well enough to travel and they are very anxious to return home." Jane smiled at Robert. "I certainly understand their desire to put London far behind them."

18 JULY 1810

Yesterday Fitzwilliam and I at last celebrated the third anniversary of our first sight of each other. We began by walking through Hyde Park to our bench. What a difference in the man I spotted that day and the one who looks upon me now, such a beautiful smile, and warm, happy eyes. Yes, there was sadness, too, but he confessed that the images that distracted him were ones of lost loved ones who never had the opportunity to meet me. That was regret that I can bear.

After we enjoyed a picnic and our servants retrieved our things, we went on to take a very long walk through Kensington Gardens. It was exhausting for both of us, despite our tightly enforced recovery. Perhaps that is why we defiantly left the house and stayed away so long. We met many acquaintances as we walked, and were grateful for their kindness, whether it was a tip of the hat and nod, or a fervent handshake and inquiry after our health. The response was welcome, although we truly did wish for our privacy. We at least know what to expect when we venture to church for the first time on Sunday. The incident was breathlessly covered in the papers, it seems, so it is no secret what occurred. By the time that we reached the end of our stroll through the gardens, neither of us had the heart to ask the other to walk all the way home. My dear Fitzwilliam gallantly offered to find us a cab, and I insisted that we stop and enjoy some ice cream before our return. His eyes lit up like a little boy to share our treat, and he was determined to tell Georgiana about it!

When we arrived at home, we were fussed over by our worried staff. As soon as he was strong enough, about two weeks after the incident, Fitzwilliam had them assemble in the ballroom and expressed his appreciation and gratitude for their loyalty and service to our family. Foster stated that the gifts were unnecessary, but Fitzwilliam would not hear of it. He firmly believes that their action is what saved me. He refuses to be reminded that had he not appeared and fought, nothing would have saved me or our dear daughter, and my foolishly not heeding his command to run is why I was struck at all. You, my love, are the one who protected us, so let me thank you here, and now I will say no more.

I worry so much over Fitzwilliam, and am almost grateful for my injury because he has no desire to be far from me, which in turn forces him to be still, as the physician recommends. He will not tell me how he feels, but I can see that he is sometimes a little bewildered, and struggles to remember simple things, but he is definitely improving, I know. My injury was painful, but it is clearly visible that the wound is nearly healed. My stitches were removed yesterday, a process that I did not anticipate at all. My dear husband plied me with some sort of drink before the surgeon arrived, and I should have known not to trust him. Never should I trust that man with a glass of anything if he hands it to me with a twinkle in his eye. It most certainly was not lemonade as he claimed. He made mention of the drink to Richard, and he nearly spat out his after-dinner port in response, and asked me what I thought of the Irish lemonade. It was only later that I sat upon Fitzwilliam's lap and refused to move until he admitted his scheme. It took endless methods of persuasion, but at last he admitted that I was drinking whiskey. No wonder I felt no pain! Fitzwilliam was rather pleased with himself, entirely too pleased if you ask me. I will most certainly have to teach him a lesson. I shall set my mind to work and take him unaware one day. Why do I have a feeling that he will not mind one bit?

Darcy smiled a little and set down the journal, then kissed Elizabeth's temple. They were resting together in the library after a long morning of catching up with their correspondence. "Are you still sleeping, love?" He wrapped both arms around her and resting his chin in her hair, focussed on the landscape he had purchased for her anniversary gift, and was now hanging over the fireplace. They had just received word that Wickham's hearing before the judge would take place in two days, if he lived that long. No trial was necessary, the result was almost a foregone conclusion after his actions, but still the process must be observed. Feelings of guilt and regret welled up in Darcy's heart, and he clutched Elizabeth tightly. "I am so sorry, love."

"ELIZABETH, PLEASE TAKE A SEAT!" Lady Matlock commanded.

"How can I sit when Fitzwilliam is in the same room with that monster?" Elizabeth paced. "I should have gone with him."

"Do not be ridiculous! Your presence would add to the spectacle! Darcy is not alone."

Yes he is. Elizabeth said to herself and paused to stare out of the window, thinking of the tension that had increased since they learned of the hearing date. That morning when they had at last risen from their bed after a night of fitful sleep, they had mechanically gone through the routine of preparing for the day. Very little had been said between them, instead it was their looks, and their tightly gripped hands, that communicated their worry and care for each other. Although no physical danger was in store, they both felt as if they were willingly going to be submitted to yet another violation by the devil.

"I need to take a walk." She announced.

"Well then, we all will go." Laura offered. "We can stroll through the park, that should be distracting, it is a beautiful day."

"Mrs. Harwick, when my sister says that she needs to take a walk, she is not suggesting a stroll." Mary smiled at Elizabeth. "I will walk with you, Lizzy."

"Can you keep up?" She smiled a little.

"Probably not, but I will try." She stood to join her. "You are not as quick on your feet as you are normally."

"I will come as well." Georgiana hurriedly rose.

"Well, if you are planning to speed around the park, I am afraid that I will have to forgo the pleasure, if I did not have boats for feet, I would say differently." Evangeline looked ruefully down at her shoes.

Elizabeth walked over and gave her a hug. "Well then, we will claim our bonnets, and . . . I presume you are remaining, Aunt Helen?"

"I am, and I hope Laura, that you will take care to keep these young ladies in check." She saw Elizabeth's brow rise. "Mrs. Darcy, you are under scrutiny just now."

"Lady Matlock, I committed no crime, and if walking with purpose is viewed as shameful, then I am glad to part company with this town and return to the wilds of Derbyshire where I and my family belong. Excuse me."

Elizabeth left the room, closely followed by Mary and Georgiana. Laura hung back to speak to Lady Matlock and Evangeline. "If I were at home, I would be going to saddle my pony. She is simply trying to relieve the stress."

"I know that, Laura." Lady Matlock sighed and glanced at the clock. "I know well Elizabeth's need to walk when she is parted from her husband. Just be sure to have her back here before too long. I have no desire to face Darcy's return with her not at home. I suspect they will be back in the next two hours or so."

Evangeline smiled. "I was wondering why you were being so particularly caustic towards her today, Lady Helen. Surely you know that Elizabeth is hardly one to fight shy, and would respond to you with energy."

"Certainly." She smiled. "I admire that young woman very much."

"So you are giving her something else to occupy her mind?" Laura suggested. "She is angry with you and your rules?"

"Precisely, my dear." Lady Matlock nodded. "And I know that she will need to return to her child before long, because as you say, she has her own rules."

"And I intend to follow her lead with them. Richard and I admire the Darcys very much." Evangeline said and stroked her hand over her growing baby. "So you may as well learn to live with that information now."

"Mrs. Fitzwilliam, I may not have the authority to speak to Mrs. Darcy about her choices, but I do have it to speak to you." Lady Matlock said seriously.

Sitting up as straight as she could, Evangeline smiled sweetly. "Do you honestly believe that I am afraid to take you on? Your son does not cause me any trepidation, and he is armed with more than his tongue."

"My son is a gentleman." She sniffed.

"In every sense of the word." Evangeline agreed.

"I am glad to be departing before the fur begins to fly!" Laura looked between mother and daughter and quickly left the room to join the sisters in the foyer. "Is Rosalie well?"

Elizabeth looked at her with surprise. "How did you know that I went to check on her?"

"Oh . . . I suppose that I have some motherly instincts, too." Laura slipped her arm in Elizabeth's. "Now, show me just how fast a country girl can walk, and we can talk about the battle royal that is about to take place in your drawing room!"

"Oh, what is going to happen?" Georgiana asked worriedly and looked back up the stairs.

"I think that at least three are required for a battle royal." Mary corrected quietly. "It began with the Romans and the gladiators."

Elizabeth laughed. "What have you been reading in Fitzwilliam's library, Mary?"

She blushed. "I . . . Fitzwilliam suggested that I start reading history, and when I did not know where to begin, Captain de Bourgh talked about visiting Rome and how fascinating it was to wander around the ruins. He has seen so much of the world, and can describe places so clearly that you almost feel that you are there."

Laura and Elizabeth exchanged glances and stepping outside, they began to walk. "Captain de Bourgh has certainly made the most of his education at sea."

"Oh he has! He said that he did not read very well when he was first in the navy, but on long voyages, when there was no work to do, one officer passed the time teaching him and a few other boys, then lent him books. And then whenever they travelled to a new port, he always had a little time on the land to wander about. The older men would look for entertainment in taverns, but the boys would see the sights. Then as he grew in rank, he had more important things to do, but he always made time to look at the places where they travelled, and let his imagination be free to wander." She sighed. "He has opened my eyes to the world beyond the little I have seen."

"I wonder if he is satisfied to be on dry land, now." Elizabeth smiled at the little sparkle of admiration she could see dancing in her sister's eyes.

"I . . . I do not know. We have not spoken of it." She blushed. "He told me that he enjoyed telling his sisters tales of his travels, but now that they are to be married, he was happy to find another sister to entertain."

Laura laughed. "I am sure that he will enjoy embellishing his tales, as well."

"Oh, do you think that he lies?" Georgiana asked. "His stories seem so real!"

"Well if he is anything like your cousin Richard, I think there is room for a wink in anything he says." Elizabeth hooked her hand over her arm. They walked around the path by the Serpentine and talked of the fashions they saw and their opinions of the ladies they knew, anything to avoid talking about the subject that was most on their minds.

"GEORGE WICKHAM, you stand convicted of the following heinous crimes: murder, prison escape, attempted kidnapping, and attempted murder. This Court doth adjudge that you be returned to Newgate. You will reside in the cells of the condemned until Wednesday next when you are to be taken to the place of execution, and there hanged by the neck until you are dead; after which your body is to be publicly dissected and anatomised. May God Almighty have mercy on your soul."

The judges' gavel struck and the sound was lost in the wave of conversation and catcalls that filled the courtroom. Wickham, battered and emaciated, stared across to where Darcy sat staring back at him unflinchingly, his cold blue eyes spearing him with barely contained fury. On either side of Darcy sat the men of his family, Fitzwilliam and Lord Matlock. Behind him in the gallery were Bingley, Harwick, and de Bourgh. Stewart stood before the bench. All bore the same expression, none felt compassion. Darcy waited, his hands balled into fists, nearly daring Wickham to speak, to taunt him once more, but no sound came. Wickham stared at him blankly, then was silently led away. Darcy closed his eyes and let his breath go.

"Come Darcy, we must vacate." Stewart said quietly and nodded to Fitzwilliam who nudged him. Gripping Darcy's elbow, he urged him to his feet and steadily guided him forward until he awoke from his haze, and moved under his own power.

They left the courtroom as the next prisoner was led in. People swirled around them, faces staring in curiosity, a cacophony of voices, questions. It was a blur of activity, finger pointing, and noise. Darcy's jaw set and the group of protectors surrounded him as they took the steps rapidly towards the street and their carriage. They did not stop until all were safely aboard and underway. Only then did Lord Matlock speak.

"It is nearly done, Son. Are you well?"

Darcy said nothing, only staring out at the passing scenery. Fitzwilliam saw that clenched in his hand was the small box containing Elizabeth's hair. "He did not even try to defend himself."

"No, but he did not seem to have a voice, either. His neck still bears the signs of your grip, Darcy. It was a powerful display." Lord Matlock looked at his son and questioned him with his eyes. Fitzwilliam shrugged and continued to try and read his cousin.

"There was no point in defending himself. Although there was no witness to him murdering the man in the alley, Wickham's prison garb certainly was damning evidence. Even without that, the escape and the attack at Darcy House was enough to bring the sentence, he knew it." Stewart licked his lips and looked around at the men who were focussed on Darcy's expression. "I am sorry that I believed it was he that had died. If I had only . . ." His apology, delivered countless times over the past weeks, was stopped when Darcy met his gaze and shook his head. Stewart bowed his down and looked at his hands.

Bingley broke the oppressive silence. "Is there any word on Mrs. Younge?"

"She has disappeared." Fitzwilliam said unhappily and lifted his chin towards Darcy. "I was sure that my good cousin was going to send Mrs. Banks running from the room in tears if he kept glaring at her as he was. I swear Darcy; you should have been in law. You would have made an innocent proclaim herself as open as the most popular whore in Covent Garden with your questioning. I daresay the woman fainted when we left." He looked for a reaction and saw nothing. Sighing, he returned to Bingley. "She conveniently received word that she had a sick relative and resigned her position, got a glowing recommendation, packed her things and was gone. We know now that a man was seen visiting one night, but he was also seen departing, so raised no suspicion. The spinster in the next room reported odd noises coming from her chamber over several days . . ." He glanced around to see the eyes rolling, "but he was never actually seen again. If it was him or some other man, we can never know, but she *is* gone from Georgiana's school."

"I have made so many mistakes." Darcy finally spoke. "I should have exposed Wickham for what he was in the first trial. I tried to protect Elizabeth by not allowing her near-rape to be public knowledge. That gave him a lesser sentence, a permeable prison, ended an innocent man's life, and brought him to my door."

"Darcy, the atmosphere at the time . . ."

"Is no different than it is now." He said bitterly. "How much gossip have we suffered?"

"The gossip was Creary, his cronies, and a few disappointed cats. The great majority of London is on your side, they are just fascinated with the tale of a member of the first circles being attacked by an escaped prisoner. All of our voices have taken care of the opinions of our friends and society, and what do you care of those who are lower?" Lord Matlock's brow rose. "They see it as entertainment, not life and death, and their thoughts are not worthy of your notice."

"Caroline has been supportive of you." Bingley offered. "How close she came to an untimely end as his wife! It has sobered her in extraordinary ways, I assure you. Not enough to make me wish to cancel my tour to avoid living with her and her husband, of course . . ." The men smiled and he looked to see Darcy still lost in his frown.

"I should have seen Mrs. Younge dismissed."

Fitzwilliam spoke with frustration, "I agreed with the plan to watch her, Darcy. Your kindness served us, we knew where she was."

"But she surely entertained him when he escaped; we all know what that spinster overheard even if she did not, and how coincidental that it was heard on days when he was free. No, somehow she maintained contact, and he knew it was safe to go to her. You said yourself she should be brought to trial!"

"I doubt that she knew what he had planned. I imagine she envisioned running away with him, nothing more." Lord Matlock offered.

"Do not placate me, Uncle. I have failed my family. I nearly killed my wife and daughter." Darcy carefully placed the box containing Elizabeth's hair into his waistcoat and went to work twisting his ring.

"If you wish to take that attitude, then what of your father's culpability?" Lord Matlock instantly felt his nephew's burning glare. "He began this by indulging him."

"Do not dare to speak against my father!" Darcy's voice was almost a growl. "He was a mourning man who Wickham used. I am the one who should have stopped this. I am the one who knew what he was."

"I am not insulting your father; I am trying to make you see reason! As much as you wish to shoulder this responsibility alone, you cannot do that. The guards at the prison I hold responsible above anyone. If they had been doing their work, Wickham would be on his way to Australia as we speak!" Lord Matlock's voice rose as Darcy's expression showed his stubborn refusal to listen. "We all advised you, we all supported these decisions. Richard is no babe in the woods, I am no wide-eyed youth. We all agreed on the plans."

"You told me I was either a fool or brilliant. We know which it was." Darcy spat.

Lord Matlock spoke sharply. "Mrs. Younge did not attack you."

"But she harboured Wickham, I know that she did. I should have shouted his guilt to the world!" Darcy said angrily. "Why, why, did I not expose him!" He pounded his fist on the side of the coach, making the others jump. "And now I have subjected . . ." He fell back into his guilty thoughts.

Harwick broke the uncomfortable silence. "I know that you value your privacy deeply, Darcy. I know that you did not care to have this exposed to the world the first time. I believe that Elizabeth sees this hearing today as yet another violation just as you do, and feels as ill as you." Darcy turned to him and his torment was clearly visible. Harwick continued quietly, "But she does not blame you for what happened; she puts the blame where it belongs, with Wickham. He alone is at fault. Elizabeth loves you, deeply and unconditionally. Do not insult her love by becoming bitter for actions that you did not take and crimes that Wickham did."

Darcy stared into Harwick's eyes and nodding, closed his own tight. "Thank you." He drew a deep breath and held his stomach. "I feel as if I will be sick."

"Hang on, Son." Lord Matlock gripped his arm while Bingley hurriedly opened the window. "We will be home soon."

Taking some time to calm, he sighed and rubbed his temples. "Thank you, all of you, for your care for us these past weeks. I know that I am given to dark contemplation, and as much as I appreciate your solid support today, I am afraid that the fraternity is not what I require to be relieved of my burden. I need my wife. The tension of the past weeks, and then knowing for certain that this day was coming, despite knowing the inevitable conclusion, has been nearly unbearable. Without her by my side, I do not know that I could have been kept from running mad. I cannot possibly explain how it felt to be forced to sit calmly across from him, knowing what he meant to achieve. She is well, and it is over." He breathed heavily again, clearly trying to convince himself of the fact. Slowly the colour began to return to his pale features.

"It is not quite over. Will you attend the hanging, Darcy?" De Bourgh asked.

"No." He shook his head, and his deadened eyes gradually became sharp and focussed once again. "My initial thoughts remain. I have no desire to see him drop, nor tolerate the spectacle of the crowd or witness the deaths of the other criminals who will meet justice that day. I saw that he was beaten, a shadow even of the man who attacked us four weeks ago. That he survived to face his sentence is surprising, and to witness his resignation upon hearing it was . . .dissatisfying. I do not know why."

De Bourgh watched him and put forth his argument, "But to see the sentence carried out, would that not be satisfying? To know for certain that he no longer walks the earth, and can never touch you or your family again?"

Darcy spoke without emotion. "There is no question in my mind that he is forever gone from us, that was decided when he attacked. I know what will happen. I saw a man hung in Lambton; Father insisted that I witness it. He wished me to understand that it was not meant to be entertainment, but a deterrent."

Turning his head to stare out of the window, he spoke quietly, "I saw a highwayman dressed in his very best, bowing to the crowd, a glass of brandy in his hand as he was led to the gallows. I saw the nightcap of his favourite prostitute drawn over his face, and the noose tightened around his neck. I heard the invocation of the vicar and then heard the creak and slam as the floor dropped out from below his feet. I saw his legs kick, heard his desperation to breathe, the gurgle in his throat, and saw the twitching and struggle of his body as his bound hands rose and his fingers clawed at the rope." He swallowed and clasped his hands. "I watched him strangle for *twenty* minutes before he at last succumbed. And there he swung; twisting in the air for another hour to be sure the sentence had succeeded. All this while the crowd cheered and ate treats as if they were at a fair." Darcy stared at his boots. "I watched his family fight to claim his body and fail. I saw it dipped in tar and hung on chains at the crossroads, and I saw it for years as it rotted away. No, I know what this sentence looks like. I thought that I would wish for Wickham to suffer in anticipation of it. To look at him today, I believe that he will welcome it. He knows what he lost. He knows that he should never have come to me again. He knows that the day I gave him Father's money, he should have listened when I told him to never come near my home again. He has learned his lesson at last."

"Too late." Fitzwilliam murmured. "He was never a good man, not even a good boy, Darcy. Perhaps he was not destined for the noose, but I have no doubt that he was never destined for the life your father tried to give him."

"I know, and I believe that is what has left me so dissatisfied, the waste. The waste of my father's love and attention . . ." Darcy turned to feel the breeze from the open window. "The whole time as I sat through the hearing, I imagined having to face that bastard, to still be alive, and my Elizabeth gone." He drew another deep breath and closed his eyes, "I cannot begin to contemplate having to return to Darcy House after this with her not there." He opened his eyes to find Harwick's steady gaze. "How did you ever survive?"

"I lived for my children." He said simply. "I had no will for anything else, not for years. But I did go on, and now I am happy again." Harwick smiled softly, "And to be a father, again. Life goes on."

"A baby." Darcy at last relaxed. "You will have your baby with Laura; I cannot begin to express my happiness for you both." His sentiments were echoed by the other men and Harwick accepted handshakes from them all.

"Thank you, she is thrilled as am I, and we cannot wait to tell our girls that a sibling is coming to join them. I suspect you will have another child with your Elizabeth before too long. Stop dwelling on what might have happened, and rejoice in what you have. She is well, and as gloriously wonderful as I have ever seen her. If I had seen her first . . ."

"Now, Harwick, I would have taken that opportunity, I was at the ball before you." Fitzwilliam winked.

"But I saw her at the dance in Cheapside before that!" Bingley reminded them.

"And if I had not been an idiot about far too many things, I would have had her as my bride long ago." Stewart smiled to see the deep frown that formed on Darcy's face. "But then I would not have my beautiful Julia."

"Nor I my Eva."

"Nor I my Laura."

"Nor I my . . . Well, my nameless angel, one fine day." Bingley smiled to see Darcy's expression soften, and heard him chuckle slightly.

"So friend, when you enter your home, what will you do? Present this glorious creature with that thunderous frown of yours, or greet her with the joy you feel to have her alive in your arms, and she feels to have you in hers?" Harwick looked pointedly at the ring beneath Darcy's fingers and saw a slight lift come to his lips. "She needs you to be strong for her, and she will take her cue from the first sight of your face. I do not say to bounce into the house with a song on your lips, but perhaps a sense of relief would do just as well."

"*HIGH DIDDLE DIDDLE, the cat and the fiddle, the cow jumped over the moon. The little dog laughed to see such sport, and the dish ran away with the spoon.*"[9] Elizabeth sang and rocked as Rosalie fed. She did not notice the nursery door open and close until Darcy was by her side and reaching out to tenderly caress the baby's cheek. Rosalie looked at him and kept drinking. "Leave some for Papa." He said softly.

"I think that she needs it more than you do." Elizabeth took his hand and he met her eyes. "Is it over?"

"It will be Wednesday." He kissed her palm and sat down beside her. "I do not wish to bear witness, but I do not wish to leave town until it has taken

---

[9] Mother Goose's Melody, "High Diddle Diddle," 1765.

place." He closed his eyes. "I cannot . . .bear the crowds. There will be five others that day. You know how they love the spectacle."

"I understand; I would not wish to see it either. There was a gibbet outside of Meryton once."

He caressed his lips over her fingers, then held her hand to his pale cheek. "I plan to wait at Surgeon's Hall and see the body before it is . . . examined. Stewart will take us to the door where it will be brought in so we do not need to be near the crowd that witnesses the procedure."

"Are you sure?"

"Yes." He opened his eyes to see the concern and love in hers. "I need to witness that proof with my own eyes. I need to know that you are safe forever." Leaning forward, he kissed her lips, and gently traced over them with his tongue. "I need you." He whispered and kissed her cheek, and then her ear. Tenderly, he caressed his mouth over her throat. "Please."

"Is everyone still here?" She asked when he settled his face on her shoulder.

"No." Darcy murmured against her pulse. "Please."

Rosalie let go and Elizabeth lifted her up to stroke her back. Darcy kissed his daughter's cheek and touched Elizabeth's. "I will be right there, Fitzwilliam. I need you, too."

"Thank you, love." He kissed her lips and rose to his feet. "I will be waiting."

"SEEMS YOU HAVE AN ADMIRER WICKHAM." The guard announced as the door to his cell was unlocked.

"Who?" He whispered and looked at the box that was set down on his cot. The area was littered with empty bottles, and remnants of meals. The condemned were afforded every indulgence from the day their death warrant was signed to the moment they walked up the steps to the gallows that were in clear view from their windows, and most of them preferred to indulge in drink.

"Dunno, woman." He lifted the lid. "Ahhhh, well, well, won't you be looking fine on your walk?" He held up the topcoat and lawn shirt.

"Dotty." Wickham was left alone with the box and picked up the yellow feather that was tucked in the coat. There was no note, she could not risk it. He sank down on the cot and stared at the clothes, and remembered how he was going to save them to wear when they started over in America. A loud noise caught his attention and the cries of the other men in the condemned yard filled the air. He looked up and saw that the gallows were being tested. He began to shake as the tolling of the bells began.

"Wickham." The guard returned. "Better get dressed; it's almost time for services."

Swallowing, he stood and mechanically began removing his clothes and putting on the fine suit. It hung off of him. From the next cell he heard another man. "God forgive you, Wickham."

"You, too." He choked and ran to the corner where he retched.

The door opened, "Let's go."

His hands bound, he was led to the chapel and sat down. Hearing a chorus of voices, he looked up to see the leering faces of the spectators, then glanced once at the open coffin by his side, then up the aisle to see the line of coffins for his fellow travellers to justice that day. The room began to spin and he felt his stomach clench. He closed his eyes and thought of his father, and how he had laughed at the good man, then Mr. Darcy's kind eyes appeared in his mind. "Fool." He whispered. Darcy's face appeared, haggard with the pain of his father's death, and he heard his own voice sneering at him when he demanded more money, and Darcy's, warning him to stay clear of his family. "I am a stupid fool." He looked up to see the vicar delivering his words of comfort to the condemned. He attempted to listen, for once in his life. "Too late." He muttered.

Outside the sounds of the gathering crowds grew. He felt a hand on his arm and he was pulled to his feet. "It is time." He heard a woman pleading to be let go, claiming that it was all a mistake. He heard her being dragged along, screaming for someone to help her. A man behind him cursed her for not facing it with dignity. Everything else around him was lost in the buzz of noise and the sickening fear that was welling up in his chest. The doors opened, the prisoners were lined up, and the slow march forward began.

"George!" Wickham searched the crowd of people lining the narrow passageway leading to the gallows, and spotted the woman dressed in blue with the bright yellow feathers in her hair. "Dotty." He croaked. He kept his eyes on hers as the guard led him forward and felt her hand on his arm when he passed. Numbly, he followed the four men and one woman up the steps, and stood before the dangling noose. Licking his parched lips, he searched the milling crowd until he spotted the feathers again, and kept his eyes on her until the black hood and the noose were slipped over his head. Somehow it was not quite so frightening in the dark; was it? Within seconds, the floor dropped out from under him.

Fitzwilliam watched every step of Wickham's last walk, and noticed the woman with the feathers. He marked her location and murmured to de Bourgh to keep his eye on Wickham while he watched her, and saw her hands fly to her face when he heard the bodies simultaneously drop and the crowd's cheer as the woman's skirt flew upwards to expose her flailing legs. Noting Wickham's progress, he turned his attention back to the woman in the crowd. "I believe that may be Mrs. Younge."

Lord Matlock, happy to look at some other scene, leaned over. "Where?"

Pointing, Fitzwilliam indicated the woman. "Shall we?"

"We will never get there through this crowd." De Bourgh said as they observed the party atmosphere.

"I can get through anything." Fitzwilliam stepped down from their prime viewing spot, and with the authority born of leading men into battle, easily parted the way so that they were eventually standing behind the woman. They heard her sob, then watched as she pulled the feathers from her hair and dropped them to the ground. De Bourgh nudged him and they saw that clutched in one hand was a handbill describing Wickham's crimes. By now his body was still, and twisted gently while two others continued to strangle and twitch.

Lord Matlock glanced at Fitzwilliam and nodded. He touched her shoulder and she turned, and recoiled, recognizing him. "Mrs. Younge? We have been looking for you." Fitzwilliam's cold gaze travelled down her face and stopped. "What is this?" He touched the pendant hanging around her throat, a butterfly made of blue sapphires. "Father?"

Leaning forward, Lord Matlock's eyes narrowed. "I know this necklace. It was a favourite of my sister's. She wore it when she was being courted by her future husband, George Darcy."

"I believe that Darcy presented this Fitzwilliam heirloom to Georgiana in exchange for the pearl, Father." Richard watched her. "You know, Georgiana Darcy, your student?"

"I . . . I do not know what you mean . . ." She stuttered.

"Well, we will just see what the magistrate has to say about that."

25 JULY 1810

I am sitting on our bed right now, carefully balancing this journal over my legs, and hoping that I do not drip ink over the sheets as I write. Beside me lies Fitzwilliam. His eyes are closed, but I know that he does not rest. On his chest is our sleeping daughter. It was all that he wanted when this day at last ended, to come to our rooms and be together.

The events of this day will live on in all of our minds, and to record them will only force us to refresh our memories of images none us care to recall. Fitzwilliam put on a stoic front when he returned, but the mask he wore over his emotions did not fool me. He had left the viewing only to find himself with a magistrate. He left the magistrate only to interview Georgiana, who in turn admitted that she feared his disappointment when her mother's necklace disappeared, and so never told him it had been lost. She remembered too late his warning to watch her purse when school began, and was careless with it. Fitzwilliam had the necklace in his hand as she spoke, and when she finished, he gave it to me. It will be given to Rosalie now, when she is old enough to appreciate the gift.

"Lizzy." He whispered. "Are you finished?"

"I can be." Elizabeth set the pen down and closed the inkpot and book. "What do you need?"

"Perhaps it is time to put Rosa to bed." He opened his eyes and kissed the baby's curls. "I wish to sleep with you."

She smiled and carefully picked her up. "Come, baby." Rosalie protested losing her pillow and immediately curled up in Elizabeth's arms.

Darcy caressed her back and smiled at his girls. "Is she too much? Should I rise?"

"No, I can manage." Elizabeth carried her to the nursery and when she returned, she found him waiting with the covers pulled back.

Darcy sighed when she enveloped him in her embrace. "It is over, and I never want to think or talk about it again."

"Very well, what shall we talk about? It has been an exceptionally long day. I am so proud of you, Will. How do you feel?" She lifted her head from his hair and kissing his brow, gently rubbed his back.

"So very tired." He closed his eyes and buried his face against her shoulder. "I was not prepared to have to face this drama with Mrs. Younge after having to look upon . . .him. I suppose that wearing the necklace was a symbol of defiance."

"What an enormous risk she was taking."

"One that nearly succeeded. I gather that she was planning to leave London immediately. She admitted her address and all that was found were her packed trunks and a large sum of money. She claimed that she had saved it from her wages and the settlement from her husband." Darcy's voice was incredulous. "Her husband was an army lieutenant!" His eyes squeezed shut and he exhaled noisily when her hands moved to massage his shoulders. "Stop it Darcy, Uncle Henry will handle this. No more! I do *not* want to talk about it!"

Elizabeth kissed his hair and watching him carefully, decided to bring up the next subject while his headache was young. "I spoke to Georgiana about the necklace."

Still trying to calm, he spoke angrily, "I told her to be careful of her purse at school for just this reason. I knew that it might be stolen. Why would she be so careless? Would she not value her mother's jewels? Does she not know their importance?"

"She was thirteen, Will." He grunted and she continued, "And then when the necklace disappeared soon after arriving at school, she decided not to tell you. It did not occur to her that you might one day ask her why she never wore it." Elizabeth kissed his cheek and gently began rubbing his temples. "I like your decision not to return it to her."

"Yes, but what sacrifice is it for her? She has been without it for months already. We will have to think of something more." He tried again to relax and failed. "Rosalie will like that necklace one day, and hopefully Georgiana will learn to care for and appreciate her possessions. Beyond the monetary value, the connection to her mother should have been precious to her."

"But she does not have any memory of her mother."

"It is no excuse for not honouring her." He said stubbornly.

"You are correct, and I am not making excuses for her. Will she return to that school?"

"No. I have asked Aunt Helen to identify one for us." Opening his eyes, he asked Elizabeth helplessly, "Are we too soft with her?"

"We have hardly seen her to be anything at all." He moaned. "I did not say that to make you feel guilty! You know that schooling is essential for her progress, and it is not as if we left her alone, if anything she has experienced the strictest of upbringings living with your aunt and uncle. No wonder she wished to be with us! But now, I think that witnessing all that we endured has her frightened. We must reassure her that we will be well." Elizabeth heard his deep sigh when he nestled further into her embrace. "I know as much about parenting as you, dear. We are both learning as we go. It would have been easier to start at the beginning with Rosalie instead of in the middle with Georgiana." She laughed softly when he nodded fervently.

"I am deeply grateful to have you with me on this journey. What would have become of her if I was alone?" He looked up and saw her smile. "What would I be doing now?"

"Oh, probably preparing to attend another gala ball, escorting some lovely young girl for an evening of dancing."

He snorted. "Hardly."

"Married?"

"I pray not." He smiled to receive her kiss, and closed his eyes. "No, I would be at Pemberley."

"Happily enjoying your solitude and becoming increasingly cantankerous in the process." Elizabeth laughed when he sat up and kissed her hard. "Bad-tempered, difficult, grumpy . . ."

"Are you through?"

"No. Argumentative, arrogant, and thoroughly disagreeable." She finished and squealed when he pushed her back and lay over top of her. "See! My point is proven; you would have been a hermit. Likely toothless." She added for good measure.

"Would I have grown a long beard and frightened the tenant's children?" He growled and began nipping at her throat.

"Oh certainly, and you would have chased them away when you angrily brandished your walking stick!"

He chuckled and looked up from his nibbling. "You have me sounding as if I were an old man!"

"So you would be, without your lively wife by your side to prod you from black moods." Elizabeth's eyes sparkled up at him. Darcy settled more comfortably over her and smiled, brushing back her hair, and looking over her face. "What are you thinking?"

"I do not doubt your prediction of my sad existence without you, and I am grateful that you have come to prod me." Darcy kissed her, then said seriously,

"I want to go home and be the good husband and master my father was. I want him to be proud of me."

"Well then Mr. Darcy, what may I do to help you to achieve this admirable goal?" Elizabeth ran her fingers through his hair and made a show of thinking deeply. He laughed softly when she kissed his nose. "I know."

"What?" He smiled and twisted a curl around his finger.

"Come here, dear man." She drew his head towards her and slowly kissed him.

Darcy moaned, whispering when she licked his parted lips, "Oh love . . ."

"Shhhh." Her lips travelled to nibble just below his ear. "I love you, my Fitzwilliam."

"Sweet love." He sighed and turned so he held her safely in his arms. As his eyes closed and he succumbed to sleep, he murmured, "No more regret, from this moment on."

Chapter 22

"Now, you will write to us." Elizabeth ordered.

"Yes, I promise." Bingley held his hands up and hid from her stern glare. "I will!"

"And you will be careful, and behave, and enjoy yourself." Her commands continued.

"Now, Mrs. Darcy, you need to make up your mind, am I to behave or enjoy myself?" He chuckled when she hit his arm. "Ow! Darcy! Control your wife!"

"No chance of that, she is simply saying what I am thinking." Darcy held out his hand, then the men embraced and clapped each other's backs before drawing away with awkward smiles and shining eyes. "I am very proud of you taking this step, Bingley. I think that it will good for you, and I look forward to seeing you again, ready to take on the rest of your life."

"Is that what the tour did for you?" He laughed and rubbed his thumb over his eye.

"No." Darcy chuckled and shrugged. "But it was an experience that I am grateful to have had."

"And what will I find when I return?" Bingley smiled at Elizabeth. "What wonders will you have begun?"

"Do you know something that I do not?" She looked back at Darcy then returned to Bingley. "I am hoping for a peaceful time of simply being a good wife and mother, and seeing what I can do with all Fitzwilliam has given me."

"That sounds dangerous." Bingley winked and grinned at his friend.

"It does, rather." Darcy's eyes twinkled at her.

She groaned and turned her back to him. "Well, we need to be on our way if we are to be at Longbourn on time. We should have left at sunrise." Elizabeth wrapped her arms around Bingley's waist and hugged him tightly. His eyes opened wide and he saw Darcy's frown, but he closed them and hugged her just as tightly back. Elizabeth let go and holding his face in her hands, kissed his cheek. "You know that we all love you, and want you to come home soon."

"Oh." He took her hands and squeezed them as his eyes welled up, and he sniffed. "How am I supposed to leave now?" Bingley kissed her cheek and hands, then placed one into Darcy's palm. "Thank you."

Darcy's smile returned when she squeezed his hand, and he helped her up into the coach. He then turned to shake Bingley's hand once more. "She speaks from the heart, and for all of us. But I am not going to kiss you."

Laughing, Bingley nodded. "Thank God for small favours." He paused and said softly, "I feel the same. Be careful on your journey home."

Darcy nodded and biting his lip, took a book from his coat and handed it to him. "You might want to look at this before you leave for Dover. It is a very good book. A *very* good book." He looked at Bingley meaningfully.

"Very well." Bingley smiled and glanced at it.

Elizabeth called out. "It really is a very good book, Mr. Bingley. It is full of excellent suggestions. Some that you should consider before your plans are set."

"Thank you." He gave them both a bemused smile and watched as Darcy stepped up into the coach and Bingley closed the door after him. A footman moved the steps back and Bingley leaned into the open window. "Miss Darcy, I have been practicing my writing, I hope that you will be able to read my letters."

"I certainly hope so, Mr. Bingley, I will be glad to see the evidence of your endeavours." She glanced at Elizabeth who smiled and nodded. "And . . .and I hope, we hope to hear from you very soon." She blushed when he flashed her a warm smile.

"I am sure that you will." He smiled at Mary. "And I hope that you enjoy Pemberley, Miss Mary. It is a magical place."

"I know that I will, sir." She smiled a little and glanced out of the window. "Oh!"

"Good, you did not depart yet!" De Bourgh leapt down from his horse and tossed the reins to a footman as he strode to the carriage. "I wished to give this to you, Miss Mary." He handed a battered journal through the window. "I sent for it from Rosings. I will not be nearby to fill your head with tales, so you may read this until we meet again. Take good care of it, now. It is precious and full of my memories as a young lad." Seeing Darcy's brows rise, he winked. "Young *lad* Cousin, you might say, a boy. Does that satisfy?"

"It does." Darcy grinned.

"Thank you, sir." Mary clutched it to her chest. "I will take good care of it."

He kicked down the step and leaned further into the window. "See that you do, Miss Mary. I look forward to hearing your impressions when next we meet." Their eyes held for several moments and his confident smile wavered briefly before it returned brighter than before. Smiling around at the group he hopped back down. "Safe journey!" De Bourgh looked up at the coachman and waved his hand. "Away!" With that the Darcy and servants' carriages pulled forward, with more farewells called from all.

"So, do I see something between you and Miss Mary?" Bingley asked as he moved towards his horse and mounted.

De Bourgh smiled and climbed up on his own. "What do I see with you and Miss Darcy?"

"She is a little girl!" Bingley cried. "You cannot be serious! I have no intention of waiting, good heavens, at least another three years!"

"Perhaps you will find some exotic Miss on your travels." De Bourgh cocked his brow. "How are your languages? Perhaps you should stick to England."

"They are not that terrible." Bingley chuckled and relaxed. "In any case, I will find a good English lass to be mine one day."

"Too bad my sisters are married." He rubbed his chin.

"No, no matchmaking. I have taken the vow to abstain from machinations for one year." Bingley said seriously. "In one year, I will find my angel."

"OH JANE, YOU ARE A BEAUTIFUL BRIDE!" Kitty sighed.

"And Robert is so happy." Charlotte stood behind her and buttoned the gown. "He is nervous, though."

"What did he do?" Mrs. Gardiner smiled and picked up the bonnet to plump the spray of white roses that adorned the brim.

"He had his waistcoat buttoned all wrong, and the valet had to ask Papa to come in and have a word with Robert because he kept untying his neck cloth, claiming he could not breathe!"

The ladies all laughed and Jane blushed. "I hope that is not a sign that he thinks he is making a mistake."

"I think that is a sign that he would rather have a quiet ceremony in the parlour instead of this spectacle your mothers have devised." Mrs. Gardiner patted her hand. "Your patience with their competition has been saintly."

"It is one day in a lifetime." Jane sighed at her aunt's praise. "We can endure it. The result is all that matters." She glanced out of the window. "Is there any news of Lizzy?"

"I know that they will be here, dear. The past days have been very trying for them, you cannot imagine the interest they suffered, or the stress they endured; they may have had a later start than anticipated, no matter their desire to leave and put it behind them." Mrs. Gardiner heard Lydia's voice in the background and saw Kitty grimace. "Are you excited to be attending school with Miss Darcy this autumn, Kitty?"

She nodded and looked at her hands. "I hope that I do not embarrass her."

"I am certain that you will not." Jane gave her a hug. "If you like, I can teach you all of the things that Lady Matlock taught me about how to behave in her society." Kitty bit her lip and nodded. "Mary did very well at that school, so I am sure that you will, too."

"Mary is much smarter than I am. I do not have any talent for music or reading." Lydia's whining grew louder. "But I am happy to be leaving." She whispered. "Is Miss Darcy nice?"

"She is very nice." Jane assured her. "You met her once, although I think that she was a little overwhelmed by our family at the time."

"She is nice, Kitty." Mrs. Gardiner smiled. "But you must remember that she is very young and might benefit from your experience as well."

Her eyes widened. "My experience? I have none!"

"That is not true at all. You are older, you have grown up seeing behaviour that you now understand is unappealing, and hopefully you will appreciate this opportunity to learn and improve your future." Mrs. Gardiner gave her a slight embrace. "Keep in mind that Miss Darcy has been denied very little, not only because of her wealth, but because she lost her parents."

"Lydia is indulged." Kitty said thoughtfully.

"She is, but what I think would benefit Miss Darcy is to see how you embrace the opportunity you have been given with this education. This is truly a gift for you; it would be good for her to appreciate what she has as a matter-of-course."

They heard a loud screech from downstairs and looking to the window, they saw the two Darcy carriages rumbling into the drive. "Thank heaven." Jane sighed and stood at the window to watch Darcy step down, hand out Mary and Georgiana, and finally Elizabeth. He said something to her and she laughed, standing on her toes to kiss him and caress his cheek. They both turned to see Mrs. Robbins approaching with Rosalie. Mrs. Bennet flew out of the door, practically prostrating herself before Darcy in her excited welcome. Mrs. Gardiner's brow rose nearly to her hairline and she turned to look at Jane for an explanation.

"Fitzwilliam had his lawyer draw up an agreement stating that he will provide a home and any additional reasonable income for Mama and any unmarried daughters upon Papa's death if it was necessary, no matter whether she outlives Elizabeth. Papa showed it to Mama; and ever since then, Fitzwilliam has become her saviour, and Elizabeth has made the most brilliant of matches, as she has always deserved to have." Jane sighed. "And . . . She has forgiven me my choice."

"Oh Jane, I am sorry." Mrs. Gardiner hugged her. "It is very good of Mr. Darcy to do such a thing."

"Robert is . . . he feels unhappy that he cannot offer such a grand gesture, but Papa explained to me that Fitzwilliam has not done this out of the goodness of his heart, it is an obligation and will keep her from his door." She hung her head. "Now I see Mama through Lizzy's eyes."

"If it makes you feel better Jane, Mama is very happy to gain you as her daughter. She said that after she had thought about it for awhile, she could not think of another girl she would want to share her home with, or give it to someday." Charlotte smiled. "And since I will be leaving in a few months to marry Michael, she will need to have another sensible daughter at home, because we all know that Maria it just too shy to speak her mind!"

"Thank you, Charlotte." Jane wiped her eyes and hugged her new sister. They heard a carriage pulling away and knew that it was Darcy going over to

Lucas Lodge with Mr. Gardiner. Since his brothers were so young, Lucas had asked Darcy to stand up with him in church. There was a knock and Elizabeth peeked around the door. "Lizzy! I was so afraid you would be late!"

"I am sorry, Jane." She hurried in and hugged her. "We tried to leave early, but Rosalie was not cooperating, and then Mr. Bingley stopped to say goodbye once more, and Captain de Bourgh stopped . . . It was just impossible to leave!" Elizabeth stood back and held her hands. "Everyone sends you their love and best wishes. I have gifts for you from the Matlocks, Harwicks and Stewarts. Mr. Bingley wishes you joy and happiness." She smiled when Jane's eyes went to the floor. "Now, what are you doing wearing this gown?" She looked over the blue dress that she had given her. "This was not supposed to be a wedding gown!"

"Oh Lizzy, how could it not be? When will I ever have another gown from Madame Dupree? And . . ." She bit her lip and whispered, "It does match my eyes." She laughed and the sisters hugged. "I promise, I will wear it over and over again, but I confess that I cannot wait to see Robert's face when he sees me!"

"Well I shall be sure to watch him instead of you." Finally they let go and Elizabeth greeted everyone else, hugging Charlotte and congratulating her on her very recent engagement to Michael de Bourgh, then kissed Kitty's cheek and felt her sister hug her hard.

"Are you truly well, Lizzy?" Kitty asked worriedly. "I was so frightened! Is Mr. Darcy well?"

"We are both so much better, I promise." She saw Charlotte's concern over Kitty's shoulder and laughed. "I am truly well, just very sore, but I refuse to wear a sling to the wedding. And my dear Fitzwilliam is much better, too. Now we will speak no more of it. This is Jane's day."

"Where is Rosalie?" Mrs. Gardiner asked when she at last received her hug.

"Yes! I want to meet my niece!" Kitty cried.

"Mrs. Robbins has her in my old room, Papa took her over as soon as we arrived and showed the way upstairs. I think that he is smitten with his granddaughter! Mama greeted us and was back in the house so fast that she did not have a chance to meet her yet." Elizabeth's smile faltered then she fixed it to her lips and continued, "I cannot say that I blame her, I am not going near Rosa until after the wedding. We took separate coaches so that our clothing remained clean and our nerves were not frayed." She laughed. "And I see that you took your own advice and left our cousins at home!"

"I am not a fool, Lizzy. They will do just fine without us for a few days." Mrs. Gardiner patted her hand. "Now, I will go check on my sister. I understand that she is very pleased with your husband."

"Yes." Elizabeth sighed and shrugged. "And my husband was very glad to leave before his poor nerves were frayed too much by her attention. I suppose his kindness has won me some approbation, at last."

"Your mother has been worried for her future for twenty years." Mrs. Gardiner said gently.

"Then why would she not be happy for me from the beginning?" Elizabeth held up her hand. "No, do not answer; I have no desire to discuss it. This is Jane's day."

"I agree. And now we should see what sort of spectacle is being prepared downstairs." Mrs. Gardiner left and was joined by the other girls, leaving Elizabeth and Jane alone.

"Are you well?"

"Yes." Jane sighed and twisted her hands. "Aunt gave me another little talk last night." She looked at Elizabeth pointedly. "It was not quite the same as yours."

"Mine was a little more hopeful, I presume?" She sat down on the bed and Jane joined her. "I received four talks before my wedding night, each one had a bit of truth, but in the end, it was a night that nobody could possibly have predicted for me." Elizabeth smiled and squeezed Jane's hand. "Has Robert reassured you?"

"Yes. He is very eager, but I know that he will be very kind." Biting her lip she blushed. "And he is going to thank Fitzwilliam for the wedding trip. He said that after listening to his little brothers arguing in their bedchamber, he . . . he was looking forward to the freedom and privacy we will experience outside of his family home."

Elizabeth started to laugh, and raised her hand to her mouth. "Forgive me, Jane. But to hear you speak of privacy at an inn . . . I am sorry. I am spoiled living at our quiet homes." She giggled. "I wonder if you and Robert will be shushing each other in the middle of the night as Fitzwilliam and I do!"

"Lizzy!"

"Oh Jane, just wait, you will understand the joy of loving your husband very soon, and the magnification of every little sound when you are trying to be quiet." Elizabeth picked up the bonnet and placed it over Jane's hair, then tied the ribbons. Finishing, she hugged her. "You are lovely. Are you ready?"

Jane nodded and taking Elizabeth's hand, they walked down the stairs. Mr. Bennet was waiting with a smile. "Well, it seems that sense will dwell in this house for the last time." He sniffed and took Jane's hand. "I am happy for you, Daughter."

"Thank you, Papa." Her brow wrinkled. "Who is playing?"

"Oh, Georgiana and Mary have prepared several duets for entertaining your guests." Elizabeth smiled. "They have been working very hard."

Mr. Bennet cocked his head. "I am overwhelmed with the change in Mary's skill. Perhaps she should stay here and entertain her father instead of going with you to Pemberley?"

"Papa, you would not do that to her would you? She is so excited to see our home!"

"Lizzy, you have been gone from Longbourn too long if you do not recognize my teasing." He said sadly.

"Forgive me, Papa, it has been a difficult time." Elizabeth's eyes welled up and she was grateful to be distracted by her mother's arrival.

"Jane!" Mrs. Bennet pulled Jane to her side and began to fuss over the gown. Elizabeth stood next to her father and watched the scene.

"So Mama thinks that I am wonderful now?" She asked quietly.

"She will probably never forgive you for marrying better than Jane, but she is certainly happier knowing for certain that despite everything, your husband is an honourable man and will look after all of his family. Even the members he does not wish to know." Mr. Bennet looked over his shoulder at Lydia. "I am growing uncertain about school for her."

"Why? Is she protesting?" She looked over to her pouting sister. "I suppose that she is upset with the attention that Jane is receiving, and is making her unhappiness known?"

"Loudly." He shrugged. "I have taken away every privilege and it makes no difference. I fear that by the time school begins, she might just run away." He looked at Elizabeth meaningfully, "I think that her precocious development is doing her no favours. The men of the neighbourhood are quite taken with her look, and her youthful exuberance is very appealing to their imaginations."

"Her figure is fully formed." Elizabeth noticed with surprise. "When did that happen?"

"I hardly know. But Mr. Collins has certainly made note of it. He is a leering fellow, and the way your mother dresses her is no help in discouraging that. I appreciate how Miss Darcy actually appears to be dressed appropriately for her age, despite her wealth. Your mother does not care; you were all dressed as women at that age." He shrugged helplessly. "Lydia knows what it is to feel a man's admiration, and how to draw it." He looked at her with resignation. "Mr. Collins is no man I would care to call Son, but it could be the best offer Lydia might expect, and it would save the estate and your mother, as well as your husband from responsibility he should not bear if I fail to provide for her."

"Oh Papa, she is not fifteen!"

"We will see." He met her eyes and smiled sadly. "Better married young than wandering the streets of London and selling herself if she runs away." Elizabeth's horrified look made him tilt his head. "Surely you are not innocent to these things? Not after the time you just experienced?"

"No Papa, but I never considered it for my family. Do you really think that Lydia would be seduced by someone?"

"That man who tried to end your life, was he not a known seducer? Darcy told me that he had fathered at least two children with servant girls during his years at Cambridge. Darcy cleaned up more than his old debts to spare his father from knowing what his ward was truly like; he found homes for the foundlings, and new situations for the girls." Elizabeth's eyes grew wide. "He spared you, as well? Forgive me for telling you then, it was not my news to relate. Perhaps though it will help you to understand better why he was so upset with himself for not exposing Wickham sooner." Mr. Bennet patted her hand when understanding appeared in her eyes.

"Lizzy, I held Rosalie many times while you and Darcy slept, and as I looked down at her, I thought of how I had failed my family, and how I knew that my granddaughter would never face want because of her father's neglect. I know that Lydia is incorrigible, and I also know that it is probably too late to change that. She is overindulged and indolent. I see her as facing a very hard and short life after running away from school in London; or married to her dream of a soldier who will likely abuse her, or leave her to her own devices when he goes to war. Marrying a foolish minister who will worship her beauty and feel himself lucky to have such a pretty young woman to satisfy his desires might just be the best that she can expect, and she would have a home." He looked around him and patted her back. "Well that is a decision for another day; now let us see your sister married to the man of her heart."

DARCY CROSSED HIS ARMS and his lips pursed back the little smile that kept trying to appear. "You *can* breathe, you know."

"It feels like a noose!" Lucas complained and glanced at Darcy. "Forgive me."

"No, no. I understand, but a noose implies that you are unwilling, why not call it a yoke and your beloved is the burden?" He chuckled to see Lucas' eyes roll. "Come now, you endured Professor McMaster's literature course."

"I did, and I thought I was free of his fanciful thinking. You do not impress me as a poet, you are far too staid."

"I leave that to my lovely bride to answer." He smiled and laughed to see Lucas blush and look back up at him.

"Umm, thank you for the wedding trip."

"You are welcome. What convinced you?"

"The bit about actually enjoying the honeymoon without . . .holding back." Lucas shrugged when Darcy's smile grew. "I wish we were leaving tonight!"

"No, you should enjoy your first night in your home, even if it must be quiet, and is not your home yet. It is a memory that will never be replaced. You will mark that place as your own, for the rest of your days."

Lucas smiled and nodded at his feet. "Did . . . Bingley have anything to say?"

"Best wishes and joy." Darcy assured him. "He is off to find his way. I just hope that he takes the correct path."

"I hope that he finds it, and, I am grateful that he let her go." Lucas stared down the aisle of the church and watched the guests filter in. "He would have made her a very good husband."

"He would have been the most prudent choice." Darcy nodded and smiled when he received a sharp look. "You are the better one, the one who loves all of her, as she does you."

"Thank you." Lucas drew a long deep breath and both men chuckled when Sir William toddled up the aisle, shaking hands and slapping backs. "He should have been in politics."

"Well as the magistrate for the neighbourhood, he is. Surely Mr. Bennet does not want the position."

"No, no, that is surely true." Sir William stepped up and beamed at them. "Is everything ready, Father?"

"It is; it is! The ladies are just arrived; your brothers are escorting them down the aisle now!" He grinned and bobbed. "A great day! Capital day!" He shook Darcy's hand and hugged his son. "Good show, Son!" He happily flew back down the aisle to escort Lady Lucas, and at last all of the guests were in place. The vicar appeared along with Mr. Collins, who attempted to address Darcy, but was given no more than a curt nod. Instead Darcy focussed on Elizabeth walking towards him, and smiled at her dancing eyes. He saw her glance unhappily at Collins, then turn to watch Lucas. Darcy's brow creased until he heard his sharp intake of breath and looked to see Jane, a vision in blue, walking towards him. Darcy looked to Elizabeth, and matched her smile. Jane and Robert held hands and took their vows, as every happy couple in that church silently renewed their own. When it was over and the names were affixed to the register, the blushing couple happily settled into a borrowed barouche and enjoyed their first kiss as man and wife.

Removed from the noisy group of family and friends, Darcy at last took his bride's hand in his and kissed it. "Now, Mrs. Darcy. Now may we go home?"

"I beg for some cake, love. I want something sweet." She laughed as his eyes lit up with a memory.

"Something to hold in your mouth?" He whispered against her ear.

"I want to taste you." She whispered back.

"But we will be at an inn tonight."

"I have been given a new perspective about lovemaking and inns today." Her eyes sparkled with mischief. "It seems that anonymity may be the key to freedom."

"Lizzzzzzzzzzzzzy." He said heatedly.

"Mr. Darcy, I think that it is time that our bed was the one to keep our neighbours awake all night." Elizabeth kissed that certain spot below his ear then drew away. "What do you think?"

Darcy's eyes were dark and his tongue slowly moistened his lips. He glanced around to be sure nobody was looking, and leaning forward to bite the identical spot below her ear, whispered, "I think that it is time that you had some cake."

"HOW IS MR. DARCY?" Caroline asked and noticing the pointed look from her husband, added, "and Mrs. Darcy? Are they feeling quite well?"

"I believe so." Bingley sat down heavily on a sofa in the Hursts' drawing room and picked up a pillow to hold. "They seemed in good spirits, glad to be leaving, and to be attending Miss Ben . . ." He glanced at the clock, "Mrs. Lucas's wedding."

"Do not tell me you were standing in some tavern as the church bells rang, toasting your lost love." Robinson laughed and received a glare from both his wife and brother. "You broke it off, Bingley."

"I said nothing of my feelings. You have a desire for discovering gossip that is not actually in existence." Looking down at the pillow, he played with the tassels. "I am only missing my friends. It is difficult to imagine that I will not see them again for so many months."

"Perhaps you will." Hurst entered the room with a letter in his hand, and took a seat. "This just arrived from Mr. Tate."

"Your tour guide?" Caroline looked at the letter curiously. "Is something wrong with your plans?"

"No, nothing is wrong with the plans, but there is something wrong with the Continent. Napoleon, to be exact." He sighed and shrugged. "I am afraid Bingley, that it is still too dangerous to undertake the journey."

"But we were not going to travel through France." He took the letter and looked at it. "So travel through Switzerland in inadvisable as well? Could we take a ship to Italy and bypass the war?"

"We could, but it would not be an easy journey. You have travelled to Spain enough times, Robinson. How is the journey?"

Becoming serious, he sat up. "Well, if you have no stomach for it, I would say it is hell. Disease, cramped quarters, stomach in your throat. Not for the casual traveller. There is the possibility of pirates and shipwreck, too. I have done it overland and by sea, neither is easy, but I am glad to have merchants to do the travelling for me now, and men to take care of my business in the south."

"We will not be travelling there this winter?" Caroline asked.

"Not unless you can sprout wings and fly." Robinson laughed. "Perhaps we will be shifting our attention to other locations."

"To the islands?" She asked with wide eyes. "We will cross the ocean?"

"If we do we may not return." He sighed. "Perhaps this estate was a good purchase." He mused and shrugged. "Well I won't be solving this problem today."

"I think that we should reevaluate our plans." Hurst turned to Bingley. "What do you say?"

"Darcy gave me a book today, a travel book of Britain . . .by Gilpin." He started to laugh. "He suggested that I give it a look, very soon."

Hurst smiled and began to laugh. "I see that your friend is trying very hard not to direct you."

"And yet he does not stop caring for me at every turn. And his wife was just as concerned." He looked up with a smile. "Perhaps we should read this book and speak to our guides."

"And plan another trip." Louisa said with relief. "I would rather not die at sea."

"I cannot help but agree with you." Hurst agreed.

"I will write to Darcy and let him know that his message was received." Bingley laughed softly. "And understood."

"GOOD HEAVENS." Darcy said flatly. "Did a garden explode in here?"

"It is rather colourful, isn't?" Mr. Gardiner chuckled and took a sip of the punch. "The end result of two very strong-willed ladies with entirely different visions."

"Jane could not stop it?" He whispered and looked around in awe.

"Jane is a mediator at heart." Mr. Gardiner laughed at his incredulous look. "You have not seen Jane at her best, Son. I think that Jane Lucas will be truer to form than Jane Bennet ever was." He winked and lifted his chin to where Lucas stood with Jane on his arm. "Look at him, the man is desperate to leave."

Darcy watched Lucas's fixed smile then his eyes travelled down to where he gripped Jane's hand. "If he is not careful, she will be crying with pain soon."

"I am afraid that her cheeks will be that shade of red for many days to come."

"Does she blush over the anticipation or the antics of the mothers?" Darcy mused. "Lady Lucas seems calmer than Mrs. Bennet."

"My sister has always been of an excitable bent." Mr. Gardiner sighed. "My mother may not have been educated, but she certainly knew how to marry off her most troubling girl."

"What was Mrs. Bennet like as a child?" Darcy forced his eyes away from the sight of his mother-in-law extolling the virtues of her daughter to her neighbours. *Two daughters married!* was shrilled across the room.

"Ah, well turn and watch your sister, and you will see the identical model." Mr. Gardiner pointed his glass to a corner and laughed at Darcy's alarm. "Not Miss Darcy, Lydia. No, no, Father saw Bennet sniffing around her, Mother knew an opportunity when she saw it . . . ah that poor man was engaged before he knew what happened to him. Oh well, he has at least three girls who do not make men cringe, and with some work and luck, perhaps he will have four. Not bad, that."

"I suppose not." Darcy sighed and looked at Georgiana. "I hope that I do well by my sister."

"You will, Son. I cannot offer you advice for a girl her age, though. I have not lived it yet."

"No, all I have are my aunt and uncle for this." He looked back to the wedded couple, free at last from Mrs. Bennet. "Look, they are making a move to escape."

Mr. Gardiner watched as Lucas guided Jane to a doorway, sent a backwards glance into the room, and with a smile, slipped into the hallway. The two men watched the window and saw them hidden behind a lilac bush just outside the door. Darcy and Mr. Gardiner chuckled and raised their glasses in toast. "Well done, Lucas."

"She will not let him stay out there for long." Darcy observed. "Just long enough to make him . . ."

"Desperate." They laughed and Mr. Gardiner nudged him. "Lizzy seems to be bearing the attention of the neighbours well."

A smile came to his eyes as he watched Elizabeth introducing Rosalie around. "She is doing that on my behalf. I warned her that I would not do well with a crowd. I am grateful for your tolerating my company for so long."

"You know that it is a pleasure, Son. And it is probably for the best to keep you apart from the curious. I am afraid that news of your experience did come here, courtesy of Mr. Collins."

"Collins?" Darcy's good mood evaporated and he glared over to the little man in the corner of the room who was eagerly talking to Mr. Bennet. "Why would he be interested?"

"He was nearly the recipient of the living at Hunsford, via the great Lady Catherine de Bourgh, the esteemed aunt of you." He snorted and performed a mock bow.

Darcy stared. "Speaking of bending over backwards to create a connection!"

"And he is the heir of this estate; it will be run into the ground within a year." Mr. Gardiner sighed. "Particularly if my brother does as he proposes, and allows a marriage between Collins and Lydia."

"She is fourteen! Has he proposed? Surely he has not agreed!"

"It would not be for several years, but she would be promised to him. It smells of my father's desperation to marry off Fran before Bennet realized what he had done." Mr. Gardiner appreciated Darcy's affront. "You do not approve?"

"Sir, I do not care for Miss Lydia, but I would not wish such a marriage on any child! She should have a choice, at least when she is old enough to know her heart and mind, even if Collins likely is the best offer she will ever receive. My sister is nearly the same age and I would not trust her judgement with such a decision, and would without question refuse my permission. I realize that I fell in love with Elizabeth when she was but fifteen, but . . . we *did* wait! After Lydia has received her schooling . . ."

"Ah well that is it, Bennet now thinks that it is hopeless to try. He envisions Lydia running wild through London and coming to a sad end. Marriage, he thinks, is the only hope."

"He will not send her? What has changed? We discussed this! He must at least try! If ever there was a girl in need of discipline . . ." He waved his hand over the gaudy display of decoration and the groaning buffet table laid out with two competing tastes in food, watched as Lydia giggled and flirted with some gawking youths, and stuttered, "Sir, whatever you and your wife did to correct my Elizabeth from thinking this is attractive, and formed her behaviour, I am forever indebted." Darcy looked with great appreciation to where Elizabeth stood, and then noticed that she was showing signs of fatigue. "Excuse me sir, she needs me." Striding across the room, he ignored the looks of curiosity and admiration that he inspired and touched Elizabeth. "Shall I relieve your burden, love?"

"Oh, thank you!" She handed over Rosalie, who squealed to be in her father's firm grip. "I did not think I would tire so soon." She reached up and smoothed over Rosalie's dress and smiled at him while he smiled widely at his baby. "I think you would rather speak to her anyway."

"I will not lie about that." He looked around the room. "Would you mind if I take her for a breath of air?"

Elizabeth laughed and caressed his cheek. "No Fitzwilliam, not at all. Have a good long talk with her." Darcy bent and kissed her softly. Hearing giggles behind him, he blushed. "Another." She whispered. Smiling, he happily kissed her again, then turned and escaped.

"Lizzy!" Kitty whispered. "Mr. Darcy is a rake!"

"No, Mr. Darcy is a gentleman." She sighed at his retreating form. "My gentleman." She turned back to Kitty. "Where is Georgiana, you two should be getting to know each other while you have this opportunity."

"She is with Mary." She pointed to the pianoforte. "I . . . I do not know music."

"Well she does not know much of drawing, so you can teach each other." Elizabeth took her by the hand and started over to the girls. Kitty resisted. "What is it?"

"What will I say to her?"

"She will be just as tongue-tied as you I promise, now come on." She gave her a hand a tug and led the way, pausing to roll her eyes at Jane as she passed.

"Are you happy, Jane?" Lucas said quietly. "You did not want to remain outside with me."

Jane turned away from watching her sisters and gave him a glowing smile. "Oh, so very happy! I am sorry, Robert, but our mothers worked very hard for this, we could not hide away, no matter how pleasant the occupation."

"Pleasant indeed. You have me tied up in knots." He whispered, and taking her hand, kissed it. "I am in desperate need of a distracting occupation."

Seeing her blush, he groaned and looked around the room for something to discuss. "Our mothers *have* gone rather . . . honestly Jane, our mothers have shown no restraint whatsoever. It is embarrassing how gaudy this is. I am sorry."

"I expected nothing less from my mother." Jane smiled and shrugged. "She was denied the big society wedding with Lizzy and Mr . . .Fitzwilliam. And your mother is marrying off her eldest son and the heir. If you think about it they have been competing with each other since they became neighbours."

"So they have." He smiled at her desire to declare peace between the families, and looked around. "I suppose that if I ever drive you to run away from me, you will certainly know the path home."

"Why would I want to leave you?" Jane said softly and looked at her hand in his. "I am yours forever now. Home is with you."

"Yes, but home is so full of people." He let out a frustrated breath. "I am anxious to go anywhere but here, and beyond the lilac bush would be preferable."

"I am afraid that we have no choice but to stay, for a little while anyway." She blushed at the intensity of his gaze. "Robert, you must not look at me so!"

His smile returned. "How am I looking at you?"

"Like . . ." She glanced around and turned back to him, "Like a ravenous wolf about to devour a lamb."

He burst into laughter and raised her hand to his lips. "Well, it is certainly how I feel. I wish that we were leaving on our journey this moment, but since we are not, perhaps when the guests depart, you and I can take our good time returning home."

"And what will we do?" Jane sighed.

"Oh . . . I will think of something appropriate." Lucas smiled when she blushed. "Something private. I think that we will be walking home, and taking a very circuitous route."

"Oh!"

He nodded and looked at her intently. "In fact, I do believe that I know just the place for us to visit."

"It is private?" He nodded. "Then I look forward to it." Jane smiled to see his eyes light up. "What have I done?"

"You have given your husband a spectacular gift." He winked and stood tall. "Thank you."

"A toast to the happy couple!" Sir William raised his glass. "May you always be as happy as you are today!"

"Hear, hear!"

"May you have many healthy children and long lives!"

"Hear, hear!"

"And may you live in peace with your relatives." Mr. Bennet winked and raised his glass. The guests laughed and he noticed Elizabeth walking quickly from where she had been standing with her sisters, a hurt look marred her face. He then noticed his wife was busy talking to a group of ladies nearby. Turning his head, he saw through the window that Elizabeth had left the house and was headed into the garden where Darcy was sitting on a bench with the baby. His brow creased, he walked towards his wife and listened to the conversation.

"I have never seen a man take such an interest in his child!" Mrs. Goulding commented. "Why Mr. Darcy seems besotted!"

"My husband certainly never carried my girls about." Mrs. King agreed.

"Well she is a pretty thing." Mrs. Bennet allowed. "But his behaviour amazes me, a man as rich as Mr. Darcy with his great estate was surely disappointed in the birth of a girl. You heard me tell Mrs. Darcy how she failed him." She nodded her head, "Well, she will just have to tolerate his attentions until she gets him that son, there is no escaping it. He needs his heir."

"I doubt that it is a trial." Mrs. Long noted as she gazed at the handsome man striding angrily towards the house.

"Mrs. Bennet, a word?" Mr. Bennet said quietly.

"What is it, Mr. Bennet, I do not have time for such things, oh look here comes Mr. Darcy!" She beamed. "Mr. Darcy, we were just speaking of you!"

"Mrs. Bennet, I would like to speak to you, privately." He spoke in very soft voice, and glanced at Mr. Bennet, "And you, sir."

"Well, come to my bookroom, then." He took Mrs. Bennet's arm and leading her to the room, closed the door.

Darcy paced for a moment then looked out of the window to where Charlotte sat with Elizabeth and Rosalie. While he watched his wife wipe her tears, he began to speak. "Madam, my wife has told me that once again, you have informed her of how she has disappointed me with the birth of our daughter. Who are you to claim to know my mind and heart enough to chastise her and further, to expound upon it to the neighbourhood?" He turned to glare at her and spoke in a low, angry voice. "I know of your reaction to the news of our injuries, and it was selfish in the extreme! You made my wife cry needlessly over hurt from you at a time when we were both fighting for our lives! Your behaviour infuriates me, and your callous machinations to benefit from your daughters' marriages disgust me. I am a liberal master, so I have been told. I take great pride in caring for those who depend upon me, and although it is done unwillingly, I have agreed to provide for you should Mr. Bennet predecease you. I do this not for you, but for my wife, who despite your neglect, still feels obligated to respect her parents. She has forgiven you time and again in the hope of one day receiving a hint of praise from you. Why she would seek it from such a woman as you is beyond me, but it only proves that her heart is good and her loyalty absolute. However, madam, I will tell you here and now, if I EVER hear of one more disparaging, unkind, or dishonest remark directed towards or about my wife, my children, or my family from you, I will burn that agreement and see you escorted to the poor house rather than help you again! And do not think that I will not hear, madam. I will."

He turned to Mr. Bennet. "As for you, sir. If you do not even make the attempt to rescue your youngest daughter from the purgatory of ignorance where you have cast her and do not send her to school, I will pledge to wash my hands of the agreement and this estate, as well. How you could consider losing this opportunity to correct your mistakes with that wild child you have created is negligence of the highest order!" Darcy fumed. "Perhaps marriage *is* her only salvation, but to that . . .weakling heir of yours? At least wait for an age when her reason may make that decision. At fourteen your daughter would have him bent to her will in days, and likely off with a far more satisfying man within weeks. I do not know if schooling will improve her, but a strong hand that you clearly lack is needed to save her, and no, it will not be mine." Darcy stopped and squeezed his eyes shut, and gasped; raising his hand to his head, then grasped the back of a chair. The room was spinning and his head was pounding. "Elizabeth."

"Mrs. Bennet, fetch Lizzy!" Mr. Bennet took Darcy by the shoulders and helped him to sit down. "There, sir, you are overwrought, you are not ready for such demonstrations." Darcy held his head in his hands and said nothing, trying to breathe through the pain. Elizabeth flew in and knelt by his side.

"Fitzwilliam? What happened?"

"I . . . I . . . Elizabeth." He reached out and she held him, stroking back his hair and kissing his lips. She looked up to her father.

"He was delivering an impassioned speech, and was felled with pain." Mr. Bennet said quietly. "I am sorry to have inspired it. Mr. Darcy," He touched his shoulder, "it will be as you say."

Darcy nodded and squeezed his eyes shut as they welled up with tears. Elizabeth held back from asking anything of what happened, but her glare at her father and hovering mother spoke of the years of anger she had never expressed. "Would someone please locate Mr. Darcy's valet and ask him to bring his elixir?"

"Yes, yes of course!" Mrs. Bennet cried and scurried away.

"No, dearest, I . . . I am well now." He breathed deeply. "It is fading."

"Fitzwilliam Darcy, you cannot lie to me or anyone else." Elizabeth hugged him and kissed his forehead. "A little bit will not hurt you, and we will be leaving soon so you may sleep in the carriage." She kissed his cheek and then his nose. "We will shock our sisters with our cuddling."

Laughing softly when she ruffled his hair, he opened his teary eyes to see the concern in hers. They kissed again. "I love you, too."

"Lizzy?" Jane entered with Robert. "What is wrong? We saw you run in here. Charlotte said that Fitzwilliam is ill?"

"Oh, Fitzwilliam just has a little headache, and you know me, always jumping to conclusions that it is worse than it is. Do not let us spoil your celebration." She smiled and he nodded, and tried to hide his grimace. Both Jane and Robert looked at them doubtfully. Adams entered with a glass of wine. She thanked him and held it to Darcy's lips. "There Jane, here is a lesson for you. This is how you treat an obstinate husband."

Darcy sipped and shuddered. "Terrible."

"I agree." She watched him finishing the drink and took the glass away. "Adams, could you please have the coach prepared and let Mrs. Robbins know that she will be taking charge of Rosalie for the trip to the inn?"

"Yes, Madam." He bowed and left.

"Better?" She said softly when he smiled a little, and with her help stood then drew her into his arms, but it was she who was supporting him.

"Thank you, love." They kissed and Robert slipped his arm around Jane's waist and looked at her.

"I like this lesson we have been given today, even if I suspect the cause." He glanced at his new in-laws, then leaned forward and kissed her. "I plan to emulate our brother and sister."

"Well, just wait until you come to Pemberley, and nobody will question you." Darcy said quietly, and they were all relieved to see the colour gradually returning to his face. "When should we expect you?"

"As much as I wish to follow you this afternoon, we will have to wait a week or so. Father wishes me to be at hand when the Reverend de Bourgh presents his settlement."

"I understand; I would do the same for my sisters. Their futures should not be left to the four winds." He glanced at Mr. Bennet, who nodded.

"Well, let us say our farewells and gather our sisters, and be on our way before you drop off." Elizabeth said softly. I will just have a word with my parents and be right with you."

"Should I remain?" He took her hand and squeezed.

"No." She kissed him and everyone left, Jane took Darcy's arm to offer support and he quietly thanked her. Lucas closed the door behind them. Drawing herself up, Elizabeth thought of Lady Matlock and how she would expect her to behave. "Mama, Papa, I do not know what was said here, but I suspect that Fitzwilliam was fighting a battle for me. It is time that I did that for myself. Mama, I respect you as my parent, but I will no longer tolerate any remark or behaviour on your or my sisters' part that is disparaging of me, my husband, or child. I am Elizabeth Darcy, and I take the care of my husband's name and reputation very seriously. Your behaviour reflects upon my family. Papa, I expect you to follow through with your plans, please do not disappoint me." She kissed his cheek and then turned to her mother and kissed hers. "We will see you in September."

She stepped out of the bookroom to find Darcy leaning against a wall and waiting for her. He smiled and she took his hands. *"Now* we may go home."

Chapter 23

A bump of the carriage woke Darcy with a start. Squeezing his eyes shut again, he became aware of the dull throb in his head that seemed to be a constant companion since they began the journey home, and was worsened at the wedding breakfast. It was something he hoped would eventually become a thing of the past; at least it did not seem to bother him when he was walking anymore. Slowly, he reopened his eyes and found that Elizabeth's curls had been his pillow. He kissed her forehead and peeked down to see that she appeared to be asleep against his shoulder, and felt her arms wrapped around his waist. Another bump and he looked out of the window. Recognizing the terrain, he knew they were soon to be entering Pemberley's outer perimeter. He felt a great sense of relief flood over him.

"You seem happy, Fitzwilliam." Mary said shyly.

"Mary, forgive me for not noticing you." He smiled and noticed that Georgiana was asleep on her shoulder. "I see that we are both serving as pillows."

"Yes, she dropped off not long after you and Lizzy did." She smiled. "I do not mind."

"We are nearly home." He pointed. "Do you see that old house there? Whenever I spot that, I know we will be at Pemberley's gate within a half-hour. I cannot say enough how happy we are to go home." Looking back at her, he saw trepidation. "You are frightened."

"It shows?" She said worriedly.

"I am afraid that you are not accomplished at hiding your feelings. And you have a sister who knows you very well, and who is proficient at reading emotions that frankly, I miss on a regular basis." He laughed softly and kissed Elizabeth's brow when he felt her hug him and he hugged her back. "As my wife reminds me often." Seeing Mary's blush, he tilted his head. "You may as well become used to us displaying our affection, Mary. I will never hold back from my wife in my home. At a public event, certainly we will observe decorum and propriety, but in the privacy of our family setting, I *will* express my love." He looked at her straight in the eye. "Do you understand?"

"Yes, sir." She bit her lip. "It is strange to me."

"I understand that, even to our closest family it is strange, but it is our choice. Now, tell me what of Pemberley frightens you."

"Jane told me how overwhelming it is."

"Jane was uncomfortable with it, that is true. It is, as Elizabeth says, just a home, a very large and well-appointed one, but still, a home. It has family, servants, furniture, and decoration." He saw her head shaking and shrugged. "I have perhaps a biased opinion, as does Georgiana, but we grew up there. Elizabeth was overwhelmed at first, but she was determined to learn all that she could, and is now much loved by our staff and supremely confident in her role. She can teach you a great deal if you let her, it will undoubtedly be useful one day when you marry."

"I do not think that I will marry anyone who owns a mansion!" She blushed, and looked at her hands. "But . . . I do like to expand my mind."

"Excellent! Then take in Elizabeth's instruction. You never know." He glanced at de Bourgh's journal. "Speaking of which, what has the captain's scribbling taught you?"

"Oh!" Mary blushed brighter than ever. "This was written when he was but a boy of fifteen. It is full of wonder, and tales of hardship. He narrowly escaped so many perils."

"Storms?"

"Yes, and disease, and . . . pirates!" She whispered. "He was in battles!"

"I imagine that he was much more frightened than he admits in the tales he recorded." Darcy nodded. "Can you read between the lines of his boyhood bragging?"

Mary smiled shyly then touched the book fondly. "Yes. He was very lonely, and appreciative of the companions he had, and the few officers who treated him kindly. He saw much of the world, but he longed to go home and live in a house."

"And now some ten-odd years later his dreams are come true." Darcy smiled. "Rosings is similar to Pemberley, not as large, but still a mansion and significant estate. It has been a great adjustment for him. It is like nothing he had ever known before, and he has done remarkably well with the transition. He is a very determined and grateful man." Seeing her thinking it over he added, "You will have a taste of his life living with us. When next you meet, you might discuss it with authority, and tell him if you like it, and how you adjusted to the change from Longbourn and school. It is an experience that you will have in common."

"I . . . I suppose that I might." Mary bit her lip and looking up at him, whispered. "He likes me, I think."

"I think so, too."

"I agree." Elizabeth said softly.

"Are you eavesdropping, love?" Darcy looked down to smile at her.

"You can hardly call me out for eavesdropping when you are aware of my presence." She sat up and smiled at Mary. "I like him, too."

Darcy pinched her and she jumped. "We are nearly home." He said innocently and jumped when she pinched him back.

"I thought so; I noticed the fence with the broken gate a few moments ago." She laughed at his surprise. "You have your landmarks, and I have mine." She sat up and stretched. "Oh, there is Lambton! Georgiana!" She gave her a little kick and startled her sister awake. "Look!"

"Oh!" She sat up and nudged Mary. "See! There is the book shop I told you about, and the baker, and oh, look! There is the wishing well!"

"Wishing well?" Darcy looked out and back to her. "It is the village water well, I did not know of wishes being granted there."

"Well, you are a boy." She said with exasperation. "It only works for girls."

"Of course." He chuckled. "And who told you this?"

"Nanny Kate."

"Ah." His brow creased and he looked at Elizabeth. "Does Rosa need a nanny yet?"

"Well, not yet." She laughed and smiled. "She does little else than eat and sleep, with occasional performances for our entertainment."

"Georgiana's governess, Mrs. Somers, left us last year to care for her father; I understand from Mrs. Mercer that he died a few months back." He looked at Georgiana then to Elizabeth. "Perhaps she might want to return and settle in with us again? I thought that Mrs. Robbins will wish to find a new family, now that we are well and Rosa sleeps through the night." They read each other's eyes. A trusted nanny to help with Georgiana until she returned to school, then to help with their children as their family grew might be just the thing until Georgiana was ready for a companion. "Shall I contact her and see if she is available?"

"I think that would be a wonderful idea, although, we may want to keep Mrs. Robbins so that we may have time together, now that we are home. After all, she expected to be here for a year. Perhaps Mrs. Somers can continue Mary's education while she waits for Rosalie to grow up a bit more." Elizabeth laughed when his eyes lit up with the thought of them having long adventures around the estate, then turned when she heard a squeal and saw Georgiana's delight. "I think that you have no objections?"

"Oh no!" She cried. "I have missed her."

"Good then, I will write to her tomorrow." Darcy glanced at Elizabeth. "Please remind me."

Elizabeth squeezed his hand and caressed his brow. "I will, Fitzwilliam." He looked down and entwined his fingers with hers, and sighed.

"EXCELLENT!" Layton grinned. "They are home, they are well, and they invite us to visit soon." He set down the letter from Darcy and smiled at Alicia. "Pack your trunks my dear, we are to Pemberley! And they invite us to bring Margaret, as well."

"Oh how wonderful!" She read the letter and laughed. "He is ecstatic to be home."

"I cannot possibly imagine why." He said dryly. "Reading of their adventures is like following a serial in the newspaper. It is torture waiting for the next letter from anyone with news. I was glad to be of service to Audrey and Singleton, but I was torn, wishing to return to London."

"There is little we could have added, dear." She kissed the top of his head and settled on the arm of his chair. "We will take over sending information to Richard. When do your parents return?"

He consulted another newly-arrived letter. "Father expects the trial for Mrs. Younge to take place in the next week or so before court ends its quarter session. Parliament will close Friday, so he is fully available to testify whenever they get the word. She will undoubtedly be convicted. Then they will return to Matlock. Unless they look in at Ashcroft on the way, I suppose that they will . . . no, Audrey and Singleton will likely join us at Matlock." He rubbed his chin. "Perhaps we will all be meeting up at Pemberley. Hmm."

"What is it?"

"I was just thinking, Pemberley may be hosting quite a large party soon, he mentions Elizabeth's sister and her new husband will be passing through on their wedding trip. I wonder if they are well enough for it. Perhaps we should wait to visit after they return from taking Georgiana to school? Give them a chance to heal some more?"

"Oh, you know that Elizabeth and Darcy will happily send their guests off to occupy themselves if they are not feeling well, but your mother seems to think they are fine." She smiled and kissed him when he looked up. "We are hardly demanding guests. Give you a horse and a gun and you will be happy chasing birds, as will the rest of the men. We ladies have a whole world of children to discuss now. I am looking forward to it, very much."

"Well then, let us start the planning." He handed her a second sheet and smiled. "Oh, and here is their advice for travelling with a baby. Leave it to Darcy to think of everything! It never occurred to me to have the baby in our coach!"

"I MAY AS WELL PLACE A COT here and take up residence." Fitzwilliam glanced around the courtroom and muttered to his father.

"Quiet." Lord Matlock stared across at Mrs. Younge as she sniffed into her handkerchief, and shielded her face from the bright glare of the sun beaming into her eyes from the suspended looking glass. "What do you think she will get?"

"Transportation or hard labour." Fitzwilliam shrugged. "Although I vote for hanging. She could join her dear Wickham."

"Picking oakum is a worthy task." De Bourgh winked.

"Always thinking of your ships." Fitzwilliam snorted.

"hmmm." Shifting his gaze to the arguing jury, Lord Matlock watched as they muttered. Suddenly the gavel knocked out its signal.

"Has the jury reached a verdict?" Asked the judge.

"Guilty, sir."

"Very well then." Mrs. Younge was pulled to her feet and the judge addressed her. "Dorothy Younge, you are found guilty of theft, you are hereby sentenced to seven years transportation." He banged the gavel. "Next!"

Mrs. Younge sobbed, "NO!!!" A guard led her from the room and Stewart turned to smile at Lord Matlock and Fitzwilliam.

"It was not the rope, which is what she deserves. But she will not be back."

"What becomes of women over there?" Fitzwilliam asked as they made their way out.

"Well, they get assignments, perhaps as servants to landowners, or work in the factories. Lucky for her she was a sewing mistress, eh?" De Bourgh shrugged. "I was on a couple of transport ships before the privateers took it over. Hellish conditions. If she's smart, she'll offer herself to an officer or some convicted man for protection. It's a long journey; she'll keep him happy, if she stays alive. She isn't a whore now, they don't send them over, but she will be considered one by the time she arrives. Maybe the officer will marry her, or if she behaves and is not pregnant when she arrives, she'll be made available to the colonists." He laughed. "I remember being aboard a ship, and the docks were swarmed by colonists fighting over the women. Too many lonely men, not enough women in that land."

"Well they want it to be a colony, not just a prison." They made their way out of the Old Bailey and stood on the steps. "Thank you again for your help." Lord Matlock shook Stewart's hand and offered him an envelope. He held up his hand.

"No, no thank you."

"Oh, I am sorry; I should have given it to the solicitor." He looked around and Stewart cleared his throat.

"No . . . I . . . This was for Darcy." He smiled and the other men nodded. "I made too many errors, it is the least I can do."

"What are your plans now?" Fitzwilliam leaned on a wall and crossed his arms. "Mrs. Stewart brought an estate with her to the marriage."

"Yes, she did." He looked at his boots and back up to the building. "I am undecided. I have come far and done well. I just might continue here for a bit, maybe see if I can be a judge one day." He shrugged. "Be my own man, I guess."

"Really?" Lord Matlock smiled. "Proving yourself?"

"I suppose. Anyway, if I grow weary of it, or do not find enough paying customers," the men laughed, "I can settle down with my lovely bride and be a landowner, and live the life of ease you all enjoy." Fitzwilliam cleared his throat loudly. "Well, that most of you enjoy."

"I am glad that you corrected yourself." Fitzwilliam took a deep breath. "Well, who will write to Darcy?"

"I will, I have other things to tell him." Lord Matlock smiled. "And we will be at Pemberley soon."

"Well I have another case, so if you will excuse me, gentlemen?" Stewart bowed and disappeared inside.

"And it seems that my work is done as well." De Bourgh smiled. "Back to Rosings to prepare for my new sister. I am having the parsonage repaired for Michael."

"Will you come to Pemberley?" Lord Matlock asked and winked at his son. "Miss Mary, excuse me, Miss Bennet will be there."

De Bourgh coloured and looked at his boots. "Thank you, but . . . I have my own estate to run. Miss Mary . . ." He smiled and looked back up. "Perhaps I will see her when she returns to town with her sisters."

"She comes out in the spring." Fitzwilliam nudged him.

"I know." He shrugged and laughed, raising his hand. "Farewell, gentlemen."

Father and son watched him stride confidently away. "What do you think?"

"I do not see the attraction, but who am I to say anything? He did not grow up expecting an heiress, and he clearly is not one to see only surface beauty. There is something there for him. Besides, she is Elizabeth's sister, and that has its merits. He is a very eligible bachelor with a target on his back, and he does not care in the least what the society ladies have to offer."

"Would you have offered for Elizabeth if Darcy had not been about?" Lord Matlock asked. "Be honest, it is just we two."

Fitzwilliam smiled and met his eye. "I will not answer that. I respect and love my wife."

"Did I teach you all these gentlemanly principles? I did an outstanding job!" Lord Matlock clapped him on the back. "Come, home to the ladies, they are undoubtedly itching for the news."

5 AUGUST 1810
Grosvenor Street
London

Dear Darcy,
I am hopeful that not only will this letter be somewhat legible, but also that it finds you and your wonderful family very well. I also hope that you are prepared to affix your smug smile of satisfaction upon your face when you learn that yes indeed, your subtle prodding was a success. I will not be taking a tour of the continent, nor of any select portions of it. It seems that a small man with a large ego has curtailed my plans, and it further seems that I am not alone in my suffering, as only the most adventurous or foolhardy are undertaking these pleasure excursions at present. Tell me, is it to be the habit of all members of your family to take such circuitous routes to my education? Would it not be simply better to tell me from the outset that my idea is harebrained? I do not mind being directed directly! Well obviously that is

the point, I suppose. You hoped that I would dampen my enthusiasm before I had taken my plans so far. You would think that the tour guide would have said something, but I suppose they were hoping to receive a deposit, non-refundable, I imagine, prior to giving me the sad news. At least your interference, because that is what it was, saved me from that expense.

Well to make a long story short, my grand tour will still be completed, but it will not be quite so grand. I will spend the next months wandering the wilds of England, Scotland, and Ireland. I suppose that this is probably not the most preferable time of the year to be moving north, but considering where I was raised, I imagine an Irish winter may not seem so terrible. Perhaps we might swing down through the Peaks 'round Christmas, if you would care to put up three weary travellers who would undoubtedly welcome the change of companions by then? I enclose our itinerary, so please post your reply and I will hopefully find it waiting for me one day.

Thank you for looking after me, please thank your wonderful wife, I feel her stealthy hand in this. I miss you all, and it has only been a few days. Please give my regards to your sisters, and if you can bear it, a kiss to Rosalie.

Sincerely,

Charles Bingley, Esq.

"Good for you, Bingley. You figured it out." Darcy sighed with a mixture of satisfaction and relief. The day that Bingley had announced his plans for a grand tour, Darcy knew that it was an impossible enterprise. His own tour had been fraught with too many harrowing experiences to imagine his far less-protected friend taking the journey. *How many times were we held up?* He mused, and was grateful for the letters of credit he carried instead of actual funds. He told Elizabeth of one such attempted robbery by desperate men, and she made him swear to never speak of it again, so frightened she was for his well-being over an experience that had long been over. Smiling to himself he reread the letter. "You will do well on this excursion, Bingley, and yes, we will be glad to host you and the Hursts at Christmas." Chuckling, the thought of Caroline's affront with that news made him eager to find Elizabeth and hear her laughter at the scheme. *Elizabeth.* His smile fell away. She should not have to be found, she should be there in her chair by his side, laughing over the letter now, and praising its legibility. Instead he was left there alone to stew over their argument. The dull throb in his head reasserted itself and he closed his eyes, and rubbed his temples.

Darcy paused and listened to the sound of the pianoforte as Georgiana, or perhaps Mary, they both were such excellent performers, played. The sound drifted through the floor, down the stairs, and into his study. He had spent the morning quietly working, immersing himself in the progress of the crops and the needs of his tenants, as well as the innumerable other details that came with Pemberley and his prolonged absence, and trying hard to concentrate and not miss anything. It was frustrating. His memory was still not quite the same, and little details seemed to escape him, but it *was* improving, he was sure.

Earlier that morning, when Elizabeth gently suggested that he consider hiring a secretary, he had reacted poorly, fearing that she saw him as weakened, and hating hearing his own fears voiced by her. Obviously his attempts to hide his continued headaches and dizzy spells had not fooled her either. As usual when he did not think through his words, he said the wrong thing. She did not attempt to reassure him, only leaving him to fume.

Of course she was correct. His father had no secretary, but then again, he also had no wife, and when Anne Darcy died, Fitzwilliam was at school. Georgiana was a baby and then a little girl, and had no contact with him other than brief visits until she was older, so George Darcy shut himself away in his study or rode out onto the estate, and worked to fill the time. Fitzwilliam Darcy had not only a vivacious wife whose company he craved, but also a daughter he did not relegate permanently to the nursery, and two nearly grown sisters who needed a male's influence. He also had just experienced the shadow of death, and vowed to not waste a moment of his life. Looking over the stack of correspondence that awaited him, and then out the window to see Elizabeth walking in the garden alone, he nodded and knew where he wished to be. He drew forward his journal to write to his wife.

10 August 1810
How is it that Elizabeth knows me better than I know myself? How can she know what is best for me, but present it in such a way that I think I have made the decision when deep down, we both know that she is the one pulling the strings? Well, my love, I kneel and offer my sword. You are correct, after nearly two weeks back at home, I am ready to concede to your observations. I need help, and I have no desire to spend my life in my study. I cannot, will not, give up control, nor will I give up my personal responses to most correspondence, or my personal contact with my tenants, nor will I give up the time that I spend with my love alone in this study, working quietly together on our common duties, I treasure that far too much. But, what I will do is accept the addition of a secretary to my life, a trusted man beyond my steward to ease the burdens of this estate and my business affairs so that I may enjoy the sweet burden of my family. I trust that my dear wife will in turn relax the determined grip she has formed over our homes since she assumed her duties. She has proven herself capable in every capacity, she has undoubtedly earned the respect and love of our staff, and now that she is indeed established firmly as a worthy owner of the title Mistress of Pemberley, I wish for her to allow our people to do their duties. We have our new butler in Bernard, we have our new House Steward in Matthews, and we have Mrs. Reynolds and Nichols. You, my love, I hope, will follow your own advice to me.

Smiling, he set down his pen and read over his contrition and pointed dig at Elizabeth, and imagined her face as she read changing from satisfaction to resignation. "We are the same, love. Stubborn as mules." Darcy wrote a note to his uncle, asking for a recommendation for a secretary, then sealing it, stood from his desk and walked outside to join Elizabeth, who was now speaking with the head gardener. "What plans have you devised to torture Mr. Green, Mrs. Darcy?" He asked as he approached.

"Sir!" The elder man with the ruddy complexion and permanently muddy knees bowed. "Mrs. Darcy was asking the origins of the rose garden. I recall it was Mrs. Darcy, Mrs. Colin Darcy, your grandmother, who had it planted here."

"I believe that you are correct." He smiled and turned to Elizabeth. "Your rose bush came from a cutting of her favourite bloom. Mr. Green and his father before him have been propagating that variety for as long as they have been at Pemberley."

"Aye, sir! And I was just telling the mistress, I have a new one in the hothouse, I think it will be a great success, would you like to see it now?" He looked eagerly between the two.

Elizabeth laughed and Darcy smiled at her. "I would love to see it. Why have you not planted it in the garden?"

"Madam, this is your garden, I was waiting for you to come home and choose the spot. If you will just wait here, I will fetch it out and you can show me where it belongs." He stopped and turned. "It will be needing a name, now. It's an orphan."

He strode quickly away and Darcy took Elizabeth's hand, and kissed it. "An orphan rose, something rather poetic in that."

"Hmm." Elizabeth gave no resistance when he tugged and drew her into his arms. "We will have to see it to know its identity."

"I already know." He whispered and kissed her ear. "And as master, I will decide."

"I thought the garden was mine!" She looked up to see his eyes twinkling at her. "What are you doing out here, you said that you have a mountain of work."

"I do."

"And?"

"I would rather be with you. If you will not work with me, then I will come to you." He rested his chin in her hair and hugged her. "Do you object?"

"No. But you know that I would be glad to return with you and help if you wish." She smiled, hearing his whispered apology for his behaviour, and responded with a kiss to his nose. Darcy laughed and then furrowed his brow when her expression changed.

"Lizzy? Is there a reason beyond our disagreement that you were out here alone?" Waiting, he said softly, "I may not be accomplished at reading others' emotions, but I think that I am an expert at reading yours."

Elizabeth sighed and leaned into his embrace. "Standing here in our garden, it is as if everything that happened in London was nothing more than a terrible dream."

"What is wrong?" He leaned down to look at her eyes as they welled up. "We are safe, dearest. We are well. Well, we are improving. What brought on your sadness? Surely it is something besides my bullheadedness?"

"I do not know." She sniffed and shrugged, then turned in his arms. "Thank you for coming outside to be with me."

Darcy hugged her to him and rubbing her back, thought of how to drag her worries from her. "We have much to do. We have been here nearly two weeks and have not gone riding, we have not visited your tree, we have not gone swimming . . ."

"Swimming! Oh no, Fitzwilliam Darcy, you will not dunk me in that cold water again!" Elizabeth declared and wiped her eyes when he nodded vehemently and smiled. "You make it sound as if we have done nothing but sit and stare at each other! We both had much to do after being away, there is the harvest approaching for you, and so much with the tenants and the house, and soon we will have guests coming. And then of course there is Rosalie."

"All the more reason to enjoy this time today." He kissed her gently. "I do not want you to be overtired. You need to go slowly."

"What of our sisters?" Elizabeth asked worriedly. "I have been trying to give them as much attention as I can, Mary seems to be happy learning from me as I work, but Georgiana seems unhappy with my occupation."

"They are not infants to be entertained, they can observe you and learn, or they can enjoy our home. Soon our nanny will arrive, and that should help, we are doing the best that we can." Darcy kissed her wrinkled brow. "You and I need our own occupation, alone." He looked off into the distance and kissing her throat, pointed to the cliff where they had spent many hours looking out over the estate. "You need to go up there."

"Do I?" She leaned back against his chest. "And what will be my pursuit?" Darcy said nothing and she looked up to him. "Will?"

"Here you are!" Mr. Green appeared, a boy with a wheelbarrow was behind him, and another carried a spade. "What do you think?" He asked eagerly.

"Oh, it is . . . lavender!" Elizabeth sighed. "I have never seen such a shade!"

Puffing his chest, he grinned. "I have been fiddling with this for years. Give it a sniff, madam!"

Laughing, she leaned to smell the rose in the wheelbarrow and smiled. "Heavenly."

"Sir?"

Darcy leaned and smelled it. "It reminds me of the loveliest woman I know. It shall be named Elizabeth."

"Fitzwilliam!"

"Do you agree; is that fitting enough for your triumph, Mr. Green?"

"Aye sir!" He looked at the garden, "And where shall we place Mrs. Darcy?"

"Wherever she will be admired the most." He ordered, and smiled to see Elizabeth blushing and staring at her feet. "Now then, my dear, shall we visit Rosalie's namesake?" He held out his arm and they walked out along the path to their glen. "You are still blushing." Darcy laughed.

"What has come over you?" She continued to look at her feet as they walked.

He studied her. "A very wise woman once commanded me to think of the past only as it gives me pleasure." Darcy stopped and lifting her chin, caressed his thumb over her lips. "What is it?"

Elizabeth looked up at him and he bent to kiss her. "I walked around the house before I went outside, and found myself in the library. I was sitting in the chair that your father favoured and . . . I noticed the little collection of mementoes that were nearby." She drew a breath and continued. "I found a miniature portrait of Wickham when I was looking at some drawings Georgiana had made when she was younger." Darcy stopped and saw her swallow hard then start to sob. He pulled her into his arms and held her tightly. "It is so accurate! It was like he was looking at me from beyond the grave, and telling me that we are not safe, not even here, not even with him buried! He has caused so much damage to us."

"Oh love." Darcy sighed and kissed her hair. "I forgot all about that . . . thing. I should have destroyed it years ago. Father had that made when my portrait was painted, a concession I suppose for the jealousy that Wickham expressed to see my anointment as the heir when I came of age. Father was not a foolish man, but when it came to being manipulated, he was so ripe for Wickham." He hugged her. "I am so very sorry, love. Do not tell me that you are going to allow such fancies to rule you? You know he is gone and cannot touch our family ever again? Does not your father call you his most sensible daughter?"

"It was such a shock, especially when we had just argued because of what he caused. It was as if he was laughing at us." Her voice cracked.

"Lizzy." He whispered and hugged her again. "We argued because I am frustrated and want to be myself faster than my body will let me, and you worry and are determined to make me slow down and accept help, which is something that I want you to do as well." Drawing away, he kissed her again. "Now, where is it?"

"In my bodice." She said against his chest.

"Well, that will not do. I will not have Wickham anywhere near the flesh that belongs only to me." He kissed her and let go. "Give it over." He held out his hand. She removed it and he glanced at the face, and recalled his last sight of the man after his death. Grimly, he clutched it in his fist. "Come."

"Where are we going?" She took his hand and they headed off across the lawn. "You are not going to throw it in the lake are you?"

"No!" He stared at her. "Pollute our lake with his image? I think not!" They strode rapidly along, and eventually the stables came into view. "I think that Richard should have the honour of destroying him."

"Richard?" She laughed and wiped her eyes. "The horse?"

"The gelding." He grinned and kissed her hand. "Shall we run?"

"Run?" Elizabeth cried out when his strides grew and he pulled her along. "Will!!"

"Can't keep up, lovie?" He stopped and scooped her up in his arms and smiled down at her. "You, my dear, are slowing me down."

"You, sir, are clearly still addled!" She declared and kissed him. "And I love it."

"I do, too." He smiled and dropped her down to her feet. "Nothing, and I mean nothing, is going to get in the way of our love again." They reached the stables and walked up to Richard's stall. "Hello, Cousin." He reached out and rubbed his forelock. "We will give you a good ride tomorrow."

"Where will we be going?" Elizabeth asked and watched as Wickham's image was positioned in the stall.

"Does it matter?" He looked up at her and raised his brows.

"No. It does not at all."

He stood and gently nudged Richard forward, and the crunch of the porcelain beneath his enormous hoof was satisfying in its absolute finality. Moving back, they looked upon the powder that remained. "Dust to dust." Darcy murmured.

"Will?"

"Hmm?" He kicked the residue into the dirt and looked up. "Yes, love?"

"Did you notice that none of the staff is here?"

"I imagine they are eating." He took out his pocket watch and glanced at the time, then gasped to see her slowly raising her skirt up, exposing her ankles. "Lizzy!" He quickly stepped out of the stall. She just giggled and raised it up to her calves. "Stop that!" Up it went to her thighs and then to her waist. "*Elizabeth . . .*" Glancing around, he wrapped his arm around her waist and lifted her up onto the ladder to the hayloft, and smacked her bottom. "Up! Now!" Happily he waited below, watching her hips sway as she climbed, and groaning as she lifted her skirts above her bare bottom when she reached the top. She turned around to smile at him.

"Are you coming?"

"*Get up there, woman.*" He growled and started after her. With a squeal she climbed over the hay towards a corner, but not fast enough. Darcy snagged her ankle and pulled her back on her belly. "You cannot escape me."

"When did I ever say that I wanted to?" She laughed when he flipped her over; her skirts had slid up, exposing all of her for him. Elizabeth giggled when he leaned down to rub his face over her belly and breathed in her scent.

"My lavender rose." He said happily, then grinning, he deftly opened his breeches and kneeled over her, kissing her lips. "Are you a temptress or a wanton?"

"Can I not be both?" Elizabeth asked as she fondled his most admirable pride, delighting in his groan as she weighed his stones, and squealed again when he took an ankle in each hand and lifted her legs high and wide. "What are you going to do?"

"Now that is the most redundant question you have ever asked me." His smile relaxed and he bent down to kiss her lovingly. Elizabeth held his face in her hands and their mouths and tongues slid and embraced, leaving them both breathless and wanting. Shakily, Darcy drew back and stroked his hands from her waist to her ankles, and seeing her impatient desire, laughed. Looking down with his tongue firmly caught between his teeth, he manoeuvred his hips, took aim, and with great precision, speared her with one mighty thrust. "Oh Lord, YES!" He roared and resting her legs on his shoulders, proceeded to satisfy his ravenous need. "Harder?" He rasped.

"Deeper. Faster." Elizabeth demanded and stared up at his jet black eyes, feeling his warm pants waft over her face as he rutted determinedly. Very, very quickly, his intense rush of pleasure began. There was no way to stop it and Elizabeth thrilled with the sight of his eyes squeezing shut, his face transforming, his body shuddering, and hearing him cry out and gasp desperately as he shot into her repeatedly. At last he calmed and let her legs down, collapsing beside her in the straw with his arm lying limply across his brow.

"*That* . . . was . . . bloody fantastic."

Elizabeth giggled and rolled to her side to kiss him. "You did seem to voice your enjoyment."

"Did I?" He laughed and rolled to face her. "Did you enjoy it? I was too fast, you did not find satisfaction."

"Of course I did." Elizabeth caressed him and they kissed. "You were loving me."

"I was ravishing you." Darcy sighed and drew her to him. "We have been so careful to be quiet, I . . . I just could not hold back. I will love you properly tonight."

"I know." When he did not say anything she looked up to see his eyes slowly blinking shut. She caressed his hair and smiled when he settled his cheek on her head. "You needed to prove yourself, Will. I know. But you need to rest even more." Below her, she heard the sound of the staff returning to their duties. She blushed and carefully moved to rebutton his breeches, and smoothed down her skirt before cuddling back to his chest. Darcy murmured something and wrapped his arms around her. She smiled and kissed his chin. "I wonder how long we will be up here."

"WHAT DO YOU THINK?" Nichols picked up his fork. "He's not quite right."

"He is just fine." Mrs. Reynolds said tersely. "Mr. Darcy is just the same as always and I don't want to hear another word about it." She glared around the table. "And Mrs. Darcy is as well."

"Mrs. Darcy is worried about him. Do you see how they look at each other?" Bernard said quietly.

"How, like moon calves?" Adams chuckled. "They are fine, not perfect, but fine." He smiled at Millie and Mrs. Robbins. "We have been with them throughout. You are new to this. Believe me, if you wanted to see a couple of people who were unwell, you should have seen them seven weeks ago."

"The man cannot ride." Nichols said. "Not like he could before."

"Let's see your head crack open and we'll see how well you can ride! Come now, the master nearly died!"

"Do not speak of it!" Mrs. Reynolds declared. "He is fine! That no good Wickham, I always thought Mr. Darcy senior was wrong to let him cosy up. He should have been paying attention to his own, that is what I thought!"

"Some thought that he *was* his own." Mr. Green said from behind his teacup. He saw the glares and curiosity and shrugged. "I never believed it, but you know how tongues wag. Jealous ones I always thought, why would one servant's child get the master's favour when the rest did not?"

"Hmmm. I hadn't thought of that." Nichols rubbed his chin. "I wonder if Mr. Darcy would do such a thing?"

"He was newly married then, that's why I never believed it." Mr. Green noted. "I didn't think I would ever see a man more besotted until I saw our master with his Mrs. Darcy." The staff all laughed and agreed.

"I knew Wickham's father, obviously, I worked under him. He was a very good man. His mother was the problem, always looking for more. More money, more gifts from the master . . . I heard her one time, *Go on Georgy, go smile at Mr. Darcy.*" Nichols shook his head. "She's the one that made him jealous of our master. The boy didn't know when to say thank you and leave well alone."

"And he swung for it." Adams said with satisfaction. "I went down to see it. Me, Foster, all the boys, we went down to the prison. We didn't stay to see him cut down, we needed to get back home before the master returned, but . . . we wanted to be there."

"Well it was likely better than being in the house. Poor Mrs. Darcy was beside herself all that time waiting for the master to come home." Millie whispered. "She just held onto the baby, didn't she, Mrs. Robbins?"

"Yes, I had to pry her away. Then she went walking and oh, that magistrate came home with the men. I think that Mrs. Darcy was ready to throttle the lot of them and throw them out the door, she was so desperate to get to her husband." Adams and Millie exchanged glances and did not add to the conversation.

Matthews entered the servant's dining room and took a seat. "So is this a regular session?"

"Nightly for the senior staff, except Mrs. Robbins when she has the duty." Adams nodded to her and winked. "But her work is much lighter now; she gets to sleep as well."

"Not for long, she's teething. Her papa will be sharing his laudanum with her." Mrs. Robbins sighed. "And we'll see how long Mrs. Darcy continues her duty once she starts getting bitten."

"My mother used whiskey." Mr. Green recalled.

"I hope Mrs. Darcy stops feeding her soon, it is time for an heir to come along." Mrs. Reynolds fretted.

"He'll come in his own good time." Adams chuckled.

"I was upstairs." Matthews began and all eyes turned to him. "Um, Miss Darcy . . . Is she given to wandering the halls at night?"

"What?"

"I was just looking over the nursery for the guests, and when I came down to the family wing, I spotted Miss Darcy outside the master's chambers. Lingering a bit." He shrugged and looked at his hands. "It's none of my business."

"She did that at Darcy House, too." Millie said softly.

"I wouldn't think too much on it." Mrs. Robbins stood and smoothed her gown. "She was distraught when they were hurt, and as you point out, Mr. Nichols; they are not quite healed yet. It just shows how fortunate we are to have such good employers. Everyone worries over them."

"COME ALONG!" Darcy called.

"Slow down!" Elizabeth cried and gave Emma a nudge. "I have not been on a horse for nearly a year!"

"Forgive me, love. My enthusiasm overtook my good sense." He reined in Richard and waited for her to catch up. "You are doing remarkably well. What a shame."

"A shame?" She laughed. "And why is that?"

"If you had forgotten everything, then I would have to teach you all over again." Darcy leaned over to bestow a kiss. "Do you remember sharing Richard?"

"I do." They kissed again then laughed as the horses moved them apart. Elizabeth squealed when she lost her hold, but Darcy's steady hand caught her in time. "Perhaps one horse would have been better."

"Perhaps. Are you comfortable?"

"I will not be in the morning, I am certain." They laughed and started walking again. "So we have no destination?"

"No." He smiled and looked around. "We have not had a chance to just be ourselves for so long. Let us explore and see what has changed. There is no hurry to return, is there?"

"No, none at all." She watched him and saw that he was fine; the gentle pace did not affect him like galloping would. "Although it should probably be before sunset so the household does not panic again." Her laughter bubbled up and he grinned. "Who knew how dedicated the stable staff is!"

"I suppose that we could have come down." Darcy smiled and looked at her fondly. "But it was so much nicer hiding up there with you."

"I cannot believe you talked me into . . . with them just below!"

"It was rather thrilling." He confessed. "Almost being caught." Elizabeth gasped. "I know, I know, I would have been mortified, but . . . It is your fault!"

"Mine!"

"Yes! How do you expect a man to behave, trapped in a hayloft, starving for food and comfort?"

"Comfort, you found comfort, *that* is certain!"

"And you did not?"

"My jaw was tired." She said with a poorly hidden smile.

"I ached for more." Darcy's hand reached out and took hers. "You cannot possibly know what that kiss means to me."

"Oh, I have an idea." Darcy blushed and kissed her hand. "I have an idea for more kisses."

"More?" He sighed. "Where?"

"All over you." Seeing a slow smile appear, she leaned over and whispered. "But I will not tell you when."

"Anticipation." He sat up straight and confidently looked out over their land. "I cannot wait."

Chapter 24

"I have to tell you Georgiana, your playing is beautiful. I have enjoyed listening to you this morning while I toiled away with plans for our guests." Elizabeth smiled. "I am quite envious!"

"Oh Elizabeth, stop." She blushed. "You play very well."

"You are being far too kind. I just do not seem to have enough hours in the day to practice anymore, perhaps this winter when there is much less to accomplish. At least I can sing wherever I am, and your brother may hear me and find some modicum of pleasure." She laughed and reached for her account book for the household. "I may just sing as I check these figures, which is fortunate, for the funds spent still astound me, and I am much more likely to be shocked into silence at the sight of them."

"Will you teach me as you have been teaching Mary? How to be a mistress?" She said quietly.

Elizabeth stopped her work and looked up. "Of course. Surely you are not wishing to be burdened with this duty yet? Mary will be out in the spring, and that means she is ready to be a wife. I am simply preparing her for what will come with some man. With the connection to our family, she will be desired, despite her small dowry."

"But will not Brother give her more?"

"He will present her a gift upon her wedding, just as he did for Jane." She smiled and squeezed Georgiana's hand. "Your brother made a great sacrifice in marrying me. I brought little into this marriage, and I am young. If we have many children, he will not have my dowry to help provide for the girls. As much as we would love to settle large sums on my sisters, we have to be prepared for our own children should they come and hopefully survive to marry one day."

"Oh Elizabeth! I cannot imagine you losing any children!" Georgiana cried.

"I have no desire to imagine it either, but it does happen, as you know." Seeing her downcast eyes, she tilted her head. "Now, why are we discussing such a sad subject? What brings you here? Or do you just miss me?"

"Of course I miss you. You are always with Fitzwilliam or Rosalie, and now Mary . . . And Jane is coming. And everyone else." She looked at her hands. "I thought it would be different."

Turning in her chair, Elizabeth gave her full attention to her. "You thought that we would be alone more often? You wish that we were not hosting our family?"

"That is petty, is it not?" She looked up and bit her lip.

"To be honest with you, neither your brother nor I are really ready to host people for an extended period, but this is family. Your cousins have been very worried about us. They will only be here a short time before leaving for Matlock. It will not be so bad."

"But then there is harvest."

"And the Harvest Home." Elizabeth smiled. "You enjoy that."

"But then I will leave and Mary will get to return with you." She looked back down at her hands.

Immediately, Elizabeth understood. "It will be a new school. Does that worry you? You do understand why we would not send you back to Mrs. Banks?"

"Yes." She said quietly. "I will have to make new friends all over again."

"You know how to now. And you will have Kitty there with you, so you already will have a friend."

Georgiana said nothing then spoke to her shoes. "Mary yelled at me today."

"Did she? That does not sound like her. What did you do to draw my sister from her shell?"

"She . . . she compared me to Lydia, doing things to draw attention. I . . . I do not do that do I?" She looked up worriedly. "She is so loud and pouty, I . . . I am really very shy. But Mary said that I am purposely taking forever to finish the reading assignment that Fitzwilliam gave me because then I have to discuss what I have done and spend time with him. And that I follow you around asking questions all the time to distract you from everyone else."

"Is that what you are doing?" She studied her. "Mary is very observant; I have a feeling that she is not too far off the mark." Elizabeth bit her lip and decided on her course. "I do not think that you are like Lydia. She draws attention to herself because she has heard nothing but praise since the moment she entered the world, and craves it constantly. Nobody ever said no to her until very recently, and I am afraid that it will lead her to a very unhappy future one day. No amount of schooling will likely touch what has become of her. You, I think, are frightened, and have been since your papa died."

Tears welled up in her eyes and she fell into Elizabeth's arms. "What will I do if I lose you?"

"We are well, Georgiana, we are!" She hugged her. "And even if we are very busy with all of our responsibilities, you are never far from our minds and we are always ready to talk to you." Drawing back she wiped her cheek. "Your papa never said no to you, did he?"

"No."

"And Fitzwilliam tried to continue that, but found that he was incapable of being a lax parent." She laughed when Georgiana sighed. "And your aunt and uncle were very strong examples for you, and then I came along. And I am wicked."

"No you are not!" She sat up and stared at her.

"I just work in collusion with your evil brother?" She suggested.

"He is not evil, either."

"And your aunt and uncle, and the rest of the family?"

"I suppose that they are just looking out for me, and want me to be a girl that Papa would be proud of."

"A *woman* your papa would be proud to give over to a very special gentleman one day." Elizabeth smiled.

"Fitzwilliam is not well yet, is he?"

Sighing, Elizabeth took her hand. "No, but he is a little better every day. Is that frightening for you?" Georgiana nodded. "Well it is frightening for all of us, but I have faith that all will be fine."

"Are you better?"

"Yes, as long as I do not try to lift anything or hold Rosalie very long." She watched her carefully, and saw that Georgiana was unconvinced. "What else frightens you?"

"When you fight."

"Hmm, well our fights are not that terrible, are they? No china gets thrown! Oh, Georgiana, I know that you want endless harmony and bliss, but even two people who deeply love each other can get on each other's last nerve from time to time, especially when we are frightened about something." She smiled when Georgiana's eyes opened wide. "Now, back to you and this call for attention that your shy self insists on displaying. What are we going to do about it?"

"Stop it, I suppose." She sighed. "I guess it is what you said once, I am not a woman, but I am not a little girl anymore."

"So the woman in you needs to recognize when you are behaving like a little girl." Elizabeth studied her and nodded. "I think that you need an occupation beyond your music and your brother's little reading assignments. We will talk to him and discuss how you can fill your time really studying and not worrying so much about us. Mrs. Somers will be back with you soon and she can keep you working."

"Oh."

"Not quite what you had in mind?" Elizabeth laughed.

"No, but I suppose it is the right thing to do." She stared back down at her hands.

"I suppose." Elizabeth stood and gave her a hug, and wondered what else they could do. She would have to talk it over with Darcy. With all their worries and responsibilities, it seemed that Georgiana had been feeling very neglected. Kissing her cheek, she whispered. "See? You are not like Lydia at all; she never would have asked these questions or worried about anyone else."

Georgiana left Elizabeth's study and walked slowly down the hallway, lost in thought. "They fight when they are frightened." She glanced up the stairs. Darcy had gone up earlier and it was worrying. She feared that he was about to suffer another terrible headache and had felt it coming on. Despite Elizabeth's assurances, she felt afraid that he was very ill. He was always so hard to understand, so serious and quiet, except when Elizabeth was near. His slight smile could mean almost anything, or that he was hiding almost anything.

She found herself by the door to Darcy's study, and paused, looking at it. Rarely did she enter, and never uninvited. But not long ago, this had been her father's study, and since Darcy had changed virtually nothing since his death, it was where she felt closest to him.

She stepped inside and closed the door. Walking around the desk, her hand ran over the polished wood, then looking back to the doorway, she settled into her father's chair, and thought of how much she missed him. With her eyes closed, she rested her hands on the leather arms and in her mind begged him to look after Darcy and Elizabeth. Many times since the attack she had awakened, and scared, crept into the hallway to stand outside of their chamber door, listening to hear some sign of life to assure her that they were well. If it was very late, it might be her brother's soft snoring. If it was early, it might be the sound of their muffled voices; or the creak of the bed as they moved, just something to confirm that they were breathing. Since returning to Pemberley though, she had lingered longer and longer, wondering what they talked about and why they laughed so much and so differently than when they were with other people, and why they did not do *something* about their bed, and if the moans she sometimes heard were caused by pain from their wounds, or something else . . .

She opened her eyes to see the miniature portraits on her brother's desk, and wondered what he thought about when he looked upon them. Then she wondered about the journals they kept. How many times had she found him before he married, staring at the pages? And how many times had she seen them both writing in them, then sharing them with each other, sometimes with smiles, and sometimes with tears.

Urgently needing to know if he was well, she left the room and mounting the stairs, found herself outside of the master's bedchamber. Not hearing anything, she moved up the hallway to listen at the sitting room door. "Perhaps he is ill." She thought worriedly and opened the door, stepping inside. It was empty, as were the bedchambers. She was about to leave when she spied their journals sitting on the writing desk. The temptation to understand this part of their marriage was irresistible. She walked forward and picked one up. It naturally fell open to a page, and as she began to read, she did not notice the knot of ribbon that fell to the floor.

21 May 1809

Hearing voices in the hallway and a door closing, Georgiana startled and straightened, listening . . . then bent her head and started to read again.

21 May 1809

I can barely manage to put into words the joy I feel this night, no this morning! And when the sun rises at last, and if I miraculously calm enough to find sleep, I will awaken knowing that I am no longer alone. My Elizabeth, my love, the subject of so many dreams and desires said yes to me. She will be my own for the rest of our lives. I know that many things, no doubt momentous, happened at the ball, perhaps things that will affect our lives for months, even years to come. But all that I know, all that I care to remember, are those precious moments alone in my uncle's garden, where my dearest, loveliest, Elizabeth fell into my arms and confessed that her heart was mine for eternity. She nearly took back her yes; she offered me a chance to change my mind, to escape if I had spoken in haste. Foolish, wonderful, woman! Three times she offered me release, and she questioned me, demanding why I would want her, and not accepting anything less than the absolute truth. Twice, I was required to propose. She cares not of what I have, but only wants me! Oh what a glorious woman! We will not have a marriage of quiet complacency. We will knock heads and make love. We will enjoy every moment and I know already that we will fight for each other in times of trouble. I know it, I feel it, we will have a marriage like no other I have ever known, and it all began with her saying yes to me. I cannot wait to begin, my Elizabeth, the taste of your lips is fresh on my tongue, the scent of your perfume has infused my soul, and the feel of your body under my hands makes me feel weak and powerful all at once, and I crave more. So much more. Thank you, my love.

"ohhhh." Georgiana's heart was racing, and eagerly, she turned the page to read his next entry when she heard the door opening. Panicking, she closed the book and dashed into Darcy's bedchamber, but stayed behind the door to see who was there.

"Is everything ready?" Darcy asked and closed the door.

"Mmmmm. I think so, as ready as it will be until we find out what was missed." Elizabeth laughed and he chuckled. "Did you enjoy your talk with Rosalie?"

"You know full well that I did." He sighed happily. "She had many important facts to impart."

"Really? Concerning her gentleman callers?" Elizabeth laughed.

Darcy groaned. "Do not even jest about that, love. I am not looking forward to that time at all."

"I was already certain of that, but you have many years to practice your protective glower." Georgiana giggled into her hand and heard them kiss. "I cannot wait to see Jane."

"I hope that Lucas handles it well. Darcy House overwhelmed him, but I suppose that Jane has him thoroughly prepared." There was the sound of a body settling into one of the chairs near the fireplace. Georgiana peeked through the keyhole and spotted Elizabeth's slippers standing between Darcy's boots. "Come here."

There was a swish and a cry. "Unhand me you ruffian!"

Darcy's low laugh filled the air. "mmmm, do you wish for a ruffian? Would you like a handsome highwayman to accost your carriage, fair maiden?"

"Only if my far more handsome husband came riding to my rescue on his jet black steed." She said softly. The room quieted and the soft sound of kisses and sighs filled the air. "Oh Will."

"Your scent is driving me mad, love." There was the rustle of a gown. "Your legs are so soft; your thighs beg to be tasted." Georgiana pressed her hands to her mouth. Darcy's breathing became unsteady and Elizabeth moaned. "So warm."

"Willlll, oh more."

"Another?" He whispered.

"Rub . . . Oh yes, slower."

"I will be sticky with you." He sighed. "I want to make you wet with me." He drew a sharp breath and moaned, "OH, Lizzy, what ohhhh, love, please, yes, oh yes, kiss me there!"

Georgiana cracked open the door and saw that Elizabeth was in Darcy's lap, his hand was under her skirt, and she was kissing his throat. Mesmerized, she stayed glued to the spot and watched. Elizabeth drew away and Darcy's dark eyes met hers. They wrapped their arms around each other and kissed deeply and slowly. "I want you so badly." Darcy murmured against her ear, and kissed down her throat while his hands caressed her body. "Do we have time?"

"How long could it take?" Elizabeth asked breathlessly.

Darcy laughed, "Oh love, at this point I would say seconds."

A knock at the sitting room door startled them and he cursed softly. "Damn."

Elizabeth kissed him and called out. "Yes?"

"The carriage has been spotted on the ridge, madam."

"Thank you, we will be right there." She smiled and looked back at Darcy. "Too late."

"Oh, no, you cannot leave me this way." He took her hand and placed it over his arousal. "It is cruel! We have time. Come . . . just let me . . ." He reached to lift her skirts.

She laughed and gave him a firm squeeze, then slipping off to stand, held his face to kiss him lovingly. "Later, love."

"Elizabeth!" He whined and took her hands to place them back where they were, "Please! We have time; we have at least twenty minutes . . .please?"

"Guests, Mr. Darcy."

"I do not care."

"My goodness, are you going to pout? Shall I compare you to Lydia?" Elizabeth held out her hands and helped him to his feet.

Darcy immediately wrapped her up in his arms, kissing that spot below her ear. "I do not think I am as bad as that."

Elizabeth sighed and melted against him. "No, but Georgiana thinks that she is. I just had a talk with her about her fears, I am afraid that she feels that we have forgotten her." Georgiana leaned closer to listen.

Darcy spoke into Elizabeth's hair and moulded her against his body while his hands rubbed continually over her back. "We are hardly ignoring her. She certainly knows how much work I have always had to do."

"We are both busy." She tried to gently push him away, but he resisted. "She has not been here since we had Rosa, and running Pemberley is not the same commitment as Darcy House for me, especially with family coming and having to care for the baby, the tenants' worries, catching up with all that has been done, and teaching Mary . . ."

"And looking after me." He kissed her softly, unwilling to be distracted from his desire. "How often have we been able to be alone? In the daylight, I mean."

She touched his cheek and looked into his passionate eyes. "Not nearly enough, Will. Things will settle down, soon. Our family just wants to check on us for a short while then we can get to the business of truly recovering." Elizabeth kissed him and caressed his shoulders. "You know that you are always the most important person for me."

"As you are for me, love."

"I know. I need you, too." She sighed as he resumed nibbling over her throat, and tried again to refocus his attention. "What do we do with Georgiana? If she turns into Lydia, I will feel like such a failure. I cannot imagine what Aunt Helen would say. What would your father think?"

"Father would be devastated, as would I." Darcy murmured and at last seemed to give up his quest. "Why do you think she is so insistent that we be with her all of the time? Why does she demand attention this way? She seems to be getting younger, not maturing."

"She said that she has been frightened since we were injured, we are her parents, Fitzwilliam. She has been orphaned once already."

"I do not know what to do. Perhaps Uncle Henry can give me some advice when they arrive. We are doing our best, but this so hard. A mistake on our part could change her irrevocably." She hugged him and Darcy laid his cheek on her hair, and looked out of the window.

Georgiana listened with her hand at her mouth. *I am being like Lydia. She is horrible! Am I horrible?*

"It seems that my conversation has thoroughly discouraged you."

"We did not have enough time anyway." He sighed and kissed her forehead. "I do not want to rush." He pressed his lips to her ear. "But I am still so ready for you."

"I would love to have you." They rested in each other's arms and swayed.

Darcy finally drew a calming breath and opened his eyes. His brow creased. "Elizabeth?"

"Hmm?"

"What is that on the floor?" He let go and bent down, picking up the lover's knot. "Did you drop this when you read the journal this morning?"

Stepping closer, she touched it. "No, I put it in its usual spot. I suppose you have not touched it?"

"No." He picked up the journal and opening it to the last entry, put the ribbon where it belonged. He flicked through the pages and noticed that one was creased. Reading the entry, his eyes softened. Elizabeth leaned against his arm and read it.

"Oh, Will." She smiled up at him.

"You had not seen that one?" He said quietly and kissed her.

"No." She kissed his cheek. "But I did see what you wrote on my entry that day."

They kissed again, then looked back at the ribbon. "Who has been reading our journals? The staff? How many of them can read?"

"Adams and Millie can, but they would never touch them. The other maids certainly cannot read, or at least not well. Perhaps they were dusting and it fell out, or they were curious?" Darcy looked at her with raised brows and she nodded, knowing that was unlikely. "Who then?"

He looked at the journal and spoke angrily, "I am not sure, but when I find out, that person will be dismissed. I will not tolerate *anyone* invading our privacy. Reading our journals is as despicable as Wickham's invasion of our home and the injury just as deep. It is as if someone was watching us love each other."

Georgiana gasped and ran from the room. In the hallway, she leaned against the wall and hugged herself. Wiping the tears that had fallen down her cheeks, she started moving towards the stairs. "He would never forgive me if he knew!"

"Georgiana!" Elizabeth called and noted how her sister jumped. "Were you looking for us? We were just going to meet Jane and Robert." She turned to see Darcy joining her.

"Oh, oh yes, I thought that I would come to find you, but did not think you were there, I did not hear anything." She spoke quickly and smiled a little.

"Are you well? Have you been crying?"

"Oh . . . I am fine." She whispered.

"Are you sure, dear?" Darcy walked over and wrapped her up in a hug. "Elizabeth told me that you had a talk. We are going to be fine. Please do not worry about us. We feel better and better every day." He smiled a little and let go. "Come, we have to find Mary and greet our guests. You will have to play for them! I am not sure if they really had a chance to listen at the wedding breakfast."

"Yes, Brother. I will be happy to." She swallowed and looked up to him and to Elizabeth. "I want you to be proud of me."

"We already are, Georgiana." Elizabeth smiled and took her hand. "And we both look forward to you becoming a wonderful woman."

"I will. I promise." She said fervently and hugged her. "I am so sorry!"

"For what?" Elizabeth asked and looked to see Darcy's concern. He put his hand on Georgiana's shoulder.

"For . . . for . . . being so insensitive to your . . . responsibilities."

"Oh." They looked at each other and smiled. "Perhaps we are too caught up in them." Elizabeth hugged her. "We are going to try to give up more of them to our staff and make more time for you."

"No." Georgiana let go and wiped her eyes. "I am being foolish and selfish." She stood up straight and tried to smile. "You are going to be well, and I am going to stop being so silly and worry about my future instead."

"Well!" Darcy smiled and looked at Elizabeth. "That was quite a talk you two had!"

Studying her for a few moments, Elizabeth turned to Darcy. "Fitzwilliam, you go ahead, I want to speak to Georgiana."

Darcy smiled and nodded, sure that she would get to the bottom of the situation. "Certainly, I will chase Mary from the library."

Elizabeth watched him go then opened the sitting room door and looked at her sister expectantly. Georgiana walked past her and jumped when the door closed. She watched her nervously. Elizabeth picked up the journal; and turned to frown at her sister. "Were you reading this?" The guilt was written clearly on her face. "How could you invade your brother's privacy? Our privacy?"

"I . . . I did not mean to." She whispered. "Please do not tell him!"

"Oh, yes, I will." Elizabeth stated flatly. "He will be very angry, and I will support whatever punishment he determines is suitable."

"Yes, Elizabeth." She cast her eyes down. "I am sorry. I was just checking to see if Fitzwilliam was well and . . . It was an impulse. I am sorry. I forgot how many responsibilities you both have. I hate knowing that he thinks that I am not maturing."

"Maturing? How can you speak of . . . You were listening to us!" Elizabeth gasped. "Were you *watching* us?"

"I . . . I . . . I heard my name."

Stepping close, she spoke in a low, fuming voice. "IF I *EVER* CATCH YOU SPYING ON YOUR BROTHER AND ME AGAIN, I WILL NOT ONLY LET HIM KNOW, BUT I WILL DARKEN YOUR DAYLIGHTS MYSELF!! DO I MAKE MYSELF CLEAR?"

"OH!!!" Georgiana's hands flew to her face in mortification.

"Now get yourself downstairs, plaster a pleasant look on your face, and if you know what is good for you, you will not give a hint of what you saw to your brother. It would devastate him to know how terribly you invaded our privacy, and I do not know that he would easily forgive you. After all that we have suffered from a man who thought nothing of entering our home and taking from us our security and health, how terribly do you think we will feel this violation? From you!" Elizabeth turned away to calm and heard Georgiana's sob. Furious, she turned back and faced her. "And young lady, starting tomorrow, you will have a regular schedule of work. You will practice your piano, you will study your languages, you will read histories and poetry, and you will report to us daily what you have accomplished. You will not waste any more time, and you will not enter this room again without invitation. I *will* speak to him about your reading his journal. Obviously our talks of the past have left no impression on you. Very well then, if you choose to behave as a child, you will be treated as one. You are going to appreciate what you have been given, and if all of this work is not enough for you, and your brother's decisions are not effective, I will find you something more stimulating to occupy your time."

"What do you mean?" She squeaked.

"I will just let you think about it." Elizabeth stormed out of the door, horrified that Georgiana had nearly witnessed them making love.

Georgiana followed meekly and barely looked up when they arrived in the courtyard. Darcy was watching for the carriage to appear and turned to smile at them. He read Elizabeth's expression and looked at Georgiana's downcast eyes. "What happened?"

"Forgive me, Fitzwilliam."

"Forgive you?" He looked to Elizabeth. "And what am I to forgive?"

"Well, I was going to wait to discuss this, but since Georgiana has chosen to speak . . ." She looked at him and said quietly, "I found who was reading your journal." He stared. Elizabeth saw Mary's jaw drop open. "I have already informed her that her idleness has come to an end and that she will be expected to fill her time with her studies, however education is a reward in my opinion."

"I agree." Darcy said quietly. "We have spoken to you before about privacy. What is your excuse?"

"I . . . You went upstairs and looked so grim that I wished to see if you were well, and . . . When I did not see anyone in the sitting room, I . . . I have always wondered why those journals seemed so important to you." She said to her shoes.

Darcy was speechless and took a moment to think of an appropriate response. "While I appreciate your concern and can understand the pull of curiosity, it is not an excuse for reading my journal."

"No, sir."

Darcy looked to see Elizabeth's expression, there was more to it than this, he was sure, rarely was she so angry. Without further knowledge, it was difficult to judge what to do, but as he was the master of the house, it was up to him to make a decision. "Well, since you choose to behave as a child, you will be treated as one. In addition to your studies, you will be taking your meals in the nursery until further notice. Clearly Aunt Helen was correct in her assertion that you should remain there until you are seventeen."

"But . . . but this is family coming to visit!" She cried.

"Yes, and they will certainly appreciate seeing their mother's ways adopted here. We have been too lenient, it seems." He then took Elizabeth's hand and felt her squeeze his in approval. He squeezed back and turned to address Mary. "How was your exploration of the library?"

She was watching Georgiana and startled. "Oh, it was fascinating! I never really had the opportunity to explore Papa's bookroom. I only entered when he was present and I was invited." She glanced at Georgiana. "But I think that I could be lost for years amongst the volumes of your library. Right now I am simply trying to learn where everything is."

He smiled at her. "Perhaps you should consult the map hanging on the wall by the door."

"A map." Mary shook her head. "Of course."

"There is a book below it that has every title recorded, as well as its location and category." Elizabeth added.

"Well. I have learned my lesson, the next time I will ask." Again she looked at Georgiana and then back to see Darcy smiling at her, and blushed with his approval.

A carriage that had seen better days entered the courtyard and came to a rest before them. Footmen appeared, opening the doors, and immediately began taking down the luggage. Lucas stepped out and shaking his head, looked at the mansion before him, then with a smile, handed out Jane. She flew into Elizabeth's arms and the sisters began talking over each other. Mary joined them for more hugs and Georgiana hung back until Elizabeth pulled her hand to join them. Darcy blew out his cheeks and walked over to shake Lucas' hand.

"Welcome."

"Thank you." He gestured to the woods. "I thought we would never clear the trees! When we entered the drive and heard the three shots from the gatekeeper, I nearly hit my head on the roof I jumped so high! Then to hear it repeated twice more as we continued to travel . . . How far is it from the gate to here?"

"About three miles." Darcy said softly then lifted his hand to rub his temple. "So you understand the need to repeat the signal."

"I do." His gaze travelled over the building. "It is beyond anything I have ever seen, Jane's description clearly was not fanciful as I supposed." Lucas' smile faltered when he noticed Darcy's pained expression. "We are forever indebted to you for this gift."

Darcy saw his concern and straightened. "You are enjoying your privacy?"

"I cannot begin to describe it."

"You do not need to, I surely understand." Darcy looked to the women and smiled. "And I hope that you know; you are under no obligation to spend your time with us. Please take full advantage of our home and enjoy your honeymoon. There are many wonderful places to explore, inside and out. Stay as long as you like or move on to the Peaks and stay with us afterwards. There is no agenda."

"What a congenial host you are!" Lucas laughed.

"I remember the early days of our marriage, and occupation with people other than my wife was frustrating. Admittedly, it remains that way." Darcy noticed Georgiana was looking at him sadly and his smile fell away. His disappointment appeared before he managed to mask it.

Lucas looked between the siblings. "Mother suggested bringing Charlotte along as a companion to Jane. Although she would have loved the trip, especially to visit Eliza, I know that this time alone with her is a rare and precious gift."

"You value your privacy." Darcy murmured.

"When you live in a small home with six other family members, yes you do."

"You value it when you live in a mansion as well."

LOOKING BEHIND HIM as they rode away, Lucas saw the expression of relief on the men's faces. He faced forward again then spoke to Darcy. "I am overwhelmed."

"What has amazed you?" He nodded to Nichols, who moved forward to join his assistants and left the brothers alone.

"Forgive me, I did not mean to interrupt your work."

"No, Nichols was just confirming some information." Darcy smiled a little and adjusted his seat. "As you saw, I was merely asking Mr. Johnson's expectations for the harvest."

"You were reassuring your tenant that you are well." Lucas glanced back to see the men gathered and watching them ride off. "I imagine that there was great concern over the fate of Pemberley should you have died."

"I imagine that you are correct." Darcy stared ahead and let the horse set the pace. "Pemberley goes to Elizabeth upon my death, to be held for our daughter for now, or to our eldest son should he one day come."

"Eliza?" Lucas was surprised. "Is there no entailment?"

"It was broken when I came of age, Father did not prepare a new one before he died, I am not sure why. I am grateful though, since I was free to assure her that this was her home for life. I have written the agreement to assure that a child of Darcy blood would always be in this home. No husband will come along and assume its ownership, so should we only have daughters, Rosalie's eldest son will inherit, or her eldest daughter will maintain possession until she has a son. Eventually some child of Darcy blood is bound to be a boy." He glanced over to Lucas with a small smile. "I will not suffer as Mr. Bennet does, with no heir."

"That is an interesting solution you have devised."

"I see the results of a family in crisis because of uncertainty daily in the example of Elizabeth and Mary, and soon enough I will have another sister to look after in Kitty. I will not let my family be without a home merely due to their sex."

"I will remember this when we have our children. My father knows nothing of these things, and nothing has been prepared for our little home." Lucas mused. "Thank you." He saw that Darcy only nodded and cleared his throat. "And I . . . thank you for tolerating my company as you look after your estate. It has been a great experience."

"I am rather surprised that you want to be away from Jane."

"Oh, well." Lucas blushed a little and cleared his throat. "I thought she could use the rest." Darcy's chuckle made him smile. "I was dying to leave home."

"I am sure of that." Darcy said quietly and continued to stare forward.

"I mentioned before that Mother thought Charlotte should come with us, to provide comfort to Jane, after my . . .attentions. I said that we would be here in just days so she could probably tolerate me that long before Eliza could . . ." Lucas heard another chuckle and his face reddened again. "Well she clearly is quite well. Did you have a companion?"

"No, we just came here." Darcy smiled and looked over to him. "We discouraged the thought of bringing anyone along even though Mrs. Bennet offered her services several times."

"What a nightmare *that* would have been!" Lucas' eyes widened and he laughed. "I have to tell you, after that set down you delivered at the wedding breakfast; she has been silent, well, quieter."

"I lost my temper." He murmured.

"It was time that someone did." Lucas looked out over the beautiful landscape. "Your sister Georgiana is being punished, I gather?"

"Yes."

"Jane and I talked about it last night. She does not know the circumstances, Eliza would not speak of them, but she did admire you, both of you, for remaining steadfast, despite your dislike of the decision." Darcy turned to him and saw Lucas nodding. "The Bennets grew up without direction; they were left on their own to understand the rules of proper behaviour. My parents are silly in so many respects, but they *are* shrewd or Father's business would not have been a success. One thing that Mother taught us was that children like to know the rules. They may test them, but they feel better knowing what they are."

"And how long should a punishment for violating them carry on?"

"I would say no more than a week would be sufficient for this banishment to the nursery. Your family arrives tomorrow?" Darcy nodded. "Well, missing the welcoming dinner would surely let them know that she had done wrong."

"And then let her back in, knowing that they all know." Darcy smiled and relaxed. "Very well, I shall do just that."

LAYTON AND ALICIA exchanged glances. Audrey nudged her mother and raised her brows. Lady Matlock shrugged and stared at her husband, who looked between Darcy and Elizabeth. Singleton watched the exchange of looks and focussed on the empty chair between Mary and Lucas. Jane cleared her throat and took a sip of wine.

"All right, what is the story?" Lord Matlock pointed his fork at the empty chair. "If this was Matlock, we would not blink at a child being excluded from the table, but this is Pemberley where we have been told repeatedly that you live by your own rules." He sniffed and smiled. "What did she do?"

Darcy spoke quietly. "She is living with the consequences of her actions for a period of time."

"How long?" He nodded to his wife. "Punishment is only effective if it is not a pittance, and yet not a lifetime."

"I intend to end it tomorrow." He looked at Elizabeth to see her nod. "It has been four days. And I wanted her to miss the first dinner with the whole family here before it was over."

Lord Matlock chuckled. "Well done, Darcy."

"I hope so."

"Is she shooting daggers at you?"

"I have not noticed."

"Well you would not; it would be behind your back." Layton grinned. "That was your method, was it not, Audrey?"

"Stephen!"

"Oh, that explains it." Singleton laughed. "I have felt the prick of your gaze when I raise your ire, my dear."

"You, raise my ire? How could that be, you are perfect." Audrey's lips twitched and she took a bite of her venison. "As I tell you constantly."

"Is *that* what you were whispering about last week?"

"No, I was encouraging you to tell me how perfect I am."

Alicia laughed. "Oh my, listen to you two, fighting like an old married couple!"

The rest of the table burst into laughter and Darcy looked to Elizabeth, who smiled at him and shrugged. Lady Matlock looked between the two, and read their eyes. "It is sometimes harder to be the one who does the punishing than the one who receives it." She smiled at her son and daughter. "Of course they would disagree."

"Mother, I do not wish to discuss your punishments. Let us just say Darcy, Georgiana is doing quite well with only a tongue-lashing and exile." Layton saw Audrey nodding. "Of course, Richard never was punished."

"That is so true." Audrey agreed. "He could get away with anything."

"Children, how old are you? Still holding on to these petty protests when the man is not here to defend himself? I am of a mind to forbid you dessert." Lord Matlock winked when they groaned. "Mr. Lucas, you have been silent, tell us of your father's methods."

Lucas startled in mid-chew. "Oh, Father left it to Mother."

"And Jane?" All eyes turned to her.

"Oh . . .we . . ." She looked at Elizabeth.

"We governed ourselves." She answered. "Which is perhaps why I take it so seriously now."

"But as tomorrow is Elizabeth's birthday, the exile shall end. I do not wish to separate the family on such a special day." Darcy's eyes smiled. "Our point has been made."

"Your birthday! Oh will you have fireworks again this year?" Alicia asked.

"Fireworks?" Lucas said softly and saw Jane's open mouth.

"Yes." Darcy noticed Elizabeth's surprise. "I could not resist the temptation."

"Fitzwilliam, it is not necessary, but thank you." She looked over to Mary who seemed as stunned as Lucas. "This will be your first time seeing them, will it not Mary? Well your birthday is in three days, so we will share the celebration."

"Oh." Mary blushed.

"Oh no, Mary will have her own celebration." Darcy smiled. "Your day is just as important to us."

"Oh!" Her eyes welled up with tears, and standing, she put her napkin down and walked over to kiss his cheek. "Thank you, Fitzwilliam!" She ran down to Elizabeth and hugged her. "Thank you. Excuse me." Hurriedly, she left the silenced room.

Lord Matlock cleared his throat. "Mary's birthday did not receive much notice in the past, I presume."

"No." Jane and Elizabeth said together.

"She will be out this spring?" Lady Matlock asked casually.

"Yes, and we will not push her." Elizabeth looked at her pointedly.

"I have no idea what you mean."

LORD MATLOCK STROLLED into the library after dinner, and clasping his hands behind his back, began perusing the shelves. Hidden away in a corner, Georgiana sat at a table by a window, staring fixedly at a book. He kept one eye on her as he casually went around the room. "So many tomes." He said, musing out loud. Not expecting any acknowledgement, he continued his wandering, taking down a title, flipping through the pages, pushing it back in place, then moving on. "hmm." He stopped and bent, then pulled an oddly shaped book from its place. "ahhhh. I knew it was here." Satisfied, he came over to Georgiana's table, set down the book, noisily pulled out a chair and sat down with a grunt. "Haven't looked at this in at least five and twenty years, perhaps longer. Depends on when Anne last made me." He chuckled and saw Georgiana's eyes flick over it. "Quite a woman she was." He moved the book to his lap, sat back and started looking through it, chuckling as he turned the pages.

"What is it?" Georgiana finally said.

"Hmm?" He looked up. "Why Georgiana! I did not know you were there! You are quiet as a mouse!"

"Uncle, you were talking to me."

"I was talking to myself." He said pointedly. "You were eavesdropping." Seeing her blush scarlet, he sat up and put the book back on the table. "Now, tell me what is on your mind, since your brother and sister are doing their best to understand. Their talks on privacy seem to fall on deaf ears."

"I did not mean to listen or read the journal."

"Was someone threatening you with death if you did not? Were the doors sealed? Could you not leave the room?"

"No, Uncle." Georgiana sighed.

"Then may we establish that you do in fact know better? That your reading the journal and remaining to spy on them in their private rooms was indeed intentional? And that your brother's punishment is nothing like what you would have received at Matlock?" He looked at her sternly.

"Yes, sir."

"I am not interested in dissecting what you did or why. I imagine it has something to do with worry and plain curiosity, mixed with opportunity and fearlessness." He watched her fidget. "I realize that Darcy and Elizabeth have spoken to you about what you saw and heard, but do you know how *deeply* you have hurt your brother?"

"I hurt him?" She looked up to him with wide eyes.

"They came home to find peace and recover, not to have your astonishing lack of respect weigh them down with more worries about doing well by you. He carries the weight of the world on his shoulders. Heaven knows that I have tried my damndest . . . Pardon me, I have tried very hard to convince him that he cannot be responsible for everyone and everything. He does not listen, though. He fears that he has failed you."

"How?"

"He fears that he is not capable of instilling an appreciation for your heritage in you, or for the values that he holds dear. The necklace . . ."

"I was careless, I know." She said quickly.

"Tell me something. I walked past your chambers earlier, and on your bed there is a doll, rather old and much repaired. Who gave that to you?"

"Nanny Kate."

"Ah." He nodded. "And if you had lost it?"

"I would *never* lose that!"

"Because she was your mother and you respect her." His brows rose and he smiled to see her surprise. "In the course of two years, you lost your father, and the woman who had served as your mother. Your brother tried to fill both roles, your aunt and I tried to as well, but none of us quite hit the mark, did we?" She said nothing. "And then Darcy finds Elizabeth, who undoubtedly had his attention. And you found yourself thrown out of the way and in school. Abandoned." Still she said nothing. "Do you like Elizabeth? Or is it that you like her so much that you do not like sharing her with your brother, much less Mary?"

"I love them both." She whispered.

Nodding, he reached into his pocket and pulled out the sapphire butterfly, and laid it on the table. She stared at it. "Which means more to you? This necklace or that doll?" Georgiana began to cry, and he ignored it. Instead, he pulled forward the book, and opened it. "This is your mother." He held out a drawing. "As you can see, the artist was not accomplished. My sister did not practice." He saw her look up. "Your aunt, Catherine."

"Oh."

"Do you notice what she wears?" He pointed.

"A blue butterfly."

"Yes." Picking up the necklace, he looked at it sadly. "Father gave this to your mother when she was about your age. Our mother had died, you see, and she was feeling very sad. He was hoping to cheer her with a gift because demonstrating affection was something that he did not do readily. Would you like to hear the history of the necklace?" Georgiana nodded silently. "Anne wore this constantly, and it would have drawn attention if it were not for the fact that she was a girl, and therefore was never seen in company, and when out with the family, was silent and demure. She never called attention to herself, and certainly was never asked for her opinions or desires. Her life was church and the schoolroom. Rather different from yours, eh?"

He saw her nod and continued. "Well, one day we were holding a ball at Matlock House. I was married to your aunt, Catherine was enjoying her second Season, and your mother was just old enough to attend a private ball but not dance, she would be out the next year. She dressed in her best new gown and of course wore her butterfly." Lord Matlock noticed that Georgiana's eyes had moved to focus on some miniatures on a shelf next to a great chair. He stood and walked over. "ahhh." There was a portrait of Anne Darcy as a girl, and around her neck was the butterfly. He picked it up and set it on the table. "Yes, that is how she appeared then, and how she was that night when George Darcy spied her for the first time. Besotted, he was. He had no idea who she was, either." He laughed. "All night he danced with the girls who were out, but watched Anne. Catherine was quite intrigued with him, but she wanted a title so focussed on de Bourgh. In any case, your father noticed that Anne's necklace had disappeared. He put on his best Darcy smile, got up his nerve, and asked Father for an introduction."

"And they fell in love?"

He smiled. "Love at first sight seems to run in the Darcy blood! Well, at some point, when they were through the preliminary awkward conversation, he managed to remember his excuse for speaking to her, and told her that the butterfly was missing. Anne was distraught, and George, besotted fool that he was, spent the rest of the evening following Anne from room to room, searching for it. By the time that they found it in a corner of the ballroom, I would say that the match was made." Georgiana's eyes were shining with tears and she held her mother's portrait in her hand. "Father made them wait, of course, but he spoke to Mr. Darcy and the arrangement was made. The delay gave them time to know each other, although their hearts were set that first night. Much as your brother's was when he fell in love with Elizabeth." Lord Matlock sighed and picked up the necklace, and watched the jewels sparkling in the light of the setting sun. "Do you understand why Darcy chose this piece to give you in exchange for the pearl? Do you understand how angry he felt that you would be so careless with it? This necklace is what inspired your father to speak to your mother."

"I did not know." She sobbed. "Papa would be so hurt if it was gone!"

"And your mother, too." Lord Matlock wiped the tear that was in his eye. "Respect, Georgiana. That is what we are trying to teach you. Respect for your heritage, respect for your family, respect for the people who love you and are doing their very best to help you grow. Every time that you spy on your brother and sister, every time that you do not listen, every time that you behave in a way that you know is wrong, you show disrespect. I realize that you never knew your mother, and that your affection for a servant is stronger, but she lost her life giving you yours. Remember that, and make her proud of you for her sacrifice." Picking up the necklace, he carefully put it into his pocket. "Perhaps one day you might earn this back."

"Really?" She wiped her eyes and hugged herself. "But Fitzwilliam said that it would go to Rosalie."

"He wanted it to go to you. Make him see that you are worthy of it." Pushing the book to her side of the table, he opened the cover. "This is a sort-of memory book your mother kept. She made me look at it with her from time to time." He sighed heavily. "Well for a boy it was not the most fascinating thing, but I remember her enthusiasm fondly. It made for good story-telling." He smiled and caressed it, then wiped his eye when a tear appeared. "Look it over, and get to know your mother."

"Thank you." Georgiana whispered.

Lord Matlock stood and pushed his chair in. "Those journals Darcy and Elizabeth keep. Rather intriguing, wouldn't you say? Every entry is a love letter." Seeing her startle and stare at him, he nodded. "You know now why they protect them so fiercely."

"*You* read them?"

"When I sat waiting for word from the surgeon and physician after Wickham's attack, I sought to distract myself from my worry. I picked up a book that lay on the writing desk; it opened to that day's entry. The moment I realized what I was reading I put it down. I picked up the other book to try again, only to find that it was another journal. I was ashamed for reading it, knowing how private your brother is. But I was glad I had as well, because it helped me to understand a relationship that is nearly unfathomable to me." He could tell that she understood, and leaned forward to make his point. "I, however, did *not* know what I was to read. I did not set out to pry. *You* did." He watched her blush. "And then you remained."

"Respect." She whispered.

"They are going to be well someday, Georgiana, stop worrying over that. Enjoy the incredibly loving home and example they are providing for you. I cannot stress enough how unique they are. If you stop wallowing in what you have not and embrace what you have been given, you might find something similar one day." He kissed her forehead and touched her hair. "Do not disappoint the family again."

"I will not, sir." She whispered.

"Or I will send your aunt to deal with you." He nodded and raised his brows. "Although, I have a feeling that Elizabeth left to her own devices could be just as effective." He saw her swallow hard and walked to the doorway. "By the way, your brother has a message. You will be permitted to rejoin the family beginning tomorrow. It is Elizabeth's birthday. I have no doubt that there will be a grand celebration."

"Thank you, Uncle."

"Thank your brother and sister." He knocked on the doorframe and clasping his hands behind his back, set off down the hallway.

Georgiana took a long deep breath, then gathering up the book and the miniature of her mother, went upstairs to her chambers. She looked at the doll, and picking it up, moved it to a chair in the corner, and set up the portrait on the table next to her bed. There was a knock on the door and she cautiously approached and opened it. Mary was standing outside.

"Oh."

"Were you expecting someone else?" She asked.

"I thought that maybe Fitzwilliam and Elizabeth . . ."

"I just saw them going into the nursery. They will probably just retire for the night, Fitzwilliam's eyes looked pained." Mary watched Georgiana's face fall, and closed the door. "I thought you had only read their journals, but now I know why Fitzwilliam has been so deeply troubled and worried. Elizabeth has fretted, sending him out on the estate, hoping it would distract him from the pain of his headaches, she has spent the last days nearly glued to the window watching for his return, he was never gone from her for long." Mary asked quietly, "How could you?"

"You know everything?" Georgiana gasped and sat down on the bed. Mary took a seat beside her.

"I was in the library when you came in. Lord Matlock saw me when he was walking around." Mary stared at her. "You watched them expressing private love to each other. Between a man and wife." Georgiana looked down but not before she saw the disappointment in Mary's face. "Lizzy has spoken to me of what happens privately between a married couple. She has told me of the physical experience, but she has spoken more to me of the emotional one, from her words, I sense that what they display before our family is nothing to what she and Fitzwilliam share when they are alone. How could you trespass on that?"

"I . . . I just could not walk away." She sniffed.

Tears slowly tracked down Mary's face. "Did you know that Fitzwilliam is going to hold a celebration for my birthday? For *me*. I am . . . I am not a *shadow* to him! Elizabeth and Jane tried to encourage me, but living in Longbourn it was so hard to be anything special. It was not until Elizabeth found Fitzwilliam, and she changed so much that I . . . I got to feel a little bit of the love they share. They love me. I cannot in any way express how . . . The gratitude I feel for them, taking me into their home, giving me an education, giving me a family who cares for me . . . How can you treat that like . . . like . . . chattel!" Mary stood. "You are jealous of the time that they wish to be alone? Do you not understand that their strength comes from their time alone? They have conquered too much to . . . to . . .bend to the will of a spoiled girl." She sniffed and turned to the door. "You have a wonderful family. You should be grateful. You could have grown up in mine." Mary walked out and closed the door behind her.

15 AUGUST 1810

Georgiana has just left us. She came to the nursery door and asked for permission to enter. I admit that I was of a mind to send her away, Fitzwilliam was suffering so, but in the end, I thought he would rest easier having the conversation now. So I sat with Rosalie in my arms and Fitzwilliam sat beside me while Georgiana stood before us and apologized. I do believe that this time it was sincere. I sensed genuine sorrow and shame, and perhaps a clear grasp of the root of our disappointment. It would be unreasonable to expect her to love a mother she never knew, and Fitzwilliam understands that, but it is not wrong to expect her to value this woman, and more so her father, who she did love and esteem.

I believe that so much of Fitzwilliam's hurt comes because he feels his duty to his family so deeply. So deeply in fact that he came a hairsbreadth from rejecting his love for me for fear of disappointing his father. Fitzwilliam feels that duty, honour, impeccable behaviour and honesty are hallmarks of the Darcy name. While I have only been a Darcy for a brief time, I too value those qualities, but more so, I have seen first-hand what the effect of poor behaviour unchecked can bring, and I would be devastated to see Georgiana become what my sister and mother are.

We did not ask for promises or make demands. We listened to her, told her that we love her, but that we expect her to prove to us she has learnt her lesson, and that she has to earn our trust again. Fitzwilliam told her that she is fortunate that my birthday fell as it did, otherwise she would not be back at the dinner table so soon. I believe that she understood that all is not forgiven until she demonstrates her improvement.

This has been exceptionally difficult for us to address. We are very grateful for Uncle Henry's offer of intervention. We are learning more every day how to be parents.

Darcy leaned over her shoulder and kissed her cheek. "It is our own fault, you know."

"What is?" Elizabeth turned to look up at him.

"We took her out of the nursery, we encouraged her to be part of our lives, and not be relegated to being silent and demure until she was deemed old enough to marry a man."

"Marry a man to whom she is silent and demure." She laughed and stood up to hug him. "Never ever tell your husband of the troubles you had all day while he was away. Give him a perfect home, a perfect meal, a lovely countenance, and a willing body." He chuckled and rested his cheek in her hair. "Then leave him to enjoy his bed alone."

"Sounds ideal." He yelped when she pinched him. "I believe that was not in the handbook you read, and by the way, that surely is not the life your father enjoys."

"Definitely not, nor will you." Elizabeth sighed and she looked up to him. "How do you feel?"

"Better." She kissed his brow and smoothed his hair. "I do, love. I think that we understand each other."

"I think that we caught it just in time."

"What do you mean?" Darcy's brow creased. "What do your fear might have happened?"

"I do not know dear, but unchecked, who knows what Georgiana may have done?"

Chapter 25

"Good morning." Darcy whispered.

Elizabeth turned in his arms and kissed him. "Good Morning."

"May I be the first to wish you a very happy birthday?"

"You may." She laughed when he nuzzled his face against her throat. "Fitzwilliam! That tickles!"

"Does it?" He rubbed his bristly cheek over hers.

"Will!" She gasped and writhed when his hands fell upon her waist and he began to tickle her. "Fitzwilliam Darcy!"

"I love you." He grinned and kept at it as she squealed and started tickling him back. "Oh no, my girl!" He rolled on top of her and pinned her hands above her head. He kissed her and they lay breathing heavily and smiling. "I love you."

"What are you about, Mr. Darcy?"

He chuckled and kissed her slowly. "I love you."

"I love you." She laughed and wrapped her arms around him as he slipped his under her shoulders. "What are you plotting?"

"Hmm." He kissed his way down her throat and started nibbling. "I have never tasted a woman of nineteen years before." His head popped up and his eyes twinkled. "I *have* tasted one of eighteen years many times, I am delighted with the change."

Elizabeth pinched him and he pressed his hips against her. "You grew bored with the child you tasted before?"

"Nooooo." He returned to his nibbling, working his way down her body. "Hmmm, thirsty."

"Ohhh." Elizabeth's back arched as he licked and suckled, then burying his face between her breasts, he sucked hard. "Ow!"

"I am simply making sure that everyone knows you are mine." Admiring the strawberry he had left, he licked it and kissed the mark. "Mine."

"Nobody but Rosalie and Millie will ever see that." Elizabeth cried out when his eyes lit up and his teeth nipped below her ear. "That does not give you permission to bite my neck!" He blew on her throat and resumed his kissing. "Oh Will." She sighed.

"Relax." Darcy whispered and sitting back on his heels, he stroked his hands down over her belly, "I want to give you your first birthday gift." He touched her. "If you want me?" Elizabeth sat up and stroked over him with both hands. Darcy's eyes closed. "I am supposed to be pleasuring you."

"Take me to our glade." She whispered as he leaned forward and pressed her into the pillows. "Ohhh, love me by our tree." Darcy settled comfortably and caressed her hair while they kissed. "This is so nice." Elizabeth sighed when he moved to taste her shoulder. Their hips moved in lazy circles, and she rested her feet on his thighs. "Will?"

"hmmm?" He smiled as her hands massaged over his shoulders and down to his buttocks. "That feels so good, love." She laughed and he finally lifted his head. "You were saying?"

"I was saying . . . Oh, I asked you to love me by our tree, but it seems that you preferred not to wait." Her eyes sparkled and he chuckled. "No?"

"Do you mean to say that you would not like me in both places? Only one time today? It is your birthday, whatever you want, you shall have. Even if I am forced to perform endless acts of love today." Darcy groaned when she caressed his bottom and he drove his hips forward, making her gasp. "And do not think for a moment that I could not meet your demand."

"I never had a doubt." They kissed and settled back into the steady motion of their embrace.

Elizabeth suckled his throat while he moaned and moved his lips to her ear. "I made a terrible mess of your birthday last year. This year, I intend to do very well by you." Darcy raised his head from where it rested on her shoulder to see her eyes smiling at him, while his smiled in return. Slowly they rocked together and sighed. "A gift we both will enjoy."

LUCAS AND JANE walked hand and hand down the hallway, and passing the master's chambers, he paused. A smile spread over his face and Jane blushed, and tugging his hand, pulled them along. "Shame on you!"

"I am not the one moaning, that is our brother." He laughed and turned his head when the sound of laughter filtered through the door. "Can you imagine us making such noises at home?"

"Oh Robert, do not speak of it!" Jane whispered and hurried them out of the hallway and away from the family bedchambers. "Not in public!"

"My dear Jane, who do you see?" He spread his arms and stood at the top of the marble staircase. "Only the echo of our voices is here. Nobody rises early except servants and our hosts." He turned and slipped his arms around her for a hug. "And it seems that they have risen quite nicely."

"What has come over you?" She laughed when he let go and they started down the steps. "You are different."

"How so?" Lucas kissed her hand and they walked into the breakfast room. "I am happy."

"Well of course, but it is something else." Jane shrugged and they stood together lifting lids and looking at the offerings. She took some buttered toast and chocolate, and he opted for something more substantial. They sat down and enjoyed the solitude. A maid silently went about her duties and a footman stood outside of the door. "You are growing used to Pemberley."

"I am. It is such a beautiful place. It is not just a house, you can feel . . . Can't you feel it, Jane? There is a rhythm here, a heartbeat." He laughed. "I sound ridiculous, I know, but when I stepped in the door that first day and saw for myself the splendour I . . . I was tempted to turn tail and run back into that carriage. Those three shots when we entered the gate were disconcerting enough."

"I told you that the park is ten miles around."

"Yes, and with the surrounding farmland it is more. Darcy could spend an entire week doing nothing but riding about the estate, and still not see it all."

"Yes." Jane sighed. "It is a little overwhelming."

"Just a little." He smiled and looked around the beautiful room, then out of the open French doors. "I thought that Netherfield was grand. It is nothing to this. I now understand what Pemberley is all about. The responsibility, the dedication, the care that this place requires, it makes me appreciate all that our brother has on his shoulders."

"It is quite . . . large."

"Large?" Lucas turned to her and laughed. "You have a gift for understatement, my dear. It is magnificent; it is ponderous in its enormity. As soon as we cleared the trees and gazed down upon it, I understood exactly your feelings of discomfort. I can only agree that I feel completely inadequate within these walls, and it makes my admiration for Darcy grow."

"I feel differently now."

"Why, my dear?" Lucas smiled and took her hand. "Has it grown on you?"

"I am here with you." She blushed. "I suppose that it makes all the difference in the world."

"Last time you had Bingley." He frowned. "That is not something that I like to know."

"But I did not feel comfortable here until it was with you. Does that not bring you relief?"

"Of course." He held her hand possessively. "I am foolish, I know, for being jealous of a man who ultimately rejected you. I suppose that I never thought that I would have my chance once you left Longbourn. You cannot imagine . . . Well, of course you can. Your mother's tongue."

"Planning my future." Jane sighed.

"All those rich men who apparently did not trip over you." He smiled and shrugged. "Forgive me Jane; I still cannot believe my good fortune."

"Who would you have chosen if I had found a rich man?" She smiled and he looked down at his plate. "Come Robert; give me someone to glare at when we go home."

"You cannot glare."

"You know that I can, you told me it was a quality you wished to see in me." He laughed. "You wanted a country girl. Who would have won you?"

"I am no fool, Jane." He kissed her hand. "Nobody."

"I do not believe you."

"Believe whatever you like." A maid entered with a basket of freshly baked buns and they grew quiet. Lucas watched yet another servant delivering a tray, and sighed to himself.

"Oh!" Georgiana entered nervously. "Am I interrupting?"

"No, not at all. Please join us." Jane smiled and Lucas found his. "Did you sleep well?"

"Oh, no, not really." Georgiana took her usual chair and nibbled on a bun. "I have a great deal to think about." She glanced out at the hallway. "Do they all hate me?"

"Hate?" Lucas turned to Jane.

"That is a rather strong word. I would say that they love you, which is why they feel so much concern." She smiled kindly. "We are not privy to what occurred, but I would say that . . . The discipline you are receiving is . . . appropriate." Georgiana only blushed.

"It is your brother's position as your parent to tell you what is expected." Lucas added.

"Your parents set boundaries for you?" Jane asked him.

"Oh, yes." He laughed. "Father and Mother did not tolerate disrespect, even if they themselves have a knack for foolishness. Their sins were of . . . I suppose ignorance of social skills for the society they had entered, and enthusiasm on my father's part that is boundless." He saw Jane's nod and Georgiana's confusion. "Mother gossips and Father is a busybody. I learned my proper behaviour at school."

Mary entered the breakfast room. "Good morning."

"Good morning." Jane watched as she took some toast and sat down away from Georgiana. "Did you sleep well?"

Mary opened her mouth to quote scripture and stopped. "I slept well enough."

Lord Matlock and Layton appeared together, and greetings travelled the room. He made a point of greeting Georgiana. "It is good to see you with us."

"Thank you, Uncle." She whispered.

Settling with a large plate of food, the elder man looked pointedly at the empty master's chair. "So, any wagers on when our hosts will arrive?"

"We are to enjoy our morning without them." Jane informed him. "Fitzwilliam has plans for Lizzy, and we will see each other this evening."

Layton smiled and winked at Lucas. "I can imagine what these plans involve."

"Whatever it is, I am sure it will be precisely the gift Eliza wished to receive." Lucas said stiffly.

Lord Matlock studied him. "Will you come shooting with us this morning, Lucas? Without Darcy or my son Richard along, we have a fighting chance of actually bagging a few birds." He smiled at Jane, "Of course, if you would rather be honeymooning, I certainly understand."

Lucas looked at Jane then turned back to the Earl. "If you do not mind then, sir, I would prefer the opportunity to enjoy the peace of this estate with my bride."

"You would be a damned fool if you did not." Lord Matlock laughed and coughed at the wide-eyed look he received from Jane. "Forgive me. Somehow I forgot that you ladies were here."

"Well that is not a surprise." Lady Matlock said from the doorway.

"Good morning, my dear." Lord Matlock stood and kissed her cheek. "Was your night restful?"

"Of course."

"Of course, how can one not sleep well at Pemberley?" He declared. "Ah, but we will be home before much longer."

"Did you see my wife?" Layton asked worriedly when she did not appear.

"She will be along soon." Lady Matlock met his eye. "She is a little peaky."

"She is ill?" He immediately stood and left the room.

"Ill?" Lord Matlock watched his wife carefully. "With anything of a lasting nature?"

"It will end when the time is right, I suspect." She smiled and he raised his brows. "Time will tell."

"So soon." He shook his head and cleared his throat when he noticed all eyes were on them. "Well Lucas, Jane, I understand you are to continue on your journey? Perhaps you might join us at Matlock for a few days before going to the Peaks?"

Jane and Lucas exchanged glances. "We would not think of trespassing . . ."

"Why not, we will be?" Singleton laughed when he and Audrey entered. "We will be there for a few months."

"It will be nice to be at Matlock again." Audrey smiled and sat next to Jane. "It would be so good to have your company; we have not really had a chance to know each other well."

"Thank you, but . . . Mr. Lucas and I were considering remaining here for the length of our visit." She looked over to him and he lifted his head and smiled. "I am afraid that we will rarely have such an opportunity to be with the Darcys, and if they will tolerate us, then we will remain for a few weeks before we need to journey home."

"Hmm, and to the reality of your lives." Lord Matlock mused.

"Sir?" Lucas bristled.

"Oh, I meant no harm, Lucas. It is simply an observation. Visiting Pemberley to us is as much a holiday as it is to you. Returning home means facing all the work I have left to my stewards, despite Layton's presence." He nodded to his son. "I have not been at Matlock since Christmas. I imagine you will have things waiting for your attention as well. The honeymoon is over, and the marriage will begin in earnest."

"Of course." Lucas observed the staff moving around the room. "It will certainly be different."

"How are your investments going with Gardiner? I must say I am well-pleased."

"They are very encouraging, sir. And I am following Darcy's advice, and investing a portion of my grandfather's bequest in a few companies that show promise with their manufacturing capabilities." He smiled and looked at Jane. "I hope to do well by my family."

Lord Matlock nodded thoughtfully. "That is excellent! I like a young man who prepares for the future. Perhaps you might even use a bit of this income to help your mother? Perhaps hire her a servant or two? I understand that your elder sister will soon be leaving home to marry? And your younger brothers will soon be apprenticed or off to the navy?"

"Yes, I . . . That is true, I might be able to afford a girl for the kitchen." He sat up straight. "And perhaps another for the household."

"It is not necessary, dear." Jane assured him and took his hand under the table.

"Yes." He nodded. "Yes, it is."

Lady Matlock smiled with approval. "Now then, Miss Lucas will marry Reverend de Bourgh, when?"

"In a little over a month, madam. They wished for it to be sooner, but Mother wished for a bit of a rest after our wedding before planning the next." They all laughed and Jane blushed. "But it works out nicely. Darcy told me last night that they will adjust their travel plans for London so that they may be present. It will give them extra time to purchase a new wardrobe for Miss Kitty, and augment yours, Miss Darcy." He smiled at her and she nodded when the eyes turned to her. "Of course Captain de Bourgh and his mother will be attending, as well."

"Oh!" Mary whispered and blushed.

Lady Matlock smiled. "Well I am certain that it will be a lovely occasion, and enjoyed by all."

"BABA." Elizabeth cooed at Rosalie.

Rosalie giggled and shook her rattle.

"Dada." Darcy leaned down and smiled at her. "Dada."

"Dada! Dadadadadadababababa." Rosalie finished her speech with bubbles and another cry of delight at her rattle's noise.

He looked up at Elizabeth and laughed. "Well, something for each of us." They were walking alongside the baby carriage. Darcy held the reins for the pony in one hand, and clasped Elizabeth's hand in the other.

"It is not a competition, Will."

"No, but . . . I long for the day when she calls me Papa." He looked into the carriage when a stream of babbling erupted again.

"Grace seems to almost be saying that, although she calls Stephen, Mama." Elizabeth laughed. "She is a little confused."

"Did you see Margaret? She was sitting up by herself; it will not be long before she is crawling." Darcy said with awe. "That will be Rosa very soon."

"And then we will be in trouble. I can see her dashing through the halls now, being chased down by her nursemaids. Poor Mrs. Somers will regret returning to Pemberley." Elizabeth looked up to him and lifted her hand to brush back his hair. "You look so relaxed today; this is the best gift of all. Will you accept Uncle Henry's suggestion that Matthews could be your personal secretary as well as house steward?"

"No, I want our house steward to look after the physical aspects of our home, not the staff or finances. We have enough staff to help with that. If I engage a secretary he will be dedicated solely to my affairs. I will meet a man in London Uncle Henry knows and will be in need of a position soon." He smiled at her sceptical look. "All right, love, not *if* I hire a secretary, but when. However, I do feel better this morning; perhaps it is the very pleasant start to our day that is influencing me." Darcy kissed her hand, and slipped his arm around her waist. "Perhaps it is relief that Georgiana's behaviour may be addressed. I think that you were correct in what you were saying last night; she was on the cusp of some great mistake. I hope that she understands now that we did not send her to school to get her out of the way."

"I imagine though that a great many of her schoolmates were."

"No doubt. How many did we see arrive with only a servant as escort? I am sure that some of her behaviour was influenced by them." He sighed and watched Rosalie entertaining herself. "I suppose that in some ways, that was why I put her in school to begin with, when Mrs. Somers left us, it seemed to be the best solution to continuing her education. I just felt so helpless when Father died. I know that I was trying to buy her happiness with gifts and indulgences. I had no idea what to do. I knew that Father would want her to be educated, and learn how to be with her peers. I tried. I thought I had tried." He looked down to his feet. "I am so grateful for you coming to my rescue. Lord knows what may have become of her."

"I did not rescue you; I think that your aunt and uncle did that."

"They helped, but I believe that whatever they did was perhaps not taken as seriously as it should." He looked back to her. "She knew that it was only a brief time in their care, she would be eventually returned to me and all would be easy again." He sighed. "You saw what we chose not to."

"I merely recognized Lydia."

Darcy leaned down and kissed her. "At last Lydia has done some good for another."

"Hmm, well hopefully Lydia will see the value of what she is about to receive. I fear that she will fight it, vehemently."

"Yes, and I am afraid that she is in for many remonstrations by her new teachers and classmates."

"I wonder if she will be more likely to listen to her peers and strangers." Elizabeth watched him tying the pony to a tree and taking out the picnic basket they had stored. She reached into the carriage and lifted up Rosalie.

"Are you sure that you can carry her?" He asked worriedly when he saw her grimace. "I can manage the basket and the baby."

"No, I am fine." She smiled and started walking. "Coming?" Darcy sighed and followed her down the path through the trees and then down the trace to their glade. "Look sweetheart, look, this is where you were born." Elizabeth walked around the grass and showed Rosalie the elm. "See, this is our tree, and here," She bent and showed her a pink rose, "This is your namesake." The baby reached and grabbed the stem, and screamed when her finger was snagged by a thorn. "Ohh, shhh, shh."

Darcy dropped the blanket he was spreading and swooped over. "Shhh, love, shhh." He wiped the big tears rolling down her face. "Shh, my Rosa." Elizabeth handed her over and immediately he cuddled her up in his arms and kissed her, then kissed her fingers, nibbling on them and making her laugh. "There my Rosa, all is well."

"You are so lost to her. I see now that you will definitely need me to keep you both in check." Elizabeth hugged him and went to set out their meal.

Darcy just smiled and walked around as she worked, singing softly. "*I gave my love a cherry that had no stone. I gave my love a chicken that had no bone. I told my love a story that had no end. I gave my love a baby with no crying.*"[10]

Rosalie cooed and he caressed her cheek with his finger. "What shall we give Mama today?" He asked her. "What would she like the best? A new necklace?" She stuck her tongue out at him. "No? But I thought that jewels were the way to a woman's heart? Hmm." He lifted her up in the air and laughed when she squealed. A glob of drool fell on his nose. Hearing Elizabeth laughing behind him he settled the baby on his shoulder. "So you suggest some new handkerchiefs, then?" Elizabeth laughed harder and came over to wipe his face. They kissed and she returned to the basket. "I think that I can do much better than that. I suggest this." He whispered in Rosalie's ear and received a hand in his mouth in return. "It is settled." He turned and grinned at Elizabeth. "She agrees with me."

"When has she not?" Elizabeth settled on the blanket and he handed her the baby. He sat and pulled off his boots, and leaned on a tree, then held out his arms to her. Scooting backwards, she leaned on his chest, and opened her gown to feed Rosalie. Darcy's arms wrapped around them both, and they

---

[10] "Riddle Song", 15th century lullaby.

watched her suckle and slowly drift to sleep. "What did you agree upon? What is my gift?"

"Oh . . . I seem to remember you asking if our next child will be conceived right here." Darcy's eyes lit up when she blushed. "I know that you are not able to yet, love, nor am I in any hurry, but I surely do hope that I may fulfil that wish for you right here, one day."

Elizabeth placed their sleeping daughter inside of the empty basket with a blanket, then returned to Darcy's arms. "I hope that you do, but for now, shall we practice?"

He peeked at Rosalie. "Have we enough time?"

"Let us find out."

16 AUGUST 1810
The celebration of Elizabeth's birthday was glorious in its simplicity. I believe this was the easiest day we have spent in, I cannot say, months, perhaps. We spent hours in our glade. We loved each other while Rosalie slept, and then shared the picnic Cook had prepared. We returned to the house to find our guests well-occupied and seemingly oblivious to our absence. It was wonderful.

Following dinner we all moved outdoors. Torches had been lit and out at the edge of the lake, we could see the figures of men moving in the dusky light, and then suddenly, the sky was ablaze with brilliant colours and the shattering sounds of the fireworks echoed over the hills. My love is not so frightened of them now, but she remained in my arms, staring up in awe at the display, and jumped back with each explosion deeper into my embrace, finally letting go to laugh at herself. I did not let her escape my arms for very long. Behind and around us, we heard ohhs and applause, the staff had come out to see the display as well, and I am glad to have given them the pleasure. I had to laugh, Lucas was a novice and his fascination was amusing, to say the least, pointing and exclaiming to Jane. His face was lit with wonder, and she had to hold his hand to keep him still. I know that he feels moments of incredible inadequacy in the face of all that Pemberley is and what he can give to Jane, but I hope that what he takes away from their visit here is a sense of welcome and belonging in our family, and pride in what his hard work can give his own.

Georgiana was reticent and polite. All of the family chose to treat her as usual, perhaps more watchful, except for Mary who like us, seems to need evidence of repentance before granting forgiveness. She played for us, and her gift to Elizabeth was a promise to make a dozen dresses for children in the workhouse before she leaves for school. It is a tall order, but she said that if Elizabeth can spend her time sewing for them, then there was no reason why she could not do the same. When Elizabeth hugged her, I do not believe there was a dry eye in the room. Mrs. Somers arrives tomorrow; it will be good to have her back.

"WHEN WILL YOU MOVE Rosalie into this nursery, Elizabeth?" Audrey walked around the large bright room and looked over to the corner where her daughter was reaching for toys held by Mary. "Grace has been in the nursery at Ashcroft from the beginning."

"Yes, so has Margaret at Matlock." Alicia sat in a rocker and watched her daughter rake some blocks her way.

"Well, Rosa will remain in the little nursery next to the mistress's chambers until she is weaned, at least, or perhaps until we have our next child. It is not as if she is in need of the schoolroom yet. Besides, I do not have any desire to go traipsing up the stairs in the middle of the night." Elizabeth spoke from her position on the floor, and smiled at her baby who was babbling and leaning against her leg.

"But you have Mrs. Robbins for night time duty." Audrey sat on a little bed. "There is no need for you to worry about it."

"Yes, but it is also convenient for me and Fitzwilliam to have her near our rooms during the day. We both go up to visit with her." Elizabeth stroked her hair. "He has private talks with her as often as possible."

Audrey and Alicia exchanged glances and shook their heads. "And what is said?"

"Oh, sometimes they talk about the estate, but mostly they talk about me." She lifted her head and smiled. "She reassures him that he is doing well by me."

"Is he doing well?" Alicia asked quietly and saw Elizabeth's smile fall away. "Forgive me, I should not pry."

"It is just that we have been so worried about both of you." Audrey said quickly.

"What do you see?" Elizabeth looked down at Rosalie and handed her a rattle. "You have known him far longer than I."

"Nothing . . . He is just . . .different." Audrey looked at Alicia helplessly. "As are you."

"Well, we are bound to be." Elizabeth sighed. "I suppose that Lady Matlock told you everything that happened."

"And Evangeline."

"Then there is no need to rehash it now." She smiled and lifted Rosalie to her shoulder, wincing a little, but not stopping the movement. "I think that it is safe to say that we are much better, and we have more pressing things to worry over. For example, your mother has identified a girls' school well away from the influence of London for my sister, Lydia."

"Oh, the school run by Miss Edwards." Alicia nodded. "Yes, it is . . . Well, let us say that they brook no nonsense there."

"I knew a girl who attended Mrs. Banks' school with me, and she snuck out of her window one evening to meet a gentleman . . .well a purported gentleman, for a rendezvous." Audrey saw the ladies' eyes widen and glanced to the corner where Georgiana sat silently listening. "Fortunately, a footman had stepped outside for a breath of air and noticed the girl dropping down onto a low roof, and the man waiting with a cart just below. Well, he raised the alarm, the man drove off and the girl was left standing on the roof, too far from the window to climb back, and too high off the ground to jump. Her parents had her removed and sent to Miss Edwards within the week."

"Oh my!" Alicia cried.

"That is exactly what we fear Lydia might do. She would go to town and disappear, not liking the rules she lived under." Elizabeth sighed. "The temptation would be great and she has no fear or even a concept of anyone using her ill. I hope that living in an atmosphere of little indulgence will save her from . . . a fate worse than death."

"Is that possible?" Audrey asked and glanced at Georgiana to see if she understood. "Would she go that far?"

"She is a flirt, she knows she is pretty, and men react viscerally to her, despite her age." Elizabeth closed her eyes and kissed Rosalie's head. "Mama's ideas on her wardrobe are not helpful."

"She does not dress demurely as Georgiana does?" Alicia smiled at her.

"No, so she will be in for a great shock when she finds the trunk of appropriate clothing waiting for her at the school, and the dresses Mama had made for her hidden away at Lucas Lodge until she is older." Hearing the peals of laughter, Elizabeth opened her eyes again. "Papa will be glad to be well away from the school by the time that the discovery is made."

"Well, are you shocked at this subterfuge, Georgiana? What of you Mary? This is your sister!" Audrey asked with a smile.

"I think that it is the wise course to follow." Mary said quietly. "Neither do I wish for my sister to be a bad influence on other girls with her dress, nor do I want her to call any more attention to herself than she already will."

Elizabeth nodded and looked at Georgiana. "What do you think, Georgiana?"

She blushed and bit her lip. "I . . . I think that Lydia is fortunate that she has family that cares enough for her to try and save her before she makes any terrible mistakes. I . . . I certainly heard girls talking about men and . . . things. It was . . . it gave me thoughts."

"Would you act upon them, though?" Alicia asked. "You know the difference between acting on an impulse and just entertaining a thought."

Georgiana looked at Mary then over to Elizabeth. "I believe that I have learned that lesson. I hope that Lydia does as well."

"I hope so, too." Elizabeth smiled and Georgiana smiled shyly in return. "I truly do."

"WELL?" Elizabeth prodded Jane the next afternoon. They were sitting on a blanket alone; watching the family moving across the lawn after Mary's birthday picnic had been cleared away. "So how do you find marriage?"

"It is quite satisfactory."

"Ohhhh, that does not sound good at all!" She laughed and drew her knees up to her chest and hugged them. "Surely you can find a better word than that! Robert is beaming. I would guess that he finds it far better than *satisfactory*."

"Well." Jane smiled and watched him amongst the men as they gathered the cricket equipment and argued about teams. "I would say it is . . .quite wonderful."

"Now *that* is much better!" Elizabeth squeezed her hand and looked over to where Georgiana and Mary sat with the babies. "He seems to be more comfortable with the men now."

"He is. It took him a few days. He was not quite so uncomfortable with Lord Matlock since they met before, but Viscount Layton and Mr. Singleton were new and I am afraid that he once again felt his inadequacy."

"It is only inadequacy if he lets it be, Jane. You know that in Meryton, he is quite the important man. He will be taking his father's place one day, perhaps he will be magistrate."

"Whoever takes Netherfield . . ."

"Will be too busy to want to meddle in local affairs. He will pay his taxes, and concern himself with his estate and his pleasures."

"Is that what Fitzwilliam does?" Jane said with her brow raised.

"No." Elizabeth sighed. "He concerns himself with everything. Except politics. I am glad that he will soon begin working with a secretary, he takes on too much."

Jane nodded and drawing a breath, closed her eyes and began a conversation that embarrassed her to her bones. "You share your bed with Fitzwilliam."

Surprised, she turned to her. "Yes, you know that. I assumed that you did the same? Lucas Lodge surely cannot have room for two chambers for you?"

"Oh, no, we share out of necessity. He has apologized." Seeing Elizabeth's confusion, she said hurriedly, "Neither of us wish to be separated, it is just his desire to give me everything that a married gentlewoman should have, at least in his estimation."

"I certainly hope that you set him right on that!" Elizabeth said pointedly and waved at the scattered family. "Believe me, all of those people you see before us were shocked that we share our bed, and I am willing to bet that the majority of them were jealous. I have not pried, but I wager that there is only one bed to be made up each morning in some chambers."

"Lizzy!"

"What is it, Jane?" She said with exasperation. "Please get to the point!"

Jane stared down at her tightly clasped hands. "How often does Fitzwilliam . . . do his duty?"

"*Duty?* Elizabeth bit her lip to hold back her laugh and spoke as seriously as she could. "Often. I will not elaborate."

"Mama said . . ."

"Jane do not dare to quote Mama's advice when it comes to husbands and how to treat them. She sets a fine table, leave her advice at that." Elizabeth took her hand. "Does he demand too much? You are newly married, it will likely change with time."

"No, no, it is not that I do not desire him . . . I just notice how . . .pleased Fitzwilliam is to look upon you, even after a year and a baby." Jane closed her eyes again. "Lizzy . . . could you . . . teach me . . ." She peeked to see Elizabeth's wide eyes. "I . . . just . . ."

"Nobody taught me Jane, and nobody taught Fitzwilliam." She spoke sincerely. "And that light you see in Robert's eyes is the joy of discovery with you. Do not pretend to be more than you are, he fell in love with Jane Bennet, not a courtesan. You have a lifetime to learn together." The sisters hugged. "Do you understand?"

"Thank you." They drew apart and Jane shrugged. "I just want him to be happy. He is so very wonderful, I just want to see him pleased with me."

"Look." Elizabeth pointed at the man laughing and trying to catch Jane's eye. "I think that he is."

"Henry! If you cannot bowl properly then give the ball over to someone who can!" Lady Matlock picked it up and tossed it away from the chair where she sat under a tree.

Bowing deeply, he apologized. "Forgive me dear, I do not know my own strength."

"A likely story." Layton grinned and retrieving the ball, gave it back to his father. "Come on Father, try again!" He took his position and nodded to Darcy, who turned back to see if Elizabeth was watching him.

She laughed and nudged Jane, calling out, "Is he not the most *handsome* player you have ever seen?"

"I think that my husband is far more handsome." Jane disagreed.

"Hear that Darcy? We have a competition brewing!" Lucas laughed.

"Shall we have the sisters duel it out? A game of battledore and shuttlecocks to the death?" He chuckled and squaring his shoulders, lifted the bat. "Come on, Uncle!"

Lord Matlock stepped into his stride, spun his arm and delivered the ball, right back into Lady Matlock's lap. "Henry!"

"Forgive me dear, I am clearly drawn to your beauty."

"Robert!" Lady Matlock cried.

Lucas and Singleton both startled and looked her way. "Yes?"

She waved her hand. "Not you, Mr. Lucas, my son, Singleton! You played in school, please take over before my husband does me an injury."

"Sir?"

"No, no, I can do this. Stand down, sir!" Lord Matlock took back possession of the ball. "It is a matter of pride, now." He stepped back into place. "Prepare yourself, Darcy."

"I have been prepared for some time, Uncle, and yet all I have felt is the breeze as the ball flies by." Darcy grinned as the family laughed. He saw his uncle's glare and pursing his lips returned to his stance. "Very well, have at it."

Lord Matlock aimed, spun his arm and gasped. "Darcy!"

"Will!" Elizabeth cried and flew to his side. Darcy lay on the ground, holding his head. Despite the proximity of the men, she reached him first, and kneeled by his side. "Dear Fitzwilliam, speak to me, please!" She lifted his head and rested it on her knees. "Will?" She caressed his face and looked at him anxiously.

Slowly he blinked open his eyes. "Is it safe?"

"Safe?" Elizabeth sniffed and tried to see him through her tears.

"Uncle is no longer holding a ball?" He smiled a little and reached for her shoulders, pulling her down and kissing her. "I am well, love."

"You are? You are sure?"

Lord Matlock stopped and hung his head, breathing a sigh of relief. "Good Lord, Son, do not scare me like that, you took ten years from me when you fell!"

"You took my breath, so it is only fair. Who knew that a ball so light could do such damage? Your aim was perfect, Uncle." Darcy slowly sat up, rubbing his back. "I will be black and blue before long." He looked around at the family gathered around him and smiled reassuringly at Georgiana who was standing and clutching Rosalie. "I am fine."

"He did not strike your head?" Elizabeth examined him closely; he had held his head, not his back, when he fell. She ran her fingers through his hair, searching for a lump.

"No love, my brain is no more addled than it already was." Darcy smiled reassuringly into her disbelieving eyes. He at last lowered his in contrition and murmured, "I am well dearest, truly."

"NO more cricket!" She proclaimed and hugged him.

"Ahhhh, there you go, she's going to be all motherly now." Layton picked up the bat and leaned on it. "Never play before the ladies, they get too emotional."

"So true." Singleton winked. "Come on Darcy, are you going to laze about there all day? We have a game on!"

"Hardly." Lucas smiled. "With his lordship bowling, we will be at sunset before the first run is made."

"I take exception to that!" Lord Matlock huffed, and scooping up the errant ball handed it to him. "Here, if you are so ready to criticize, you take over."

"I?" He looked at the ball.

"No, no Robert, I do not want you to play." Jane came to his side. "I cannot bear to see you injured."

"Ahhhh, Honeymooners. Come, you do not see our wives worrying over us, look they are assured and have returned to their racquets!" Layton waved at Alicia, and Audrey laughed.

"You were never in danger, dear." Alicia waved back.

"We would not mind seeing them suffer a bit, go ahead, play on!" Audrey called.

"You see? The bloom is gone." Singleton said sadly.

"It is dangerous." Elizabeth said worriedly.

"It is not." Darcy stood and pulled her up. "I will prove it. Singleton, would you bowl to my wife, please?"

"Fitzwilliam!" He smiled and taking the bat from Layton stood with his arms around her. "Like this, love." He whispered and kissed her ear. They both held the bat and took a practice swing. "Just like this."

"You are shocking our sisters." She whispered.

"I probably am." He whispered back, then called to Singleton, "Go on, lob it!" The ball was pitched, and watching, Darcy drew back their arms. "Watch the ball, Lizzy." He swung and they hit it. Elizabeth cheered and he laughed. "There, you did it!" He kissed her cheek. "Now, try again."

This time he stepped away, and Robert threw. She managed to hit it, and turned to grin. "I did it!"

"Yes, now run!" He shoved her and watched her take off. Darcy stood with his hands on his hips and laughed, and held his arms out to catch her when she returned. "Well done, love, well done." He picked her up and they spun.

"No sense of decorum whatsoever." Lord Matlock sighed.

"They are at their home, Henry; they can do whatever they wish before us." Lady Matlock shrugged. "It is not for us to criticize."

"I am not, I am envious." He looked over to where Georgiana and Mary had returned to playing with the babies. "How are they getting on?"

"Their conversation seems to be limited to the children, but is warming."

"I was glad that Mary was in the library and took the initiative to speak to Georgiana. Nothing like a peer telling you off to get your attention." He watched them chasing baby Grace back onto the blanket and then Georgiana grabbed Margaret's foot when she rolled off in another direction. "They will be fine."

"Of course they will, sisters have spats and make up all the time. I am sure that Anne and Catherine did."

"Well, mostly Catherine did the spitting and Anne did the reconciling. She was a lovely girl." He smiled sadly and looked at her twin in Georgiana. "I was glad for the opportunity to share the story of George and Anne's first meeting with Georgiana. I was very surprised to learn when I returned the necklace to Darcy that he did not know it either; he simply treasured a symbol of his mother. No wonder he never understood George telling him that it was acceptable to fall in love at first sight." He saw his wife's sad smile. "I am sure that our children will treasure such symbols of you, dear."

"I hope so." She shrugged and sniffed, then looked down with surprise when she felt his hand clasp hers, and smiled when he bestowed a kiss. "This is a beautiful day."

"It looks like rain is approaching." He looked to the gathering clouds. "We need to pack it in." Seeing her head shake he kissed her hand again and stood. "I know, my dear. It is a beautiful day." He helped her up and called. "Children, gather your playthings, we need to return to the house!"

Layton looked over to Audrey. "Now that sounds familiar."

THAT EVENING AFTER DINNER, the family gathered in the music room. When everyone was comfortably seated, Georgiana spoke up. "I . . . I have a song that I would like to play in honour of Mary's birthday."

"Oh." Mary smiled. "How nice!"

"Would you help me to turn the pages?" She asked quietly.

"Of course." Mary joined her at the bench and they all watched and listened to the challenging and emotional piece. "It was beautiful! I do not know this song."

"I do." Darcy smiled at Elizabeth. "It is my birthday song."

"Yes it is." She laughed when curious looks came their way. "Fitzwilliam gave Georgiana the sheet music for this song when he returned from his tour."

"And coincidentally, Elizabeth was learning it at the same time." He smiled at her, and kissed her hand.

"Oh!" Mary's hand went to her mouth. "I remember, Lizzy! You seemed so determined to learn this!" Darcy looked down and blushed.

Elizabeth entwined her fingers in his and squeezed. "I did, something drew me to it, but it certainly never sounded as beautiful as it does when Georgiana plays." The sisters' eyes met. "Thank you for the pleasure of hearing it played properly again."

"I thought it could be a traditional song to play for family birthdays." She whispered.

"I like that idea very much." Darcy nodded and stood. "Mary, Elizabeth and I have a few gifts for you, as well."

"Oh . . . I do not . . ."

"Hush." Elizabeth stood and brought over a package wrapped in silk. "Open it."

Fumbling a little, Mary pulled the ribbon and parted the fabric. "Books!"

"I chose the histories, so that we might discuss them when you are finished. Elizabeth chose the novels to broaden your mind," the family laughed, "and you will notice that there is a journal there as well. Now that you are a woman, you should start recording the events of your life." He smiled and touched the volume. "You will treasure your foolish thoughts one day, and wonder at how you have grown."

"Thank you." She whispered and touched the books. Darcy cleared his throat and she looked to him. "And since you *are* now a woman, you should dress as one. When we are in town, you will visit Madame Dupree and order a new wardrobe, and," he handed her a velvet pouch, "you should begin to acquire your jewels."

"Jewels?" She gasped, and with a trembling hand, pulled the drawstring. Elizabeth took the bag and tipped it so that the simple pearl necklace and earrings tumbled into Mary's palm. "oh."

"Mary." Elizabeth said softly and touched the pendant around her throat. "This pearl that I am wearing?" Mary nodded. "This pearl is named Richard, and was a treasured reminder of a young nephew who broke Mrs. Darcy's strand of pearls. Your necklace, as you see, has three. The centre pearl comes from that same broken strand, and represents your place in our family. The two smaller pearls on either side represent your past and your future. As Fitzwilliam said, today you are seventeen, and you leave your childhood behind."

"Oh." She whispered and stood to hug Elizabeth, then turned to see Darcy waiting with his arms open. He hugged her and kissed her forehead. "Thank you. So much." He squeezed her and let go. "Thank you."

"We love you, Mary." Elizabeth smiled and took her hand. "Just imagine what the next year might bring, and where you might wear this!"

"Oh . . . I . . ." She paused and bit her lip. "I cannot imagine."

15 SEPTEMBER 1810
The annual Harvest Home was a wonderful success, due in no small part to our wonderful staff. Georgiana and Mary's enthusiastic assistance over the past month was such a great help to me. I know that it would not have been the same without them. Fitzwilliam was delighted with the entire event; and he danced with both of them. Dear Mary was approached by several young men for more dances throughout the evening. Her face was perpetually blushing, and Fitzwilliam assured her that she was lovely. Georgiana naturally did not dance with any other men, but she seemed content to watch Mary and remind her to smile and breathe each time she came near. Of course, Fitzwilliam danced every other set with me. There was no persuading him otherwise, and I admit that I did not try very hard. It was wonderful to stand across from him again, and look into his twinkling eyes. It has been far too long since we have danced. It is something that I intend to correct in our future.

Tomorrow we depart for Hertfordshire. We have planned our travel so that we will stay at an inn only five miles from Meryton. We will arrive in good time for Charlotte and Reverend de Bourgh's wedding, and then travel on to London. We received word today confirming what we already suspected, Alicia is with child. Fitzwilliam has begun his fretting, of course, and he told me countless times today that he is grateful he did not stop me from feeding Rosalie. He professed that he

could not imagine the worry he would feel to see me carrying another child so soon after giving birth, no matter how much he would dearly love another.

Our dear baby seems to be growing and learning more with every day, and has added a second tooth to her first. We celebrated, of course, and gave her some new toys to chew. We celebrated for another reason as well. Fitzwilliam has spent an entire week without a debilitating headache. His head continues to throb, but he is determined to only allow me to know when it becomes too much to bear, he does not wish to be regarded as an invalid. The improvement has given him confidence that one day perhaps he will be completely recovered. Our journey will be a great test; the long carriage ride, and particularly our visit to Longbourn will surely challenge his well-being. I pray that they do not set him back.

Darcy laughed when he read her entry and closing the book, laid it on the bedside table and blew out the candle. He turned back and spooning his body to hers, kissed her neck. "Dearest, if your family makes my head ache, I do believe that you will knock theirs together."

Elizabeth laughed and held the hands that rested over her waist. "I cannot disagree with you, not one little bit."

Chapter 26

"Captain de Bourgh, it is my great honour to greet you again, and on such an auspicious occasion! Your brother, marrying the lovely daughter of my cousin's neighbour, what a find, and how fortunate he is to have met her! Surely being your brother you would wish more for him than merely serving as the humble clergyman for your magnificent estate! Should the living at Hunsford come open once again, please know that I would be honoured to be granted that most coveted position." He bobbed and bowed, then presented a coy smile. "I am the ideal choice, having spent so much time with the congregation and their needs, and most importantly, I know how to serve my benefactors, and I would be glad to provide a fine example of behaviour, not only as a guide to our neighbours, but as a proper husband when I take my cousin to wife."

"Your cousin, Mr. Collins?" De Bourgh said coldly to the pest, and wondered if he offered him a guinea he would go away. "You have made an arrangement?"

"Indeed! I intend to offer for one of my poor cousins and thereby assure the ladies of a home when their father passes. The family is naturally grateful for my generosity. It is the least I can do; after all, I am aware of the tragedy of their circumstances, as is the entire neighbourhood." He paused and made a sad face. "However, I would require a better living to provide for my wife and children until that tragic day arrives, as my hopes for Hunsford were dashed." Glancing at de Bourgh he saw that his gaze remained icy and cleared his throat delicately. "Although it was certainly understandable why you might offer it to your unmarried brother."

"Who is now a married man in need of this living you covet. Your concern over his future and welfare is astonishing, as well as your solution." De Bourgh flicked his eyes over Collins, and decided to let the fool prattle on while he maintained his vigil for the Darcy carriage. The mix of flattery and gall amazed him. "Your in-laws would not welcome the heir into their home? It would be but one more mouth to feed, and your income as a curate would surely pay your keep there."

Collins' face coloured an unbecoming shade of pink. "Ahem, I . . .well; my father is actually the heir."

"I see." De Bourgh smiled when he heard his brother's snort from his position behind Collins in the sitting room at Lucas Lodge. "And has a cousin has accepted you?"

"None as yet, but I am certain that it will be easily arranged. The gratitude of the family for my condescension will be great." Seeing de Bourgh's disgust, he became petulant. "I *am* to be the master of their estate one day."

"As you just confirmed, two men must die before that happens, and you may very well leave this earth before them." De Bourgh glared then noticed Lydia, who was giggling and disturbingly, sending inviting looks directly at him. He shook his head and looked back at Collins. "So who is this fortunate woman?"

"Mrs. Bennet has graciously suggested her eldest unmarried girl. I intend to stay near her as much as possible today. She has recently reached seventeen years; you will agree that is quite the acceptable age for marriage!" He started when he heard de Bourgh's hiss.

"*Miss Mary Bennet?*"

Collins nodded and spoke cautiously. "She has not the beauty of her sisters, she is not as . . .robust, however, she seems to have the proper demeanour that makes her an ideal helpmate as a vicar's wife and will provide the perfect example of deference that her husband would require. I took the opportunity to observe her at my cousin, Mrs. Lucas' wedding. She is shy, which is a lovely testament to her delicacy, and I know that she will serve me well, and with her mother's sanction, I cannot help but see her by my side very soon. Certainly her father would agree." Misreading the man's blank face for approval, he continued on with his quest. "However, we return to my concern, I would require a better position and abode before taking her. Will you consider my offer to accept the living at Hunsford when you give your brother his own estate? After all, we are family."

"FAMILY?" De Bourgh's hands twitched. "By what convoluted formula do you arrive at that?"

Collins' attention was distracted by the sound of Mrs. Bennet calling out excitedly. He bobbed. "Ah, my cousin arrives. I must approach Mrs. Bennet so that she may arrange the proper introduction to my future wife."

"Collins!" The vicar called, and the small man immediately changed directions.

Lucas leaned in. "If you follow through and take him off to Kent, I would be greatly appreciative. I have no desire to have him as neighbour, let alone brother."

"Well that display certainly explains the opinions of my parishioners and their relief at my appointment. What a fool he is!" Michael de Bourgh said in amazement as he joined the conversation. "Of course if you wish to split Rosings, I will not turn down the offer." He chuckled and then looked at his brother whose anger was displayed in his bared teeth and focussed gaze. "Peter?"

"*Wife?*" De Bourgh finally spoke. "He insults her! Miss Mary will do far better than the likes of him, of that you may be sure. He is fortunate I do not carry my sword any longer or he would feel the flat of the blade across his back!" De Bourgh's eyes bore into the retreating figure of the scurrying man. Breathing heavily, he regained control of himself, and looked up when he heard an increase in the volume of conversation around the front of the house. The Darcys had arrived, "What took them so long? It is only a mile from the church!" He watched the family greetings and nodded to Darcy when he looked up and smiled, but his eyes fixed on Mary. He had gazed at her as much as he dared during the service, but the family had quickly disappeared afterwards and he only hoped they would come to the breakfast. "She has changed."

Michael looked at her and laughed at his brother. "She *is* different. Perhaps she is a slowly blooming rose."

"I saw her come to life at Pemberley." Lucas felt Jane come to stand by his side. "Do you not agree, my dear? Mary changed there?"

"Yes, she did. She embraced everything that she was given. She chose not to be intimidated by the greatness of the estate." Jane looked down as Lucas entwined his fingers with hers. "She is changing inside and out."

"She is already lovely." De Bourgh murmured.

"And you are lost." Nudging him, Michael managed to draw his attention. "Well?"

"She is far too young."

"Our sisters married at seventeen and eighteen."

"They were far too young, and you know it." He smiled at Mary's blushes. "And I am so old."

"Yes, I hear your bones creaking now. There is a chill in the air; shall I find you a comforter?" Michael laughed. "You are only ten years older."

"Eleven." He sighed. "She deserves better. She deserves a chance to see what Darcy's name can give her."

"Peter, I realize that you are still adjusting to living on land, but someday the truth will dawn on you that you are master of a great estate, and the de Bourgh name is hardly one to be avoided. You have as much or more to offer her as any man." He gave him a shove. "Go."

Before de Bourgh could respond, their mother swooped over and whispered, "Good heavens Peter, if you do not wipe that silly besotted look off of your face, Darcy will die trying to contain his laughter and that poor child you have fixed upon will die of embarrassment!"

"What?" De Bourgh jumped and Michael laughed.

"Now, take me over there and introduce me to her."

"Mother . . . I . . ." He spluttered.

"Oh very well, go greet her on your own, but I will be waiting." She raised her brows. "I want to meet Mrs. Darcy, as well." She turned around to Michael. "Where is your wife?"

He started. "She is . . ." He glanced around to see Charlotte hugging Elizabeth and relaxed. "Come Mother, I will introduce you to Mrs. Darcy."

Mrs. de Bourgh looked at her eldest son. "Peter!"

He startled again and straightening his coat, he walked through the crowd to find Darcy watching his progress. De Bourgh's focus fell on Mary. He drew in a deep breath and smiled at her, and delighted in the instant and becoming blush spreading over her cheeks. His smile grew, and he called out to his cousin.

"Darcy!"

"I was wondering when you would encourage your feet to move." The men clasped hands and clapped backs. "Are you well? You look as if you have just gone ten rounds with Tom Cribb!"

"I hope not, then I would be on the losing end of things." He smiled. "What took you so long? The church is not in London." Examining Darcy's contracted pupils, he nodded. "I take it that preventative measures were necessary?"

Darcy's smile reduced and he murmured, "It seems that crowded circumstances are to be challenging for me." He sighed and shrugged. "I just hope to stave off anything debilitating, it is not so bad right now and if we were at home I would not have taken a dose, but my in-laws seem to inspire the worst. I have had a good run of things for a little over a week. However that is not the reason for our delay. We needed to address a problem with my wife's dress and stopped off at Longbourn." He laughed at the single man's confusion and thought of Elizabeth begging him to relieve the pressure in her painful and leaking breasts while Millie hurriedly had a fresh gown pressed, and how he bargained with her to relieve her need if she relieved his.

"Oh." De Bourgh studied the warmth that radiated from his expression. "I see. So you are feeling well?"

"Better." He corrected and saw that Charlotte had at last relinquished Elizabeth and moved on to greet Mary and Georgiana. Elizabeth came to Darcy's side and wrapped her hand around his arm.

De Bourgh smiled to see her assessing her husband, and the expression displaying satisfaction when Darcy's chuckle rumbled through his chest. "Mrs. Darcy, you look very well indeed, the time at Pemberley seems to have done both you and your husband a great deal of good."

Elizabeth laughed when he bowed to kiss her hand. "It was precisely the rest we needed, but we were poorer for not having your company. I do hope that you might choose to visit us there one day?"

"I will, just as I would enjoy your company at Rosings; however this summer I felt that I should experience my first harvest on the spot, instead of through the post." He saw Darcy's approval. "I knew you would appreciate that."

Darcy pursed his lips and contained his smile. "And I have no doubt that it was stated purely to test my reaction."

De Bourgh chuckled then noticed Collins making his way over to the Bennets. "Darcy, may I have a word in private for a moment?"

"Certainly, Elizabeth . . ."

"I will just go and greet my parents." Elizabeth smiled.

"No." De Bourgh interrupted. They turned to look at him. His face coloured, and leaning to the couple, he whispered. "Collins is planning to approach Mrs. Bennet to ask for an introduction to his future wife, Mary." He looked at his boots. "I would not wish such a match on any good woman."

"I see." Darcy saw Elizabeth's wide eyes. "Perhaps you and I should speak to Mr. Bennet?"

"Darcy, I am not ready to . . .begin . . ."

"Yes, but we must let him know that one day you will be." Darcy's gaze met de Bourgh's. "Correct?"

"I . . . I will not push her. She must know that surely there are others who would care." He looked back to her talking with Charlotte and smiled a little. "She is so young."

Darcy sighed. "Do you wish to leave her vulnerable? A daughter married to Collins would guarantee that Bennet blood remains at Longbourn, somewhere in that man there must be some pride for his heritage." Darcy inwardly groaned at de Bourgh's reticence. "I will speak to him if you are not prepared."

"Yes." De Bourgh nodded at last. "That is fine."

"And I am sure that Mama will be delighted to witness such a rich gentleman speaking to my sisters, and will shoo away Mr. Collins." Elizabeth smiled and lifted her brow.

"Perhaps to one sister more than the other?" De Bourgh laughed and relaxed. "Thank you, I shall take your advice." He turned around and offered his smile first to Georgiana. "Miss Darcy, your trip was pleasant?"

"Oh, yes sir. It was." Georgiana smiled. "I hope that your journey was as well?"

De Bourgh tilted his head and studied her. "It was; thank you, the roads are very good between here and Rosings." Catching Georgiana looking to Elizabeth, he noticed her warm smile and nod of approval, then turned at last to Mary. "Miss Bennet." He bowed low, and gazing into her eyes, took her hand. "May I wish you a very happy belated birthday? I am sorry, but I only just learned of your freedom from childhood."

"Oh." Mary blushed. "Thank you."

"I should have known by the beautiful gown you wear, this shade of green is very becoming." He let go and his smile grew. "How did you know this was my favourite colour?"

"It was in your journal." She saw the delight in his eyes and blushed anew. "Lizzy . . . She thought I could use a new dress for the wedding and I . . ." Mary halted and cast her eyes down.

"It is beautiful. And if it was for my benefit, I thank you." Rewarded by her gaze returning to his, he sighed. "My memory has not done you justice, or is it that you have changed so much since we last met? You also seem to have benefitted by your time at Pemberley. I look forward to hearing all of your adventures."

"I hardly had adventures sir, unless you mean the ones that I enjoyed within the abundance of books I had the opportunity to read." She bit her lip. "It was a wonderful education to learn so many things of the world. I . . . I decided to . . . follow your travels."

"You did?" He laughed, and without thought slipped her hand onto his arm and looked at her eagerly. "Tell me!"

"Oh." Mary blushed and stared at his gloved hand resting over hers, then up to his eyes. She caught Elizabeth watching and nodding encouragingly. "It . . . it was Lizzy's idea. She told me that last winter when Fitzwilliam kept her from her walking; she took the journal from his grand tour and followed his progress with an atlas, and read travel books and histories about the places he visited." She saw de Bourgh smile and nod, and continued. "And when he learned what she was doing, he joined her, and they spent months going through each journal entry, and he would tell her stories of his adventures. They plan to continue this winter."

De Bourgh looked up to find Darcy listening. "How long was your trip?"

"Nine months." Darcy smiled.

His brow furrowed. "And . . .where are you in your storytelling?"

Elizabeth leaned on Darcy's shoulder. "I believe that we have just reached the Alps? On your way south." Darcy nodded and de Bourgh stared.

"You must be full of adventures or your storytelling defies the paucity of your conversation with anyone other than your fair wife."

Darcy smiled and raised Elizabeth's hand to his lips. "I am easily distracted by a very willing pupil."

"Who is eager to be educated." She laughed.

De Bourgh cleared his throat and darted a glance at Mary. She was smiling at the couple, but he was unsure if she understood why they were glowing. "I would enjoy hearing your analysis of my travels as a young lad."

"I would like to know of your travels in the years since then." Mary said softly. "You have had such wonderful opportunities."

"I have, and seen things I can scarcely describe. I believe it was a far richer education than I might have earned in years of formal schooling." He paused and looked down at his boots. "Surely you did other things than concentrate on my boyish musings."

"She danced." Georgiana offered and gave Mary a nudge. Darcy and Elizabeth laughed when de Bourgh's head snapped back up. "She was asked to dance by many young men at the Harvest Home last week. She wore this gown there, as well. Just to try it out." Georgiana giggled when Mary glared at her and blushed. "Oh, there is Kitty, I think I will go and see her." She dashed off and Mary looked up to see an unfamiliar look in de Bourgh's eyes.

"Did you enjoy your dances?" He said carefully.

"I . . . It was my first opportunity to apply what I had learned at school."

"Of course. Schooling for you would be an equal adventure to mine at sea."

"I was thinking, de Bourgh, we will be in town for about a fortnight before the girls start school. Perhaps you might join Elizabeth and me in escorting Mary around for a few evenings? Perhaps take in a performance or two?" Darcy felt Elizabeth's foot step on his boot and resting his hand on the small of her back, he rubbed. "Just to round out the group?"

De Bourgh turned to Mary and smiled brilliantly. "I would be honoured to partner you, Miss Bennet."

Her smile lit up her face. "I . . . I would . . . I would like that, sir."

Across the room, Lydia watched the couples smiling at each other. "What is Captain de Bourgh doing smiling at Mary?"

Kitty leaned and looked. "Oh, he is so handsome! I stared at him the whole time he was standing up with his brother. I know that Maria was hoping that he would smile at her during the service, but she was too shy to look up to this face."

"He is lovely." Georgiana sighed. "But he is also sweet on Mary."

"What?" Kitty and Lydia turned and stared at her.

Georgiana smiled. "He is."

"What would any handsome man want with her? What a joke!" Lydia declared, then an idea struck her. "He just does not know any better." Adjusting her skirts she started to move forward. Kitty's eyes widened and she looked at Georgiana.

"What are you going to do?" Georgiana asked. "They obviously missed seeing each other. Please leave them alone."

"Oh, Mary will have him bored to tears in a minute. I will just rescue him." Lydia set off before they could stop her.

"Kitty, I know that she is your sister, but I am so glad that she is not going to school with us." Georgiana said fervently.

"Well, soon you will see why I am glad, too." Kitty watched her sister's hips start to sway and closed her eyes.

"Captain de Bourgh!" Lydia arrived and stood directly in front of him. Mary instantly let go of his arm and clasped her hands before her. De Bourgh frowned and turned his gaze to the girl. "Maria Lucas said that you are a sea captain."

"I was, yes."

"Where is your uniform? I love to see a man in a fine uniform; it makes him so much more handsome."

"I am retired."

"Oh." She glanced at Mary, and took his arm. "Will you escort me to the refreshment table?"

"I was having a conversation with your sister, Miss Lydia. You interrupted us." He said sternly and removed her hand.

"What can she have to say that is interesting? All she speaks about is sermons, she goes on and on about such boring subjects, it makes your head spin! I *never* listen to her! Now, Mama said that you are very rich and have a great house. Is it nearby? You must give a ball! We can go and dance and dance! I would be very happy to dance with you!"

"Miss Lydia, you are far too young to attend a ball, a lady waits to be asked to dance, and fortunately my home is too far away to chance your arriving unexpectedly." Seeing her beginning to pout he grew annoyed. "Your sister Mary has undoubtedly learned a great deal and you would do well to listen, she can teach you how to behave like a lady, as she does. And your sisters Elizabeth and Jane can do the same."

"All Jane cares about is Mr. Lucas, I see them all over the place, making eyes at each other and kissing. At least they are fun to watch." Georgiana blushed and looked at her feet as Lydia continued on. "Lizzy is rich, but she never buys me anything." She glared at her. "And she did not invite me to town when they were there this summer."

"Your sister and brother were very ill, Miss Lydia." De Bourgh said coldly.

"Oh, I know. Mama went on and on about how we would be thrown in the hedgerows because Lizzy was going to die and Mr. Darcy would not take care of us." She nodded and Darcy, hearing his name, turned and stared at her. "He is hateful."

"Miss Lydia." De Bourgh's voice was low. "Curb your voice."

"But everything will be fine now that Mary is to marry Mr. Collins."

"What?" Mary's hands flew up to her mouth.

De Bourgh looked at Mary quickly and turned to her sister. "Miss Lydia, you have no business repeating unfounded gossip."

"It is not gossip!" She said stubbornly. "Mama said that he would marry her and save Longbourn. After all it is just Mary . . ."

Darcy saw that Elizabeth was about to blow and de Bourgh's hands were clenched. Mary was in tears and turned to run from the room. Georgiana took her hand and they left together. Furious, de Bourgh leaned down and spoke in a heated whisper near Lydia's ear. "How dare you spread lies like this? You are an unthinking, hurtful, selfish little girl. You dress like a trollop, and you have the unchecked mouth of a common waif!" Lydia gasped and he would have continued except for the feel of Darcy's hand on his shoulder. He stood and seethed. "Someone speak to her! Get through the wool that inhabits her mind!" Spinning away, he went in search of Mary.

Elizabeth took Lydia by the arm and walked her, protesting, across the room to her mother and father. "Papa, Mama, Lydia was repeating opinions that I sincerely hope are not your own?"

"Mama, tell her to let me go!" Lydia twisted.

"Hold still and lower your voice, you are making a scene!" Elizabeth hissed.

"I am not!"

"Miss Lydia." Darcy's deep voice cut through her cries. "Enough." Lydia stared up at his intense glare and her mouth snapped shut. He turned to Mrs. Bennet and said in a barely audible, but undeniably angry voice. "I need to clarify two points. First, Mary is not, and will not be attached to Mr. Collins. She will not be forced to accept his suit any more than this spoiled brat that you call daughter will." Mr. Bennet watched the reactions of mother and daughter, and met Darcy's furious glare. "Second, I assume, correctly I hope, that the views espoused by this uneducated, indulged, and intellectually neglected child are the remnants of old conversations that remained in her memory because of their vehement and endless repetition by her mother, and are no longer the topic of current conversation."

"I assume that these are the topics that we discussed in our last meeting, sir?" Mr. Bennet said quietly.

"They are."

"I can assure you that they have not been repeated, but it seems that although one source of noise has been silenced, another equally loud one has not." He looked at Lydia tiredly. "But she will very soon be on her way to school."

"I will not go." She said flatly. Darcy glared at her again and she was silenced.

"You know the conditions of our agreement, sir." He nodded to Elizabeth, who let her go. "I will add another. My family's name is linked to yours, your disgrace is mine. I will not have centuries of my family's honour ruined by the behaviour of this foolish girl." His eyes closed and he drew a breath. "Excuse me."

Elizabeth looked after him and saw that he was moving towards the front door and silence. She turned to her parents. Without a hint of emotion, she spoke quietly. "It seems that we cannot come to visit here without some sort of confrontation occurring, I am only grateful that the noise and activity of this joyous event has kept the neighbourhood from witnessing our shame. However, I will not risk the health of my husband by subjecting him any longer to this situation. Please say your goodbyes to Kitty, we will be leaving for London within the half-hour."

"Lizzy, please understand that we have not made any promises to Mr. Collins regarding Mary." Mr. Bennet said softly.

"The only one whose name has not been proposed for him has been Kitty's, and thankfully she will be in school."

"Why does she get to go to London?" Lydia whined.

"Because she wants to get away from you." Elizabeth said coldly. Lydia searched the room and saw Kitty standing with Maria, as far away from her as possible. "Did you hear how Captain de Bourgh described you?"

"yes." She muttered.

"Did you hear how Mr. Darcy described you?"

"yes."

"Those are two very good, and very wealthy men expressing their opinions. Do you think that any other decent man would have one that is different?" Greeted with silence, Elizabeth took Lydia's hand and waited for her to look her in the eye. "This is your one opportunity, Lydia. Listen to me. Take it and improve, or," She turned her sister to look at Collins, "that could be the best future you can hope for." Lydia recoiled and looked at her father, who nodded.

Elizabeth let go. "I must go and find my husband. Excuse me." She walked away and her progress was followed by Mr. Bennet.

"Quite the formidable woman, Mrs. Darcy is." A voice with an approving tone spoke from behind him. "She is how old? Nineteen? My goodness, I will enjoy knowing her very much." Mrs. de Bourgh smiled when the Bennets turned to her. "Forgive me for listening, but I could not help it, my son was distressed because of this child's behaviour, and I am rather protective of my own." She cast a disgusted look at Lydia, nodded and moved away.

"Mr. Bennet, why would Mrs. de Bourgh worry over her son's distress over Lydia?" Mrs. Bennet fretted.

"He was trapped talking to Mary before I went over to rescue him." Lydia sniffed and Mrs. Bennet's eyes widened as the impossible chance of a match struck her.

"You will not speak to another man again until you are out." Mr. Bennet informed her. "Thank heaven you will soon be in a school populated solely by women."

"Mama . . ."

Fresh from her realization she spoke vehemently. "No Lydia, you must go. Lizzy spoke the truth. Captain de Bourgh is a rich man and he was unhappy with you. You must go to school and learn how to attract one yourself." She glanced sadly at Jane with Lucas. "You are so beautiful."

Outside on a bench beneath the shade of an oak tree, Darcy sat with his eyes closed, and tried to let the gentle sounds of the clucking chickens wash away the growing pain in his head. Elizabeth approached and standing behind him, gently massaged his neck and shoulders. "How are you?"

"The preventative dose was an excellent suggestion, love." He said softly and leaned into her touch. "It is not as bad as it probably would have been." He sighed. "I do not know that I can comfortably come here again. I have been feeling so much better, but the anticipation of . . . well just about anything occurring . . ." He tried to smile through the throbbing of his head. "Even our little tryst did not manage to overcome it."

"Then we will just have to relax you again when we arrive at home." She kissed his nose and he leaned back against her breasts. "Peter is talking to Mary and Georgiana."

"Is he?" Darcy smiled and snuggled his head against his pillows, relaxing into her gentle caress. "What are they doing?"

"He has them laughing." Elizabeth smiled. "He is a bit of a rake."

"He is very shy."

She leaned down and kissed his ear. "I know. He reminds me of you." Darcy chuckled. "ahhh, that is better."

"Is everything well?" Jane asked as she and Lucas approached them. "I could not hear it, but I saw Lydia's face."

"Could anyone else hear?"

"No." Lucas leaned against the tree and studied Darcy's face, his eyes remained closed. "There is enough noise in there to block out her whining." Jane looked at him and he shrugged. "I am calling a spade a spade, my dear. It is no secret that your sister is in need of discipline." He laughed, "And it seems that it took Darcy and de Bourgh to swoop in and deliver it, the evil brother and the handsome stranger."

"Evil?" Darcy said softly.

"You do not bring her gifts." Jane said before Lucas could answer.

He glanced at her and looked back at Darcy. "After Elizabeth left, I spoke to Mr. Bennet. I told him that I will not tolerate the poor example of behaviour that Lydia presents for my younger siblings, and that he either check it, or I would speak to my father about denying her access to them and our home."

"That was well done." Darcy smiled slightly. "You do not have the authority to dictate to Mr. Bennet since you are not master, but you do have the authority to threaten. And surely Mr. Bennet knows well enough that you are the one who truly is in charge of this home." He grimaced and held his breath for a moment, and slowly let it go. Elizabeth continued to gently rub his neck. "And she will soon be gone to school, so it is unlikely that you will need to carry through with it. I think that the important point is that you are making it clear that you are not to be taken lightly."

"I have had an excellent teacher." Lucas said softly and Darcy did not respond.

"Jane, you must decide on your response, as well. If Mama complains . . ."

"I will follow whatever my husband and Sir William state are the rules of our home, Lizzy." Jane spoke quietly. "And I know that I must determine what we will do when Kitty and Lydia are gone. Mama will not like keeping her own company, but she will not be able to spend her days here, either."

"Are you certain you do not have any tenancies available at Pemberley?" Lucas smiled and Darcy chuckled. "I know, I know, this is our home."

"You will do well by it."

"Eliza?" They looked up to see Charlotte approaching with Michael. "Are you . . ." She stopped when they came around the gathering to see Darcy's position. "Are you well, Mr. Darcy?"

"I will be." He slowly blinked open his eyes and grimaced with the light. "Eventually."

"So are we all chaperoning my brother?" Michael laughed and looked over to the other gathering. "He has been a bundle of nerves in anticipation of our wedding." He smiled at Charlotte, "and it was not out of concern for me."

"Leave them be, Michael."

"What sort of brother would I be if I did not harass him? Just because I am a vicar, it does not mean that I am without humour." He laughed. "Collins was lobbying to see me ousted, though."

"What?" Darcy stared. "It is a life appointment!"

"He suggested that Peter break up Rosings and give me half." He saw Darcy's eyes roll. "Even I know that the estate must be intact to keep the family strong."

"Exactly." He murmured. "When our son is born, we will ensure that for Pemberley."

"Lizzy, are you?" Jane asked excitedly.

"OH!" Elizabeth blushed. "No, no." Darcy looked up to her with a little smile. "We are in no hurry."

"Well, we are going to say our farewells." Charlotte smiled at them all. "And depart for Hunsford. It is a long journey."

"You are welcome to stay at Darcy House tonight." Elizabeth offered and Darcy took her hand to kiss. "It would make your journey easier, would it not?"

"Well, yes," Michael smiled, "but my brother has already invited us to join him and mother at his townhouse for a week of honeymooning."

"He did?" Charlotte gasped.

"Did I not tell you?" He winked and raised her hand to his lips. "Surprise."

"Maybe Collins could fill in for you." Lucas offered to the collective groans of the friends. He laughed and took Jane's hand. "It was just a thought."

25 SEPTEMBER 1810
The Globe Inn
Dumfries

Dear Darcy,
Well here we are at last. How many times have you told me of the angling by the shore, and the amazing variety of fish to be had? I have enjoyed myself immensely

here this past week. Hurst's skill with a rod is rather frightening, he can but glance at the water and already his line is tugging with a furious dogfish or bass. Naturally, staying at an inn, we do not have much use for our catch, so we simply turn it in to the innkeeper, and he is pleased with the gift. By the way, I picked up a memento for you. Mrs. Darcy mentioned your fondness for the poet Burns once and lo above our table last night, I saw a plaque applied to the wall saying this is where he sat writing his verse! Last night we were treated to a round of his songs by a lusty group of drunken Scotsmen. I would have lent my voice to the chorus, had I understood what they were saying, however, I was glad to drink along with them. I hunted about for a souvenir for you, a book of poetry that I actually chose as opposed to those sonnets your fair wife found for you. Do you still carry that about?

Louisa wished to tour a bit so the other day we wandered off to Gretna Green, settled in a tavern and watched a fair number of weddings across the way at the blacksmith's and then a few more couples came in and declared themselves to the witnesses within the tavern. Hurst and I had a good time, wagering on which couple would pay the extra fee to take advantage of the bed in the next room, then we bet on how fast the bride and groom would reappear, properly consummated. It is a fascinating and doubtless quite profitable industry! I was regarded with great interest at first, it seems that gentleman pay a particularly high fee for the privilege of eloping, and after many times being given the long face for having been jilted, eventually Hurst and I just played along, and accepted their offers of whiskey.

Mrs. Darcy, I hereby offer my sincerest apologies if I have offended you, I only wish to make your stoic husband smile. I hope that you both continue to heal and that this new journey to London assures you that the town is not cursed; it only contains a few cursed inhabitants. I wish you very well, I hope that your sisters are happy in their new school, I hope that my sweet Rosalie is growing and taking an even firmer grip upon her papa's heart, and I want you to know that I miss you all deeply. My visit to Pemberley cannot come soon enough.

Sincerely yours,

Charles Bingley, Esq.

Elizabeth wiped a tear that appeared in her eye. "He is such a dear man. We must find him someone to love."

"Lizzy."

"I know."

"So you are not offended with his story?" Darcy took the letter from her hand and set it down on the table beside the sofa.

"No." She laughed and snuggled into his chest, "He is just seeking that elusive smile."

"Hardly elusive when I have my girls in my arms." He looked down at Rosalie's peaceful face. Elizabeth adjusted the ribbons on her little cap and he kissed her hair. "No caps for you, love."

"Mama is apoplectic about it."

"Your mother is apoplectic about everything." He sighed. "Indulge me. I will provide funds for feathers, hats, jewels and pins, but please love, no caps."

"Bonnets?"

"If you must."

"I love your hats." She looked up to his smile. "I like your top hats the best."

"I do, too." They kissed until Rosalie squirmed as their bodies pressed against her and she protested. "I am sorry, little love." Darcy hurriedly readjusted her, while Elizabeth covered her again. The couple's eyes met and they resumed their kissing. "Lizzy?"

"hmm?" She sighed as his lips fixed under her ear. "When do you wish to begin again?"

"You mean, try and have another child?"

"Yes." He lifted his head and smiled into her eyes. "Whenever you are ready, I will be, too."

"Is this because Alicia is with child?"

"No." He sighed and looked at their baby. "I . . . I do not know. Maybe I am becoming more confident."

"As a father, or that we can survive anything that comes our way?" She caressed his brow. "You are feeling better."

"Yes." They kissed again. "Yes to everything. Whenever you are ready, dear. Whenever Rosa is ready." He looked back at her and leaned down to nuzzle his nose against her. Rosalie's hand reached up to hold it and he chuckled.

"Now you are doomed to remain there." Elizabeth laughed.

"No, no. I cannot kiss you from this position. Forgive me love." He pulled away and the baby yawned. "There."

"When I cannot bear her teeth any longer . . ." She offered and he laughed. "She does not have your tender tongue."

"Hmmm. I would dearly enjoy the touch of yours." His eyes met hers. "Shall we bid our daughter good night?"

"And what of our sisters?" She whispered when he leaned to kiss her again.

Darcy's mouth hovered over hers and he watched the tip of her tongue as it travelled slowly over her lips. "I think they will benefit from their evening alone." He captured her mouth. "Elizabeth . . ." He whispered warmly in her ear.

"Ba!" They jumped. "Baabababa babababaaaadadadadada." His head rested in Elizabeth's hair while they both started to laugh. "Maybe we should divest ourselves of our daughter before we continue."

"I think that she wants to play."

"I want to play." Darcy declared, and stood. "And I want you to play with me." Elizabeth leaned forward and kissed the arousal proudly straining at his breeches, then mouthed it to the sound of his groan.

"If you insist." She stood and took the baby from his arms. "But I pick the game."

"WHAT IF I DO NOT DO WELL?" Kitty looked up from the trunk and watched as another new gown was placed inside. "Lizzy, I am not like these girls." She darted a glance at the door and whispered, "I sometimes do not know what Georgiana is talking about."

"What is she telling you?"

"Oh . . . she said that she is remembering when Mary started school and all of the things that confused her, and she gives great speeches on what to do and how to look at people, walking and talking, how to eat . . . Oh Lizzy, what am I going to do? I will probably cut some duke's daughter and will not know that I did it! I should have gone to Lydia's school!"

"No, Kitty. Lydia's school is for girls who do not respect rules and behave badly." Elizabeth took her hand and they sat together on the bed. "I know that you are relieved to be separated from her, especially after her behaviour at the wedding." She studied her sister's downcast eyes. "I always believed that you just followed along with Lydia."

"Well." She glanced at the door again. "Mary did not want me."

"Mary probably did not know that you would want her. I think that all five of us found different ways to survive our upbringing."

"But I did not know that there was anything wrong with it!" Kitty cried. "Not until you left and did not return, and Jane returned without a husband, and . . . Mama was so upset all of the time! Papa just suddenly started making us study and I realized that something was wrong with us." She sighed. "And when I tried to talk to Lydia about it, she would just laugh at me. She does not really listen to me. It is . . . It is as if I am nothing more than a doll to play with."

"And she throws you aside when she is bored." Elizabeth held her hand. "So why would you want to go to school with her?"

"I guess it is because I know what to expect from her." She shrugged and started to wipe her eyes with her hand and felt a handkerchief pressed into her palm. "Oh Lizzy, what will I do in this school for rich girls?"

Elizabeth brushed back the curls that fell across her face. "You will learn how to be the best Kitty you can. You will leave there in two years just as rich in knowledge as they are. What happens after that is up to you. We offered Mary a home with us at Pemberley, and we will be happy to have you come to us there when you are finished as well."

"You would let me come?" Kitty looked up hopefully.

"Of course." Elizabeth smiled and kissed her. "Poor Fitzwilliam, another woman in the house!"

"Then you will have to have a boy next!" Kitty giggled. "And we can spoil him!"

"I have a feeling that he will need spoiling after his papa fills his head with talk of duty and honour." Elizabeth laughed. "Now, are you still frightened?"

"Yes."

"I think that we should go and talk to Mary. She can tell you everything about how to fit in with these rich girls." She tugged Kitty's hand and they stood. "And I think that I might have a few things to tell you, too."

"But you are a rich girl now, Lizzy." Kitty followed her out of the room.

"I suppose I am." She laughed and gave her a hug. "But once upon a time, I was just as silly as you."

"I CANNOT REACH MY ARMS AROUND YOU!" Fitzwilliam laughed.

"Richard, do *not* toy with me!" Evangeline warned him. "I am not in a playful mood."

"I am!" He rested his chin on her shoulder and kissed her neck. "So tell me my dear, what may I do to improve yours?"

"Carry your child for me." Evangeline closed her eyes and sighed. "I am so tired."

"I know sweet girl." He whispered in her ear. "It is nearly over."

"It is not." She let her weight rest against his chest. "It is two months away."

"But that is less than nine." He hugged her and laid his hands over her belly. "He is kicking me."

Tiredly, she sighed. "Me, as well."

Chuckling, he took her hand. "Come along, dear. Darcy and Elizabeth will be here very soon, that should cheer you."

"I wish that I could visit them." She looked at her swollen feet. "What am I saying; I wish that I could walk."

"You do just fine, and I like always knowing where you are." He chuckled at her glare. "And think of the money we save without you shopping!"

"Richard Fitzwilliam, if you think that you are cheering me . . ."

"No, I know I am infuriating you." He winked and led her to a sofa, eased her down and lifted her legs so that they rested on pillows. Leaning down, he kissed her. "Better?"

"Yes." She said reluctantly.

"Good." He settled behind her back and rubbed her shoulders. "I love you."

"You think that makes up for everything?"

"Everything? You mean making you so lovely?" He chuckled when she groaned and kissed her cheek. "Indeed!"

"Sir, the Darcys have arrived." A footman announced and soon showed them in.

"Forgive us for not standing." Fitzwilliam smiled as they entered and shook hands with Darcy. "Where is Mary?" He craned his neck to the doorway. "Did she lose her way?"

"No." Elizabeth kissed them both and sat down next to Darcy. "She and Aunt Gardiner are enjoying tea at the de Bourgh townhouse."

"With Mrs. de Bourgh and son." Darcy chuckled.

"Oh ho!" Fitzwilliam rubbed his hands together.

"Keep your oh ho's to yourself, Richard." Evangeline nudged him. "Is it a match?"

"You are as bad as your husband." Elizabeth laughed. "Or Lady Helen!"

"I am not!" She declared.

Darcy stepped in. "No match. Not yet. He has this ridiculous sense of honour or duty or something, wanting to wait until she is sure and truly ready." Fitzwilliam and Evangeline, exchanging glances, blushed.

Fitzwilliam cleared his throat. "Rather admirable, that."

"Hmm." Darcy's hint of a smile graced his mouth.

"And the girls, they are settled at school?" Darcy's smile disappeared. "Come on, man, you know it is best for them."

"I know."

"They are just in Queen's Square; Kitty wondered why they could not just walk there from Darcy House every day." Elizabeth smiled when Darcy relaxed against her. "We explained that would defeat the purpose of a boarding school."

"It is hardly a stroll down the lanes to move between Mayfair and Bloomsbury." Fitzwilliam laughed. "Country girls."

"Richard, do not test my ire so soon in our visit." Elizabeth warned. He raised his hands over his head in surrender.

Darcy cleared his throat. "They were soundly warned about walking alone. I am not so afraid for Georgiana, but Kitty . . ."

"Kitty is a follower; she will do whatever Georgiana says." Elizabeth assured him. "She will do whatever is necessary to fit in to her new circumstances, and if the Misses Stevenson give her praise, she will be loyal to them forever."

"Sounds like an ideal wife." Fitzwilliam winked at Darcy. "You know, hanging on your every word, rushing to provide you a drink, a rub, any bit of comfort."

"And without protest." Darcy added when Fitzwilliam yelped from Evangeline's pinch, and sent a sidelong glance at Elizabeth. "I feel the heat of your glare, my love, and it warms my soul."

"That is not the only thing that I should be warming on you." She declared and crossed her arms.

"Oh ho!" Fitzwilliam cried.

"Richard!"

"She baits him, my dear!" He sat forward, "Come man, return the strike!"

"I will not fight my wife for your entertainment, Cousin." Darcy stated and smiled to see Elizabeth let down her stance. "I do that for my own."

"Fitzwilliam Darcy!"

"Touché!" Richard declared. "Good Lord, Darcy. It is good to see you back in top form again. It has been far too long!"

Darcy looked down at Elizabeth's fingers entwining with his and smiled. "We are not there yet, Cousin, but we have learned how to tame the beast."

"And how is this done?" Evangeline watched them supporting each other.

"We have accepted our weaknesses and have learned when to accept help." Elizabeth looked into Darcy's smiling eyes then turned to see understanding in theirs. "And we are ready to move on."

Chapter 27

"What do you think of Mrs. de Bourgh?" Mrs. Gardiner asked Mary.

"She seems rather brusque. But I believe that she means well." Mary added quickly.

Elizabeth hid her smile in her teacup. "She reminded me of Lady Matlock in some ways, she does not mince words. But I agree, she means well, she is very protective and does not tolerate foolishness."

"I could see that she liked you, Mary, she was just seeing what sort of a girl you are." Mrs. Gardiner smiled and sighed when Mary's eyes widened. "She wanted to see if you are genuine. I am certain that her son has begun attracting attention. He is a handsome young man who has control of a large estate, he is going to be desired by a great many women. He is no innocent fool, but Mrs. de Bourgh will be vetting any woman who smiles at him, and more, any who he chooses to smile at in return."

"But I . . . I am not chasing him, I would not know how to chase a man!"

Elizabeth sighed. "That is not what she said, Mary. But surely you can understand how protective Mrs. de Bourgh will feel about him? He has been away from home since he was a very young boy, and now he has returned at last to have all of these riches and responsibilities thrust upon him. She is just protecting him now in the way she could not do all those years when he was at sea."

"Oh."

"I know; that is something you and I find hard to understand, since it is so different from our own experience. But I will certainly be just as protective with my children." She smiled.

Mrs. Gardiner nodded and turned to Mary. "She has not had an easy life, and she needed to be very strong to see her family safely to adulthood. She has been a widow for a long time, and had to rely on the kindness of family to help them get by on the little she had from her husband until Captain de Bourgh began earning enough to send home to her. You know that is why her younger son was not in the navy, do you not? Captain de Bourgh was so terribly lonely as a boy, he insisted that part of the funds he sent be saved to send his brother to school, and to keep him from the sea."

"How good of him!" Mary whispered. "I did not know. I knew that he was lonely, he wrote about it, but . . ." She fell into thoughtful silence. "His journal was his friend."

"Just as my journal was mine, and Fitzwilliam's was his." Elizabeth saw that she understood and smiled. "Captain de Bourgh is a very modest man, and to speak of that would be promoting himself, even to his journal. He reminds me of Fitzwilliam in many ways. He is a very dedicated family man. It is something to be admired."

"How do you know so many details about him?" Mary asked her aunt. "I can see why Lizzy would but, how do you know?"

"Well I had of course met him before, so I was able to talk to his mother about some little observations I had made. And then it was just two mothers speaking about a favourite child. How do you feel about him?"

"Oh, he is so very kind to me. Why?"

Elizabeth laughed. "Well clearly he finds you disgusting and wishes to fill his imagination with images of you to laugh about when you are gone."

"Lizzy!"

"Truly Mary! The way he stares at you! I am certain that he is amazed continually that such a poor creature as you can breathe, let alone engage in intelligent discourse! Oh yes, you are a curiosity, a freak at a fair." Elizabeth nudged her and smiled.

"You are teasing me." Mary said to her hands.

"Of course I am! Mary! Oh, do you not recognize the smile in his eyes when he looks upon you? He has come sightseeing with us so many times this week! Why do you think that is? He is very sly, not smiling too much, not hovering too much, but his pleasure cannot be entirely disguised. Just wait until we take Fitzwilliam to the theatre, you will be in your new gown, your hair beautifully dressed, wearing . . . oh I have a lovely necklace you must borrow, and when we come down the stairs together, I am sure that the expression on his face will give away all of his thoughts."

Mrs. Gardiner sighed at her playful niece and took Mary's hand. "What do you think of him?"

"He is very kind. And he seems genuinely interested in me." Mary smiled shyly. "I like learning all about him."

"Well that is only natural, and you are fortunate that he has a very pleasant voice that he is not afraid to use." Elizabeth laughed and clapped when she saw Mary blushing again. "Do you like him?"

"Yes, of course." She looked up to see her sister's eyes sparkling. "Lizzy, what has come over you?"

"Oh Mary, cannot I feel happy for you?" Elizabeth laughed. "Captain de Bourgh is a dear man, he is loyal, he is considerate, and he is becoming a confident master. How can you not admire such a man? And what I like best of all about him, he likes you. That shows excellent taste." She stood to hug her sister. "I am sorry to sound like a matchmaking mama, I simply like him and love you."

"Thank you, Lizzy." She sighed. "I confess, I have thought of how he has become master of an estate, and how different it is from what he has known for so long. I wonder if he will change as he becomes more comfortable." She looked to her sister. "Fitzwilliam cares little for society, and he would be just as happy to be at home at Pemberley all of the time. Captain de Bourgh, he has so many opportunities ahead of him."

"He does, and he is taking his time. I know that he spoke to Fitzwilliam about wanting to be confident in his new position, and confident in the world where he now lives. He wants to do well for his family."

"And to meet some lady of society." Mary deflated. "I understand."

"No, Mary, you do not." Mrs. Gardiner touched her knee. "Watch him at the theatre, see where his attention rests, see how he responds to the ladies who undoubtedly know who he is and what he has, and then you will perhaps understand him better."

"Lizzy!" Benjamin Gardiner ran into the room and threw his arms around her waist. "Lizzy!"

"My goodness! Look how you have grown!" Elizabeth cried and gasped at the force of his hug. "How did you escape your governess?"

"I heard you laughing. I waited until she was not looking and snuck downstairs. She is busy with Amy." He beamed at her. "I have not seen you for so very long!"

"I know, and I missed you, dear." She hugged him and kissed his blonde curls. The sound of boots in the hallway was followed by the arrival of Darcy and Mr. Gardiner. Benjamin kept his tight grip on Elizabeth and frowned at Darcy.

Mr. Gardiner spoke sternly. "Son, why are you scowling at Mr. Darcy?"

"He always takes Lizzy away."

Darcy's eyes widened and he bit back a smile when she started to laugh. "Forgive me; I did not know there was a rival for my affection!"

"You always go back in the parlour and close the door." Benjamin accused. Darcy's eyes met Elizabeth's and they both blushed.

"We have very fond memories of that room, Benjamin, and a visit to your home would not be complete without a moment spent there." He smiled and ruffled his hair. "I am happy to know how fond you are of your cousin."

"Now you know how I feel, since your affections belong to another woman." Elizabeth hugged the little boy and he snuggled in closer. Darcy smiled to see her eyes dancing. It had been a long time since they both felt so good.

"I think, Mrs. Gardiner, that it is time that our boy was breeched." Mr. Gardiner tilted his head and looked over his son. "Time to remove the petticoats and make him a man."

"Oh Edward, must we?" Mrs. Gardiner sighed. "He is so young."

"He is six." He met her eye. "Breeches. It is time. We probably should have done it a few years ago."

"Yes dear." She looked sadly at Elizabeth. "He is a child no more."

Darcy watched the scene and looked up to Mr. Gardiner. "I remember my first pair of breeches. I was six, I think. I do not remember my mother's reaction, but my father was undoubtedly very proud. I remember being glad to be out of stays." He laughed to see Elizabeth's obvious sigh. "They gave me a little party to celebrate, that I remember, but then as soon as I was in my skeleton suit, my education of all that is Pemberley began in earnest. I would join Father as he rode the estate. It was not always easy, though. I remembered sometimes wishing that my lessons with him were finished so that I could escape to the schoolroom." He smiled at Benjamin still embracing Elizabeth. "Will you begin taking your son with you?"

"Of course, but his schooling is very important as well." Mr. Gardiner's chest puffed. "I am very proud of what I can provide for him."

"As you should be." Darcy nodded. "I look forward to passing on my pride to our son one day." He met Elizabeth's smiling eyes. "Well, eventually."

"WHERE ARE YOU GOING, MRS. BENNET?" Mr. Bennet's voice floated from his bookroom. "I certainly hope that you are not bound for Lucas Lodge again."

"You make me sound as if I am a pest! I am visiting our daughter!" She entered the room and started fussing over her bonnet. "She needs me."

"To do what, exactly? She is living in another woman's home; she is learning her role as wife and future mistress from the person whose place she will one day assume. A friendly call once or twice a week is sufficient enough disruption from you." He looked at her pointedly. "You heard Lucas. He was serious. He would deny access to his home if he felt that the behaviour of our family was a bad influence on his own."

"He was speaking of Lydia." Mrs. Bennet sniffed.

"He implied us all." He said sternly. "Lydia is a product of her education."

"Oh my poor dear girl! Tell me again how she cried for me when you left her at that horrible school!"

Rolling his eyes and sighing, he set down his paper. "She cried for herself, but Miss Edwards made it perfectly clear in the first moments of their meeting that she will brook no nonsense from her. That woman has years of experience with spoiled girls, she reminded me of Darcy with her ability to silence with a look. As if I did not already feel that I am a failure as a parent by those two young men chastising me, after seeing how quickly that woman handled our daughter, I was humbled and embarrassed for having to present her as mine."

"Poor Lydia; exposed to all of those awful girls! I do hope that she is not influenced by them." She sighed and when Mr. Bennet did not respond, she looked up to see the disbelief in his face. "Why do you stare so?"

"Mrs. Bennet, Lydia may have an opportunity to improve herself. Do you not see what schooling has done for Mary?"

"Mary attended the same school as Miss Darcy. Besides she always had her nose in a book." She sniffed. "Just like Lizzy."

"Yes, and Lizzy has done so poorly." Mr. Bennet sighed.

"Ever since Lizzy married Mr. Darcy, all of our girls have been taken away." Mrs. Bennet played with her bonnet ribbons. "If he had not taken her, there never would be this need for schooling. You would not have thought of it."

"No, I did not, despite Lizzy's pleas for it, and I have done our daughters and our families no favours for being so negligent. Mrs. Bennet, surely you are not holding a grudge against Mr. Darcy for urging that our daughters be improved? Without proper education, Elizabeth has made an exceptional match, as has Jane. And if Captain de Bourgh continues to admire Mary, she will be extraordinarily wed. I could never have imagined such fortune for her, for any of our girls. You should be overjoyed, and I am overwhelmed that you are not. And now Kitty will have the opportunity to meet men through Elizabeth, and if Lydia works very hard, she may just win someone better than my heir. How can you not be pleased, what happened to your cries of triumph to have two daughters wed?"

She burst into tears and wailed, "I am alone! What am I to do now?" She sniffed and fell into a chair, waved her handkerchief and sobbed into it. "Oh, Mr. Bennet!"

"If you had succeeded in marrying them off at the age of fifteen they would all be gone now, too!" Sighing, he waited for a break in her gasps and spoke quietly. "Mrs. Bennet, now do you understand where we have been deficient parents? We have provided a poor example to our daughters of marriage and drifted apart. Now that it is just you and I, we are lost. We have nothing in common. I can keep myself busy forever with the estate and my books, but you must find somewhere to put your time, and I do not see you embroidering for the remainder of your days."

"Oh no!" Her eyes grew wide.

"Neither will you spend your days visiting Jane. There must be more for you than gossiping with your sister and the neighbours because you will not be spending my savings on frippery, it will go to pay my steward as he deserves and to save for my family's survival past my death. Lizzy sent me a letter; would you care to hear what she has to say?" He held it up.

"I suppose." She sniffed and eyed the fine stationary.

"It says, first that they are well, and Rosalie is sitting up by herself now." He saw her nod. "She enjoyed taking the girls shopping for their new dresses, and Mary has several lovely ones now. They were waiting for her new gowns to be finished before they went out with Captain de Bourgh. Mr. Darcy's birthday is this week, and they will take in a performance at Covent Garden in celebration."

"Oh." Mrs. Bennet looked envious. "I would love to go to town. Perhaps we . . ."

"Mrs. Bennet, *we* are not going anywhere." He said sternly. "However, she was thinking of how you might be feeling at a loss now that the house is empty, and suggests that you might do as she when she first became Mrs. Darcy." He licked his lips and braced himself. "She suggests that you begin to visit our tenants and learn their needs." Mrs. Bennet opened her mouth and he held up his hand. "It is not an unreasonable plan. You have never really concerned yourself with them. Neither have I, and I think that Longbourn is poorer for it. She also said that gardening is all the rage in London and she thought you might like to spend the winter planning out how you would reinvigorate our small park, perhaps making sketches to give to our steward." Before she said more, he continued, "And she suggested that you and I could read together and . . . talk about what we read."

"Read!" Her eyes grew wide.

"It is an admirable way to pass the time, Mrs. Bennet. It might just improve our minds." He sighed. "Lizzy is trying to think of activities that you might possibly entertain willingly. She would undoubtedly hope that you would take greater interest in becoming an outstanding mistress of this estate and provide a sound example to our remaining children. Visiting tenants would give you the contact with others that you enjoy, improving the garden will give you pride in something you have accomplished." Once more he tried to impress her with their failure to their children. "I am certain that she wonders why she has had to take on the duties of mother to Mary and Kitty." Seeing her brow furrow, he took some slight comfort at the sight. "I am open to suggestion; perhaps that is how you might spend your time today. Thinking."

STEWART NUDGED DARCY when he walked past his chair at the club and sat down. "What brings you here?" He grinned. "And looking so well?"

"Which causes you the most consternation?" Darcy smiled and putting down his paper, waved off the servant who immediately appeared at his elbow with glasses of port. Stewart accepted one and sat back.

He gestured with his glass. "I am not criticizing. I am just pleased to see it. So the girls are settled?"

"Yes." Darcy sighed. "We will remain the rest of this week just to be sure that all is well, then return straight home."

"No visits to the in-laws." Stewart winked. "Can't say that I blame you. We have been without the Henleys since August." He took a sip and grinned. "Bliss!"

"They are not so very bad."

"Darcy, I know your mother-in-law and you know mine. Enough said."

Darcy lifted his hand in defeat. "Say no more. How is Mrs. Stewart?"

"Very well. Lovely and wonderful." He sighed and laughed at Darcy's satisfied smirk. "You will have to bring Elizabeth by to visit."

"I believe that she is doing that as we speak. She was to spend the day making calls to a few friends, and then tomorrow we will go to the theatre."

"Ah . . ." Stewart's brow creased. "Tomorrow is your birthday!"

"How on earth, and further, why would you remember that?" Darcy laughed.

"Oh, well, a year ago, it was not marked so well." He saw the frown appear and shook his head. "Forgive me."

"No, it was also the day that I learned Elizabeth was with child." He shrugged and his smile returned. "A long year that I am glad to call over."

"So what brings you here today? A chance to enjoy some time amongst men for a change?"

Darcy glanced around the sparsely populated room. "Most of the men are in the country. Why are you still here, by the way?"

"Our parents are going to be with Laura and Harwick, she is due next month, and well honestly, I have no desire to go to Moreland and spend the autumn with my brother." He shrugged when Darcy's lips lifted in a smile. "Next week we will be heading to our little estate and remain until court begins again. So, what brings you here?"

"Always the barrister. Well I met a friend of Lord Wolcroft's who knew his private secretary. Arthur Conrad, do you know him?"

"Conrad." Stewart closed his eyes. "I know that name. Older fellow, about forty?"

"About that." Darcy nodded. "He was with Lord Wolcroft for nearly twenty years before he died and the estate was inherited by a distant cousin. He chose not to continue Conrad's employment."

"Ah, Wolcroft, he was a playmate of your father's." Stewart smiled to see Darcy's head shake. "Well then, his credentials are impeccable."

"Which is why he is being considered for this position." He sighed. "Not that I wish to have him."

"Loosen up the reins, Darcy."

"I know, I know. Perhaps I can talk Elizabeth out of it though. I so enjoy working with her." He shrugged and smiled. "I wish that she would be my secretary. I trust her beyond anyone."

"I cannot imagine my father or brother entertaining such a thought." Stewart laughed. "But I can see Mrs. Darcy rising to the challenge."

"That is just it, she already has, and proven to be a very worthy helpmate. Her letters are far more palatable than mine. Well, she will meet him and then we will decide." Seeing Stewart's grin he sighed. "What?"

"She will decide."

"I am the master."

"You are with everyone but Mrs. Darcy." Seeing Darcy's eyes cast down and a blush appear, Stewart stopped his teasing and adjusted his seat. "The judge moved into Netherfield with his party last week."

"Oh?" Clearly relieved with the change in subject, Darcy looked back up. "And have you heard any opinion?"

"His nephew is with him, he's a barrister as well, and he sent me a note that his uncle loves the place. They attended an assembly there and Sir William Lucas welcomed them with open arms."

"No doubt. My brother Lucas was likely in the background both cringing and marvelling."

"I am sure. The beauty of his wife was mentioned."

"Lucas will have to watch that." Darcy mused. "She never attracted me, but I am not blind, and neither are any of the other men who might take that estate and try to take advantage of her."

"Mrs. Lucas would never . . ."

"No, of course not, but I do not trust the men who will look around that neighbourhood and be disappointed in the quality of the available ladies. You know full well that chasing birds and fox is not the only sport they will pursue."

"Rather cynical view, Darcy. Was someone looking over Elizabeth recently?" He smiled and raised his brow. "Feeling a bit of jealousy?" When he received no response, Stewart laughed. "That is it, someone approached her and what, asked for a dance and you did not like to share?" When there was still no response, Stewart laughed harder. The thought of Elizabeth ever being tempted was impossible. "What will you do at the theatre?"

"Hopefully everyone is off in the country." He stared at his hands then glanced up at the clock. "I think that it is time for me to wend my way home." The men stood and shook hands. "If you need any help with the estate, just let me know."

"I will Darcy." Stewart smiled. "Thank you."

2 OCTOBER 1810

This morning I awoke in the most pleasant manner possible, that kiss, my Elizabeth, that kiss is a gift! Rarely bestowed but so gratefully received! Pleasanter still is her promise to be tucked to sleep this evening in a manner that has me wishing time away. I have no idea what is planned, but the gentlest of kisses, the slight trace of her fingertips, and her whisper has me on fire. I will undoubtedly follow my love around the house like a hound today, seeking out the pleasure I know she will bestow, and I am so ready to receive. More darling, more, I beg of you!

Calm, I must calm. Dearest, I can see your eyes dancing as you read this, a triumphant gleam lighting them. I know you, I know you well. You enjoy torturing the innocent man that I am. You siren! Calm Darcy, calm. It is useless, what is the time? Only eight in the morning! Hours and hours to go, a whole day! An evening at the theatre, dinner, friends, birthday celebrations, I want none of it! I want my promise! I am at last feeling myself, and I want to feel this! Torturous, enticing woman!

Elizabeth's hand went to her mouth and she failed to contain her laughter. Its sound bubbled and drifted from the sitting room to where Darcy sat being shaved. His eyes opened and he smiled.

"Sir." Adams said patiently.

"Ah, yes." Darcy schooled his features and tried to maintain a smooth countenance when Elizabeth's voice lowered and an imitation of his own floated through the door.

"Here I stand in cap and gown, stolid merchant of this town.
What's before me, shall restore me; hourglass hurry on the time!
Heartbeat pounding, hope resounding, as I await the wedding chime!"

Darcy sighed and bit back his smile as she continued in her own lilting voice,

"Here I am, my face is plain, rouge would ply its charm in vain.
Jesus heed me-Does he need me? What is running through his head?
Dowry offers for his coffers, can he love me as he said?"

Adams chuckled this time and when Darcy's eyes met his, he shrugged. Back came the male voice,

"Here she comes with veil in place, would that I could see her face!
Oh I've missed her, never kissed her; since the day when first we spoke.
Wife I'll make her, I would take her, had she nothing but her cloak!"

"Good man, that." Adams said appreciatively as he swiped off the last of the whiskers. Darcy held up his hand to silence him and both men paused to listen as Elizabeth's true voice resumed,

"Here I stand, before our God, hand in hand, I find it odd.
World is shifting, him I'm gifting, with my life and all I be!
And in his eyes, I recognise; that he has honest love for me."

Darcy stood and smiled, drawing a deep satisfied breath, and slipping on his coat, walked to the sitting room where he stood and watched her writing in her journal. She finished her scratching and sang the end of her song,

"Here we are, we've made our vows, ahead is all that love allows.
Joy is winging, our hearts singing, though we're plain and middle aged.

Bells are pealing, live revealing, beauty found in every page."[11]

Moving behind her, he rested his hands on her shoulders and kissed her throat. She rested back against his chest while he reached forward to move the journal so that he could read.

2 October 1810
My dear Fitzwilliam has reached another birthday this morning, and he impatiently awaits his gift. What could it be, I wonder? He seems to think it is a gift of love, well so it shall be, but what form will it take? He thinks it should be of a physical nature. So like a man, thinking of his pleasure, does he not know that the celebration of his birth should be one of celebrating life? Hardly an occasion for la petit mort, *as the French so happily describe that moment of absolute release. That joyous, shattering, melting moment when our hearts and bodies sing and are joined together in . . . oh, but I digress. Pleasure, he speaks of pleasure. Will he not find pleasure in the sound of our daughter's giggle? The joy of the musician's songs, or the conversation and company of our dearest friends and family? No? Selfish man. What do you anticipate, love? You speak of that kiss, that one you adore, is it the kiss to your lips or the one to your . . . oh, that is the one, the one you desire? Is it truly so rarely bestowed or is it that you crave it so much? What else shall I kiss, love? You will tell me, will you not? You will whisper and take my hands, show me what you want me to touch, and I will take care of you, I will love you, today and always.*

Darcy stood absolutely still and silent. His grip on Elizabeth's shoulders tightened, and he bent to gently kiss then rest his face against her cheek. She heard an unsteady intake of breath and suddenly he let go and bellowed, "How woman, how do you expect me to survive the remains of this day? Do you know what you say when you write these things? Do you? You are no naive child anymore; you are not a blushing bride!" Darcy turned her around and kissed her hard. "Tease!" He stamped out of the door and down the stairs, the music of her laughter followed him all the way, and when he reached his study, he took a deep breath and looked up at the landing to smile widely before turning and closing the door.

CAROLINE STARED FROM THE WINDOW of the tea room and watched the stream of shoppers as they slowly wandered down Bond Street. She sipped her tea and made comments to herself, waiting for her husband to return from the conversation he was holding with an acquaintance in the corner. Her gaze came to rest on the long overcoat of a very tall man, his broad shoulders and trim

---

[11] Sally Odgers, "The Wedding of Henry and Joan," 2004.
http://sallyodgers.50megs.com/lals.htm

waist made her sigh. Then as her eyes travelled down to his backside, he turned, his unbuttoned coat opening with the movement, and she was treated to a view of his muscular thighs, encased in tight, well-tailored breeches. "Oh my." She breathed. Before she could catch his face, he turned again, and held out his elbow to a small woman, dressed impeccably in the latest of fashion. "Naturally, he is married." She glanced down at her glove to see the outline of her ring beneath the fabric. "So am I."

Robinson's voice cut across the room and she studied him for a moment. He was not without his looks; he wore his clothes well, and certainly was enthusiastic in their bed, always wishing to try something new, undoubtedly something that he learned from his various courtesans. It was only once or twice a week, she could not complain, and if her suspicions were correct, that would be ending for some time, as well. Again her eyes moved to spot the couple across the street. A carriage passed and after it had moved on, she gasped. The couple had turned towards each other and she witnessed a slow smile lighting the man's face, and a gloved hand covering the woman's mouth as she laughed. "Mr. Darcy." She whispered. Darcy took his wife's hand and wrapped it around his arm. She leaned onto his shoulder and they entered the bookshop they had been examining. When they disappeared, she deflated and jumped when Robinson sat down.

"Took you by surprise?" He laughed and picked up his cup, took a sip and made a face. "Cold!"

"Oh. I had not noticed." She saw his surprise. "I was watching the people passing."

"Hmm." He signalled for fresh water and watched the foot traffic. "Anyone of interest out there?"

"No." She looked at the bookshop. "Nobody at all." They finished their tea and Robinson was about to pay the bill when he noticed her sit up. Following her gaze, he looked across the street to see Elizabeth emerge from the shop and turn with a smile to see Darcy ducking his head down so that he could exit the low door. He was carrying a small package, but still managed to hold it and take his wife's hand to place on his arm. Displaying the package, he smiled and bent to speak in her ear, then they continued on their way, only to disappear into a pastry shop.

"Nobody at all." He snorted and she looked quickly away from the window. "Did I tell you I received a letter from Hurst?"

"No, but I suppose it was more of the same, a count of fish and birds taken, and a list of towns they had visited." She sniffed. "Such a waste of money. I find it difficult to believe that Louisa is having as fine a time as she claims."

"Perhaps not, but she will certainly enjoy her Christmas plans."

"Oh, and what god-forsaken Irish town will they choose to visit?"

"I am not sure exactly what town it is near, but they will be spending several weeks at Pemberley before returning here for the little Season." He saw her choke on the biscuit she was nibbling. "It seems that Darcy is welcoming them with open arms."

Caroline coughed. "What!"

"Imagine that." He smirked and stood. "Too bad it is the beginning of the orange season or I might propose that we join them." He walked to the doorway and rolled his eyes at her continued immobility. "Mrs. Robinson. Are you coming?"

She stood and wiped the crumbs from her gown. "Yes, Mr. Robinson." When they passed the pastry shop she peered in the window in time to see Elizabeth laughingly feeding a spoonful of ice cream to Darcy, and his barely contained smile. Feeling her husband laughing at her, she coloured and looking straight ahead, kept walking.

DARCY OFFERED DE BOURGH a glass of port and smiled to see the liquid slosh slightly when he took the glass. "Steady."

"I am fine. I have spent too many years standing on a pitching deck not to remain upright in your study." He glanced around and fixed upon the Pemberley landscape, then startled when he heard the ring of crystal when the stopper was replaced on top of the decanter. "Why are you nervous?"

"I am fine." Darcy took a long sip, and de Bourgh raised his brows. "It has been a long day."

"Oh? I would think that Mrs. Darcy would have planned every detail." He turned and studied him. "What duties have you been forced to perform?"

"None at all." He smiled to his boots. "She took me shopping."

"That sounds like a gift to herself." De Bourgh laughed.

"No, no. Her gift was her undivided attention. We visited every bookshop within walking distance of this house. No carriages today. We enjoyed tea, she took me for pastry. We purchased enough books to keep us well-entertained this winter," he sighed, "it was the most wonderful day."

"But . . ."

He continued to smile at his boots. "The day contained its pleasures, the evening promises its own."

"And you must live through this performance to arrive at another?" Darcy said nothing and de Bourgh smiled, raising his glass to his lips, "A fortunate man indeed."

"Are you prepared for the evening?"

"In what way? I am neither married nor courting." Darcy's eyes rolled. "Not until spring."

"What is so magic about spring?"

"It seems proper." He sighed. "Leave me alone, Darcy. I have enough to do right now."

"I will not push you." He was silent and studied his companion. "You remember Bingley?"

"Of course."

"He played matchmaker between me and Elizabeth." Seeing de Bourgh's interest, he continued. "By the greatest of coincidences he met her and realized our mutual attraction. If it were not for him, I might have never had the courage to speak to her when we at last met, and then if it was not for Fitzwilliam's pushing I still might not have displayed the courage of my convictions and chased her all the way to the Gardiner's home." Darcy smiled. "Elizabeth refers to it as *Charlotte's Rule.*"

"My new sister?" De Bourgh asked with a bemused smile.

"The very woman. She always told Elizabeth that sometimes a woman must display her feelings to the gentleman, to *help him along.*"

Laughing, de Bourgh took a sip of his port. "Well she certainly knew what she was about with my brother. He did not know what happened, he was attached before he knew it, not that he isn't happy beyond anything he has ever known. They began as friends, but I suspect it will be more before long. So, Miss Lucas set her trap and snared him."

"Yes."

"And you tell me this for what purpose? You had matchmaking friends helping you along . . ."

"I did." Darcy smiled and seeing Foster standing by the doorway, he took a last sip and set down his glass. "Come friend, let us away." He took de Bourgh's elbow and pointed him to the door, took the glass out of his hand, and gave him a push.

"And you are helping me, now?" He said with amusement as Darcy moved him around.

"Your hand shakes for a reason." Darcy shrugged. "I am not pushing you, but I do wish to point out the obvious. I needed it, so I do it for you."

De Bourgh's lips lifted in a smile. "I understand. And I appreciate it." They walked out to the foyer and gazed up the stairs. "Oh my." De Bourgh murmured.

"So lovely." Darcy breathed and watched the sisters descend. He took Elizabeth's hands and smiled down at her. "You torture me tonight, love." He bent and kissed her cheek, closed his eyes and breathed in the delicate scent she had applied to her bare shoulders. Speaking in her ear, he whispered, "You do this on purpose."

"Of course I do." She laughed and caressed his cheek. "It is only fair; I am just as taken by you."

De Bourgh stood in flustered silence. Mary stared at her slippers, sending desperate glances to Elizabeth and Darcy, and seeing no help coming from that quarter, finally chanced a look up at the blushing man before her. "Sir, are you well?"

"Mary, Miss Mary, Miss Bennet!" He gulped and breathed. "You, you are . . . what have you done to yourself?"

She recoiled. "What is wrong? I thought you would like it!"

"No!" He said desperately and reached out to snatch her hand as she turned to run back up the stairs. Darcy and Elizabeth turned to watch in disbelief. "Mary, no, I . . . You are . . . You are . . . You take my ability to speak." He blushed and gripped her hand, then gently tugged her forward. "Forgive me, please, I am never tongue-tied, but . . . You have managed to inspire it quite nicely. Please, let us leave for the theatre; I want all who are there to see me with the loveliest woman I have ever known on my arm." He beamed at her and she blushed. "Beautiful, so very beautiful."

"Oh." She watched as he bent and kissed her hand. "Oh my!"

"You must have a coat, a shawl?" He looked around and saw a maid standing nearby and signalled her. Mary's shawl was slipped over her shoulders, her reticule was placed in her hands, and he had her hand on his arm and was headed for the door before he stopped. "Are you coming?" He demanded of Darcy and Elizabeth.

They laughed and Darcy helped Elizabeth with her things. "Right behind you."

ARRIVING AT COVENT GARDEN, they entered the Theatre Royal and moved up the stairs to the private boxes. Most of London society had moved to the country, but enough remained to make progress slow and conversation necessary. Mary remembered her aunt's advice. She looked at the women who admired de Bourgh, then looked to see where his attention was focussed, and invariably it was on her. Elizabeth and Darcy were too much of a novelty and important to affect an anonymous entrance, and soon they were surrounded by people, asking after their health and wanting an opportunity to extend invitations that were immediately, and with Elizabeth's skill, graciously declined. De Bourgh followed the direction of Darcy's chin indicating a door, and entered the box reserved for them. Showing Mary to a chair, he sat beside her.

"Well that is an experience I do not care to repeat." He smiled and made a show of wiping his brow. "Do your sister and brother have to run the gauntlet each time they show their faces?"

"I do not know; they have not really been out all that much." She relaxed when she saw that his nervousness had dissipated, and the friendly, confident man had reappeared. "I think that you were drawing your own share of attention."

"Me?" He laughed. "Who would want me?"

"You are too modest, sir. Your value as a suitor is surely well known by now." She looked down at her hands and back up to his smiling eyes. "What did I say?"

"What precisely is my value as a suitor? Can you put a price on it?" He crossed his arms.

"No! I only mean that . . . The more mercenary would . . . You have Rosings!"

"I do. I still can hardly believe it." He shrugged. "I have Rosings, but it is just a big empty house, well except for Mother. At least my brother is nearby and I have Charlotte now. And then there is Lady Catherine."

"Oh, I have heard that she is quite the harridan." Her hand went to her mouth.

De Bourgh chuckled. "So she is."

"Does she make your life difficult? The stories I heard of her seemed rather frightening."

"No, she is no more difficult than an overinflated admiral who expects his boots to be . . ." He stopped. "She has been reduced to the life she always feared living and therefore she fights it all the more. She is not meek, she is not kind, she will never change."

"What a shame." Mary shook her head and saw that he awaited an explanation. "I just mean that forgiveness may be granted if she tried."

"You are very good." Unable to stop himself; he continued, "You are very loyal, that is something that I like about you very much."

"Oh." She blushed. "I like that about you, too."

Encouraged, he spoke on, "I . . . I liked how you cared for Darcy and Elizabeth through their trials and tribulations."

"I . . . I liked how you did, too." Mary stared down at her tightly entwined fingers.

He flushed with her assurance, and let his mouth run away. "I . . . I like how you . . .are trying so hard to do everything right." He smiled when she looked up. "Now that I have seen your origins, I am doubly impressed with the woman you have become."

Mary frowned and his smile faltered. "That is not my doing."

"Whose was it then?"

"Lizzy, Aunt Gardiner, the school . . ."

Shaking his head, he stopped her. "None of that would mean a thing if you were not open to it, Miss Mary." Their eyes met again and he saw the surprise and pleasure in hers. Lost in the glow, he drew a breath and licked his lips. "I . . ." Mary felt her heart begin to race. "I . . ."

"Yes, Captain de Bourgh?" She whispered.

"I . . ." He closed his eyes and thought of Darcy and his nudging. "Miss Mary, I . . . Want you to know that I . . ." He swallowed. "I like you."

"oh." She breathed, and gazing into his eyes, saw the slight hopeful smile, and said softly. "I like you." Instantly his eyes lit up and he smiled widely. "Oh, I said the right thing!"

"Yes." He let out a relieved breath. "Yes, you certainly did."

Just then Darcy and Elizabeth entered the box. Instantly both Mary and de Bourgh straightened, they had been leaning closer and closer with each declaration. "I thought that we would never get away from them." Elizabeth noted their blushes and smiled at Darcy, who winked at her. "Did we miss anything?"

"No." They said in unison.

"Oh, well, that is good to know." Darcy helped Elizabeth to her chair and sat down. "By your flushed faces, I would have thought it was warmer. Here love, you should keep your shawl, I have no desire to see you ill."

He carefully wrapped her up and as the lights fell, he leaned to her ear. "Were we too soon?"

"Something happened." Elizabeth whispered. He chuckled and kissed her cheek. "We must behave."

"I think not." He slipped his arm around her shoulder and drew her to his side. "I must warm you."

"I am already warm."

"So am I." Darcy whispered.

"Shhhh, later."

"Teasing woman!" Darcy kissed her ear and drew her to rest against his shoulder, occasionally kissing her hair, and entwining his fingers with hers as they lay against her waist.

De Bourgh could just barely make out the shape of Darcy's shoulders in the dark, his black suit made him nearly disappear, but he knew that they were embraced. He smiled and looked over to Mary, who seemed engrossed in the music of the orchestra. *She likes me! Now what do I do? She is to return to Pemberley in days. I will not see her for months, how many? April, good Lord, six months!* His heart sank. *It is your own fault, you said spring. Why, why did I speak? Is she as affected as I? She seems so serene!* The music stopped and he realized that the intermission had come. The Darcys were unmoving and he noticed that the lamps were being lit. He nudged Darcy with his boot, and startled, his head popped up.

"Oh!" Elizabeth said softly when he moved. "I must have fallen asleep!"

"I joined you." Darcy chuckled. "All that walking you made me do today."

"Oh, it was such a trial!" She laughed and sat up to look around at Mary. "Are you enjoying yourself?"

"Yes, it is beautiful; I wish that we could be at home and listen to such music." She saw de Bourgh's head tilt. "I am happiest at home."

"Is that so? I thought that I detected a woman who enjoyed learning about the world?" He smiled.

"I do, I want to learn about places and I enjoy seeing the sights, I suppose though that I . . . I am not a girl who likes balls. I am fonder of conversation than dancing." She bit her lip. "I suppose that is unfashionable."

"Perhaps, but to be honest with you, I never had a chance to learn the dances, so I would most likely stand in a corner observing rather than participating. I suppose that I will have to learn one or two. I will need to if I am to beg your brother to escort you this spring." His smile grew when she blushed again, and reassured of her reception, he looked over to Darcy. "Could I have a word with you?"

"Certainly." Darcy stood and smiled at Elizabeth before following de Bourgh out into the hallway.

Elizabeth scooted over to Mary's side. "What happened?"

"We talked a little." She bit her lip and stared at her hands then back up to see her sister's encouraging smile. "He told me that he likes me! Oh Lizzy!" The sisters hugged. "And I told him that I like him, too!"

"Oh how wonderful!" Elizabeth laughed. "Do you know how long it takes some people to just say something as simple as that? Why, it took Fitzwilliam years to tell me!"

"But Fitzwilliam did not know where you were!" Mary protested.

Elizabeth pushed a curl back over Mary's shoulder and smiled. "Oh, he could have found me." She looked back to her face. "I am so glad that you and Peter are friends, and admit it. Now, what happens next?"

"Next?"

Elizabeth took her hand and gave it a squeeze. "hmm. I wonder what he is speaking to Fitzwilliam about."

"Darcy." De Bourgh took him to stand by the windows and stared out at the busy street below. He watched as Darcy nodded at an acquaintance and impatiently waited for another to shake his hand and enquire after his health. At last he had his attention. "I have made a tremendous error. I told Mary my feelings."

Darcy's face did not mask his surprise. "You told her you *love* her?"

"NO!" He glanced around and lowered his voice. "I like her."

"Oh." Darcy relaxed. "And?"

"I . . . I realized that I will not see her again until you return to town." He looked miserable. "Why did I speak my feelings?"

"Because you would burst if you did not." Darcy smiled and crossed his arms. "Easter is in mid-April, we will be coming for the Season probably at the end of March. I seem to recall you stating mere hours ago that you wished to wait for spring to court her?"

"I am an idiot."

"Well that goes without saying, so what are you going to do about it now?"

"What do you suggest?" He sighed. "Six months!"

"No longer than a little journey to America and back?"

"You are laughing at me."

"You are not a man to be laughed at. Although I find it amusing that a man who can take a battleship against Napoleon without flinching is so flustered by telling a seventeen-year-old girl that he likes her." Darcy chuckled as de Bourgh glared. "What do you want me to do? Ask the Gardiners to put her up for the winter? Then you could come and court her?" Seeing his eyes light up, Darcy shook his head. "No."

"What the devil do you mean; no? YOU pushed me!"

"Maybe. I just told you a story and encouraged you to realize your feelings. I did not tell you to pour out your deep professions of *like* for Mary." He tilted his head. "I think that waiting would be good for you. Make your heart grow fonder and all that." Darcy laughed. "Come, it cannot be so easy, the path to true love is never easy. Then you will not appreciate it when you finally achieve your heart's desire. I was an idiot, pining over Elizabeth for years. You will be an idiot pining for a girl who knows you like her and are waiting for her."

"Please Darcy, let her stay in London." He begged. "I promise I will . . ."

"What?" Darcy looked at him sternly.

"God alone knows." He sighed. "I know nothing of this world of courtship. I have no desire to be part of the whirl of society or be prey to the mamas. I found the girl for me; can I not leave it at that?"

"Say no more tonight." Darcy said quietly. "We will speak to Mary and see what she desires, then we will speak to Mr. Gardiner. I make no promises."

"But . . ."

He sighed and nodded. "Very well. I accept that. I have held these feelings for months, I only realized what they were at the wedding, when she . . . she was no longer a girl in my eyes."

"Yes." Darcy said softly. "I remember each time I saw Lizzy over the years. Each time I had to imprint a new vision of her in my mind, she was changing, growing lovelier." He saw de Bourgh's nod and clapped his back. "And yes, I married her at the tender age that Mary is now, so I am not the one to make this decision. I leave it to Mr. Gardiner. Agreed?"

"Agreed." The gong sounded and de Bourgh smiled. "What do you think the sisters were talking about?"

Chuckling, Darcy led the way to the box. "I am sure that I will find out soon enough."

DE BOURGH AWKWARDLY SAID HIS GOODBYES to Mary and she ran up the stairs to be alone in her room. "He wants her to stay." Elizabeth said thoughtfully when they reached their rooms at last after eating the cold supper the staff had left for them.

"Yes. He has finally let his mind listen to his heart." Darcy closed the door behind him and taking off his coat, deftly removed the knot from his neck cloth. He hopped and struggled, but managed to remove his boots with some semblance of grace. Hearing her giggle, he whispered, "Shoes, yes, love, I know."

Elizabeth kissed his frown. "How can we help them along?" Still frowning, he turned her around and lifting her hair out of the way, caressed the silky skin of her shoulders, and gently kissed her throat. Slowly, he eased out each button on the back of her gown. Adams appeared in the doorway of the dressing room, and seeing his master's activity, did an about-face and disappeared for the night. The gown gave way and shifted, slipping into a puddle of silver, glimmering in the firelight. Immediately Darcy's hands went to work on her stays, and he sighed when they came loose and fell, and his hands were free to trace over the nearly transparent chemise. The fullness of her breasts and the tight buds beneath his fingertips made the aching of his desire almost painful to endure. "Oh love." He whispered. "No more talk of anyone but us tonight. It is still my birthday."

"Only for another ten minutes." Elizabeth leaned back against his chest, and purred when he caressed his hands over her curves. "Then I can ask . . ."

"No." He commanded. "*My* birthday, *my* night, *my* love. You promised, Lizzy. You promised me hours and hours ago. I have been barely hanging on all day." He breathed out a long groan and buried his face in her hair while her body shook again with laughter. "You are a cruel woman."

"I suppose that my next task is to change your mind." She pressed her bottom against his straining breeches. "Tell me how I should do that."

"Oh love," he turned her around and lifted off the chemise, and smiled at his wife clad only in stockings and garters. "Oh love." He simply stood and stared.

"Will?"

"hmm?"

"Hopeless." One by one, his shirt buttons were released, then the fine fabric was slipped from his shoulders. Elizabeth kissed his chest, still fragrant with his musky cologne, rubbed her cheek over the dark nest of hair, then gently suckled his small tight nipples. He groaned and laid his cheek on her head while his hands traced over her shoulders, invariably pausing over the scar, and as always, moving him to clutch her and demand a deep and satisfyingly long kiss. Elizabeth's hands were not idle; they opened his breeches and slipped them and his small clothes down to the floor. They stood smiling at each other, both nude but for their stockings. "You look silly." Elizabeth laughed and squealed when he lifted her up and onto the bed. "I am supposed to be the one in charge!" She protested.

"I would like to see you carry me." Darcy kneeled above her and ran his hands down her body. "Then again, you would likely drop me on my head."

"Very likely, and I would be crushed by your formidable weight."

"I would like to crush you under my weight right now." He leaned forward to kiss her and she scooted out, pushing him down on his belly. "Where did you go?"

"Silly man." Elizabeth rubbed her hands over his broad back and down his spine to firmly run over his firm, round bottom, then back up and down, massaging away any hint of tension that resided in his body. Darcy moaned.

"You will have me asleep soon."

She leaned and licked his bottom then nipped the flesh, and he jumped. "mmmm, delicious."

"Elizabeth . . ."

She lay on his back and nibbled on his ear. "Tell me where you want me to touch."

"You know where." He said hoarsely.

She slipped off and rolling over, Darcy watched her smile and kiss her way down his chest, "Here?" She whispered from his naval, licking the small dent and making him sigh.

"Lower." He said hoarsely.

"Oh." Moving lower, she kissed between his legs and traced her tongue over his thighs. "Here?"

"Higher please, Lizzy." He looked at her. "Please kiss me." The moment her tongue found his heated velvety skin, he closed his eyes. She could not help smiling as he sighed and sank back in the pillows. "I love this. I will never get enough of this kiss." Elizabeth pleasured him until a great shiver ran through his body. Darcy opened his eyes and pulled her shoulders towards him. "Come up here."

She lay over his chest and kissed his nose. "Why did you want me to stop?"

Darcy caressed her hair and smiled. "You would do anything to make me happy."

Elizabeth laughed and suckled his lips and tongue. "Within reason."

He laughed softly. "What would you consider as unreasonable?"

"Hmm, let me think." She gasped when he rolled her over so they faced each other. They kissed as he lifted her leg over his hip, entwining their arms and joining their bodies, relaxing into their embrace. "Ohhhhh." Darcy cupped her breast and kissed it, then suckled as she sighed. He lifted his face to kiss her and moaned softly when her mouth found its way down his throat.

"Oh love." He whispered and opened his eyes when she laughed. He thrust harder in response and she gasped then took his face in her hands to kiss his lips. The tempo increased and he rolled them over. Elizabeth laughed when he moved to kiss her throat and tasted a mouthful of hair instead. Frustrated, he pushed it away and stared down at her sparkling eyes. "All I wanted today was to spend every moment being loved by you."

"And that was exactly what you received." She drew his face back down to kiss while they steadily began to move again. She looked into his happy passionate eyes. "This gift was a pleasure to bestow." They kissed slowly and she ruffled his hair. "Happy birthday, Fitzwilliam."

Chapter 28

"I am sorry." Mr. Gardiner said to de Bourgh. "I think that it is in Mary's best interests to return to Pemberley."

"Best interests?" He stood and paced the study. "You make it sound as if I mean to do her harm!"

"No." Mr. Gardiner sat back and watched his movement. "You admit freely that you have only just realized your feelings for my niece."

"Yes, should we not be able to explore this, to develop our feelings? How can that be accomplished from such a distance? At least if she were in London . . ."

"She would be left to sit and wait for your attention at your pleasure and convenience. You are returning to Rosings. What will Mary do here? She is not in school. Yes, she could help my wife, but in the meantime, what would she do to occupy her time besides sitting in the window and waiting for you to come? That is not fair to her, and I do not believe it is what you truly want either. You did tell Darcy that you wanted to wait for spring, did you not?"

De Bourgh threw out his weak argument. "Mrs. Darcy spent a great deal of time living with you before she married Darcy."

"Yes, but that is the point, she was *living* here. Our home, our routine, was hers. She joined us in our social engagements, perhaps looking for a mate, and escaping a home life at Longbourn that was frankly untenable for her. Pemberley offers riches to Mary that we can only wish for here. She has access to an exceptional library, grounds for walking, safety, and not only that; she will have the invaluable education of how to be mistress to an estate." He smiled kindly. "Captain I am not discouraging your suit, I am simply pointing out the facts to you. I think that you and Mary will be an ideal match. You are both steadfast, and have grown up in lonely circumstances. You found a way to recognition. You have proven yourself and have done very well, even before becoming master of Rosings. Mary has the limitations of her sex and her youth to keep her from succeeding; however, she has grasped the opportunities that the Darcys have given to her with passion. I have no doubt that you will do very well together."

"But not until I can devote all of my time to her." He said softly.

"She deserves all of your attention, especially at the start of your relationship. And do you not want her to be anticipating seeing you as much as you wish to see her?" Mr. Gardiner smiled. "She is overwhelmed with the knowledge that you like her, what will she do if you proclaim love?"

"I am not ready to do that yet, sir."

"And she is not ready to hear it. That is why I will not allow her to spend six months waiting for the rare visit from you." Mr. Gardiner stood and put his hand on de Bourgh's shoulder. "I want you to come together this spring when you can visit her every day, take her around London, and give this courtship the attention it deserves. And I believe that since this was your first thought as expressed to Darcy, you know that it is right."

"Is this Mary's decision as well, sir?"

"Mary will do as she is told." Mr. Gardiner said quietly. "She has grown up without any guidance from her parents, and now she has Darcy, and to some extent, me. She has sought our advice. She is not Elizabeth; you cannot look at her sister and think that you will see Mary." Seeing de Bourgh's dejection he squeezed his shoulder. "Mary wants to stay." De Bourgh's eyes closed in relief. "But she has not the strength to sit and wait, see you and then have to wait again. As I said, she is not Elizabeth."

"All or nothing." His head came up and he smiled. "Very well. I can accept that. I like that. May I write to her, sir?"

"That is very irregular. You know that a single man does not write to the object of his affection without an engagement in place." Mr. Gardiner smiled sympathetically when de Bourgh's eyes cast down. "I will speak to Darcy about this; and recommend that since your intentions are clear, he allow letters to be addressed to Mary. However, you should know that the letters will be shared with all of the family. Keep to subjects that Darcy can read without wishing to strangle you."

De Bourgh smiled and relaxed. "No love letters. I can bear that."

"NO, NO, LOVE." Darcy said with a strangled cry. "Let go."

"Mamamamaba!" Rosalie proclaimed and grabbed his neck cloth with renewed energy.

"Rosa!" He said sternly. "NO!" She blinked at him and burst into tears. Darcy sighed and he held her close, rubbing her back while she wailed.

"Now what do you do?" Fitzwilliam asked anxiously. "Does she understand what you said?"

"I do not think she knows the word yet; it is the tone of my voice, or maybe my expression. If I say no to her when she is calm and without force, she just merrily continues with her activity." He bounced slightly and kissed her head. "It is different week to week, we have one behaviour figured and she turns around and has something new. I cannot tell you how many times we have run to check our journals to see what worked in calming her, or what some mysterious symptom that appears actually means."

"I am scared to death." Fitzwilliam cautiously touched her back. "I am afraid that I cannot be like you, Darcy. I will leave it to the women." He felt the baby tremble under his hand. "She is so small."

"Yes." Darcy kissed her forehead and she sucked her hand.

"Ma."

Chuckling, he whispered, "Mama?"

"Baba."

"I thought as much." He walked around the room. "You know, strangling your father is just not done, dear. No matter how pleasing it is to see Papa's face turn purple."

Fitzwilliam laughed and relaxed. "I cannot believe that Elizabeth has not run in here to rescue you."

"No, she trusts me." He tilted his head when he heard a sigh. "Sleeping?"

"It seems so." Fitzwilliam looked at her shyly. "May I?" Carefully Darcy handed her over and awkwardly Fitzwilliam cuddled her. "Oh Lord, help me."

"So will you model your parents, leave it to the nursemaid and the governess?" Darcy folded his arms and watched as his cousin stared in wonder. "Never pick her up when she cries, visit for minutes a day, hold her at arm's length?"

"no." He whispered and gently kissed her cheek. "I want to be like you. I will try, even though I know it is not the done thing. I suppose I will not know until the baby is here. Perhaps I can be a bit of both you and Father." Walking around the room, he moved to the window and watched Elizabeth holding Eva's arm and walking her slowly around the garden. "Eva is so tired, Darcy. She is truly suffering through this. I fear for her life, I fear for the child." He looked up and sought his reassurance. "She must be well."

"I pray that she will be." Darcy said helplessly. "Your parents will come soon?"

"Late next month." Richard watched the women walking and blinked back the tears pricking his eyes. "How did you survive this? You delivered this child!"

"Trust me; it was not something I hoped to do. I planned to remain with Elizabeth, but I expected to do that fighting a midwife in her chambers, not in a glade with nothing but my coat to lie on and my pocket knife to . . ." He saw Fitzwilliam's face grow white. "I intend to keep her near the house from the last month on next time."

"You plan for another."

"Of course." Darcy caressed Rosalie's back. "I love my wife, it will come one day. It is inevitable."

"I think that this will be our only child."

"Why?"

"Did you know that she delivered a stillborn boy after Carter died?"

"No." Darcy's brow creased.

"No, you were not in London when she told Mother." Fitzwilliam paced. "If she lives through this, I swear, I will never risk her health again, I will never touch her."

"Yes, you will."

"Darcy, no."

"She loves you, Richard; she loves you like my mother loved my father. She would not let him consider not touching her, even after she lost four babies and he could not bear to face losing another or putting her through it again, they continued to love each other."

"And she died."

"Yes." Darcy sighed. "There is no guarantee that all will be well, but please, do not let your fear ruin this for both of you. She is probably as frightened as you, and she needs you more. If you have fears, you know there are ways to reduce the likelihood of pregnancy." He blushed and looked at his feet. "I attempt to practice them, but I admit that I often become carried away. However at this point diligence is not necessary. Perhaps after our fourteenth child when she wants to lock me out of her chambers." He looked up and smiled. "We talk about these things, and share our concerns. Elizabeth will tell me when we need to become serious."

"I wish you would be here when it is her time." Fitzwilliam smiled a little. "I can just imagine what Father will decide is appropriate conversation to distract me."

Darcy laughed softly. "Well you can always stay with her."

"No." He shook his head. "I do not care to have her cries be the last sound of her voice that will haunt me if . . ."

"I understand." They exchanged glances and looked at Rosalie.

Fitzwilliam smiled when Rosalie yawned and opened her eyes for a moment. "Hello, little girl." Looking back out of the window, he saw Elizabeth pointing up at them. Evangeline saw him standing with the baby and smiled widely. Elizabeth said something and both women started to laugh. He chuckled and shook his head. "I am the butt of some joke it seems."

Darcy peered out of the window and saw them wiping tears, they were laughing so hard. "It is a good one." He smiled and clasped his cousin's shoulder. "Perhaps she is not as ill as your mind tells you. She is tired, she is miserable, she is moody and weary of the process, but she will be fine."

"She will."

"I am the pessimist in the family, you are the optimist."

"That is true; you do have a streak of gloom about you." Fitzwilliam blinked away the moisture in his eyes. "A cloud that follows you about."

"Not lately, have you noticed that we managed an entire visit to London and no major mishaps occurred?" Darcy stood tall, "I am rather proud of that!"

Fitzwilliam laughed heartily and made a face when Rosalie woke again. "Any minor mishaps?" He whispered.

"Well, there was the moment when Elizabeth entered my study while I was interviewing my new secretary. He was very surprised when she began searching through my desk and removed a stack of letters, gave an opinion for how to respond to one of them and departed. I watched his discomfort and casually mentioned that my wife's opinion was often sought."

"I bet that he nearly suffered a stroke!"

"He certainly scrambled to say that he fully understood and thought it was a sensible idea." Darcy shook his head. "He does not know what he is getting into with Elizabeth. Or me for that matter. He is a man set in the ways of his former employer."

"Perhaps he is not the best choice, then. He will forever be saying *that is not how it was done with* . . ."

"That crossed my mind, but he is too good to pass up. Since Elizabeth is forcing my hand . . ." He laughed at Fitzwilliam's smile. "It is hard to give up total control, but I know that she wishes it for my well-being." Sighing, he shrugged. "It was my decision, of course, but she was pleased that I saw the sense in her hopes for me. I will learn to delegate. But I *will* remain in charge of it all."

"I know; that is why I am not retiring anytime soon. At least in my work, I am the man in charge, until some idiot General orders me to do something." He glanced at Darcy. "They suggested that I return to battle."

"What?" Darcy startled. "Are they serious?"

"I guess some fool saw me on horseback and thought I looked just fine, and wanted to know why I was not on the continent." He closed his eyes. "If he had seen me dismount after a day in the saddle and try to walk . . ."

"Surely your superiors would say something? They know your condition."

"Yes, of course." He sighed. "It . . . My injuries are not immediately visible, so it is sometimes assumed that I am shirking my duties or that I am a gentleman's son who bought my way to the comfortable position I have. It is galling!" He growled and Rosa's eyes opened. "Forgive me, little girl." He kissed her and found himself calming. "It is the ones who do not know me." He sighed and shrugged. "I have never in my life shirked duty, and I earned my rank. I could work behind the lines, I suppose, but that is what I do now. Perhaps it is just someone influential below me who wants to move up."

"Could you leave it?" Darcy asked quietly. "Can you afford to live on your pension? This home is yours."

"I do not have enough years in yet, but Eva's money is invested for more income. I have an allowance from Father." Fitzwilliam raised his head and shrugged. "If push came to shove, I would leave. It is just . . . I suppose they need experienced leadership. Perhaps I should be flattered."

"Perhaps. If you need anything . . ."

"I am fine, Darcy. I am just sounding off to you. We have seen too little of each other."

"I have missed you as well." Both men stared at Rosalie. "I feel much better." He said quietly.

"I am glad of it."

"We will return in March." Darcy assured him. "And you will be holding a baby in your arms and have a beautiful, happy wife by your side."

Fitzwilliam nodded. "Yes."

"It will be well."

"Keep telling me that." He looked up smiled. "Good Lord, we are more emotional than the women!"

"Do not let them know." Darcy laughed. "We would never hear the end of it!"

"THERE." De Bourgh presented four journals to Mary. "My formative years for your reading pleasure."

She smiled and taking them from his hands, clutched them to her chest. "But what of your years as an adult? I want to know all of your adventures."

Seeing Darcy's crossed arms and stern expression, he shook his head and smiled before turning back to her. "I think that those are best left for another time, perhaps when I can sit beside you and supervise which passages are acceptable."

"I do not understand."

"I do not care to frighten you with some of my experiences." He said carefully and noticed Darcy's eyes roll.

"Oh, stories of battles." Mary nodded seriously. "I am certain that they were terrible."

"Yes, battles of a sort." De Bourgh nodded and hearing Darcy's snort he sighed. "You are no help to me, Darcy."

"I am not supposed to be." He smiled. Elizabeth appeared at his side holding Rosalie.

"Well, I think that the house is in order. I have everything on my list." She looked around the hallway. "I think."

"We can always send for anything we have left behind, dearest."

"I know." She sighed and biting her lip, she handed him the baby. "I will be right back."

They watched her dash up the stairs. "What is wrong?" Darcy murmured and handing Rosalie to de Bourgh, he followed her.

Bemused, de Bourgh juggled the squirming child and looked at Mary helplessly. She laughed and setting down the journals, held out her arms to accept her niece. "There Rosa, I will take you." Finding herself in confident arms, she relaxed and babbled while playing with the ribbons on Mary's bonnet. She laughed and smiled at him. "See, it is not so difficult."

"I have never held a baby before." He stared at the girl. "I am amazed at Darcy's assurance."

"I think that it just comes with practice." She bounced and cooed at Rosalie and glanced up the stairs. "I wonder what is wrong."

"She simply forgot something, I am sure." He relaxed and gazed at her holding the baby. "You look very comfortable. Do you hope for many children?"

"Oh." Mary blushed. "I hardly hoped to ever leave Longbourn."

"Well you have certainly managed that. Now you need a new adventure. Darcy has accepted my invitation to spend Easter at Rosings, something that he did most of his life. Of course you will come with him and Elizabeth, and Miss Darcy." He touched the baby's cheek and she grabbed his finger. Laughing he looked to see Mary's blush. "I look forward to showing off the estate to you."

"Your home."

"Yes, I hardly believe it, but after nearly a year, I suppose that it is." He shook his head. "It is overwhelming." Glancing up the stairs and around the hall, he touched Mary's hand. "I have been given permission to write to you."

"I know." She watched his fingertips slip under hers and started to tremble.

"I . . . I hope that by the time we meet again, we will know each other well enough to . . ." He swallowed, "to be very good friends."

Mary blushed and stared at their fingers. "Why do you want to be friends with me?"

"Mary . . ." He smiled and glancing around to see that they were still alone, he took her hand and kissed it. "I am just a man who joined the Navy and fortune smiled on me. I am barely comfortable on land, let alone on my estate. I do not ever want to be part of the social whirl. Do you?"

"No." She smiled at the warmth in his voice, and watched him tuck her hand back over Rosalie. "I look forward to spring so much." Hearing footsteps they turned and looked up the stairs. Darcy and Elizabeth were walking together; his arm was around her waist. The expression on their faces was difficult to read, but when they arrived, they both smiled. "Is everything well?" Mary handed Rosalie back over to Elizabeth.

"Yes." She looked up Darcy. "I think that it is."

He nodded and smiled while caressing Rosalie's back. His eyes met Elizabeth's. "I think so, too." Clearing his throat, he gestured to the door. "Let us go home."

"OH LOOK, A LETTER!" Kitty saw the envelope on her bed and picking it up, spoke excitedly. "It is from Lydia! I have not heard from her since she went to school. They must be very busy there, I have written to her at least twice a week since we left Longbourn, and I told her all about things here." Georgiana reserved her opinion and sank down on her bed to watch as she read. The expression of anticipation on Kitty's face died and soon became one of disappointment.

"Anything interesting?" She asked cautiously.

"She does not seem to miss home at all." Kitty bit her lip and blushed. "Or any of the family, except for Mama."

"Not you?"

"She says nothing at all of missing me. She only misses how easy it was at home." She looked up to Georgiana with tears in her eyes. "I guess that I was just someone to occupy her when she was bored."

"No, she would not be writing to you if that was the case. She must want to share her new experiences with you." Thinking hard for something good to say, Georgiana added, "I had the impression that she is not used to expressing feelings of affection for people."

Kitty sniffed and shook her head. "She is very good at expressing dislike for people, anyone who did not let her have her way. She says she has a friend who likes to have fun as she does, the girl she shares her room with, Jessica Simkins." Kitty was quiet as she read and turned the page over. "Jessica this, Jessica that, it is all about this girl. She asks nothing of how you and I get on, or anything of our school."

"Well, I guess that means that she is making friends, at least one." Georgiana tilted her head. "That is good, is it not? She is occupied with her school."

"I guess, but it seems like this girl is the only one she likes." She looked up. "She calls all the other ones dreadfully dull, all listening to Miss Edwards, the headmistress, and afraid of putting a toe out of line. I guess that she is fairly strict. And all of the other ones have been in trouble before. I have a feeling that they are not kind to her. She said they are always shushing her and telling her to pay attention and do her work. Some of them make fun of her manners, but Jessica tells her that they do not need those pompous brats anyway."

"It sounds like Jessica is the one in charge and Lydia is following her. She is a bad influence."

"Just like Lydia was to me." Kitty's eyes filled with tears and Georgiana stood up to hug her. "Thank you for helping me here. I do not know how I would have gotten along without your friendship."

"You would have been fine." Georgiana whispered. "Have we not met many nice girls here? There are many snobby ones, but we only have to be polite to them. Elizabeth taught me that I do not have to imitate anyone whose behaviour I do not like just to fit in."

"She did?" Kitty wiped her face. "When did she do that?"

"Oh, that was just from living with her and Fitzwilliam. They are wonderful." Kitty smiled to hear that description. "You will see."

"I should imitate Lizzy."

"I can hear her saying now that you should be yourself."

The girls laughed and Kitty relaxed and looked back at the letter. "Lydia does not like the headmistress at all."

"Well that is no surprise, she tells her no, after all." Georgiana sat back down and hugged a pillow. "I bet she is nothing compared to the Misses Stevenson." The girls rolled their eyes and laughed.

Kitty sat down beside her. "Oh no."

Georgiana sat up. "What is it?"

"A militia unit has made camp in the village where the school is located and she and this Jessica are spending their free time walking in to look at them. A few of the officers come over to talk to them whenever they do. They lied and told them they were older." The girls exchanged worried glances. "She has always been fond of men in uniform. Mama put that in her head. She says it is all good fun but Miss Edwards and the other teachers have seen them at it and warned them off. Oh . . . They were given extra work to occupy their time, but it has only made them more determined to speak to the men again."

"Surely Lydia knows not to speak to a strange man in a flirtatious manner!" Georgiana gasped. "Brother would . . . Oh I cannot imagine the tongue lashing he would give me, oh and Elizabeth!" She shivered.

"Has Lizzy yelled at you?" Kitty put down the letter for a moment.

"Oh." Georgiana blushed. "Yes."

"Me, too." Kitty looked down. "It was frightening, but after I thought about it, well after I stopped glaring at her, I knew that she was correct."

"Yes, I thought the same."

"What did you do?"

"What did *you* do?"

"Something bad enough for Lizzy to yell." Kitty said with a smile.

"Yes, and Fitzwilliam, and Uncle Henry, oh and Mary."

"Oh my!" Kitty put her hand to her mouth. "I never would have guessed you could . . ."

"Well, I learned my lesson." Georgiana looked at the letter. "Lydia seems not to care about people in authority. I wonder if you wrote to her to stop being friends with this girl and listen to her teachers she might pay attention?"

"I doubt it. She only seems to listen to Mr. Darcy and Mr. Lucas. Should we say something to them? It sounds like her teachers know about it, so they would tell Papa if there is a problem, would they not?"

"Yes." Georgiana shrugged. "I guess that I was thinking that of all the people who yelled at me, it was Mary who really got my attention first. She . . . she made me realize what a selfish, stupid fool I was. I do not know, but it was hearing it from a friend that made me understand how I hurt everyone else and grow up, I guess."

"Mary is so different now." Kitty said softly. "So confident."

"I do not know if she is confident, but she is no longer a shadow, as she called herself." She grinned, "And she has a handsome man looking at her!"

"If I could attract a man as handsome as Captain de Bourgh someday, I would feel confident, too!" Kitty giggled along with Georgiana. "Well, if Mary's talk helped you, I suppose it would not hurt to write to Lydia." She stood and walked over to the writing desk. "Help me to decide what to say."

Georgiana read the letter through, and rolling her eyes, put it down. "How about, this? Dear Lydia, stop being such a fool?"

"Act your age?"

"Grow up?"

"Behave yourself or you will be married to Mr. Collins!" They giggled and bent their heads together to write her a sensible letter that was sure to be ignored.

"HANG ON, SON." Lord Moreland put his hand on Harwick's shoulder as they walked away from the birthing chamber. Hearing Laura cry out, Harwick stopped and stiffened; then turned to go back to her. Lord Moreland took a firm hold of his arm. "No, you said your farewells, now you will do her no good to stay, come along."

"She needs me." He said stubbornly.

"She needs the women who are with her." Guiding his son-in-law towards the stairs, they both looked up when the sound of running feet caught their ears and suddenly Ella and Margaret appeared at the top of the next landing.

"Papa!" Margaret flew down to hug him, Ella followed, a little slower. "What is wrong with Mama? Why does she cry?"

Harwick looked at Lord Moreland and drew on his resolve to speak calmly. He knelt and wrapped his arms around his little girls. "Mama is well, she is just . . ." He hugged them tightly and buried his face in their hair.

"Papa, you are holding me too tight!" Margaret cried.

"Forgive me dear." He blinked hard and kissed her, then kissed Ella who remained silent, but clutched his sleeve. "I love you both very much, and so does Mama." The governess arrived and he looked up. "Please keep them busy."

"Yes sir, I am sorry." Taking their hands, she led them away downstairs to the library, where they might be insulated from Laura's cries.

Please do not leave me a widower again. He prayed and slowly rose to his feet. Lord Moreland stayed by his side and they made their way to the study where they waited in silence as Harwick paced. The hours ticked slowly by while the shadows moved across the room. Harwick maintained his silent vigil, not drinking, not reading, only staring from time to time at the portraits of each of his wives. Lord Moreland read a book, watched the pacing man, and made no attempt to reassure him. Eventually he sank down into a chair and closed his eyes, waiting. At last the door opened and Lady Moreland appeared.

Both men jumped to their feet. "Congratulations." She smiled wearily. "You have a beautiful, healthy son."

"Oh." He breathed. "And . . . Laura?"

"She is exhausted, but well." She smiled and grasped his hands. "She is well, dear. She asks for you. Go to her."

"Yes." He wiped his face and kissed her cheek. "Thank you!" Turning, he pumped his father-in-law's hand then flew out of the room, ran up the stairs, and finally arrived in his wife's chamber. She lay on the bed, her hair brushed but still damp, her face pale, but graced by a tired smile. In her arms was a tightly wrapped bundle. He stopped in the doorway and just drank in the scene, then with a glance, sent the servants from the room. He slowly entered, and closed the door behind him.

15 NOVEMBER 1810
Meadowbrook
Leicester

Dear Darcy,
I have waited one week just to be sure that all is well before I announced our wonderful news. My beautiful Laura has delivered us a son. He has proven himself to be healthy, and by his lusty cries, I know that he is strong. My Laura is doing well, and if it takes a dedicated staff of stern maids, she will stay abed for the duration of her recovery. I will not take the chance of losing her. She protests but it falls on deaf ears. Every recommendation for her will be followed, and when my dear wife recovers, we will celebrate with an appropriate holiday, perhaps to Bath, perhaps to London, if it were summer we would go to the sea. I would have welcomed any child, you know that, Darcy. But a son, I have a son! My family will live on in Stewart Archer Harwick. I know that you understand, I pray that you and Elizabeth will be so blessed one day. Our daughters are delighted with their new brother, I could not be prouder of my family.
Thank you again for your unflagging support and letters of reassurance. I am grateful for your friendship, as I know that Laura is thankful for Mrs. Darcy's. Please express Laura's appreciation to her. No, I will not allow her to sit at a desk to write yet, either. She will run away in utter frustration before long, but fortunately, my hunting skills are excellent and I will bring her home.
Sincerely,
Jeffrey Harwick, Esq.

Darcy closed his eyes in a silent prayer of thanksgiving. "A son." He looked up to the landscape of Pemberley that hung across the room and stood to examine it. "An heir." His chin lifted and he nodded. "Well, now that Lizzy's body seems to be ready to bear a child again, perhaps we might have another soon." Thinking of Rosa's newly acquired crawling skills, he chuckled to himself. They had spent the previous afternoon sitting on the carpet before the fire in the music room, taking turns sending their giggling girl crawling back and forth between them while Mary played every lullaby and children's song she knew. By the time they had stopped, Rosalie was curled up and asleep on Elizabeth's lap, and he had scooted over to embrace them both. "Another girl would be wonderful, too." He sighed. "As long as the child is healthy, and my Elizabeth is too, I do not care."

A knock came to the door and he turned to see his newly-arrived secretary. "Sir, I have finished going over the accounts and familiarizing myself with the system you have employed here."

"Yes?" Darcy's face became that of the master, and he walked back to his desk to sit down. "Do you have any recommendations?"

"To be honest with you sir, no. It is efficient and if followed precisely, there is no chance of missing collecting income or paying your obligations in a timely manner."

"My father spent some years developing it." Darcy said quietly and looked at the account book on his desk. "I am glad to know that it passes your scrutiny."

"Yes sir, I . . . Sir what role do you wish me to take here? You have made it clear that you wish to maintain your correspondence."

"I have been debating your role, I . . ." He looked up when he heard a soft, "oh."

Elizabeth just stopped at the doorway to the study and the secretary was on his feet and bowing low as Darcy was still rising. He smiled. "Mrs. Darcy."

"Mr. Darcy, forgive me, I am not used to your having a secretary." She smiled a little to him and felt herself being assessed by a two pairs of intelligent eyes. The blue pair was reading every detail of her face.

"It is an honour, madam." Conrad bowed again and looked to Darcy, apparently waiting for him to dismiss his wife.

Darcy studied the older man and understood his posture, then smiled at Elizabeth. "Will you not join us?" He took her hand and led her to the chair immediately to the right of his; then taking his seat again looked up expectantly at Conrad. "Shall we continue?"

Conrad's open mouth snapped shut and he sat down gracefully. "Certainly, sir."

"Perhaps I should clarify something from the start, Conrad. Mrs. Darcy is aware of all of my business, she reads much of my correspondence, and while she may not know every detail, she is cognizant of my affairs. I told you before that I value her opinion. Besides that, I wish for her to be prepared for any possibility." He smiled at her frown. "Even I am susceptible to the occasional cold, Mrs. Darcy."

"A cold I will accept." She nodded. "However, I do not care to discuss anything else."

"Of course." Darcy looked back to his new employee. "Is this clear?"

"Yes, Mr. Darcy. Forgive my surprise."

"Not at all." Darcy smiled at Elizabeth. "Is there anything that I can do for you?"

"It is a matter of a personal nature." She said softly and he saw that her smile had entirely disappeared. Darcy's brow knit, and he noticed that she held a letter.

He nodded and addressed Conrad. "My wife is in need of my attention, perhaps you might take this opportunity to look over the letter I received from Reverend Evans."

"Yes, sir." He looked at his notes.

"I will call for you when we are through." Darcy said quietly, but the dismissal was clear in his voice.

"Yes, sir." Conrad stood and bowed, then left the room, closing the door behind him.

"Lizzy?" Darcy held out his hand and took hers. She responded to the tug and rising, sat in his lap where she wrapped her arms around his neck and began to sob. "Dearest, what is wrong? Is it the letter?"

"Yes." She sniffed and he rubbed her back. Taking it from her, he opened the paper and read the short note from Layton. "Oh." He said softly. "Alicia might have lost the baby."

"She slipped and fell down the stairs." Elizabeth's sobs returned and he held her tightly. "Oh Will, how many times did you chase me down when I insisted on walking in the snow? How many times did I fall? How did you ever endure me?"

"Dearest, nothing happened to you, and Alicia will be well. She only twisted her ankle. I imagine that she is just very ungainly."

"Of course she is." Resting her head on his shoulder, she tried to relax. "I am sorry, I do not know why I . . . I read this letter and just needed to see you."

"I understand, love. We have been talking a great deal about children lately. I imagine that you simply saw yourself in her place." He whispered. "Please do not cry. The baby is not lost; Alicia will not be like Eva."

"Eva?" She looked up and he closed his eyes. "Eva lost a baby this way? When?"

"Not by falling. It was to her first husband, a boy."

"Oh, Will."

"Dearest you cannot let this overwhelm you, or you will be as nervous as I the next time you are with child. This family can only bear one nervous parent." Darcy kissed her and they held each other tightly. Resting his forehead on hers, he resumed rubbing her back; then spotted the letter from Harwick on his desk. "Here." He managed to reach it, and pressed it into her hand. "Read this."

"I cannot see." She wiped her eyes and took a shuddering breath. "What is it?"

"It is the joyous announcement of the birth of Master Stewart Harwick." He smiled a little and blinking back his own emotion, kissed her cheek. "He and Laura are well."

"Thank heaven." Elizabeth sighed and burrowed into his arms. "Forgive me for . . ."

"Nothing." Darcy whispered.

"TAKE A SEAT MR. CONRAD." Mrs. Reynolds indicated a chair. "The senior staff takes their meals here."

"Thank you. I appreciate your help in getting me settled, Mrs. Reynolds." He sat and nodded to the others around the table. "You are the house steward, I understand?"

Matthews drew a bowl of potatoes towards him and speared a few. "I am." Pushing the bowl back he laughed, "It is not quite what I thought it would be."

"Being Mr. Darcy's secretary is not quite what I expected either." The two men glanced at each other. "You should be his secretary."

"I work for Mrs. Darcy and I look after the house. I see that repairs are made, and look after the staff that are involved in its physical upkeep, from collecting rainwater to maintaining the cesspits." He shrugged. "It leaves Nichols free to worry over the tenants and business of the land."

"And what of you?" He addressed Bernard. "In my last position, the butler was head of all the staff."

"I am head of the male staff. And of course I look after the silver, spirits and wine cupboard, and make sure that any and all needs of Mr. and Mrs. Darcy beyond their chambers are met."

"And you, Mrs. Reynolds?" He said quietly. "You seem to have the most straight-forward role."

"I care for the female staff, and the cleanliness of the house, and *I* have the keys." The men around the table chuckled.

"Rather proud of those keys, Missus." Mr. Green winked at her.

"She who has control over the tea leaves has more power than the one with the key to the port." Nichols laughed.

Mrs. Reynolds sniffed but looked rather pleased. "I also have seniority."

"Yes, yes, you have been here since the master was but four." Nichols rolled his eyes while the men chuckled.

"And you are the wet nurse?" He addressed Mrs. Robbins.

"Yes, and Mrs. Somers is the governess-in-waiting." Again the room filled with laughter.

"I am quite occupied being companion to Miss Bennet and continuing her education." Mrs. Somers smiled. "I am certain to have Miss Rosalie under my care before long, though."

"And I hope to have a new little one under my care before too long." Mrs. Robbins sighed. "I hope; I have no desire to leave this place."

"It is the young ones that seek their fortunes in town." Mrs. Reynolds said disapprovingly and glanced at the girl who was serving them. "Stay in the country, I say, but off they go."

"Finding a hard time defining your role?" Matthews glanced at Conrad and dug into his plate of food. "Well, it is what you make of it. Mr. Darcy is of an independent bent."

"And the mistress is not?" Nichols sighed and took a swig from his tankard of ale. "Look Conrad, the master bringing you on is a huge concession to his wife, and an even greater one to what he feels his duties are. He has no desire to turn over responsibility to his servants, he wants to know everything, and is very well-respected by staff, tenants, neighbours and all who are associated with him. He is a good man. You are lucky to have been chosen."

"I am not suggesting that I am not!" Conrad said defensively.

Nichols held up his palm. "Forgive me, but I have seen him tackle his birthright with great purpose since his father died, and I am very impressed, not to mention admiring how he and Mrs. Darcy have endured everything else that has come their way. I suggest that you observe him, he has a way of hiding things, but watch his face, when his chin is up, he is angry or proud, when his lips are pressed together, he is thinking hard, and when his brow is knit, he is stressed. *That* is when he needs help."

"I am to read his mind?" Conrad said incredulously.

"Yes." They all said in unison.

"He will not ask for aid." Nichols said simply. "He takes it on himself to the exclusion of others, save his wife. You must anticipate him, and trust me, it is a rare trick when you can, but the pleasure in his expression of praise is worth the effort."

At last Adams cleared his throat. "Conrad, Mr. Darcy asks that you sort his business correspondence, stay away entirely from his personal letters, write letters for him based on the notations he will leave, accept the intake of income from the tenants, pay the bills, and keep his appointments organized. You are to remind him of details that can easily be forgotten. You will accompany him on occasion to meetings where note-taking would be difficult. Mr. Darcy will always check over your work, so do not take offence, he will not accept anything to do with his estate at face value. Your role is to relieve the everyday burdens so that he and Mrs. Darcy might enjoy their time alone and with their family." He picked up his knife and fork and looked around at the staff. "Mr. Darcy, as you all will likely agree, is much returned to himself, however I will betray his confidence this one time. His headaches continue, his memory remains slightly impaired, and Mrs. Darcy wants the stress reduced so that he might continue to heal." Turning back to Conrad he pointed his knife. "Your position is to make damn sure that our master continues on that path to recovery. If you feel underutilized, then leave, we will take care of them." With a glance at Millie, he nodded. "Do not ever betray Mrs. Darcy's confidences. Do not follow my example."

"I never have betrayed her, sir." She whispered.

"I know." He began to eat while the others glanced around at each other. "Will you stay?"

"How can I not? I see before me a staff so loyal to a couple who are half my age, that I feel you would have me drawn and quartered were I to let them down." Conrad shook his head. "I have never seen the like."

"Well of course not!" Mrs. Reynolds' chin rose. "This is Pemberley."

26 NOVEMBER 1810
I received a letter today from Alicia at last. Fitzwilliam and I wrote to her and Stephen immediately, expressing our worry over her well-being, and were discouraged not to have received any further news since Stephen's first brief note. Of course now we understand why. Lord and Lady Matlock had departed for London to attend to Richard and Eva during her confinement; and Stephen wished to wait and see what might transpire. He had alerted the midwife and she came to examine Alicia, proclaiming her well, but chastising her severely for falling. If the baby had been lost, Alicia would naturally be blamed for her carelessness. Would they not have enough sadness without that burden? When Fitzwilliam heard my exclamation, I explained to him that whenever a woman miscarries, it is always blamed on her; just as excessive pain during labour is seen as deserved. Fitzwilliam was furious, crying against the wisdom of the so-called educated. Hearing him defend her made me feel so very proud to have him as my husband.

I spoke to our local midwife at church and asked her why my courses have returned, despite my still feeding Rosa, and she said that because we have offered her solid food and I am not feeding her as often, my body is making ready to have another child. We have read of ways to delay pregnancy, and have tried them all, so far successfully, it seems! However, despite our worries and fears, I anticipate our next child greatly. Soon our little girl will be eight months old. She knows her name, now. My dear Fitzwilliam keeps prompting her to say, "Papa." It will come, love. Patience!

"Patience." He smiled and closed his eyes. "I suppose that when she begins to speak we will wax fondly on the days when she was silent." Chuckling, he thought of Elizabeth's subtle message. "So my love, you are ready to be a mother again." He drew out the little box containing her hair and caressing the long curl, kissed it before putting it back in place. "Very well, then. We shall see what heaven brings us." He then set to work writing his entry for the day.

26 November 1810
Conrad and I are gradually becoming used to each other. It is not easy and I am happy to have established him in a small office near the library so that he is no longer sitting in my study. I admit that his daily list of reminders on my desk has become a very welcome addition to my routine. Where I would remember appointments by making notes, Conrad has augmented that to include thoughts that I seem to randomly express as I discuss them. The reminders have been quite useful, surprising even, as I often have no recollection of stating them. As much as I hate to admit it, I needed this aid.

Yes Elizabeth, you were correct, now please dear, stop smirking and think of a proper method of informing this new servant when you have joined me in the study. I have no desire to repeat the scene when he opened the door to find us entwined. Never has my pride shrunk so quickly, and this is from a man who enjoys swimming in the lake! Thank God it was only a kiss he observed, but given time, I would have had you spread over the top of my desk, and would have been enthusiastically working to make us parents again, although admittedly, at that moment, parenthood was hardly the uppermost thought in my mind. Either we lock the door when you come in, or I suggest that you tie another of your admirable love knots to hang on the handle. Perhaps I should have him practice knocking, and I should practice grunting orders to go away while spearing you? Would you like that love? I surely would. Blessed heaven, I feel so much better! We must take advantage of our relative seclusion, Bingley and the Hursts arrive in a matter of days, what say you to a tour of the house, love? How many rooms are there? We may walk with difficulty, and blush incessantly, but I am game if you are!

"Fitzwilliam Darcy!" Elizabeth cried and stared at him with her hand over her mouth. Grinning, he spun around from the writing desk, and wrapping his arms around her waist drew her tightly to him. He rested his chin on her breasts and looked up while his fingers traced over her bottom. "Ninety-two rooms in five days?" She raised her brow. "Your proposal is awe-inspiring, not to mention your stamina."

Laughing, he kissed her cleavage, then unbuttoning the front of her gown, he began suckling a nipple. "I was thinking of just the public and family rooms."

"Oh." She smiled and caressed her fingers through his hair as his nose pressed against her soft flesh, and his twinkling blue eyes looked up at her. "So that brings us down to . . .half?"

"Hmm. Forty six." He let go and opened the other side of her gown to suckle the neglected nipple. "Divided by five . . ."

"I do not see this happening."

"Perhaps we can make this an adventure, whenever we tire of our guests, we can slip away to check another location from the list." Darcy chuckled. "I shall put Conrad to work drawing one up for us!"

"Oh my!" Elizabeth laughed and he buried his face between her mounds to blow a raspberry, then looked up to stare at her mouth. "And what explanation will you offer?"

"Hmm." Licking his lips he studied hers. "You and I are taking an in-depth survey of the . . ."

"Decoration?"

"Hmm."

"Warmth?"

"I like that." He lifted her skirts and ran his hands up and between her legs. "Comfort?"

"Oh, I so like that." Unbuttoning his breeches, he helped her to sit astride, and sighing, kissed her lips at last. Darcy smiled and rocked his hips a little as she laughed and rotated hers, and wrapped her arms around his neck. "So I suppose that this room may be left off the list?"

"Oh no, my secretary will likely feel that I forgot it with my addled memory. We will simply have to revisit this place." They began kissing and moving in earnest when a knock came to the door. Darcy gasped and called out, "Begone!"

A girl squeaked and footsteps were heard running away. Elizabeth dissolved into laughter and Darcy, too far gone to stop, lost his tenuous control within moments, burying his face on her shaking shoulder while he tried to regain his breath and composure. When he lifted his head he was met by her delighted smile. "You need to work on your delivery."

"My delivery was just fine, love." He smacked her bottom and groaned when she lifted off then bent to kiss him. With a contented sigh, he stood and fixed his breeches, then took her hand to pull her from the room. "How many more rooms to go? Let's get cracking!"

Chapter 29

"Do you still love me?" Bingley said with a smile when he released Elizabeth from his embrace. She held his face in her hands, and studied his warm green eyes. They closed when she kissed his cheek.

"Of course I do. We all do." She felt Darcy touch her shoulder and took his hand. He drew her to his side and slipped his hand possessively around her waist. "I cannot wait to hear of your adventures."

"In the wilds of Ireland!" Bingley noted the glint in Darcy's eye, despite his welcoming smile, and laughed. "Well, I could go for a taste of that fine port you keep, Darcy. What say you, Hurst?"

"I would be delighted to join you!" He rubbed his arms. "I would be delighted to feel my limbs again!"

The group laughed as Elizabeth and Mary escorted Louisa up the stairs to her chambers and Darcy led the way to his study. "Thank you for allowing my hug, Darcy." Bingley winked when the men settled into their chairs. "I know that you did not like it."

"No, I did not. But I also know that it is simply genuine care for a brother and sister. Besides, I would say that you embraced me nearly as tightly."

"But in a manly way." Bingley lift his chin and Hurst snorted.

"I have seen more affection displayed in your foyer today than I have between my entire family in decades." He lifted his glass and toasted them. "To sentiment."

Darcy smiled and crossed his legs. "Well, are you finished? Are you prepared to return to society, full of adventures and ready to take on your life?"

"You make it all sound so dramatic, Darcy! We were hunting, fishing, and eating very well. We saw a great many ruined castles, an extraordinary number of sheep," Darcy chuckled, "and in general, simply enjoyed the scenery. It was a solid and dramatic change from London, and I think it helped me to be comfortable with my own company. I encouraged Hurst and Louisa to go off on their own frequently and I was left to my own devices. I met many fascinating characters, rode over territory that was amazing in its beauty, well, I suppose that I did all of the things that you told me to do, and appreciated this opportunity that will likely never come again once I am settled." Drawing a deep breath, he sat back in his chair and looked fondly around the room. "I am ready, I believe. I have had enough of wandering aimlessly. Hurst and I were talking about continuing our travels when the weather warms, perhaps moving south and exploring the coast, Ramsgate or Brighton, and at the moment we were speaking, I felt a great deal of enthusiasm for it. After all, Brighton is quite the popular resort." He shrugged and sighed. "And then we drove into Pemberley."

"And?" Darcy's lips twitched and he sipped his drink. "How has my home ruined your plans?"

"That is just it, Darcy. I felt all the relief and comfort of coming home." He glanced at Hurst. "As much as I appreciate the rooms you lend me in London, I am truly ready to acquire rooms of my very own, where I can . . ." He glanced at the Pemberley landscape and waved, "Put a picture on the wall and nobody can protest where I place the hook."

"Your walls. Your home." Darcy nodded.

"Until you take a wife and she is the one who will dictate your decoration." Hurst noted.

"Not in my study." Bingley declared and drank in the masculine atmosphere. "Well, I must find a study first."

Darcy studied him and sat up a little. "Well, I have kept my eyes open for estates in this area, and I am afraid that nothing suitable for your needs has presented itself. There are a few that I am watching, and perhaps in a year or so . . . well, that does nothing for you now. Netherfield remains available. I understand from Lucas that the judge will not renew his lease. However the owner has at last seen the wisdom of improving his land, so the productivity of the estate should be increasing."

"Is that so?" Bingley nodded thoughtfully. "Perhaps I should write to him and put in my request to lease it now, no hemming and hawing this time."

"When would you take it?" Hurst asked.

"Well it would be foolish to take it before Michaelmas; I will be in town for the Season."

"Is there any hesitation about living so close to Lucas Lodge?"

Bingley looked up to a spot in the corner of the room. "No." He smiled back at Darcy. "None at all. She was not the girl for me." He sat forward and rubbed his hands together. "Now, you have our company for the next month, whatever will you do with us?"

Darcy sighed and smiled. "Why do I look forward to New Year already?"

"No, no, Darcy, we will be perfect guests. Louisa is looking forward to telling Caroline all about Pemberley."

He groaned. "Wonderful. How is your sister?"

Hurst smiled at Bingley. "Pregnancy does not sit well with her, but she already has the nursery decorated, undoubtedly by the time we return she will have the appropriate staff in place. She will see this child long enough to show off to visitors and then go back to her affairs. I believe that she has told Robinson that she expects a long holiday afterwards."

"For performing her services." Darcy sighed. "I cannot imagine my wife being so cold."

"Mrs. Fitzwilliam is nearing her moment, is she not?" Bingley smiled. "How is your cousin? The stoic soldier? I wager that he will not even perspire, he has faced so much."

"They expect the baby sometime in the next few weeks, near Christmas." Darcy glanced at a letter on his desk from Fitzwilliam that contained an endless list of questions and endless worries. "He will be fine."

"MMMM, SO NICE. Good morning." Fitzwilliam murmured while rubbing Evangeline's shoulders. He then firmly massaged his way down her spine and back up again.

She stretched like a cat and sighed. "What has you so pleased?"

"Oh my dear, have I ever told you how much I enjoy bothering you?" He nuzzled his lips to her throat. "I do, you know."

"I believe that I have noticed." Eva closed her eyes and melted back into the relief his mammoth hands gave her aching body. "But this is not in any way a bother."

"No?" Kissing her ear, he slipped his hands around to caress her breasts. "Is it possible that these have grown in the night?"

"Richard . . ."

"Seriously love, look at them!" He adjusted his position kneeling behind her on the bed, took a breast in each hand, and began to juggle. "They are orbs!"

"They always were." She opened her eyes and looked at how they spilled out of his palms. "Although they seem rather obscene."

"Oh, no!" Fitzwilliam said vehemently. "No, no, no!" He smiled when she laughed softly. "How do you feel?"

"I am a mass of emotion. I am tired, anxious, oh Richard, all I can think about is . . ." She looked up to see his face resting on her shoulder. "You."

"Me?" Sitting up, his smile expressed his delight. "Really?"

"Oh yes, please?"

"I am a gentleman, I would not think of leaving a lady in distress." Happily, he laid her on her side and was just going to settle behind her when she gasped. "Eva? I have not begun yet."

She clutched her belly and laid her head back on his chest. "Richard you silly idiot, I am not that numb. I know when you have begun! I just felt a pain."

"A pain?" He said in confusion then the light of dawn flooded his mind. His desire melted as his heart started to pound. "What kind of pain? Your back is sore?"

"Yes, but . . ." She sighed and felt his hands slip around her protectively. "It was a labour pain."

"No." He said flatly.

"I am afraid so." She turned back and felt her heart lurch to see fear registering in his eyes. "It was going to happen sometime."

"No."

"Richard Fitzwilliam. Stop denying this, I am going to bear this child, and it seems that it will be today." She felt his increasing tension as his body stiffened behind her, and in some way, she was grateful for it. Being strong for him would force her to push her own worries aside. "I think that we need to notify the accoucher."

"Oh no." He clutched her possessively. "No."

"Do *you* wish to deliver me?"

"Good God, no!" He stared.

"Then please alert the staff, and . . . ohhhhhh." She squeezed her eyes shut. "Ohhhh."

"EVA!"

"Dear, I am well; it could be many, many hours."

"Elizabeth delivered in no time!" He said as panic rose in his voice.

"So you need to get to your duties! Notify the staff and send a note to your parents."

"My parents?" He said blankly. "Why?"

"So that your father can keep you sane and your mother will come and fight with me." She laughed at his absolutely lost expression. "Oh Richard, you resemble a little boy who has dropped his candy in the mud."

"What?" He blinked and saw her smile. "I am not that lost!"

"How did you ever ride into battle?"

"Oh love. I cared for my boys, but it is nothing to holding my life in my arms." He sighed and kissed her. "Forgive me." Carefully, he rose to his feet and stood to pull the bell. He watched her try to sit up and rushed to her side. "Where are you going?"

"I am going to walk."

"No."

"That seems to be a favourite word of yours today." She laughed a little then squeezed her eyes shut when another pain came and went. "Oh my."

"Is it worse?" He said anxiously.

"No. Now help me to stand." Eva ordered her hopeless husband.

"Must you? I do not care to see our baby drop from you as you stride about the room."

"Richard Fitzwilliam, I sincerely doubt that giving birth to your child will inspire such nonchalant behaviour on my part. Besides, if anything, I will waddle." She grasped his hands and stood, then leaned into his arms. A knock at the door came and he gave the orders to send for the male mid-wife and to notify Matlock House of the imminent birth.

"Now, what must we do?" He said softly as he slowly walked her around the chambers. "Shall I tell you how much I love you?"

"I have yet to hear you stop telling me. It is in everything you say and do." Evangeline caressed his worried face. They held each other and kissed until the chamber door opened and their staff began the business of preparing for the baby to arrive. Fitzwilliam felt himself being relegated to the doorway as they took over his wife's care. "I love you." Evangeline said softly. Nodding and kissing his fingers, he held up his palm before walking away.

"MRS. DARCY." Bernard said quietly from the doorway. "Some visitors have arrived and ask for permission to see the house."

"Oh, I thought that it might be the Henley's carriage. They have been threatening to visit." Elizabeth's brow creased then she smiled when she heard Hurst chuckling. She saw Louisa's shaking head and addressed her, "We have not had anybody since summer. It is an odd time to be touring."

"I would not say that." Bingley smiled. "Look at us."

"That is true." Elizabeth shrugged.

Bernard cleared his throat. "One lady claims some acquaintance with you, Madam. She is the former Miss Long."

"Sarah!" Elizabeth cried and jumped up. Bingley and the Hursts exchanged curious glances while Mary followed her down the stairs to the foyer where a man and two women stood in utter awe as they gaped at the magnificent hall. "Sarah Long!"

"Oh!" A young woman wearing a simply tailored gown and coat ran forward, "Elizabeth! Oh and Mary! Oh, just look at how beautiful you are!" She stopped her advance suddenly when she took in their fine gowns, and obviously fully realized the difference in their stations. She blushed when she glanced down at her dress.

Elizabeth smiled reassuringly, "I was just about to say the same of you. You are glowing!"

Sarah stood a little taller and turned to the others. "Mrs. Darcy, Miss Mary Bennet, this is my husband, Mr. Andrew Wilcox, we were married three weeks ago, and we are on our wedding trip."

"I did not know that you had married already! Forgive me; I am due a letter from Jane. I am sure that she will include the wonderful news. Congratulations to you both." Elizabeth smiled and looked to the other woman. "And . . . You look so familiar."

"They tell me that I bear a striking resemblance to my Aunt Long." The pretty young woman with auburn hair and green eyes smiled and curtseyed.

"Mrs. Darcy, this is my cousin Miss Abbey Martin, she accompanied us on our trip. Mr. Wilcox is from Derbyshire and we have been visiting his family." She looked up at him with an adoring smile. "And now we are on our way back home."

"Mr. Wilcox, I hope that you found your family well?"

"Yes, Mrs. Darcy, very well." He said softly. "I must say that it is a great pleasure to visit Pemberley, thank you for tolerating us. I have grown up hearing of the estate. My family owns a small estate, Nevillewood, not too far from Matlock."

"Mr. Wilcox has the living at Langley." Sarah said proudly.

"Congratulations, sir. That is a wonderful achievement!" Elizabeth smiled. "I suppose that was how you met; Langley is not far at all from Meryton."

"We met at an assembly." He smiled at Sarah. "She somehow coaxed me to dance."

"I believe that she planted herself in front of you until you noticed her." Abbey laughed and Elizabeth turned to her with a sparkle in her eye. "Forgive me, I could not resist."

"Not at all, I am very fond of teasing the ones I love, as my sister can attest." She nudged Mary and raised her brows.

Taking the cue to speak, Mary nervously turned to Abbey. "Are you from Langley, Miss Martin?"

"No, I live in London, but last year I began to spend the autumn in the country, better air, Mama said," she bit her lip and continued, "my father is in trade." She glanced at Elizabeth and was relieved to see that she was not in the least disgusted. "He purchases fabric from the mills in Yorkshire, and has several shops around town. He is very successful."

"Well that is a pleasant coincidence; one of our houseguests owns several mills. Perhaps he will know your father. I will introduce you when your tour is completed."

"You have friends in trade?" Abbey said with surprise and unconsciously glanced around at the splendour before her.

Elizabeth leaned forward and said in a conspiratorial whisper, "Miss Martin, I am proud to say that I have *family* in trade."

"Oh." She smiled and laughed. "Forgive me, but I resisted visiting here, despite the slight connection that my cousin can claim, I feared that . . . well that we would be looked at without favour. Mr. Wilcox has been very verbose in his stories of Pemberley, it has a very long history and great influence in the county, it seems. And he *is* a student of history." She smiled at him.

Wilcox blushed. "It was Mr. Lucas who suggested that we might take in the estate when we were in the area. He said it was not to be missed, and that you are most welcoming."

"Oh yes, and after hearing your mother go on and on about it, we simply had to see if she was, well, you know." Sarah blushed.

"Oh, I know." Elizabeth smiled. "Well, here it is. My housekeeper will be glad to show you around, and when you are finished, please join us for tea." She noted Abbey's surprise and she smiled at her. "Where are you staying?"

"In Lambton." Wilcox said quickly. "We depart for home in the morning. We wish to be there to celebrate Christmas."

"Well then, Mrs. Reynolds?" Elizabeth turned and nodded to her, then looked back at the party. "I will see you in about an hour."

"You will not join us?" Sarah asked.

"Oh no." She laughed. "How can you comment on the decoration if I am standing by your side? Come and join us when you are through. As I said, we have some other guests and I will be glad to introduce you to them. Go ahead and enjoy yourselves."

Elizabeth and Mary walked back up the stairs and Mrs. Reynolds cleared her throat. "Now then, the master of Pemberley is Mr. Fitzwilliam Darcy, he is . . ."

"I am surprised that you did not stay with them, Lizzy." Mary whispered and sent a backwards glance as they disappeared down the hallway towards the dining room. "I do not really know the Long family, but you used to talk to the girls."

"I did, but I cannot be expected to drop everything to be a guide to people who essentially arrived uninvited and unannounced. Like it or not, I have a position to maintain, and Fitzwilliam expects me to do so. I am not being superior; I am simply being the mistress of Pemberley. Sarah is a very nice girl and she is clearly very proud of her new husband, and wanted to please him by showing her connection to an estate he admired. Undoubtedly she also has the desire to satisfy her curiosity courtesy of our mother's imagination. Now Sarah can tell the gossips the truth of our home, and hopefully Mama will be silenced as she has never seen it." She saw Mary's eyes widen in admiration and said quietly. "However, I invited them for tea because of our acquaintance. That is a significant honour, and I believe that Miss Martin recognized it; she seems to be educated, and certainly well-off. I wonder if her father has invested in her future as Mrs. Hurst's father did."

"I can hardly believe how many things you took into consideration in that short interview, Lizzy! I was just trying to think of something sensible to say. Is being so conscious of behaviour and position the way of all mistresses when people come to the home?" Mary asked as they made their way back to the sitting room.

"I cannot speak for everyone, but this was a topic that Lady Matlock discussed with me when we were all together here, and Fitzwilliam and I were newly married. It seemed there was almost a daily influx of visitors, and I felt compelled to meet them. She corrected me. If I am available I will speak to them, but I do not interrupt my work if I am busy, and Fitzwilliam never has. I am not sure if Rosings has ever accepted visitors. You will have to ask Captain de Bourgh in your next letter." Elizabeth smiled when Mary blushed. "It will not be long before his next comes."

"I miss him."

"Good." Elizabeth laughed. "Oh Mary, can you imagine how much I missed my Fitzwilliam? And I did not even know if he cared for me."

"Lizzy." Mary stopped and looked at her hands. "May I write a private letter to him?"

"What would you want to say that is so private? You are not courting, Mary." Elizabeth studied her. "And if you do write him a private letter, how could he respond? You know that his letters are read by us all."

"I do not wish for a response." Mary said softly. "I only wish to express my impressions of his journals, so that he knows that I understand why he gave them to me." She looked up and spoke pleadingly. "I promise it will be just this once, and I will beg him not to respond, but I want him to know, to really know that I . . . care."

"Oh Mary."

"Please.

"I will ask Fitzwilliam."

"He will say no." She said sadly.

"You could ask him." Elizabeth said with a smile. "He is especially easy to persuade if you give him a hug."

"I could not just hug him!" Mary gasped. "I could not!"

"Then play his favourite songs."

Mary shook her head and Elizabeth took her hand and squeezed. "I am sorry, Mary. I know that you might want to express something that would be embarrassing for us, especially for Fitzwilliam to read. I propose that you write your letter, and I will read it. Fitzwilliam will accept my judgement on this. We simply do not want either of you to be expressing inappropriate thoughts. Would that be acceptable?"

"I only want him to know that I understand so much of him. We are so much alike." Mary saw Elizabeth's head nodding. "You really do understand."

"Yes, I truly do. Fitzwilliam and I are very similar."

Relaxing, Mary decided it was time for her to tease. "I think that he wishes for you to play for him." She said and saw Elizabeth's surprise. "He looks at the pianoforte and back to you often."

"He does?" Elizabeth blushed. "Oh, since you and Georgiana took over the music room, I am afraid that I have not felt accomplished enough to compare with you, and have shirked my playing. He has not played for me either, I should point out."

"Then practice for him. I think that he would enjoy it very much." Mary giggled. "And you *must* sing!"

She laughed. "I do that all of the time."

"Yes, and he looks so lost!" Mary sighed. "I want to see Peter . . . Captain de Bourgh look lost."

"He does, Mary. You just have to stop looking at your hands and into his eyes, he will love it." She squeezed her hand and smiled.

"Are you two going to join us?" Bingley appeared at the doorway and grinned. "Or will you continue this fascinating discussion of love in the hallway where any and all can listen?"

"You cannot hear us unless you do it on purpose, Mr. Bingley." Elizabeth said with her hands on her hips. "What are you about?"

Chuckling, he stepped back into the room and waited for the sisters to pass. "Your husband has abandoned me for the estate, what do you expect?"

"I expect you to entertain your brother and sister."

His head wagged. "No, I have done that for months."

"You should have accompanied Fitzwilliam."

"No, this was a meeting about his money, and none of my business." He grinned. "Try again."

"Well we will shortly have three visitors joining us for tea. Perhaps you might act the gracious host while my dear husband is occupied?" She tilted her head and smiled.

"I get to play master of Pemberley?" He puffed his chest. "Why, I feel the mantle of responsibility falling on my shoulders as we speak! I am taller, I am prouder, I am Darcy!" He drew an imaginary sword and slashed the air. Laughing, he led her by the hand to a sofa and sat beside her. "Does this mean that I get to assume all husbandly duties?"

"Charles." She said sternly.

"Yes, dear Elizabeth?" He batted his eyes and kissed her hand. "Tell me you care for me."

"Like a brother and a friend." Her lips twitched.

"*Not* the answer I wanted." He sighed dramatically and gave her a rueful smile. "Darcy would rightly kill me if he heard this. Forgive me."

"I know that you mean no harm. In any case, you had your chance."

Bingley's brow furrowed and he sat up straight. "When?"

"When you asked me to dance." Elizabeth grinned and Louisa laughed. "Remember, I had no idea of Fitzwilliam's interest. You sir, made me aware, you shot yourself in the foot. You could have swept me off of my feet that very night." She placed her hand to her heart.

Louisa shook her head. "Do not listen to her teasing, Charles; she is paying you back for your insolence. Besides, Caroline would not have let you. She would have conspired to separate you."

"Definitely. Once she heard that the estate was small, she was ready to move you on to greener pastures." Hurst nodded

Bingley sat back and laughed. "Do you mean to say that if I had stuck by your side that evening I would have stood a chance?"

Elizabeth's eyes sparkled. "What do you think?"

"I think that you spoiled your chance." Hurst chuckled.

"I think that Mrs. Darcy's heart was decided long before she ever favoured me with a smile, and she has never led me or any other man on. Her focus has always been on one particular person, just as her beloved husband's was on her, whether either of them knew it or not." Bingley smiled when Elizabeth's eyes cast to the floor. "There Mrs. Darcy, I can tease back."

"You were not teasing. You are always a gentleman, and very sweet." She looked back up at him and saw his cheeks were pink. "Someday a wonderful girl will see that, too."

"Pardon me Mrs. Darcy; we have finished the tour of the open public rooms." Mrs. Reynolds announced.

"Oh, I forgot how much of the house is closed for winter. Please show our guests in, and have some fresh tea sent up. If Mr. Darcy is available, please let him know that we have some guests from Hertfordshire." The group entered and Elizabeth and the others stood. "Mr. and Mrs. Hurst, Mr. Bingley, may I introduce Mr. and Mrs. Wilcox, and Miss Martin."

"It is a great pleasure." Bingley bowed to them and looked to Abbey as a slow smile spread over his face. Blushing, she smiled shyly and curtseyed, greeting the Hursts along with her cousins.

"Please take a seat." Elizabeth glanced at Bingley and fought back her smile. "How did you find the home? Did it live up to the acclaim you have heard?"

Wilcox's eyes were travelling over the room and came back to hers. "Absolutely, I look forward to writing to my family of the experience. There was much speculation over the interior, I admit, and I am pleased to say that we were all so incorrect."

"Really?" Elizabeth laughed. "What was the debate?"

"Oh you know, dripping with ornamentation." Abbey said and blushed when she saw that Bingley was completely focussed on her.

Elizabeth nodded. "I have been to a few houses like that, and I was pleased when my husband first showed me his homes to find that they are an excellent reflection of his personality."

"Thank you, Mrs. Darcy." Darcy said from the doorway. Immediately the guests stood and Elizabeth rose with them.

"Mr. Darcy, may I introduce Mr. and Mrs. Wilcox and Miss Martin."

"It is a pleasure; I understand that you are from Hertfordshire?" He smiled slightly and glanced at Bingley, who smiled and moved from his seat by Elizabeth to take one on the sofa occupied by Abbey.

"Yes, sir." Sarah breathed as she stared at the imposing man. "You probably do not remember me, but I was at Jane Bennet's wedding."

"Oh, well forgive me, but I was . . ." He looked at Elizabeth.

"We were a little preoccupied that morning." She smiled and he nodded, having no recollection of her, let alone most of the day.

"So were many other girls." Sarah sighed. "Many were disappointed to see Mr. Lucas marry, but none were surprised it would be to Jane, we all saw how he looked at her, even as the other girls wished he would look our way."

Bingley turned to regard her. "So he was a desired suitor in the neighbourhood?"

"Oh yes. After all he is heir to Lucas Lodge, and there are not so many suitors of his worth in the neighbourhood. Of course I met my Mr. Wilcox so I was completely satisfied." She smiled up at her blushing husband.

"Nobody needs to hear that, Mrs. Wilcox."

"Oh, let her be happy with you, Reverend." Elizabeth smiled and slipped her hand into Darcy's grasp. "There is no shame in caring for your spouse."

He saw their entwined fingers and smiled. "I suppose not."

Darcy looked at her sparkling eyes and smiled warmly. "Thank you, dear."

"There were those gentlemen who occupied Netherfield this autumn." Sarah continued on. "The judge and his nephews. They departed just before our wedding."

"What did you think of them?"

"Not much." Abbey said and rolled her eyes. "I was there for several weeks before Sarah's wedding and ran across that group of rakes at a few functions. One at Lucas Lodge." She said thoughtfully. "Why the label of gentleman gives a man permission to behave so ungentlemanly, I will never understand."

"I understand precisely what you are saying." Elizabeth laughed and she saw Darcy's brow crease.

"You do?" Darcy asked her.

"Of course, think of the men who approach a lady with a silver tongue and an empty conscious, or worse, one who thinks so well of himself that he not only informs them of their inferiority, but explains that they must be grateful for his condescension to address them." She watched his brow furrow further and squeezed his hand.

"I see." He said softly as the memory of Creary flooded back. "I know men like that. And men who are no longer like that."

"So do I. We have certainly met a few." Elizabeth's grip tightened and she turned to Sarah. "What did these men do? Surely they did not behave too badly?"

"Oh . . . I suppose not. But when rich men come into the neighbourhood you know that their every move is watched. If I was not engaged to my Mr. Wilcox, I know that Mama would have been eyeing them for me." She smiled up at her husband and looked to her cousin. "She was pushing you towards one was she not, Abbey?"

"Yes." She sighed. "It was embarrassing."

"Were they rakish, then?" Mrs. Hurst smiled, "Or just a little more charming than the neighbourhood was accustomed to seeing?"

"I heard of a great deal of galloping through the neighbourhood." Abbey smiled. "They had a certain charming way about them, perhaps it was just something in their air and manner of walking that made the hearts flutter. And perhaps it was a great deal of wishful thinking by some romantic girls."

"I think that there is much in that. I remember the giggling of girls when we would attend the assemblies." Elizabeth smiled when Darcy squeezed her hand

and moved his leg to touch hers. "Now, Miss Martin tells me that her father is in trade, and that they purchase fabrics from mills in Yorkshire. Could you be in business with her father, Mr. Bingley?"

"Oh." Bingley startled from his preoccupation of studying Abbey and blinked. "Martin." He chewed his lip and then nodded slowly. "I believe that I do business with a man named . . . Auggie." He laughed when Abbey blushed. "Forgive me, Mr. August Martin. Is he your father?"

"Yes." She smiled. "That is Papa. He is Auggie to very few."

"I am not so involved with the daily affairs of the business as I should be, but I have met him occasionally when our paths crossed at the mills." Bingley's eyes looked off in the distance and he chewed his lip again. "I remember . . . I was home on holiday, I believe it was the first break from Cambridge . . . Father took me around the mill, showing me off, you know, the first Bingley to attend." He blushed and looked down and back up to see Abbey watching him. "Well, Father saw that Auggie, Mr. Martin, was there and went into his spiel, and then Aug . . . Mr. Martin said that he wanted to have his girls attend a proper finishing school. He asked Father where my sisters attended." He looked to Louisa and she rolled her eyes.

"Mrs . . ." Louisa began.

"Farnsworth." Abbey finished. All eyes turned to her and she stared at Bingley. "Your father is the reason we had to go to that terrible woman?"

"She was a harridan." Louisa agreed.

"No, calling her a harridan is an insult to harridans!" Abbey proclaimed and then catching a twinkle in Bingley's eye she blushed and looked down, then back up. "You knew that."

"I certainly heard enough stories from Louisa and Caroline." He smiled at her and looked to Louisa. "Did I not?"

"I think that they were entirely justified." Louisa sniffed. "Miss Martin, I congratulate you for surviving. I am only amazed that the school remains standing. You cannot be long from it?"

"I left there when I was eighteen." She said softly and again found Bingley's gaze on her. "Two years ago."

"And her mother is frantic to marry her off!" Sarah proclaimed. "She will not let her other sister come out until she is settled. Much different from your mother, is she not?" She smiled at Elizabeth.

Darcy squeezed her hand. "Yes, quite." Elizabeth then smiled at Abbey and changed the subject. "For your father to be known by such an endearing nickname, he must be a wonderful man."

"Oh, he is a dear." She said tactfully.

Bingley chuckled. "He is a gifted tradesman, born to sell, I remember thinking. I believe that he could sell a tired mule to a gentleman and convince him he was buying a stallion." He looked at Abbey and she shook her head at her hands, but had a wide smile on her face.

The rest of the company laughed, and Darcy lifted his chin. "Sounds as if he is the perfect customer for you, Bingley."

Bingley nodded, but did not take his eyes off of Abbey. "Yes, I am sure that he is. Well if I give it all up, whoever purchases will be glad to have his business."

"Give it up?" Abbey looked back up to him. "Why would you do that?" She saw his warm gaze travelling over her again and pulled herself together in the face of the handsome man's attention. "I mean, that would be a shame to have such a good business relationship die."

"It would." Bingley agreed. "However I am to purchase an estate."

"Oh." She nodded and realized at once the difference between them. "I see, and you need capital."

"Precisely." Tilting his head, he smiled. "And perhaps I might improve the general neighbourhood in Hertfordshire and take Netherfield."

"Really?" Sarah cried delightedly. "Oh, what news! May I tell everyone?"

"Mrs. Wilcox, no agreement has been reached with the owner; this is still speculation on Mr. Bingley's part." Darcy said quietly and sent his friend a stern and pointed look.

Sighing, he nodded at his friend. "Yes, of course, but I admit that I have been considering the estate for some time. Perhaps next autumn I will be the annoying gentleman at the dances making eyes at the young ladies."

"And raising the speculation of the Mamas." Hurst said with a twitch of his lips.

Louisa sighed. "Oh my, why do I see us spending the autumn in Hertfordshire? You will need a hostess, Charles."

"I will, indeed, thank you for volunteering Louisa!" He laughed. "You may put to work all of those skills you learned from Mrs. Farnsworth."

Abbey and Louisa both sighed and smiled at each other. "Come now Miss Martin, let us commiserate together."

"Oh Mrs. Hurst, please, I prefer to put the past behind me!"

"My goodness Mary, I think that you must have done very well with Mrs. Banks!" Elizabeth smiled and encouraged her. "Or have you been keeping your woes to yourself?"

"I enjoyed my schooling very much, Lizzy." She said diplomatically, but seeing Abbey's smile, she looked to her hands and murmured, "But I was glad to see it end, too."

"Ah, I believe that we all share that sentiment, Miss Mary." Bingley nodded.

Sarah sat quietly and Elizabeth, noting her silence, leaned towards her. "You know Sarah, I think that listening to all of this talk, you and I are the fortunate ones."

She sat up a little and saw her husband's gentle smile. "Yes, we are."

"Now tell us all about your honeymoon." Elizabeth turned and gave her full attention to the bride. "And if you do not mind waiting a bit after we finish our tea, I would be grateful if you could deliver a letter to my family?"

"Oh!" Sarah smiled. "I would be honoured, Mrs. Darcy!"

"Thank you, Mrs. Wilcox." She saw Darcy's small smile and felt his hand squeeze hers again. "I am so happy that you came to visit us today."

"LYDIA! YOU ARE HOME!" Kitty flew into the bedroom where Lydia stood staring at her open trunk. "I am sorry I was not home when you arrived. I was visiting Maria, they are decorating Lucas Lodge for the dance tonight and . . ." She stopped. "What is wrong?"

"Where did you get *that* dress?" Lydia walked over to Kitty and touched the fine fabric.

"Oh." Kitty smiled. "Lizzy bought it for me. We went to the modiste that she and Georgiana like and she bought me some new things for school. Is it not pretty? Georgiana got one that is similar, but hers is in a shade of blue that nearly matches her eyes, it is so pretty! We went on an outing one day and I know that she was the prettiest girl there! We went to the museums and took our papers and crayons and drew, and we go to performances, and . . . Well you know, it is all in my letters. I wish that she could have come home with me for Christmas, but she is staying with Lord and Lady Matlock. Did you get the letter we sent? We were so worried about you and that girl Jessica; you really have to start minding your teachers."

"Lizzy *bought* you that?" Lydia grabbed at the gown and Kitty pulled away. Immediately she ran out the door and into the bedchamber formerly occupied by Jane and Elizabeth, and tore open the closet, grabbing a gown from a peg. "All of these are yours? From Lizzy?" She screeched.

"Lydia!" Kitty ran and played tug of war with her. "Stop it!"

"What on earth is happening in here?" Jane demanded from the doorway. Mrs. Gardiner was by her side. "Lydia put down that dress at once!"

"No! Lizzy bought her lots of fancy new dresses, and all of the dresses that Mama had made for me are gone! I have to wear this!" She glared at her simple gown.

"There is absolutely nothing wrong with that gown and for your information, Lizzy bought all of your school gowns, too! There is no difference in the style from Kitty's gowns." Jane took back the now hopelessly wrinkled dress and set it aside. "So stop this noise!"

Lydia stared at her. "Where are Mama's gowns?"

"You may have them back when you are a woman."

"I *am* a woman!"

"Have you learned nothing at that school?" Mrs. Gardiner asked.

"Jessica said it is a waste of time, Jessica said . . ."

"Jessica! We wrote to you and told you to get away from her!" Kitty cried. "She is bad!"

"Who is this Jessica?" Mrs. Gardiner asked and crossed her arms.

"She is . . ."

"My best friend." Lydia said positively. Kitty stared at her and turned away. Jane put her hand on her shoulder.

Kitty sniffed and raised her chin. "She is her roommate and she flirts with the officers. Lydia does, too." Lydia stared at her sister's betrayal.

"Lydia!"

"They smile at me!" She shrugged and tried to look nonchalant. "Oh it is just a joke. We do it to get back at the headmistress. She has chaperones following us and we play a game, taking turns distracting them, while the other slips away into the shops to meet the soldiers for a few moments. They think it is funny. One of them said he had a really wonderful hiding place that he will show us when we return."

"You will do no such thing." Mrs. Gardiner declared. "I will go now and speak to your parents, but hear me now, young lady. Do not even think of approaching another man again or I will make sure that you spend the rest of your days reading aloud to the children in the poor house." She glared and left the room.

Jane looked between the sisters. "What else happens at your school, Lydia? Are you learning anything at all? Do the other girls talk to you?"

"We do lessons, and they are so dull! Handwriting, letter writing, sewing, languages, *reading*. So deadly dull! The only lessons I like are dancing." Her face brightened. "I always pay attention there."

"Everything that they are teaching you is important, Lydia." Jane sat her down. "You are too old now to behave as a child. You must prepare for your future."

"I will marry a soldier." She said dreamily.

"And he will expect you to keep house for him. There will be no money for servants to do all of the work. You will have to help." Jane saw the surprise in Lydia's eyes. "If you do not improve yourself, you will not find a man with the means to provide all of the luxuries you enjoy at Longbourn. You have to understand this!"

"You sound like all of the other girls at school." Lydia pouted. "Nobody wants to have fun."

"It is not a matter of having fun, it is survival." Jane tried to impress her sister and sighed when nothing seemed to make a dent. There was a soft knock at the door and Lucas was there. Lydia's eyes grew wide.

"Your aunt looked very upset, is there something wrong?" He spoke to Jane but his eyes were on Lydia. "I hope that I do not need to repeat the admonishment that you heard from our brother Darcy, Sister?"

"No, sir." Lydia whispered.

"I hope that I do not need to repeat the words from Captain de Bourgh, which I believe you did understand."

"No, sir, I mean, yes, sir." She looked down.

"Do we need to have Mr. Collins pay a visit? He is only too happy to expound on the proper behaviour of a young lady." Lucas folded his arms.

"No, sir."

"Lydia." Jane took her hand. "Think. If all of your teachers, and all of the girls at your school are behaving one way, and only Jessica is behaving like you, who do you think is in the right?"

"Please do not waste this opportunity, Lydia." Kitty said quietly. "I will not."

"I am not wasting anything. I am going to go see Mama." Lydia hurried past Lucas and out of the room.

Kitty hung her head and Jane put her arm around her. "We will try again another time when she is calm. But in the meantime, let us get that dress pressed, you are coming to the dance tonight."

"AHHHHH." LUCAS SMILED. "At last a dance with the most beautiful . . ."

"Robert, I have begged you not to call me beautiful." Jane smiled into his happy eyes. "You enjoy teasing me too much."

"No, I love teasing you." He clasped her hand and they stepped forward and back. "However, I am not alone in proclaiming your beauty. I believe the men of Netherfield looked at you with entirely too much admiration. I am glad that they are gone."

"I did not ask for it!" She protested. "And not one of them ever suggested anything to me."

"No, not to you, but their eyes gave them away." He passed behind her. "They saw what I do."

"Robert." Jane blushed and he laughed softly. "Please stop."

"Am I not permitted to be possessive of you?" He whispered as they clasped hands again.

"If I may speak of the girls who persist in their admiration of you." She lifted her chin and he chuckled.

"Well done, dear." They smiled and danced without speaking until the song ended. Clapping, they looked to the musicians then back to each other, waiting for the next. "I understand that the judge will not renew the lease for the spring."

"I believe that you are correct. Mama heard . . ."

"Naturally." He winked and they began to move again. "She knows all."

"Well she has found a whole new source of untapped gossip in the tenants." Jane smiled and they both looked over at Mrs. Bennet talking excitedly with her sister. "Papa will have to buy another horse and gig so that she can visit on her own."

"I do not see your mother driving a gig by herself." Lucas laughed. "And woe to the man on foot when she is driving down his lane!"

"Fitzwilliam bought Lizzy a barouche to drive."

"Of course he did. I cannot believe he gave in to her prodding." He saw that Jane was biting her lip. "What is it?"

"Well . . . He does not know that it was purchased for her yet." Jane saw his brows rise. "She expressed admiration and he . . ."

"So he will be hoodwinked to teach her, no doubt by some convincing feminine ploy." Lucas smiled, already knowing the truth that Darcy let Elizabeth think she was charming him.

"I have no idea what you are talking about!" Jane huffed and spun away from him to join hands with another man down the line. When she returned, he was smiling at her. "What are you thinking?"

"I am thinking that I would rather enjoy you trying to convince me of something by using your wiles." He bent to her ear. "Is there anything you desire?"

"I can tell there is something that you desire." Jane saw that his eyes had darkened and she felt his hand tighten over hers. "Robert, we have a houseful of guests!"

"My parents do." He whispered. "And they are all occupied and very noisy." He looked at her intently. "Come Jane, we have not had a chance in days! With your family arriving for Christmas and all the other engagements," speaking urgently he whispered, "Nobody would hear . . ."

"Your brothers are upstairs."

"My brothers need to find apprenticeships." He growled. Jane smiled up at him and his glare softened. "Tonight?"

"Yes." She smiled. "Any night."

"Any?" He startled and stared. "And I . . ." He smiled and shaking his head, laughed when their movement ended. "I do not care what you say, Jane Lucas, you do know how to tease."

"Bennet."

"Sir William."

"Care to wager on a grandchild?" He winked and looked towards the couple.

"Most unseemly, gentlemen." Mr. Gardiner joined in. "This should be done over port." The men laughed and he looked across the room. "Kitty is a different girl; we had a very pleasant journey with her. She is learning some things at school. Has she shown you her drawings?"

"No." Mr. Bennet looked over to her standing with Maria and watching the dancers. "She has not mentioned them."

"Hmm." Mr. Gardiner clasped his hands behind his back. "Perhaps you should ask. I imagine that she is unsure of your interest and shy of showing her accomplishments." He noted Mr. Bennet's brow crease and moved on. "Lydia was put out that Kitty would attend this evening."

"As you know, Lydia was in high dudgeon before the subject arose." He saw his brother's eyes roll and glanced at Sir William, and kept the gossip to himself. Looking over to Kitty, he lifted his chin. "She is sixteen, and Jane spoke to me, telling me that it was entirely proper for a girl to attend a private dance at that age, to get a feel for the situation so that when she is out, she will be comfortable. She is not permitted to dance, but she may observe. Lydia was angry to be left behind, and when she told Kitty that she could not go, Kitty ignored her."

"Really?" Mr. Gardiner smiled. "Well Kitty is thinking for herself, not following her younger sister's orders."

"Yes." Mr. Bennet smiled with the realization. Kitty saw his approval, and nearly dropped her cup of punch. "I think that for the first time, Kitty has something that Lydia does not."

"But she does not lord it over her." Sir William noted. "She *is* different, come to think of it." He rubbed his cheek. "Perhaps I should look into a school for Maria. She is so shy."

"Well Kitty's school certainly does well by her. I spoke to the headmistress of Lydia's school when I went to collect her this morning. It seems that there is a militia unit in the village, catching the girls' eyes."

"I understand that Meryton may get one next autumn." Sir William offered. "Mixed opinion on that, good for business but lock up your daughters!" Mr. Gardiner and Mr. Bennet exchanged glances and kept their opinions to themselves.

"WELL?" BINGLEY APPEARED in Darcy's study the next morning.

"Well what?" Darcy glanced at Conrad and he gathered his papers and disappeared.

"Miss Martin, man!" He plopped into a chair and sat forward to stare at Darcy with bright eyes.

"You seemed to get along nicely." Darcy smiled. "Actually I was extremely impressed. You were confident, self-assured, in fact, you were everything that you are not now."

Bingley sat back and laughed. "Oh. I was doing my best, Darcy. The term "puppy" is very clear in my memory. I like her."

"She was very nice, and you seem to have a great deal in common."

"Yes!" Sitting forward again he spoke eagerly. "I lay abed all last night thinking of that. We share a common appreciation for the work of our fathers; and in many ways come from similar worlds. I cannot tell you how refreshing that is!"

"So the ladies raised in the thick of the *Ton* did nothing for you?" Darcy smiled and stretched his arms over his head.

"Oh, I would not say that." Bingley winked at him. "It is just, well they are just so damned, I do not know, full of themselves. I think that I could be rich as Midas and still they would look down on me." Shrugging, he sat back again. "I suppose that was the attraction to Mrs. Lucas, well and Mrs. Darcy, too." Seeing Darcy's face lose expression, he smiled. "Sorry, I just enjoy seeing that scowl."

"Do you want my help or not?" Darcy glared.

"I would say he does." Hurst strolled in and took a chair. "I like her, Bingley. Louisa did, too. And that is saying something, she used to hold a great ambition to see you married to royalty, her expectations have dropped a bit."

Darcy rolled his eyes. "That sounds more like Mrs. Robinson than Mrs. Hurst."

"Well, perhaps." Hurst tilted his head. "I think though that I do see a bit of the puppy about you this morning, what say you, Darcy?"

"Well . . ." He sighed and looked directly at Bingley. "At least he did not call her an angel." Hurst laughed and Bingley blushed. "You do make a habit of having your head turned easily. She is a nice girl, but I do not think that you need to set your agenda around her. Telling her you would take Netherfield . . . you are too quick, Bingley. Take your time; you have a whole Season ahead of you before you become a landowner, or renter, rather. There is no hurry to fall in love with the first pretty girl who crosses your path."

"I had not really thought about that. I . . . I suppose that I was . . ." Bingley shrugged. "It was nice to actually have a real conversation with a girl instead of just staring at her."

"That is because you share common experiences. You have learned something with that, have you not?" Darcy smiled when understanding appeared in his friend's eyes. "She was putting on a brave front in here, when she managed to tear her eyes from yours. It reminds me of you once." Bingley smiled to his boots then rubbed his nose. "Far be it from me to tell you who to love, but I think that you are seriously jumping the gun."

"Is this one of those moments when I should take my friends' advice and follow my gut?"

"Ah, well. No, actually I am being quite serious. I am not hoping to teach you by subterfuge this time." Darcy leaned forward and spoke seriously, "If you happen to still remember her name when you are back in town and the Season has begun, you have an excellent excuse in re-establishing contact by paying a call to her father. You could mention meeting Miss Martin here and enquire after her health. I suspect a dinner invitation would soon follow."

"*If* he remembers her is the salient point here." Hurst said with a twitch to his lips. "I lay odds that she will be gone from your mind the moment another young lady smiles at you."

"Am I that fickle?" Bingley cried. His companions said nothing and simply looked at him. "Well, it is time to put a stop to that!"

"Good for you, Bingley." Darcy laughed and put a sheet of paper and a pen in front of him. "Now, I suggest that you write to the owner of Netherfield before your plans go awry once again."

"SO THERE YOU WERE, standing in the middle of the lawn, searching everywhere for those pearls." Lord Matlock chuckled and put the stopper back in the top of the nearly empty decanter of port. "A more pathetic sight I have never witnessed. I must say it took all of me to remain stern."

"I seem to remember Mother had no problem at all being quite stern." Richard said in a flat tone as he stared at his clasped hands hanging between his legs. "She meted out punishment most effectively."

"Ah well, spare the rod, spoil the child." He resumed his seat opposite his son. "Although I imagine that you thought it was a beating worthy of the criminals in the pillory, I would say that your lashings were no more painful than a quick crack of the hand. I think the lashings of the tongue were more memorable."

"They both sting, Father."

He shrugged. "They were meant to, but they did you no harm."

"You were much kinder to Audrey and Stephen." He said to his hands.

Laughing, he sipped his drink. "That statement is in direct contrast to how they feel about *your* supposedly lax punishments."

"What?" He looked up. "I . . ."

"All three of you were punished the same way, and might I add, none of you was ever hurt. I think that the anticipation was more effective in curbing you." He chuckled. "Well that and a few turns at mucking out the stables."

"But I enjoyed that." Fitzwilliam managed a smile.

"And Stephen did not." He sighed. "No for you, the trick was to set you to work writing out your lessons. Audrey . . . Well, she never really did anything wrong. She would not dare disappoint her mother."

"I miss her, but it is good to see her so happy with Singleton now."

"Yes, that was one of the greatest regrets I have ever had, giving her to that beaten boy. Now that is an example of parental discipline gone horribly wrong. I did not know; I had no idea that Singleton was such a terrible mess. He seemed an ideal suitor and they got on so well." He shook his head. "That bastard of a father of his."

"I look at all of the examples of fathers and . . . I worry over how I will be to my child." Fitzwilliam glanced up at the ceiling then back to his hands. "I admire so many things in you, but I . . . see the non-traditional behaviour of Darcy and I wish to emulate him."

"And your brother?" Lord Matlock asked softly.

"He walks a tightrope, I think. He wishes to be as free as Darcy, but enjoys the comfort of convention. I would say that he holds Margaret much more than you ever held us, and they spend more time with her, but they both feel the burden of their position and do not feel comfortable straying too far from what is expected. I am no Viscount, and that gives me freedom of a sort."

"Yes, and Darcy is the same in a way, although once he realized what his father had tried to teach him about his expectations, he also felt that freedom you speak of to follow his own path." Lord Matlock smiled. "Your brother, however, does have that title, and he will always bear scrutiny, so he must be more careful. Therefore, Margaret is neither coddled nor neglected. They have set their rules and your mother and I endeavour to stay out of it. They are very happy, and soon there will be another." He sighed contentedly. "Hopefully the heir."

"I hope that you do not make them feel that they have failed if it is not." Richard said pointedly.

"No, no, but it is to be expected." He shrugged. "Then again, if there is not one, the estate would go to you and yours."

"I am hardly counting on that." Fitzwilliam sighed and looked at the clock. "Twenty hours since this began! Why is it taking so long?"

"I imagine your wife is expressing the same sentiment." He smiled and leaned forward to grasp his shoulder. "She will be well."

"Yes. I keep telling myself that." He sighed again and searched for a distraction. Rubbing his temples he murmured, "What ever happened to those pearls?"

Lord Matlock smiled. "Ah, odd you should ask, since apparently two of them have turned up."

"What?" Fitzwilliam's head lifted. "Where? Did Darcy find them? After all of these years? I admit to searching every time I am at Pemberley."

Chuckling, Lord Matlock sat back in his chair. "Let me tell you the story of your evil cousin . . ."

"Richard." Both men were on their feet and in front of Lady Matlock. She looked very weary. "No news yet, dear. Evangeline was worried about you, and asked me to come and see how you are." She caressed his face. "You look exhausted."

"I am sure that it is nothing to my wife." He took his mother's hand. "How is she, really?"

"She is doing fine."

Fitzwilliam searched her eyes and dropped her hand. "No, she is not. You are here for a reason; you are preparing to tell me something horrible." He drew himself up and looked to the door. "Excuse me."

"Richard, no, remain here!" Lady Matlock ordered and he shook his head.

"I am going where I should have been all along. What kind of a man am I?" He strode from the room and Lord Matlock touched his wife's hand. She turned and fell into his open arms.

"*Is* anything wrong?" Lord Matlock asked urgently.

"No, Evangeline and I have been arguing for the last few hours. She wants Richard, and finally threatened to keep the baby from me if I did not go and find him." She smiled and leaned on his chest. "I truly love that young woman."

Lord Matlock squeezed her and kissed her forehead. "But you told him to stay."

"Well I wanted to make sure that he would go." Lady Matlock sighed and her husband laughed softly and held her. "I know my stubborn boy."

Without stopping to consider his actions, Fitzwilliam followed the sound of his wife's voice, and opened the door to the bedchamber. She lay on her side, her back to the man sitting next to the bed. His eyes widened at the sight of another man seeing his wife so indecently dressed, but continued in. "Sir . . ." the midwife stood and Fitzwilliam glared at him.

"Stand down and do your job."

"Richard." Evangeline whispered and he came around to see her face, kneeling on the floor to hold her hands. "You came . . . ohhhhhhhh."

"This is where I belong." He picked up a cloth and wiped her brow. "You are a magnificent soldier."

She smiled a little, gasped again, clutched his hands, then screamed. He resisted every desire he was feeling, wanting to run away, wanting to strangle the mid-wife, wanting to curse nature for making her suffer, but instead he said how much he loved her, and stared into her eyes.

"I am so tired." She said as her voice cracked.

"Your grip belies that statement." He smiled and flexed his fingers before giving his hands back over to her. "Come love, you can do this."

"You are there, Mrs. Fitzwilliam, the head is crowning." The man checked again. "The next push should do it."

"Oh heaven help me I hope so." She gasped and beared down once more then screamed. Richard looked when he heard the cry of triumph from the midwife and stared as the baby's head appeared.

"Oh Eva!" He felt her relax then she clutched him again and pushed. "Oh love, you did it!" He watched as the baby was delivered and the midwife went about the business of rousing and cleaning the child. "A girl!" Richard turned and kissed her. "We have a baby girl!"

Evangeline wiped the tears pouring down his face and she sobbed. He kissed her hands and her lips. "A beautiful, beautiful," the baby started squalling and he laughed, "noisy, fearsome little girl! Thank you, my love." He sighed and hugged her. "Thank you."

Chapter 30

A slow smile spread over de Bourgh's face when he sorted through the stack of post. "Mary." He sighed and looked at her handwriting carefully. "Your hand shook when you addressed this." The thought of her being nervous when she wrote his name made his heart leap. His hand shaking now, he broke the seal and read. When he reached the end, he closed his eyes then returned to the beginning to read it through again. An hour later his mother found him still at his desk, the letter in his hand but now his eyes stared out at the rain sheeting down the window.

"Quite a storm." She smiled and took a seat. When he did not respond she glanced at the letter, but unable to tell anything other than the surety that the hand was that of a woman, she studied his faraway look. "Days like this make me think of your father."

"Oh?" He said softly. "Thinking of him at sea?"

"Yes." She said just as softly. "It was the closest I could come to understanding the life he led, I am sure that his letters never told me the complete truth." De Bourgh smiled a little and kept his gaze with the trees bending in the wind. Mrs. de Bourgh tilted her head and recited softly,

> *"How can my poor heart be glad,*
> *When absent from my sailor lad;*
> *How can I the thought forego-*
> *He's on the seas to meet the foe?*
> *Let me wander, let me rove,*
> *Still my heart is with my love;*
> *Nightly dreams, and thoughts by day,*
> *Are with him that's far away.*
> *On the seas and far away,*
> *On stormy seas and far away;*
> *Nightly dreams and thoughts by day,*
> *Are aye with him that's far away."*[12]

"You have become a student of poetry?" De Bourgh asked with a hint of a laugh.

---

[12] Robert Burns, "O'er the Hills and Far Away," 1794.

"I found comfort in the words that I could not express myself, waiting for my boys to come home." She smiled and saw his wistful appearance. "Do you miss it?"

He finally looked to her. "Sometimes, which amazes me. I spent so much time in that tiny, miserable cabin, wishing to be on land, away from the danger, the regulation, the spit and polish, the hierarchy . . . And then I think of the thrill of the ocean, the power of command, the purpose of battle, the opportunity to see the world. And then I know what a fool I am for missing any of that life. I have an exceptional home, one I never dared dream about, and it comes with its own set of regulation, polish, and power. But I have no anchor here." He sighed and looked back down. "Mary wrote me a letter."

"Mary? Not Miss Bennet?" She admonished gently and he smiled and shook his head. "Mary, then. And what was this entirely improper letter about? I take it that this is different from the family letters you have been exchanging."

"Mrs. Darcy approved it, Mother." He closed his eyes. "She understands me, Mary does. She read my journals from the age that she is now. She never felt at home at Longbourn. She describes it as a feeling of being a permanently unwelcome guest, but not having the means to move on to better accommodations, not until Elizabeth escaped and facilitated her own." He looked back to his mother who was nodding slowly. "Rather like Anne de Bourgh escaped her miserable existence and rescued me from . . ."

"Your father was very lonely at sea, too."

"Yes." He looked at the letter, then handed it over to her. Mrs. de Bourgh read it through and smiled. "She has fallen in love with you."

"Do you think so? We have barely had time together."

"Yes, but you have shared yourself with her through your journals." She studied him as he thought. "She is no empty-headed fool, Peter. The girl has plenty of good sense and you said yourself that she can be rather fierce when driven to it. You have told her more of yourself than most men ever tell their wives." He shrugged and Mrs. de Bourgh handed back the letter and sat up straight. "Then again, you were not educated the way most men are. Well? What is the problem? You are in love with her."

"I hardly know . . ."

"Of course you do." She became business-like. "I paid great attention to her when we were at Michael's wedding. Her sister Elizabeth impressed me very favourably, but she is married and a mother, hardly a fair comparison. But I saw potential and most of all; I saw how you ran after her when she was hurt by her younger sister's callousness."

"I did." He smiled and blushed, thinking of how much he had wanted to wrap her up in his arms and kiss that hurt away, and assure her that she would be forever safe with him. "How did this happen?" He said almost to himself.

Mrs. de Bourgh laughed to see the bemused look in his eye. "Oh my son, you have been wishing for a home and a family since you were a little boy."

"I suppose that I have. I have a pile of invitations here, asking us . . ." He laughed as her eyes rolled, "Well, asking me to come to the neighbour's homes to enjoy an evening."

"With their daughters."

"Naturally." He sat up and looked at the stack. "Do you see them at church? Thank heaven that Michael delivers a sensible and short sermon, I can stay awake and escape before the mama's greedy fingers latch onto my arm and drag me over to greet the girls."

"They are rather anxious." Mrs. de Bourgh smiled. "Lady Catherine was spitting mad last week. She overheard one group of ladies discussing strategies to capture you before the Season began and you were lost to the social whirl of London. She pronounced them all fools."

"Lady Catherine supported me?" He stared in surprise. "I find that hard to believe!"

"I believe that she has a personal agenda. She failed at installing Darcy as her daughter's husband and owner of the estate, but I have no doubt that she is feeding tidbits of information to selected friends about you, to give their daughters a leg up in their charming your favour."

"What a conniving idea! What have you heard?"

Mrs. de Bourgh warmed to her subject and leaned forward. "Well, I have it on the best authority that she has sent her maid to gossip with our staff to learn your favourites in food, drink, activities, and even reading selections." De Bourgh's mouth hung open. "What her ultimate goal is, I could not say. Perhaps she hopes for a pliable mistress to be installed so that she can make her own circumstances more comfortable."

"Play on the lucky girl's gratitude for winning such a magnificent husband?" He growled. "The woman disgusts me, Mother. A year after her daughter's death; and she still grasps at what she never had."

"Yes!" Mrs. de Bourgh's eyes grew bright as she smiled widely. "And I cannot wait to see her with the Darcys!"

"Mother, behave." He admonished sternly.

"Can you just imagine how put out she will be when you marry the sister of the woman who stole Darcy?" She laughed and clapped.

"You are enjoying yourself far too much, Mother." De Bourgh laughed at her and shook his head, "And you assume too much."

"Do I?" She stood and walked around the desk to kiss his cheek and put Mary's letter on the blotter. "Will your hand shake as much as hers when you respond to this letter?" Seeing his astonishment, she caressed his hair and strolled from the room, humming a little love song as she went.

"KITTY, PLEASE JOIN ME IN THE BOOKROOM." Mr. Bennet stood up from his seat at the dining room table and waiting for her to precede him, followed her to his sanctuary and closed the door. "Please take a seat."

"Yes, sir." She whispered.

He cleared his throat and walked around the room, looking at his books and hoping for inspiration. He noticed that her face was turning pink and her hands were twisting. "I looked through your sketch book last night. You have a talent I never knew of before. I am sorry that I have missed enjoying it until now." Kitty's bewilderment was clear and he closed his eyes before stopping and patting her shoulder. "I am sorry that praise from me brings surprise, as well."

"Oh, I . . ."

He took a seat behind his desk and held up his hand. "No, there is no need to say a thing. Now then, I am assured from all that I have seen of you over this holiday that you are indeed benefitting from your schooling, and I must say that I am even more greatly pleased to see that you have resisted Lydia's attempts to domineer you."

"I am trying, sir." She whispered. "I have found better examples at school and elsewhere."

"Yes." He took a moment to think of how to approach this daughter he barely knew. Seeing her nerves increasing, he dove in. "I am concerned about your sister. She still seems to be resistant to the direction and threats that she has received from all of us. You know her best, has anything we have said reached her?"

Kitty stared down at her clasped hands and thought about Lydia. At last she looked up to see her father's expectant expression. "I think that she is confused, especially when Mama told her to stop complaining and to pay attention to the teachers so that she could marry very well."

"Yes." Mr. Bennet smiled. "I was rather surprised at that. Mrs. Wilcox's visit to Pemberley and her vivid description of the estate and the graciousness of Lizzy and Darcy made quite an impression on her." He saw Kitty's confusion and waved it away. At last his wife understood that her behaviour had denied her access to her daughter's world. "So, do you think that she will continue to flirt with these soldiers?"

"I do not know, Papa. I think that she might forget all that was said to her as soon as she is back with her friend."

"I thought as much." He nodded and looked down at the letter he had received from the headmistress. "Very well, then. I know what I must do."

"What is that, Papa?"

He smiled. "Be a parent, my dear. Now then, you return to London and learn all that you can. Lizzy wrote that they will be there in March. If you like, you may accompany her family to Rosings for Easter rather than returning home, it is up to you."

"Oh." She smiled happily. "I . . . I would like very much to be with them. And Rosalie."

"Of course." He nodded, and felt the heaviness of his failure weigh on his heart. "Well, off with you, I am sure that you have packing to do before morning." She stood and was about to leave when he said quietly, "I am very proud of the young woman you are becoming, Kitty."

"Oh." She blushed and looked at her feet. "Thank you, Papa."

"Please ask Lydia to come to me." He watched the door close behind her and sat back in his chair. "Well, let us see if I can summon the strength of my sons."

"I THOUGHT THAT THEY WOULD NEVER LEAVE!" Jessica rolled her eyes at the backs of the retreating servants and closed the door with a bang. She turned to where Lydia sat on her bed and smiled widely. "How long have you been here?"

"A few hours. Papa wished to speak to Miss Edwards before he left."

"Oh." Jessica studied her and sat on her bed. "Are you in trouble?"

"No." She lied. "Did Miss Edwards write to your father?"

"What about?"

"The militia."

"Oh that." She shrugged. "He said that Miss Edwards is well-paid to look after me. He looks at her like another governess, someone to keep me out of his way. I do not know what she is so worried about. All of our soldiers are so very lovely to us." She giggled. "I have been begging him to let me go to Brighton this summer! Lieutenant Tike said that all of the soldiers go there then, the place is just *teeming* with officers! You have to ask your father if you can come with me! What fun we will have! I so want to marry an officer!" She stood up and started going through Lydia's closet, held up a new dress to herself, wrinkled her nose and tossed it on the bed. "Only one new dress? I got five."

"Papa would not let me get more than one." Lydia started to whine. "He said that he has to save money for when I come out."

"Only one more year for me!" Jessica crowed and grabbing Lydia's new bonnet; stuck it on her head and spun around the room. "And I will have dresses and jewellery and slippers, and all of the men will look at me!" She took off the bonnet and tossed it in the air. "Papa will give me anything I want."

"Why?" She grabbed her bonnet from where it landed on the floor and held onto it.

"Because I am so pretty! And I ask him very nicely." She smiled. "My sisters are so jealous. They tell me to settle down all of the time, but they do not get dresses and ribbons and the men do not look at them like they look at me. So I must be the one in the right! They will all be old maids, and I will have the handsomest husband." She sighed.

"Mama wanted us all married at fifteen, but my older sisters changed her mind. She said that I have to pay attention to what they did to capture their husbands. Even Mary might have found one." She shook her head in disbelief.

"Oh, I asked Papa if he knows about the Darcys." She sat on the bed and stared eagerly at Lydia. "They are VERY rich. You must go to London with them, and they will buy you anything you want."

"I do not think so." Lydia glanced at her closet and felt her anger rising. "Kitty is going to spend the Season with them."

"What about you?" Jessica demanded. "Why does *she* get everything?"

Lydia shrugged. "Lizzy likes her. She goes to school with Georgiana Darcy."

"Oh, that's right." Jessica thought. "I bet that she is spoiled."

Lydia thought about the last time she saw Georgiana and how shy she was. "I do not think . . ."

"I cannot wait to see Lieutenant Tike." She sighed. "I spotted him when our carriage came through the village. He saw me and he smiled so widely, then he made the secret sign that we have. I will meet him tomorrow!"

"Oh . . ." Lydia bit her lip. "Miss Edwards told Papa about us speaking to the soldiers."

"So? That was in her letter to my Papa, too. He asked me what I was about and I said that we were just talking in the shops and he was satisfied." She smiled slyly. "I think I might let him kiss me."

"But what about the chaperones?"

"What about them?" Jessica demanded. "You will distract them!"

"I think that they might know about that." Lydia cringed when she saw Jessica's glare. "Papa said something about that."

"Well I do not know how they found out, but nothing is going to keep me from seeing Lieutenant Tike!" She folded her arms and stared off into a corner. There was a knock on the door and Miss Edwards entered.

"Ladies, we have decided to separate you. Miss Simkins, follow me. You are going into the empty chamber near the sitting room."

"Why?" Lydia and Jessica demanded.

"I do not owe you any explanation." She sniffed at them and looked to Jessica. "Come along."

Jessica turned to Lydia and whispered, "That room has a window right above the roof for the kitchen!"

"What are you going to do?"

"I do not know, but . . . something." She glared at Miss Edwards' back. "Nobody will tell *me* what to do!"

30 JANUARY 1811
Grosvenor Street
London

Dear Darcy,
Is it rude to proclaim joy at the departure of one's flesh and blood? Well then Hurst, Louisa, and I must be the most uneducated, uncouth lot of relatives to live on this earth because I would say no more than five minutes after we assured ourselves that the Robinson's carriage had turned the corner, we were standing in the parlour with glasses in hand and toasting our good fortune. I rather imagine the staff was undoubtedly doing the same in the kitchen. All that remains of them is a larder full of marmalade. Well whatever decorating was accomplished at the Robinson home, I sincerely hope that they enjoy it. I cannot imagine what it would have been to endure all that time with them at home. The fights!

Beyond that happy news, I also wish to confirm that I am set to lease Netherfield beginning at Michaelmas. I am delighted and excited to at last take this definite step forward in fulfilling Father's dreams. I hereby invite your wonderful family to join us there. At last I have the opportunity to return the gift of hospitality. And will not Mrs. Darcy enjoy seeing her sister and perhaps her parents again? Well, I leave that for your private discussion.

I look forward more than I can say to your arrival in town. I hope to steal a dance or two during the Season from the lovely ladies of Darcy House. By the way, rumours abound about the new master of Rosings. De Bourgh should be wary, they have the prey in their sights! Perhaps after I have Netherfield I will be just as desired? Oh, a young man's dream!

Please offer my love to all three of your ladies. I miss you all.
Sincerely yours,
Charles Bingley, Esq.

Darcy shook his head and set down the letter. "No mention of Miss Martin."

"Are you surprised?" Elizabeth smiled and he shrugged. "I imagine that if their paths crossed it would be different. They simply live in such different worlds. He would have to seek her out."

"And that is unlikely when he undoubtedly has the attention of many ladies. He is not as undesired as he claims; word is travelling about him as well. What do you think of his warning to de Bourgh?"

"It is perfectly reasonable that he would attract attention, however I believe that his heart is set on course." Elizabeth laughed when his eyes rolled. "I cannot resist the nautical terms."

"Can Mary?" He chuckled and nudged her slipper with his boot. She threw a bit of paper at his nose and hit him. Darcy picked the ball out of his neck cloth and aimed it back at her nose. "Your aim is improving."

"Snowballs." She laughed and he gave a long sigh then smiled at her.

"What of Netherfield?"

She let out her own dramatic sigh. "I want to support him, but . . . Well we would not be at Longbourn."

"What shall I tell him, love?" Darcy leaned forward. "I leave it to you. My headaches are nearly gone."

She spoke very seriously. "If my family dares hurt you . . ."

Darcy took her hand and kissed it. "I think that it will be . . .tolerable." Elizabeth caressed the fringe of hair from his eyes and he kissed her lips gently. "He needs us."

"Very well. I cannot deny the truth of that."

"GOOD MORNING BABY GIRL." Fitzwilliam whispered and smiled happily when her fist wrapped around his finger. "Good morning my little Annabel Pearl. And good morning my beautiful wife."

"You are a silly fool, Richard." Evangeline whispered. They kissed and looked down at their baby.

"Do you know what today is?" He wiggled his brows.

"I believe that it is the fourth day of February." She protested when his lips began nibbling her throat. "Richard, behave!"

"What, my good wife, is the significance of this day?" He pressed his nose to hers and kissed her lips.

"This is our daughter's Christening day. It is so kind of Stephen and Alicia to agree to be her godparents. It is a miracle that he is allowing her to travel to the church, with her due anytime this month."

"You are toying with me. Very well then, I will play your game." He sat up straight. "Well, since we are the godparents to Margaret I suppose that it was only right to ask them for Annabel. Perhaps we might ask Darcy and Elizabeth next time." He beamed at her and fell back to nibbling her neck. "And happy day, we may begin working on that miracle this very afternoon!"

Evangeline batted him away. "I sincerely hope you are not serious!"

"What do you think?" He chuckled and kissed her. "Oh Eva, I have missed you. Have you not missed me?"

"Maybe a little." She said grudgingly and laughed when he immediately covered her face in kisses. "Yes, you mountain of a man, I have missed you. I am anticipating the churching ceremony as much as you." He kissed her soundly. Annabel let go and yawned. "Good girl." She lifted her up and stroked her back. "Your mother has not said a word about my feeding her."

"Why, I wonder." He peeked around her shoulder and made faces at the baby, who blinked and closed her eyes.

"I think that I made a great many threats to her while I was labouring." Evangeline laughed at his antics. "She is not interested, dear."

"Let me hold her." He asked and held out his arms. Carefully the transfer was made and he cuddled her to his chest. "My pretty girl." He looked up and sighed. "Everyone should be this happy." Suddenly his brow creased and he made a face. "Eva . . ."

"Yes, dear?" She pursed her lips.

"Um . . . she is . . . oh Eva she is wet!"

She peeked over at their soundly sleeping baby and looked up at his disconcerted face. "So she is."

"What do I do?"

"Maybe we should call the maid?"

"Um . . . Eva?"

"Hmm?"

"It is not just wet now." He looked very uncomfortable.

Evangeline kissed him and stood. "Come, Papa."

"Eva . . ." He held out the baby. "Please?" She laughed and walked away. Fitzwilliam sighed and rose to his feet. "I have learned a lesson, I think."

"WHOA!" Darcy cried and grabbed his hat before it flew from his head. "Slow down, Lizzy!"

"Oh for heaven's sake, we are barely crawling along!" She turned her head to smile at him and he gently turned her head forward. "Yes dear, the horse goes where I am looking."

"Precisely." Darcy smiled at her warmly and watched as she flicked the reins. "You are making me quite proud."

"I am?"

He watched the blush spreading up over her already pink face. "Oh yes. You have taken to driving very quickly." He firmly pulled her arms down and smiled at her glance. "There is no need to raise your arms, love, you are properly seated. I do not want you to be sore when we return home."

"I know." She sighed and looked out over the head of the trotting pony. "I look forward to the spring when we may try the barouche."

Darcy chuckled and rubbed her back, encouraging her to sit straight. "I do, too. Although I think that I should probably start you with a gig."

"Why?" She demanded.

"Because it is much less expensive to replace."

"Do you think that I will have an accident?" She turned and stared.

"No . . . Well, if you do not stop staring at me and pay attention to the path, you just might wind up in the lake. Fortunately it is frozen." He went to grab the reins of the sleigh and she gasped as he redirected the animal and blushed again. "Sit tall, love."

"Yes, Fitzwilliam." She peeked at him to see that he was still wearing his little smile. "I do like this."

"I know, but you must promise me again that you will never ever go alone." He moved next to her and slipped his arm around her waist. "You could not have done this a few years ago. You lacked the confidence. And you need that to assure the horse that you are in charge."

"I am confident now?"

"Oh yes my wonderful mistress of Pemberley. I find it extraordinarily attractive." Darcy whispered warmly against her ear, then expertly, he took the reins out of her grasp, snapped them and they took off at a much faster and smoother pace across the snow, heading for the edge of the woods where he brought the horse to a halt. "Care to visit your tree?"

"I would, very much." He tied off the horse and helping her down, they walked along the path through the silent forest. "It seems only the deer and rabbits have been here." She nestled against his thick coat as his arm held her securely to his side. "I feel that we are intruders in a silent cathedral. It is so beautiful."

"I love how the sunlight glistens off of the ice." He whispered. "It sparkles like your eyes." Pausing, he dipped his head to gently caress her lips, then turning, lifted her chin to stare at her before kissing her pink cheeks and press his lips to her cold nose. She laughed and he smiled before returning to her mouth. Moulding their bodies together, their lips and tongues tasted and explored. They ended the kisses embraced and with her head resting against his chest. Darcy drew a long deep breath and stared out at the endless trees. "I am so glad that we came out here today. This is a very welcome day of warmth. I have missed our little adventures."

"I have, too." Elizabeth murmured and he laughed when she kissed his chin. "What is it?"

"Ohhhh that nose is very cold."

"So is yours, but I am not complaining. After all, yours is so much larger than mine!"

"Careful, love. I might just have to run my cold hands up your warm legs!" He threatened.

Elizabeth gave him a pointed look of warning and he held up his hands in contrition. "Do you know what I would like to do when we return?" They started walking again. "I want to sit in front of the fire in the library, some scandalously fortified hot toddy at our sides," he chuckled, "a few good books and a warm blanket nearby, and curl up in your arms, ignore it all, and kiss you silly."

"And how will you know when I have been sufficiently kissed to be declared silly?"

"I think that when our jaws ache as much as our desire."

"I think that I am quite there, now." They kissed and he saw her brows rise. "I would love that. What of Mary?"

"She is not invited."

"Thank you." He laughed softly and they exchanged smiles. "De Bourgh is counting the days until we arrive at Rosings."

"He has six weeks to go."

"A little more. We have to wait for the girls to be free of school for Easter." Darcy focussed and thought. "Easter is the fourteenth of April."

"Yes." Elizabeth smiled and saw the flicker of relief appear in his eyes for remembering. "So you would like to arrive at the end of March?"

"Yes, that gives us time with whatever we need to accomplish before you have all of the girls, and I can take care of a little business, catch up with our friends and family, then we may go on. Everyone is in town now."

"For Alicia." Elizabeth said softly and he nodded, looking ahead to the glade.

"Ah, there it is." He looked down and smiled. "You see, the tree is quite safe, and taller than ever. Do you remember insisting that we come out here and visit last year? It took everything in me to hold my tongue and bear with you. I wonder if all of your pregnancies will make you so . . ." He stopped when she looked up at him. "Fascinating."

"That was not the word at the tip of your tongue."

Darcy wrapped her up in his arms and kissed her. "Taste my tongue and see what word comes to you." They spent many long minutes kissing in the warmth of the bright sunshine that flooded their private sanctuary. Darcy felt her shiver, and opening up his coat, helped her inside, enclosing her in the safety of its folds while she clung to him and they continued to kiss. At last they stopped for air and he held her tightly, rubbing her back, and wondering how to start the conversation. "I received another letter from Richard."

"I saw that." She whispered and drank in his warm, comforting scent. "Is he still silly and ecstatic?"

"He is ridiculous in his joy. At seven weeks of age, Annabel has him lost. I would laugh at him, except that I am equally guilty of being a ridiculously proud Papa. I fear that our letters from now on will contain only passing references to news and instead be filled with competing declarations over the wonders of our daughters and the glory of our wives." Darcy felt her squeeze and he chuckled. "He still was going on over being present at the birth, I suppose that is because Layton and Alicia arrived for her confinement, and it brought back his memories of wonder." He looked at the tree where Elizabeth had reclined and remembering Rosalie's birth; hugged her tightly and swallowed hard. "Wonder hardly describes what we experienced here."

Elizabeth lifted her head and they kissed again. He tasted tears on her cheeks and kissed them away before she settled back against him. He sighed and continued. "He reminded me of the wager we have amongst the cousins, who will have the first boy." She stiffened and his eyes closed. "I suppose that it is up to Alicia in the next few weeks to see if it still stands. I read your journal, you laugh at us men."

She spoke against his chest. "How can I not? Betting on the sex of a baby!"

"Oh come, love, it is a fascinating wager!" Darcy hugged her, rocking them a little. "Months of anticipation!"

"And what does the winner receive?"

"A son, of course." He smiled and felt her squeeze.

"I see through you, now." Elizabeth looked up at him. "You heard me talking to Rosa about a baby brother."

"Yes." Darcy loosened his hold enough to look down at her. "What concerns you, love?"

His soft gaze was all she needed to let her worries come pouring out. "For some strange reason, I felt relief that Eva had a girl, but now it is Alicia's turn again . . . Again, Fitzwilliam! Their daughter is not even a year old and she is about to give him . . . Mr. Harwick was so happy to have a son. He said that he would love any child, but I remember when he first wanted to court Jane, he said that he wished to marry solely to have an heir." Darcy's brow creased. "And that is my most important duty, to give you your heir."

"Your most important duty is to love me. Whatever follows is a blessing." Elizabeth caressed his cheek. "Fitzwilliam, I know that you wish for a son."

His gaze stayed with her eyes. "I do, and maybe he will come one day, and if you gift me with any more children I will be thrilled whatever the sex. I will gladly love a second girl; after all, I am forever grateful for the second daughter I married." He smiled and then looked down when he saw Elizabeth's eyes well up. "Lizzy." He lifted her chin and kissed her, then wiped the tear away with his thumb.

"Sometimes Will, you say something that melts my heart."

"Well then I will have to work to say things that melt you more often." He kissed her nose and her cheek and smiled while caressing her jaw. He spoke softly. "I wish for a son. Of course I do. What do you ask, love?"

"When?"

He laughed. "Today." Seeing her serious expression, he sighed. "Whenever it happens. I hope that you do not feel pressure because of my wishing."

"I *know* that I must give you a son."

"Elizabeth . . ."

"No Will, I must. I am not parroting Mama, I know that it is what Pemberley requires." She looked at the tree where Rosalie was born. "I will stop feeding Rosa entirely."

"No, dearest." He shook his head. "You will feed her as long as you wish; I do not believe that the few times a day that you still feed our baby has any effect on your ability to become with child anymore. Besides this is your desire to feed her for one year; if I was so concerned I never would have agreed to you doing this in the first place. I would have listened to those supposedly learned men at the Foundling Hospital who proclaimed that a woman is not fit enough to understand how to manage the feeding of her own child." [13]

"What foolish man said that?" She gasped. "A woman does not . . . oh that is ridiculous! Must everything of me be managed by a man?" Darcy looked down and she sighed. "Forgive me."

"I do not make the laws or even agree with them all, Elizabeth."

"And I was not grouping you with them. Oh Will I just feel obliged to try."

"I think that we try quite often. And I fully intend to be trying quite vigorously when we return home, what better way is there to warm?" He smiled and kissed her when her cold pink cheeks blushed warm and red. "What has you worried? Is it Alicia?"

"She did not feed Margaret, and here she is about to give birth again."

"May I point out that Audrey is not in the family way and she did the same as Alicia?"

"Yes." She sighed.

"And Jane is not with child and she has been married for well over half a year?"

"Yes."

"Well then? There is no hurry, Elizabeth. Stop worrying and just love the baby we have now. If a son comes, I will be overjoyed. If I have a houseful of women . . ." He laughed, "Well then I will be taking many long rides alone."

"We would just come after you." She sniffed.

Darcy smiled and hugged her. "You know, to see you so weepy in this particular spot, I would be willing to wager that you are with child again this very moment. After all, you did spend a solid nine months sobbing into your handkerchief. Or my coat; or whatever other convenient bit of cloth was available." He laughed when she looked up and glared at him. "You see? You have been holding this worry inside of you and it grew. Stop worrying, our child will come." He kissed her soundly. "And I promise to be insufferably proud of little Fitzwilliam."

"Oh . . . Will, I dearly love your name, but one Fitzwilliam in the family is quite enough." She smiled and he stared at her with his eyebrows raised. "Truly love, what would we call him? Willie?"

"NO!"

"Well, it would have to be distinguished from you. I suppose that William would do."

"William is a common name." He sniffed.

---

[13] "*It is with great pleasure that I see at last the Preservation of Children become the Care of men of Sense. In my opinion this business has been too long finally left to the management of women, who cannot be supposed to have a proper knowledge to fit them for the Task.*"
Cadogan, Essay (for Nurses), London Foundling Hospital, 1756.

"But think of all the great men we know who possess that name!" Elizabeth warmed to the subject as his reassurance filled her heart. "There is Sir William Lucas, and William Collins, and . . ."

"I am utterly convinced, NO." He ran his hands over her back and they kissed again. "Dearest, is it too cold to try to conceive a baby right now?"

"In the snow?" She gasped and looked around them. "You are not serious?"

He pressed his hips forward and rubbed. "What do you think?"

"Will . . ."

"Over here!" He pulled her across the glade to a fallen tree and stood behind her. "I will keep you very, very warm." Darcy's eyes were dark but they twinkled.

"I cannot believe . . . Fitzwilliam Darcy, you are insane!" Elizabeth laughed as he pulled off one glove with his teeth and opened his breeches, then lifted the back of her coat and skirt. "Ohhhh, it is cold!"

"Shhhh!" Securing his feet in the snow, he leaned forward and slid home. "Sooooo warm!!!" He growled while he manoeuvred his hips and let his coat cover them both. "Dearest stop laughing!" He laughed and hugged her. "Lizzy!"

"I cannot help it, Will!" She looked back to him and he kissed her. "This is the silliest thing we have ever done. This not going to work, it is too cold!"

"I know." He smiled and sighed; reluctantly moving away from her. "However, I succeeded in my goal. I got you to laugh. Do you feel better, love?"

"How could I not?" Elizabeth turned and fixing their clothes, settled into his arms. They remained in the clasp, kissing as steady puffs of their breath froze and swirled around their heads.

"Are you warm now?"

"Sooooooooo warm." Snuggling against him, she whispered. "Let us go home."

"Before the warmth wears off?" He murmured and tightened his embrace.

"No, so that we get cold again." Elizabeth's eyes were sparkling and she laughed to see his brow crease. "So that we have to warm again."

"Toddies in the library?"

"mmm, and Fitzwilliam in the bedchamber."

"I will drive." He said immediately and started pulling her towards the path. When she laughed, he grinned. "Come on!"

"WHERE IS SHE, MISS LYDIA?" Miss Edwards demanded.

Lydia sat still on the straight backed chair in the headmistress' office and clasped her hands. "I have no idea."

"Miss Lydia, you are Miss Jessica's only friend, surely she told you."

"She just left that note." Lydia pointed at the desk. "That is all I know. She has not been telling me things so much since you moved her out of my room. She found out that my sister told my father about meeting the soldiers." Lydia sniffed twisted her handkerchief. "She did not trust me to keep her secrets."

Miss Edwards saw genuine distress in Lydia's eyes. Since returning to school, she had found herself largely unwelcomed by the other girls who were making sincere efforts to improve. Jessica had felt the same disdain, and without Lydia always by her side, she had turned her thoughts to the friendly welcome that she received from Lieutenant Tike. "The window in her room was open."

"oh." Lydia whispered.

"Well?"

"She noticed it was over the roof to the kitchen."

"Who was she meeting, Miss Lydia? Her parents need to know so that she might be found before it is too late."

"For what?" Lydia looked up with wide eyes.

"Before she is raped, Miss Lydia." Miss Edwards said angrily.

"What?" Lydia's hand went to her mouth. "She wants to marry Lieutenant Tike!"

"And a fine match it would be." She said sarcastically and looked around the office. "When news of this gets out I will have to close. Well maybe not." She looked at Lydia. "This is a school for wild girls." She swept out of the room to send a footman to summon the magistrate and the colonel of the militia. Lydia remained on the chair and listened to the buzzing of the gossip as the news travelled like wildfire around the school. Over and over she heard the words, "She is ruined!"

"NO, ROSA." Elizabeth admonished.

"Teeth?" Darcy peeked over her shoulder and looked at her sympathetically.

"Look at her, she knows what she does." She gave her daughter a stern stare. "No." Immediately Rosalie began feeding again.

"She reminds me of you." Darcy smiled. "That same mischievous glint is in her eye."

"I know." Elizabeth laughed softly. "It frightens me."

"She will mind us, dear. We will watch over that." He raised his brows at his daughter. "You will be a perfect little Miss."

"Oh where is the fun in that?"

He sighed. "You are no help."

"Would you have wanted me if I was perfect?" She tilted her head.

"No more than you would have wanted me." Bending down he kissed her and stroked Rosalie's cheek. "Fine, we will aim for humanity, not perfection."

"Now that I can appreciate." Elizabeth smiled and lifted the baby up to her shoulder.

There was a quiet knock at the door and Mary peeked inside. "May I join you?"

"Certainly." Darcy moved away from Elizabeth and awkwardly sat down on the child sized bed, low to the floor. Elizabeth laughed and he blushed. "Not very dignified."

"No dear, but very amusing."

"Ha, ha." He said dryly and looked to Mary who was attempting to remain serious. "What can we do for you?"

"Oh, a letter came from Rosings." She held it out. "I . . . I thought it might be important."

"Oh?" Elizabeth caught Darcy's eye. "Well we should read it straight away!"

"Absolutely." He broke the seal and read silently and without expression. Then folding it up went to place it in his coat.

"Wait!" Mary cried. "What did it say?"

"Hmm? Oh, the letter." He drew it back out and reopened it. "8 March, 1811, Rosings, Kent . . ."

"Fitzwilliam!" Mary cried.

He lifted his brow and looked at her blankly, but could not hide his twinkling eyes. "De Bourgh is wishing to confirm our travel dates, and suggests meeting up in London instead of waiting to see each other at Easter. He will be at his townhouse next week, it seems, and . . . Oh he hopes to receive word of our arrival . . ." He peered at the letter then held it up to Elizabeth. "What does that say?"

"Um, the instant we arrive." She said flatly.

"Ah, yes, the instant." His lips twitched and he glanced at Mary, whose face was pink. "He mentions something of wishing to spend a great deal of time in our company, as well."

"Oh?" Mary breathed.

"He further mentions that he has accepted invitations to several balls and wishes to confirm a minimum of two sets with you at each, he will escort you, of course, and although you are fonder of conversation than dancing, he hopes that you will bear with his unprecedented desire to explore the world of communication through," Darcy cleared his throat, "demonstration."

Elizabeth burst into laughter and Darcy could no longer hold himself in. Confused, Mary looked between them and Elizabeth waved to Darcy to handle it. "Mary, the man is besotted and wants to hold your hand."

"Oh!" Her hands went to her face. "Really?"

Rosalie started squirming and Elizabeth set her down on the floor. They watched her happily crawl away and Elizabeth gasped when she reached and pulled herself up to stand. Rosalie jabbered and stared at them with wide eyes. Darcy grabbed Elizabeth's hand and squeezed. Mary gasped and clapped.

"Good girl, Rosa!" He cried and they watched her let go, wobble, and fall. Darcy stood and then bent to scoop her up and spin her around the room. "What a good girl you are!"

"Ahaaaaa!" She cried and beamed.

"I love you dear girl!" Darcy kissed her.

"Mama!" Rosalie patted his cheek and he sighed as Elizabeth stood to stroke her hair. "You love Mama, I know. He looked her in the eye. "Papapapapapapapa."

"Papa!" She crowed. "Papapapapapapaaaaaaaa!"

Darcy turned to Elizabeth and beamed. "She knows me!" He looked back at Rosalie. "Shall I buy you a pony, dear?"

"Fitzwilliam!" Elizabeth cried.

Darcy kissed his wife and immediately Rosalie wanted to be back down on the floor. They watched her scoot away and try to stand again. Slipping his hand around Elizabeth's waist, he spoke proudly. "I was just seeing if you were paying attention." Their eyes met and joy radiated from his. "Papa!"

The story continues in Volume 3 of the Memory Series,
How Far We Have Come

Books by Linda Wells:
Chance Encounters

Fate and Consequences

Perfect Fit

Memory
Volume 1: Lasting Impressions
Volume 2: Trials to Bear
Volume 3: How Far We Have Come